EX LIBRIS

VINTAGE CLASSICS

THE DEATH OF IVAN ILYICH AND OTHER STORIES

Leo Tolstoy was born in central Russia in 1828. In 1852 he published his first work, the autobiographical *Childhood*. He served in the army during the Crimean War and his *Sevastopol Sketches* (1855–6) are based on his experiences. His two most popular masterpieces are *War and Peace* (1865–9) and *Anna Karenina* (1875–8). He died on 20 November 1910.

Richard Pevear and Larissa Volokhonsky have been nominated for the PEN Translation Prize three times and have won it twice. They live in Paris.

OTHER MAJOR WORKS BY LEO TOLSTOY

LEO TOLSTOY

The Death of Ivan Ilyich and Other Stories

TRANSLATED, ANNOTATED AND INTRODUCED BY

Richard Pevear and
Larissa Volokhonsky

VINTAGE BOOKS
London

Published by Vintage 2010

2 4 6 8 10 9 7 5 3

Translation © Richard Pevear and Larissa Volokhonsky 2009
Introduction © Richard Pevear 2009

This translation has been made from volumes X, XII and XIV of *Collected Works in
Twenty-two Volumes* by Leo Tolstoy (Moscow, 1982-83)

First published in the United States by Alfred A. Knopf in 2009-08-12
First published in Great Britain by Vintage in 2009

Vintage
Random House, 20 Vauxhall Bridge Road,
London SW1V 2SA

www.vintage-classics.info

Addresses for companies within The Random House Group Limited can be found at:
www.randomhouse.co.uk/offices.htm

The Random House Group Limited Reg. No. 954009

A CIP catalogue record for this book
is available from the British Library

ISBN 9780099541066

The Random House Group Limited supports The Forest Stewardship Council (FSC),
the leading international forest certification organisation. All our titles
that are printed on Greenpeace approved FSC certified paper carry the
FSC logo. Our paper procurement policy can be found at
www.rbooks.co.uk/environment

Printed and bound in Great Britain by
Clays Ltd, St Ives plc

Contents

INTRODUCTION

THERE MAY BE SUCH A THING as an "O. Henry story"; there may even be such a thing as a "Chekhov story"; but, as readers of this collection will discover, there is no such thing as a "Tolstoy story." From the narrative simplicity of *The Prisoner of the Caucasus* to the psycho-pathological density of *The Kreutzer Sonata*, from the intense single focus of *The Death of Ivan Ilyich* to the kaleidoscopic multiplicity of *The Forged Coupon*, from the rustic immediacy of *Master and Man* to the complex (and still highly relevant) geopolitical reality of *Hadji Murat*, from the rough jottings of *The Diary of a Madman* to the limpid perfection of *Alyosha the Pot*, Tolstoy was constantly reinventing the art of fiction for himself.

The eleven stories in this collection were written, with one exception, after 1880—that is, in the last thirty years of Tolstoy's long life (1828–1910). The one exception is *The Prisoner of the Caucasus*, which dates to 1872, the period between *War and Peace* and *Anna Karenina*, when Tolstoy busied himself with the education of the peasant children on his estate. Dissatisfied with the textbooks available, he decided to write his own, producing in the same year both an ABC and a reader which included, among other things, *The Prisoner of the Caucasus* and *God Sees the Truth but Waits*. Twenty-six years later, in his polemical treatise *What Is Art?*, laying down the principles for distinguishing between good and bad art in our time, he stated that there are only two kinds of good art: "(1) religious art, which conveys feelings coming from a religious consciousness of man's position in the world with regard to God and his neighbour; and (2) universal art, which conveys the simplest everyday feelings of life, such as are accessible to everyone in the world." In a note he added: "I rank my own artistic works on the side of bad art, except for the story *God Sees the Truth,* which wants to belong to the first kind, and *The Prisoner of the Caucasus,* which belongs to the second." We have included *The Prisoner* here, first, on its own merits. It shows very well how Tolstoy, for all the constraints his pedagogical and polemical intentions placed upon him, never lost that "gift of concrete evocation" which the French scholar and translator Michel Aucouturier rightly calls "the secret of his art." And, second, because it balances nicely with the last piece in the collection, also set in the Caucasus, the novella *Hadji Murat,* finished in 1904 and published posthumously in 1912.

The stories written for his school reader were Tolstoy's first attempt, after the immense inclusiveness of *War and Peace,* to purge his art of what he came to regard as its artistic pretensions and superfluous detail. The same attempt was repeated time and again later in his life, testifying to the constant conflict within him between his innate artistic gift and the moral demands he made upon himself, the conflict, as he understood it, between beauty and the good. In his *Reminiscences of Tolstoy,* Maxim Gorky repeats a story told him by his friend Sulerzhitsky about the elderly Tolstoy in Moscow which shows how alive that conflict remained:

Suler tells how he was once walking with Lev Nikolaevich in Tverskaya Street when Tolstoy noticed in the distance two soldiers of the Guards. The metal of their accoutrements shone in the sun; their spurs jingled; they kept step like one man; their faces, too, shone with the self-assurance of strength and youth. Tolstoy began to grumble at them: "What pompous stupidity! Like animals trained by the whip . . ."

But when the guardsmen came abreast with him, he stopped, followed them caressingly with his eyes, and said enthusiastically: "How handsome! Old Romans, eh, Lyovushka? Their strength and beauty! O Lord! How charming it is when man is handsome, how very charming."

By 1873 Tolstoy had dropped his pedagogical efforts and plunged into work on a new novel, *Anna Karenina*, equally filled with "superfluous detail and artistic pretensions," and equally limited to the lives of the Russian aristocracy, not in history now but in his own time and milieu. Here the conflicting claims of art and moral judgement strike a very difficult balance, and its precariousness is strongly felt. The novel marks a major turning point in Tolstoy's life, the end of what might be called his idyllic period. D. S. Mirsky, in *A History of Russian Literature*, notes in *Anna Karenina* "the approach of a more tragic God than the blind and good life-God of *War and Peace*. The tragic atmosphere thickens as the story advances towards the end." And it is not only the tragedy of Anna herself. By 1877, when he was writing the final chapters, both Tolstoy and his hero and likeness, Konstantin Levin, found themselves in a profound spiritual crisis. The novel "ends on a note of confused perplexity," writes Mirsky; it "dies like a cry of anguish in the desert air." The note is struck in Levin's reflections once he has attained all he wanted in life, all that the younger Tolstoy thought a man needs for happiness—a good marriage, children, a flourishing estate. He is haunted by doubts: "What am I? And where am I? And why am I here?" These questions, which bring Levin close to suicide, find an answer in his reconciliation with the Church. Levin asks himself, "Can I believe in everything the Church confesses?" And decides, rather hastily, that "there was not a single belief of the Church that violated the main thing—faith in God, in the good, as the sole purpose of man." "Serving the good instead of one's needs" became Levin's watchword, as it became Tolstoy's. But for Tolstoy, at least, the reconciliation was an uneasy one, undermined by latent contradictions, and it did not last long.

In 1879, only a year after the publication of *Anna Karenina*, he began work on a book to which he gave the title *A Confession*. This was not a novel; it was a sustained and rhetorically powerful exposition of the spiritual crisis he had lived through and the "conversion" (his own term) it had brought about in him, a conversion to what he called "true Christianity" as opposed to "Church Christianity." *A Confession* was the first, and the most personal and compelling, of the series of polemical works Tolstoy wrote over the next twenty years, culminating in *What Is Art?* (1898), in which he expounded his new religious views and their philosophical, social, and aesthetic consequences. These works made Tolstoy world famous, not as an artist but as a moral teacher; they led to what became known as "Tolstoyism," an anti-State, anti-Church, egalitarian doctrine of the kingdom of God on earth, to be achieved by means of civil disobedience and non-violent resistance, which brought him adherents such as Rainer Maria Rilke, Romain Rolland, Mahatma Gandhi, and the founders of the kibbutz movement in Palestine, among many others. It also brought him some of his first English translators.

The stories collected here have a complex and ambiguous relation to Tolstoy's moral teaching; some, like *Hadji Murat*, were even written, as he admitted, "in secret from himself" and contrary to his notions of "good art." But they all have a direct relation to the crisis he describes so forcefully in *A Confession:*

> My life stopped. I could breathe, eat, drink, sleep, and could not help breathing, eating, drinking, sleeping; but there was no life, because there were no desires whose satisfaction seemed reasonable to me . . . I could not even desire to know the truth, because I guessed what it consisted in. The truth was that life was an absurdity . . . The idea of suicide came to me as naturally as ideas for improving my life had come to me before. This idea was so tempting that I had to use tricks with myself so as not to carry it out at once.

> . . .

> My question, the one which brought me, at the age of fifty, to the verge of suicide, was the simplest of questions, the one that every man carries in the depths of himself, from the stupidest child to the wisest old man—the question without answering which life is impossible, as I indeed experienced. Here is that question: "What will come of what I do now, of what I will do tomorrow— what will come of my whole life?" Formulated differently, the question would be the following: "Why should I live, why desire anything, why do anything?" It can also be put like this: "Is there a meaning in my life that will not be annihilated by the death that inevitably awaits me?"

For all his ambition to change the world by his teaching, Tolstoy shows in his later stories how deeply troubled he remained by these questions, which he tried repeatedly to answer for others. Late in life he remarked to Gorky: "If a man has learned to think, no matter what he may think about, he is always thinking of his own death. All philosophers were like that. And what truths can there be, if there is death?" It was this unappeasable anguish, and not the settled positions of his tracts, that nourished Tolstoy's later artistic works, in which the conversions are not rational and collective but mystical, sudden, unique, and the "answers" are almost beyond the reach of words.

In 1882 the imperial censorship refused to allow publication of *A Confession*, which Tolstoy had finished in 1880, but it was already circulating in thousands of handwritten copies and was eventually printed in Geneva in 1884, through the efforts of Vladimir Chertkov, Tolstoy's first and most active disciple. Chertkov, a wealthy young landowner and horse-guards officer, met Tolstoy in 1883 and immediately fell under the influence of his new ideas. After *A Confession*, Tolstoy had begun to write moral tales intended for the people. The first was *What Men Live By* (1881), a parable set in realistic peasant circumstances, in which the archangel Michael, exiled temporarily by God, can only return to heaven once he has learned three things: what is given to man, what is not given to man, and what men live by. Some of the other stories have equally moralizing titles: *Where Love Is, God Is; Evil Allures, but Good Endures; A Spark Neglected Burns the House; How Much Land Does a Man Need?* In 1885, on Tolstoy's initiative, Chertkov founded and financed a publishing house called The Mediator in order to make the stories available to the people in inexpensive illustrated editions.

These stories were meant to embody simple Christian moral principles in the simplest style possible, but in fact they cost Tolstoy a great deal of work. Thirty-seven manuscript versions of *What Men Live By* were found among his papers. He was, in a sense, relearning his craft. Like *The Prisoner of the Caucasus*, the popular tales occupy a middle position between his earlier expansive and inclusive realism and the later stories collected here. They were experimental, the work on them dominated by questions of form. That may seem surprising in the light of Tolstoy's obsession with truth and scant respect for formalists and formalism in the arts ("You're an inventor," he once said to Gorky, meaning it as a criticism). But he was always concerned with form and formal innovation, though never for its own sake. There is a revealing comment in his diary for 20 January 1890: "Strange thing this concern with perfection of form. It is not in vain. Not in vain when the content is good.—If Gogol had written his comedy [*The Inspector General*] summarily, weakly, it would not have been read by a millionth of those who have now read it. One must sharpen an artistic work so that it penetrates. And sharpening it means making it artistically perfect . . ." Mirsky comments in his *History:* "It is quite wrong to affirm that in any literary sense the change that overcame Tolstoy about 1880 was a fall. He remained forever, not only the supreme writer, but the supreme craftsman of Russian letters."

Tolstoy's later ideal, the model of "universal ancient art" by which he proposed to measure all narratives, including his own, was the story of Joseph from the book of Genesis. In *What Is Art?* he explains why:

> In the narrative of Joseph there was no need to describe in detail, as is done nowadays, Joseph's blood-stained clothes, Jacob's dwelling and clothes, and the pose and attire of Potiphar's wife when, straightening a bracelet on her left arm, she said, "Come to me," and so on, because the feeling contained in this story is so strong that all details except the most necessary—for instance, that Joseph went into the next room to weep—all details are superfluous and would only hinder the conveying of the feeling, and therefore this story is accessible to all people, it touches people of all nations, ranks, ages, has come down to our time, and will live on for thousands of years. But take the details from the best novels of our time and what will remain?

Yet Tolstoy was unable to achieve that ideal even in the plainest of his later stories. On the contrary, everywhere in them we find the most precisely observed details of time and place, a concentration on the particular, on sights and smells, on the gestures and intonations of characters—on all that was so specific to Tolstoy's genius, to his extraordinary sensual memory and gift of concrete realization. If that were taken away, there would indeed remain a core of universal human experience—Tolstoy was not interested in the topical issues of his time and almost never wrote about them—but there would not be that poetry of reality which characterized his artistic works from the very beginning and reached perhaps its highest point in his last major work, *Hadji Murat.*

In *What Is Art?* Tolstoy discards "the all-confusing concept of beauty" and defines art as "that human activity which consists in one man's consciously conveying to others, by certain external signs, the feelings he has experienced, and in others being infected by those feelings and also experiencing them." The metaphor of infection has a quality of physical closeness, even of impingement, about it: infection does not require the consent of the infected. But art is also the creation of an image held up for contemplation, and contemplation implies distance and the freedom of the contemplator. The formal qualities of the work create the distance necessary for contemplation. In *The Kreutzer Sonata*, a story that dramatizes an attempt at "infection" in Tolstoy's sense, distance is created by the narrator, a fellow passenger on the train, a curious but passive listener, who throws the would-be infector, Pozdnyshev, into high relief. And it is the vivid, contradictory, pathetic figure of Pozdnyshev that Tolstoy finally holds up to us (and to himself) as a sign.

Even *The Prisoner of the Caucasus*, a story meant for peasant school-children, is more self-consciously literary than it seems. It is a deliberately anti-romantic retelling of Alexander Pushkin's romantic poem of the same title, written in 1822. Pushkin tells the story of a world-weary, Byronic Russian officer taken prisoner by the Caucasian mountaineers. When a beautiful Circassian girl falls in love with him, he is too jaded to respond. In the end she helps him to escape and then throws herself into a mountain torrent and drowns. Tolstoy's hero is a sturdy, practical fellow with the rather crude, physiological name of Zhilin, which comes from the word for sinew. His fat fellow prisoner is Kostylin, whose name comes from the word for crutch. The Circassian beauty is turned into the thirteen-year-old Dina, who likes Zhilin because he makes dolls for her. The polemic of this near-parody has little to do with educating peasant children and much to do with Tolstoy's own literary stance and temperament.

The second piece in the collection, *The Diary of a Madman,* also borrows its title from an earlier literary work, Nikolai Gogol's hallucinatory tale of the petty clerk Mr. Poprishchin. But they have only the title in common. In fact, Tolstoy first called his story *The Diary of a Non-madman,* to mark his distance from Gogol and assert the actual sanity of his self-declared madman. The theme and the experience behind it were of profound significance for him. The first draft dates to 1884. He returned to it a number of times between 1887 and 1903, but left it unfinished. The fragment, which Mirsky considered "the most genuinely mystical" of Tolstoy's writings, recounts a crisis close to the one described in *A Confession*, but closer still to something that actually happened to Tolstoy in 1869, when he, like his hero, was cheerfully travelling to Penza to buy an estate and stopped for the night in Arzamas. Tolstoy wrote to his wife on 4 September 1869: "The day before yesterday I spent the night in Arzamas, and an extraordinary thing happened to me. At two o'clock in the morning, a strange anxiety, a fear, a terror such as I have never before experienced came over me. I'll tell you the details later, but never have I known such painful sensations . . ." In the story, Tolstoy develops that one incident and attempts to find a resolution for its metaphysical anguish. There was an even earlier experience, however, that was a prelude to the night in Arzamas and the crisis of *A Confession*. This was the death of his brother Nikolai in the southern French town of Hyères, where he was being treated for tuberculosis. In September 1860 Tolstoy visited him and in a letter described his death and burial as "the most painful impression of my life." The confrontation with the mystery of death became a central theme of his later work.

Rumination on the same themes, places, and even moments over long stretches of time is typical of Tolstoy. The presence of the Caucasus in his work is a good example of it. He first went to the Caucasus as a volunteer in 1851, to join Nikolai, who was on active duty there. He happened to be in Tiflis in December of that same year when the Avar chief Hadji Murat came over to the Russians, an act he condemned at the time as base. In 1853 he wrote his first story about the war in the Caucasus, *The Raid*, describing the destruction of a Chechen village by the Russian army; in 1855 he described another Russian tactic against the mountaineers in *The Woodfelling*. From 1852 to 1862, he worked at his novel *The Cossacks*, portraying the failed attempt of a self-conscious young Russian officer to enter into the unreflecting, natural life of the Cossacks who manned the line of fortresses against the Chechens in the mountains. In 1872 he returned to the same setting in *The Prisoner of the Caucasus*. And, finally, in 1896 he began work on *Hadji Murat*, which, incidentally, contains another version of the raid that formed the subject of his first story (the earlier version had been somewhat cut by the censors).

The Devil (1889), a story of sexual obsession, also had roots in

Tolstoy's past: the relations of his hero Irtenev with the peasant woman Stepanida are based on Tolstoy's own relations, described in detail in his diary, with a married peasant woman on his estate, in the years prior to his marriage in 1862. Similarly, the brief story *After the Ball*, written in 1903, was based on an incident that had occurred with Tolstoy himself when he was living in Kazan in the 1840s. So, too, the blizzard in *Master and Man* (1895) is a variant of *The Snowstorm*, written in 1856.

Tolstoy's religious ambitions, which came to dominate his public life after 1880, were also not the result of his "conversion," but had long been brewing in him. As early as March 1855, he wrote in his diary:

> Yesterday a conversation on the divine and faith led me to a great, an immense thought, to the realization of which I feel capable of devoting my life.—This thought is to found a new religion corresponding to the evolution of humanity, a religion of Christ, but stripped of faith and mysteries, a practical religion which promises no future blessedness, but grants blessedness on earth . . . To act *consciously* for the union of men with the help of religion, that is the basis of a thought which, I hope, will sustain me.

There could be no clearer statement of the programme he developed during the last decades of his life. Mirsky rightly observes:

> From the very beginning we cannot fail to discern in him an obstinate search for a rational meaning to life; a confidence in the powers of common sense and his own reason; contempt for modern civilization with its "artificial" multiplication of needs; a deeply rooted irreverence for all the functions and conventions of State and Society; a sovereign disregard for accepted opinions and scientific and literary "good form"; and a pronounced tendency to teach.

Of the eleven stories in this collection, only four were published in Tolstoy's lifetime: *The Prisoner of the Caucasus*, *The Death of Ivan Ilyich*, *The Kreutzer Sonata*, and *Master and Man*. The others first appeared in the volumes of his posthumous writings edited and published by Vladimir Chertkov in 1911–12. Some of the stories were finished relatively quickly (*After the Ball* and *Alyosha the Pot* each in a single day); some, like *Father Sergius, The Forged Coupon,* and *Hadji Murat,* he worked at for many years. His reluctance to publish had several reasons: disputes between his wife and Chertkov over the rights to his work; concerns about the censorship (*The Kreutzer Sonata,* written in 1887–89, was published in 1891 only after Tolstoy's wife personally petitioned the emperor); and a feeling of guilt for concerning himself with art at all (after finishing *Master and Man,* one of his most perfect stories, he wrote in his diary: "I am ashamed to have wasted my time on such stuff ").

The Death of Ivan Ilyich was the first work Tolstoy published after the crisis described in *A Confession.* Written between 1884 and 1886, at the same time as his stories for the people, it shows clearly both a continuity with his earlier work and the artistic changes that resulted from his "conversion." The power of concrete evocation is the same, but there is a new brevity, rapidity, and concentration on essentials, an increased formality of construction underscoring the main idea, and a cast of characters not drawn from Tolstoy's own social milieu. The protagonists of Tolstoy's earlier works were more or less openly autobiographical: Nikolenka Irtenev in the early trilogy *Childhood, Boyhood, and Youth,* Olenin in *The Cossacks,* Pierre Bezukhov in *War and Peace,* Levin in *Anna Karenina.* They were self-conscious men, seekers of truth, concerned with their own inner development. The protagonist of *The Death of Ivan Ilyich* is a banal and totally unreflecting man, a state functionary, and, worst of all for Tolstoy, a judge. The germ of the story came from the sudden death in 1881, at the age of forty-five, of a certain Ivan Ilyich Mechnikov, a prosecutor in the city of Tula, about eight miles from Tolstoy's estate. He had visited Tolstoy once, and in fact Tolstoy had found him an unusual man. In the story, however, he makes him "most ordinary," heaps him with scorn and irony, and then, through a simple but powerful inversion from outside to inside, brings him to an extraordinary transformation. The story ends where it began, but with everything changed. In *The Good in the Teaching of Tolstoy and Nietzsche,* the Russian philosopher Lev Shestov wrote: "*The Death of Ivan Ilyich,* as an artistic creation, is one of the most precious gems of Tolstoy's work. It is a question mark so black and strong that it shines through the new and radiant colours of that preaching by which Tolstoy wished to make us forget his former doubts."

Master and Man, written ten years later, and with an entirely different cast of characters, this time drawn from village merchant and peasant life, is a variation on the theme of *The Death of Ivan Ilyich*. It is reminiscent of the popular stories in its setting, but is told with a gripping physical intensity and, in Mirsky's words, "with a sustained beauty of construction" that makes it one of Tolstoy's masterpieces. He isolates the merchant Brekhunov, as he does Ivan Ilyich, in the most extreme human situation, and, rightly, never explains the change that comes over him as he struggles to save his servant's life. "That's how we are," he says to himself in his usual businesslike way, and suddenly bursts into tears of joy.

Pozdnyshev in *The Kreutzer Sonata* and Irtenev in *The Devil* are also examples of Tolstoy's testing by extremes, but in their case the testing leads not to "light," but to the most terrible human darkness. *The Kreutzer Sonata* caused more of a public outcry than anything else Tolstoy wrote, owing to its frank treatment of sex. Tolstoy was accused of attacking the institution of marriage and corrupting the youth. (Incidentally, the United States Post Office, with an unusual show of erudition, refused to handle by mail any publication containing a translation of the story or excerpts from it.) Tolstoy's sympathizers, on the other hand, tried to separate him completely from the character of Pozdnyshev. In a diary entry in 1890, before the publication of the story, but after it had spread in manuscript, Tolstoy jotted down this response: "They think he is some sort of special man, and, according to them, there is nothing at all like that in me. Can they really find nothing?" The struggle Tolstoy portrays in *The Kreutzer Sonata* and in *The Devil* is not against institutions and conventions, but against sensual seduction and the resulting loss of personal freedom. And he links art and especially music with sexuality as forces of seduction. He himself was strongly subject to all of them.

Father Sergius, begun in June 1890 and worked on over the next eight years, presents another kind of testing, though it has some relation to the sexual stories. It tells about a young prince who abandons society to become a monk and hermit; what is tested in his life is pride—the pride of an aristocrat enrolled in the elite Cadet Corps, the pride of intellectual and military ambition, but also the pride that seeks spiritual perfection, the pride of self-conscious humility. Lev Shestov sees Father Sergius as a reflection of Tolstoy in his later years—famous, attracting visitors and disciples from all over the world, but aware in himself of his own "unworthiness." It is a story of repeated departures, which ironically keep bringing the old monk back to where the young guards officer began. In a striking way, it anticipates Tolstoy's final departure in November 1910, leaving his estate, his family, and the "Tolstoyans" in search of solitude. After a frustrated visit to the monastery of Optino, he fell gravely ill at the railroad station of Astapovo and died in the stationmaster's house.

Father Sergius is a good example of Tolstoy's later manner, with its quick tempo and concentration on essentials. In his *Reminiscences of Tolstoy*, Maxim Gorky records a moment that reveals the "secret" artistic pleasure Tolstoy took in writing it:

> One evening, in the twilight, half closing his eyes and moving his brows, he read a variant of the scene in *Father Sergius* where the woman goes to seduce the hermit: he read it through to the end, and then, raising his head and shutting his eyes, he said distinctly: "The old man wrote it well."
>
> It came out with such sincerity, his pleasure in its beauty was so sincere, that I shall never forget the delight it gave me at the time . . . My heart stopped beating for a moment, and then everything around me seemed to become fresh and revivified.

The perfect foil for characters like Pozdnyshev and Father Sergius is the hero of the little story *Alyosha the Pot*, a simple and obedient young peasant, a sort of holy fool, who lives and dies with a purity and inner peace that forever eluded Tolstoy and most of his characters. In his diary for 28 February 1905, Tolstoy noted with characteristic dismissiveness: "Wrote Alyosha, very bad. Gave it up." When the symbolist poet Alexander Blok read the story on its first publication in 1911, he noted in *his* diary: "One of the greatest works of genius I have read—Tolstoy's *Alyosha the Pot*." Mirsky agrees with Blok, calling the story "a masterpiece of rare perfection." There actually was a servant in Tolstoy's household nicknamed Alyosha the Pot, who worked as a helper to the cook and the yard porter. Tolstoy's sister-in-law, Tatyana Kuzminskaya, confessed in her memoirs that she remembered him only as an ugly halfwit.

Unlike the other stories collected here, *The Forged Coupon* does not concentrate on a single protagonist, but presents a whole series of characters—merchants, radical students, peasants, policemen, monks, sectarians, even the Russian royal family—all linked without knowing it by the consequences of a single petty crime. It is a perfect parable, circular in structure, which goes more and more deeply into evil until it reaches a turning point and doubles back into more and more good. The structure is intentionally abstract, but the abstraction is countered by a wealth of minute particulars, and the main characters—Stepan Pelageyushkin, Marya Semyonovna, the thief Vassily—have a remarkably vivid presence. It is all told in a brisk, matter-of-fact, sometimes unexpectedly humorous tone that heightens the drama of the events, as in the description of Vassily's prison break, narrated in brief, breathless phrases—one of the best escape scenes in literature.

In his diary for 19 July 1896, Tolstoy noted that, as he was crossing the ploughed fields that day, he came upon a crimson Tartar thistle that had been broken down by the plough. "It made me think of Hadji Murat. I want to write. It defends its life to the end, alone in the midst of the whole field, no matter how, it defends it." The novella begins and ends with that same encounter. Tolstoy worked on it from 1896 to 1904, with the express wish that it not be published in his lifetime. It testifies, as Michel Aucouturier has written, to "that which is most spontaneous and most obstinate in him," his irrepressible need for artistic creation. The symbol of the Tartar thistle thus acquires a more personal, unspoken meaning.

But even before the encounter with the thistle, the events of 1851 were stirring in him. On 29 May 1895 he mentioned in his diary that he was reading and enjoying the memoirs of General V. A. Poltoratsky, published in the *Historical Messenger* in 1893. Poltoratsky began his military career in the Caucasus and was a witness to some of the events described in the novella. Tolstoy not only drew from his memoirs, but included him as a character. M. T. Loris-Melikov, who later became minister of the interior, also appears as a character. Tolstoy took long passages from the transcripts of his conversations with the Avar chief, who told him his life story. He also made use of General F. K. Klügenau's journals and his letters to Hadji Murat, and in chapter XIV he transcribed the whole of Prince M. S. Vorontsov's letter to the minister of war Chernyshov, which he translated from the French. Documentary evidence was as important to him in writing *Hadji Murat* as it had been in writing *War and Peace*. As late as 1903, he asked his cousin Alexandra Alexeevna, who had been a lady-in-waiting at court, for details about Nicholas I, though his final portrait of the emperor is far less flattering than the one she gave him.

Tolstoy likened the technique of his narrative to "the English toy called a *peepshow*—behind the glass now one thing shows itself, now another. That's how the man Hadji Murat must be shown: the husband, the fanatic . . ." (diary for 21 March 1898). Not only Hadji Murat, but all the characters and events of the novella are shown in brief flashes, taking us from the clay-walled houses of a Chechen village, to a frontline fortress, to the regional capital at Tiflis, to the imperial palace in Petersburg, and back again; portraying Russians, Tartars, Cossacks, peasants, foot soldiers, officers, statesmen, Russian princesses, Tartar wives, the imam Shamil, the emperor Nicholas I. The story of the peasant conscript Avdeev illustrates the technique in miniature. We are introduced to him in the second chapter; in the fifth he is badly wounded in a chance skirmish; in the seventh he dies; in the eighth Tolstoy goes back to Avdeev's native village, to his parents, family squabbles, his drunken brother, his unfaithful wife. No more is heard of Avdeev; he and his family are quite irrelevant to the main story; but like the social comedy of the scenes in Tiflis and Petersburg, like the village scenes among the mountaineers, they go to make up the world of the novella. The composition is as inclusive as in *War and Peace*, if not more so, but rendered with an economy of means that is the final perfection of Tolstoy's art.

Few things written about the two centuries of struggle in Chechnya are as telling as the page and a half of chapter XVII, the briefest in the novella, a terse, unrhetorical inventory of the results of a Russian raid on a mountain village. Nowhere in Tolstoy's polemical writings is there a more powerful condemnation of the senseless violence of war. Moral judgement is not pronounced in the novella; it is implicit in the sequence of events, and in the figure of Hadji Murat, with whom Tolstoy identifies himself. He is present even where he is absent, as in the scenes in Petersburg, or in Shamil's stronghold, or in the carousing of Russian officers in the fortress. He is the immanent measure of human dignity in the novella.

Hadji Murat is a new kind of hero for Tolstoy. He is not a self-conscious seeker after the meaning of life; he is not a converted sinner to whom the light is revealed in extremis; he is not sensually enslaved, but also not a holy fool or innocent. And he has no fear of death. As a military leader, he first betrays the Chechens, then the Russians; he kills without hesitation or remorse. Yet he is also not a savage: he carefully performs his ritual duties as a Muslim, he shares unquestioningly in the traditional culture of his people, and he is fiercely loyal to what is most dear to him. He is a warrior and a natural man, who, in the words of the great chorus from Sophocles' *Antigone*, finds himself "pathless on all paths." The equity of Tolstoy's portrayal of his fate lends it a transcendent beauty, set off by the indifferent singing of the nightingales. This final scene, deliberately placed out of sequence, casts its light over the whole novella, and over the whole of Tolstoy's work.

RICHARD PEVEAR

The Death of Ivan Ilyich

AND OTHER STORIES

The Prisoner of the Caucasus

(A TRUE STORY)

I

A GENTLEMAN WAS serving as an officer in the Caucasus. His name was Zhilin.

A letter once came for him from home. His old mother wrote to him: "I have grown old, and would like before I die to see my beloved son. Come to me to say farewell, bury me, and then with God's help go back to the army. And I have found you a bride: intelligent, and nice, and there is property. If she is to your liking, perhaps you will marry her and stay for good."

Zhilin fell to thinking: "And in actual fact the old woman's doing poorly; I may not get to see her again. Why don't I go; and if the bride is nice, I might just get married."

He went to his colonel, obtained leave, said goodbye to his comrades, stood his soldiers to four buckets of vodka in farewell, and made ready to go.

There was war then in the Caucasus. There was no travelling the roads by day or by night. As soon as a Russian rode or walked out of a fortress, the Tartars either killed him or carried him off into the hills. And so it was arranged that twice a week an escort of soldiers would go from fortress to fortress. The soldiers went in front and behind, and people went in the middle.

It happened in the summer. At dawn the baggage trains assembled outside the fortress, the escorting soldiers came out, and they started down the road. Zhilin went on horseback, and the cart with his belongings went with the train.

There were sixteen miles to travel. The train went slowly; now the soldiers would stop, then a cart wheel would fall off or a horse would refuse to move, and they would all stand there waiting.

The sun had already passed noon, and the train had only gone half the way. Dust, heat, a scorching sun, and nowhere to take shelter. Bare steppe; not a tree, not a bush along the road.

Zhilin rode ahead, stopped, and waited while the train caught up. He heard them start blowing the horn behind, meaning they had stopped again. And Zhilin thought: "Why don't I go on by myself, without the soldiers? I've got a good horse under me; if I come across Tartars, I can gallop away. Or maybe I shouldn't? . . ."

He stood there pondering. Then another officer, Kostylin, with a gun, rode up to him on his horse and said:

"Let's go on alone, Zhilin. I can't stand it, I'm hungry, and it's so hot. My shirt is soaking wet." Kostylin was a heavy man, fat, all red, the sweat simply pouring off him. Zhilin thought a little and said:

"Is your gun loaded?"

"Yes."

"Well, let's go then. Only let's agree not to separate."

And they went ahead down the road. They rode over the steppe, talking and looking to both sides. You could see a long way all around.

Just as the steppe ended, the road entered a pass between two hills, and Zhilin said:

"We ought to ride up the hill and look around, otherwise they may well jump us from behind it and we won't see them."

But Kostylin said:

"What's the point of looking? Let's go on."

Zhilin did not listen to him.

"No," he said, "you wait down here, and I'll just have a look."

And he sent his horse to the left, up the hill. The horse under Zhilin was a hunter (he had paid a hundred roubles for her when she was a filly in a herd and had broken her himself); she carried him up the steep slope as if on wings. He reached the crest, looked—in front of him, two hundred yards away, stood mounted Tartars, some thirty of them. He saw them and started to turn back; the Tartars also saw him and dashed towards him, drawing their guns from their cases as they rode. Zhilin went dashing down the slope as fast as his horse could carry him, shouting to Kostylin:

"Get your gun out!" and himself thinking about his horse: "Sweetheart, bring me through, don't trip up, if you stumble, I'm lost. If I reach the gun, I won't let them take me."

But Kostylin, instead of waiting, cut and ran for the fortress as soon as he saw the Tartars. He lashed his horse now on one side, now on the other. All you could see through the dust was how the horse switched its tail.

Zhilin could see things were bad for him. The gun had ridden off; nothing could be done with a sabre alone. He sent his horse back towards the soldiers, thinking to get away. He saw six of them rushing to cut him off. There was a good horse under him, but under them there were still better, and they were racing to cut him off. He began to rein in, meaning to turn back, but the horse was already making straight for them and there was no stopping her. He saw a red-bearded Tartar on a grey horse approaching him. He was shrieking, baring his teeth; his gun was at the ready.

"Well," thought Zhilin, "I know you devils: if you take me alive, you'll put me in a hole and whip me. You won't get me alive."

Zhilin, though not a big man, was bold. He snatched out his sabre and sent his horse straight at the red Tartar: "Either trample him with my horse, or cut him down with my sabre."

But the horse did not carry Zhilin that far; he was fired at from behind and his horse was hit. The horse crashed to the ground at full speed, pinning down Zhilin's leg.

He tried to get up, but two stinking Tartars were already sitting on him, twisting his arms behind his back. He tore loose, threw them off, but three more jumped from their horses and started hitting him on the head with the butts of their guns. His eyes went dim and he reeled. The Tartars seized him, took spare saddle girths, tied his arms behind his back with a Tartar knot, and dragged him to the saddle. They knocked his hat off, pulled off his boots, felt him all over, took his money, his watch, tore his clothes. Zhilin turned to look at his horse. She, the dear thing, lay on her side as she had fallen and only thrashed her legs—they could not find the ground. There was a hole in her head and dark blood was spurting from it; the dust was wet with it for two yards around.

One of the Tartars went to her and started to remove the saddle. She kept thrashing—he drew his dagger and slashed her throat. There was a whistling in her windpipe, the horse shuddered, and steam came out.

The Tartars removed the saddle, the bridle. The red-bearded Tartar mounted his horse, the others seated Zhilin behind him on the saddle, strapped him to the Tartar's waist with a belt so that he would not fall off, and took him into the hills.

Zhilin sat behind the Tartar, swaying, his face knocking against the stinking Tartar back. All he saw in front of him was that robust Tartar back, a sinewy neck, and a shaved nape showing blue under the hat. Zhilin's head was wounded, blood had clotted over his eyes. And he could neither straighten up on the horse nor wipe off the blood. His arms were twisted so much that it hurt his collarbone.

They rode for a long time from hill to hill, waded across a river, came out on a road, and descended into a hollow.

Zhilin wanted to make note of the road they took him by, but his eyes were covered with blood and he could not move.

Dusk was falling. They crossed another river, started climbing a rocky hill, there was a smell of smoke, a barking of dogs.

They arrived at an aoul.* The Tartars all got off their horses, Tartar children came, surrounded Zhilin, squealed joyfully, started throwing stones at him.

A Tartar chased the children away, took Zhilin off the horse, and called for a hired man. A Nogai came, high-cheekboned, in nothing but a shirt. The shirt was in tatters, his whole chest was bare. The Tartar gave him some order. The man brought shackles: two oak blocks fixed to two iron rings, one ring with a clasp and padlock.

They untied Zhilin's arms, put the shackles on him, and led him to a shed, pushed him in and locked the door. Zhilin fell on dung. He lay there for a while, felt around in the darkness for a softer spot, and lay down.

* See glossary of Caucasian mountaineer words following *Hadji Murat*.

II

ZHILIN HARDLY SLEPT all that night. The nights were short. He saw light through a chink. Zhilin got up, dug at the chink to make it bigger, and began to look.

Through the chink he could see a road going downhill, to the right a Tartar saklya, beside it two trees. A black dog was lying on the threshold, a goat with kids was walking about, the kids wagging their little tails. He saw a young Tartar woman coming from the bottom of the hill in a loose, bright-coloured shirt, trousers, and boots, her head covered with a kaftan, and on her head a big tin jug of water. She walked, her back swaying, flexing, and led by the hand a little Tartar boy with a shaved head, in nothing but a shirt. The woman went into the saklya with the water, and yesterday's Tartar with the red beard came out, in a silk beshmet, at his belt a silver dagger, with shoes on his bare feet. A tall, black lambskin hat was pushed back on his head. He came out, stretched, stroked his red beard. He stood for a while, said something to the man, and went somewhere.

Then two boys rode by to water their horses. The horses had wet muzzles. Other little boys with shaved heads ran out in nothing but shirts, without drawers, gathered in a bunch, went to the shed, took a twig and began to poke it through the chink. Zhilin hooted at them: the little boys shrieked and went dashing away, their bare knees gleaming.

Zhilin was thirsty, his throat was dry; he thought, "If only they'd come and look in on me." He heard the shed being unlocked. The red Tartar came, and with him another man, smaller, darker. Bright black eyes, red cheeks, a small, trimmed beard; a merry face, always laughing. The dark one was still better dressed; his deep-blue silk beshmet was trimmed with braid. The dagger at his waist was big, silver; his shoes were of red morocco, also trimmed with silver. And over his thin shoes there were other, thicker ones. His hat was tall, of white lambskin.

The red Tartar came in, said something that seemed like abuse, and stood there; he leaned against the doorpost and kept fidgeting with his dagger, looking sidelong at Zhilin from under his eyebrows like a wolf. And the dark one—he was brisk, lively, moving as if on springs—went straight up to Zhilin, squatted down, bared his teeth, patted him on the shoulder, started jabbering something very quickly in his own language, winked, clucked his tongue, and kept repeating: "Kood uruss! Kood uruss!"

Zhilin understood nothing and said:

"Drink, give me a drink of water!"

The dark one laughed.

"Kood uruss," he kept jabbering in his own language.

Zhilin showed with his lips and hands that they should give him a drink.

The dark one understood, laughed, looked out the door, called someone:

"Dina!"

A girl came running, slight, thin, about thirteen years old, and her face resembling the dark one's. It was clear she was his daughter. Her eyes were also black, bright, and her face was pretty. She was dressed in a long, dark-blue shirt with wide sleeves and no belt. The hem, the bodice, and the sleeves were trimmed with red. Trousers on her legs, little shoes on her feet, and over the shoes other shoes with high heels; on her neck a necklace all of Russian fifty-kopeck coins. Her head uncovered, her braid black, and in the braid a ribbon, and the ribbon hung with charms and a silver rouble.

Her father told her to do something. She ran off and came back bringing a little tin jug. She gave Zhilin the water and squatted on her heels herself, all doubled up so that her shoulders were lower than her knees. She sat, opened her eyes wide, and looked at Zhilin as he drank, as if he were some sort of animal.

Zhilin handed the jug back to her. She leaped away like a mountain goat. Even her father laughed. He sent her somewhere again. She took the jug, ran off, brought flatbread on a round board, and again sat doubled up, not taking her eyes off him—looking.

The Tartars left and locked the door again.

A short time later, the Nogai came to Zhilin and said:

"Aida, master, aida!"

He also did not know Russian. Zhilin understood only that he wanted him to go somewhere.

Zhilin went in his shackles, hobbling, unable to take a step, his feet turning aside all the time. Zhilin followed the Nogai out. He saw a Tartar village, some ten houses, and their church with a little tower. Three saddled horses were standing by one house. Some boys were holding them by the bridles. The dark Tartar sprang out of that house and waved his hand for Zhilin to come to him. He laughed, kept saying something in his own language, and went back indoors. Zhilin went into the house. The room was nice, the walls smoothly covered with clay. By the front wall lay multicoloured feather beds, on the sides hung costly carpets; on the carpets—guns, pistols, sabres, all inlaid with silver. One wall had a small stove in it at floor level. The floor was earthen, clean, like a threshing floor, and the whole front corner was spread with felt; over the felt, carpets, and on the carpets, down pillows. And on the carpets sat Tartars in just their indoor shoes: the dark one, the red one, and three guests. They all had down pillows behind their backs, and before them, on a round board, millet pancakes, and melted cow's butter in a bowl, and Tartar beer—bouza—in a little jug. They were eating with their hands, and their hands were all covered with butter.

The dark one jumped up, ordered Zhilin to be seated to the side, not on a carpet, but on the bare floor, went back to the carpet, and offered his guests pancakes and bouza. The man seated Zhilin in his place, took off his outer shoes, put them by the door next to where the other shoes stood, and sat down on the felt closer to the masters; he looked at them eating and wiped his watering mouth.

The Tartars finished eating the pancakes, and a Tartar woman came in wearing the same kind of shirt as the young one and trousers; her head was covered by a scarf. She took away the butter and pancakes, and brought a nice little basin and a jug with a narrow spout. The Tartars first washed their hands, then folded them, sat on their heels, blew in all directions, and recited prayers. They conversed in their own language. Then one of the Tartar guests turned to Zhilin and began speaking in Russian.

"You were captured by Kazi Muhammed," he said, pointing to the red Tartar, "and he gave you to Abdul Murat," he pointed to the dark one. "Abdul Murat is now your master."

Zhilin was silent.

Abdul Murat began to speak, and he kept pointing to Zhilin, and laughing, and saying:

"Soldier uruss, kood uruss."

The interpreter said:

"He tells you to write home a letter, to have ransom sent for you. When the money comes, he will let you go."

Zhilin thought a moment and said:

"How much does he want as ransom?"

The Tartars talked it over, then the interpreter said:

"Three thousand coins."

"No," said Zhilin, "that I cannot pay."

Abdul jumped up, started waving his arms, and said something to Zhilin—still thinking he could understand. The interpreter translated, saying:

"How much will you give?"

Zhilin thought a moment and said:

"Five hundred roubles."

Here the Tartars began talking quickly, all at once. Abdul started shouting at the red one; he jabbered so that saliva sprayed from his mouth. But the red one only narrowed his eyes and clucked his tongue. They fell silent; the interpreter said:

"For the master five hundred roubles small ransom. He paid two hundred roubles for you himself. Kazi Muhammed owed him money. He took you for debt. Three thousand roubles, he cannot allow less. And if you do not write, in hole they put you, punish you with whip."

"Eh," Zhilin thought, "the more timid I am with them, the worse it gets." He jumped to his feet and said:

"And you tell that dog that if he tries to scare me, I won't give him a kopeck, and I won't write at all. I was never afraid of you dogs and never will be!"

The interpreter translated, and again they all began talking at once.

They jabbered for a long time, then the dark one jumped up and went over to Zhilin.

"Uruss," he said, "dzhigit uruss, dzhigit!" ("Dzhigit" means "fine fellow" in their language.) And he laughed. He said something to the interpreter, and the interpreter said:

"Give one thousand."

Zhilin stood his ground.

"I won't give more than five hundred roubles. And if you kill me, you won't get anything."

The Tartars talked for a while, sent the man somewhere, and kept glancing now at Zhilin, now at the door. The man came back, and behind him walked someone fat, barefoot, and in tatters. His feet were also shackled.

Zhilin gasped—he recognized Kostylin. He, too, had been captured. They were seated side by side; they began talking to each other, while the Tartars kept silent and looked on. Zhilin told what had happened to him; Kostylin told how his horse had stopped under him and his gun had misfired, and this same Abdul had caught up with him and taken him.

Abdul jumped up, pointed at Kostylin, and said something.

The interpreter translated that they both now had one master and that the one who paid the ransom first would be released first.

"See," he said to Zhilin, "you keep getting angry, but your comrade is peaceable; he wrote a letter home, they will send five thousand coins. And he will be fed well and will not be harmed."

Zhilin said:

"My comrade can do as he likes; he may be rich, but I am not rich. It will be as I said. Kill me if you wish, there won't be any profit in it for you, but I won't write more than five hundred roubles."

Silence ensued. Suddenly Abdul jumped up, fetched a little chest, took out a pen, a scrap of paper, and ink, pushed them towards Zhilin, slapped him on the shoulder, and pointed: "Write." He agreed to the five hundred roubles.

"Wait a minute," Zhilin said to the translator, "tell him to feed us well, clothe and shoe us properly, and keep us together—it'll be more cheerful for us—and remove these shackles."

He looked at the master and laughed. The master laughed, too. He listened to it all and said:

"I'll give them the best clothes: a cherkeska and boots fit for a wedding. I'll feed them like princes. If they want to live together, let them live in the shed. But to remove the shackles is impossible—they'll get away. I'll only remove them at night." He sprang over, patted Zhilin on the shoulder. "Yours kood, mine kood!"

Zhilin wrote the letter, but addressed it incorrectly so that it would not get there. He thought: "I'll get away."

Zhilin and Kostylin were taken to the shed, there they were given corn shucks, a pitcher of water, bread, two old cherkeskas, and some worn soldiers' boots. They must have pulled them off soldiers they had killed. For the night they removed the shackles and locked them in the shed.

III

ZHILIN AND HIS COMRADE LIVED like that for a whole month. The master kept laughing: "Yours, Ivan,[1] is kood—mine, Abdul, is kood." He fed them poorly—all he gave them was unleavened bread made from millet, baked like flat cakes, or else just unbaked dough.

Kostylin wrote home once more, kept waiting for the money to be sent, and moped. He sat in the shed for whole days and counted the days until the letter would come, or else slept. And Zhilin knew that his letter would not get there, but he did not write any more.

"Where could my mother get so much money to pay for me?" he thought. "She's lived mostly on what I send her. If she scraped up five hundred roubles, it would be the ruin of her. God willing, I'll get out of it myself."

He kept looking out, figuring out how he could escape. He walked about the aoul whistling, or sat doing some handiwork, fashioning dolls out of clay or weaving baskets from twigs. Zhilin was good at all sorts of handiwork.

Once he made a doll with a nose, arms, legs, and a Tartar shirt, and put the doll on the roof.

The Tartar women went for water. The master's daughter, Dina, saw the doll, called the women. They put their jugs down, looked, laughed. Zhilin took the doll down and gave it to them. They laughed but did not dare to take it. He left the doll, went into the shed, and watched what would happen.

Dina ran up, looked around, snatched the doll, and ran away.

The next day, at dawn, he saw Dina come out to the porch with the doll. She had dressed it in some scraps of red cloth and rocked it like a baby, singing something in her language. The old woman came out, scolded her, snatched the doll away, smashed it, and sent Dina somewhere to work.

Zhilin made another doll, still better, and gave it to Dina. Once Dina brought a little jug, set it down, squatted and looked at him, laughing and pointing to the jug.

"What's she so glad for?" Zhilin thought. He took the jug and began to drink. He thought it was water, but it was milk. He drank the milk.

"Good," he said.

How glad Dina was!

"Good, Ivan, good!" and she jumped up, clapped her hands, snatched up the pitcher, and ran away.

And after that she began to bring him milk every day on the sly. And then Tartars also made cheese cakes of goat's milk and dried them on the rooftops—so she secretly brought him these cheese cakes. And then the master also once slaughtered a sheep, so she brought him a piece of mutton in her sleeve. She dropped the things and ran away.

Once there was a big thunderstorm, and the rain poured down in buckets for a whole hour. All the rivers became muddy; where there had been a ford, the water was now seven feet deep, overturning stones. Streams flowed everywhere, the hills resounded with their noise. Once the thunderstorm passed, streams ran everywhere through the village. Zhilin talked the master into giving him a penknife, carved a shaft, some little planks, put blades on a wheel, and to the two sides of the wheel attached dolls.

The girls brought him some rags, and he dressed the dolls: one was a man, the other a woman. He tied them on and set the wheel in the stream. The wheel turned, and the dolls jumped.

The whole village gathered: boys, girls, women; the men came, too, clucking their tongues:

"Ai, uruss! Ai, Ivan!"

Abdul had a broken Russian watch. He called Zhilin, showed it to him, clucked his tongue. Zhilin said:

"Here, I'll fix it."

He took it, dismantled it with the penknife, laid out the parts; put them together again, gave it back. The watch worked.

The master was delighted, brought him his old beshmet, all in tatters, and gave it to him. He had no choice but to take it—at least it was good for covering himself at night.

After that the rumour went around that Zhilin was a master craftsman. People started coming to him from far-off villages: one to have the lock of a musket or a pistol fixed, another a watch. The master brought him tools: pincers, and gimlets, and a file.

Once a Tartar fell ill. They came to Zhilin:

"Go, treat him."

Zhilin knew nothing about treating ailments. He went, looked, thought: "Maybe he'll just get well by himself." He went to the shed, took some water, some sand, stirred it. In front of the Tartars, he whispered over the water and gave it to the sick man to drink. Luckily for him, the Tartar recovered. Zhilin began to understand their language a little. And those Tartars who got used to him would call out "Ivan! Ivan!" when they needed him, but some still looked askance at him, as at a beast.

The red Tartar did not like Zhilin. When he saw him, he frowned and turned away or swore at him. There was also an old man there. He did not live in the aoul, but came from the foot of the hill. Zhilin saw him only when he came to the mosque to pray to God. He was small, there was a white towel wrapped around his hat, his beard and moustaches— white as down—were trimmed, and his face was wrinkled and red as brick. His nose was hooked like a hawk's beak, his eyes were grey, angry, and he had no teeth, only two fangs. He used to walk in his turban, propped on a crutch, looking about like a wolf. He would see Zhilin, snort, and turn away.

Once Zhilin went down the hill to see where the old man lived. He went along the path, saw a little garden with a stone wall, behind the wall—cherry trees, peach trees, and a hut with a flat roof. He went closer; he saw beehives plaited from straw standing there, and bees flying, buzzing. And the old man was on his knees doing something by a beehive. Zhilin stepped up on something in order to see and his shackles clanked. The old man turned around—shrieked, snatched the pistol from his belt, fired at Zhilin. Zhilin barely managed to huddle behind a rock.

The old man went to Zhilin's master to complain. The master summoned Zhilin, laughed, and asked:

"Why did you go to see the old man?"

"I didn't do anything bad," said Zhilin. "I just wanted to see how he lived."

The master translated. And the old man got angry, hissed, jabbered something, his fangs stuck out, he waved his arms at Zhilin.

Zhilin did not understand it all, but he understood that the old man was telling the master to kill the Russians and not keep them in the aoul. The old man left.

Zhilin asked the master who the old man was. The master said:

"He's a big man! He was the foremost dzhigit, he killed a lot of Russians, he was rich. He had three wives and eight sons. They all lived in one village. The Russians came, destroyed the village, and killed seven of his sons. The one remaining son went over to the Russians. The old man also went over to the Russians. He lived with them for three months, found his son, killed him with his own hands, and escaped. After that he stopped making war and went to Mecca to pray to God. That's why he has a turban. A man who has been to Mecca is called a hadji and wears a turban. He doesn't like your people. He tells me to kill you; but I cannot kill you—I paid money for you; and besides, I've come to like you, Ivan; not only not kill, I wouldn't even let you go if I hadn't given my word." He laughed and kept repeating in Russian: "Yours, Ivan, is kood—mine, Abdul, is kood!"

IV

Zhilin lived like that for a month. By day he went about the aoul or did handiwork, and when night came and the aoul grew quiet, he dug in his shed. It was hard digging because of the stones, but he worked at the stones with the file and dug a hole under the wall big enough to get through. "I only need to know exactly where I am," he thought, "and in what direction to go. But the Tartars won't tell me."

So he chose a time when the master was away. After dinner, he went to the hill outside the aoul—he wanted to look around from there. But as the master was leaving, he told his son to follow Zhilin and not let him out of his sight. The boy ran after Zhilin and shouted:

"Don't go! Father told you no. I'll call people right now!"

Zhilin started persuading him.

"I won't go far," he said. "I'll just go up that hill: I need to find an herb—to treat your people. Come with me; I won't run away with shackles on me. And tomorrow I'll make you a bow and arrow."

The boy was persuaded; they went. The hill was not far by the look of it, but with shackles it was difficult; he walked, walked, and barely made it to the top. Zhilin sat down and began looking the place over. To the south, beyond the hill, he could see a hollow, a herd of horses moving about, and in the lowland another aoul. Next to the aoul, another hill, steeper yet; and beyond that hill—another. Between the hills a forest showed blue, and then more hills rising higher and higher. And above them all, white as sugar, stood the snow-covered mountains. And one snowy mountain stood higher than all the others, like a hat. To sunrise and to sunset—ever the same mountains; aouls smoked here and there in the hollows. "Well," he thought, "that's all their side." He began looking in the Russian direction: at his feet was the river, his aoul, the kitchen gardens around it. By the river, like little dolls, he could see women sitting, rinsing. Beyond the aoul a lower hill, and after it two more hills covered with forest; and between the two hills, a level space showed blue, and far, far away over this level space, something like smoke was drifting. Zhilin began to recall where the sun had risen and set when he was living at home in the fortress. He saw: our fortress must be exactly in that valley. There, between those two hills, he would have to make his escape.

The sun was setting. The snowy mountains were going from white to scarlet; it grew dark in the black hills; steam rose from the hollows, and that same valley where our fortress must be burned like fire in the setting sun. Zhilin began to peer—something was hovering there in the valley, like the smoke of chimneys. And he fancied to himself that it was from that same Russian fortress.

It was already late. The mullah was calling. They were driving the herd—the cows were lowing. The boy kept urging him: "Let's go." But Zhilin did not want to leave.

They returned home. "Well," thought Zhilin, "now I know the place; I must make my escape." He wanted to escape that same night. The nights were dark—the moon was on the wane. Unfortunately, the men returned in the evening. They usually came back driving cattle with them and in cheerful spirits. But this time they drove nothing, but brought a slain man across a saddle, the red one's brother. They came back angry; they all prepared the funeral. Zhilin also came out to watch. They wrapped the dead man in linen, without a coffin, took him outside the village, laid him on the grass under the plane trees. A mullah came, the old men gathered, wrapped towels around their hats, took their shoes off, and sat on their heels in a row before the dead man.

The mullah in front, three old men in turbans behind him in a row, and behind them more Tartars. They sat looking down, silent. They were silent for a long time. The mullah raised his head and said:

"Allah!" (that is, God). He said this one word, and again they looked down and were silent for a long time; they sat and did not move. Again the mullah raised his head:

"Allah!" and they all said, "Allah!" and again fell silent. The dead man did not stir, and they sat as if dead. None of them stirred. The only sound to be heard was that of the leaves of the plane trees turning in the wind. Then the mullah recited a prayer, they all rose, picked up the dead man, and carried him. They brought him to a hole in the ground. The hole was not an ordinary one, but dug out underneath like a cellar. They took the dead man under the arms and legs, bent him double, lowered him down carefully, tucked him under the ground in a sitting position, and folded his arms over his stomach.

The Nogai brought some green rushes, they stuffed them into the hole, quickly filled it with earth, levelled it, and placed a vertical stone at the dead man's head. They trampled down the earth, and again sat in a row before the grave. They were silent for a long time.

"Allah! Allah! Allah!" They sighed and stood up.

The red one gave money to the old men, then stood up, took a whip, struck himself three times on the forehead, and went home.

In the morning, Zhilin saw the red one leading a mare outside the village and three men following him. They went out of the village, the red one took off his beshmet, rolled up his sleeves—such enormous arms he had—drew his dagger, and sharpened it on a whetstone. The men pulled the mare's head up, the red one came over, cut her throat, laid the mare down, and began to skin her, ripping the skin off with his fists. Women and girls came and started washing the guts and the inside. Then they cut the mare up and took the pieces to the cottage. And the whole village gathered at the red one's to commemorate the dead man.

For three days they ate the mare and drank bouza, commemorating the dead man. All the Tartars were at home. On the fourth day, at dinnertime, Zhilin saw that they were preparing to go somewhere. They brought horses, made ready, and left, some ten men, including the red one. Only Abdul stayed home. The moon was newborn, the nights were still dark.

"Well," thought Zhilin, "tonight we must escape," and he said so to Kostylin. But Kostylin grew timid.

"How can we escape? We don't even know the way."

"I know the way."

"But we won't make it in one night."

"If we don't, we'll spend the night in the forest. See, I've stored up some flatbread. Why do you want to sit here? It's fine if they send the money, but what if they don't raise enough? The Tartars are angry now, because one of them was killed by the Russians. There's talk about wanting to kill us."

Kostylin thought and thought.

"Well, let's go."

V

ZHILIN GOT into the hole and dug it wider, so that Kostylin could get through; and they sat and waited until the aoul quieted down.

As soon as the people in the aoul became quiet, Zhilin crawled under the wall and got out. He whispered to Kostylin: "Crawl through." Kostylin started crawling; his foot struck a stone and made a noise. The master had a watchdog—speckled and extremely vicious; his name was Ulyashin. Zhilin had been taming him with food beforehand. Ulyashin heard the noise, started barking, and came flying, with other dogs behind him. Zhilin whistled softly, flung him a piece of flatbread—Ulyashin recognized him, wagged his tail, and stopped barking.

The master heard him and started hushing from the saklya: "Hush! Hush! Ulyashin!"

Zhilin scratched Ulyashin behind the ears. The dog became quiet, rubbed against his legs, wagged his tail.

They went on sitting around the corner. Everything grew quiet; the only sounds were of sheep coughing in the barn and water running over pebbles below. It was dark; the stars were high in the sky; over the hill the young moon reddened, its sharp horns turned upwards. In the hollows the mist was white as milk.

Zhilin stood up and said to his comrade:

"Well, brother, aida!"

They set off; they had only gone a few steps when they heard a mullah singing on the roof: *"Allah! Bismillah! Al-rahman!"*[2] It meant people would be going to the mosque. They sat down again, hiding by the wall. They sat for a long time, waiting while the people passed by. Again it grew quiet.

"Well, God help us!" They crossed themselves and went. They went through the yard, down the steep slope to the river, crossed the river, went along the hollow. The mist was dense but low-lying, and over their heads the stars were clearly visible. Zhilin could tell by the stars which way to go. The mist was cool and made it easy to walk, only their boots were worn and uncomfortable. Zhilin took his off, abandoned them, and went barefoot. He hopped from stone to stone and kept glancing at the stars. Kostylin began to fall behind.

"Slow down," he said. "Curse these boots, my feet are all sore."

"Take them off, it'll be easier."

Kostylin went barefoot—that was still worse; he cut his feet on the stones and kept falling behind. Zhilin said to him:

"If you scrape your feet, they'll heal; if they catch up with us, they'll kill us—that's worse."

Kostylin said nothing; he walked on and kept groaning. They went through the hollow for a long time. They heard dogs barking to the right. Zhilin stopped, looked around, climbed the hill, feeling with his hands.

"Eh," he said, "we made a mistake, went too far right. There's another aoul here, I saw it from the hill; we'll have to go back and to the left up the hill. There should be a forest."

But Kostylin said:

"Wait a little at least, give me a breather—my feet are all bloody."

"Eh, brother, they'll heal. Hop lighter, like this!"

And Zhilin ran back, to the left, up the hill, to the forest. Kostylin kept falling behind and moaning. Zhilin shushed at him and kept going.

They climbed the hill. There it was—the forest. They went into the forest—thorns tore the remains of their clothes. They came upon a path in the forest. They took it.

"Stop!" There was a tramp of hooves on the road. They stopped, listened. It tramped like a horse and stopped. They set off—it tramped again. They stopped—it stopped. Zhilin crept out, looked at the path where it was lighter—something was standing there. A horse or not a horse, and on the horse something strange, not like a man. It snorted—

he heard it. "What a wonder!" Zhilin whistled softly—it shot off the road into the forest and went crashing through the forest like a storm, breaking branches.

Kostylin simply collapsed from fear. But Zhilin laughed and said:

"It was a stag. Hear his antlers breaking through the forest? We're afraid of him, and he's afraid of us."

They went on. The Seven Sisters had begun to set, morning was not far off. Whether this was the way to go or not, they did not know. It seemed to Zhilin that he had been taken down this road and that they had some seven miles more to go, but there was no sure sign, and it was night—he could not tell. They came to a clearing. Kostylin sat down and said:

"As you like, but I won't make it: my feet won't walk."

Zhilin started persuading him.

"No," he said, "I won't make it, I can't."

Zhilin got angry, spat, swore at him.

"I'll go alone then. Goodbye!"

Kostylin jumped up and went on. They walked for about three miles. The mist was still denser in the forest, you could see nothing in front of you, and the stars were barely visible.

Suddenly they heard a horse tramping ahead of them. They could hear it strike the stones with its shoes. Zhilin lay on his stomach and began listening to the ground.

"It's so—there's a horseman coming here, towards us."

They ran off the road, sat in the bushes, and waited. Zhilin crept out to the road, looked—there was a mounted Tartar coming, driving a cow, and muttering something to himself under his breath. The Tartar rode by. Zhilin went back to Kostylin.

"Well, God spared us—get up, let's go."

Kostylin started to get up and fell.

"I can't—by God, I can't; I've got no strength."

He was a heavy, plump man; he broke into a sweat; and the cold mist enveloped him in the forest, and his feet were scraped—he went limp. Zhilin started forcing him to get up. Kostylin screamed:

"Ow, that hurts!"

Zhilin froze.

"What are you shouting for? That Tartar's close by, he'll hear you."

And he thought: "He really has grown weak; what am I going to do with him? It's no good to abandon a comrade."

"Well," he said, "get up, and I'll carry you on my back, since you can't walk."

He hoisted Kostylin onto his back, held him under the thighs, went out to the road, and lugged him on.

"Only for Christ's sake don't squeeze my throat," he said. "Hold me by the shoulders."

It was heavy for Zhilin, his feet were also bloody, and he was tired. He kept bending over, adjusting, tossing Kostylin to get him higher, humping him down the road.

Evidently the Tartar had heard Kostylin scream. Zhilin heard someone coming behind them, calling out in his own language. Zhilin rushed into the bushes. The Tartar snatched his gun, fired and missed, shrieked in his own language, and galloped off down the road.

"Well," said Zhilin, "we're done for, brother! That dog will gather the Tartars now and come after us. Unless we can make a couple of miles, we're done for." And he thought about Kostylin: "What the devil made me take this block of wood with me? Alone I'd have got away long ago."

Kostylin said:

"Go alone. Why should you perish because of me?"

"No, I won't, it's no good to abandon a comrade."

He picked him up on his shoulders again and trudged on. He went like that for half a mile. It was all forest and no way out to be seen. The mist was beginning to disperse, and clouds seemed to be gathering; the stars were no longer visible. Zhilin was exhausted.

He came to a little spring by the roadside set with stones. He stopped and put Kostylin down.

"Let me rest and have a drink," he said. "We can eat some flatbread. It mustn't be far now."

He had just lain down to drink when he heard a tramping behind them. They rushed to the right, into the bushes, down a slope, and lay flat.

They heard Tartar voices; the Tartars stopped at the very place where they had turned off the road. They talked, then began siccing, as if they were setting on dogs. They listened—something was crashing through the bushes, some unfamiliar dog was coming straight for them. It stopped and began to bark.

The Tartars, also unfamiliar, rode down on them; they seized them, bound them, put them on horses, and rode back.

They rode for two miles, met the master Abdul with two more Tartars. They talked for a while, put them on his horses, and went back to their aoul.

Abdul no longer laughed or said anything to them.

They were brought to the aoul at dawn and set down in the street. Children came running. They hit them with stones, with whips, and shrieked.

The Tartars gathered in a circle; the old man from the foot of the hill also came. They started talking. Zhilin heard that they were deciding what to do with them. Some said they should be sent further into the hills, but the old man said: "They must be killed." Abdul protested, he said: "I gave money for them; I'll take ransom for them." But the old man said: "They won't pay anything, they'll only cause trouble. And it's a sin to feed Russians. Kill them and be done with it."

They dispersed. The master went up to Zhilin and started speaking to him:

"If the ransom is not sent to me within two weeks," he said, "I'll flog you to death. And if you try to escape again, I'll kill you like a dog. Write a letter, a nice, good letter!"

They were brought paper, they wrote letters. Shackles were put on them, and they were taken behind the mosque. There was a hole there twelve feet deep, and they were put into that hole.

VI

THEIR LIFE BECAME quite wretched. Their shackles were not removed, and they were not allowed to see the light of day. Unbaked dough was thrown to them, as to dogs, and water was lowered to them in a jug. The hole was stinking, stuffy, damp. Kostylin became quite ill, swollen, and ached all over; he groaned all the time, or slept. Zhilin also became dejected, he saw things were bad. And he did not know how to get out of it.

He started to dig, but there was nowhere to throw the dirt; the master saw it and threatened to kill him.

Once he was sitting on his haunches in the hole, thinking about the free life and feeling dull. Suddenly a flatbread fell right into his lap, then another, and cherries came pouring down. He looked up. Dina was there. She looked at him, laughed, and ran away. Zhilin thought: "Maybe Dina will help me?"

He cleared a little space in the hole, picked out some clay, and started fashioning dolls. He made people, horses, dogs; he thought, "When Dina comes, I'll toss them to her."

Only the next day there was no Dina. But Zhilin heard horses stamping, people riding by, and the Tartars gathered at the mosque, argued, shouted, and mentioned the Russians. And he heard the old man's voice. He could not make it out properly, but he guessed that the Russians had come close, and the Tartars were afraid they would enter the aoul and did not know what to do with the prisoners.

They talked it over and left. Suddenly he heard something rustling above. He saw Dina squatting there, her knees higher than her head, her necklace hanging down, dangling over the hole. Her eyes glittered like stars; she took two cheese flatbreads from her sleeve and threw them to him. Zhilin took them and said:

"Where have you been so long? I've made a whole lot of toys for you. Here, take them!" He began tossing them to her one by one. But she shook her head and did not look at them.

"Don't," she said. She sat silently for a while, and then said: "Ivan! They want to kill you." And she put her hands to her throat.

"Who wants to kill me?"

"My father. The old men are telling him to. And I feel sorry for you." Zhilin said:

"If you feel sorry for me, bring me a long stick."

She shook her head—meaning "impossible." He put his hands together, begging her:

"Dina, please! Dinushka, bring it!"

"Impossible," she said, "they'll see me, everybody's at home," and she left.

Zhilin sat there in the evening, thinking: "What's going to happen?" He kept looking up. He could see the stars, but the moon had not risen yet. A mullah called, everything became quiet. Zhilin had already begun to doze off, thinking, "The girl's afraid."

Suddenly clay poured down on his head; he looked up—there was a long pole poking at the edge of the hole. It poked and then began to descend, moving slowly down into the hole. Zhilin was overjoyed, seized it with his hand, pulled it down. It was a sturdy pole. He had seen it before on the master's roof.

He looked up: stars glittered high in the sky; and just over the hole Dina's eyes gleamed like a cat's. She bent down, her face at the edge of the hole, whispering:

"Ivan! Ivan!" and she waved her hands before her face, meaning "quiet."

"What?" said Zhilin.

"Everybody's gone, there are only two at home."

Zhilin said:

"Well, come on, Kostylin, let's give it a last try. I'll help you up."

Kostylin would not even hear of it.

"No," he said, "it looks like I'm not going to get out of here. Where will I go, if I don't even have strength enough to turn around?"

"Well, goodbye, then, and don't think ill of me." He and Kostylin kissed each other.

He grasped the pole, told Dina to hold it, and climbed up. Twice he fell off—the shackles hindered him. Kostylin supported him, and he somehow managed to climb to the top. Dina took his shirt in her little hands, tugged him with all her might, and laughed.

Zhilin pulled the pole out and said:

"Put it back in place, Dina. If they find it missing, they'll beat you."

She dragged the pole off, and Zhilin went down the hill. He came to the bottom, picked up a sharp stone, and began prising the lock from the shackles. But the lock was strong, he could not knock it off, and it was awkward work. He heard someone running down the hill, leaping lightly. He thought, "It must be Dina again." Dina came running, took the stone, and said:

"Let me."

She knelt down and began prising at the lock. Her arms were thin as twigs, she was not strong enough. She threw down the stone and started to cry. Zhilin set to work on the lock again, and Dina squatted next to him, holding him by the shoulder. Zhilin looked around, he saw a red glow lighting up to the left, beyond the hill, the moon was rising. "Well," he thought, "I'll have to go through the hollow and reach the forest before the moon rises." He got up and threw the stone away. Even with the shackles, he had to go.

"Goodbye, Dinushka," he said. "I'll remember you all my life."

Dina held him, feeling with her hands for where to put the flatbread. He took the flatbread.

"Thank you," he said, "clever girl. Who'll make dolls for you when I'm gone?" And he stroked her head.

Dina burst into tears, covered her face with her hands, and ran up the hill, leaping like a goat. All you could hear were the trinkets in her braid clinking against her back.

Zhilin crossed himself, put his hand on the lock of the shackles so that it would not clank, and walked down the road, dragging his foot. He kept glancing at the glow of the rising moon. He recognized the road. Going straight, it would be about five miles. He only had to reach the forest before the moon rose high. He crossed the river; the light beyond the hill grew paler. He walked down the hollow, glancing all the time: the moon was not yet visible. Now the glow brightened and on one side of the hollow it became lighter and lighter. The shade moved towards the hill, coming closer and closer to him.

Zhilin went on, always keeping to the shade. He was hurrying, but the moon was coming out still more quickly; the tops of the trees to the right were already lit up. He was very near the forest. The moon came from behind the hills—all was white, as bright as daytime. Every little leaf on the trees was visible. It was still and bright over all the hills, as though everything had died out. The only noise was the stream burbling below.

He reached the forest without meeting anyone. Zhilin chose a darker spot in the forest and sat down to rest.

He rested and ate a flatbread. He found a stone and tried to knock the shackles off again. He hurt his hands, but did not succeed. He got up and went along the road. He walked a mile and was totally exhausted—his legs hurt. He took some ten steps and stopped. "No help for it," he thought, "I'll drag on as long as I have strength. If I sit down, I'll never get up. I can't reach the fortress. When it gets light, I'll lie down in the forest, spend the day, and go on again at night."

He walked all night. He only happened upon two Tartar horsemen, but Zhilin heard them from far off and hid behind a tree.

The moon had already begun to grow pale, dew fell, dawn was near, and Zhilin had not yet reached the end of the forest. "Well," he thought, "I'll go thirty steps more, turn off into the forest, and sit down." He went thirty steps and saw that the forest was ending. He came out to the edge—it was quite light; the steppe spread before his eyes, and he could see the fortress, and to the left, quite close, at the foot of a hill, there were fires burning, dying out, smoke was spreading, there were people by the fires.

He looked more closely, he saw guns gleaming, there were Cossacks, soldiers.

Zhilin was overjoyed. He gathered his last strength and started down the hill. He thought, "God forbid a Tartar horseman should see me here in the open field; it's close, but I won't get away."

He had only just thought it—he looked: to the left stood three Tartars, some hundred yards away. They saw him and started towards him. His heart sank. He waved his arms, cried out with all his might:

"Brothers! Help! Brothers!"

Our men heard him. The Cossacks leaped on their horses. They started towards him, to cut off the Tartars.

The Cossacks were far away, and the Tartars were close. Zhilin gathered his last strength, held up the shackles with his hand, and ran towards the Cossacks, beside himself, crossing himself, shouting:

"Brothers! Brothers! Brothers!"

There were some fifteen Cossacks.

The Tartars became frightened. They began to stop before they reached him. And Zhilin went running to the Cossacks.

The Cossacks surrounded him, asked him who he was, what he was, where from? But Zhilin was beside himself, he wept and kept repeating:

"Brothers! Brothers!"

The soldiers ran out to them, surrounded Zhilin; one brought him bread, another kasha, another vodka; another covered him with an overcoat, yet another broke his shackles.

The officers recognized him and took him to the fortress. The soldiers were glad, comrades gathered around Zhilin.

Zhilin told them how it had all happened to him, and said:

"That's my going home and getting married for you! No, it's clearly not my fate."

And he stayed to serve in the Caucasus. And Kostylin was ransomed for five thousand only after another month. He was brought back barely alive.

1872

The Diary of a Madman

1883. 20 OCTOBER. Today I was taken to the provincial board for examination, and the opinions were divided. They debated and decided that I am not mad. But they decided that only because, during the examination, I used all my strength to keep from speaking out. I did not speak out because I am afraid of the madhouse; I am afraid that there they would keep me from doing my mad deed. They declared me to be subject to affects and something else of the sort, but—in my right mind; they declared it, but as for me, I know that I am mad. The doctor prescribed me a treatment, assuring me that if I follow his prescriptions strictly, it will go away. Everything that troubles me will go away. Oh, what I'd give to have it go away! It's too tormenting. I'll tell you in due order how and why this examination came about, how I lost my mind, and how my madness betrayed itself. Until the age of thirty-five I lived like everybody else, and there was nothing noticeable about me. Maybe only in early childhood, before I was ten, there was something in me similar to my present state, but even then only in fits, and not, like now, constantly. In childhood it came over me a little differently. Here is how.

I remember I was going to bed once, I was five or six years old. My nanny Evpraxia—tall, thin, in a brown dress, with a cap on her head, and with the skin hanging down under her chin—was undressing me and putting me to bed.

"Let me, let me," I said, and stepped over the rail.

"Well, lie down, lie down, Master Fedenka—look at Mitya, the good boy, already lying down," she said, nodding towards my brother.

I jumped into bed still holding her hand. Then I let go, kicked my feet under the blanket, and covered myself up. And it felt so good. I quieted down, thinking: "I love nanny, nanny loves me and Mitenka, and I love Mitenka, and Mitenka loves me and nanny. And Taras loves nanny, and I love Taras, and Mitenka loves him. And Taras loves me and nanny. And mama loves me and nanny, and nanny loves mama, and me, and papa, and we all love each other, and it's good for us all." And suddenly I hear the housekeeper run in and shout something crossly about a sugar bowl, and nanny answers crossly that she didn't take it. And it's painful for me, and frightening, and incomprehensible, and terror, cold terror, comes over me, and I hide my head under the blanket. But the darkness under the blanket doesn't make me feel any better. I remember how a boy was once beaten in my presence, and how he cried out, and how terrible Foka's face was as he beat him.

"You won't, you won't," he kept repeating, and he went on beating him. The boy said, "I won't." And the man kept repeating, "You won't," and went on beating him. And then it came over me. I began to sob and sob. And for a long time no one could calm me down. This sobbing, this despair were the first fits of my present madness. I remember it came over me another time when my aunt told us about Christ. She told us and was going to leave, but we said:

"Tell us more about Jesus Christ."

"No, I have no time now."

"No, tell us," and Mitenka begged her to tell us. And our aunt began telling us again what she had told us earlier. She told us that they crucified him, beat him, tortured him, and he kept praying and did not judge them.

"Why did they torture him, auntie?"

"They were wicked people."

"Yes, but he was good."

"Well, that will do, it's past eight. Do you hear?"

"What did they beat him for? He forgave them, but why did they beat him? It was painful. Was it painful, auntie?"

"Well, that will do, I'm going to have tea."

"Maybe it's not true, they didn't beat him."

"Well, that will do."

"No, no, don't go."

And again it came over me, I sobbed and sobbed, and then started beating my head against the wall.

That was how it came over me in childhood. But from the age of fourteen, when sexuality awakened in me and I gave myself up to vice, it all went away, and I was a boy just like all boys. Like all of us, raised on heavy, overabundant food, pampered, with no physical labour and with every possibile temptation for arousing sensuality, and in a milieu of equally spoiled children, the boys my age taught me vice, and I gave myself up to it. Then this vice was replaced by another. I began to know women, and so, seeking pleasure and finding it, I lived to the age of thirty-five. I was perfectly healthy, and there were no signs of my madness. Those twenty years of my healthy life passed in such a way for me that I now remember almost nothing of them and recall them now with difficulty and loathing.

Like all mentally healthy boys of my circle, I went to school, then to the university, where I took a degree in law. Then I was briefly in government service, then I became acquainted with my present wife and got married and lived in the country, as they say, raised children, managed the estate, and was a justice of the peace. In the tenth year of my marriage, I experienced the first fit since my childhood.

My wife and I had saved money from her inheritance and my activity as a notary and decided to buy an estate. I was very concerned, as I ought to have been, with increasing our wealth and with the wish to increase it in the most intelligent way, better than others. I found out wherever estates were for sale and read all the announcements in the newspapers. I wanted to buy in such a way that the produce or timber of the estate would cover the purchase, and I would get the estate for nothing. I was looking for the sort of fool who has no sense of these things, and once it seemed to me that I had found one. An estate with large forests was for sale in Penza province. From all I could learn, it appeared that the seller was just such a fool, and the forests would cover the price of the estate. I got ready and went. We went first by railway (I went with a servant), then by stagecoach. For me it was a very cheerful trip. My servant, a young, good-natured man, was as cheerful as I was. New places, new people. We travelled, felt cheerful. The place was some hundred and fifty miles away. We decided to travel without stopping, only changing horses. Night fell; we kept going. We began to doze. I dozed off, but suddenly woke up. I was afraid of something. And as often happens, I woke up frightened, animated—it seemed I'd never fall asleep again. "Why am I travelling? Where am I travelling to?" suddenly came into my head. Not that I didn't like the idea of buying an estate cheaply, but I suddenly fancied that there was no need at all for this long trip, that I would die here in a strange place. And it felt eerie to me. Sergei, my servant, woke up, and I took advantage of that and began talking with him. I talked about the local area, he answered me, joked, but to me it was dull. We talked about home, about how we'd make the purchase. And it was astonishing to me how cheerfully he responded. For him everything was good and cheerful, while for me it was all hateful. But all the same, while I was talking with him, it was a relief for me. But besides its being dull and eerie to me, I began to feel fatigue, a wish to stop. It seemed to me that to go into a house, to see people, to have tea, and, above all, to fall asleep would be a relief. We were approaching the town of Arzamas.

"Why don't we stop here? We can rest a bit."

"Fine."

"Is it far to town?"

"Five miles from that post."

The driver was staid, precise, and taciturn. He drove at a slow and dull pace. We went on. I fell silent, feeling relieved because I was looking forward to the rest ahead and hoped that there it would all go away. We drove on and on in the darkness, it seemed terribly long to me. We neared the town. The folk were all asleep already. Little houses appeared from the darkness, there was the sound of harness bells and horses' stamping, especially resonant, as happens near houses. Large white houses came along here and there. And it was all cheerless. I was waiting for the posting station, the samovar, and rest—to lie down. We drove up, finally, to some little house with a hitching post. The house was white, but it looked terribly sad to me. So much so that it even felt eerie. I got out quietly. Sergei briskly, energetically took out all that was needed, running and stamping on the porch. And the sound of his feet drove me to anguish. I went in, there was a little corridor, a sleepy man with a spot on his cheek—that spot seemed terrible to me—showed me to the main room. The room was gloomy. I went in and it felt still more eerie.

"Isn't there some little room where I could rest?"

"There's a bedroom. It's right here."

A clean, whitewashed, square room. How tormenting it was to me, I remember, that this little room was precisely square. There was one window, with a curtain—red. A table of Karelian birch and a sofa with curved armrests. We went in. Sergei prepared the samovar and made tea. And I took the pillow and lay down on the sofa. I didn't sleep. I heard Sergei drinking tea and calling to me. It was frightening for me to get up, frightening to drive sleep away and sit in this room. I did not get up and began to doze off. And I must indeed have dozed off, because when I came to myself there was no one in the room and it was dark. Again I was as wide awake as in the cart. I felt there was no possibility of falling asleep. Why have I driven here? Where am I taking myself? What am I running away from? I'm running away from something frightful and cannot do it. I'm always with myself, and it is I who am my own torment. I, here I am, all here. Neither the Penza estate nor any other will add to or take away anything from me. But I, I'm sick of myself, I can't stand myself, I torment myself. I want to fall asleep, to forget myself, and I can't. I can't get away from myself. I went out to the corridor. Sergei was sleeping on a narrow bench, his arm hanging down, but he was sleeping sweetly, and the attendant with the spot was sleeping, too. I had gone out to the corridor hoping to get away from what tormented me. But it came out with me and darkened everything. I felt just as frightened, maybe even more. "What is this foolishness?" I said to myself. "Why am I anguished, what am I afraid of?" "Me," the voice of death answered inaudibly. "I am here." Chills crept over me. Yes, of death. It will come, it's here, but it should not be. If I were actually facing death, I could not have experienced what I was experiencing, I would have been afraid then. But now I was not afraid, but I saw and felt that death was coming and at the same time felt that it should not be. My whole being felt the need, the right to live, and at the same time the happening of death. And this inner rending was terrible. I attempted to shake off this terror. I found a copper candlestick with a burned-down candle and lit it. The red flame of the candle and its size, slightly smaller than the candlestick, all said the same thing. There is nothing in life, but there is death, and it should not be. I tried to think about what interested me: my purchase, my wife—not only was there nothing cheerful, but it all became null. Everything was overshadowed by terror at my perishing life. I had to fall asleep. I lay down. But as soon as I lay down, I suddenly jumped up from terror. And anguish, anguish, such spiritual anguish as comes before vomiting, only spiritual. Eerie, frightening, it seems you're frightened of death, but then you recollect, you think about life, and you're frightened of your dying life. Somehow life and death merged into one. Something was tearing my soul to pieces and yet could not tear it. Once more I went and looked at the sleeping men, once more I tried to fall asleep, it was all that same terror—red, white, square. Something was being torn, but not coming apart. Tormenting, and a tormenting dryness and spite, not a drop of goodness did I feel in myself, but only a level, calm spite against myself and what had made me. What had made me? God, they say, God. Pray, I recalled. I hadn't prayed for a long time, some twenty years, and did not believe in anything, though for propriety's sake I prepared for and took communion once a year. I began to pray. Lord have mercy, Our Father, Hail Mary. I began to invent prayers. I crossed myself and bowed to the ground, looking around, afraid of being seen. It was as if this distracted me, I was distracted by the fear that I might be seen. I lay down. But I had only to lie down and close my eyes for the same feeling of terror to jostle me, to get me up. I couldn't bear it any more. I woke the attendant, woke Sergei, ordered the horses harnessed, and we drove on. In the open air and in movement, it got better. But I felt that something new had settled on my soul and poisoned my whole former life.

BY NIGHTFALL we reached the place. All day I had struggled with my anguish and overcome it; but there was a frightening residue in my soul: as if some misfortune had befallen me, and I could only forget it for a time; but it was there in the bottom of my soul, and it possessed me.

We arrived in the evening. The old steward received me well, though not joyfully (he was vexed that the estate was being sold). Clean rooms with soft furniture. A shiny new samovar. Big teacups, honey with the tea. It was all very nice. But my questions to him about the estate were reluctant, as if it was an old, forgotten lesson. It was all cheerless. I slept through the night, however, without anguish. I ascribed that to the fact that I had prayed again in the evening. And then I began to live as before; but the dread of that anguish hung over me ever after. I had to live without pause and, above all, in habitual conditions, like a student who, out of habit, without thinking, repeats the lesson he has learned by heart, so I had to live in order not to fall again into the power of that terrible anguish that had first appeared in Arzamas.

I returned home safely, not having bought the estate, because I didn't have enough money, and began to live as before, with the only difference that I began to pray and go to church. It seemed to me as before, but I now recall that it was no longer as before. I lived by what had been started before, I went on rolling with the former impetus along tracks that had been laid down before, but I no longer undertook anything new. And I now took less interest in the things started before. It was all dull to me. And I became pious. And my wife noticed it and scolded and nagged me for it. The anguish did not repeat itself at home. But once I went unexpectedly to Moscow. I made ready in the afternoon and left in the evening. There was a case being tried. I arrived in Moscow feeling cheerful. On the way I got into conversation with a Kharkov landowner about farming, banks, where to stay, the theatres. We decided to stay together at the Moscow Inn on Myasnitskaya and go to *Faust* that same evening. We arrived, I went into the small room. The heavy smell of the corridor was in my nostrils. The porter brought my suitcase. The floor maid lit a candle. The candle flared up, then the flame sank, as always happens. Someone coughed in the next room—probably an old man. The maid left; the porter stood asking if he should undo the straps on my suitcase. The flame revived and threw its light on the blue wallpaper with yellow stripes, a partition, a scratched table, a small sofa, a mirror, a window, and the narrow dimensions of the whole room. And suddenly the Arzamas terror stirred in me. "My God, how am I going to spend the night here," I thought.

"Undo them, please, my dear fellow," I said to the porter, so as to keep him there. And to myself, "Get dressed quickly and go to the theatre."

The porter undid the straps.

"Please go to the gentleman in number eight, my dear fellow, the one who arrived with me, and tell him I'll be ready presently and will come to him."

The porter left, and I hurriedly began to dress, afraid to look at the walls. "What nonsense," I thought, "why am I afraid like a child? I'm not afraid of ghosts. Yes, ghosts . . . it's better to be afraid of ghosts than of what I'm afraid of. Of what? Nothing . . . Myself . . . Well, nonsense." Anyway, I put on a stiff, cold, starched shirt, inserted the studs, put on a frock coat and new shoes, and went to the Kharkov landowner. He was ready. We went to *Faust*. On the way, he stopped to have his hair curled. I had my hair cut by a Frenchman, chatted with him, bought some gloves; everything was very well. I completely forgot the oblong room and the partition. It was also pleasant in the theatre. After the theatre, the Kharkov landowner suggested that we go and have supper. That was not my custom, but when we left the theatre and he suggested it to me, I recalled the partition and agreed.

We came home past one o'clock. I had drunk an unhabitual two glasses of wine, but I was cheerful. But as soon as we entered the corridor with its dimmed lights and I was enveloped by the hotel smell, cold terror ran down my spine. But there was nothing to do. I shook my friend's hand and went into the room.

I spent a terrible night, worse than in Arzamas, and only in the morning, when the old man had already begun to cough next door, did I fall asleep, not in bed, in which I had tried several times to lie down, but on the sofa. All night I had suffered terribly; again my soul and body had been painfully sundered. "I live, have lived, must live, and suddenly death, the annihilation of everything. Why life, then? To die? To kill myself at once? I'm afraid. To wait till death comes? I'm still more afraid. To live, then? What for? In order to die." I could not get out of this circle. I would pick up a book and read. For a moment I would forget myself, and then again the same question and terror. I would get into bed, close my eyes. Still worse. God made this. Why? They say: don't ask, but pray. All right, I prayed. I prayed now, too, again as in Arzamas; but there and afterwards I prayed simply, like a child. Now my prayer had a meaning: "If you exist, reveal to me why and what I am." I bowed down, recited all the prayers I knew, invented my own, and added: "So, reveal it." And I would grow quiet and wait for an answer. But there was no answer, as if there was no one to answer me. And I remained alone with myself. And I gave myself answers in place of the one who would not answer. So as to live in the future life, I answered myself. Then why this unclarity, this torment? I cannot believe in the future life. I believed when I did not ask with all my soul, but now I cannot, I cannot. If you existed, you would tell me, tell people. But if you don't exist, there is only despair. But I don't want it, I don't want it. I was indignant. I asked him to reveal the truth to me, to reveal himself to me. I did everything that everybody does, but he would not reveal himself. "Ask, and it shall be given you,"[1] came to my mind, and so I asked. It was not comfort that I found in this asking, but rest. Maybe I didn't ask, maybe I renounced him. "You make one step forward, he makes ten steps back." I didn't believe in him, but I asked, and still he did not reveal anything to me. I settled accounts with him and condemned him. I simply didn't believe.

THE NEXT DAY I tried as hard as I could to finish all my business during the day and avoid a night in the hotel room. I did not finish everything and returned home during the night. There was no anguish. My life, which had begun to change since Arzamas, was changed still more by this Moscow night. I became still less concerned with affairs, and apathy kept coming over me. My health began to fail. My wife demanded that I be treated. She said that my talk of faith and God came from illness. But I knew that my weakness and illness came from the unresolved question in me. I tried not to give way to this question and tried to fill my life with habitual conditions. I went to church on Sundays and feast days, I pre-pared for communion, I even observed fasts, having begun to do so after my trip to Penza, and I prayed, but more as a habit. I expected nothing from it, as if I did not tear up a bill of exchange and made claims when it was due, though I knew it was impossible to get anything for it. I did it just in case. And I filled my life, not with estate management—I was repulsed by the struggle it took; I had no energy—but with reading magazines, newspapers, novels, playing cards for small stakes, and the sole manifestation of my energy was hunting out of old habit. I had been a hunter all my life. Once in the winter a neighbour came with his hounds to go wolf hunting. I went with him. We arrived at the appointed place, put on skis, and went on. The hunt was not successful, the wolves broke through the battue. I heard it from far off and went through the woods, following the fresh tracks of a hare. The tracks led me deep into a clearing. In the clearing I found him. He leaped so that I could no longer see him. I went back. I went back through a big forest. The snow was deep, my skis sank, I got tangled in the brush. It grew more and more dense. I began to wonder where I was; the snow changed everything. And I suddenly felt that I was lost. Home, the hunters were far away, nothing could be heard. I was tired and all in a sweat. Once you stop, you freeze. If you keep walking, you lose strength. I called out, all was quiet. No one responded. I walked back. Again it wasn't right. I looked around. It was all forest, no telling east from west. I walked back again. My legs were tired. I felt frightened, stopped, and the whole terror of Arzamas and Moscow came over me, only a hundred times greater. My heart pounded, my arms and legs trembled. To die here? I don't want to. Why die? What is death? I wanted to question, to reproach God as before, but here I suddenly felt that I didn't dare, that I shouldn't, that I couldn't have accounts with God, that he had said what was needed, that I alone was to blame. And I began to pray for his forgiveness, and I felt myself vile. The terror did not last long. I stood for a short time, recovered myself, went in one direction, and soon came out. I wasn't far from the edge. I walked to the edge, to the road. My arms and legs were trembling in the same way and my heart was pounding. But I felt joy. I reached the hunters; we returned home. I was cheerful, but I knew that in me there was something joyful, that I would sort it out when I was left alone. And so it happened. I was left alone in my study and began to pray, asking forgiveness and remembering my sins. They seemed few to me. But I remembered them, and they became vile to me.

SINCE THEN I began to read the Holy Scriptures. For me the Bible was incomprehensible, tempting,[2] the Gospels moved me to tenderness. But most of all I read the lives of the saints. And this reading comforted me, presenting me with examples that it seemed more and more possible for me to imitate. Since that time the affairs of my estate and family interested me less and less. They even repulsed me. It all seemed not right to me. How and what would be right I did not know, but that which had been my life had ceased to be it. Again I learned that while buying an estate. Not far from us an estate was for sale on very profitable terms. I went there, it was all excellent, profitable. It was especially profitable that the only land the peasants owned was their kitchen gardens. I realized that they would have to harvest the landowner's fields for nothing in exchange for pasture, and so it was. I evaluated it all; it all pleased me out of old habit. Then I left for home, met an old peasant woman, asked her the way, talked with her. She told me about her poverty. I came home and, while telling my wife about the profits of the estate, I suddenly felt ashamed. It became loathsome to me. I said I couldn't buy the estate, because our profit would be based on people's poverty and misfortune. I said it, and suddenly the truth of what I said lit up in me. Above all the truth that the muzhiks want to live as much as we do, that they are people—brothers, sons of the Father, as the Gospel says.[3] Suddenly something that had long been aching in me tore free, as if it had been born. My wife got angry, scolded me. But for me it was joyful. This was the beginning of my madness. But total madness began still later, a month after that. It began with my going to church, standing through the liturgy, praying well and listening and being moved. And suddenly they gave me a prosphora,[4] then we went to kiss the cross, began jostling, then at the door there were the beggars. And suddenly it became clear to me that all this should not exist. Not only that it should not exist, but that it does not exist, and if this does not exist, then there is no death or fear, and the former rending in me is no more, and I am no longer afraid of anything. Here the light shone fully upon me, and I became what I am. If none of this exists, then first of all it does not exist in me. Right there on the porch I gave the beggars all I had with me, thirty-six roubles, and went home on foot, talking with the people.

1884–1903; UNFINISHED

The Death of Ivan Ilyich

I

$\mathcal{I}$N THE BIG BUILDING of the law courts, during a break in hearing the case of the Melvinskys, the members and the prosecutor met in Ivan Yegorovich Shebek's office, and the conversation turned to the famous Krasovsky case. Fyodor Vassilievich became heated demonstrating non-jurisdiction, Ivan Yegorovich stood his ground; as for Pyotr Ivanovich, not having entered into the argument in the beginning, he took no part in it and was looking through the just-delivered *Gazette*.

"Gentlemen," he said, "Ivan Ilyich is dead!"

"Can it be?"

"Here, read it," he said to Fyodor Vassilievich, handing him the paper still smelling of fresh ink.

Inside a black border was printed: "It is with profound grief that Praskovya Fyodorovna Golovin informs relations and acquaintances of the passing away of her beloved husband, Ivan Ilyich Golovin, member of the Court of Law, which took place on the 4th of February of this year 1882. The funeral will take place on Friday at 1 p.m."

Ivan Ilyich had been a colleague of the assembled gentlemen, and they had all liked him. He had been ill for several weeks; it had been said that his illness was incurable. His post had been kept open for him, but there was an understanding that, in case of his death, Alexeev might be named to his post, and to Alexeev's post either Vinnikov or Shtabel. So that, on hearing of Ivan Ilyich's death, the first thought of each of the gentlemen assembled in the office was of what this death might mean in terms of transfers or promotions of the members themselves or of their acquaintances.

"Now I'll probably get Shtabel's or Vinnikov's post," thought Fyodor Vassilievich. "It was promised to me long ago, and the promotion means a raise of eight hundred roubles, plus office expenses."

"I must now request my brother-in-law's transfer from Kaluga," thought Pyotr Ivanovich. "My wife will be very glad. Now she won't be able to say I've never done anything for her family."

"I thought he would never get on his feet," Pyotr Ivanovich said aloud. "What a pity."

"But what exactly did he have?"

"The doctors couldn't determine. That is, they did, but differently. When I saw him the last time, it seemed to me he'd recover."

"And I haven't visited him since the holidays. I kept meaning to."

"Did he have money?"

"It seems his wife has a little something. But quite insignificant."

"Yes, we'll have to go. They live terribly far away."

"From you, that is. Everything's far from you."

"See, he can't forgive me for living across the river," Pyotr Ivanovich said, smiling at Shebek. And they started talking about the long distances in town and went back to the session.

Apart from the reflections this death called up in each of them about the transfers and possible changes at work that might result from it, the very fact of the death of a close acquaintance called up in all those who heard of it, as always, a feeling of joy that it was he who was dead and not I.

"You see, he's dead, and I'm not," each of them thought or felt. Close acquaintances, Ivan Ilyich's so-called friends, involuntarily thought as well that it would now be necessary for them to fulfil the very boring obligations of decency and go to the funeral service and to the widow on a visit of condolence.

Closest of all were Fyodor Vassilievich and Pyotr Ivanovich.

Pyotr Ivanovich had been Ivan Ilyich's comrade in law school and considered himself as under obligation to him.

Having told his wife over dinner the news of Ivan Ilyich's death and his reflections on the possible transfer of his brother-in-law to their district, Pyotr Ivanovich, without lying down to rest, put on his tailcoat and drove to Ivan Ilyich's.

At the entrance to Ivan Ilyich's apartments stood a carriage and two cabs. Downstairs, in the front hall by the coatrack, leaning against the wall, was a silk-brocaded coffin lid with tassels and freshly polished gold braid. Two ladies in black were taking off their fur coats. One, Ivan Ilyich's sister, he knew; the other was an unknown lady. Pyotr Ivanovich's colleague, Schwartz, was about to come downstairs and, from the topmost step, seeing him enter, stopped and winked at him, as if to say: "Ivan Ilyich made a botch of it; we'll do better, you and I."

Schwartz's face with its English side-whiskers and his whole slim figure in its tailcoat had, as usual, an elegant solemnity, and this solemnity, always in contrast to Schwartz's playful character, had a special piquancy here. So thought Pyotr Ivanovich.

Pyotr Ivanovich let the ladies go ahead of him and slowly followed them up the stairs. Schwartz did not start down, but remained upstairs. Pyotr Ivanovich understood why: he obviously wanted to arrange where to play vint[1] that evening. The ladies went on upstairs to the widow, and Schwartz, with seriously compressed, firm lips and a playful glance, moved his eyebrows to show Pyotr Ivanovich to the right, to the dead man's room.

Pyotr Ivanovich went in, as always happens, with some perplexity about what he was to do there. One thing he did know, that crossing oneself on such occasions never did any harm. Concerning the need to bow at the same time, he was not quite sure, and therefore he chose something in between: going into the room, he began to cross himself and to bow slightly, as it were. At the same time, insofar as his moving hand and head allowed him, he looked around the room. Two young men, one a schoolboy, nephews apparently, were crossing themselves as they left the room. A little old lady stood motionless. And a lady with strangely raised eyebrows was saying something to her in a whisper. A reader in a frock coat, brisk, resolute, was loudly reading something with an expression that precluded all contradiction; the butler's helper, Gerasim, passing in front of Pyotr Ivanovich with light steps, sprinkled something on the floor. Seeing this, Pyotr Ivanovich at once sensed a slight smell of decaying corpse. During his last visit with Ivan Ilyich, Pyotr Ivanovich had seen this muzhik in the study; he had performed the duties of a nurse, and Ivan Ilyich had especially liked him. Pyotr Ivanovich kept crossing himself and bowing slightly in an intermediary direction between the coffin, the reader, and the icons on a table in the corner. Then, when this movement of crossing himself with his hand seemed to have gone on too long, he stopped and began to examine the dead man.

The dead man lay, as dead men always lie, with a peculiar heaviness, dead-man fashion, his stiffened limbs sunk into the lining of the coffin, his forever-bent head on the pillow, displaying, as dead men always do, his yellow, waxen forehead with the hair brushed forward on his sunken temples, and his thrust-out nose, as if pressing down on his upper lip. He had changed very much, had grown still thinner, since Pyotr Ivanovich last saw him, but, as with all dead people, his face was more handsome, and above all more significant, than it had been in the living man. There was on his face the expression that what needed to be done had been done, and done rightly. Besides that, there was also in that expression a reproach or a reminder to the living. This reminder seemed out of place to Pyotr Ivanovich, or at least of no concern to him. Something felt unpleasant to him, and therefore Pyotr Ivanovich crossed himself again hastily, too hastily, as it seemed to him, to conform to decency, turned and went to the door. Schwartz was waiting for him in the passage, his legs straddled, his hands playing with his top hat behind his back. One glance at Schwartz's playful, clean, and elegant figure refreshed Pyotr Ivanovich. Pyotr Ivanovich understood that he, Schwartz, was above it all and would not succumb to depressing impressions. His look alone said: the incident of the funeral service for Ivan Ilyich could in no way serve as a sufficient motive for considering the order of the session disrupted, that is, that nothing could prevent them from cracking a newly unsealed deck of cards that same evening, while a valet set up four as yet unlit candles; in general, there were no grounds for supposing that this incident could prevent us from spending that evening pleasantly. He even said so in a whisper to the passing Pyotr Ivanovich, suggesting that they get together for a game at Fyodor Vassilievich's. But Pyotr Ivanovich was evidently not fated to play vint that evening. Praskovya Fyodorovna, a short, fat woman, who, despite all her efforts to achieve the contrary, still broadened from the shoulders down, dressed all in black, her head covered with lace, and with the same strangely raised eyebrows as the lady who had stood facing the coffin, came out of her rooms with other ladies and, accompanying them to the dead man's door, said:

"The service will begin at once; please go in."

Schwartz, bowing indefinitely, stood there, apparently neither accepting nor declining this suggestion. Praskovya Fyodorovna, recognizing Pyotr Ivanovich, sighed, went up close to him, took him by the hand, and said:

"I know you were a true friend of Ivan Ilyich . . ." and looked at him, expecting some action from him that would correspond to those words.

Pyotr Ivanovich knew that, as there he had had to cross himself, so here he had to press her hand, sigh, and say: "Believe me!" And so he did. And, having done that, he felt that the result achieved was the desired one: that he was moved and she was moved.

"Come while it hasn't started yet; I must talk with you," said the widow. "Give me your arm."

Pyotr Ivanovich offered her his arm, and they went to the inner rooms, past Schwartz, who winked mournfully at Pyotr Ivanovich: "There goes our vint! Don't complain if we take another partner. Unless you join us as a fifth when you get free," said his playful glance.

Pyotr Ivanovich sighed still more deeply and mournfully, and Praskovya Fyodorovna gratefully pressed his arm. Having gone into her drawing room, upholstered in pink cretonne and with a sullen lamp, they sat by the table, she on the sofa, Pyotr Ivanovich on a low pouf with bad springs that gave way erratically under his weight. Praskovya Fyodorovna wanted to warn him that he should sit on another chair, but she found such a warning inconsistent with her position and changed her mind. As he sat down on this pouf, Pyotr Ivanovich recalled how Ivan Ilyich had decorated this drawing room and had consulted him about this same cretonne, pink with green leaves. Passing by the table and sitting down on the sofa (generally the whole drawing room was filled with knick-knacks and furniture), the widow caught the black lace of her black mantilla on the carving of the table. Pyotr Ivanovich got up to release it, and the pouf, freed from under him, roused itself and gave him a shove. The widow began to release the lace herself, and Pyotr Ivanovich sat down again, crushing the rebellious pouf under him. But the widow did not release it completely, and Pyotr Ivanovich got up again, and again the pouf rebelled and even gave a snap. When all this was over, she took out a clean cambric handkerchief and began to cry. The episode with the lace and the struggle with the pouf cooled Pyotr Ivanovich down, and he sat scowling. This awkward situation was interrupted by Sokolov, Ivan Ilyich's butler, with the report that the plot in the cemetery chosen by Praskovya Fyodorovna would cost two hundred roubles. She stopped crying and, glancing at Pyotr Ivanovich with the air of a victim, said in French that it was very hard for her. Pyotr Ivanovich made a silent gesture expressing the unquestionable conviction that it could not be otherwise.

"Smoke, please," she said in a magnanimous and at the same time broken-hearted voice, and she began to discuss the question of the price of the plot with Sokolov. Pyotr Ivanovich, lighting up, heard her asking in great detail about the prices of various plots and determining which should be taken. Besides that, having finished about the plot, she also gave orders about the choir. Sokolov left.

"I do everything myself," she said to Pyotr Ivanovich, pushing aside the albums that lay on the table; and, noticing that the table was threatened with ashes, she promptly moved an ashtray for Pyotr Ivanovich and said: "I find it false to claim that grief prevents me from concerning myself with practical matters. On the contrary, if anything can, not comfort . . . but distract me, it is my troubles over him." She took out her handkerchief again as if she was about to cry, but suddenly, as if overcoming herself, gave a shake and began to speak calmly:

"However, I have business with you."

Pyotr Ivanovich bowed, not allowing the springs of the pouf, which at once began stirring under him, to act up.

"During the last days he suffered terribly."

"He suffered very much?" asked Pyotr Ivanovich.

"Ah, terribly! The last, not minutes, but hours, he didn't stop screaming. For three days in a row he screamed incessantly. It was unbearable. I can't understand how I endured it. It could be heard through three doors. Ah! what I've endured!"

"And can it be that he was conscious?" asked Pyotr Ivanovich.

"Yes," she whispered, "till the last moment. He said farewell to us a quarter of an hour before he died, and also asked that Volodya be taken away."

The thought of the suffering of a man he had known so closely, first as a merry boy, a schoolmate, then as an adult colleague, despite the unpleasant awareness of his own and this woman's falsity, suddenly terrified Pyotr Ivanovich. He again saw that forehead, the nose pressing on the upper lip, and he felt afraid for himself.

"Three days of terrible suffering and then death. Why, that could come for me, too, right now, any minute," he thought, and he was momentarily afraid. But at once, he did not know how himself, the usual thought came to his aid, that this had happened to Ivan Ilyich and not to him, and that it should and could not happen to him, that in thinking so he had succumbed to a gloomy mood, which ought not to be done, as was obvious from Schwartz's face. And having reasoned thus, Pyotr Ivanovich calmed down and began asking with interest about the details of Ivan Ilyich's end, as if death was an occurrence proper only to Ivan Ilyich, but not at all to him.

After various discussions of the details of the truly terrible physical sufferings endured by Ivan Ilyich (these details Pyotr Ivanovich learned only by the effect of Ivan Ilyich's sufferings on Praskovya Fyodorovna's nerves), the widow evidently found it necessary to proceed to business.

"Ah, Pyotr Ivanovich, it's so hard, so terribly hard, so terribly hard," and she began to cry again.

Pyotr Ivanovich sighed and waited while she blew her nose. When she finished blowing her nose, he said:

"Believe me . . ." and again she fell to talking and told him what was evidently her main business with him; this business consisted in the question of how to obtain money from the treasury on the occasion of her husband's death. She made it seem that she was asking Pyotr Ivanovich's advice about a pension; but he saw that she already knew in the minutest detail things that he did not know, such as all that could be squeezed out of the treasury on the occasion of this death; but that she would like to find out whether it was not possible somehow to squeeze out more. Pyotr Ivanovich tried to think up some way, but, having thought a little and, for decency's sake, having scolded our government for its stinginess, he said it seemed that more was impossible. Then she sighed and obviously began thinking up some way to get rid of her visitor. He understood that, put out his cigarette, got up, pressed her hand, and went to the front hall.

In the dining room with the clock that Ivan Ilyich was so happy to have bought in an antiques shop, Pyotr Ivanovich met a priest and several more acquaintances who had come for the service, and noticed a beautiful young lady of his acquaintance, Ivan Ilyich's daughter. She was all in black. Her waist, which was very slender, seemed more slender still. She had a gloomy, resolute, almost wrathful look. She bowed to Pyotr Ivanovich as if he were to blame for something. Behind the daughter, with the same offended look, stood a rich young man of Pyotr Ivanovich's acquaintance, an examining magistrate, her fiancé as he had heard. He bowed to them dolefully and was about to go into the dead man's room, when from under the stairs appeared the little figure of Ivan Ilyich's schoolboy son, who looked terribly like him. He was a little Ivan Ilyich, as Pyotr Ivanovich remembered him from law school. His eyes were tearful and such as are found in impure boys of thirteen or fourteen. The boy, noticing Pyotr Ivanovich, began to scowl sternly and bashfully. Pyotr Ivanovich nodded to him and went into the dead man's room. The service began—candles, moans, incense, tears, sobs. Pyotr Ivanovich stood frowning, looking at the feet in front of him. He did not glance once at the dead man and throughout did not succumb to weakening influences and was one of the first to leave. There was no one in the front hall. Gerasim, the butler's helper, sprang out of the dead man's room, rummaged with his strong hands through all the fur coats to find Pyotr Ivanovich's coat, and held it for him.

"Well, brother Gerasim?" said Pyotr Ivanovich, just to say something. "A pity, isn't it?"

"It's God's will. We'll all come to it some day," said Gerasim, baring his white, even row of muzhik's teeth, and, like a man in the heat of hard work, briskly opened the door, hailed the coachman, helped Pyotr Ivanovich in, and sprang back to the porch, as if thinking about what else he might do.

Pyotr Ivanovich found it especially pleasant to breathe fresh air after the smell of incense, corpse, and carbolic acid.

"Where to?" asked the coachman.

"It's not late. I can still go to Fyodor Vassilievich's."

And Pyotr Ivanovich went. And indeed he found them at the end of the first rubber, so that it was timely for him to step in as a fifth.

II

THE PAST HISTORY of Ivan Ilyich's life was most simple and ordinary and most terrible.

Ivan Ilyich died at the age of forty-five, a member of the Court of Law. He was the son of an official who had made a career in Petersburg in various ministries and departments, of the sort that brings people to a position in which, though it becomes clear that they are unfit to perform any sort of substantial duties, still, because of their long past service and rank, they cannot be dismissed, and therefore they receive invented, fictitious posts and non-fictitious thousands, from six to ten, on which they live to a ripe old age.

Such was the privy councillor, the unnecessary member of various unnecessary institutions, Ilya Yefimovich Golovin.

He had three sons. Ivan Ilyich was the second son. The eldest had made the same sort of career as his father, only in a different ministry, and was already drawing near that age in the service at which this salaried inertia is attained. The third son was a failure. He had spoiled things for himself in various places and was now serving with the railways; his father and brothers, and especially their wives, not only did not like meeting him, but, unless from the utmost necessity, did not even remember his existence. The sister was married to Baron Greff, the same sort of Petersburg official as his father-in-law. Ivan Ilyich was *le phénix de la famille*,* as they said. He was not as cold and meticulous as the elder and not as desperate as the younger. He was between the two—an intelligent, lively, pleasant, and decent man. He was educated together with his younger brother in law school. The younger brother did not finish and was expelled from the fifth class. Ivan Ilyich finished his studies successfully. In law school he was already what he would be throughout his later life: a capable man, cheerfully good-natured and gregarious, but strict in fulfilling what he considered his duty; and he considered his duty all that was so considered by highly placed people. He was not ingratiating, either as a boy or later as an adult, but, from the earliest age he had had this quality of being drawn, as a fly is to light, to the most highly placed people in society, of adopting their manners, their views of life,

* The pride of the family.

and of establishing friendly relations with them. All the passions of child-hood and youth went by without leaving big traces on him; he had been given to sensuality and vanity and—towards the end, in the upper classes—to liberalism, but it was all within certain limits, which were correctly pointed out to him by his instinct.

In law school he had committed acts which had formerly seemed to him of great vileness and had inspired a feeling of self-loathing in him at the time he committed them; but subsequently, seeing that such acts were also committed by highly placed people and were not considered bad, he, without really thinking them good, forgot all about them and was not troubled in the least by the memory of them.

On leaving law school in the tenth rank[2] and receiving money from his father to outfit himself, Ivan ordered clothes from Charmeur,[3] hung a little medal on his watch chain inscribed *respice finem*,* took his leave of prince and tutor, dined with his schoolmates at Donon's,[4] and with a fashionable new trunk, linen, clothes, shaving and toiletry kits, and a plaid, ordered and purchased at the very best shops, left for the provinces to take a post as official on special missions for the governor, which his father had procured for him.

In the provinces Ivan Ilyich immediately arranged as easy and pleas-ant a situation for himself as his situation in law school had been. He served, made his career, and at the same time amused himself pleasantly and decently; from time to time his superiors sent him on missions to various districts, and he behaved himself with dignity with both those above him and those beneath him, and with precision and incorruptible honesty, which he could not but be proud of, he carried out the missions he was charged with, mostly to do with the Old Believers.[5]

In matters of service, despite his youth and inclination for light merri-ment, he was extremely restrained, official, and even stern; but socially he was often playful and witty, and always good-natured, decent, and *bon enfant*,† as his superior and his wife, with whom he was like one of the family, used to say of him.

There was a liaison in the provinces with one of the ladies who fas-tened upon the foppish lawyer; there was also a milliner; there were

* Look to the end.
† A pleasant fellow.

drinking parties with travelling imperial adjutants, and little trips to a remote back street after supper; there was also subservience to his superior and even to the superior's wife; but it all bore such a lofty tone of propriety that it could not be called by any bad words: it all merely fell under the rubric of the French saying: *Il faut que jeunesse se passe.** It was all done with clean hands, in clean shirts, with French words, and above all in the highest society, consequently with the approval of highly placed people.

So Ivan Ilyich served for five years, and then came changes in the service. New legal institutions appeared; new people were needed.[6]

And Ivan Ilyich became this new man.

Ivan Ilyich was offered a post as examining magistrate, and Ivan Ilyich accepted it, though this post was in another province and he had to abandon the relations he had established and establish new ones. Ivan Ilyich's friends saw him off, had a group photograph taken, offered him a silver cigarette case, and he left for his new post.

As an examining magistrate, Ivan Ilyich was just as *comme il faut*, decent, capable of separating his duties from his private life and of inspiring general respect as he had been as an official on special missions. The work of an examining magistrate was itself far more interesting and attractive for Ivan Ilyich than his previous work. In his previous work, he had found it pleasant to walk at an easy pace, in an undress uniform from Charmeur's, past trembling petitioners waiting to be received and officials envious of him, straight to the superior's office, and sit down with him for tea and a cigarette; but there had been few people directly dependent on his will. Of such people there had been only police officers and Old Believers, when he was sent on special missions; and he had liked to treat such people, who were dependent on him, courteously, almost in a comradely fashion, had liked to let them feel that here was he, who had the power to crush them, treating them in a simple, friendly way. There had been few such people then. Now, though, as an examining magistrate, Ivan Ilyich felt that everyone, everyone without exception, the most important, the most self-satisfied people—everyone was in his hands, and he needed only to write certain words on paper with a letterhead, and this important, self-satisfied man would be brought to

* Youth must have its day.

him as an accused person or a witness, and, if he was not of a mind to let him sit down, the man would stand before him and answer his questions. Ivan Ilyich never misused this power of his; on the contrary, he tried to soften its expression; but for him the consciousness of this power and the possibility of softening it constituted the main interest and attraction of his new work. In that work itself, namely in examinations, Ivan Ilyich very quickly adopted the method of pushing away from himself all circumstances not concerned with service, and investing even the most complicated case in such a form that, on paper, the case was reflected only in its external aspects and his personal views were entirely excluded, and, above all, the required formality was fully observed. This was a new thing. And he was one of the first people to work out the practical application of the statutes of 1864.

Having moved to a new town in the post of examining magistrate, Ivan Ilyich made new acquaintances, connections, behaved in a new way, and adopted a somewhat different tone. He placed himself at a certain dignified remove from the provincial authorities, but chose the best circle of magistrates and rich nobility living in the town, and adopted a tone of slight dissatisfaction with the government, moderate liberalism, and a civilized sense of citizenship. At the same time, without changing his elegant dress in the least, Ivan Ilyich, given his new duties, stopped shaving his chin and gave his beard the freedom to grow where it liked.

Ivan Ilyich's life came together very pleasantly in this new town as well: the society that cast aspersions at the governor was close-knit and agreeable; his salary was higher, and no little pleasure was added to his life by whist, which Ivan Ilyich began to play, having a capacity for playing cards cheerfully, for calculating quickly and subtly, so that generally he always came out the winner.

After two years of service in the new town, Ivan Ilyich met his future wife. Praskovya Fyodorovna Mikhel was the most attractive, intelligent, and brilliant girl of that circle in which Ivan Ilyich moved. Among other amusements and rests from his labours as a magistrate, Ivan Ilyich established light and playful relations with Praskovya Fyodorovna.

Ivan Ilyich, when an official on special missions, had generally danced; now, being an examining magistrate, he danced only as an exception. He now danced in the sense that, while belonging to the new institutions and of the fifth rank,[7] if it comes to dancing, I can demonstrate that in that line I can do better than others. So, from time to time, at the end of an evening, he danced with Praskovya Fyodorovna, and it was mostly during that dancing that he won Praskovya Fyodorovna's heart. She fell in love with him. Ivan Ilyich had no clear, definite intention of marrying, but when the girl fell in love with him, he put the question to himself. "In fact, why not get married?" he said to himself.

Miss Praskovya Fyodorovna was of good noble stock and not bad-looking; there was a bit of money. Ivan Ilyich might have counted on a more brilliant match, but this match was also good. Ivan Ilyich had his salary; she, he hoped, would have as much. A good family; she was a sweet, pretty, and perfectly respectable woman. To say that Ivan Ilyich married because he loved his bride and found her sympathetic to his view of life would be as incorrect as to say that he married because people of his society approved of this match. Ivan Ilyich married out of both considerations: he did something pleasant for himself in acquiring such a wife, and at the same time he did what highly placed people considered right.

And so Ivan Ilyich got married.

The process of marriage itself and the initial time of married life, with its conjugal caresses, new furniture, new dishes, new linen, went so well until his wife's pregnancy that Ivan Ilyich was already beginning to think that marriage not only would not disrupt that character of life— easy, pleasant, merry, and always decent and approved of by society— which Ivan Ilyich considered the very essence of life, but would even add to it. But then, with the first months of his wife's pregnancy, there appeared something new, unanticipated, unpleasant, painful, and indecent, which it had been impossible to anticipate and which it was impossible to get rid of.

His wife, without any cause, as it seemed to Ivan Ilyich, *de gaieté de coeur*,* as he said to himself, began to disrupt the pleasantness and decency of life: she became jealous over him without any reason, demanded that he court her, found fault with everything, and made unpleasant and crude scenes.

At first Ivan Ilyich hoped to free himself from the unpleasantness of this situation by that same easy and decent attitude towards life which had rescued him before—he tried to ignore his wife's state of mind and went on living as easily and pleasantly as before: invited friends to make

* On a whim.

up a game, tried to get away himself to the club or to see colleagues. But one time his wife began to abuse him so energetically in crude terms, and so stubbornly went on abusing him each time he did not fulfil her demands, obviously firmly resolved not to stop until he submitted, that is, sat at home and was just as bored as she was, that Ivan Ilyich became terrified. He realized that marital life—at least with his wife—was not always conducive to the pleasantness and decency of life, but, on the contrary, often disrupted them, and that it was therefore necessary to protect himself against these disruptions. And Ivan Ilyich began to search for ways of doing that. His work was the one thing that commanded Praskovya Fyodorovna's respect, and Ivan Ilyich, by means of his work and the duties it entailed, began to struggle with his wife, fencing off his independent world.

With the birth of the child, the attempts at nursing and various failures at it, with illnesses, real and imaginary, of the child and the mother, in which it was demanded that he participate, but in which he could understand nothing, Ivan Ilyich's need to fence off a world for himself outside the family became still more imperative.

As his wife became more irritable and demanding, Ivan Ilyich transferred the centre of gravity of his life to his work. He came to like his work more and became more ambitious than he had been before.

Very soon, not more than a year after his marriage, Ivan Ilyich understood that marital life, while offering certain conveniences, was essentially a very complex and difficult affair, with regard to which, in order to fulfil one's duty, that is, to lead a decent life approved of by society, one had to work out a certain attitude, as one did to one's work.

And Ivan Ilyich did work out such an attitude to marital life. He demanded of marital life only those comforts of dinner at home, housekeeping, bed, which it could give him, and, above all, that decency of external forms which was defined by public opinion. In the rest he sought a cheerful pleasantness, and if he found it, he was very grateful; if he met with resistance and peevishness, he at once retired to his own separate, fenced-off world of work and found pleasantness in it.

Ivan Ilyich was valued for his good service and three years later was appointed assistant prosecutor. The new duties, their importance, the possibility of calling anyone into court and putting him in jail, the public speeches, the success Ivan Ilyich had in these things—all this attracted him still more to his work.

Children came. His wife was growing more and more peevish and angry, but the attitude to domestic life worked out by Ivan Ilyich made him almost impervious to her peevishness.

After serving for seven years in the same town, Ivan Ilyich was transferred to the post of prosecutor in a different province. They moved, there was too little money, and his wife did not like the place they moved to. The salary was higher than previously, but life was more expensive; besides, two of the children died, and therefore family life became still more unpleasant for Ivan Ilyich.

Praskovya Fyodorovna blamed her husband for all the misfortunes that occurred in this new place of living. Most of the subjects of conversation between husband and wife, especially the children's education, led to problems that were reminiscent of quarrels, and quarrels were ready to flare up at any moment. There remained only rare periods of amorousness that came over the spouses, but they did not last long. These were islands that they would land on temporarily, but then they would put out again to the sea of concealed enmity that expressed itself in estrangement from each other. This estrangement might have upset Ivan Ilyich, if he had considered that it ought not to be so, but by now he took this situation not only as normal, but as the goal of his activity in the family. His goal consisted in freeing himself more and more from these unpleasantnesses and in giving them a character of harmlessness and decency; and he achieved it by spending less and less time with his family, and when he was forced to do so, he tried to secure his position by the presence of outsiders. The main thing was that Ivan Ilyich had his work. The whole interest of life was concentrated for him in the world of his work. And this interest absorbed him. The consciousness of his power, the possibility of destroying any man he wanted to destroy, his importance, even externally, as he entered the court or met with subordinates, his success before his superiors and subordinates, and, above all, his skill in pleading cases, which he was aware of—all this was a cause for joy, and, along with friends, dinners, and whist, filled his life. So that generally the life of Ivan Ilyich continued to go as he thought it should go: pleasantly and decently.

He lived that way for another seven years. The eldest daughter was already sixteen, one more child had died, and there remained the young schoolboy, a subject of contention. Ivan Ilyich wanted to send him to law school, but Praskovya Fyodorovna, to spite him, sent him to preparatory school. The daughter studied at home and was growing up nicely; the boy was also not a bad student.

III

So went Ivan Ilyich's life during the seventeen years following his marriage. He was already a seasoned prosecutor, who had turned down several transfers in expectation of a more desirable post, when a certain unpleasant circumstance unexpectedly occurred, which all but disrupted the tranquillity of his life. Ivan Ilyich was expecting the post of presiding judge in a university town, but Hoppe somehow beat him out and got the post. Ivan Ilyich became irritated, reproached him, and quarrelled with him and his immediate superior; he was treated with coldness and at the next promotions he was again passed over.

That was in the year 1880. That year was the hardest of Ivan Ilyich's life. In that year it turned out, on the one hand, that his salary was not enough to live on; and on the other, that everyone had forgotten him, and that what seemed to him the greatest, cruelest injustice in his regard, others saw as a perfectly ordinary matter. Even his father did not consider it his duty to help him. He felt that everyone had abandoned him, considering his position with its 3,500-rouble salary as most normal and even fortunate. He alone knew that, with the consciousness of the injustice done him, with his wife's eternal carping, and with the debts he began to run up, living beyond his means—he alone knew that his position was far from normal.

In the summer of that year, to lighten his expenses, he took a holiday and went with his wife to spend the summer in the country with Praskovya Fyodorovna's brother.

In the country, without work, Ivan Ilyich felt for the first time not merely boredom, but an unbearable anguish, and he decided that it was impossible to live like that, and that it was necessary to take decisive measures.

Having spent a sleepless night, pacing the terrace the whole time, Ivan Ilyich decided to go to Petersburg to solicit for himself, and, so as to punish *them* for not knowing how to appreciate him, to transfer to another ministry.

The next day, despite all the attempts of his wife and brother-in-law to dissuade him, he went to Petersburg.

He went with one purpose: to solicit a post with a salary of five thousand. He no longer adhered to any ministry, tendency, or kind of activity. He only needed a post, a post with five thousand, in the administration, in a bank, in the railways, in the empress Maria's institutions,[8] even in customs, but he had to have five thousand and to leave the ministry where they had not known how to appreciate him.

And, lo and behold, this trip of Ivan Ilyich's was crowned with astonishing, unexpected success. In Kursk an acquaintance, F. S. Ilyin, seated himself in first class and told him about a fresh telegram received by the governor of Kursk saying that there was to be an upheaval in the ministry in a few days: Ivan Semyonovich was appointed to replace Pyotr Ivanovich.

The proposed upheaval, besides its significance for Russia, had a special significance for Ivan Ilyich in that, by bringing forward a new person, Pyotr Petrovich, and, obviously, his friend Zakhar Ivanovich, it was highly favourable for Ivan Ilyich. Zakhar Ivanovich was a colleague and friend of Ivan Ilyich.

In Moscow the news was confirmed. On arriving in Petersburg, Ivan Ilyich found Zakhar Ivanovich and received the firm promise of a post in his former Ministry of Justice.

A week later he sent a telegram to his wife: "Zakhar to replace Miller I get appointment in first memorandum."

Owing to this change of personnel, Ivan Ilyich unexpectedly received an appointment in his former ministry that placed him two steps higher than his old colleagues, with a salary of five thousand, and three thousand five hundred for moving expenses. All his vexation with his former enemies and the entire ministry was forgotten, and Ivan Ilyich was completely happy.

Ivan Ilyich returned to the country cheerful, content, as he had not been for a long time. Praskovya Fyodorovna also cheered up, and a truce was concluded between them. Ivan Ilyich told her how he had been fêted in Petersburg, how all those who had been his enemies were put to shame and now fawned on him, how they envied his post, and, particularly, how loved he was in Petersburg.

Praskovya Fyodorovna listened to all this and pretended to believe it, and did not contradict him in anything, but only made plans for a new arrangement of life in the town they were moving to. And Ivan Ilyich was glad to see that those plans were his plans, that they agreed, and that his faltering life was again acquiring its true, natural character of cheerful pleasantness and decency.

Ivan Ilyich came for only a short time. On the 10th of September he had to take up his post, and, besides, he needed time to settle into a new place, to transport everything from the province, to buy, to order still more; in short, to arrange things as it had been decided in his mind, and almost exactly as it had been decided in Praskovya Fyodorovna's heart.

And now that everything had arranged itself so fortunately, and he and his wife agreed in their aims, and, besides that, lived together so little, they became such friends as they had not been since the first years of their married life. Ivan Ilyich had first thought of taking his family away at once, but his sister-in-law and her husband suddenly became so especially amiable and familial towards Ivan Ilyich and his family that, at their insistence, Ivan Ilyich left alone.

Ivan Ilyich left, and the cheerful state of mind produced by his success and his agreement with his wife, the one intensifying the other, stayed with him all the while. A charming apartment was found, exactly what the husband and wife were dreaming of. Vast, high-ceilinged reception rooms in the old style, a comfortable and grandiose study, rooms for his wife and daughter, a schoolroom for his son—everything as if purposely designed for them. Ivan Ilyich himself took up the decoration, chose the wallpaper, bought furniture, especially antiques, which he had upholstered in an especially *comme il faut* style, and it all grew, grew and approached that ideal which he had formed for himself. When it was half done, the result exceeded his expectations. He perceived what a *comme il faut*, exquisite, and by no means banal character it would all take on when it was finished. Falling asleep, he imagined how the reception room was going to be. Looking at the as yet unfinished drawing room, he already saw the fireplace, the screen, the whatnot, and those little chairs scattered around, those dishes and plates on the walls, and the bronzes, when they were all put in place. He rejoiced at the thought of how he would astonish Pasha and Lizanka, who also had a taste for these things. They would never expect it. In particular, he managed to find and buy cheaply antique objects that endowed everything with a particularly noble character. In his letters he deliberately presented everything as worse than it was, in order to astonish them. All this occupied him so much that even his new duties, fond as he was of the work, occupied him less than he had expected. During sessions he had moments of distraction: he was pondering what sort of cornices to have for the curtains, straight or festooned. He was so taken up with it that he often pottered about himself, even moved furniture and rehung curtains himself. Once he climbed a ladder to show the uncomprehending upholsterer how he wanted the drapery done, missed his footing, and fell, but, being a strong and agile man, held on and only bumped his side on the knob of the window frame. The bruised place ached for a while, but soon stopped. All this time Ivan Ilyich felt especially cheerful and healthy. He wrote: "I feel as if I've shaken off fifteen years." He hoped to finish in September, but it took until the middle of October. The result was charming—as not only he said, but all those who saw it said to him.

Essentially, though, it was the same as with all people who are not exactly rich, but who want to resemble the rich, and for that reason only resemble each other: damasks, ebony, flowers, carpets, and bronzes, dark and gleaming—all that all people of a certain kind acquire in order to resemble all people of a certain kind. And in his case the resemblance was such that it was even impossible for it to attract attention; but to him it all seemed something special. When he met his family at the railway station, brought them to his brightly lit, finished apartment, and a footman in a white tie opened the door to the flower-decked front hall, and they then went on to the drawing room, the study, and gasped with pleasure— he was very happy, showed them all around, drank in their praises, and beamed with pleasure. That same evening, over tea, when Praskovya Fyodorovna asked him, among other things, how he had fallen, he laughed and acted out how he had gone flying and frightened the upholsterer.

"It's not for nothing I'm a gymnast. Another man might have been badly hurt, but I just got a slight knock here; it hurts when you touch it, but it's already going away; a simple bruise."

And they began to live in their new lodgings, in which, as always, once they had settled nicely, there was just one room lacking, and on their new means, which, as always, were lacking just a little—some five hundred roubles—and it was very nice. Especially nice was the initial time, when all was not arranged yet and still needed arranging: this to buy, that to order, this to move, that to adjust. Though there were some disagreements between husband and wife, they were both so content and there was so much to do that it all ended without any big quarrels. When there was nothing more to arrange, it became slightly boring and lacking in something, but by then they were making acquaintances, habits, and life became full.

Ivan Ilyich, having spent the morning in court, would come home for dinner, and in the initial time his state of mind was good, though it did suffer slightly on account of the lodgings. (Each spot on the tablecloth, on the damask, a torn-out curtain pull, annoyed him: he had put so much labour into arranging it that any damage was painful to him.) But in general Ivan Ilyich's life went on as he believed life ought to go: easily, pleasantly, and decently. He got up at nine, had coffee, read the newspaper, then put on his uniform and went to court. There the yoke in which he worked was already broken in; he fell into it at once. The petitioners, the inquiries in the chancery, the chancery itself, the court sessions—public and administrative. In all this one had to know how to exclude all that was raw, vital—which always disrupts the regular flow of official business; one had to allow no relations with people apart from official ones, and the cause of the relations must be only official and the relations themselves only official. For instance, a man comes and wishes to find something out. As an unofficial man Ivan Ilyich can have no relations with such a man; but if there are relations with this man as a colleague, such as can be expressed on paper with a letterhead, then within the limits of those relations Ivan Ilyich does everything, decidedly everything he can, and with that observes a semblance of friendly human relations, that is, of politeness. As soon as the official relations are ended, all others are ended as well. This skill in separating the official side, not mixing it with his real life, Ivan Ilyich had mastered in the highest degree and through long practice and talent had developed to such a degree that, like a virtuoso, he sometimes allowed himself, as if jokingly, to mix human and official relations. He allowed himself that because he felt himself always capable of separating the official when he needed to and of discarding the human. For Ivan Ilyich this business went not only easily, pleasantly, and decently, but even with virtuosity. During recesses he smoked, drank tea, conversed a little about politics, a little about general matters, a little about cards, and most of all about promotions. And,

weary, but with the feeling of a virtuoso who has given a perfect perfor-
mance of his part as one of the first violins in the orchestra, he returned
home. At home, the daughter and mother had been out somewhere or
had someone else with them; the son had been to school, had prepared
his lessons with his tutors, and was diligently studying what they teach in
school. All was well. After dinner, if there were no visitors, Ivan Ilyich
sometimes read a book which was being much talked about, and in the
evening he sat down to work, that is, read papers, consulted the laws—
compared testimony and applied the laws to it. For him this was neither
boring nor amusing. It was boring when there might have been a game of
vint; but if there was no vint, it was still better than sitting alone or with
his wife. But Ivan Ilyich's real pleasure was in little dinners, to which he
invited ladies and gentlemen of important social position and passed the
time with them similarly to the way such people usually pass the time,
just as his drawing room was similar to all other drawing rooms.

Once they even had a soirée with dancing. And Ivan Ilyich was merry,
and everything was nice, only a big quarrel broke out with his wife over
the cakes and sweets. Praskovya Fyodorovna had her own plan, but Ivan
Ilyich insisted on buying everything from an expensive pastry shop, and
he bought a lot of cakes, and the quarrel was about the fact that there were
cakes left over and the bill from the pastry shop was for forty-five roubles.
The quarrel was big and unpleasant, and Praskovya Fyodorovna called
him "fool" and "slouch." And he clutched his head and angrily said something about divorce. But the soirée itself was merry. The best society was
there, and Ivan Ilyich danced with Princess Trufonov, the sister of the one
famous for founding the society "Quench Thou My Grief." The official
joys were the joys of self-esteem; the social joys were the joys of vain-
glory; but Ivan Ilyich's real joys were the joys of playing vint. He admitted that after anything, after whatever joyless events there might be in his
life, the joy which, like a candle, burned before all others—was to sit
down to vint with good players and soft-spoken partners, a foursome
without fail (with a fivesome it was very painful to sit out, though one
always pretended to like it), and to carry on an intelligent, serious game
(when the cards came your way), then have supper and drink a glass of
wine. And Ivan Ilyich went to bed in an especially good humour after
vint, especially when he had won a little (to win a lot was unpleasant).

So they lived. The social circle that formed around them was of the
best sort; they were visited by important people and by young people.

In their view of the circle of their acquaintances, husband, wife, and daughter agreed completely and, without prearrangement, in the same way fended off and freed themselves from various friends and relations, ragtag people, who came flying with tender feelings to their drawing room with the Japanese dishes on the walls. Soon these ragtag friends stopped flying, and the Golovins remained surrounded by only the best society. Young men courted Lizanka, and Petrishchev, the son of Dmitri Ivanovich Petrishchev and sole heir to his fortune, an examining magistrate, began courting Liza, so that Ivan Ilyich even mentioned it to Praskovya Fyodorovna: perhaps they should arrange a ride together in a troika, or organize theatricals. So they lived. And it all went on like this without change, and it was all very well.

IV

THEY WERE all in good health. It could not be called ill health that Ivan Ilyich sometimes said he had a strange taste in his mouth and some discomfort on the left side of his stomach.

But it so happened that this discomfort began to increase and turn, not into pain yet, but into the consciousness of a constant heaviness in his side and into ill humour. This ill humour, growing stronger and stronger, began to spoil the pleasantness of the easy and decent life that had just been established in the Golovin family. The husband and wife began to quarrel more and more often, and soon the ease and pleasantness fell away, and decency alone was maintained with difficulty. Scenes again became frequent. Again only little islands were left, and few of them, where the husband and wife could come together without an explosion.

And now Praskovya Fyodorovna could say, not without grounds, that her husband had a difficult character. With the habit of exaggeration typical of her, she said that he had always had a terrible character, and it had needed all her goodness to put up with it for twenty years. It was true that the quarrels now began with him. His carping always began just before dinner and often precisely as he was beginning to eat, over the soup. He would point out that something was wrong with one of the plates, or that the food was not right, or that his son had his elbow on the table, or it was his daughter's hairstyle. And he blamed Praskovya Fyodorovna for it all. At first Praskovya Fyodorovna protested and said unpleasant things to him, but twice at the start of dinner he flew into such a rage that she realized it was a morbid condition provoked in him by the taking of food, and she restrained herself; she no longer protested, but only hurried with dinner. Her restraint Praskovya Fyodorovna set down to her own great credit. Having decided that her husband had a terrible character and made her life miserable, she began to pity herself. And the more she pitied herself, the more she hated her husband. She began to wish for his death, yet she could not wish for it, because then there would be no salary. And that irritated her against him still more. She considered herself dreadfully wretched precisely in that even his death could not save her, and she became irritated, concealed it, and this concealed irritation of hers increased his irritation.

After one scene in which Ivan Ilyich was particularly unfair and after which, talking it over with her, he said that he was in fact irritable, but that it was from illness, she told him that, if he was ill, he ought to be treated, and demanded that he go to a famous doctor.

He went. It was all as he expected; it was all as it is always done. The waiting, and the assumed doctorly importance familiar to him, the same that he knew in himself in court, and the tapping, and the auscultation, and the questions calling for predetermined and obviously unnecessary answers, and the significant air, which suggested that you just submit to us, and we will arrange it all—we know indubitably how to arrange it all, all in the same way as for anybody you like. It was all exactly the same as in court. As he put on airs before the accused in court, so the famous doctor put on airs before him.

The doctor said: Such-and-such indicates that there is such-and-such inside you; but if that is not confirmed by the analysis of this-and-that, then it must be assumed that you have such-and-such. If we presume such-and-such, then . . . and so on. For Ivan Ilyich only one question mattered: was his condition dangerous or not? But the doctor ignored this inappropriate question. From the doctor's point of view it was an idle question and not to be discussed; there existed only the weighing of probabilities—a floating kidney, chronic catarrh, or appendicitis. It was not a question of Ivan Ilyich's life, but an argument between a floating kidney and the appendix. And before Ivan Ilyich's very eyes the doctor resolved this argument most brilliantly in favour of the appendix, with the reservation that the urine analysis might give new evidence and the case would then be reconsidered. All this was just exactly what Ivan Ilyich himself had performed as brilliantly a thousand times over the accused. The doctor performed his summing up just as brilliantly, and triumphantly, even merrily, glanced over his spectacles at the accused. From the doctor's summing up, Ivan Ilyich drew the conclusion that things were bad, and that for him, the doctor, and for anyone else you like, it was all the same, but for him things were bad. And this conclusion struck Ivan Ilyich painfully, calling up in him a feeling of great pity for himself and great anger at this doctor, who was indifferent to such an important question.

But he said nothing, got up, put money on the table, and sighed.

"We sick people probably often ask you inappropriate questions," he said. "But, generally, is it a dangerous illness or not? . . ."

The doctor glanced at him sternly with one eye through his spectacles, as if to say: Accused, if you do not keep within the limits of the questions put to you, I will be forced to order you removed from the court.

"I've already told you what I consider necessary and appropriate," said the doctor. "The analysis will give further evidence." And the doctor bowed.

Ivan Ilyich went out slowly, climbed dejectedly into the sleigh, and drove home. On the way he kept going over what the doctor had said, trying to translate all those complicated, vague scientific terms into simple language and read in them the answer to the question: bad—is it very bad for me, or still all right? And it seemed to him that the sense of everything the doctor had said was that it was very bad. Everything seemed sad to Ivan Ilyich in the streets. The cabbies were sad, the houses were sad, the passers-by and the shops were sad. And that pain, the obscure, gnawing pain, which did not cease for a moment, seemed to have acquired, in connection with the doctor's vague words, a different, more serious meaning. With a new, heavy feeling Ivan Ilyich now paid heed to it.

He came home and started telling his wife. His wife listened, but in the middle of his account his daughter came in with her hat on: she and her mother were going somewhere. She forced herself to sit down and listen to this boredom, but could not stand it for long, and the mother did not hear him out.

"Well, I'm very glad," said his wife, "so now see to it that you take your medicine regularly. Give me the prescription, I'll send Gerasim to the pharmacy." And she went to get dressed.

He could not breathe freely while she was in the room and sighed heavily when she left.

"Oh, well," he said. "Maybe in fact it's all right . . ."

He began to take medicines, following the doctor's prescriptions, which were changed on account of the urine analysis. But then it just so happened that, in this analysis and in what should have followed from it, there was some sort of confusion. It was impossible to reach the doctor himself, and meanwhile what was being done was not what the doctor had said to him. He either forgot, or lied, or was hiding something from him.

But all the same Ivan Ilyich started following the prescriptions precisely and in following them found comfort at first.

Ivan Ilyich's main occupation since the time of his visit to the doctor became the precise following of the doctor's prescriptions concerning hygiene and the taking of medicines, and paying heed to his pain and to all the functions of his organism. People's illness and people's health became Ivan Ilyich's main interests. When there was talk in his presence of someone being ill, or dying, or recovering, especially of an illness similiar to his own, he listened, trying to conceal his excitement, asked questions, and made applications to his illness.

The pain did not diminish; but Ivan Ilyich tried to make himself think that he was better. And he could deceive himself as long as nothing worried him. But as soon as there was some unpleasantness with his wife, a setback at work, or bad cards at vint, he immediately felt the whole force of his illness; he used to endure these setbacks, expecting to quickly right the wrong, to overcome it, to achieve success, a grand slam. But now any setback undercut him and threw him into despair. He said to himself: I was just getting better, and the medicine was beginning to work, and here's this cursed misfortune or unpleasantness . . . And he became angry at the misfortune or at the people who had caused him the unpleasantness and were killing him; and he felt how this anger was killing him, but he could not repress it. It seems it ought to have been clear to him that this anger at circumstances and at people was aggravating his illness, and that therefore he should not pay attention to unpleasant occasions; but his reasoning was quite the opposite: he said that he needed peace, looked out for anything that might disturb that peace, and at the slightest disturbance became irritated. His condition was also made worse by his reading of medical books and consulting of doctors. The worsening went on so gradually that he could deceive himself comparing one day with another—the difference was so slight. But when he consulted doctors, it seemed to him that it was getting worse and even very quickly. And despite that, he constantly consulted doctors.

That month he visited yet another celebrity: the other celebrity said almost the same thing as the first, but put his questions differently. And the consultation with this celebrity only increased Ivan Ilyich's doubt and fear. The friend of a friend of his—a very good doctor—defined the illness in quite another way still and, though he promised recovery, his questions and conjectures confused Ivan Ilyich still more and increased his doubts. A homeopath defined the illness in still another way and gave him medicine, and Ivan Ilyich, in secret from everyone, took it for a week. But after a week, feeling no relief and losing confidence both in the former treatments and in this one, he fell into still greater dejection. Once a lady acquaintance told about healing with icons. Ivan Ilyich caught himself listening attentively and believing in the reality of the fact. This occasion frightened him. "Can I have grown so mentally feeble?" he said to himself. "Nonsense! It's all rubbish, I mustn't give way to anxieties, but choose one doctor and keep strictly to his treatment. That's what I'll do. It's over now. I won't think, and I'll strictly follow the treatment till summer. Then we'll see. These vacillations are over now! . . ." That was easy to say, but impossible to do. The pain in his side kept gnawing at him, seemed to be increasing, becoming constant; the taste in his mouth kept becoming stranger; it seemed to him that his mouth gave off a disgusting smell, and his appetite and strength kept weakening. It was impossible to deceive himself: something dreadful, new, and so significant that nothing more significant had ever happened in his life, was being accomplished in Ivan Ilyich. And he alone knew of it. Everyone around him either did not understand or did not want to understand and thought that everything in the world was going on as before. This was what tormented Ivan Ilyich most of all. He saw that his household—mainly his wife and daughter, who were in the very heat of social life—did not understand anything, were vexed that he was so cheerless and demanding, as if he was to blame for it. Though they tried to conceal it, he saw that he was a hindrance to them, but that his wife had worked out for herself a certain attitude towards his illness and held to it regardless of what he said and did. This attitude was the following:

"You know," she would say to acquaintances, "Ivan Ilyich cannot keep strictly to the treatment he's prescribed, as all good people do. Today he takes his drops and eats what he's been told to and goes to bed on time; tomorrow suddenly, if I don't look out, he forgets to take them, eats sturgeon (which is forbidden), and stays up till one o'clock playing vint."

"Well, when was that?" Ivan Ilyich would ask with vexation. "Once at Pyotr Ivanovich's."

"And last night with Shebek."

"Anyway I couldn't sleep from pain."

"Whatever the reasons, you'll never get well like this, and you're tormenting us."

Praskovya Fyodorovna's external attitude to her husband's illness, which she voiced to others and to him, was that Ivan Ilyich himself was to blame for the illness and that this whole illness was a new unpleasantness he was causing his wife. Ivan Ilyich felt that this came from her involuntarily, but that did not make it easier for him.

In court Ivan Ilyich noticed or thought he noticed the same strange attitude towards himself: now it seemed to him that he was being eyed like someone who would soon have to vacate his post; now his colleagues suddenly began to joke in friendly fashion about his anxieties, as if that terrible and dreadful unheard-of thing that was sitting in him and ceaselessly gnawing at him and inexorably drawing him somewhere was a most pleasant subject for jokes. Schwartz especially irritated him with his playfulness, vitality, and *comme il faut*-ishness, which reminded Ivan Ilyich of himself ten years ago.

Friends would come for a game, sit down. They dealt, flexing the new cards, sorting diamonds with diamonds, seven of them. His partner bid no trump and opened with two diamonds. What more could one wish for? It should all go cheerfully, briskly—a grand slam. And suddenly Ivan Ilyich feels that gnawing pain, that taste in his mouth, and it seems wild to him that at the same time he should rejoice at a grand slam.

He looks at Mikhail Mikhailovich, his partner, striking the table with a sanguine hand and refraining, politely and indulgently, from picking up the tricks, but moving them towards Ivan Ilyich, so as to give him the pleasure of collecting them without taking the trouble to reach out his hand. "Does he think I'm so weak that I can't reach that far?" Ivan Ilyich thinks, forgets about the trumps and double trumps his own, and loses the slam by three tricks, and most terrible of all is that he sees how Mikhail Mikhailovich suffers and it makes no difference to him. And it is terrible to think why it makes no difference to him.

Everyone sees that it is hard for him, and they say: "We can quit if you're tired. Get some rest." Rest? No, he is not the least bit tired, and they play out the rubber. Everyone is gloomy and silent. Ivan Ilyich feels that it is he who has cast this gloom over them, and he cannot disperse it. They eat supper and go home, and Ivan Ilyich is left alone with the consciousness that his life is poisoned for him and poisons life for others, and that this poison is not weakening but is permeating his whole being more and more.

And with this consciousness, along with physical pain, along with terror, he had to go to bed and often not sleep from pain for the better part of the night. And the next morning he had to get up, dress, go to court, talk, write, and if he did not go, stay at home with the same twenty-four hours in a day, every one of which was torture. And he had to live alone on the brink of disaster like that, without a single human being who could understand and pity him.

V

SO A MONTH went by, then two. Before the New Year his brother-in-law came to their town and stayed with them. Ivan Ilyich was in court. Praskovya Fyodorovna had gone shopping. Going into his study, he found his brother-in-law there, a healthy, sanguine fellow, unpacking his suitcase. On hearing Ivan Ilyich's footsteps, he raised his head and looked at him silently for a moment. That look revealed everything to Ivan Ilyich. The brother-in-law opened his mouth to gasp, but checked himself. This movement confirmed everything.

"What, have I changed?"

"Yes . . . there's a change."

And much as he tried after that to bring his brother-in-law around to talking about his external appearance, the brother-in-law would say nothing. Praskovya Fyodorovna came home, and the brother-in-law went to her. Ivan Ilyich locked the door and started looking in the mirror—full-face, then profile. He picked up his portrait with his wife and compared it with what he saw in the mirror. The change was enormous. Then he bared his arms to the elbow, looked, pulled his sleeves down, sat on the ottoman, and turned darker than night.

"Don't, don't," he said to himself, jumped to his feet, went to the desk, opened a brief, started reading it, but could not. He unlocked the door, went to the reception room. The door to the drawing room was shut. He went up to it on tiptoe and started listening.

"No, you're exaggerating," Praskovya Fyodorovna was saying.

"How 'exaggerating'? Don't you see—he's a dead man, look in his eyes. No light. What's wrong with him?"

"Nobody knows. Nikolaev" (this was another doctor) "said something, but I don't know. Leshchetitsky" (this was the famous doctor) "said on the contrary . . ."

Ivan Ilyich stepped away, went to his room, lay down, and began to think: "A kidney, a floating kidney." He remembered all that the doctors had told him, how it had detached itself, and how it floats. By an effort of imagination he tried to catch this kidney and stop it, fasten it down; so little was needed, it seemed to him. "No, I'll go to see Pyotr Ivanovich again." (This was the friend who had the doctor friend.) He rang the bell, ordered the horse harnessed, and made ready to go.

"Where are you off to, Jean?" his wife asked with an especially sad and unusually kind expression.

This unusual kindness angered him. He gave her a dark look.

"I must go to see Pyotr Ivanovich."

He went to see his friend who had the doctor friend. And with him to the doctor. He found him in and had a long conversation with him.

On examining the anatomical and physiological details of what, in the doctor's opinion, was going on inside him, he understood everything.

There was a little thing, a tiny little thing, in the appendix. This could all be put right. Strengthen the energy of one organ, weaken the functioning of another, absorption would take place, and all would be put right. He was a little late for dinner. He dined, talked cheerfully, but for a long while could not go and get busy. Finally he went to his study and at once sat down to work. He read briefs, worked, but the awareness that he had put off an important, intimate matter, which he would take up once he had finished, never left him. When he finished work, he remembered that this intimate matter was the thought of his appendix. But he did not give in to it, he went to the drawing room for tea. There were guests; they talked, played the piano, sang; there was the examining magistrate, their daughter's desired fiancé. Ivan Ilyich spent the evening, as Praskovya Fyodorovna remarked, more cheerfully than others, but never for a moment did he forget that he had put off the important thought of his appendix. At eleven o'clock he said goodnight and went to his room. He had slept alone since the time of his illness, in a small room by his study. He went there, undressed, took a novel by Zola but did not read it, and thought. In his imagination the desired mending of the appendix was taking place. Absorption, ejection, restoration of the correct functioning. "Yes, that's all so," he said to himself. "One need only assist nature." He remembered about his medicine, got up, took it, and lay on his back, waiting to feel the beneficial effect of the medicine and how it killed the pain. "Just take it regularly and avoid harmful influences; even now I feel a little better, a lot better." He began to touch his side—it did not hurt. "Yes, I don't feel it, truly, it's already much better." He put out the candle and lay on his side . . . The appendix was mending, absorbing. Suddenly he felt the old familiar, dull, gnawing pain, stubborn, quiet, serious. In his mouth the same familiar vileness. His heart shrank, his head clouded. "My God, my God!" he said. "Again, again, and it will never stop." And suddenly he pictured the matter from an entirely different side. "The appendix! The kidney!" he said to himself. "This is not a matter of the appendix or the kidney, but of life and . . . death. Yes, there was life, and now it is going, going, and I cannot hold it back. Yes, why deceive myself? Isn't it obvious to everybody except me that I'm dying and it is only a question of the number of weeks, days—right now, maybe. Once there was light, now there's darkness. Once I was here, and now I'll be there! Where?" Cold came over him, his breath stopped. He heard only the pounding of his heart.

"There will be no me, so what will there be? There will be nothing. So where will I be, when there's no me? Can this be death? No, I don't want it." He jumped up, wanted to light a candle, felt around with trembling hands, dropped the candle and candlestick on the floor, and fell back on the pillow again. "What for? It makes no difference," he said to himself, gazing wide-eyed into the darkness. "Death. Yes, death. And none of them knows, or wants to know, or feels pity. They're playing." (He heard through the door the distant roll of a voice and ritornello.) "It makes no difference to them, but they'll also die. Fools. For me sooner, for them later; but it will be the same for them. Yet they make merry. Brutes!" He was choking with anger. And he felt tormentingly, unbearably oppressed. It just can't be that everyone has always been condemned to this terrible fear. He sat up.

"Something's not right. I must calm down; I must think it over from the beginning." And so he began to think it over. "Yes, the beginning of the illness. I bumped my side, and then I was just the same, that day and the next; it ached a little, then more, then doctors, then dejection, anguish, doctors again; and I was coming closer and closer to the abyss. Losing strength. Closer and closer. And here I am wasted away, there's no light in my eyes. It's death, yet I think about my appendix. I think about repairing my appendix, yet it's death. Can it be death?" Again terror came over him, he gasped for breath, bent down, began searching for the matches, leaned his elbow on the night table. It hindered him and hurt him, he became angry with it, vexedly leaned still harder, and the night table fell over. In despair, suffocating, he fell on his back, expecting death at once.

The guests were just leaving. Praskovya Fyodorovna was seeing them off. She heard something fall and came in.

"What's the matter?"

"Nothing. I tipped it over by accident."

She went out and came back with a candle. He was lying there, breathing heavily and very rapidly, like a man who has run a mile, looking at her with a fixed gaze.

"What's the matter, Jean?"

"Nothing. I tipped it over." ("No use talking. She won't understand," he thought.)

In fact she did not understand. She picked up the night table, lit the candle, and left hastily: she had to see off a lady guest.

When she returned, he was lying on his back in the same way, looking up.

"What is it, are you worse?"

"Yes."

She shook her head and sat down.

"You know, Jean, I think we ought to invite Leshchetitsky to the house."

This meant inviting the famous doctor and not minding the cost. He smiled venomously and said: "No." She sat for a while, went over, and kissed him on the forehead.

He hated her with all the forces of his soul while she was kissing him, and had a hard time not pushing her away.

"Goodnight. God grant you fall asleep."

"Yes."

VI

IVAN ILYICH SAW that he was dying, and he was in continual despair.

In the depths of his soul Ivan Ilyich knew that he was dying, but not only was he not accustomed to it, he simply did not, he could not possibly understand it.

The example of a syllogism he had studied in Kiesewetter's logic[9]—Caius is a man, men are mortal, therefore Caius is mortal—had seemed to him all his life to be correct only in relation to Caius, but by no means to himself. For the man Caius, man in general, it was perfectly correct; but he was not Caius and not man in general, he had always been quite, quite separate from all other beings; he was Vanya, with mamá, with papá, with Mitya and Volodya, with toys, the coachman, with a nanny, then with Katenka, with all the joys, griefs, and delights of childhood, boyhood, youth. Was it for Caius, the smell of the striped leather ball that Vanya had loved so much? Was it Caius who had kissed his mother's hand like that, and was it for Caius that the silk folds of his mother's dress had rustled like that? Was it he who had mutinied against bad food in law school? Was it Caius who had been in love like that? Was it Caius who could conduct a court session like that?

And Caius is indeed mortal, and it's right that he die, but for me, Vanya, Ivan Ilyich, with all my feelings and thoughts—for me it's another matter. And it cannot be that I should die. It would be too terrible.

So it felt to him.

"If I was to die like Caius, I would have known it, my inner voice would have told me so, but there was nothing of the sort in me; and I and all my friends understood that things were quite otherwise than with Caius. And now look!" he said to himself. "It can't be. It can't be, but it is. How can it be? How can I understand it?"

And he could not understand and tried to drive this thought away as false, incorrect, morbid, and to dislodge it with other correct, healthy thoughts. But this thought, not only a thought but as if a reality, came back again and stood before him.

And he called up a series of other thoughts in place of this thought, in hopes of finding support in them. He tried to go back to his former ways of thinking, which had screened him formerly from the thought of death. But—strange thing—all that had formerly screened, hidden, wiped out the consciousness of death now could no longer produce that effect. Lately Ivan Ilyich had spent most of his time in these attempts to restore the former ways of feeling that had screened him from death. He would say to himself: "I'll busy myself with work—why, I used to live by it." And he would go to court, driving away all doubts; he would get into conversation with colleagues and sit down, by old habit absent-mindedly, pensively glancing around at the crowd and placing his two emaciated arms on the armrests of the oaken chair, leaning over as usual to a colleague, drawing a brief towards him, exchanging whispers, and then, suddenly raising his eyes and sitting up straight, would pronounce certain words and begin the proceedings. But suddenly in the midst of it the pain in his side, paying no attention to the stage the proceedings had reached, would begin *its own* gnawing work. Ivan Ilyich sensed it, drove the thought of it away, but it would go on, and *it* would come and stand directly in front of him and look at him, and he would be dumbstruck, the light would go out in his eyes, and he would again begin asking himself: "Can *it* alone be true?" And his colleagues and subordinates would be surprised and upset to see that he, such a brilliant and subtle judge, was confused, was making mistakes. He would rouse himself, try to come to his senses, and somehow bring the session to an end and return home with the sad awareness that his work in court could no longer, as before, conceal from him what he wanted concealed; that by his work in court he could not rid himself of *it*. And what was worst of all was that *it* drew him to itself not so that he would do something, but only so that he should look it straight in the eye, look at it and, doing nothing, suffer inexpressibly.

And to save himself from this state, Ivan Ilyich looked for consolation, for other screens, and other screens appeared and for a short time seemed to save him, but at once they were again not so much destroyed as made transparent, as if *it* penetrated everything and there was no screening it out.

It happened in this latter time that he would go into the drawing room he had decorated—into that drawing room where he had fallen, for which—as he laughed venomously to think—for the arranging of which he had sacrificed his life, because he knew that his illness had begun with that bruise—he would go in and see that something had made a scratch on the varnished table. He would look for the cause and find it in the bronze ornamentation of an album, the edge of which was bent. He would pick up the album, an expensive thing he had put together with love, and become vexed at his daughter's and her friends' carelessness—here a torn page, there some photographs turned upside down. He would diligently put it all in order and bend back the ornamentation.

Then it would occur to him to transfer this whole *établissement** with the albums to another corner, near the flowers. He would call a servant: his daughter or his wife would come to help him; they would disagree, contradict him, he would argue, get angry; but all was well, because he did not remember about *it*, *it* was not seen.

But then his wife would say, as he was moving the objects himself: "Let the servants do it, you'll do harm to yourself again," and suddenly *it* would flash from behind the screen, he would see *it*. *It* flashes, he still hopes *it* will disappear, but he involuntarily senses his side—there sits the same thing, gnawing in the same way, and he can no longer forget it, and *it* clearly stares at him from behind the flowers. What is it all for?

"And it's true that I lost my life here, over this curtain, as if I was storming a fortress. Can it be? How terrible and how stupid! It can't be! Can't be, but is."

He would go to his study, lie down, and again remain alone with *it*. Face to face with *it*, and there was nothing to be done with *it*. Only look at *it* and go cold.

---

* Establishment.

VII

How it came about in the third month of Ivan Ilyich's illness it was impossible to say, because it came about step by step, imperceptibly, but what came about was that his wife, and daughter, and son, and the servants, and acquaintances, and the doctors, and, above all, he himself—knew that for others the whole interest in him consisted only in how soon he would finally vacate his place, free the living from the constraint caused by his presence, and be freed himself from his sufferings.

He slept less and less; they gave him opium and began injections of morphine. But that did not relieve him. The dull anguish he experienced in a half-sleeping state only relieved him at first as something new, but then became as much or still more of a torment than outright pain.

Special foods were prepared for him by the doctors' prescription; but these foods became more and more tasteless, more and more disgusting to him.

Special arrangements were also made for his stools, and this was a torment to him each time. A torment in its uncleanness, indecency, and smell, in the awareness that another person had to take part in it.

But in this most unpleasant matter there also appeared a consolation for Ivan Ilyich. The butler's helper, Gerasim, always came to clear away after him.

Gerasim was a clean, fresh young muzhik, grown sleek on town grub. Always cheerful, bright. At first the sight of this man, always clean, dressed Russian-style, performing this repulsive chore, embarrassed Ivan Ilyich.

Once, having got up from the commode and being unable to pull up his trousers, he collapsed into the soft armchair, looking with horror at his naked, strengthless thighs with their sharply outlined muscles.

Gerasim, in heavy boots, spreading around him the pleasant smell of boot tar and the freshness of winter air, came in with a light, strong step, in a clean canvas apron and a clean cotton shirt, the sleeves rolled up on his bared, strong, young arms, and without looking at Ivan Ilyich—obviously restraining the joy of life shining on his face, so as not to offend the sick man—went to the commode.

"Gerasim," Ivan Ilyich said weakly.

Gerasim gave a start, evidently afraid he was remiss in something, and with a quick movement he turned to the sick man his fresh, kind, simple young face, only just beginning to sprout a beard.

"What, sir?"

"I suppose this must be unpleasant for you. Excuse me. I can't help it."

"Mercy, sir." And Gerasim flashed his eyes and bared his young, white teeth. "Why shouldn't I do it? It's a matter of you being sick."

And with his deft, strong hands he did his usual business and went out, stepping lightly. And five minutes later, stepping just as lightly, he came back.

Ivan Ilyich was still sitting the same way in the armchair.

"Gerasim," he said, when the man had set down the clean, washed commode, "help me, please. Come here." Gerasim went to him. "Lift me up. It's hard for me alone, and I've sent Dmitri away."

Gerasim went to him. With his strong arms, just as lightly as he stepped, he embraced him, deftly and softly lifted and held him, pulling his trousers up with the other hand, and was about to sit him down. But Ivan Ilyich asked him to lead him to the sofa. Gerasim, effortlessly and as if without pressure, led him, almost carried him, to the sofa and sat him down.

"Thank you. How deftly, how well . . . you do it all."

Gerasim smiled again and was about to leave. But Ivan Ilyich felt so good with him that he did not want to let him go.

"I tell you what: move that chair for me, please. No, that one, under my legs. It's a relief for me when my legs are raised."

Gerasim brought the chair, set it down noiselessly, lowering it all at once right to the floor, and placed Ivan Ilyich's legs on it; it seemed to Ivan Ilyich that it was a relief for him when Gerasim lifted his legs high.

"I feel better when my legs are raised," said Ivan Ilyich. "Put that pillow under for me."

Gerasim did so. Again he lifted his legs and set them down. Again Ivan Ilyich felt better while Gerasim was holding his legs. When he lowered them, it seemed worse.

"Gerasim," he said to him, "are you busy now?"

"By no means, sir," said Gerasim, who had learned from the townspeople how to talk with gentlefolk.

"What more have you got to do?"

"What's there for me to do? I've done everything except split the wood for tomorrow."

"Then hold my legs a little higher, can you?"

"That I can." Gerasim lifted his legs higher, and it seemed to Ivan Ilych that in that position he felt no pain at all.

"But what about the wood?"

"Please don't worry, sir. There'll be time."

Ivan Ilyich told Gerasim to sit and hold his legs, and he conversed with him. And—strange thing—it seemed to him that he felt better while Gerasim held his legs.

After that Ivan Ilyich occasionally summoned Gerasim and made him hold his legs on his shoulders, and he liked talking with him. Gerasim did it easily, willingly, simply, and with a kindness that moved Ivan Ilyich. Health, strength, vigour of life in all other people offended Ivan Ilyich; only Gerasim's strength and vigour of life did not distress but soothed him.

The main torment for Ivan Ilyich was the lie, that lie for some reason acknowledged by everyone, that he was merely ill and not dying, and that he needed only to keep calm and be treated, and then something very good would come of it. While he knew that whatever they did, nothing would come of it except still more tormenting suffering and death. And he was tormented by that lie, tormented that no one wanted to acknowledge what they all knew and he knew, but wanted to lie to him about his terrible situation, and wanted him and even forced him to participate in that lie. The lie, this lie, perpetrated upon him on the eve of his death, the lie that must needs reduce the dreadful, solemn act of his death to the level of all their visits, curtains, sturgeon dinners . . . was terribly tormenting for Ivan Ilyich. And—strangely—many times, as they were performing their tricks over him, he was a hair's breadth from shouting at them: "Stop lying! You know and I know that I'm dying, so at least stop lying." But he never had the courage to do it. The dreadful, terrible act of his dying, he saw, was reduced by all those around him to the level of an accidental unpleasantness, partly an indecency (something like dealing with a man who comes into a drawing room spreading a bad smell), in the name of that very "decency" he had served all his life; he saw that no one would feel sorry for him, because no one even wanted to understand his situation. Only Gerasim understood that situation and pitied him. And therefore Ivan Ilyich felt good only with Gerasim. It felt good to him when Gerasim held his legs up, sometimes all night long, and refused to go to sleep, saying: "Please don't worry, Ivan Ilyich, I'll still get some sleep"; or when, suddenly addressing him familiarly, he added: "Maybe if you weren't sick, but why not be a help?" Gerasim alone did not lie, everything showed that he alone understood what it was all about, and did not find it necessary to conceal it, and simply pitied his emaciated, weakened master. Once he even said straight out, as Ivan Ilyich was sending him away: "We'll all die. Why not take the trouble?"—expressing by that that he was not burdened by his trouble precisely because he was bearing it for a dying man and hoped that when his time came someone would go to the same trouble for him.

Apart from this lie, or owing to it, the most tormenting thing for Ivan Ilyich was that no one pitied him as he wanted to be pitied: there were moments, after prolonged suffering, when Ivan Ilyich wanted most of all, however embarrassed he would have been to admit it, to be pitied by someone like a sick child. He wanted to be caressed, kissed, wept over, as children are caressed and comforted. He knew that he was an important judge, that he had a greying beard, and that therefore it was impossible; but he wanted it all the same. And in his relations with Gerasim there was something close to it, and therefore his relations with Gerasim comforted him. Ivan Ilyich wanted to weep, wanted to be caressed and wept over, and then comes his colleague, the judge Shebek, and instead of weeping and caressing, Ivan Ilyich makes a serious, stern, profoundly thoughtful face and, by inertia, gives his opinion on the significance of a decision of the appeals court and stubbornly insists on it. This lie around and within him poisoned most of all the last days of Ivan Ilyich's life.

VIII

IT WAS MORNING. It was morning if only because Gerasim had gone and the servant Pyotr had come, put out the candles, drawn one curtain, and quietly begun tidying up. Whether it was morning or evening, Friday or Sunday, was all the same, all one and the same: a gnawing, tormenting pain, never subsiding for a moment; the awareness of life ever hopelessly going but never quite gone; always the same dreadful, hateful death approaching—the sole reality now—and always the same lie. What were days, weeks, and hours here?

"Would you care for tea, sir?"

"He needs order, so his masters should have tea in the mornings," he thought, and said only:

"No."

"Would you like to lie on the sofa?"

"He needs to tidy up the room, and I'm in his way, I am uncleanness, disorder," he thought, and said only:

"No, let me be."

The servant pottered around some more. Ivan Ilyich reached out his hand. Pyotr obligingly came over.

"What can I do for you, sir?"

"My watch."

Pyotr picked up the watch, which was lying just by his hand, and gave it to him.

"Half past eight. Are they up yet?"

"No, sir. Vassily Ivanovich" (that was the son) "has gone to school, and Praskovya Fyodorovna gave orders to wake her if you asked for her. Shall I do so?"

"No, don't." "Shouldn't I try some tea?" he thought. "Yes . . . bring tea."

Pyotr went to the door. Ivan Ilyich was afraid to be left alone. "How can I keep him? Ah, yes, my medicine." "Pyotr, give me my medicine." "Who knows, maybe the medicine will still help." He took a spoonful and swallowed it. "No, it won't help. It's all nonsense, deception," he decided as soon as he tasted the familiar sickly sweet and hopeless taste. "No, I can't believe it any more. But the pain, why the pain? If only it would stop for a moment." And he moaned. Pyotr turned back. "No, go. Bring the tea."

Pyotr went out. Ivan Ilyich, left alone, moaned not so much from pain, terrible though it was, as from anguish. "Always the same, always the same, all these endless days and nights. Let it be sooner. What sooner? Death, darkness. No, no. Anything's better than death!"

When Pyotr came in with the tea tray, Ivan Ilyich looked at him for a long time in perplexity, not understanding who and what he was. Pyotr became embarrassed under this gaze. And when Pyotr became embarrassed, Ivan Ilyich came to his senses.

"Ah, yes," he said, "the tea . . . good, set it down. Only help me to wash and put on a clean shirt."

And Ivan Ilyich began to wash. With pauses for rest, he washed his hands, his face, brushed his teeth, started combing his hair, and looked in the mirror. He became frightened; especially frightening was how his hair lay flat on his pale forehead.

While his shirt was being changed, he knew he would be still more frightened if he looked at his body, so he did not look at himself. But now it was all over. He put on his dressing gown, wrapped himself in a plaid, and sat down in the armchair to have tea. For a moment he felt refreshed, but as soon as he began to drink the tea, there was again the same taste, the same pain. He forced himself to finish it and lay down, stretching his legs. He lay down and dismissed Pyotr.

Always the same thing. A drop of hope glimmers, then a sea of despair begins to rage, and always the pain, always the pain, always the anguish, always one and the same thing. Being alone is a horrible anguish, he wants to call someone, but he knows beforehand that with others it is still worse. "At least morphine again—to become oblivious. I'll tell him, the doctor, to think up something else. It's impossible like this, impossible."

An hour, two hours pass in this way. But now there's a ringing in the front hall. Could be the doctor. Right, it's the doctor, fresh, brisk, fat, cheerful, with an expression that says: So you're scared of something here, but we'll fix it all up for you in no time. The doctor knows that this expression is unsuitable here, but he has put it on once and for all and cannot take it off, like a man who puts on a tailcoat in the morning and goes around visiting.

The doctor rubs his hands briskly, comfortingly.

"I'm cold. It's freezing outside. Let me warm up," he says with such an expression as if they only had to wait a little till he warmed up, and when he warmed up, he would put everything right.

"Well, how . . . ?"

Ivan Ilyich senses that the doctor would like to say "How's every little thing?" but that he, too, senses that he cannot say that, and so he says: "How was your night?"

Ivan Ilyich looks at the doctor with a questioning expression: "Will you never be ashamed of lying?" But the doctor does not want to understand the question.

And Ivan Ilyich says:

"Terrible as ever. The pain doesn't go away, doesn't let up. If you could do something!"

"Ah, you sick people are always like that. Well, sir, now I seem to be warm; even the most exacting Praskovya Fyodorovna could make no objection to my temperature. Well, sir, greetings." And the doctor shakes his hand.

And, setting aside all his earlier playfulness, the doctor begins with a serious air to examine the sick man, takes his pulse, his temperature, and then gets to the tappings, the auscultations.

Ivan Ilyich knows firmly and indubitably that this is all nonsense and empty deception, but when the doctor, getting on his knees, stretches out, putting his ear now higher, now lower, and with a most significant face performs various gymnastic evolutions over him, Ivan Ilyich succumbs to it, as he used to succumb to lawyers' speeches, when he knew very well they were all lies and why they were lies.

The doctor, kneeling on the sofa, was still doing his tapping when the silk dress of Praskovya Fyodorovna rustled in the doorway and she was heard reproaching Pyotr for not announcing the doctor's arrival to her.

She comes in, kisses her husband, and at once begins to insist that she was up long ago and it was only by misunderstanding that she was not there when the doctor came.

Ivan Ilyich looks at her, examines her all over, and reproaches her for her whiteness, and plumpness, and the cleanness of her hands, her neck, the glossiness of her hair, and the sparkle of her eyes, so full of life. He hates her with all the forces of his soul. And her touch makes him suffer from a flood of hatred for her.

Her attitude towards him and his illness is ever the same. As the doctor had developed in himself an attitude towards his patients which he was unable to take off, so she had developed a certain attitude towards him—that he had not done something he should have, and he himself was to blame, and she lovingly reproached him for it—and she could no longer take off this attitude towards him.

"He simply doesn't listen! Doesn't take his medicine on time. And above all, he lies in a position which is surely bad for him—legs up."

She told about how he made Gerasim hold his legs.

The doctor smiled with kindly disdain, meaning: "No help for it, these sick people sometimes think up such foolishness; but it's forgivable."

When the examination was over, the doctor looked at his watch, and then Praskovya Fyodorovna announced to Ivan Ilyich that, whether he liked it or not, she had invited a famous doctor that day, and he would examine him and consult with Mikhail Danilovich (as the usual doctor was called).

"Don't resist, please. I'm doing it for myself," she said ironically, letting it be felt that she was doing it all for him, and that alone gave him no right to refuse. He said nothing and scowled. He felt that this lie surrounding him was so entangled that it was hard to sort anything out.

Everything she did for him she did only for herself, and she said to him that she was doing for herself that which she was in fact doing for herself, as if it was such an incredible thing that he would have to understand it inversely.

Indeed, at half past eleven the famous doctor arrived. Again there were auscultations and significant conversations in his presence and in the next room about the kidney, about the appendix, and questions and answers with such a significant air that again, instead of the real question of life and death, which now alone confronted him, there re-emerged the question of the kidney and the appendix, which were not behaving as they should, and for which Mikhail Danilovich and the famous doctor were about to fall upon them and make them mend their ways.

The famous doctor took his leave with a serious but not hopeless air. And to the timid question which Ivan Ilyich addressed to him, raising his eyes glittering with fear and hope, whether there was a possibility of recovery, he replied that, though he could not vouch for it, there was such a possibility. The hopeful look with which Ivan Ilyich saw the doctor off was so pitiful that, on seeing it, Praskovya Fyodorovna even burst into tears as she came out of the study to hand the famous doctor his honorarium.

The boost in his spirits produced by the doctor's reassurance did not last long. Again the same room, the same paintings, curtains, wallpaper, vials, and his same sick, suffering body. And Ivan Ilyich began to moan; he was given an injection and became oblivious.

When he came to, it was getting dark; his dinner was brought. He forced himself to swallow some bouillon; and again the same thing, and again the approach of night.

After dinner, at seven o'clock, Praskovya Fyodorovna came into his room dressed for the evening, with fat, tight-laced breasts, and with traces of powder on her face. She had already reminded him in the morning that they were going to the theatre. Sarah Bernhardt[10] was visiting, and they had a box he had insisted on taking. Now he had forgotten about it, and her outfit offended him. But he concealed his offence when he remembered that he himself had insisted that they get a box and go, because it was an educational aesthetic pleasure for the children.

Praskovya Fyodorovna came in pleased with herself, but as if guilty. She sat down, asked about his health, as he could see, only in order to ask, not in order to find out, knowing that there was nothing to find out, and began telling him what she had in mind: that they would not have gone for anything, but the box had been taken, that Hélène and their daughter and Petrishchev (the examining magistrate, the daughter's fiancé) were going, and that it was impossible to let them go alone. And that otherwise she would have liked better to sit with him. Only he should do what the doctor had prescribed in her absence.

"Ah, yes, and Fyodor Petrovich" (the fiancé) "wanted to come in. Can he? And Liza."

"Let them."

The daughter came in all dressed up, with her young body bared, that body which made him suffer so. Yet she exposed it. Strong, healthy, obviously in love, and indignant at the illness, suffering, and death that interfered with her happiness.

Fyodor Petrovich came in, too, in a tailcoat, his hair curled *à la Capoule*,[11] with a long, sinewy neck closely encased in a white collar, with an enormous white shirt front and narrow black trousers tightly stretched over his strong thighs, with a white glove drawn onto one hand, and holding an opera hat.

After him a little schoolboy crept in inconspicuously, in a new uniform, the poor lad, wearing gloves, and with terrible blue circles under his eyes, the meaning of which Ivan Ilyich knew.

He had always pitied his son. And his frightened and commiserating glance was dreadful for him. Apart from Gerasim, it seemed to Ivan Ilyich that Vasya alone understood and pitied him.

They all sat down and asked again about his health. Silence ensued. Liza asked her mother about the opera glasses. An altercation ensued between mother and daughter about who had done what with them. It was unpleasant.

Fyodor Petrovich asked Ivan Ilyich whether he had seen Sarah Bernhardt. At first Ivan Ilyich did not understand what he was being asked, and then he said:

"No, have you?"

"Yes, in *Adrienne Lecouvreur*."¹²

Praskovya Fyodorovna said she had been especially good in something or other. The daughter objected. A conversation began about the gracefulness and realism of her acting—that very conversation which is always one and the same.

In the middle of the conversation, Fyodor Petrovich glanced at Ivan Ilyich and fell silent. The others glanced at him and fell silent. Ivan Ilyich was staring straight ahead with glittering eyes, obviously indignant with them. This had to be rectified, but it was quite impossible to rectify it. This silence had to be broken somehow. No one ventured to do it, and they all became frightened that the decorous lie would somehow be violated, and what was there would be clear to all. Liza was the first to venture. She broke the silence. She wanted to conceal what they all felt, but she let it slip.

"Anyhow, *if we're going*, it's time," she said, glancing at her watch, a gift from her father, and smiling barely perceptibly to the young man about something known only to them, and she stood up, her dress rustling.

They all stood up, said goodbye, and left.

When they were gone, it seemed a relief to Ivan Ilyich: there was no lie—it had gone with them—but the pain remained. The same pain, the same fear made it so that nothing was harder, nothing was easier. It was all worse.

Again minute followed minute, hour hour, always the same, and always without end, and always more frightening the inevitable end.

"Yes, send Gerasim," he replied to Pyotr's question.

IX

LATE THAT NIGHT his wife returned. She came in on tiptoe, but he heard her: he opened his eyes and hastily closed them. She wanted to send Gerasim away and sit with him herself. He opened his eyes and said:

"No. Go away."

"Are you suffering very much?"

"It makes no difference."

"Take some opium."

He agreed and drank it. She left.

Until about three he lay in tormenting oblivion. It seemed to him that they were pushing him painfully into some narrow and deep black sack, and kept pushing him further, and could not push him through. And this thing, which is terrible for him, is being accomplished with suffering. And he is afraid, and yet he wants to fall through, and he struggles, and he helps. And then suddenly he lost hold and fell, and came to his senses. The same Gerasim is sitting at the foot of the bed, dozing calmly, patiently. And he is lying with his emaciated legs in stockings placed on Gerasim's shoulders; the same candle with its shade, and the same unceasing pain.

"Go away, Gerasim," he whispered.

"Never mind, I'll stay, sir."

"No, go away."

He took his legs down, lay sideways on his arm, and felt sorry for himself. He waited only until Gerasim went to the next room, and then stopped holding himself back and wept like a child. He wept over his helplessness, over his terrible loneliness, over the cruelty of people, over the cruelty of God, over the absence of God.

"Why have You done all this? Why have You brought me here? Why, why do You torment me so terribly? . . ."

He did not expect an answer and wept that there was not and could not be an answer. The pain rose up again, but he did not stir, did not call out. He kept saying to himself: "Well, go on, beat me! But what for? What have I done to You? What for?"

Then he quieted down, not only stopped weeping, but stopped breathing, and became all attention: it was as if he were listening not to a voice that spoke in sounds, but to the voice of his soul, to the course of thoughts arising in him.

"What do you want?" was the first clear idea, expressible in words, that he heard. "What do you want? What do you want?" he repeated to himself. "What? Not to suffer. To live," he replied.

And again he gave himself entirely to such intense attention that even the pain did not distract him.

"To live? To live how?" asked the voice of his soul.

"Yes, to live as I lived before: nicely, pleasantly."

"As you lived before, nicely and pleasantly?" asked the voice. And he started to go over in his imagination the best moments of his pleasant life. But—strange thing—all those best moments of his pleasant life seemed now not at all as they had seemed then. All— except for his first memories of childhood. There, in childhood, there had been something really pleasant, which one could live with if it came back. But the man who had experienced that pleasure was no more: it was as if the memory was about someone else.

As soon as that began the result of which was he, the Ivan Ilyich of today, all that had then seemed like joys melted away and turned into something worthless and often vile.

And the further from childhood, the closer to the present, the more worthless and dubious were those joys. It began with law school. There had still been some truly good things there: there had been merriment, there had been friendship, there had been hopes. But in the higher grades those good moments had already become more rare. Then, during the initial time of working for the governor, there had again been good moments: these were his memories of love for a woman. Then it all became confused, and there was still less that was good. And further on still less of the good, and the further, the less.

His marriage . . . so accidental, and the disenchantment, and the smell of his wife's breath, and the sensuality, the dissembling! And this deadly service, and these worries about money, and that for a year, and two, and ten, and twenty—and all of it the same. And the further, the deadlier. As if I was going steadily downhill, while imagining I was going up. And so it was. In public opinion I was going uphill, and exactly to that extent life was slipping away from under me . . . And now that's it, so die!

But what is this? Why? It can't be. Can it be that life is so meaningless and vile? And if it is indeed so vile and meaningless, then why die, and die suffering? Something's not right.

"Maybe I did not live as I should have?" would suddenly come into his head. "But how not, if I did everything one ought to?" he would say to himself and at once drive this sole solution to the whole riddle of life and death away from him as something completely impossible.

"What do you want now, then? To live? To live how? To live as you live in court, when the usher proclaims: 'Court is in session!' Court is in session, court is in session," he repeated to himself. "Here is that court! But I'm not guilty!" he cried out angrily. "What for?" And he stopped weeping and, turning his face to the wall, began to think about one and the same thing: why, what for, all this horror?

But however much he thought, he found no answer. And when it occurred to him, as it often did, that it was all happening because he had not lived right, he at once recalled all the correctness of his life and drove this strange thought away.

X

ANOTHER TWO WEEKS went by. Ivan Ilyich no longer got up from the sofa. He did not want to lie in bed and so he lay on the sofa. And, lying almost always face to the wall, he suffered all alone the same insoluble suffering and thought all alone the same insoluble thought. What is this? Can it be true that it is death? And an inner voice replied: Yes, it's true. Why these torments? And the voice replied: Just so, for no reason. Beyond and besides that there was nothing.

From the very beginning of his illness, from the time when Ivan Ilyich first went to the doctor, his life had divided into two opposite states of mind, which alternated with each other: now there was despair and the expectation of an incomprehensible and terrible death, now there was hope and the interest-filled process of observing the functioning of his body. Now there hung before his eyes a kidney or an intestine that shirked its duty for a time; now there was only incomprehensible, terrible death, from which there was no escape.

These two states of mind had alternated from the very beginning of the illness; but the further the illness went, the more dubious and fantastic became the considerations of the kidney and the more real the awareness of approaching death.

He needed only to recall what he had been three months ago and what he was now, to recall how steadily he had gone downhill, for any possibility of hope to be destroyed.

In the recent time of that solitude in which he found himself, lying face to the back of the sofa, that solitude in the midst of the populous town and his numerous acquaintances and family—a solitude than which there could be none more total anywhere: not at the bottom of the sea, not under the earth—in the recent time of that dreadful solitude, Ivan Ilyich had lived only on imaginings of the past. One after another, pictures of the past appeared to him. They always began with the nearest time and went back to the most remote, to childhood, and there they stayed. If Ivan Ilyich recalled the stewed prunes he had been given to eat that day, he then recalled the raw, shrivelled French prunes of his childhood, their special taste, the abundant saliva when it got as far as the stone, and alongside this memory of taste emerged a whole series of memories from that time: his nanny, his brother, his toys. "Mustn't think about that . . . too painful," Ivan Ilyich said to himself and shifted back to the present. A button on the back of the sofa and the puckered morocco. "Morocco's expensive, flimsy; there was a quarrel over it. But there was another morocco and another quarrel, when we tore our father's briefcase and were punished, and mama brought us little pies." And again it stayed with childhood, and again it was painful for Ivan Ilyich, and he tried to drive it away and think of something else.

And again right there, along with this course of recollection, another course of recollection was going on in his soul—of how his illness had grown and worsened. The further back it went, the more life there was. There was more goodness in life, and more of life itself. The two merged together. "As my torment kept getting worse and worse, so the whole of life got worse and worse," he thought. There was one bright spot back there, at the beginning of life, and then it became ever darker and darker, ever quicker and quicker. "In inverse proportion to the square of the distance from death," thought Ivan Ilyich. And this image of a stone plunging down with increasing speed sank into his soul. Life, a series of ever-increasing sufferings, races faster and faster towards its end, the most dreadful suffering. "I'm racing . . ." He would give a start, rouse himself, want to resist; but he already knew that it was impossible to resist, and again, with eyes weary from looking, but unable not to look at what was before him, he gazed at the back of the sofa and waited—waited for that dreadful fall, impact, and destruction. "It's impossible to resist," he said to himself. "But at least to understand what for? Even that is impossible. It would be possible to explain it, if I were to say to myself that I have not lived as one ought. But that cannot possibly be acknowledged," he said to himself, recalling all the legitimacy, regularity, and decency of his life. "To admit that is quite impossible," he said to himself, his lips smiling, as if there were someone to see that smile and be deceived by it. "There's no explanation! Torment, death . . . What for?"

XI

So TWO WEEKS WENT BY. During those weeks an event desired by Ivan Ilyich and his wife took place: Petrishchev made a formal proposal. This took place in the evening. The next day Praskovya Fyodorovna came to her husband's room, pondering how to announce Fyodor Petrovich's proposal to him, but the previous night a new change for the worse had occurred in Ivan Ilyich. Praskovya Fyodorovna found him on the same sofa, but in a new position. He was lying on his back, moaning, and staring straight in front of him with a fixed gaze.

She started talking about medicines. He shifted his gaze to her. She did not finish what she had begun: such spite, precisely against her, was expressed in that gaze.

"For Christ's sake, let me die in peace," he said.

She was going to leave, but just then their daughter came in and went over to greet him. He looked at his daughter in the same way as at his wife, and to her questions about his health said drily to her that he would soon free them all of himself. They both fell silent, sat for a while, and left.

"What fault is it of ours?" Liza said to her mother. "As if we did anything! I feel sorry for papa, but why torment us?"

The doctor came at the usual time. Ivan Ilyich answered "Yes" and "No," without taking his spiteful gaze from him, and in the end said:

"You know you can't help at all, so leave off."

"We can ease your suffering," said the doctor.

"Even that you can't do. Leave off."

The doctor came out to the drawing room and informed Praskovya Fyodorovna that things were very bad and that the only remedy was opium to ease his sufferings, which must be terrible.

The doctor said that his physical sufferings were terrible, and that was true; but more terrible than his physical sufferings were his moral sufferings, and these were his chief torment.

His moral sufferings consisted in the fact that, looking at Gerasim's sleepy, good-natured, high-cheekboned face that night, it had suddenly occurred to him: And what if my whole life, my conscious life, has indeed been "not right"?

It occurred to him that what had formerly appeared completely impossible to him, that he had not lived his life as he should have, might be true. It occurred to him that those barely noticeable impulses he had felt to fight against what highly placed people considered good, barely noticeable impulses which he had immediately driven away—that they might have been the real thing, and all the rest might have been not right. His work, and his living conditions, and his family, and these social and professional interests—all might have been not right. He tried to defend it all to himself. And he suddenly felt all the weakness of what he was defending. And there was nothing to defend.

"But if that's so," he said to himself, "and I am quitting this life with the consciousness that I have ruined everything that was given me, and it is impossible to rectify it, what then?" He lay on his back and started going over his whole life in a totally new way. In the morning, when he saw the footman, then his wife, then his daughter, then the doctor—their every movement, their every word confirmed the terrible truth revealed to him that night. In them he saw himself, all that he had lived by, and saw clearly that it was all not right, that it was all a terrible, vast deception concealing both life and death. This consciousness increased his physical sufferings tenfold. He moaned, and thrashed, and tore at his clothes. It seemed to be choking and crushing him. And for that he hated them.

He was given a large dose of opium and became oblivious; but at dinnertime the same thing began again. He drove everyone away and thrashed from side to side.

His wife came to him and said:

"Jean, darling, do this for me" (for me?). "It can't do any harm and often helps. It's really nothing. Even healthy people often . . ."

He opened his eyes wide.

"What? Take communion? Why? There's no need! Although . . ."

She began to cry.

"Yes, my dear? I'll send for ours, he's so nice."

"Excellent, very good," he said.

When the priest came and confessed him, he softened, felt a sort of relief from his doubts and consequently from his sufferings, and a moment of hope came over him. He began thinking about the appendix again and the possibility of its mending. He took communion with tears in his eyes.

When they laid him down after communion, he felt eased for a moment, and hopes of life appeared again. He began to think about the operation that had been suggested to him. "To live, I want to live," he said to himself. His wife came to congratulate him on his communion; she said the usual words and added:

"Isn't it true you're feeling better?"

He said "Yes" without looking at her.

Her clothes, her figure, the expression of her face, the sound of her voice—all told him one thing: "Not right. All that you've lived and live by is a lie, a deception, concealing life and death from you." And as soon as he thought it, his hatred arose and together with hatred his tormenting physical sufferings and with his sufferings the consciousness of near, inevitable destruction. Something new set in: twisting, and shooting, and choking his breath.

The expression of his face when he said "Yes" was terrible. Having uttered this "Yes," he looked her straight in the face, turned over with a quickness unusual in his weak state, and shouted:

"Go away, go away, leave me alone!"

XII

FROM THAT MOMENT began a three-day ceaseless howling, which was so terrible that it was impossible to hear it without horror even through two closed doors. The moment he answered his wife, he realized that he was lost, that there was no return, that the end had come, the final end, and his doubt was still not resolved, it still remained doubt.

"Oh! Ohh! Oh!" he howled in various intonations. He began by howling, "I won't!" and so went on howling on the letter O.

For all three days, in the course of which there was no time for him, he was thrashing about in that black sack into which an invisible, invincible force was pushing him. He struggled as one condemned to death struggles in the executioner's hands, knowing he cannot save himself; and with every moment he felt that, despite all his efforts to struggle, he was coming closer and closer to what terrified him. He felt that his torment lay in being thrust into that black hole, and still more in being unable to get into it. What kept him from getting into it was the claim that his had been a good life. This justification of his life clutched at him, would not let him move forward, and tormented him most of all.

Suddenly some force shoved him in the chest, in the side, choked his breath still more, he fell through the hole, and there, at the end of the hole, something lit up. What was done to him was like what happens on the train, when you think you are moving forward, but are moving backward, and suddenly find out the real direction.

"Yes, it was all not right," he said to himself, "but never mind. I can, I can do 'right.' But what is 'right'?" he asked himself and suddenly grew still.

This was at the end of the third day, an hour before his death. Just then the little schoolboy quietly stole into his father's room and went up to his bed. The dying man went on howling desperately and thrashing his arms about. His hand landed on the boy's head. The boy seized it, pressed it to his lips, and wept.

Just then Ivan Ilyich fell through, saw light, and it was revealed to him that his life had not been what it ought, but that it could still be rectified. He asked himself what was "right," and grew still, listening. Here he felt that someone was kissing his hand. He opened his eyes and looked at his son. He felt sorry for him. His wife came over to him. He looked at her. She was gazing at him with a despairing expression, open-mouthed, and with unwiped tears on her nose and cheek. He felt sorry for her.

"Yes, I'm tormenting them," he thought. "They're sorry, but it will be better for them when I die." He wanted to say that, but was unable to bring it out. "Anyhow, why speak, I must act," he thought. He indicated his son to his wife with his eyes and said:

"Take him away . . . sorry . . . for you, too . . ." He also wanted to say "Forgive," but said "Forgo," and, no longer able to correct himself, waved his hand, knowing that the one who had to would understand.

And suddenly it became clear to him that what was tormenting him and would not be resolved was suddenly all resolved at once, on two sides, on ten sides, on all sides. He was sorry for them, he had to act so that it was not painful for them. To deliver them and deliver himself from these sufferings. "How good and how simple," he thought. "And the pain?" he asked himself. "What's become of it? Where are you, pain?"

He became attentive.

"Yes, there it is. Well, then, let there be pain.

"And death? Where is it?"

He sought his old habitual fear of death and could not find it. Where was it? What death? There was no more fear because there was no more death.

Instead of death there was light.

"So that's it!" he suddenly said aloud. "What joy!"

For him all this happened in an instant and the significance of that instant never changed. For those present, his agony went on for two more hours. Something gurgled in his chest; his emaciated body kept twitching. Then the gurgling and wheezing gradually subsided.

"It's finished!" someone said over him.

He heard those words and repeated them in his soul. "Death is finished," he said to himself. "It is no more."

He drew in air, stopped at mid-breath, stretched out, and died.

1884–86

The Kreutzer Sonata

*But I say to you that every one who looks at a woman lustfully
has already committed adultery with her in his heart.*

MATTHEW 5:28 (RSV)

*The disciples said to him, "If such is the case of a man with his
wife, it is not expedient to marry." But he said to them, "Not
all men can receive this saying, but only those to whom it is
given. For there are eunuchs who have been so from birth, and
there are eunuchs who have been made eunuchs by men, and there
are eunuchs who have made themselves eunuchs for the sake of
the kingdom of heaven. He who is able to receive this, let him
receive it."*

MATTHEW 19:10–12 (RSV)

I

IT WAS EARLY SPRING. We were travelling for the second day. Passengers going short distances entered and left the carriage, but three passengers, like myself, had been travelling from the very place of the train's departure: an unattractive and no longer young lady, a smoker, with a worn-out face, in a coat of mannish cut and a hat; her acquaintance, a garrulous man of about forty, with neat new things; and another gentleman who kept himself apart, of medium height, with jerky movements, not yet old, but with obviously premature grey in his curly hair, and with unusually glittering eyes quickly darting from object to object. He was dressed in an old but expensively tailored coat with a lambskin collar and a tall lambskin hat. Under the coat, when he unbuttoned it, could be seen a jerkin and an embroidered Russian shirt. A peculiarity of this gentleman also consisted in the fact that he occasionally produced strange sounds, similar to a cough or laughter begun and broken off.

Throughout the trip, this gentleman carefully avoided communicating or becoming acquainted with the other passengers. To his neighbours' attempts at conversation he responded briefly and curtly, and he either read, or smoked, looking out the window, or, taking provisions from his old bag, drank tea or ate a little something.

It seemed to me that he was weary of his solitude, and several times I was about to strike up a conversation with him, but each time our eyes met, which happened often, since we sat cater-corner to each other, he turned away and took up a book or looked out the window.

During a stop, towards evening of the second day, at a large station, this nervous gentleman went to get some hot water and made tea for himself. The gentleman with neat new things, a lawyer, as I learned afterwards, and his neighbour, the smoking lady in the mannish coat, went to have tea at the station.

During the absence of the gentleman and lady, several new persons entered the carriage, among them a tall, clean-shaven, wrinkled old man, evidently a merchant, in a skunk-fur coat and a cloth cap with an enormous visor. The merchant sat down across from the places of the lady and the lawyer and at once got into conversation with a young man, a merchant's clerk by the looks of him, who got into the carriage at the same station.

I was sitting cater-corner to them and, as the train was not moving, I could hear snatches of their conversation when no one was passing by. The merchant began by saying that he was going to his estate, which was only one stop away; then, as usual, they got to talking first about prices, about trade, talked, as usual, about how trading was done in Moscow nowadays, then talked about the Nizhny Novgorod fair. The clerk started telling about how some rich merchant they both knew had been carousing at the fair, but the old man did not let him finish and himself started telling about the former carouses in Kunavin, which he himself had taken part in. He was obviously proud of having taken part in them, and with obvious delight told how he and that same acquaintance got drunk once in Kunavin and pulled such a stunt that it had to be told in a whisper, and the clerk guffawed for the whole carriage to hear, and the old man also laughed, baring two yellow teeth.

Not expecting to hear anything interesting, I got up to take a stroll on the platform before the train left. In the doorway I met the lawyer and the lady, who were discussing something animatedly as they went.

"You won't have time," said the gregarious lawyer, "it's nearly the second bell."

In fact, before I reached the end of the train, the bell rang. When I came back, the animated conversation between the lady and the lawyer was still going on. The old merchant sat silently across from them, looking sternly before him and from time to time chewing his lips with his teeth in disapproval.

"Then she informed her husband straight out," the lawyer was saying, smiling, as I passed by them, "that she could not and would not live with him, because . . ."

And he started telling something further that I could not make out. After me more passengers came, the conductor came, a tradesman ran in, and there was noise for quite a while, which prevented me from hearing the conversation. When everything became quiet, and I could again hear the voice of the lawyer, the conversation had obviously gone on from a particular case to general considerations.

The lawyer was speaking about how the question of divorce now occupied public opinion in Europe and how with us such cases were appearing more and more often. Noticing that his was the only voice audible, the lawyer stopped talking and turned to the old man.

"There were no such things in the old days, isn't that so?" he said, smiling pleasantly.

The old man was about to make some reply, but just then the train started, and the old man, taking off his visored hat, began to cross himself and recite a prayer in a whisper. The lawyer, looking away, waited politely. Having finished his prayer and crossed himself three times, the old man set his cap on straight, pulled it down low, settled back in his seat, and began to speak.

"They happened before as well, sir, only less," he said. "These days it couldn't be otherwise. They've got so very educated."

The train, moving faster and faster, clattered over the joints, and it was hard for me to hear, but I was interested and moved closer. My neighbour, the nervous gentleman with the glittering eyes, obviously also became interested and tried to listen without moving from his place.

"What's so bad about education?" the lady said with a barely noticeable smile. "Can it be better to marry as they did in the old days, when the bride and groom hadn't even seen each other?" she went on, responding, as is the habit with many ladies, not to her interlocutor's words, but to the words she thought he would say. "They didn't know if they loved, if they could love, but married whoever happened along and suffered all their lives. Is that better, in your opinion?" she said, obviously addressing her speech to me and to the lawyer, and least of all to the old man with whom she was talking.

"They've got so very educated," repeated the old man, looking at the lady with scorn and leaving her question unanswered.

"It would be desirable to know how you explain the connection between education and marital discord," the lawyer said with a barely noticeable smile.

The merchant was about to say something, but the lady interrupted him.

"No, that time is past," she said. But the lawyer stopped her.

"No, allow him to express his thought."

"Education leads to foolishness," the old man said resolutely.

"People marry who don't love each other, and then they're surprised that they live in discord," the lady spoke hurriedly and kept glancing at the lawyer, at me, and even at the clerk, who got up from his seat and, leaning on the back, listened smilingly to the conversation. "It's only animals that can be coupled as the owner likes, but people have their inclinations, their attachments," she said, obviously wishing to sting the merchant.

"You oughtn't to talk that way, madam," the old man said. "Animals are brutes, but man's been given the law."

"Well, but how live with a person if there's no love?" the lady hastened to voice her opinions, which probably seemed very new to her.

"That wasn't gone into before," the old man said in an impressive tone. "It's only started now. There's something, and she up and says: 'I'm leaving you.' Even among muzhiks this fashion's caught on: 'Here,' she says, 'take all your shirts and trousers, and I'll go with Vanka, his hair's curlier than yours.' Well, go and talk after that. The first thing in a woman should be fear."

The clerk looked at the lawyer, and at the lady, and at me, obviously holding back a smile and ready either to laugh or to approve of the merchant's speech, depending on how it would be taken.

"What fear?" said the lady.

"This: that she fears her hu-u-usband![1] That's what fear."

"Well, my dear man, that time has passed," the lady said, even with a certain spite.

"No, madam, that time cannot pass. As she, Eve, a woman, was created out of her husband's rib, so she'll remain to the end of time," said the old man, tossing his head so sternly and victoriously that the clerk at once decided that victory was on the merchant's side and laughed loudly.

"It's you men who reason that way," said the lady, not surrendering and glancing at us. "You gave yourselves freedom, but you want to keep woman in her high chamber. And you permit yourselves everything all right."

"Nobody's got any permission, it's only that a man doesn't bring additions to the household, and a woman is a frail vessel," the merchant went on imposing.

The imposingness of the merchant's intonations was obviously winning the listeners over, and even the lady felt crushed, but still did not surrender.

"Yes, but I think you'll agree that a woman is a human being and has feelings just as a man does. What is she to do if she doesn't love her husband?"

"Doesn't love him!" the merchant repeated menacingly, working his eyebrows and lips. "She'll love him all right!"

This unexpected argument was especially to the clerk's liking, and he produced an approving sound.

"Oh, no, she won't," the lady began, "and if there's no love, it's impossible to force it."

"Well, and if a wife betrays her husband, what then?" said the lawyer.

"That's not done," said the old man, "you've got to see to that."

"But if it happens, what then? It does occur."

"With some it does, but not with us," said the old man.

They all fell silent. The clerk stirred, moved closer, and, clearly not wishing to be left behind the others, smiled and began:

"Yes, sir, there was also a scandal with one of our fellows. It's also very hard to decide. He also ended up with a loose sort of woman. And she started playing the devil. And he was a sober lad and with some development. First she went with an office clerk. He tried to talk it over nicely. She wouldn't quiet down. Did all sorts of nastiness. Started stealing money from him. And he beat her. But she got worse still. Took up with one of the unbaptised, with a Jew, if I may say so. What was he to do? He dropped her altogether. So he lives as a bachelor, and she plays around."

"Because he's a fool," said the old man. "If he hadn't given way to her from the very start, if he'd really brought her up short, she'd live with him all right. Mustn't give 'em freedom from the start. Never trust a horse in the field or a wife in the house."

Just then the conductor came to ask for tickets to the next station. The old man gave him his ticket.

"Yes, sir, the female sex has got to be brought up short way before, or else it's all lost."

"Well, and how about you yourself telling just now how married men lived it up at the Kunavin fair?" I asked, unable to restrain myself.

"That's another matter," the merchant said and sank into silence.

When the whistle sounded, the merchant stood up, took his bag from under the seat, wrapped himself in his coat, and, tipping his cap, went out to the rear platform.

II

As soon as the old man left, several voices rose in conversation.

"An Old Testament papa," said the clerk.

"A living *Domostroy*,"² said the lady. "What a wild notion of women and marriage!"

"Yes, sir, we're far from the European view of marriage," said the lawyer.

"The main thing such people don't understand," said the lady, "is that marriage without love isn't marriage, that only love sanctifies marriage, and that the only true marriage is one sanctified by love."

The clerk listened and smiled, wishing to memorize as much of the intelligent conversation as he could for future use.

In the middle of the lady's speech, a sound as of broken-off laughter or sobbing came from behind me, and, turning to look, we saw my neighbour, the solitary, grey-haired gentleman with the glittering eyes, who, during the conversation, which obviously interested him, had inconspicuously approached us. He stood, placing his hands on the back of a seat, and was obviously very agitated: his face was red, a muscle twitched on his cheek.

"What is this love . . . love . . . love . . . that sanctifies marriage?" he said, faltering.

Seeing the speaker's agitated state, the lady tried to answer him as gently and circumstantially as she could.

"True love . . . If there is this love between a man and a woman, then marriage is possible," said the lady.

"Yes, ma'am, but what is meant by true love?" said the gentleman with the glittering eyes, timidly and with an awkward smile.

"Everybody knows what love is," said the lady, obviously wishing to break off her conversation with him.

"But I don't," said the gentleman. "You must define what you mean . . ."

"Why, it's very simple," the lady said, but fell to thinking. "Love? Love is an exclusive preference for one man or woman over all the rest," she said.

"Preference for how long? For a month? For two days? For half an hour?" the grey-haired man said and laughed.

"No, excuse me, you're obviously talking about something else."

"No, ma'am, about the same thing."

"Madam says," the lawyer mixed in, pointing to the lady, "that marriage should proceed, first, from attachment—love, if you wish—and that if such is present, then only in that case does marriage present itself as something, so to speak, sacred. Hence any marriage which does not have at its base a natural attachment—love, if you wish—has nothing morally obligatory in itself. Is my understanding correct?" he turned to the lady.

The lady, nodding her head, expressed her approval of this explanation of her thought.

"Wherefore . . ." the lawyer went on with his speech, but the nervous gentleman, his eyes now burning with fire, was obviously restraining himself with difficulty and, not giving the lawyer his say, began:

"No, I'm talking about the same thing, about the preference for one man or woman over all others, only I ask: preference for how long?"

"For how long? For a long time, sometimes for a whole lifetime," said the lady, shrugging her shoulders.

"Yes, but that happens only in novels, and never in life. In life this preference for one over others may last for years, but very rarely, more often for a few months or else weeks, days, hours," he said, obviously knowing that he was astonishing everyone by his opinion, and pleased with that.

"Ah, how can you! No. No, excuse me," all three of us started speaking in one voice. Even the clerk produced some sort of disapproving sound.

"Yes, sir, I know," the grey-haired man outshouted us, "you're speaking of how it's considered to be, and I'm speaking of how it is. Every man experiences what you call love for every beautiful woman."

"Ah, it's terrible, what you're saying; but isn't there this feeling between people that is called love and that is given not for months or years, but for a whole lifetime?"

"No, there isn't. Even if we allow that a man does prefer a certain woman for his whole life, the woman, in all probability, will prefer someone else, and that's how it is and always has been in the world," he said, took out a cigarette case, and began to light up.

"But it may also be mutual," said the lawyer.

"No, sir, it may not," the man objected, "any more than it may be that two marked peas lie side by side in a cartload of peas. And besides that, it's not only a matter of improbability here, but most likely of satiety. To love one woman or one man for a whole lifetime is the same as to say that one candle will burn for a whole lifetime," he said, inhaling greedily.

"But you keep talking about physical love. Don't you allow for love based on a oneness of ideals, on spiritual affinity?" said the lady.

"Spiritual affinity! Oneness of ideals!" he repeated, producing his sound. "In that case there's no need to sleep together (forgive the crudeness). And yet people go to bed together as a result of a oneness of ideals," he said and laughed nervously.

"Excuse me," said the lawyer, "but the facts contradict what you're saying. We see that marriages do exist, that the whole of mankind or the majority of it lives in marriage, and many live honourably throughout a long married life."

The grey-haired gentleman laughed again.

"First you say that marriage is based on love, and when I express doubt about the existence of any love except the sensual, you prove the existence of love by the fact that marriages exist. But in our time marriage is nothing but deceit!"

"No, sir, excuse me," said the lawyer, "I say only that marriages did and do exist."

"They do. Only why do they exist? They did and do exist among people who see something mysterious in marriage, a sacrament that's binding before God. Among them they exist, but among us they don't. Among us people marry, seeing nothing in marriage except copulation, and the result is either deceit or violence. If it's deceit, it's easier to bear. The husband and wife only deceive people that they live monogamously, but live polygamously on both sides. That's vile, but still it goes over; but when, as most often happens, the husband and wife take upon themselves the external obligation to live together all their lives, and already hate each other after the second month, wish they were divorced, and still live together, then what comes of it is that terrible hell from which people drink themselves to death, shoot themselves, kill and poison themselves or each other," he spoke more and more quickly, letting no one put in a word, and growing more and more heated. Everyone was silent. It was awkward.

"Yes, critical episodes undoubtedly do occur in married life," said the lawyer, wishing to stop this indecently heated conversation.

"I see you've figured out who I am?" the grey-haired gentleman said softly and as if calmly.

"No, I don't have that pleasure."

"It's no great pleasure. I'm Pozdnyshev, the one to whom that critical episode occurred which you alluded to, that episode in which he killed his wife," he said, quickly glancing at each of us.

No one could find anything to say, and we all remained silent.

"Well, it makes no difference," he said, producing his sound. "Anyhow, forgive me! Ah! . . . I won't hamper you."

"No, no, please . . ." said the lawyer, himself not knowing "please" what.

But Pozdnyshev, not listening to him, quickly turned and went to his seat. The gentleman and lady were whispering. I sat beside Pozdnyshev and was silent, unable to think of what to say. It was too dark to read, and therefore I closed my eyes and pretended that I wanted to sleep. So we rode on silently until the next station.

At the station, the gentleman and lady moved to another car, which they had arranged earlier with the conductor. The clerk settled himself on a seat and fell asleep. Pozdnyshev kept smoking and drinking the tea he had made at the last station.

When I opened my eyes and looked at him, he suddenly addressed me with resolution and irritation:

"It is probably unpleasant for you to sit with me, knowing who I am? In that case I can go away."

"Oh, no, please."

"Well, then, would you like some? Only it's strong." He poured me tea.

"They say . . . And it's all lies . . ." he said.

"What are you talking about?" I asked.

"Always the same thing: this love of theirs and what it is. Don't you want to sleep?"

"Not at all."

"Then do you want me to tell you how I was led by that same love to what happened to me?"

"Yes, if it's not too painful for you."

"No, it's painful for me to be silent. Drink your tea. Or is it too strong?"

The tea was in fact like beer, but I drank a glass. Just then the conductor passed. He silently followed him with angry eyes, and began only when the man was gone.

III

"Well, then I'll tell you . . . You really want me to?"

I repeated that I wanted it very much. He paused, rubbed his face with his hands, and began:

"If I'm to tell you, I must tell everything from the beginning: I must tell how and why I married, and what sort I was before marriage.

"Before marriage I lived as everyone does—that is, in our circle. I'm a landowner and a university graduate, and was marshal of the nobility.[3] Before marriage I lived as everyone does, that is, in depravity, and, like all people of my circle, while living in depravity, I was sure I was living as one should. I thought of myself as a dear fellow and a completely moral person. I wasn't a seducer, had no unnatural tastes, did not make it the chief aim of life, as many of my peers did, but gave myself to depravity soberly, decently, for the sake of health. I avoided women who might bind me by giving birth to a child or becoming attached to me. However, maybe there were children and attachments, but I made as if there weren't any. And I not only considered that moral, but I was proud of it."

He stopped, produced his sound, as he always did, evidently, when a new thought came to him.

"And in that lies the chief loathsomeness," he cried. "Depravity does not lie in anything physical, no, depravity is no physical outrage; but depravity, true depravity, lies precisely in freeing oneself of moral relations to a woman with whom you enter into physical contact. But that freedom was just what I laid to my credit. I remember how I suffered once from not managing to pay a woman who, probably having fallen in love with me, had given herself to me. I calmed down only when I had sent her the money, showing thereby that I did not consider myself morally bound to her. Don't nod your head as if you agree with me," he suddenly shouted at me. "I know those tricks. You all—and you, you, too—at best, unless you're a rare exception, have the same views I had then. Well, it makes no difference, forgive me," he went on, "but the point is that it's terrible, terrible, terrible!"

"What's terrible?" I asked.

"That abyss of delusion we live in regarding women and our relations to them. No, sir, I cannot speak of it calmly, and not because this episode, as he put it, occurred with me, but because since that episode occurred with me, my eyes have been opened, and I see everything in quite a different light. Everything's inside out, inside out! . . ."

He lit a cigarette and, leaning his elbows on his knees, began to speak.

I could not see his face in the darkness and only heard, through the rattling of the carriage, his impressive and pleasant voice.

IV

"Yes, sir, only having suffered greatly, as I suffered, only thanks to that did I understand where the root of it all lies, understand what ought to be, and therefore see all the horror of what is.

"So kindly see how and when that which led up to my episode began. It began when I was going on sixteen. It happened when I was still in high school and my older brother was a first-year university student. I did not know women yet, but, like all the unfortunate children of our circle, I was already not an innocent boy: it was already the second year since I was corrupted by other boys; already woman, not this or that woman, but woman as something sweet, woman, any woman, woman's nakedness, tormented me. My solitude was impure. I was tormented, as ninety-nine per cent of our boys are tormented. I was horrified, I suffered, I prayed, and I fell. I was already depraved in imagination and in reality, but I had not yet taken the final step. I was perishing alone, but had not yet laid hands on another human being. But then a comrade of my brother's, a student, a merrymaker, what's known as a good fellow, that is, the greatest of scoundrels, who taught us to drink and play cards, persuaded us after a drinking party to go *there*. We went. My brother was also still innocent, and he fell that night. And I, a fifteen-year-old boy, defiled myself and contributed to defiling a woman, without any understanding of what I was doing. I had never heard from any older men that what I was doing was bad. Neither will anyone hear it from them now. True, it's in the commandments, but the commandments are needed only for answering the priest at an examination,[4] and then not very much needed, far less than the commandment about using *ut* in the Latin conditional.

"So I never heard from any older people, whose opinions I respected, that this was a bad thing. On the contrary, I heard from people I respected that it was a good thing. I heard that my struggles and sufferings would calm down after that, heard it and read it, and heard from older men that it would be good for my health; and from my schoolmates I heard that there was some sort of merit or valour in it. So that in general I could see nothing but good in it. The danger of illness? But even that had been foreseen. The solicitous government takes care of that. It keeps an eye on the correct functioning of brothels and furnishes depravity to schoolboys. And salaried doctors keep an eye on it. That's how it should be. They maintain that depravity is good for one's health, and they organize proper, well-regulated depravity. I know mothers who take care of their sons' health in that sense. Science, too, sends them to brothels."

"Why science?" I said.

"And what are doctors? Priests of science. Who corrupts young men, maintaining that it's necessary for their health? They do. And then with terrible self-importance they treat syphilis."

"But why shouldn't they treat syphilis?"

"Because if one per cent of the efforts spent on treating syphilis was spent on eradicating depravity, there would long since have been no syphilis to speak of. And yet the efforts are applied not to eradicating depravity, but to encouraging it, to ensuring its safety. Well, but that's not the point. The point is that with me, and with ninety per cent, if not more, not only of our class but of all, even peasants, that terrible thing happened, that I fell not because I yielded to the natural temptation of a certain woman's charm. No, no woman tempted me; I fell because the milieu around me saw that fall, some as a most legitimate and healthful function, others as a most natural and not only forgivable but even innocent amusement for a young man. I did not understand that it was a fall, I simply began giving myself to those half pleasures, half needs, which are proper, as had been suggested to me, to a certain age, I began giving myself to depravity as I had begun to drink and smoke. And yet there was something special and touching in this first fall. I remember feeling sad at once, on the spot, before I left the room, so sad that I wanted to cry, to cry about the loss of my innocence, about my forever-destroyed relation to women. Yes, sir, my natural, simple relation to women was destroyed forever. From then on I did not and could not have a pure relation to women. I became what's known as a fornicator. To be a fornicator is a physical condition similar to the condition of a morphine addict, a drunkard, a smoker. As a morphine addict, a drunkard, a smoker is not a normal person, so a man who has known several women for his own pleasure is no longer normal, but is corrupted forever—a fornicator. As a drunkard or a morphine addict can be recognized at once by his face, his manner, so, too, a fornicator. A fornicator may abstain, struggle; but he will never have a simple, clear, pure, brotherly relation to women. You can recognize a fornicator at once by the way he eyes a young woman and looks her over. And I became a fornicator and remained one, and that's what destroyed me."

V

"THAT'S RIGHT, sir. Then it went further and further, there were all sorts of deviations. My God, when I remember all my loathsomeness in this respect, it's horrible! That's how I remember myself, who was laughed at by my comrades because of my so-called innocence. And when I hear about gilded youth, officers, Parisians! And all these gentlemen, and I, when we thirty-year-old debauchees, having hundreds of the most various and terrible crimes on our souls with regard to women, when we, scrubbed clean, shaven, scented, in clean linen, a tailcoat or a uniform, happen to enter a drawing room or a ballroom—the emblem of purity—how charming!

"Just think of what ought to be and what is. It ought to be that when such a gentleman enters the company of my sister or daughter, I, knowing his life, should go up to him, take him aside, and quietly say to him: 'My dear fellow, I know how you live, how you spend your nights and with whom. This is no place for you. There are pure, innocent girls here. Go away!' That's how it ought to be; how it is, is that when such a gentleman appears and dances with my sister or my daughter, embracing her, we rejoice, if he's rich and has connections. Perchance, after Rigolboche,[5] he will honour my daughter as well. Even if there are traces left, a bit of illness—never mind. Nowadays there are good treatments. Why, I know several parents in high society who were overjoyed to marry their daughters off to syphilitics. Oh, oh, loathsome! May there come a time when this loathsomeness and lying are exposed!"

And he produced his strange sounds several times and took his tea. The tea was awfully strong, there was no water to dilute it. I felt particularly agitated by the two glasses I had drunk. He, too, must have been affected by the tea, because he was becoming increasingly excited. His voice was growing more and more melodious and expressive. He constantly shifted his posture, took his hat off, put it on again, and his face kept changing strangely in the semi-darkness in which we were sitting.

"Well, that's how I lived till the age of thirty, not for a moment abandoning the intention of marrying and setting up for myself the most lofty and pure family life, and to that end I was looking for a suitable girl," he went on. "I wallowed in festering depravity and at the same time kept an eye out for girls whose purity would make them worthy of me. I rejected many precisely because they weren't pure enough for me; at last I found one whom I deemed worthy. She was one of two daughters of a once very rich but now ruined landowner from Penza province.

"One evening, after we had gone for a boat ride and were returning home at night by moonlight, and I was sitting beside her and admiring her shapely figure in a close-fitting jersey and her tresses, I suddenly decided that she was the one. It seemed to me that evening that she understood everything, everything I felt and thought, and that I felt and thought the most lofty things. Essentially, it was only that the jersey was especially becoming, as were the tresses, and that after a day spent in closeness to her I desired still greater closeness.

"It's an astonishing thing how complete the illusion can be that beauty is the good. A beautiful woman says stupid things, you listen and don't see the stupidity, you see intelligence. She says and does vile things, and you see something sweet. And when she doesn't say stupid or vile things, but is beautiful, you think she's a marvel of intelligence and morality.

"I returned home in ecstasy and decided that she was the height of moral perfection and that therefore she was worthy to be my wife, and the next day I proposed.

"What a tangle it is! Of thousands of marrying men, not only among our kind, but unfortunately also among the people, there is hardly one who has not been married ten times already, or else a hundred, a thousand, like Don Juan, before his marriage. (True, there are, as I've heard and observed, pure young men, who feel and know that it's not a joke but a great matter. God be with them! But in my time there wasn't one like that in ten thousand.) And everybody knows it and pretends not to know. In all novels there are detailed descriptions of the heroes' feelings, of the ponds and bushes they walk by; but, while his great love for some girl is described, nothing is said about what he, the interesting hero, did before: not a word about his visits to houses, about chambermaids, kitchen maids, other men's wives. If there exist such improper novels, they are not put into the hands of those who most need to know—the young girls. First we pretend before young girls that the licentiousness that fills half the life of our cities and even villages, that this licentiousness doesn't exist. Then we get so used to this pretence that finally, like the English, we ourselves begin sincerely to believe that we're all moral people and live in a moral world. As for the girls, the poor things believe it in all seriousness. So my unfortunate wife also believed. I remember how, when I was already her fiancé, I showed her my diary, from which she could learn at least a little of my past, mainly about the last liaison I had, which she might have learned of from others, and of which I therefore felt it necessary to tell her. I remember her horror, despair, and bewilderment when she learned and understood. I saw that she wanted to drop me then. And why didn't she!"

He produced his sound, paused, and took another sip of tea.

VI

"No, anyhow, it's better, it's better like this!" he cried. "It serves me right! But that's not the thing. I wanted to say that it's only the unfortunate girls who are deceived here. The mothers know it, especially mothers educated by their husbands, they know it very well. And while pretending to believe in the purity of men, in reality they act quite differently. They know what bait will catch men for themselves and their daughters.

"For it's only we men who don't know, and don't know because we don't want to know, while women know very well, that the most lofty, poetic love, as we call it, depends not on moral qualities, but on physical intimacy and, with that, on hairstyle, the colour and cut of a dress. Ask an experienced coquette who has set herself the task of captivating a man which she would sooner risk: to be convicted, in the presence of the man she is trying to charm, of lying, cruelty, even licentiousness, or to appear before him in a poorly made and unattractive dress—she will always prefer the first. She knows that we men all lie about lofty feelings—we need only her body, and therefore we'll forgive any vileness, but will not forgive an ugly, tasteless, bad-tone dress. A coquette knows that consciously, but every innocent girl knows it unconsciously, as animals know things.

"Hence those loathsome jerseys, those things slapped on behind, those bare shoulders, arms, all but bare breasts. Women, especially those who have gone through the men's school, know very well that conversations about lofty matters are—conversations, but that a man needs their body and all that presents it in the most alluring light; and that's what gets done. If only we cast off the habit of this outrage, which has become second nature to us, and look at the life of our upper classes as it is, with all its shamelessness, it's one continuous brothel. You don't agree? Allow me to prove it," he went on, interrupting me. "You say that women in our society live by other interests than women in brothels, and I say no, and I'll prove it. If people differ in their goals in life, in the inner content of their life, that difference will inevitably be reflected in externals as well, and externally they will be different. But look at those unfortunate despised ones and at ladies of the highest society: the same outfits, the same fashions, the same perfumes, the same bared arms, shoulders, breasts, and tight-fitting, thrust-out behinds, the same passion for little stones, for expensive, glittering things, the same amusements, dancing, and music, and singing. As those use every means to allure, so do these. No difference. To define it strictly, one need only say that the short-term prostitutes are usually despised, the long-term prostitutes respected."

VII

"Yes, so it was these jerseys, and tresses, and slapped-on bits that caught me. To catch me was easy, because I had been raised in conditions in which amorous young men are forced like hotbed cucumbers. For our stimulating, excessive food, along with total physical idleness, is nothing other than a systematic exciting of lust. Surprising or not, it's true. And I myself saw none of it until recently. But now I've seen it. That's why it pains me that nobody knows it, and they say stupid things, like that lady.

"Yes, sir, this spring some muzhiks were working on a railway embankment near me. Ordinary food for a peasant lad is bread, kvass, and onion; he's alive, vigorous, healthy, and does light field work. He goes to work on the railway, here his grub is kasha and a pound of meat. But then he gets rid of that meat working sixteen hours a day with a thousand-pound cart. And so it's just right for him. Well, but we who consume two pounds of meat, game, and all sorts of strong food and drink—where does all that go? Into sensual excesses. And if it does go there, and the safety valve is open, everything's fine; but close the valve, as I did temporarily, and at once you get an excitement which, passing through the prism of our artificial life, will express itself in a love of the purest water, sometimes even platonic. And I fell in love as everybody does. It was all there: the raptures, the tenderness, the poetry. But in fact this love of mine was the product, on the one hand, of the activity of the mama and the dressmakers, and, on the other, of the excess of food I consumed in my idle life. If, on the one hand, there had been no boat rides, no dressmakers with their tight waists, and so on, and my wife had been dressed in a shapeless housecoat and sitting at home, while I, on the other hand, had been living in normal human conditions, consuming as much food as was needed for my work, and if my safety valve had been open—because it somehow chanced to be closed at that time—I wouldn't have fallen in love, and nothing would have happened."

VIII

"WELL, but this time it all fell together: my condition, and a pretty dress, and a successful boat ride. Twenty times it hadn't succeeded, but this time it did. Like a trap. I'm not laughing. Marriages are set up that way now, like traps. Isn't it only natural? The wench is ripe, she must get married. It seems so simple, when the wench is not ugly and there are men who wish to marry. That's how it was done in the old days. The girl comes of age, the parents arrange the marriage. That's how it was done and is done in all mankind: among the Chinese, the Hindus, the Mohammedans, among our folk; that's how it's done in at least ninety-nine per cent of the human race. Only one per cent or less of us, the profligates, found it no good and invented something new. And what is this new thing? The new thing is that the girls sit there, and the men, as in a marketplace, walk about and choose. And the wenches wait and think, but don't dare to say: 'Me, dear man! No, me. Not her, but me: look what shoulders I've got, and other things.' And we men stroll about, look them over, and are very pleased: 'I know, I won't fall for that.' They stroll about, they look them over, very pleased that it's all set up for them. Watch out, don't get careless—snap, that's it!"

"Then how should it be?" I said. "Should the woman make the proposal?"

"I really don't know how; only if it's equality, then it's equality. If they think matchmaking is humiliating, this is a thousand times more so. There the rights and chances are equal, but here the woman is either a slave in a marketplace or bait in a trap. Tell some mother or the girl herself the truth, that the only thing she's busy with is snaring a husband. God, what an insult! Yet they all do only that, and there's nothing else for them to do. And the terrible thing is to see quite young, poor, innocent girls sometimes busy with it. And again, if it was done openly, but it's all deceit. 'Ah, the origin of species, how interesting! Ah, Liza's so interested in painting! Will you be at the exhibition? How instructive! And troika rides, and the theatre, and the symphony! Ah, how wonderful! My Liza's mad about music. Why don't you share these convictions? And boating! . . .' And just one thought: 'Take, take me, my Liza! No, me! Well, try at least! . . .' Oh, the loathsomeness! the lies!" he concluded, and finishing the last of his tea, he began to put away the cups and plates.

IX

"YOU KNOW," he began, putting the tea and sugar in his bag, "the domination of women from which the world suffers—it all comes from this."

"How do you mean, the domination of women?" I said. "The rights and advantages are on the men's side."

"Yes, yes, that's just it," he interrupted me. "That's just what I want to tell you, that's what explains the extraordinary phenomenon that, on the one hand, it is completely correct that woman is reduced to the lowest degree of humiliation, and, on the other hand, that she dominates. Just the same as the Jews, as they pay back for their oppression by monetary power, so with women. 'Ah, you want us to be merchants only. Very well, we merchants will own you,' say the Jews. 'Ah, you want us to be objects of sensuality only. Very well, as objects of sensuality we will enslave you,' say the women. The absence of women's rights is not in the fact that she cannot vote or be a judge—to be occupied with such things does not constitute any sort of right—but in the fact that, to be equal to man in sexual relations, she must have the right to use the man or abstain from him as she wishes, to choose a man as she wishes and not to be chosen. You say that's outrageous. Very well. Then a man should not have those rights either. But now a woman is deprived of the right the man has. And so, to make up for that right, she acts upon the man's sensuality, through sensuality she so subjects him that his choice is merely formal, and in reality it is she who chooses. And once she possesses this means, she misuses it and acquires terrible power over people."

"But where is this special power?" I asked.

"Where? Everywhere, in everything. Go through the shops in any big city. There are millions there, the human labour invested there is inestimable, but look at ninety per cent of these shops—is there anything in them for the use of men? All the luxury of life is required and maintained by women. Count up all the factories. A huge number of them make useless adornments, carriages, furniture, trinkets for women. Millions of people, generations of slaves perish at this hard labour in the factories only for women's whims. Women, like queens, keep ninety per cent of the human race in the bondage of slavery and hard labour. And all because they've been humiliated, deprived of equal rights with men. And so in revenge they act upon our sensuality, they catch us in their nets. Yes, it's all from that. Women have made of themselves such an instrument for arousing sensuality that a man cannot deal with a woman calmly. As soon as a man approaches a woman, he succumbs to her spell and gets befuddled. Even before, I always felt awkward, eerie, when I saw a woman decked out in a ball gown, but now I'm downright scared, I see something downright dangerous for people and against the law, I want to call the police, to ask for protection against the danger, to demand that the dangerous object be taken away, removed.

"Yes, you laugh!" he shouted at me. "But this is not a joke. I'm sure the time will come, and maybe very soon, when people will understand it and will be surprised at the existence of a society which allowed for acts so disturbing to the public peace as those bodily adornments downright provoking of sensuality which women are allowed in our society. It's the same as setting all sorts of traps along paths and promenades—even worse! Why is gambling forbidden, while women in prostitutionous, sensuality-arousing costumes are not? They're a thousand times more dangerous!"

X

"WELL, so that's how I got caught. I was, as it's called, in love. I not only imagined her to be the height of perfection, I also imagined, during the time of my engagement, that I, too, was the height of perfection. For there's no scoundrel who, if he searches, can't find some scoundrels worse than himself in some respect, and who, therefore, can't find a reason to feel proud and be pleased with himself. So it was with me: I didn't marry money—gain had nothing to do with it—unlike the majority of my acquaintances, who married for money or connections. I was rich, she was poor. That's one thing. Another, which I was proud of, was that others married with the intention of continuing in the future to live in the same polygamy they had lived in before marriage; while I had the firm intention of keeping to monogamy after the wedding, and there were no limits to the pride I took in that. Yes, I was a terrible swine and imagined that I was an angel.

"The time of my engagement did not last long. I cannot recall that time now without shame! What vileness! It's supposed to be a time of spiritual love, not sensual. Well, if love is spiritual, a spiritual communion, then that spiritual communion should be expressed in words, conversation, dialogue. There was none of that. It used to be terribly difficult to speak when we were left by ourselves. Like some sort of labour of Sisyphus. You think up something to say, say it, and again must be silent and think. There was nothing to talk about. Everything that could be said about the life ahead of us, the arrangements, the plans, had already been said, and what then? If we had been animals, we would simply have known that we weren't supposed to talk; but here, on the contrary, talking was necessary and yet pointless, because we were concerned with something not to be resolved in conversation. And with that there's also this hideous custom of eating confectionery, crude gluttony on sweets and all these loathsome preparations for the wedding: talk about the apartment, the bedroom, bed linen, coats, dressing gowns, underwear, costumes. You must understand that, if people marry according to the Domostroy, as that old man said, then the feather beds, the dowry, the linen are only details accompanying the sacrament. But with us, when out of ten men who marry there's scarcely one who not only believes in the sacrament but also believes that there's a certain obligation in what he is doing, when out of a hundred men there's scarcely one who wasn't married before, and out of fifty one who wasn't preparing beforehand to betray his wife on every convenient occasion, when the majority looks at the trip to church only as a particular condition for possessing a certain woman—think what a terrible significance all these details acquire from that. It turns out that that's the whole thing. It turns out as something like a purchase. An innocent girl is sold to a debauchee, and the purchase is surrounded by certain formalities."

XI

"THAT'S HOW everybody marries, and that's how I married, too, and the much-praised honeymoon began. The name alone is so base!" he hissed spitefully. "I once went around all the shows in Paris and stopped to look at one advertising a bearded lady and a water dog. It turned out to be nothing more than a man in a woman's low-cut dress and a dog stuck into a walrus skin and swimming in a tub of water. It was all of very little interest; but as I was leaving, the showman politely saw me out and, addressing the public at the entrance, pointed to me and said: 'Here, ask the gentleman whether it's worth seeing. Come in, come in, one franc per person!' I was ashamed to say it wasn't worth seeing, and the showman was probably counting on that. It's probably the same with those who have experienced all the loathsomeness of a honeymoon and don't want to disappoint others. I also did not disappoint anyone, but now I don't see why I shouldn't tell the truth. I even think it's necessary to tell the truth about it. Awkward, shameful, vile, pitiful, and, above all, dull, impossibly dull! It was something like what I experienced when I was learning to smoke, when I wanted to throw up, and the saliva flowed, and I swallowed and made it look as if I found it pleasant. The enjoyment of smoking, as of the other, comes later, if it comes at all: the spouses must educate themselves in this vice in order to derive enjoyment from it."

"Why vice?" I said. "Aren't you talking about the most natural human property?"

"Natural?" he said. "Natural? No, I'll tell you, on the contrary, I've come to the conviction that it's un . . . natural. Yes, absolutely un . . . natural. Ask children, ask an uncorrupted girl. My sister was married very young to a man twice her age and a debauchee. I remember how surprised we were on her wedding night when she ran away from him, pale and in tears, and, shaking all over, said she would not for anything, not for anything, that she couldn't even speak of what he wanted from her.

"Natural, you say! It's natural to eat. And from the very beginning eating is delightful, easy, pleasant, and not shameful; but this is loathsome, and shameful, and painful. No, it's unnatural! And an unspoiled girl, I've become convinced, always hates it."

"How then," I asked, "how then is the human race to go on?"

"Yes, so long as the human race doesn't perish!" he said with spiteful irony, as if expecting this familiar and unfair objection. "Preach abstention from childbearing in the name of letting English lords go on with their gluttony—that you can do. Preach abstention from childbearing in the name of having more pleasure—that you can do; but stammer something about abstaining from childbearing in the name of morality—good heavens, what an outcry! It's as if the human race may come to an end because a dozen or two want to stop being swine. But forgive me. I find this light unpleasant, may I shade it?" he said, pointing to the lamp.

I said it made no difference to me, and hastily, as he did everything, he climbed up on the seat and drew the woollen curtain over the lamp.

"All the same," I said, "if everybody recognized it as their law, the human race would come to an end."

He did not reply at once.

"You say, how will the human race go on?" he said, sitting down again across from me, with his legs spread wide and his elbows resting low on them. "Why should it go on, this human race?" he said.

"Why? If it didn't we wouldn't exist."

"And why should we exist?"

"Why? In order to live."

"And why live? If there's no goal at all, if life is given for the sake of life, there's no need to live. And if so, then the Schopenhauers, and the Hartmanns, and all the Buddhists[6] are perfectly right. Well, but if there is a goal in life, it's clear that life should come to an end once that goal is achieved. And that's how it turns out," he said with visible excitement, obviously cherishing his thought greatly. "That's how it turns out. Note that if the goal of mankind—goodness, kindness, love, as you wish—if the goal of mankind is what is said in the prophecies, that all men will be united by love, that spears will be beaten into pruning hooks, and so on, what is it that hinders the achieving of that goal? Passions hinder it. Among the passions the strongest, and most evil, and most stubborn is sexual, carnal love, and therefore, if the passions are annihilated, including the ultimate, the strongest of them, carnal love, then the prophecy will be fulfilled, people will be united, the goal of mankind will be achieved, and it will have nothing to live for. As long as mankind lives, an ideal stands before it, and, of course, not the ideal of rabbits or pigs, which is to multiply as much as possible, and not of simians or Parisians, which is to enjoy the pleasures of sexual passion with the greatest possible refinement, but the ideal of the good, achieved through temperance and purity. People have always striven and still strive for it. And see how it turns out.

"It turns out that carnal love is a safety valve. If the generation of mankind living now has not achieved its goal, then it hasn't achieved it only because there are passions in it, including the strongest of them— the sexual. But if there is sexual passion, then there will be a new generation, meaning that there is the possibility of achieving the goal in the next generation. If the next one doesn't achieve it, again there's the next one, and so on until the goal is achieved, the prophecy is fulfilled, and people are united together. Otherwise how would it turn out? Let's allow that God created people for the achievement of a certain goal, and created them mortal, without sexual passion, or eternal. If they were mortal, but without sexual passion, how would it turn out? They would live for a time and die without achieving the goal; and for the goal to be achieved, God would have to create new people. If they were eternal (though it's more difficult for the same people than for new generations to correct mistakes and approach perfection), then suppose that after many thousands of years they achieved the goal—what use would they be then? What to do with them? It's best of all precisely the way it is . . . But maybe you don't like this form of expression? Maybe you're an evolutionist? Then, too, it turns out the same. The highest breed of animals—

people—in order to hold out in the struggle with other animals, should join together, like a hive of bees, and not multiply endlessly; just like the bees, it should raise sexless ones, that is, again, should strive for continence, and by no means for the inflaming of lust, towards which the whole order of our life is directed." He paused. "The human race will come to an end? But can anyone, however he looks at the world, question that? It's as unquestionable as death. According to all the teachings of the Church, the end of the world will come, and according to all scientific teachings, it is inevitably the same. Why is it strange, then, that for moral teaching it turns out the same?"

He was silent for a long time after that, drank more tea, finished smoking his cigarette, and, taking new ones from his bag, put them into his old, soiled cigarette case.

"I understand your thinking," I said. "The Shakers maintain something similar."

"Yes, yes, and they're right," he said. "Sexual passion, whatever its circumstances, is an evil, a terrible evil, which must be fought, not encouraged, as with us. The words of the Gospel, that whoever looks at a woman with lust has already committed adultery, refer not only to other men's wives, but precisely—and above all—to one's own."

XII

"YET IN OUR WORLD it's just the reverse: even if a man still thought of continence while a bachelor, once married they all think that now continence is no longer necessary. These trips after the wedding, the secluded places the young people go to with parental permission—why, it's nothing else but a permission for debauchery. But the moral law avenges itself once it's violated. Hard as I tried to arrange the honeymoon for myself, nothing came of it. The whole time was vile, shameful, and dull. But very soon it also became painfully oppressive. That started very soon. I think on the third or fourth day I found my wife looking dull, began asking her why, began to embrace her, which in my opinion was all she could have wished for, but she pushed my arm away and burst into tears. About what? She couldn't say. But she felt sad, oppressed. Probably her exhausted nerves urged upon her the truth about the vileness of our relations; but she couldn't say it. I began to question her, she said something about feeling sad without her mother. I thought it wasn't true. I started reassuring her, ignoring her mother. I didn't understand that she simply felt oppressed, and her mother was only an excuse. But she became offended at once that I passed over her mother in silence, as if I didn't believe her. She said she could see I didn't love her. I reproached her for being capricious, and suddenly her face changed completely, instead of sadness it expressed irritation, and she began to reproach me for egoism and cruelty in the most venomous words. I looked at her. Her whole face expressed the utmost coldness and hostility, almost hatred towards me. I remember how horrified I was to see it. 'How? What?' I thought. 'Love is the union of souls, and instead of that there's this! No, it can't be, it's not her!' I tried to soften her, but ran into such an impenetrable wall of cold, venomous hostility that, before I could turn around, the irritation had seized me, too, and we said a heap of unpleasant things to each other. The impression of that first quarrel was terrible. I've called it a quarrel, but it wasn't a quarrel, it was only the uncovering of the abyss that actually lay between us. Amorousness had been exhausted by the satisfaction of sensuality, and we were left facing each other in our actual relation to each other, that is, two egoists totally alien to each other, wishing to get as much pleasure as possible each from the other. I've called what happened between us a quarrel; but it was not a quarrel, it was only the uncovering of our actual relation to each other as a result of the cessation of sensuality. I didn't understand that this cold and hostile relation was our normal relation, did not understand it because this hostile relation of the first days was very soon concealed from us again by a newly arisen 'rectified' sensuality, that is, amorousness.

"And I thought that we had quarrelled and made peace and that it wouldn't happen any more. But during this same first honeymoon the period of satiety came again, and again we ceased to need each other, and again there was a quarrel. This second quarrel struck me more painfully than the first. So the first wasn't accidental, and this is how it has to be and will be, I thought. The second quarrel struck me the more in that it arose from the most impossible cause. It was something about money, of which I am never sparing and really could not be sparing with my wife. I remember only that she somehow turned the matter in such a way that some remark of mine came out as the expression of my wish to dominate her through money, which I supposedly declared to be my exclusive right—something impossible, stupid, base, unnatural both to me and to her. I became irritated, started reproaching her for indelicacy, and she me, and off it went again. In her words and in the expression of her face and eyes I saw again the same cruel, cold hostility that had so struck me before. I remember quarrelling with my brother, my friends, my father, but there had never been that peculiar, venomous spite between us that there was here. But some time went by, and again this mutual hatred was hidden by amorousness, that is, sensuality, and I still comforted myself with the thought that these two quarrels were mistakes that could be corrected. But then came a third, a fourth quarrel, and I realized that this was not accidental, but that it had to be and would be that way, and I was horrified at what faced me. With that I was also tormented by the terrible thought that I alone had such a bad life, so unlike what I had expected with my wife, while for other married couples it was not that way. I didn't know then that this was the common lot, but that, like me, they all thought it was their exclusive misfortune, and concealed this exclusive, shameful misfortune not only from each other, but from themselves, not admitting it to themselves.

"It began with the first days and went on the whole time, and kept growing more intense and embittered. In the depths of my soul I felt from the first weeks that I was *caught,* that what had turned out was not what I had expected, that marriage is not only not happiness, but something very oppressive, yet, like everyone else, I did not want to admit it to myself (I wouldn't even now if it weren't for how it ended) and concealed it not only from others, but from myself. I am astonished now that I did not see my real situation. I could have seen it, if only because the quarrels began from such causes that afterwards, when they were over, it was impossible to remember what they were. Reason had no time to fit sufficient causes to the constantly existing hostility towards each other. But still more striking was the insufficiency of the pretexts for reconciliation. Sometimes there were words, explanations, even tears, but sometimes—oh! it's vile to remember it now—after the cruellest words to each other, suddenly there were silent looks, smiles, kisses, embraces . . . Pah, loathsome! How could I not see all the vileness of it then . . ."

XIII

TWO PASSENGERS CAME IN and started settling themselves on a seat far from us. He was silent while they settled themselves, but as soon as they quieted down, he went on, obviously not losing the thread of his thought for a minute.

"What is filthy above all," he began, "is that it's supposed in theory that love is something ideal, lofty, but in practice love is something loathsome, swinish, which it is even loathsome and shameful to speak of or remember. There must be some reason why nature made it loathsome and shameful. But if it's loathsome and shameful, that's how it should be understood. But here, on the contrary, people pretend that the loathsome and shameful is beautiful and lofty. What were the first signs of my love? That I gave myself to animal excesses not only without being ashamed of them, but for some reason taking pride in the possibility of these physical excesses, and that without giving the least thought not only to her spiritual life, but even to her physical life. I wondered where our anger against each other came from, yet the thing was perfectly clear: that anger was nothing other than the protest of human nature against the animal that was overwhelming it.

"I was astonished at our hatred for each other. But it couldn't have been otherwise. That hatred was nothing other than the mutual hatred of accomplices in a crime—both for instigating and for sharing in the crime. How could it not be a crime, when she, the poor thing, became pregnant in the very first month, and our swinish intercourse continued. You think I'm digressing from my story? Not in the least! I'm telling you all about how I killed my wife. They asked me at the trial how and with what I killed my wife. Fools! They think I killed her then, with a knife, on the 5th of October. I didn't kill her then, but much earlier. Just as they all kill now, all, all . . ."

"But with what?" I asked.

"That's the astonishing thing, that nobody wants to know something that's so clear and obvious, something that doctors should know and preach, but are silent about. It's a terribly simple thing. Man and woman are created like the animals, so that after carnal love pregnancy begins, then nursing—conditions in which carnal love is harmful for the woman as well as for her child. There are an equal number of women and men.

What follows from that? It seems clear. It takes no great wisdom to draw the conclusion from it that animals draw, that is, continence. But no. Science has gone so far as to find some sort of leukocytes that run in the blood, and all sorts of other useless nonsense, but this it's been unable to understand. At least you don't hear it said.

"And so there are only two ways out for a woman: one is to make herself into a freak, to destroy or keep on destroying in herself, as need be, the capacity for being a woman, that is, a mother, so that the man can calmly and continuously enjoy himself; or the other way out, even not a way out, but a simple, crude, outright violation of the laws of nature, which takes place in all so-called honest families. Namely, that the woman, contrary to her nature, should be at the same time pregnant, and a nurse, and a lover—should be that which no animal descends to. And she may not have strength enough. Hence the hysterics and bad nerves in our life, and among the people—shriekers.[7] Note that among young girls, among pure ones, there are no shriekers, but only among peasant women, and among peasant women, it's those who live with their husbands. So it is with us. And it's exactly the same in Europe. The hospitals are all filled with hysterical women who violate the law of nature. But the shriekers and Charcot's patients[8] are completely disabled, while the world is filled with half-crippled women. Just think what a great thing is being accomplished in a woman when she conceives or nurses the child born to her. That which will continue and replace us is growing. And this sacred thing is violated—by what? It's dreadful to think! And they talk about the freedom and rights of women. It's the same as if cannibals fattened up their captives for eating and along with that assured them that they were concerned with their rights and freedom."

All this was new and I was struck by it.

"But how then? If that's so," I said, "then it turns out that a man can make love to his wife only once in two years, but for a man . . ."

"For a man it's necessary," he picked up. "Again our dear priests of science have persuaded everybody. I'd order these magicians to perform the duties of the women who, in their opinion, are necessary to men. What would they say then? Impress it upon a man that vodka, tobacco, opium are necessary to him, and it will all be necessary. It turns out that God didn't understand what was needed, and therefore, without asking the magicians, arranged it all badly. Kindly note that the thing just

doesn't jibe. Man has the need and the necessity, so they decided, of satisfying his lust, and here childbearing and nursing go mixing in, interfer-
ing with the satisfying of that want. What to do? Turn to the magicians,
they'll arrange it. And they came up with something. Oh, when will
these magicians and their deceptions be dethroned? It's high time! It's
gone so far that people lose their minds and shoot themselves, and all
because of that. How could it be otherwise? Animals seem to know that
their offspring continue their kind and keep to a certain law in that
respect. Only man doesn't know and doesn't want to know it. And he's
concerned only with having as much pleasure as possible. And who is
he? Man, the king of nature. Note that animals couple only when they
can produce offspring, but the filthy king of nature—any time, just for
the pleasure of it. And what's more, he exalts this apelike occupation into
the pearl of creation, love. And in the name of this love, that is, this
muck, he ruins—what?—half of the human race. Of all women, who
should be helpers in mankind's movement towards truth and goodness,
he, in the name of his pleasure, makes not helpers, but enemies. Look,
what slows mankind's forward movement everywhere? Women. And
why so? Only because of that. Yes, sir, yes," he repeated several times
and began to stir, took out his cigarettes and smoked, obviously wishing
to calm down a little.

XIV

"THAT'S THE SORT of swine I was," he went on again in his former
tone. "Worst of all was that, living that nasty life, I imagined that, since I
wasn't tempted by other women, I was therefore living an honest family
life, that I was a moral person, and was to blame for nothing, and that if
we had quarrels, then she, her character, was to blame.

"The one to blame was, of course, not she. She was the same as
everybody, as the majority. She had been brought up as the position of
women in our society demanded, and therefore as all women of the well-
to-do classes, without exception, are brought up, and cannot help but be
brought up. There's talk of some sort of new women's education. All
empty words: the education of women is exactly what it should be under
the existing—not feigned, but real—general view of women.

"And the education of women will always correspond to men's view of them. We all know how a man looks at a woman: *'Wein, Weiber und Gesang,'** and so poets speak in verses. Take all poetry, take all painting and sculpture, beginning with love poetry and naked Venuses and Phrynes, and you'll see that woman is an instrument of pleasure, so she is on the Truba and on the Grachevka,⁹ and at the court ball. And note the devil's cunning: well, enjoyment, pleasure, so then let it be known that it's pleasure, that woman is a sweet morsel. No, at first the knights assert that they deify woman (deify, but still look at her as an instrument of enjoyment). Now they assert that they respect woman. Some yield a seat to her, pick up a handkerchief; others acknowledge her right to occupy all posts, to participate in the government, and so on. They do all that, but the view of her is still the same. She is an instrument of enjoyment. Her body is a means of enjoyment. And she knows it. It's the same as slavery. Slavery is nothing other than the use by a few of the forced labour of many. And therefore, to be rid of slavery, people should stop wanting to use the forced labour of others, considering it sinful or shameful. Yet meanwhile they abolish the external form of slavery, arrange it so that it's no longer possible to purchase slaves, and imagine and persuade themselves that there is no more slavery, and they don't see and don't want to see that slavery continues to exist, because people, just as before, like and regard as good and just the use of the labour of others. And once they regard it as good, people will always be found who are stronger or more cunning than others and will be able to do it. The same with the emancipation of woman. The slavery of woman consists only in that people wish, and regard it as a very good thing, to use her as an instrument of enjoyment. Well, and so they liberate woman, give her various rights equal to man's, but go on looking at her as an instrument of enjoyment, and educate her as such from childhood and by public opinion. And so she is still the same humiliated, depraved slave, and man is still the same depraved slave owner.

"They liberate woman in schools and law courts, but look at her as an object of enjoyment. Teach her, as she is taught among us, to see herself in the same way, and she will forever remain an inferior being. Either she will prevent the conception of a fetus, with the help of

---

* Wine, women, and song.

scoundrelly doctors, that is, will be an outright prostitute, who has descended not to the level of an animal, but to the level of a thing, or she will be what in most cases she is—mentally ill, hysterical, and wretched, which is in fact the case, with no possibility of spiritual development.

"Schools and courses cannot change it. It can be changed only by a change in men's view of women and women's of themselves. It will change only when women regard the state of virginity as the highest state, and not as now, when the highest condition of a human being is shame and disgrace. As long as that's not so, the ideal of every girl, whatever her education, will be to attract as many men, as many males, as possible, so as to have the possibility of choice.

"And the fact that one of them knows a little more mathematics and another can play the harp changes nothing. A woman is happy and achieves everything she can desire when she enchants a man. And therefore a woman's chief task is to know how to enchant him. That's how it has been and will be. That's how it is in a girl's life in our world, that's how it continues to be in her married life. In a girl's life it's necessary for the sake of choice, in married life for the sake of power over the husband.

"One thing that stops or at least suppresses this for a time is children, and then only if the woman is not a freak, that is, if she nurses them herself. But here again there are the doctors.

"With my wife, who wanted to nurse herself and did nurse the next five children, it happened that the first baby was unwell. These doctors, who cynically undressed her and palpated her everywhere, for which I had to thank them and pay them money—these dear doctors discovered that she ought not to nurse, and in that first time she was deprived of the sole means that could save her from coquetry. The baby was nursed by a wet nurse, that is, we took advantage of this woman's poverty, need, and ignorance, we lured her away from her own baby to ours, and for that put a kokoshnik[10] with gold braid on her head. But that's not the thing. The thing is that at that time of freedom from pregnancy and nursing, the previously dormant feminine coquetry awakened in her with particular force. And, correspondingly, there appeared in me with particular force the pangs of jealousy, which tormented me ceaselessly throughout my married life, as they cannot but torment all husbands who live with their wives as I did, that is, immorally."

XV

"THROUGHOUT MY MARRIED LIFE, I never ceased to experience the torments of jealousy. But there were periods when I suffered from it especially sharply. And one of those periods was when the doctors forbade her to nurse after the first child. I was especially jealous at that time, first, because my wife then experienced that specific maternal restlessness which must be provoked by the causeless disruption of the regular course of life; second, because, seeing how easily she cast aside the moral duty of a mother, I concluded, correctly though unconsciously, that it would be as easy for her to cast aside her marital duty, the more so as she was perfectly healthy and, despite the prohibition of the dear doctors, nursed the succeeding children herself and nursed them perfectly well."

"Anyhow, you don't like doctors," I said, noticing the especially spiteful expression in his voice every time he so much as mentioned them.

"It's not a matter of liking or not liking. They ruined my life, as they have ruined and are ruining the lives of thousands, of hundreds of thousands of people, and I can't help connecting effects with causes. I understand that they want to make money, just as lawyers and others do; I would willingly give them half my income, and anyone, if he understood what they do, would willingly give them half his property, only so that they not interfere in your family life, so that they never come near you. I haven't gathered information, but I know dozens of cases—there's no end of them—when they have either killed the child in a mother's womb, insisting that the mother was unable to deliver, though afterwards the mother delivered perfectly well, or killed the mother under the pretext of some sort of surgery. No one counts up these murders, just as no one counted up the murders of the Inquisition, because it was supposed to be for the good of mankind. There is no counting the crimes they commit. But these crimes are all nothing compared to the moral depravity of materialism that they introduce into the world, especially through women. I'm not even talking about the fact that, if they only follow their directions, then, owing to the infections everywhere, in everything, people must go not towards unity, but towards disunity: according to their teaching, everyone must sit separately and never take the carbolic acid sprayer out of their mouths (though they've discovered that that, too, is no good). But that, too, is nothing. The main poison is the corruption of people, especially women.

"Nowadays it's impossible to say: 'You live badly, live better'— impossible to say it to yourself or to anyone else. If you live badly, the cause is an abnormality of the nervous functions, and so forth. And you must go to them, and they prescribe you thirty-five kopecks' worth of medicine at the pharmacy, and you take it. You'll feel still worse, then there'll be more medicine and more doctors. An excellent trick!

"But the thing isn't that. I only said that she nursed the children perfectly well herself and that only this bearing and nursing of children saved me from the torment of jealousy. If it hadn't been for that, it all would have happened sooner. The children saved me and her. In eight years she bore five children. And she nursed them all herself."

"And where are your children now?" I asked.

"My children?" he repeated fearfully.

"Excuse me, perhaps it's a painful memory for you?"

"No, never mind. My sister-in-law and her brother took them. They wouldn't let me have them. I gave them my fortune, but they wouldn't let me have them. I'm something like a madman. I'm coming from them now. I saw them, but they wouldn't let me have them. Because I'd bring them up so that they wouldn't be like their parents. But they must be like them. Well, what to do! It's clear that they won't let me have them and won't trust me. And I don't know if I'd be able to raise them. I think not. I'm a ruin, a cripple. There's just one thing in me. I know. Yes, it's true, I know something that people will not learn soon.

"Yes, my children are alive and growing up to be the same savages as everyone around them. I've seen them, three times I've seen them. There's nothing I can do for them. Nothing. I'm going to my place in the south now. I have a little house and garden there.

"Yes, it won't be soon that people learn what I know. How much iron and what sort of metals there are in the sun and stars—that may soon be learned; but as for what exposes our swinishness, that is difficult, terribly difficult . . .

"You at least listen, and I'm grateful for that."

XVI

"You've JUST BROUGHT children to mind. Again, what terrible lying goes on about children. Children are God's blessing, children are a joy. That's all a lie. Once it was all so, but now there's nothing like that. Children are a torment, and nothing more. The majority of mothers feel that directly and sometimes inadvertently say it directly. Ask the majority of mothers of our circle of well-to-do people, they'll tell you that they don't want to have children for fear their children might get sick and die, do not want to nurse them once they're born, so as not to become attached to them and suffer. The delight afforded them by a child's charm, by those little hands, the little feet, the whole little body, the pleasure afforded by a child is less than the suffering they experience—to say nothing of the illness or loss of a child—simply from fear alone of the possibility of illness and death. On weighing the advantages and disadvantages, it turns out that it is disadvantageous and therefore undesirable to have children. They say it directly, boldly, imagining that these feelings in them come from their love for children, a good and praiseworthy feeling which they are proud of. They don't notice that by this reasoning they reject love outright and assert only their own egoism. For them the pleasure of a child's charm is less than the suffering from fear for it, and therefore they don't want a child they would love. They don't sacrifice themselves for the sake of a loved being, but a being to be loved for themselves.

"Clearly this is not love, but egoism. But one cannot raise a hand to condemn them, the mothers from well-to-do families, for this egoism, when one remembers what they suffer over their children's health, again owing to those same doctors, in our upper-class life. When I so much as remember, even now, my wife's life and state in the early days, when there were three or four children, and she was entirely taken up by them—it's terrible. There was no life of our own at all. It was some eternal danger, salvation from it, again imminent danger, again desperate efforts, and again salvation—constantly a situation like that of a sinking ship. Sometimes it seemed to me that she was doing it on purpose, that she was pretending to worry about the children in order to defeat me. So tempting it was, so simply it resolved all questions in her favour. It sometimes seemed to me that everything she did and said on those occasions, she did and said on purpose. But no, she herself suffered terribly and constantly accused herself on account of the children, their health and ill-nesses. It was a torture for her and for me also. And she couldn't help suf-fering. For the attachment to her children, the animal need to feed, pamper, and protect them, was the same as in the majority of women, but what animals have—the lack of imagination and reason—was not there. A hen is not afraid of what may happen to her chick, she doesn't know all the illnesses that may befall it, does not know all the means that people imagine may save it from illnesses and death. And children for her, for a hen, are not a torment. She does for her children what is fitting and joyful for her to do; her children are a joy for her. And when a chick falls ill, her cares are well defined: she keeps it warm, feeds it. And in doing that, she knows she's doing all that's needed. If the chick drops dead, she doesn't ask herself why it died or where it has gone, she clucks a little, then stops and goes on with her life as before. But for our wretched women and for my wife it was not so. To say nothing of illnesses and how to treat them, she heard and read on all sides endlessly varied and constantly changing rules about how to raise and educate children. Feed them like this or that; no, not this, not that, but like this; how to dress, give to drink, bathe, put to bed, take for a walk, give fresh air—we, mostly she, learned new rules about it all every week. As if children began to be born yesterday. And if a child is not properly fed, not properly bathed, or at the wrong time, and falls ill, it turns out that she is to blame for not doing what had to be done.

"That's while they're healthy. And it's a torment even so. But if the child falls ill, that's the end. Perfect hell. It's supposed that illness can be treated and that there is this science, there are these people—doctors—and they know how. Not all, but the best of them know how. And here the child is sick, and one must hit upon this very best, that is, the one who can save, and then the child is saved; but if you can't get hold of this doc-tor or you don't live in the same place where this doctor lives—the child is lost. And this faith is not exclusively hers, it is the faith of all the women of her circle, and on all sides she hears only this: Ekaterina Semyonovna's two children died, because they did not call Ivan Zak-harych in time, but Marya Ivanovna's older girl was saved by Ivan Zakharych; and the Petrovs followed the doctor's advice in time and sep-arated their children in different hotels, and they stayed alive, but with those who didn't separate them, the children died. And this woman had a weak child, they moved to the south on the doctor's advice—and saved the child. How can she not be tormented and worried all her life, if the lives of her children, to whom she has an animal attachment, depend on her learning in time what Ivan Zakharych says about it? And what Ivan Zakharych is going to say nobody knows, least of all he himself, because he knows very well that he knows nothing and cannot help in any way, and only shifts about at random, only so that they don't stop believing that he knows something. For if she were wholly an animal, she would not be so tormented; and if she were wholly a human being, then she would have faith in God, and she would speak and think as believing peasant women do: 'God gave, and God has taken away, there is no escape from God.' She would think that the life and death of all people, as well as of her children, is beyond the power of people, and in the power of God alone, and she would not be tormented by thinking it is within her power to prevent the illness and death of her children, but that was not what she did. Her situation was this: she was given these most fragile, weak beings, subject to countless calamities. For these beings she feels a passionate, animal attachment. Besides, these beings are entrusted to her, and at the same time the means of preserving these beings are hidden from us and revealed to total strangers, whose services and advice can be obtained only for a lot of money, and not always then.

"Our whole life with the children was for my wife, and therefore for me, not a joy but a torment. How could she not be tormented? She was tormented constantly. It would happen that we had only just calmed down after some scene of jealousy or simply a quarrel, and thought we could live, and read, and think; I would start doing something, and suddenly the news would come that Vasya was throwing up, or Masha had blood in her stool, or Andryusha had a rash, and, of course, life was over. Where to gallop, for which doctor, how to isolate the child? Enemas, thermometers, mixtures, and doctors would begin. Before it was all over, something else would begin. There was no regular, firm family life. There was, as I've said, a constant attempt at salvation from imaginary and real dangers. That is so in the majority of families now. In my family it was especially pronounced. My wife was child-loving and gullible.

"So the presence of children not only did not improve our life, but poisoned it. Besides that, the children were yet another occasion of discord for us. Ever since there were children, and the more so as they grew up, the more often did the children themselves become the means and object of discord. Not only the object of discord, but they were tools of struggle; we fought each other, as it were, using the children. Each of us had a favourite child—a tool for fighting. I fought more using Vasya, the older boy; she using Liza. Besides, when the children began to grow up and their characters defined themselves, they became allies, whom we drew each to his own side. They suffered terribly from it, poor things, but we, in our constant war, never got around to thinking of them. The girl was on my side; the eldest boy, who resembled my wife and was her favourite, was often hateful to me."

XVII

"Well, sir, that's how we lived. Our relations grew more and more hostile. And we finally reached the point where it was no longer discord that produced hostility, but hostility that produced discord: whatever she said, I disagreed with in advance, and she did just the same.

"In the fourth year it was somehow decided by itself on both sides that we could not understand each other or agree with each other. We now stopped all attempts at talking things over to the end. About the simplest things, especially about the children, we inevitably remained each with his own opinion. As I now recall, the opinions I defended were not at all so dear to me that I couldn't have given them up; but she was of the opposite opinion, and to yield meant to yield to her. And that I could not do. Nor could she. She probably always considered herself completely in the right before me, and I, in my own eyes, was always a saint before her. Together we were almost condemned to silence or to such conversation as I'm sure animals can conduct between themselves: 'What time is it? Time for bed. What's for dinner today? Where shall we go? What's in the newspapers? Send for the doctor. Masha has a sore throat.' It was enough to step a hair's breadth outside this impossibly narrow circle of conversation for irritation to flare up. There were confrontations and expressions of hatred about the coffee, the tablecloth, the droshky, a game of vint[11]—all things that could not have any significance for either of us. I, at least, often seethed with terrible hatred for her! I sometimes watched how she poured tea, swung her leg, or put a spoon to her mouth and slurped, sucking in the liquid, and hated her precisely for that, as for the worst of actions. I didn't notice then that the periods of anger arose in me with perfect logic and regularity in correspondence to the periods of what we called love. A period of love—a period of anger; an energetic period of love—a long period of anger; a weaker show of love—a short period of anger. We didn't understand then that this love and anger were one and the same animal feeling, only from different ends. To live that way would have been terrible if we had understood our situation; but we didn't understand or see it. In that lies both the salvation and the punishment of man, that, when he doesn't live in the right way, he can befog himself so as not to see the grievousness of his situation. That was what we did. She tried to forget herself in intense, always hurried cares of the household, decoration, clothing, her own and the children's, their studies, their health. I had my own drunkenness—the drunkenness of work, hunting, cards. We were both constantly busy. We both felt that the busier we were, the angrier we could be at each other. 'It's fine for you to make faces,' I'd think, 'you tormented me with scenes all night, and I have a meeting.' 'That's fine for you,' she not only thought but said, 'but I stayed up all night with the baby.'

"That's how we lived, in a perpetual fog, not seeing the situation we were in. And if what happened hadn't happened, I would have lived the same way into old age and thought, at my death, that I had lived a good life, not very good, but not bad either, just like everybody else; I would not have understood the abyss of unhappiness and vile lies in which I wallowed.

"We were two convicts, hating each other, bound by one chain, poisoning each other's life, and trying not to see it. I didn't know then that ninety-nine per cent of all married couples live in the same hell I did and that it cannot be otherwise. I didn't know it then either about others or about myself.

"It's astonishing what coincidences occur in a regular and even in an irregular life! Just when the parents make life unbearable for each other, city conditions become necessary for educating the children. And the need to move to the city appears."

He fell silent and once or twice produced his strange sounds, which now were very much like restrained sobs. We were approaching a station.

"What time is it?" he asked.

I looked. It was two o'clock.

"You're not tired?" he asked.

"No, but you are."

"I'm suffocating. Excuse me, I'll take a walk and drink some water."

And he walked unsteadily through the carriage. I sat alone, going over all he had told me, and so deep in thought that I did not notice he had come back by the other door.

XVIII

"YES, I keep getting carried away," he began. "I've thought over many things, I look at many things differently, and I want to tell it all. Well, so we started living in the city. Unhappy people live better in the city. In a city a man can live for a hundred years and not notice that he died and rotted long ago. There's no time to sort things out for yourself, you're always busy. Business, social relations, health, art, the children's health, their upbringing. Now we must receive these and those, visit these and those; now we must look at her, hear him or her. For in a city at any given moment there is one celebrity, or else two or three at once, who can't be missed. Now you must have yourself treated, or this one or that one, then there are teachers, tutors, governesses, but life is as empty as can be. Well, that's how we lived, and the pain of our common life was less felt. Besides that, at first we had a wonderful occupation—getting settled in a new city, in a new apartment, and another occupation—going from the city to the country and from the country to the city.

"We lived through one winter, and the next winter the following circumstance occurred, inconspicuous and seemingly insignificant, but which produced all that happened later. She was unwell, and the scoundrels told her not to have children and taught her the means. To me it seemed disgusting. I fought against it, but she, with light-minded stubbornness, stood her ground, and I gave in: the last justification of our swinish life—children—was taken away, and life became still more vile.

"A muzhik, a workman, needs children. It's hard for him to feed them, but he needs them, and therefore his marital relations are justified. But for people like us, who have children, more children aren't needed—extra care, expense, co-inheritors, they're a burden. And for us there's no justification for our swinish life. We either get rid of the children artificially, or look upon them as a misfortune, the result of carelessness, which is still more vile. There's no justification. But we're so fallen morally that we don't even see the need for justification. The majority of today's educated world is given to this depravity without the slightest remorse of conscience.

"There can be no remorse, because there is no conscience in our life, apart from, if it may be called so, the conscience of public opinion and criminal law. And here neither the one nor the other is violated. There's no sense in being conscience-stricken before society: *everybody* does it, both Marya Pavlovna and Ivan Zakharych. Why breed paupers or deprive oneself of the opportunity of social life? To be conscience-stricken before criminal law or afraid of it is also senseless. It's outrageous wenches and soldiers' wives who throw babies into ponds and wells; they, to be sure, should be put in jail, but with us it's all done in a timely and clean way.

"We lived like that for another two years. The treatment the scoundrels gave her obviously began to work; she throve physically and grew pretty as the last beauty of summer. She sensed it and looked after herself. In her there developed a sort of provocative beauty that disturbed people. She was in the full vigour of a well-nourished, excited woman of thirty who is not bearing children. Her appearance was disturbing. When she passed among men, she drew their eyes. She was like a stable-bound, well-nourished harness horse whose bridle has been taken off. There was no bridle at all, just as with ninety-nine per cent of our women. And I sensed it and was frightened."

XIX

HE SUDDENLY GOT UP and moved over to the window.

"Excuse me," he said and, turning his eyes to the window, sat silently like that for some three minutes. Then he sighed deeply and again sat down facing me. His face had become quite different, his eyes were pathetic, and some strange almost-smile puckered his lips. "I'm a little tired, but I'll tell it to you. There's still a long time, it's not daybreak yet. Yes, sir," he began again, lighting a cigarette. "She had gained weight since she stopped giving birth, and this illness—the eternal suffering over the children—began to go away; not exactly go away, but it was as if she recovered from a drinking bout, came to her senses, and saw that there was the whole of God's world with its joys, which she had forgotten about, but which she didn't know how to live in, God's world, which she had never understood. 'Don't miss it! Time is passing, it won't come back!' That's my notion of what she thought, or rather felt, and it was impossible for her to think or feel otherwise: she had been brought up to think that there is only one thing worthy of attention in the world—love. She had married, had got something of that love, but not only far from what had been promised, what was expected, but also many disappointments, sufferings, and then an unexpected torment—the children! That torment wore her out. And here, thanks to the obliging doctors, she learned that she could do without children. She was glad, tried it, and came alive again for the one thing she knew—love. But love with a husband befouled by jealousy and all sorts of anger was not the right thing. She began to imagine some other, clean, new love, or at least so I thought. And so she began looking around, as if expecting something. I saw it and couldn't help being alarmed. Time and again it would happen that, talking to me, as usual, by means of others, that is, talking with outsiders but addressing her speech to me, she would boldly declare, not aware that an hour before she had said the opposite, would declare half seriously that maternal cares were a deception, that it's not worthwhile giving your life to children when you're young and can enjoy life. She occupied herself less with the children, not as desperately as before, but more and more with herself, her appearance, though she tried to conceal it, and her pleasures, and even her accomplishments. She again enthusiastically took up the piano, which before had been completely abandoned. This was the beginning of it all."

He again turned his weary gaze to the window, but, clearly making an effort with himself, went on again at once.

"Yes, sir, this man appeared." He hesitated and produced his peculiar sounds a couple of times through his nose.

I could see that it was tormenting for him to mention this man, to remember him, to speak of him. But he made an effort and, as if tearing through the obstacle that hindered him, resolutely went on:

"In my eyes, in my estimation, he was a trashy little man. And not because of the significance he took on in my life, but because he really was so. Anyhow, the fact that he was no good only served as proof of how unreasoning she was. If it hadn't been him, it would have been someone else." He again fell silent. "Yes, sir, he was a musician, a violinist; not a professional musician, but a semi-professional, semi-society man.

"His father was a landowner, my father's neighbour. He—his father—was ruined, and the children—three boys—all got taken care of; this one, the youngest, was sent to his godmother in Paris. There he was sent to the conservatory, because he had a talent for music, and he came out of it a violinist and played in concerts. As a human being, he was . . ." He was obviously going to say something bad about him, checked himself, and said quickly: "Well, I don't really know how he lived, I only know that he came to Russia that year and came to me.

"Moist, almond-shaped eyes, red smiling lips, a little waxed moustache, hair done in the latest fashion, the face of a banal prettiness, the sort women refer to as not bad, weakly built, though not ugly, with an especially developed behind, as with women, as with the Hottentots, so they say. They say they're also musical. Tending towards familiarity as far as possible, but sensitive and always ready to stop at the slightest resistance, with an observance of his external dignity, and with high-buttoned shoes of that special Parisian shade, and bright-coloured neckties, and other things that foreigners adopt in Paris, and that in their singularity and novelty always work with women. In his manners an affected, external gaiety. That manner, you know, of speaking of everything in hints and fragments, as if you know it all, remember it, and can fill in the rest yourself.

"So he and his music were the cause of everything. At the trial the case was presented as if it had all happened out of jealousy. By no means; that is, not by no means, but it was and wasn't so. At the trial it was decided that I was a deceived husband and that I had killed in defence of my insulted honour (that's what they call it). And that's why I was acquitted. At the trial I tried to explain the meaning of the thing, but they took it as if I was trying to rehabilitate my wife's honour.

"Her relations with this musician, whatever they were, had no meaning for me, nor for her either. What has meaning is what I've told you about, that is, my swinishness. It all came about because between us there was that terrible abyss I told you about, that terrible intensity of mutual hatred, in which the first occasion was enough to produce a crisis. The quarrels between us had recently become something dreadful, and were especially striking in that they also gave way to intense animal passion.

"If he hadn't shown up, someone else would have. If the pretext hadn't been jealousy, it would have been something else. I insist that all husbands who live as I did must either become profligate, or separate, or kill themselves or their wives, as I did. If there are some with whom this hasn't happened, it's a rare exception. For before I ended as I did, I was on the verge of suicide several times, and she also tried to poison herself."

XX

"Yes, that's how it was, and not long before the end.

"We lived as if in peace, and there was no reason at all to disturb it. Suddenly a conversation begins about how such-and-such a dog won a medal at a show, I say. She says: 'Not a medal, but an honourable mention.' An argument begins. There begins a jumping from one subject to another, reproaches: 'Well, yes, we've known that for a long time, it's always that way: you said . . .' 'No, I didn't.' 'In other words, I'm lying! . . .' You feel that that terrible sort of quarrel is about to begin in which you want to kill either yourself or her. You know it's going to begin, and you fear it like fire and want to restrain yourself, but anger takes possession of your whole being. She is in the same state, even worse, she deliberately misconstrues your every word, giving it a perverse meaning; each of her words is soaked with venom; she needles just where she knows it will hurt me most. And the further it goes, the worse it gets. I shout: 'Shut up!' or something like that. She rushes out of the room and runs towards the nursery. I try to hold her back, to finish talking, to prove something, and I seize her by the arm. She pretends I've hurt her and shouts: 'Children, your father is beating me!' I shout: 'Don't lie!' 'It's not the first time!' she shouts, or something like that. The children rush to her. She calms them down. I say: 'Don't pretend!' She says: 'For you everything's a pretence. You'd kill a man and say he's pretending. Now I understand you. That's what you want!' 'Oh, why don't you drop dead!' I shout. I remember how horrified I was by those awful words. I never expected I could say such awful, crude words, and I'm astonished that they could just leap out of me. I shout these awful words, run to my study, sit down and smoke. I hear her go to the front hall on her way out. I ask where she's going. She doesn't answer. 'Well, to hell with her,' I say to myself, go back to the study, lie down again and smoke. Thousands of different plans of how to take revenge on her and get rid of her, and how to set it all to rights and make it as if nothing had happened, come to my head. I think about it all and smoke, smoke, smoke. I think of running away from her, hiding, going to America. I reach the point of dreaming of how I get rid of her, and how wonderful it will be, and I will become intimate with another beautiful woman, a completely new one. I'll get rid of her by her dying, or my divorcing her, and I try to think how to do it. I see that I'm confused, that I'm not thinking what I should, but it's for that, so as not to see that I'm not thinking what I should, that I smoke.

"And life at home goes on. The governess comes and asks, 'Where is *madame*? When will she be back?' A servant asks whether tea should be served. I come out to the dining room; the children, especially the eldest, Liza, who already understands, look at me questioningly and with hostility. We have tea in silence. She's not home yet. The whole evening goes by, she doesn't come, and two feelings alternate in my soul: anger against her for tormenting me and all the children by her absence, which is bound to end by her coming back, and fear that she won't and will do something to herself. I could go looking for her. But where? At her sister's? But it's stupid to come and ask. God be with her; if she wants to torment, let her be tormented herself. Because that's what she expects me to do. And the next time it will be worse still. And what if she's not with her sister, but is doing something or has already done something to herself? . . . Eleven, twelve, one o'clock. I don't go to the bedroom, it's stupid to lie there alone and wait, yet I lie down right here. Then I want to do something, to write letters, to read; I can't do anything. I'm sitting alone in my study, tormented, angry, and listening. Three, four o'clock—she's still not here. I fall asleep towards morning. I wake up— she's not here.

"Everything in the house goes on as before, but they're all bewildered and look at me questioningly and reproachfully, supposing it's all because of me. And in me there is the same struggle—between anger at her for tormenting me, and anxiety over her.

"Around eleven her sister comes as an ambassador from her. And the usual thing begins: 'She's in a terrible state. Well, what is it!' 'But nothing's happened.' I say she has an impossible character and I haven't done anything.

" 'But it can't be left like this,' says the sister.

" 'It's all her doing, not mine,' I say. 'I won't make the first step. If it's separation, it's separation.'

"My sister-in-law leaves with nothing. I had said boldly that I wouldn't make the first step, but once she's gone and I come out and see the children, pathetic, frightened, I'm now ready to make the first step. I'd be glad to make it, but I don't know how. Again I pace, smoke, drink vodka and wine at lunch, and achieve what I subconsciously desire: I don't see the stupidity, the meanness of my position.

"At around three she arrives. Meeting me, she says nothing. I imagine she's giving in, I begin to say that I felt challenged by her reproaches. She, with the same stern and terribly pained face, says she did not come to discuss things, but to take the children, that we cannot live together. I begin to say that it's not my fault, that she drove me out of my wits. She looks at me sternly, solemnly, and then says:

" 'Don't say any more, you'll regret it.'

"I say that I can't stand comedies. Then she exclaims something I can't make out and runs to her room. The key clicks behind her: she's locked herself in. I shove at the door, there's no response, and I walk away angrily. Half an hour later Liza comes running in tears.

"What? Has something happened?"

"I can't hear mama."

We go. I pull at the door as hard as I can. The door is not well bolted, and the two halves open. I go over to the bed. She's lying awkwardly on the bed, in her petticoats and high boots, unconscious. On the table an empty vial of opium. We bring her back to consciousness. More tears and, finally, reconciliation. Not even reconciliation: in the soul of each of us there is the same old anger against the other, with the added irritation of the pain caused by this quarrel, which each of us lays to the other's account. But it all has to be ended somehow, and life goes on as before. Such quarrels and worse happened constantly, once a week, or once a month, or every day. It was always the same thing. One time I had already obtained a passport to go abroad—the quarrel had lasted for two days—but then there was again a half talk, half reconciliation—and I stayed."

XXI

"So THAT's the sort of relations we had when this man appeared. He—his name was Trukhachevsky[12]—came to Moscow and appeared at my place. It was in the morning. I received him. We had once been on familiar terms. He tried to address me somewhere between formally and familiarly, tending towards the familiar, but I straight away set a formal tone, and he submitted at once. I disliked him intensely from the first glance. But, strangely, some sort of strange, fatal force drew me, not to spurn him, not to keep him at a distance, but, on the contrary, to become closer to him. What could have been simpler than to talk with him coldly, say goodbye, not introduce him to my wife? But no, as if on purpose, I began to speak about his playing, said I had been told that he had abandoned the violin. He said that, on the contrary, he now played more than ever. He began to recall that I used to play. I said that I no longer played, but that my wife played well.

"Amazing thing! My relations with him from the first day, from the first hour of my meeting him, were such as they could have been only after what was to happen. There was something strained in my relations with him: I noticed every word, every phrase spoken by him or myself, and ascribed significance to them.

"I introduced him to my wife. They at once struck up a conversation about music, and he offered his services in playing with her. My wife, as always lately, was very elegant and alluring, disturbingly beautiful. She clearly liked him from the first glance. Besides, she was glad that she would have the pleasure of playing with a violin, which she liked so much that she had even hired a violinist from the theatre, and this joy was expressed on her face. But, seeing me, she at once understood my feeling and changed her expression, and the game of mutual deception began. I smiled pleasantly, pretending I was very pleased. He, looking at my wife as all fornicators look at beautiful women, pretended that he was interested only in the subject of the conversation—precisely that which no longer interested him at all. She tried to appear indifferent, but my falsely smiling jealous man's expression, so familiar to her, and his lascivious gaze obviously aroused her. I saw that from the very first meeting her eyes began to glitter in a special way, and, probably owing to my jealousy, something like an electric current was at once established between them, giving rise to a similarity of expressions, gazes, and smiles. She blushed—and he blushed; she smiled—he smiled. We talked about music, Paris, various trifles. He got up to leave and, smiling, stood with his hat on his twitching thigh, looking now at her, now at me, as if waiting for what we would do. I remember that moment precisely because, at that moment, I might not have invited him, and then nothing would have happened. But I glanced at him, at her. 'Don't go thinking I'm jealous over you,' I mentally said to her, 'or that I'm afraid of you,' I said mentally to him, and invited him to bring his violin some evening so as to play with my wife. She glanced at me in astonishment, flushed, and, as if frightened, began to refuse, saying that she didn't play well enough. This refusal of hers irritated me still more, and I insisted still more. I remember the strange feeling with which I looked at his nape, at his white neck, in contrast to his black hair brushed forward on both sides, when he left us with his hopping, somehow birdlike gait. I couldn't help admitting to myself that this man's presence tormented me. 'It's up to me,' I thought, 'to make it so that I never see him.' But to do so would mean acknowledging that I'm afraid of him. No, I'm not afraid of him! That would be too humiliating, I said to myself. And just then, in the front hall, knowing that my wife could hear me, I insisted that he come that same evening with his violin. He promised and left.

"In the evening he came with his violin and they played. But it took them a while to get started, they didn't have the scores they needed, and those they did have my wife couldn't play without preparation. I loved music very much and sympathized with their playing, set up the music stand, turned the pages. And they played this and that, some songs without words and a little Mozart sonata. He played excellently, and he had in the highest degree what's known as tone. And fine, noble taste besides, not at all in keeping with his character.

"He was, to be sure, much better than my wife, and helped her, and at the same time politely praised her playing. He bore himself very well. My wife seemed to be interested only in the music and was very simple and natural. While I, though pretending to be interested in the music, suffered constantly from jealousy all evening.

"From the first moment that his eyes met my wife's, I saw that the beast who was sitting in them both, outside all conventions of position and society, asked, 'Possible?'—and replied, 'Oh, yes, very much so.' I saw that he had never expected to meet such an attractive woman in my wife, a Moscow lady, and he was very glad. Because he had no doubt at all that she would agree. The whole question was only whether the obnoxious husband would be a hindrance. If I had been a pure man, I wouldn't have understood that, but I, like the majority of men, had thought that way about women before I married, and therefore I could read his soul like an open book. I was especially tormented because I saw unquestionably that she had no other feelings for me than a constant irritation, only rarely interrupted by habitual sensuality, and that this man with his external elegance and novelty, and, above all, with his unquestionable musical talent, with the intimacy that comes from playing together, with the influence that music produces on impressionable natures, especially the violin—that this man was bound not only to please her, but unquestionably, without the slightest hesitation, to conquer her, crush her, twist her, tie her in knots, do whatever he wanted with her. I couldn't help seeing it, and I suffered terribly. But, despite that, or maybe owing to it, some power forced me against my will to be not only especially polite, but even amiable with him. Whether I was doing it for my wife's sake or for his, to show that I wasn't afraid of him, or for my own, so as to deceive myself—I don't know, only from my first relations with him I couldn't be simple. In order to resist the desire to kill him right then, I had to be amiable with him. I served him expensive wine at supper, I admired his music, I talked to him with an especially amiable smile and invited him to dine with us the next Sunday and play more with my wife. I said I'd invite some of my acquaintances, music lovers, to listen to him. And so it ended."

And in strong agitation, Pozdnyshev shifted his position and produced his special sound.

"It was strange how the presence of this man affected me," he began again, obviously making an effort to be calm. "I return home from an exhibition two or three days after that, come into the front hall, and suddenly feel something heavy, like a stone, press down on my heart, and I can't figure out what it is. This something was that, in passing through the front hall, I noticed something that reminded me of him. Only in my study did I realize what it was, and I went back to the front hall to check. Yes, I was not mistaken: it was his overcoat. You know, a fashionable overcoat. (I noted with extraordinary attention everything that concerned him, though I didn't realize it.) I ask—it's so, he's here. I pass, not through the drawing room, but through the schoolroom, to the reception room. Liza, my daughter, is sitting over a book, and the nanny is standing by the table with the baby, spinning some sort of lid. The door to the reception room is closed, and through it I hear the measured sounds of an arpeggio and voices, his and hers. I listen but can't make anything out. Obviously, the sounds of the piano are purposely meant to drown out their words, maybe their kisses. My God, what rose up in me then! When I merely remember the beast that lived in me then, I'm horrified. My heart was suddenly wrung, stopped, then began to pound like a hammer. The main thing, as always in any anger, was pity for myself. 'In front of the children, of the nanny!' I thought. I must have looked frightful, because even Liza looked at me with strange eyes. 'What am I to do?' I asked myself. 'Go in? I can't, God knows what I'll do.' But I can't go away either. The nanny looks at me as if she understands my position. 'It's impossible not to go in,' I said to myself and quickly opened the door. He was sitting at the piano, making those arpeggios with his big, white, upturned fingers. She was standing at the curve of the grand, over some open scores. She was the first to see or hear, and she glanced at me. Either she was frightened and pretended not to be, or she was in fact not frightened, but she did not stir or give a start, but only blushed, and that later.

" 'I'm so glad you've come; we haven't decided what to play on Sunday,' she said in a tone in which she would not have spoken to me if we had been alone. That and the fact that she said 'we' about herself and him made me indignant. I greeted him silently.

"He shook my hand and at once, with a smile that seemed downright mocking to me, began to explain that he had brought some scores to prepare for Sunday and now there was a disagreement between them about what to play: a more difficult and classical thing, namely, a Beethoven sonata for violin, or some small pieces? It was all so natural and simple that it was impossible to find fault with it, but at the same time I was certain that it was all untrue, that they had been arranging how to deceive me.

"One of the most tormenting relations for a jealous man (and in our social life all men are jealous) is certain social conventions which allow for the greatest and most dangerous closeness between a man and a woman. One would make oneself a laughing stock among people if one objected to closeness at balls, the closeness of doctors with their lady patients, closeness in the making of art—painting and, above all, music. Two people are taken up with the most noble of arts, music; for that a certain closeness is required, and there is nothing reprehensible in that closeness, and only a stupid, jealous husband could see something undesirable in it. And yet everybody knows that it is precisely by means of these same occupations, especially music, that the greater share of adulteries occur in our society. I obviously embarrassed them by the embarrassment that showed in me: for a long time I couldn't say anything. I was like an upended bottle from which the water will not pour because it's too full. I wanted to curse at him, to throw him out, but I felt that again I had to be polite and amiable with him. And so I was. I pretended that I approved of everything and again, following that strange feeling that made me treat him the more amiably the more painful his presence was for me, I told him that I relied on his taste and advised her to do the same. He stayed a while longer, as long as it took to smooth over the unpleasant impression I had made by suddenly coming into the room with a frightened face and then saying nothing—and left, pretending that it was now decided what to play the next day. I was fully convinced that, compared with what preoccupied them, the question of what to play was a matter of complete indifference.

"I saw him to the front hall with particular politeness (how can one not see off a man who has come to disturb the peace and destroy the happiness of a whole family!). I pressed his soft, white hand with particular affection."

XXII

"FOR THAT WHOLE DAY I didn't speak to her; I couldn't. Her closeness called up such hatred for her in me that I feared for myself. Over dinner, in front of the children, she asked me when I was leaving. I had to go to a district session the next week. I told her when. She asked if I needed anything for the road. I said nothing and sat silently at the table, then silently went to my study. Lately she never came to my room, especially at that time. I was lying in my study and feeling angry. Suddenly I heard familiar footsteps. And the frightful, monstrous thought comes to my head that she, like Uriah's wife,[13] wanted to conceal the sin she had already committed, and that was why she was coming to see me at such an inopportune hour. 'Can it be she's coming to me?' I thought, listening to her approaching footsteps. If it's to me, it means I'm right. And an inexpressible hatred for her rises in my soul. Closer and closer the footsteps. Can it be she won't pass by and go to the reception room? No, the door creaked, and in the doorway her tall, handsome figure, and in her face, in her eyes—timidity and fawning, which she wants to conceal, but which I see and the meaning of which I know. I held my breath so long that I nearly suffocated, and, continuing to look at her, I seized the cigarette case and began to smoke.

" 'Well, what is it, I come to sit with you, and you start smoking'—and she sat down close to me on the sofa, leaning against me.

"I drew back so as not to touch her.

" 'I see you're displeased that I want to play on Sunday,' she said.

" 'I'm not at all displeased,' I said.

" 'As if I don't see!'

" 'Well, I congratulate you on seeing. I see nothing, except that you're behaving like a cocotte . . .'

" 'If you're going to swear like a trooper, I'll leave.'

" 'Leave then; only know that, if you don't value the honour of the family, then I don't value you (devil take you), but I do the honour of the family.'

" 'But what is it, what is it?'

" 'Clear out, for God's sake, clear out!'

"Either she was pretending that she didn't understand what it was about, or she really didn't understand, but she became offended and angry. She got up, yet didn't leave, but stood in the middle of the room.

" 'You've become decidedly impossible,' she began. 'Such a character even an angel couldn't get along with.' And, as always, trying to sting me as painfully as possible, she reminded me of how I had behaved with my sister (there had been an occasion when I had lost my temper and said all sorts of rude things to my sister; she knew it tormented me and needled me on that spot). 'After that nothing from you would surprise me,' she said.

" 'Yes, insult me, humiliate me, disgrace me, and put all the blame on me,' I said to myself, and suddenly such terrible anger against her came over me as I had never yet experienced.

"For the first time I wanted to express that anger physically. I jumped up and moved towards her; but just as I jumped up, I remember becoming aware of that anger and asking myself if it was good to give way to that feeling, and at once answered myself that it was good, that it would frighten her, and at once, instead of resisting that anger, I began to heat it up in myself and rejoiced that it blazed more and more in me.

" 'Clear out or I'll kill you!' I shouted, going up to her and seizing her by the arm. I consciously intensified the angry tone of my voice as I said it. And I must have been frightening, because she grew so timid that she couldn't even leave, and only repeated:

" 'Vasya, what is it, what's the matter with you?'

" 'Get out!' I roared still louder. 'Only you can drive me into a rage. I can't answer for myself!'

"Having given free rein to my rage, I revelled in it, and I wanted to do something extraordinary, showing the extreme degree of this rage of mine. I wanted terribly to beat her, to kill her, but knew it was impossible, and therefore, to unleash my rage, I seized a paperweight from the desk and, shouting, 'Get out!' once more, hurled it to the floor, missing her. I had aimed very well so as to miss. Then she started out of the room, but stopped in the doorway. And right then, while she could still see (I did it so that she could see), I began taking things from the desk—candlesticks, an inkstand—and throwing them on the floor, continuing to shout:

" 'Get out! clear off! I can't answer for myself!'

"She left—and I stopped at once.

"An hour later the nanny came and said that my wife was in hysterics. I went; she was sobbing, laughing, couldn't say anything, and was shaking all over. She wasn't pretending, she was genuinely ill.

"Towards morning she calmed down, and we made peace under the influence of the feeling we called love.

"In the morning, when I confessed to her, after our reconciliation, that I was very jealous of Trukhachevsky, she was not embarrassed in the least and laughed quite naturally. It even seemed so strange to her, so she said, the possibility of fancying such a man.

" 'Could a decent woman possibly feel anything towards such a man apart from the pleasure afforded by music? If you like, I'm prepared never to see him. Even on Sunday, though everybody's invited. Write to him that I'm unwell, and that's the end. It's only disgusting that anyone, mainly he himself, might think he's dangerous. And I'm too proud to allow that to be thought.'

"And she wasn't lying, she believed what she said; she hoped to call up scorn for him in herself by these words and to protect herself from him that way, but she didn't succeed. Everything went against her, especially that cursed music. So it all ended, and on Sunday the guests assembled, and they played again."

XXIII

"I THINK it's superfluous to say that I was very vain: if you're not vain, then there's nothing to live by in our ordinary life. Well, so on Sunday I began tastefully organizing the dinner and the evening with music. I myself bought the things for dinner and invited the guests.

"By six o'clock the guests had assembled, and he, too, had appeared in a tailcoat with diamond studs in bad tone. He behaved casually, replied hastily to everything with a little smile of agreement and understanding, you know, with that particular expression that whatever you say or do is exactly what he expected. All that was improper in him I now noticed with particular pleasure, because it was all supposed to calm me down and prove that he stood on such a low level for my wife that, as she said, she could not lower herself to it. Now I no longer allowed myself to be jealous. First, I had already suffered through that torment and needed a rest; second, I wanted to believe my wife's assurances and did believe them. But, though I wasn't jealous, I was still unnatural with him and with her during dinner and the first half of the evening, before the music began. I still followed the movements and glances of them both.

"The dinner was like all dinners, dull, affected. The music began rather early. Ah, how well I remember all the details of that evening; I remember how he brought the violin, opened the case, took off a cover some lady had embroidered for him, took out the violin, and started tuning up. I remember how my wife sat down with an affectedly indifferent look, behind which I could see she was concealing great timidity—timidity mostly to do with her own skill—sat down at the grand with an affected look, and there began the usual A on the piano, the pizzicato of the violin, the setting up of the scores. Then I remember how they glanced at each other, looked around at the people taking their seats, said something to each other, and it began. He struck the first chord. His face became serious, stern, sympathetic, and, listening to his own sounds, he carefully plucked the strings with his fingers, and the grand answered him. And it began . . ."

He stopped and produced his sounds several times in a row. He was about to start speaking, but snuffed his nose and stopped again.

"They played Beethoven's Kreutzer Sonata. Do you know the first presto? Do you?!" he cried. "Ohh! . . . That sonata is a fearful thing. Precisely that part. And music generally is a fearful thing. What is it? I don't understand. What is music? What does it do? And why does it do what it does? They say music has an elevating effect on the soul—nonsense, lies! It affects one, affects one fearfully, I'm speaking of myself, but not at all in a soul-elevating way. It affects the soul neither in an elevating nor in an abasing way, but in a provoking way. How shall I put it? Music makes me forget myself, my true situation, it transports me to some other situation not my own; under the influence of music it seems to me that I feel what, in fact, I do not feel, that I understand what I do not understand, that I can do what I cannot do. I explain it by the fact that music works like yawning, like laughter; I'm not sleepy, but I yawn looking at a yawning man, I have no reason to laugh, but I laugh hearing someone else laugh.

"It, music, at once, transports me directly into the inner state of the one who wrote the music. I merge with him in my soul and, together with him, am transported from one state to another, but why I do that I don't know. The man who wrote, let's say, the Kreutzer Sonata— Beethoven—knew why he was in such a state. That state led him to certain actions, and therefore that state had meaning for him, while for me it has none. And therefore music only provokes, it doesn't conclude. Well, they play a military march, soldiers march to it, the music achieves its end; they play a dance tune, I dance, the music achieves its end; they sing a mass, I take communion, the music also achieves its end; while here there's only provocation, but what's to follow from that provocation isn't there. And that's why music sometimes has such a fearful, such a terrible effect. In China music is a state affair. And that's how it should be. As if it can be allowed that anyone who likes should hypnotize another or many others and then do what he likes with them. And, above all, that this hypnotist should be the first immoral man who comes along.

"Otherwise it's a terrible means in the hands of anyone who comes along. Take, for instance, this Kreutzer Sonata, the first presto. How can that presto be played in a drawing room among ladies in décolleté? It's played, they applaud a little, and then eat ice cream and talk about the latest scandal. These things can be played only in certain important, significant circumstances, and when there's a demand to accomplish certain important actions in accordance with that music. Play it and do what the music attunes you to. Otherwise the calling up of an energy, a feeling, that accords neither with the place, nor with the time, that is not manifest in anything, can only have a pernicious effect. On me, at least, this thing had a terrible effect; it seemed to me as if completely new feelings, new possibilities, which I hadn't known until then, were revealed to me. It was as if something were saying in my soul, 'So it's like that, not at all as I thought and lived before, but like that.' What this new thing was that I had learned, I couldn't explain to myself, but the consciousness of this new state was very joyful. All those same persons, including my wife and him, appeared in quite a new light.

"After that presto they went on to play a beautiful but ordinary, not new, andante, with banal variations and quite a weak finale. Then, at the request of the guests, they went on to play Ernst's Elegy, then various little things. It was all good, but it didn't produce one hundredth of the impression on me that the first piece produced. It all occurred against the background of the impression produced by the first piece. I felt light and gay all evening. As for my wife, I had never seen her the way she was that evening. Those shining eyes, that severity and significance of expression while she played, and that complete melting away, the weak, pathetic, and blissful smile after they finished. I saw it all, but I ascribed no other significance to it than that she was experiencing the same things as I, and that to her, as to me, new, never-experienced feelings had been revealed, or as if recalled. The evening ended well, and everybody went home.

"Knowing that in two days I was to go to a session, Trukhachevsky, on taking his leave, said that he hoped on his next visit to the city to repeat the pleasure of that evening. From that I could conclude that he did not consider it possible to come to my house in my absence, and that pleased me. It turned out that, as I would not return before his departure, we would not see any more of each other.

"For the first time I shook his hand with genuine pleasure and thanked him for the pleasure. He also took leave of my wife. The way they said goodbye seemed to me most natural and proper. Everything was fine. My wife and I were very pleased with the evening."

XXIV

"TWO DAYS LATER I left for the district, having said goodbye to my wife in the best and calmest of moods. In the district there was always no end of business and a totally special life, a special little world. For two days I spent ten hours a day in the office. On the second day a letter from my wife was brought to me in the office. I read it on the spot. She wrote about the children, the uncle, the nanny, some purchases, and among other things, as if of a most ordinary thing, that Trukhachevsky had come, brought the promised scores, and promised to play more, but that she had refused. I didn't remember him promising to bring scores: it seemed to me that he had said his final goodbye, and therefore it struck me unpleasantly. But there was so much business that there was no time for thinking, and only in the evening, on returning to my place, did I reread the letter. Besides the fact that Trukhachevsky had come once more in my absence, the whole tone of the letter seemed strained to me. The enraged beast of jealousy growled in its kennel and wanted to leap out, but I was afraid of that beast and quickly locked it up. 'What a vile feeling jealousy is!' I said to myself. 'What could be more natural than what she writes?'

"And I went to bed and began to think about the business ahead of me tomorrow. It always took me a long time to fall asleep during these sessions, in a new place, but this time I fell asleep very soon. And as it happens, you know, suddenly there's an electric shock and you wake up. So I woke up, and woke up with the thought of her, of my carnal love for her, and of Trukhachevsky, and of how they had concluded it between them. Horror and anger wrung my heart. But I started reasoning with myself. 'What nonsense,' I said to myself, 'there are no grounds, there's nothing and never was. How can I so humiliate her and myself by supposing such horrible things. Some sort of hired fiddler, known to be a trashy fellow, and suddenly an honourable woman, the respected mother of a family, *my* wife! How preposterous!' presented itself to me on one side. 'How else could it be?' presented itself to me on the other. How could there not be that same simple and understandable thing in the name of which I married her, that same thing in the name of which I lived with her, which was the one thing I wanted from her and which others, therefore, also wanted, including this musician? He's an unmarried man, healthy (I remembered him crunching on the gristle in a cutlet and putting his red lips greedily to a glass of wine), well-nourished, smooth, and not only without principles, but obviously with the principle of availing himself of such pleasures as come along. And between them the connection of music, that most refined lust of the senses. What could hold him back? Nothing. On the contrary, everything entices him. She? Who is she? She's a mystery, as she was, so she is. I don't know her. I know her only as an animal. And nothing can, nothing should hold back an animal.

"Only now did I remember their faces that evening, when, after the Kreutzer Sonata, they played some passionate little thing, I don't recall by whom, some piece sensual to the point of obscenity. 'How could I leave?' I said to myself, remembering their faces. 'Wasn't it clear that everything had been accomplished between them that evening? And wasn't it obvious that already that evening there not only was no barrier between them, but that they both, and mainly she, experienced a certain shame after what had happened with them?' I remember how she smiled weakly, pathetically, and blissfully, wiping the sweat from her flushed face, when I went up to the piano. Already then they avoided looking at each other, and only at supper, when he poured water for her, did they glance at each other and smile slightly. I now remembered with horror that glance of theirs that I had intercepted with its barely perceptible smile. 'Yes, it's all concluded,' one voice said to me, and at once another voice said something quite different. 'It's something that's come over you, it can't be,' said that other voice. It felt eerie to me lying there in the dark, I lit a match, and it felt somehow frightening to me in that little room with yellow wallpaper. I lit a cigarette and, as always happens when you turn around in the same circle of unresolved contradictions— you smoke, and so I smoked one cigarette after another, in order to befog myself and see no contradictions.

"I didn't sleep all night, and at five o'clock, deciding that I couldn't remain in this tension any longer and would leave at once, I got up, woke the caretaker who served me, and sent him for horses. To the meeting I sent a note saying that I had been summoned to Moscow on urgent business and therefore asked to be replaced by another member. At eight o'clock I got into the tarantass and drove off."

XXV

THE CONDUCTOR CAME IN and, noticing that our candle had burned down, put it out, not replacing it with a new one. Outside it was growing light. Pozdnyshev was silent, sighing deeply all the while the conductor was in the carriage. He went on with his story only when the conductor was gone and in the semi-dark of the moving carriage only the rattle of the windows and the regular snoring of the clerk could be heard. In the half-light of dawn I could no longer see him at all. I could hear only his more and more agitated and suffering voice.

"I had to go twenty miles by carriage and eight hours by rail. The carriage ride was wonderful. It was a frosty autumn with bright sun. You know that season, when horseshoes imprint themselves on the butterlike roadway. The roads are smooth, the light bright, and the air invigorating. It was good to be riding in a tarantass. When it grew light and I set out, I felt easier. Looking at the horses, at the fields, at the passers-by, I would forget where I was going. Sometimes it seemed to me that I was simply riding, and that nothing of what had called me back existed. It was especially joyful for me to forget myself like that. When I did remember where I was going, I said to myself: 'Don't think, we'll see later.' On top of that, an event occurred midway that held up my journey and distracted me still more: the tarantass broke down and had to be repaired. This breakdown had great significance in that it made it so that I arrived in Moscow not at five o'clock, as I had planned, but at midnight, and at home towards one o'clock, since I did not catch the express and had to go by regular passenger train. Going for a cart, the repairs, the payment, tea at the inn, talking with the innkeeper—all that distracted me still more. Towards evening everything was ready, and I set off again, and it was still better riding by night than by day. There was a young moon, a little frost, again a beautiful road, horses, a merry driver, and I rode along and enjoyed it, almost not thinking at all about what awaited me, or especially enjoying it precisely because I knew what awaited me and was bidding farewell to the joys of life. But this calm state, the ability to suppress my feelings, ended with that ride. As soon as I got on the train, something quite different began. That eight-hour train trip was something terrible for me, which I won't forget all my life. Either because, on settling in the carriage, I vividly imagined myself arriving, or because the railroad has such a stirring effect on people, once I sat down in the carriage, I could no longer control my imagination, and it began ceaselessly painting for me, with an extraordinary vividness, pictures that inflamed my jealousy, one after another, and one more cynical than the other, all about the same thing, about what was happening there without me, and how she was betraying me. I burned with indignation, anger, and some peculiar feeling of intoxication with my humiliation, as I contemplated those pictures, and I couldn't tear myself away from them; I couldn't help looking at them, couldn't erase them, couldn't help evoking them. Not only that, but the more I contemplated those imaginary pictures, the more I believed in their reality. It was as if the vividness with which those pictures presented themselves to me served as proof that what I imagined was a reality. Some devil, as if against my will, invented and urged upon me the most terrible considerations. A long-past conversation with Trukhachevsky's brother came to my mind, and in a sort of ecstasy I tore my heart with that conversation, referring it to Trukhachevsky and my wife.

"It was very long ago, but I remembered it. Trukhachevsky's brother, I remembered, once replied to the question of whether he visited brothels by saying that a respectable man wouldn't start going where he might get sick, and where it was dirty and vile, when he can always find a respectable woman. And so he, his brother, found my wife. 'True, she's no longer in her first youth, there's a tooth missing on one side, and there's a certain puffiness'—I was thinking for him—'but no help for it, one must avail oneself of what's there.' 'Yes, he's condescending to her in taking her as his mistress,' I said to myself. 'Besides, she's safe.' 'No, it's impossible! What am I thinking!' I said to myself in horror. 'There's nothing, nothing like that. And there aren't even any grounds for supposing anything like that. Didn't she say to me that even the thought that

I could be jealous of him was humiliating for her? Yes, but she's lying, it's all a lie!' I cried—and it started again . . . There were only two other passengers in our carriage—an old lady and her husband, both very untalkative—and they got off at one station, and I remained alone. I was like a beast in a cage: now I jumped up, went to the windows, then, staggering, I began to pace, trying to speed up the carriage; but the carriage, with all its seats and windows, went rattling along just like ours . . ."

And Pozdnyshev jumped up, took a few steps, and sat down again.

"Oh, I'm afraid, I'm afraid of railway carriages, terror comes over me. Yes, it's terrible!" he went on. "I said to myself: 'I'll think about other things. Well, say, about the owner of the inn where I had tea.' Well, so, in the eyes of my imagination appears the innkeeper with his long beard and his grandson—a boy the same age as my Vasya. My Vasya! He'll see the musician kiss his mother. What will that do to his poor soul? But what is it to her! She's in love . . . And the same thing rose up. No, no . . . Well, I'll think about the inspection of the hospital. Yes, how that patient yesterday complained about a doctor. The doctor had a moustache like Trukhachevsky's. And how insolently he . . . They deceived me when he said he was leaving. And again it began. Everything I thought about had a connection with him. I suffered terribly. The suffering lay mainly in ignorance, in doubts, in splitting apart, in not knowing whether I must love her or hate her. My sufferings were so intense that I remember having a thought that I liked very much, of getting out on the way, lying down on the rails under the carriage, and ending it. Then at least you won't hesitate and doubt any longer. The one thing that kept me from doing it was pity for myself, which at once immediately called up hatred for her. Towards him there was some strange feeling of both hatred and consciousness of my humiliation and his victory, but towards her a terrible hatred. 'I can't put an end to myself and leave her; she must suffer if only a little, if only to understand what I've suffered,' I said to myself. I got out at every station in order to distract myself. At one station I saw people drinking in the buffet, and I at once drank some vodka myself. Next to me stood a Jew, also drinking. He got to talking, and, only so as not to remain alone, I went with him to a dirty, smoke-filled third-class carriage strewn with the shells of sunflower seeds. I sat beside him there, and he chattered a lot and told anecdotes. I listened to him, but couldn't understand what he was saying, because I went on thinking my own thoughts. He noticed it and started demanding that I pay attention to him; then I got up and went back to my carriage. 'I must think over,' I said to myself, 'whether what I think is true, and whether I have grounds for tormenting myself.' I sat down, wishing to think it over calmly, but, instead of calmly thinking it over, the same thing began again: instead of reasoning—pictures and imaginings. 'So many times I've been tormented like this,' I said to myself (I remembered similar fits of jealousy in the past), 'and it all ended in nothing. So now, too, maybe, even certainly, I'll find her peacefully asleep; she'll wake up, be glad to see me, and by her words, her glance, I'll feel that there was nothing and it was all nonsense. Oh, how good that would be!' 'But, no, that's happened too often, and now it will no longer be so,' some voice said to me, and it began again. Yes, here's where the punishment lay! I wouldn't take a young man to a syphilis clinic to rid him of the desire for women, but to my own soul, to look at the devils that were tearing it apart! The terrible thing was that I recognized for myself the full, unquestionable right over her body, as if it were my body, and at the same time I felt that I couldn't own that body, that it was not mine, and that she could dispose of it as she wished, and she wished to dispose of it not as I wished. And I could do nothing either to him or to her. Like Vanka the Steward at the foot of the gallows,[14] he'll sing a little song about how he kissed her sugary lips and so on. And he's on top. And still less can I do anything with her. If she hasn't done it but wants to, and I know it, then it's worse still: it would be better if she had done it, so that I knew it, so that there'd be no uncertainty. I couldn't have said what I wanted. I wanted her not to wish for what she must wish for. It was total madness!"

XXVI

"AT THE NEXT to last station, when the conductor came to take our tickets, I gathered up my things and went out to the rear platform, and the consciousness that it was close, that the resolution was here, increased my agitation still more. I was cold, and my jaws trembled so much that my teeth chattered. I left the station mechanically with the crowd, hired a cab, got in and drove away. I rode along looking at the rare passers-by, and the yard porters, and the shadows cast by the street lamps and my droshky, now in front, now behind, without thinking about anything. After going half a mile, my feet felt cold, and it occurred to me that I had taken off my woollen socks on the train and put them in my bag. Where's the bag? Is it here? It is. But where's the wicker trunk? I remembered that I had forgotten all about my baggage, but remembering and taking out the check, I decided that it wasn't worth going back and rode on.

"Hard as I try now, I simply can't remember my state then: what was I thinking? what did I want? I know nothing. I remember only being conscious that something frightening and very important in my life was being prepared. Whether the important thing came about because I thought that way, or because I had a foreboding of it—I don't know. It may also be that, after what happened, all the moments leading up to it took on a dark shade in my memory. I drove up to the porch. It was past midnight. Several cabs stood near the porch, expecting customers because of the lighted windows (the lighted windows were in our apartment, in the reception room and drawing room). Not accounting to myself for why there was still light in our windows so late, in the same state of expecting something dreadful, I went up the steps and rang. Our footman—the kind, assiduous, and very stupid Egor—opened the door. The first thing that caught my eye, hanging among other clothes on the stand in the front hall, was his overcoat. I should have been astonished, but I wasn't, it was just what I expected. 'That's it,' I said to myself. When I asked Egor who was there and he named Trukhachevsky, I asked if there was anybody else. He said:

" 'No one, sir.'

"I remember him saying it with such an intonation as if he wished to make me happy and disperse my doubts about there being anyone else. 'No one, sir. So, so,' I seemed to say to myself.

" 'And the children?'

" 'They're well, thank God. Asleep long ago, sir.'

"I couldn't breathe and couldn't stop the trembling of my jaws. 'Well, so it's not as I thought: before I thought it was a misfortune, but it would all turn out well, as formerly. Now, though, it's not as formerly, now it's everything I imagined to myself, and thought I was only imagining it, but here it all is in reality. Here it is . . .'

"I almost burst into sobs, but at once the devil prompted me: 'Cry, turn sentimental, and they'll quietly part, there'll be no evidence, and you'll doubt and suffer forever.' And at once the sensitivity towards myself vanished and a strange feeling appeared—you won't believe it— a feeling of joy that my torment was now over, that now I could punish her, could rid myself of her, could give vent to my anger. And I gave vent to it—I became a beast, an angry and cunning beast.

" 'Don't, don't,' I said to Egor, who was about to go to the drawing room. 'Here's what to do: quickly take a cab and go; here's my baggage check, fetch my things. Off with you.'

"He went down the corridor for his coat. Fearing he might frighten them off, I went to his little room with him and waited while he got ready. From the drawing room, two rooms away, came the sounds of talking and of knives against plates. They were eating and hadn't heard the bell. 'If only they don't come out now,' I thought. Egor put on his coat trimmed with Astrakhan lamb and left. I let him out and locked the door behind him, and it was eerie for me when I felt that I was left alone and that I had to act at once. How—I didn't know yet. I only knew that it was all over now, that there could be no doubt of her guilt, and that I would punish her at once and end my relations with her.

"Before I had been hesitant, I had said to myself: 'Maybe it's not true, maybe I'm mistaken'—now it was no longer so. It was all decided irrevocably. In secret from me, alone with him, at night! This was a complete forgetting of everything. Or worse still: such deliberate daring, such boldness in crime, so that the boldness served as a sign of innocence. It was all clear. There was no doubt. I feared only one thing, that they might make a run for it, invent yet another deception, and thus deprive me of obvious evidence and the possibility of punishment. And, so as to catch them the sooner, I went on tiptoe to the reception room, where they were sitting, not through the drawing room, but through the corridor and the nurseries.

"In the first nursery the boys were asleep. In the second nursery the nanny stirred, was about to wake up, and I imagined what she would think when she learned everything, and was so overcome with self-pity at this thought that I couldn't hold back my tears, and, so as not to wake the children, I ran out on tiptoe to the corridor and to my study, collapsed on the sofa, and burst into sobs.

"I—an honourable man, I—my parents' son, I—who all my life dreamed of the happiness of family life, I—a man who has never betrayed her . . . And look! Five children, and she embraces a musician, all because he has red lips! No, she's not a human being! She's a bitch, a loathsome bitch! In the next room from her children, whom she has pretended to love all her life! And to write what she wrote to me! And to throw herself on his neck so insolently! But what do I know? Maybe it's been this way all the while. Maybe it's with lackeys that she's been making all those children that are considered mine. And I'd come tomorrow, and she, with her hair done up, with that waist of hers and her lazy, graceful movements (I've seen all of her attractive, hateful face), would meet me, and this beast of jealousy would forever be sitting in my heart and tearing it to pieces. What will the nanny think? And Egor? And poor Lizochka! She already understands certain things. And this insolence! and this lie! and this animal sensuality, which I know so well,' I said to myself.

"I wanted to get up, but I couldn't. My heart was pounding so hard that I couldn't keep on my feet. Yes, I'll die of a stroke. She'll kill me. That's what she wants. Well, so, should she kill me? No, that would be too much to her advantage, I won't afford her such pleasure. Yes, and I'm sitting here, and they're eating and laughing there, and . . . Yes, despite the fact that she's no longer in her first freshness, he didn't scorn her: anyhow she's not bad, and, above all, she's at least safe for his precious health. 'Why didn't I strangle her then?' I said to myself, remembering the moment a week ago when I pushed her out of my study and then smashed things. I vividly remembered the state I was in then; not only remembered it, but felt the same need to smash, to destroy, that I had felt then. I remember how I wanted to act and how all considerations except those needed for action left my head. I got into the state of a beast or a man under the influence of physical excitement at a time of danger, when a man acts precisely, unhurriedly, but without losing a moment, and all only with one definite goal."

XXVII

"THE FIRST THING I did, I took off my boots and, in my stockinged feet, went up to the wall above the sofa, where I had guns and daggers hanging, and took a curved Damascus dagger, which had never been used and was terribly sharp. I drew it out of the scabbard. I remember the scabbard falling behind the sofa and remember saying to myself: 'I must find it afterwards, otherwise it will get lost.' Then I took off my coat, which I had had on all the while, and, stepping softly in just my stockings, went there.

"And stealing up quietly, I suddenly opened the door. I remember the expression on their faces. I remember that expression, because that expression gave me a tormenting joy. It was an expression of terror. That was just what I wanted. I'll never forget the expression of desperate terror that appeared in the first second on both their faces when they saw me. He had been sitting at the table, I believe, but on seeing or hearing me, he jumped to his feet and stood back to the cupboard. On his face there was the quite unquestionable expression of terror alone. On her face there was the same expression of terror, but there was something else as well. If there had been only the one, maybe what happened wouldn't have happened; but in the expression of her face, or at least it seemed so to me in the first moment, there was also chagrin, displeasure, that her amorous passion and happiness with him had been disrupted. As if she needed nothing now except that her happiness not be interfered with. The one expression and the other remained on their faces only for an instant. The expression of terror on his face was replaced at once by the expression of a question: Can we lie or not? If we can, we'd better begin. If not, something else will begin. But what? He looked at her questioningly. On her face, when she looked at him, the expression of vexation and chagrin was replaced, as it seemed to me, by a concern for him.

"I stood in the doorway for a moment, holding the dagger behind my back. At the same moment, he smiled and in a ridiculously indifferent tone, began:

" 'And we've been making music . . .'

" 'This is a surprise,' she began at the same time, submitting to his tone.

"But neither of them finished what they were saying: the same rage I had experienced a week ago came over me. Again I experienced that need for destruction, violence, and the ecstasy of rage, and gave myself up to it.

"Neither finished what they were saying . . . That other thing which he had been afraid of began, at once breaking off all that they were saying. I rushed at her, still hiding the dagger so that he wouldn't prevent me from striking her in the side under the breast. I had chosen that spot from the beginning. The moment I rushed at her, he saw and—something I never expected from him—seized me by the arm, shouting:

"'Come to your senses! What are you doing! Help!'

"I tore my arm free and silently turned on him. His eyes met mine, he suddenly went white as a sheet, even his lips, his eyes flashed somehow peculiarly, and—something I also never expected from him—he darted under the piano and through the door. I rushed after him, but there was a weight hanging on my left arm. It was she. I gave a jerk. She hung on even more heavily and wouldn't let go. This unexpected hindrance, the weight, and her loathsome contact with me inflamed me still more. I felt that I was totally enraged and must be frightening, and I was glad of it. I swung my left arm as hard as I could, and my elbow struck her right in the face. She cried out and let go of my arm. I wanted to run after him, but remembered that it would be ridiculous to go running after my wife's lover in my stockinged feet, and I didn't want to be ridiculous, I wanted to be frightening. Despite the terrible rage I was in, I was aware all the time of the impression I was making on others, and that impression even partly guided me. I turned to her. She had fallen on the sofa and, holding her hand to the eyes I had hurt, was looking at me. In her face were fear and hatred of me, of her enemy, as in a rat when you pick up the trap it's caught in. At least I saw nothing in her except that fear and hatred of me. It was a fear and hatred of me that must be caused by her love for another man. But I might still have restrained myself and not have done what I did, if she had kept silent. But she suddenly began to speak and snatch with her hand at my hand holding the dagger.

" 'Come to your senses! What are you doing? What's the matter with you? There's nothing, nothing, nothing . . . I swear!'

"I might have delayed longer, but those last words, from which I concluded the opposite, that is, all that had happened, called for a response. And the response had to correspond to the mood I had driven myself into, which was steadily in crescendo and had to go on rising in the same way. Rage also has its laws.

" 'Don't lie, loathsome woman!' I screamed and seized her arm with my left hand, but she tore herself free. Then, still holding the dagger, I seized her by the throat with my left hand, threw her on her back, and began to strangle her. What a tough neck it was . . . She seized my hand with both hands, trying to tear it from her throat, and, as if that was just what I was waiting for, I struck her as hard as I could with the dagger in the left side below the ribs.

"When people say they're not aware of what they're doing in a fit of rage—it's nonsense, not true. I was aware of everything and never for a second ceased to be aware. The more I turned up the steam of my rage, the more brightly the light of consciousness glowed in me, in which I couldn't help seeing all that I was doing. I knew what I was doing every second. I can't say I knew beforehand what I was going to do, but in the second when I was doing it, even, I think, a little before, I knew what I was doing, as if to make repentance possible, as if to be able to tell myself that I could have stopped. I knew I was striking below the ribs and that the dagger would go in. At the moment I was doing it, I knew I was doing something horrible, such as I had never done before, and which would have horrible consequences. But that consciousness flashed like lightning, and the act followed immediately after that consciousness. And the act became conscious with an extraordinary vividness. I felt and remember the momentary resistance of her corset and something else, and then the knife sinking into something soft. She seized the dagger with her hands, cut them, but couldn't hold it back. For a long time afterwards, in prison, after the moral turnabout was accomplished in me, I thought of that moment, remembering what I could, and reflecting. I remember for an instant, only for an instant, preceding the act, the terrible awareness that I was killing and had killed a woman, a defenceless woman, my wife. I remember the horror of that awareness, and therefore I conclude and even vaguely remember that, having stuck in the dagger, I immediately pulled it out, wishing to repair what I had done and stop it. For a second I stood motionless, waiting to see what would happen and whether it could be repaired. She jumped to her feet and cried:

" 'Nanny! He's killed me!'

"The nanny, who had heard the noise, was standing in the doorway. I went on standing there, waiting and not believing it. But then blood gushed from under her corset. Only then did I understand that it couldn't be repaired, and at once I decided that there was no need, that this was the very thing I wanted and the very thing that had to be done. I waited until she fell and the nanny rushed to her crying, 'Good God!' and only then did I throw the dagger aside and walk out of the room.

" 'I mustn't get agitated, I must know what I'm doing,' I said to myself, not looking at her or the nanny. The nanny cried out, calling the maid. I went down the corridor and, having sent the maid, went to my study. 'What must I do now?' I asked myself and at once knew what. Going into the study, I went straight to the wall, took down a revolver, examined it—it was loaded—and put it on the table. Then I got the scabbard from behind the sofa and sat down on the sofa.

"I sat like that for a long time. I didn't think of anything, didn't remember anything. I heard them fussing with something there. I heard someone come, then someone else. Then I heard and even saw Egor bring my wicker trunk to the study. As if anybody needed it!

" 'Have you heard what happened?' I said. 'Tell the yard porter to inform the police.'

"He said nothing and left. I got up, locked the door, and, taking out cigarettes and a match, began to smoke. I hadn't finished smoking before sleep seized me and overpowered me. I must have slept for two hours. I remember dreaming that she and I were friends, quarrelled, but made peace, and that something interfered slightly, but we were friends. I was awakened by a knock on the door. 'It's the police,' I thought, waking up. 'I did kill, it seems. But maybe it's she, and nothing has happened.' There was another knock on the door. I didn't respond, I was settling the question of whether it had happened or not. Yes, it had. I remembered the resistance of the corset and the knife sinking in, and a chill ran down my spine. 'Yes, it did. Yes, now I must kill myself as well,' I said to myself. But I knew as I was saying it that I wouldn't kill myself. However, I got up and took the revolver in my hands again. But, strange thing: I remember how I had been close to suicide many times in the past, how that day even, on the train, it had seemed easy to me, easy precisely because I was thinking how struck she'd be by it. Now I not only couldn't kill myself, but couldn't even think about it. 'Why should I?' I asked myself, and there was no answer. There was more knocking on the door. 'Yes, first I must find out who's knocking. I still have time.' I put down the revolver and covered it with a newspaper. I went to the door and slid back the bolt. It was my wife's sister, a kindly, stupid widow.

" 'Vasya, what is it?' she said, and poured out her ever-ready tears.

" 'What do you want?' I asked rudely. I saw there was no need or reason to be rude with her, but I couldn't come up with any other tone.

" 'Vasya, she's dying! Ivan Zakharych said so.' Ivan Zakharych was the doctor, her doctor and adviser.

" 'So he's here?' I said, and all my anger against her rose up again. 'Well, what of it?'

" 'Vasya, go to her. Ah, it's so terrible,' she said.

" 'Shall I go to her?' I put the question to myself. And at once replied that I should go to her, that it's probably always done that way, that when a husband kills his wife, as I had done, he's obliged to go to her. 'If that's how it's done, I must go,' I said to myself. 'Yes, if need be, I'll always have time,' I thought about my intention to shoot myself, and followed after her. 'Now there'll be phrases, grimaces, but I won't give in to that,' I said to myself.

" 'Wait,' I said to her sister. 'It's stupid without boots, let me at least put on my slippers.' "

XXVIII

"AND, amazing thing! Again, when I left my study and walked through the familiar rooms, again the hope appeared in me that nothing had happened, but the smell of that medical muck—iodine, carbolic acid—struck me. No, it had all happened. Going down the corridor past the nursery, I saw Lizonka. She looked at me with frightened eyes. It even seemed to me that all five children were there and they were all looking at me. I went up to the door, and the maid opened it for me from inside and stepped out. The first thing that caught my eye was her light-grey dress on the chair, all dark with blood. She was lying with her knees drawn up on our double bed, on my side even, because it was easier to get to. She was lying slightly propped on pillows, in an unbuttoned bed jacket. The wounded place had been covered with something. There was a heavy smell of iodine in the room. First and most of all I was struck by her swollen face, with blue bruises on part of the nose and under the eye. That was the result of the blow of my elbow, when she had tried to hold me back. Of beauty there was none, but it seemed to me that there was something vile in her. I stopped in the doorway.

" 'Go, go to her,' said her sister.

" 'She probably wants to repent,' I thought. 'Should I forgive her? Yes, she's dying, and I can forgive her,' I thought, trying to be magnanimous. I went up close. With difficulty she raised her eyes to me, one of which was bruised, and with difficulty, faltering, said:

" 'So you've done it, you've killed . . .' And her face, through physical suffering and even the proximity of death, expressed the same old, familiar, cold, animal hatred. 'But the children . . . I won't . . . let you have . . . She (her sister) will take . . .'

"Of what was the main thing for me, of her guilt, her betrayal, she seemed to consider it not worth making mention.

" 'Yes, admire what you've done,' she said, glancing at the door, and she sobbed. In the doorway stood her sister with the children. 'Yes, this is what you've done.'

"I looked at the children, at her bruised, swollen face, and for the first time I forgot myself, my rights, my pride, for the first time I saw in her a human being. And all that had offended me, all my jealousy, seemed so insignificant to me, and so significant what I had done, that I wanted to press my face to her hand and say, 'Forgive me!'—but I didn't dare.

"She fell silent, closing her eyes, obviously unable to speak further. Then her disfigured face quivered and winced. She pushed me away weakly.

" 'Why did all this happen? Why?'

" 'Forgive me,' I said.

" 'Forgive? That's all nonsense! . . . Only let me not die! . . .' she cried, raised herself slightly, and turned her feverishly glittering eyes to me. "Yes, you've done it! . . . I hate you! . . . Aie! Ah!' she cried, obviously in delirium, frightened at something. 'Well, kill, kill, I'm not afraid . . . Only all of them, all of them, and him, too. He's gone, he's gone!'

"Her delirium continued from then on. She didn't recognize anyone. That same day, towards noon, she died. Before that, at eight o'clock, I was taken to the police station and from there to prison. And there, sitting for eleven months awaiting trial, I thought over myself and my past and understood it. I began to understand on the third day. On the third day I was taken there . . ."

He wanted to say something, but, unable to hold back his sobbing any longer, he stopped. Then, gathering his forces, he went on:

"I began to understand only when I saw her in the coffin . . ." He sobbed, but at once hastened on: "Only when I saw her dead face did I understand all that I'd done. I understood that I, I had killed her, that it was from my doing that she who was once alive, moving, warm, and had now become motionless, waxen, cold, and that never, nowhere, nothing could repair that. No one who hasn't lived through that can understand it . . . Ohh! ohh! ohh!" he cried several times and quieted down.

We sat for a long time in silence. He kept sobbing and shaking silently in front of me.

"Well, forgive me . . ."

He turned away from me and lay down on the seat, covering himself with a plaid. At the station where I was to get out—this was at eight o'clock in the morning—I went over to him to say goodbye. He was either asleep or pretending, but he didn't stir. I touched him with my hand. He uncovered himself, and it was clear that he had not been asleep.

"Goodbye," I said, giving him my hand.

He gave me his and smiled faintly, but so pitifully that I wanted to weep.

"Yes, forgive me," he repeated the same word with which he had ended his whole story.

1889

The Devil

> *But I say to you that every one who looks at a woman lustfully has already committed adultery with her in his heart.*
>
> *If your right eye causes you to sin, pluck it out and throw it away; it is better that you lose one of your members than that your whole body be thrown into hell. And if your right hand causes you to sin, cut it off and throw it away; it is better that you lose one of your members than that your whole body go into hell.*
>
> MATTHEW 5:28–30 (RSV)

I

A BRILLIANT CAREER AWAITED Evgeny Irtenev. He had everything it took. An excellent education at home, brilliantly completed studies in the law school of Petersburg University, connections with the highest society through his recently deceased father, and even a start at service in a ministry under the patronage of the minister. There was also a fortune, even a large fortune, but a dubious one. His father had lived abroad and in Petersburg, giving six thousand to each of his sons—Evgeny and the elder one, Andrei, who served in the horse guards—and he and the mother had run through quite a lot. He used to come to the estate only for two months in the summer, but did not concern himself with running it, leaving all that to the glutted manager, who also did not concern himself with the estate, but in whom he had full confidence.

After the father's death, when the brothers started dividing things up, there turned out to be so many debts that their attorney even advised them to renounce the inheritance, keeping for themselves the grandmother's estate, which was valued at a hundred thousand. But their neighbour on the estate, a landowner who had had dealings with the old Irtenev, that is, who had a promissory note from him and came to Petersburg on that account, said that, in spite of the debts, they could still straighten out their affairs and hold on to the large fortune. All that was needed was to sell the woodlot and some sections of waste land, and hold on to the main goldmine—the Semyonovskoe estate with its fifteen hundred acres of black earth, sugar factory, and seventy acres of water meadows—if one devoted oneself to the business, settled in the country, and managed things intelligently and economically.

And so Evgeny, having gone to the estates in spring (his father died during Lent) and examined everything, decided to go into retirement, settle in the country with his mother, and occupy himself with management, so as to hold on to the main estate. With his brother, with whom he was not on very friendly terms, he made the following bargain: he undertook to pay him four thousand a year or a lump sum of eighty thousand, for which his brother would renounce his share of the inheritance.

That was what he did, and, settling in the big house with his mother, he ardently, but at the same time prudently, took up the management of his estates.

It is commonly thought that the most usual conservatives are the old, and the innovators are young people. That is not quite correct. The most usual conservatives are young people. Young people who want to live, but who do not think and have no time to think about how one should live, and who therefore choose as a model for themselves the life that was.

So it was with Evgeny. Having settled now in the country, his dream and ideal was to resurrect the form of life that was, not under his father—his father had been a bad manager—but under his grandfather. And now, in the house, and in the garden, and in farming, with the changes proper to the time, of course, he tried to resurrect the general spirit of his grandfather's life—all on the grandest footing, with prosperity for all around, and order, and good organization, and yet it took a lot to organize that life: it was necessary to satisfy the demands of creditors and banks, and for that he had to sell land and postpone payments; it was necessary to obtain money in order to continue, with hired workers or his own, carrying on the immense farm work in Semyonovskoe, with its fifteen hundred acres of ploughland and its sugar factory; it was necessary to run the house and garden so that they did not look neglected and gone to seed.

There was much work, but Evgeny also had much strength—physical and spiritual. He was twenty-six, of medium height, strongly built, with muscles developed by gymnastics, a sanguine man with a bright flush all over his cheeks, with bright teeth and lips, and with not thick but soft and curly hair. His only physical flaw was nearsightedness, which he had developed in himself by wearing eyeglasses, and now he could no longer go without a pince-nez, which was already making little creases above the curve of his nose. That is how he was physically, while his spiritual image was such that, the more one knew him, the more one loved him. His mother had always loved him most of all, and now, after her husband's death, she concentrated on him not only all her affection, but all her life. But it was not only his mother who loved him like that. His comrades at high school and the university had always felt not only love but also a particular respect for him. He always had the same effect on all strangers. It was impossible not to believe what he said, impossible to suspect any deceit or falseness given such an open, honest face and, above all, eyes.

In general his whole personality helped him greatly in his affairs. The creditor who would have refused someone else, trusted him. The clerk, the headman, the muzhik who would have done a nasty turn and deceived someone else, forgot all deceit under the pleasant impression of having to do with a kind, simple, and, above all, open man.

It was the end of May. Evgeny had somehow worked out an affair in town to do with freeing the waste land from mortgage so that he could sell it to a merchant, and had borrowed money from that same merchant to renew his stock—that is, horses, oxen, carts. And, above all, to begin the necessary construction of a farmstead. Things got going. Timber was transported, carpenters were already at work, and manure was brought in eighty carts, but so far it all hung by a thread.

II

IN THE MIDST of these cares a circumstance occurred which, though not important, tormented Evgeny a bit at the time. He had spent his youth as all young, healthy, unmarried men do, that is, he had had relations with various sorts of women. He was not a libertine, but neither was he, as he used to say to himself, a monk. He had given himself to it only insofar as it was necessary for his physical health and mental freedom, as he used to say. It had started when he was sixteen. And so far everything had gone well. Well in the sense that he had not given himself up to depravity, had not once been carried away, and had not once been sick. At first he had had a seamstress in Petersburg, but then she went bad, and he made other arrangements. And this side was so well provided for that it did not disturb him.

But here it was the second month that he had been living in the country, and he decidedly did not know what to do. His involuntary abstinence began to have a bad effect on him. Should he go to town for that? And where? How? This alone troubled Evgeny Ivanovich, and as he was convinced that it was necessary and that he needed it, it actually became a need for him, and he felt that he was not free and against his will he followed every young woman with his eyes.

He considered it wrong for him to take up with a woman or girl from his own village. He knew by hearsay that in this respect his father and grandfather had stood completely apart from other landowners of that time and had never started any intrigues with serf women at home, and he decided not to do that; but later, feeling himself more and more bound, and imagining with horror what might happen to him in a small town, and realizing that they were not serfs now, he decided it could be done even here. Only do it so that nobody knows, and not out of depravity, but only for the sake of health, as he said to himself. And once he had decided it, he found it still more disturbing; talking with the headman, with muzhiks, with the cabinetmaker, he involuntarily brought the conversation around to women, and if the conversation got on to women, he kept it there. At women themselves he looked more and more intently.

III

BUT TO RESOLVE the matter in himself was one thing, to carry it out was another. To approach a woman himself was impossible. Which one? Where? It had to be through someone, but to whom should he turn?

Once he happened to stop for a drink of water in a forest watch-house. The forester was his father's former huntsman. Evgeny Ivanovich fell to talking with him, and the forester began telling oldtime stories about carousing during the hunt. And it occurred to Evgeny Ivanovich that it would be good to arrange it here, in the watch-house or in the forest. Only he did not know how, or whether old Danila would undertake it. "Maybe he'll be horrified by such a suggestion, and I'll be put to shame, or maybe he'll quite simply agree." So he was thinking as he listened to Danila's stories. Danila was telling how they had stopped at the deacon's wife's place in an outlying field, and he had brought Pryanichnikov a peasant woman.

"I can," thought Evgeny.

"Your father, may he rest in peace, wasn't given to such foolishness."

"I can't," thought Evgeny, but to explore further, he said:

"Then why did you do such bad things?"

"What's so bad about it? She's glad, and my Fyodor Zakharych is pleased as can be. It's a rouble for me. Otherwise what's he going to do? He's got life in his bones, too. Bet he drinks wine."

"Yes, I can say it," thought Evgeny, and he set out at once.

"You know," he felt himself flush crimson, "you know, Danila, it's tormenting for me." Danila smiled. "I'm not a monk after all—I'm used to it."

He felt that everything he had said was stupid, but he was glad, because Danila approved of it.

"Why, you should have said so long ago. It can be done," he said. "Only tell me which sort."

"Oh, really, it's all the same to me. Well, of course, so long as she's healthy and not ugly."

"Understood!" Danila clinched. He fell to thinking. "Ah, there's a nice little piece," he began. Evgeny blushed again. "A nice little piece. You see, sir, they married her off in the autumn," Danila began to whisper, "and he can't do anything. To a fancier that's worth something."

Evgeny even winced from embarrassment.

"No, no," he began. "That's not at all what I want. On the contrary" (what could be the contrary?), "on the contrary, I want only that she be healthy and not much trouble—a soldier's wife or the like."

"I see. That means I put Stepanida at your disposal. Her husband's away in town, she's the same as a soldier's wife. And she's a nice, clean woman. You'll be pleased. I even told her the other day—go on, but she . . ."

"Well, so when?"

"Oh, tomorrow even. I'll be going for tobacco and I'll stop by, and at dinnertime you come here or to the bathhouse behind the kitchen garden. There's nobody around. Anyway, folk all sleep at dinnertime."

"Well, all right."

Terrible excitement seized Evgeny as he was going home. "What will it be like? What is a peasant woman? Something suddenly ugly, terrible. No, they're beautiful," he said to himself, remembering those he liked to look at. "But what will I say, what will I do?"

For the whole day he was not himself. At noon the next day he went to the watch-house. Danila was standing in the doorway and silently made a significant nod towards the woods. The blood rushed to Evgeny's heart, he felt it, and he went to the kitchen garden. No one was there. He went to the bathhouse. No one. He looked in, came out, and suddenly heard the crack of a snapping twig. He turned to look—she was standing in a thicket across a little gully. He rushed across the gully. There were nettles there which he did not notice. He got stung and, the pince-nez having fallen off his nose, ran up the slope on the other side. In a white embroidered apron, a reddish-brown woollen skirt, and a bright-red kerchief, barefoot, fresh, firm, beautiful, she stood there and smiled timidly.

"There's a little path around here, you could've gone that way," she said. "I came long ago. A good while."

He went up to her, looked around, and touched her.

A quarter of an hour later they parted, he found his pince-nez and went to Danila's, and in answer to his question, "Are you pleased, master?" gave him a rouble and went home.

He was pleased. There had been some shame only at the beginning. But then it went away. And it was all good. Above all, it was good in that he now felt light, calm, cheerful. As for her, he had not even made her out very well. He remembered that she was clean, fresh, not bad-looking, and simple, without pulling faces. "What's her family?" he said to himself. "Did he say Pechnikov? Which Pechnikov is it? There are two households. She must be old Mikhaila's daughter-in-law. Yes, that must be it. His son lives in Moscow. Someday I'll ask Danila."

After that this formerly important unpleasantness of country life—involuntary abstinence—was removed. Evgeny's freedom of thought was no longer disturbed, and he could freely occupy himself with his affairs.

And the affairs Evgeny had taken upon himself were far from easy: sometimes it seemed to him that he could not hold out and would end by putting the estate up for sale anyway, all his labours would be wasted, and, above all, it would show that he had not held out, had been unable to finish what he had taken upon himself. That troubled him most of all. He barely had time to plug one hole, before a new, unexpected one opened up.

During all this time more and more of his father's debts, previously unknown, came to light. It was clear that in his later years his father had borrowed wherever he could. At the time of the division in May, Evgeny had thought he finally knew everything. But suddenly, in the middle of summer, he received a letter from which it followed that there was still a debt of twelve thousand to the widow Esipov. There was no promissory note, there was simply a receipt, which, according to his attorney, he could contest. But it would never have entered Evgeny's head to refuse to pay a real debt of his father's merely because the document could be contested. He only had to know for certain whether it was a real debt.

"Mama, who is this Kaleriya Vladimirovna Esipov?" he asked his mother when they met, as usual, at dinner.

"Esipov? She's your grandfather's ward. Why?"

Evgeny told his mother about the letter.

"I'm surprised she's not ashamed. Your father gave her so much money."

"But do we owe her?"

"Well, how shall I put it? There is no debt. Papa in his infinite kindness . . ."

"Yes, but papa considered it a debt."

"I can't tell you. I don't know. I know how hard it is for you."

Evgeny saw that Marya Pavlovna did not know what to say herself and was as if drawing him out.

"From that I can see it must be paid," her son said. "I'll go to her tomorrow and discuss the possibility of postponing it."

"Ah, I'm so sorry for you. But, you know, it's better that way. Tell her she'll have to wait," said Marya Pavlovna, obviously reassured and proud of her son's decision.

Evgeny's position was especially difficult, also, because his mother, who lived with him, had no understanding of his position. All her life she had been used to living so grandly that she was unable even to imagine the position her son was in, which was such that from one day to the next his affairs could turn out so that they would have nothing left, and her son would have to sell everything and live and support his mother by work alone, which in his position might bring him some two thousand roubles at most. She did not understand that they could be saved from that position only by cutting their expenses for everything, and therefore she could not understand why Evgeny was so pinched in trifles, in paying for gardeners, coachmen, servants, and even food. Besides that, as with most widows, her feeling of reverence for the memory of the deceased, so unlike the feelings she had had for him while he was alive, did not admit of the thought that anything the deceased had done or started could be bad or changed.

Evgeny maintained with great effort both the garden and the greenhouse with two gardeners and the stable with two coachmen. And Marya Pavlovna naïvely thought that by not complaining about the food prepared by the old cook, or that the paths in the park were not all being swept, or that instead of footmen there was just one boy, she was doing everything possible for a mother who was sacrificing herself for her son. And so in this new debt, in which Evgeny saw almost a fatal blow to all his undertakings, Marya Pavlovna saw only an occasion manifesting Evgeny's nobility. Marya Pavlovna also did not worry much about Evgeny's material situation, because she was sure he would find a brilliant match that would straighten everything out. He could indeed make a most brilliant match. She knew a dozen families who would be happy to give him their daughters in marriage. And she wished to arrange it as soon as possible.

IV

EVGENY WAS DREAMING of marriage himself, only not in the same way as his mother: the thought of making marriage a means of straightening out his affairs was repugnant to him. He wanted an honest marriage, out of love. He kept an eye on the girls he met and knew, tried to picture himself with them, but his fate would not get decided. Meanwhile his relations with Stepanida went on, which he had not expected at all, and even acquired the character of something established. Evgeny was so far from being dissolute, it was so hard for him to do this secret and—as he felt—wrong thing, that he made no sort of arrangements, and even after the first meeting hoped never to see Stepanida again; but it turned out that some time later the restlessness came over him again, which he attributed to the same cause. And this time the restlessness was no longer impersonal: he imagined precisely those dark, shining eyes, the same chesty voice saying "a good while," the same smell of something fresh and strong, and the same high breast rising under the apron, and all that in the same grove of hazels and maples bathed in bright sunlight. Embarrassed as he was, he again turned to Danila. And again a meeting was arranged in the woods at noon. This time Evgeny looked her over more, and everything in her seemed attractive to him. He tried to talk with her, asked her about her husband. In fact, it was Mikhaila's son, and he lived as a coachman in Moscow.

"Well, then, how is it . . ." Evgeny wanted to ask how it was that she betrayed him.

"How is what?" she asked. She was obviously intelligent and quick-witted.

"How is it that you come to me?"

"Go on," she said gaily. "I suppose he's running around there. So why not me?"

She was obviously affecting casualness, bravado. And Evgeny found that sweet. But all the same he did not fix a meeting with her himself. Even when she suggested that they get together without Danila, towards whom she was somehow ill-disposed, Evgeny did not agree. He hoped that this meeting was the last. He liked her. He thought that such relations were necessary for him and that there was nothing bad in it; but in the depths of his soul he had a more strict judge, who disapproved of it and hoped this would be the last time, or if he did not hope, then at least he did not want to participate in this affair and set it up for himself another time.

So the whole summer went by, in the course of which he saw her some ten times and each time through Danila. There was one time when it was impossible for her to come, because her husband was there, and Danila offered him another woman. Evgeny refused in disgust. Then her husband left, and the meetings went on as before, first through Danila, but later he simply fixed the time himself, and she came with the peasant woman Prokhorov, because it was impossible for a peasant woman to go about alone. Once, at the very time fixed for their meeting, a family came to see Marya Pavlovna with the girl she wanted Evgeny to marry, and Evgeny could not get away. As soon as he was able to leave, he made as if to go to the threshing floor and then took a roundabout path to the place of their meetings in the woods. She was not there. But in the usual place everything was broken as far as the arm could reach—bird cherry, hazels, even a young maple as thick as a stake. She had become upset and angry while she waited and, playfully, had left a reminder for him. He stood and stood, then went to Danila and asked him to invite her for the next day. She came and was the same as ever.

So the summer went by. The meetings were always set up in the woods and only once, towards fall, in the threshing barn in their back-yard. It never entered Evgeny's head that these relations had any mean-ing for him. About her he did not think at all. He gave her money and nothing more. He did not know and did not think that the whole village already knew about it and envied her, that at home they took the money from her and encouraged her, and that her notion of sin, under the influ-ence of money and sympathy at home, had been totally obliterated. It seemed to her that, since people envied her, what she was doing was good.

"I simply need it for my health," thought Evgeny. "Suppose it's wrong and, though nobody says anything, everybody knows, or a lot do. The woman she comes with knows. And if she knows, she must have told others. But what to do then? I'm behaving badly," thought Evgeny, "but what to do, it won't be for long."

The main thing that troubled Evgeny was the husband. At first he imagined for some reason that her husband must be a poor sort, and it was as if that partly justified him. But he saw the husband and was struck. He was a fine fellow and a dashing one, certainly no worse and probably better than himself. At the next meeting he told her that he had seen her husband and it was a pleasure to look at such a fine fellow.

"There's not another like him in the village," she said with pride.

That surprised Evgeny. Since then the thought of the husband had tormented him still more. He happened once to be at Danila's, and Danila fell to talking and said to him straight out:

"The other day Mikhaila asked me whether it was true that the master was living with his son's wife. I said I didn't know. Then too, I said, better with the master than with some muzhik."

"Well, and he?"

"Never mind, he said: just wait till I find out, I'll give it to her."

"Well, if the husband came back, I'd drop it," thought Evgeny. But the husband lived in town, and for the time being the relations continued. "When need be, I'll break it off, and there'll be nothing left," he thought.

And that seemed unquestionable to him, because in the course of the summer he was intensely occupied with many other things: the setting up of the new farmstead, and the harvest, and construction work, and, above all, paying off his debt and selling the waste land. These were all subjects which consumed him entirely, which he thought about going to bed and getting up in the morning. This was all real life. The relations— he did not even call it a bond—with Stepanida were something quite inconspicuous. True, when the desire to see her came over him, it was so strong that he could think of nothing else, but that did not last long; a meeting would be arranged, and he would forget her again for weeks, sometimes even for a month.

In the autumn, Evgeny frequently went to town, and there became close to the Annensky family. The Annenskys had a daughter just out of boarding school. And here, to Marya Pavlovna's great regret, it happened that Evgeny sold himself cheap, as she used to say, fell in love with Liza Annensky, and proposed.

From then on the relations with Stepanida ceased.

V

WHY EVGENY CHOSE Liza Annensky is impossible to explain, as it is always impossible to explain why a man chooses this rather than that woman. There were a multitude of reasons, both positive and negative. There was the reason that she was not a very rich bride, such as his mother had found for him, and that she was naïve and pathetic in her relations with her mother, and that she was not a beauty who attracted attention, and yet not bad-looking. But the main thing was that the closeness with her began at the moment when Evgeny was ripe for marriage. He fell in love because he knew he would marry.

At first Evgeny merely liked Liza Annensky, but when he decided that she would be his wife, he felt much stronger feelings for her, he felt that he was in love.

Liza was tall, slender, long. Everything about her was long: her face, her nose, not thrust out but down the face, her fingers, her feet. Her complexion was very delicate, white, yellowish with a delicate flush, her hair was long, light brown, soft and wavy, and she had beautiful, clear, trusting eyes. Those eyes especially struck Evgeny. And when he thought of Liza, he always saw before him those clear, meek, trusting eyes.

So she was physically; spiritually he knew nothing about her, but only saw those eyes. And those eyes seemed to tell him everything he needed to know. The meaning of those eyes was the following.

While still at boarding school, from the age of fifteen, Liza had constantly fallen in love with all attractive men, and was animated and happy only when she was in love. Having left boarding school, she fell in love in the same way with all the young men she met, and naturally fell in love with Evgeny as soon as she made his acquaintance. It was this lovingness that gave her eyes that special expression which so captivated Evgeny.

That winter she had already been in love with two young men at the same time, and she blushed and became agitated not only when they entered the room, but when their names were spoken. But later, when her mother hinted that Irtenev seemed to have serious intentions, her love for Irtenev intensified so much that she became almost indifferent to the two earlier ones, and when Irtenev began to call on them, or at a ball or a gathering he danced with her more than with others, and obviously wished to know only whether she loved him, then her love for Irtenev became something morbid, she saw him in her sleep and awake in a dark room, and all the others disappeared for her. And when he proposed and they were given the parental blessing, when they kissed and became engaged, then she had no other thoughts than him, no other desires than to be with him, to love him and be loved by him. She was proud of him, she was moved by him and by herself and their love, she swooned and melted all over for love of him. The more he came to know her, the more he loved her. He had never expected to meet with such love, and that love intensified his feeling still more.

VI

Before spring he came to Semyonovskoe to look things over and give orders about the farming, and above all about the house, which was being decorated for the newlyweds.

Marya Pavlovna was displeased with her son's choice, but only because the match was not as brilliant as it might have been, and because she did not like Varvara Alexeevna, the future mother-in-law. Whether she was good or wicked she did not know or decide, but that she was not a respectable woman, not *comme il faut*, not a lady, as Marya Pavlovna said to herself—that she had seen from their first acquaintance, and it had distressed her. Distressed her because she valued this respectability out of habit, knew that Evgeny was very sensitive to it, and foresaw much distress for him on account of it. But she liked the girl. She liked her mainly because Evgeny liked her. She had to love her. And Marya Pavlovna was prepared for that, and quite sincerely.

Evgeny found his mother joyful, content. She was arranging every-thing in the house and getting ready to leave herself as soon as he brought his young wife. Evgeny tried to talk her into staying. And the question remained unresolved. In the evening, after tea, Marya Pavlovna was playing patience as usual. Evgeny sat helping her. This was the time of the most intimate talks. Having finished one game and not yet started a new one, Marya Pavlovna glanced at Evgeny and, somewhat hesitantly, began thus:

"I wanted to tell you, Zhenya. Of course, I don't know, but generally I wanted to advise you that before marrying you absolutely must put an end to all your bachelor affairs, so that nothing can trouble you or, God forbid, your wife. Do you understand me?"

And indeed Evgeny understood at once that Marya Pavlovna was alluding to his relations with Stepanida, which had ceased since the autumn, and, as solitary women always do, ascribed to them a much greater significance than they had. Evgeny blushed, not so much from shame as from vexation that the kindly Marya Pavlovna was meddling— out of love, true—but meddling all the same where she should not and in what she did not and could not understand. He said that he had nothing that needed to be concealed, and that he had always behaved himself in precisely such a way that nothing could interfere with his marriage.

"Well, that's splendid, my dear. Don't be offended with me, Zhenya," Marya Pavlovna said abashedly.

But Evgeny saw that she had not finished and had not said what she wanted to. And so it turned out. A little later she began telling him how, in his absence, she had been asked to stand godmother by . . . the Pchelnikovs.[1]

Now Evgeny blushed, not from vexation and not even from shame, but from some strange sense of awareness of the importance of what he was about to be told, an awareness that was involuntary, in total disagreement with his reason. And it turned out as he expected. Marya Pavlovna, as if she had no other purpose than conversation, said that only boys had been born that year, a sign of war.[2] At the Vasins and the Pchelnikovs, the young women's firstborn were both boys. Marya Pavlovna wanted to tell it inconspicuously, but she became embarrassed herself when she saw the colour on her son's face and him nervously taking off, clicking, and putting back on his pince-nez and quickly lighting a cigarette. She fell silent. He was also silent and could not think up any way to break the silence. So they both understood that they had understood each other.

"Yes, above all, in the country there must be fairness, so that there are no favourites, as at your uncle's."

"Mama," Evgeny said suddenly, "I know what you're getting at. You needn't worry. My future family life is so sacred a thing for me that I wouldn't violate it under any circumstances. And what there was in my bachelor life is all quite finished. And I've never entered any sort of bonds, and nobody has any rights over me."

"Well, I'm glad," said his mother. "I know your noble thoughts."

Evgeny took these words of his mother's as his due and said nothing.

The next morning he went to town thinking about his bride, about anything in the world except Stepanida. But, as if on purpose to remind him, as he drove near the church, he began to meet people walking or driving from there. He met old Matvei and Semyon, some children, some young girls, and here are two women, one older and one dressed up, wearing a bright-red kerchief, and somewhat familiar. The woman is walking lightly, briskly, a baby on her arm. He came even with them, the older woman stopped and made an old-fashioned bow, but the young one with the baby only inclined her head, and familiar, smiling, merry eyes flashed from under the kerchief.

"Yes, that's her, but it's all over, and there's no point in looking at her. And the baby may be mine," it occurred to him. "No, what non-sense! The husband was here, she went to see him." He did not even start calculating. He had made the decision that it was necessary for his health, he had paid money, and nothing more; there neither was, nor had been, nor could be, nor should be any sort of bond between them. He was not suppressing the voice of his conscience, no, his conscience simply said nothing to him. And he did not recall her once after the talk with his mother and that meeting. And not once did he meet her after that.

On the Sunday after Easter Evgeny was married in town and immedi-ately left for the country with his young wife. The house had been set up as is usual for a young couple. Marya Pavlovna wanted to leave, but Evgeny, and above all Liza, persuaded her to stay. She only moved to the wing.

And so a new life began for Evgeny.

VII

THE FIRST YEAR of family life was a difficult year for Evgeny. It was dif-ficult in that affairs he kept putting off somehow during the time of his engagement, now, after his marriage, all suddenly fell on him.

To extricate himself from debt proved impossible. The summer house was sold, the most crying debts were covered, but more debts remained, and there was no money. The estate brought good income, but he had to send some to his brother and pay for the wedding, so that there was no money, and the factory could not go on and had to be stopped. The only way to disentangle himself was to use his wife's money. Liza, having understood her husband's position, demanded it herself. Evgeny agreed, but only on condition that half of the deed for the estate be made out in his wife's name. And so he did. Not for his wife, of course, who was offended by it, but for his mother-in-law.

These affairs, with various changes, some successful, some unsuccessful, were one thing that poisoned Evgeny's life in that first year. Another was his wife's poor health. In the autumn of that first year, seven months after their marriage, a misfortune befell Liza. She went in a charabanc to meet her husband, who was returning from town, the quiet horse acted up, Liza became frightened and jumped out. The jump was rather fortunate—she could have been caught by a wheel—but she was already pregnant, and that same night she began to feel pain and had a miscarriage, and for a long time she could not recover. The loss of the hoped-for child, the wife's illness, the disruption of life caused by it, and, above all, the presence of his mother-in-law, who came as soon as Liza fell ill—all this made that year still more difficult for Evgeny.

But, despite these difficult circumstances, towards the end of the first year Evgeny felt very well. First, his heartfelt intention to restore his declining fortune, to renew his grandfather's life in new forms, was, though slowly and with effort, being realized. Now there could be no talk of selling the entire estate for debt. The main estate, though transferred to his wife's name, was saved, and, if only the beet crop turned out well and the price was good, by the next year the situation of want and strain could be replaced by complete well-being. That was one thing.

The other was that, however much he had expected from his wife, he had never expected to find in her what he did find: it was not what he had expected, it was something much better. The moving scenes, the loving raptures, though he tried to set them up, did not come off, or came off very feebly; but something quite different did come off, so that life became not only more cheerful and pleasant, but also easier. He did not know why it happened, but it was so.

It happened because she decided right after their betrothal that of all the people in the world there was only one Evgeny Irtenev, who was higher, cleverer, purer, nobler than all, and therefore it was the duty of all people to serve this Irtenev and do his pleasure. But since it was impossible to make them all do it, she had to do it herself as far as she could. And so she did, and therefore all her inner forces were always directed at finding out, at guessing what he liked, and then doing that very thing, whatever it was and however difficult it might be.

And there was that in her which constitutes the chief delight of relations with a loving woman, there was in her, owing to her love for her husband, a second sight into his soul. She sensed—often, it seemed to him, better than he himself—every state of his soul, every shade of his feelings, and acted correspondingly, and so she never offended his feelings, but always soothed the painful feelings and strengthened the joyful. But not only his feelings, she also understood his thoughts. The subjects of agriculture, the factory, the appraisement of people, foreign as they were to her, she understood at once, and could be not only his interlocutor, but often, as he himself told her, a useful, irreplaceable adviser. She looked at things, at people, at everything in the world only with his eyes. She loved her mother, but, seeing that Evgeny was displeased with his mother-in-law's interference in their life, she at once took her husband's side, and with such resoluteness that he had to restrain her.

On top of all that, there was in her no end of taste, tact, and, above all, tranquillity. Everything she did, she did inconspicuously, conspicuous were only the results of what she did, that is, cleanliness, order, and elegance in all things. Liza understood at once what her husband's ideal of life was and tried to achieve and succeeded in achieving in the arrangement and order of their house the very things he wished. They had no children, but there was hope for that as well. In winter they went to an accoucheur in Petersburg, and he assured them that she was quite healthy and could have children.

And this wish was realized. By the end of the year she was pregnant again.

One thing that did not so much poison as threaten their happiness was her jealousy—a jealousy which she restrained and did not show, but which often made her suffer. Not only could Evgeny not love anyone, because there were no women in the world worthy of him (whether she was worthy of him or not, she never asked herself), but therefore neither could any woman dare to love him.

VIII

THEY LIVED like this: he got up early, as always, and went to the farm, to the factory, where work was going on, or sometimes to the fields. By ten he came home for coffee. Coffee was taken on the terrace by Marya Pavlovna, an uncle who lived with them, and Liza. After conversation, often very animated, over coffee, they dispersed until dinner. They dined at two. After that they went for a walk or a ride. In the evening, when he came from the office, they had late tea, and he sometimes read aloud, she worked, or they played music or talked when there were guests. When he went away on business, he wrote and received letters from her every day. Occasionally she accompanied him, and that was especially merry. On his and her name days, guests assembled, and it pleased him to see how she was able to organize everything so that they all felt good. He saw, and also heard, how everyone admired her, the sweet young hostess, and he loved her still more for that. Everything went splendidly. She bore her pregnancy easily, and the two of them, still timorously, began to plan how they would bring up their child. The way of upbringing, the methods, were all decided by Evgeny, and she only wished obediently to do his will. Evgeny had read himself up on medical books and intended to bring up the child by all the rules of science. She naturally agreed to everything and, in preparation, sewed sleeping sacks, both warm and light, and prepared the cradle. So came the second year of their marriage and the second spring.

IX

IT WAS the eve of Pentecost.³ Liza was in her fifth month and, though careful, she was cheerful and active. Both mothers, hers and his, were living in the house on the pretext of looking after and protecting her, and only bothered her with their bickering. Evgeny was taken up especially ardently with farming, a new method of processing beets on a large scale.

On the eve of Pentecost, Liza decided that the house needed a thorough cleaning, which had not been done since Holy Week,⁴ and to help the servants she summoned two peasant women as day labourers to wash the floors and windows, beat the furniture and rugs, and put on slipcovers. These women came early in the morning, heated kettles of water, and set to work. One of the women was Stepanida, who had only just weaned her boy, and through the clerk, whom she now ran around with, had offered herself as a floor scrubber. She wanted to have a good look at the new mistress. Stepanida lived alone as before, without her husband, and carried on, as she had before with old Danila, who had caught her taking firewood, then with the master, now with a young fellow—the office clerk. Of the master she did not think at all. "He's got a wife now," she thought. "But I'd be pleased to have a look at the mistress and how she runs things. They say it's done up nicely."

Evgeny had not seen her since he met her with the baby. She did not go to do day labour, because she had a baby, and he rarely passed through the village. That morning, on the eve of Pentecost, Evgeny got up early, before five o'clock, and left for the fallow field, where phosphorites were to be spread, and he left the house before the women, who were busy with the kettles at the stove, came in.

Cheerful, content, and hungry, Evgeny came back for breakfast. He got off his horse by the gate and, handing it over to a passing gardener, walked to the house, lashing the tall grass with his whip and repeating, as often happened, a just-uttered phrase. The phrase he kept repeating was: "Phosphorites will justify"—what, to whom?—he did not know and did not think.

On the lawn they were beating a rug. The furniture had been brought out.

"Good heavens, what a cleaning Liza's begun! Phosphorites will justify. See what a housewife. A dear little housewife! Yes, a dear little housewife," he said to himself, vividly picturing her in her white housecoat, her face beaming with joy, as it almost always did when he looked at her. "Yes, I must change my boots, otherwise phosphorites will justify, that is, smell of dung, and my dear little housewife is in a certain condition. Why in a certain condition? Yes, a new little Irtenev is growing inside her," he thought. "Yes, phosphorites will justify." And, smiling at his thoughts, he put his hand to the door of his room.

But before he had time to push on the door, it opened of itself, and he ran smack into a peasant woman coming out with a bucket, barefoot, her skirt tucked up, her sleeves rolled high. He stepped aside to let her pass, she also stepped aside, straightening with a wet upper arm the kerchief that had slipped to one side.

"Go on, go on, I'll leave if you . . ." Evgeny began and, recognizing her, suddenly stopped.

She, smiling with her eyes, glanced at him gaily. And, straightening her skirt, she went out the door.

"What's this nonsense? . . . What is it? . . . It can't be," Evgeny said, scowling and waving his hand as at a fly, displeased that he had noticed her. He was displeased that he had noticed her, and yet he could not tear his eyes from her body, swayed by the strong, agile gait of her bare feet, from her arms, her shoulders, the beautiful folds of her blouse, and the red skirt tucked up high over her white calves.

"What am I staring at?" he said to himself, lowering his eyes so as not to see her. "Yes, anyhow I've got to go in and take another pair of boots." And he turned back to his room, but, before he went five steps, himself not knowing why and on whose order, he glanced around again, so as to see her one more time. She was turning the corner and at that moment also glanced back at him.

"Ah, what am I doing?" he cried in his soul. "She might think something. It's even certain she already does."

He went into his wet room. Another woman, old, skinny, was there and still scrubbing. Evgeny tiptoed over the dirty puddles to the wall where his boots stood and was about to leave when that woman also left.

"She's gone and the other one, Stepanida, will come—alone," someone suddenly started reasoning within him.

"My God! What am I thinking, what am I doing!" He seized the boots and ran with them to the front hall, put them on there, brushed himself off, and went out to the terrace, where the two mothers were already sitting over coffee. Liza was obviously waiting for him and came to the terrace through the other door at the same time he did.

"My God, if she, thinking me so honest, pure, innocent, if she knew!" he thought.

Liza, as always, met him with a beaming face. But that day she seemed to him especially pale, yellow, long, and weak.

X

OVER COFFEE, as often happened, that particular sort of ladies' conversation was going on, in which there was no logical connection, but which was obviously connected in some way, since it went on without interruption.

The two ladies bickered, and Liza skilfully manoeuvred between them.

"I'm so vexed that they didn't manage to have your room scrubbed before your return," she said to her husband. "But I did so want to tidy things up."

"Well, how are you, did you sleep after I left?"

"Yes, I did, I'm fine."

"How can a woman in her condition feel fine in this unbearable heat, when her windows are all on the sunny side," said Varvara Alexeevna, her mother. "And without blinds or awnings. I've always had awnings."

"Why, it's shady here by ten o'clock," said Marya Pavlovna.

"And you get fever from that. From the dampness," said Varvara Alexeevna, without noticing that she was saying the exact opposite of what she had just said. "My doctor always said it's never possible to determine the illness without knowing the character of the sick woman. And he knows, because he's a leading doctor and we pay him a hundred roubles. My late husband did not believe in doctors, but to me he never grudged anything."

"How can a man grudge anything to a woman, when her life and the baby's may depend on it . . ."

"Yes, when the means are there, then the wife need not depend on her husband. A good wife is obedient to her husband," said Varvara Alexeevna, "only Liza is still too weak after her illness."

"Not at all, mama, I feel perfectly well. Why didn't they serve you boiled cream?"

"There's no need. I can do with fresh."

"I asked Varvara Alexeevna. She declined," said Marya Pavlovna, as if to vindicate herself.

"No, I don't want any today." And, as if to stop the unpleasant conversation and yield magnanimously, Varvara Alexeevna turned to Evgeny. "Well, did you spread your phosphorites?"

Liza ran to fetch the cream.

"But I don't want it, I don't want it."

"Liza! Liza! Slowly!" said Marya Pavlovna. "These quick movements are harmful for her."

"Nothing's harmful if there's inner peace," said Varvara Alexeevna, as if hinting at something, though she herself knew that her words could not hint at anything.

Liza came back with the cream. Evgeny was drinking his coffee and listening sullenly. He was used to such conversation, but that day he was particularly annoyed by its meaninglessness. He would have liked to think over what had happened to him, but this chatter hindered him. Having finished her coffee, Varvara Alexeevna left in an ill humour. Liza, Evgeny, and Marya Pavlovna remained alone. And the conversation was simple and pleasant. But Liza, made sensitive by love, noticed at once that something was tormenting Evgeny and asked him whether anything unpleasant had happened. He was not prepared for this question and hesitated slightly as he said there was nothing. And this answer made Liza ponder still more. That something was tormenting him, and tormenting him very much, was as obvious to her as a fly in the milk, but he would not tell her what it was.

XI

AFTER BREAKFAST they all went to their rooms. Evgeny, following the usual order, went to his study. He did not start reading, did not write letters, but sat and began to smoke one cigarette after another, thinking. He was terribly surprised and upset by this nasty feeling that had unexpectedly appeared in him, from which he had considered himself free ever since he married. Since then he had never once experienced that feeling either for her, the woman he had known, or for any other woman except his wife. In his soul he had rejoiced many times at this liberation, and here suddenly this incident, seemingly so insignificant, revealed to him that he was not free. He suffered now, not because he was again subject to that feeling, because he desired her—that he did not even want to think of—but because that feeling was alive in him and he had to guard against it. There was no doubt in his soul that he would suppress that feeling.

He had one unanswered letter and a paper that had to be composed.

He sat down at his desk and began to work. Having finished, and forgetting entirely about what had alarmed him, he left to go to the stables. And again, as ill luck would have it, whether accidentally or on purpose, the moment he stepped out to the porch, the red skirt and red kerchief came from around the corner and, arms swinging and hips swaying, walked past him. Not that she merely walked, she ran past him, as if frolicking, and caught up with her companion.

Again the bright noonday, the nettles, the back of Danila's watch-house, and in the shade of the maples her smiling face, nibbling some leaves, arose in his imagination.

"No, it can't be left like this," he said to himself and, waiting until the women disappeared from sight, went to his office. It was just dinnertime, and he hoped to find the steward still there. And so it happened. The steward had just woken up. He stood in the office, stretching, yawning, and looking at a herdsman, who was telling him something.

"Vassily Nikolaevich!"

"At your service."

"I'd like a word with you."

"At your service."

"Finish with him first."

"So you won't bring it in?" Vassily Nikolaevich said to the herdsman.

"It's heavy, Vassily Nikolaevich."

"What is it?"

"A cow has calved in the meadow. Well, all right, I'll order a horse hitched at once. Tell Nikolai to hitch up Lysukha, to the dray maybe."

The herdsman left.

"You see," Evgeny began, blushing and aware of it. "You see, Vassily Nikolaevich. When I was a bachelor, I had some sins here . . . Maybe you've heard . . ."

Vassily Nikolaevich smiled with his eyes and, evidently feeling sorry for his master, said:

"It's about Stepashka?"

"Well, yes. So here's the thing. Please, please, don't send her to do work in the house . . . You understand, it's very unpleasant for me . . ."

"Yes, it must be the clerk Vanya arranged it."

"So please . . . Well, what, are they going to spread the rest?" said Evgeny, to conceal his embarrassment.

"I'll go right away."

And so it ended. And Evgeny calmed down, hoping that, as he had lived through a year without seeing her, it would be the same now. "Besides, Vassily will tell the clerk Ivan, Ivan will tell her, and she will understand that I don't want it," Evgeny said to himself, and rejoiced that he had taken it upon himself and told Vassily, hard as it had been for him. "Yes, anything's better, anything's better than this doubt, this shame." He shuddered at the mere memory of this mental crime.

XII

THE MORAL EFFORT he had made to overcome his shame and tell Vassily Nikolaevich calmed Evgeny. It seemed to him that it was all over now. And Liza noticed at once that he was completely calm and even more joyful than usual. "Surely he was upset by this bickering between our mothers. In fact, it is painful, especially for him with his sensitivity and nobility, to keep hearing these unfriendly and bad-toned hints at something," thought Liza.

The next day was Pentecost. The weather was splendid, and the peasant women, going to the woods as usual to make wreaths, came to the manor house and started to sing and dance. Marya Pavlovna and Varvara Alexeevna came out to the porch in smart dresses and with parasols and went to the round dance. Evgeny's uncle, who was living with them that summer, a flabby profligate and drunkard, came out with them in his Chinese jacket.

As always, there was one multicolored, bright ring of young women and girls in the center, and around it, from different sides, like broken-away planets and satellites circling them, were young girls holding hands, the new calico of their sarafans rustling, and little boys snorting at something and running up and down after each other, and bigger boys in blue or black jackets and peaked caps and red shirts, constantly spitting sunflower-seed shells, and the household servants, and strangers looking at the round dance from a distance. The two ladies went right up to the ring, followed by Liza in a light blue dress and ribbons of the same colour in her hair, with wide sleeves from which her long, white arms with their angular elbows appeared.

Evgeny did not want to go out, but it was ridiculous to hide. He also came out to the porch with a cigarette, greeted the boys and muzhiks, and got to talking with one of them. The women were bawling a dance song with all their might and snapped their fingers and clapped along as they danced.

"The lady's calling," a lad said, coming up to Evgeny, who had not heard his wife's call. Liza called him to look at the dancing, and at one of the dancing women whom she liked most of all. It was Stepasha. She was wearing a yellow sarafan, a velveteen vest, and a silk kerchief—a broad, energetic, ruddy, merry woman. She must have danced very well. He saw nothing.

"Yes, yes," he said, taking off and putting on his pince-nez. "Yes, yes," he said. "So it's impossible for me to get rid of her," he thought.

He was not looking at her, because he feared her attractiveness, and for that very reason what he saw fleetingly seemed especially attractive to him. Besides, he saw from the glance she flashed at him that she saw him and saw that he admired her. He stood there as long as was necessary for propriety, and, seeing that Varvara Alexeevna had called her over and had said something awkward and false to her, calling her "sweetie," he turned and walked away. He walked away and went back to the house. He left so as not to see her, but, going upstairs, not knowing how and why himself, he went to the window, and all the while the peasant women were by the porch, he stood at the window looking, looking at her, revelling in her.

He ran downstairs while no one could see him and went slowly to the balcony, and on the balcony lit a cigarette, and went to the garden, as if for a stroll, in the direction in which she had gone. He had not gone two steps down the alley before a velveteen vest over a yellow sarafan and a red kerchief flashed behind the trees. She was going somewhere with another woman. "Where are they going?"

And suddenly passionate lust seared him, clutching his heart like a hand. As if by someone else's alien will, Evgeny glanced around and went after them.

"Evgeny Ivanych, Evgeny Ivanych! I'd like to talk with Your Honour," a voice spoke behind him, and Evgeny, seeing old Samokhin, who was digging a well for him, came to his senses, turned quickly, and went towards Samokhin. While talking with him, he turned sideways and saw the two women walk down, evidently to the well or on the pretext of the well, and then, after lingering there for a while, run off to the round dance.

XIII

AFTER TALKING with Samokhin, Evgeny went back home crushed, as if he had committed a crime. First of all, she understood him, she thought he wanted to see her, and she wished it, too. Second of all, this other woman—this Anna Prokhorov—obviously knew about it.

The main thing was that he felt defeated, that he had no will of his own, and there was another force that moved him; that today he had been saved by a lucky chance, but if not today, then tomorrow, or the day after tomorrow, he would perish all the same.

"Yes, perish"—he understood it no other way—to betray his young, loving wife, on the estate, with a peasant woman, for everyone to see, was that not really perdition, a terrible perdition, after which it was no longer possible to live? "No, I must, I must take measures."

"My God, my God! What am I to do? Can it be that I'll perish like that?" he said to himself. "Is it really impossible to take measures? I must do something. Do not think about her," he ordered himself. "Do not think!"—and at once he began to think, and saw her before him, and saw the shade of the maples.

He remembered having read about an old monk who, tempted by a woman he had to lay hands on in order to heal her, put his other hand in a brazier and burned his fingers. He remembered that. "Yes, I'm ready to burn my fingers rather than perish." And, looking around to see that there was no one in the room, he lit a match and put his finger in the flame. "Well, think about her now," he addressed himself ironically. He felt pain, withdrew the sooty finger, dropped the match, and laughed at himself. "What nonsense. That's not what needs to be done. I must take measures so as not to see her—go away myself or send her away! Yes, send her away! Offer her husband money so that he'll move to town or to some other village. People will find out, they'll talk about it. Well, it's still better than this danger. Yes, I must do it," he said to himself and went on looking at her without taking his eyes away. "Where is she going?" he suddenly asked himself. It seemed to him that she had seen him at the window and now, glancing at him, had joined arms with some woman and was going towards the garden, briskly swinging her arm. Not knowing why or what for himself, all because of his thoughts, he went to the office.

Vassily Nikolaevich, in a dapper frock coat, pomaded, was sitting over tea with his wife and a guest in a paisley shawl.

"Might we have a talk, Vassily Nikolaevich?"

"It's possible. If you please. We've had our tea."

"No, better that you come with me."

"Just a moment, let me take my cap. You, Tanya, cover the samovar," said Vassily Nikolaevich, coming out cheerfully.

It seemed to Evgeny that he was a bit drunk, but there was nothing to be done; maybe it was for the better, he would be more sympathetic with his situation.

"It's about the same thing again, Vassily Nikolaevich," said Evgeny, "about that woman."

"What about it? I told them not to bring her."

"No, here's generally what I thought and what I wanted to consult you about. Couldn't they be sent away, the whole family?"

"But sent away where?" Vassily said, with displeasure and mockery, as it seemed to Evgeny.

"What I thought was to give them money or even some land in Koltovskoe, only so that she's not here."

"How can you send them away? His roots are here—where will he go? And what is it to you? Is she in your way?"

"Ah, Vassily Nikolaevich, you understand, it would be terrible for my wife to find out."

"But who's going to tell her?"

"But how can I live under this fear? And generally it's painful."

"What are you worried about, really? Let bygones be bygones. Who's sinless before God or guiltless before the tsar?"

"Even so, it would be better to send them away. Couldn't you talk with the husband?"

"There's no point talking. Eh, Evgeny Ivanovich, what is it to you? It's all past and forgotten. What doesn't happen? And who's going to say anything bad about you now? Everybody sees how you are."

"But tell him even so."

"All right, I'll have a talk with him."

Though he knew beforehand that nothing would come of it, this conversation calmed Evgeny somewhat. Above all, he felt that in his anxiety he had exaggerated the danger.

Had he really gone in order to meet with her? That was impossible. He had simply taken a stroll in the garden, and she had just happened to run out there, too.

XIV

ON THAT SAME DAY of Pentecost, after dinner, while walking in the garden and going from there to the meadow, where her husband took her to show her the clover, Liza stumbled and fell as she was stepping over a small ditch. She fell softly on her side, but she gasped, and in her face her husband saw not only fear but pain. He wanted to lift her up, but she pushed his hand away.

"No, Evgeny, wait a little," she said, smiling weakly and looking at him from below somehow guiltily, as it seemed to Evgeny. "My foot just slipped."

"That's what I always say," Varvara Alexeevna began. "How can someone in your condition jump over ditches?"

"But it's nothing, mama. I'll get up right now."

She got up with her husband's help, but at the same moment she turned pale and her face showed fear.

"Yes, I'm not well," and she whispered something to her mother.

"Ah, my God, what have we done! I told you not to go," Varvara Alexeevna shouted. "Wait, I'll bring servants. She mustn't walk. She must be carried."

"You're not afraid, Liza? I'll carry you," said Evgeny, putting his left arm around her. "Hold me by the neck. There."

He bent down, took her under the legs with his right arm, and lifted her up. Never afterwards could he forget the suffering and at the same time blissful expression on her face.

"I'm heavy for you, dear!" she said, smiling. "Mama's run off, tell her!"

And she leaned towards him and kissed him. She obviously wanted her mother to see how he carried her.

Evgeny called out to Varvara Alexeevna not to hurry, because he would carry Liza. Varvara Alexeevna stopped and began shouting still more.

"You'll drop her, you're sure to drop her. You want to destroy her. You have no conscience."

"I'm carrying her splendidly."

"I won't, I can't watch how you kill my daughter." And she ran around the corner of the alley.

"Never mind, it will pass," Liza said, smiling.

"If only there are no consequences, like last time."

"No, I don't mean that. That's nothing. I mean mama. You're tired, rest a little."

But though she was heavy, Evgeny carried his burden with proud joy to the house and did not hand her over to the maid and the cook, whom Varvara Alexeevna had found and sent to meet them. He carried her to her bedroom and put her on the bed.

"Well, go now," she said, and, pulling his hand to her, she kissed it. "I'll manage with Annushka."

Marya Pavlovna also came running from the wing. Liza was undressed and put to bed. Evgeny sat in the drawing room with a book in his hand, waiting. Varvara Alexeevna walked past him with such a reproachfully gloomy look that it frightened him.

"Well, so?" he asked.

"So? Why ask? The very thing you wanted when you made your wife jump over moats."

"Varvara Alexeevna!" he cried. "This is unbearable. If you wish to torment people and poison their life"—he was about to say, "then take yourself somewhere else," but he restrained himself. "Isn't it painful for you?"

"It's too late now."

And, tossing her bonnet triumphantly, she walked through the door.

The fall had indeed been a bad one. Her foot had slipped awkwardly, and there was a danger of miscarriage. Everyone knew that it was impossible to do anything, that it was only neccesary to lie quietly, but even so they decided to send for the doctor.

"Much-esteemed Nikolai Semyonovich," Evgeny wrote to the doctor, "you have always been so kind to us that I hope you will not refuse to come and help my wife. She is in . . ." and so on. Having written the letter, he went to the stables to give orders about the horses and carriage. They had to prepare horses to bring the doctor, and others to take him back. Where the management was not on a grand footing, that could not be arranged all at once, but had to be thought out. Having seen to it all personally and sent the coachman off, he returned home past nine o'clock. His wife was lying down and said she was fine and nothing hurt; but Varvara Alexeevna sat by a lamp shielded from Liza by a musical score, knitting a big red blanket with a look which said clearly that after what had happened there could be no peace. "And whatever anybody else may do, I at least fulfil my duty."

Evgeny saw it, but, to make it look as if he had not noticed, tried to assume a cheerful, carefree look, and told how he had prepared the horses and how the mare Kavushka went very well in the left trace.

"Yes, of course, it's just the time to break in horses, when help is needed. The doctor will probably also get thrown into a ditch," said Varvara Alexeevna, looking at her knitting from under her pince-nez as she brought it close to the lamp.

"But somebody had to be sent. And I did what seemed best."

"Yes, I remember very well how your horses drove me straight under a train."

This was her long-standing fiction, and now Evgeny committed the imprudence of saying that that was not quite how it was.

"Not for nothing have I always said, and I said it so many times to the prince, that the hardest thing is to live with untruthful, insincere people. I'll put up with anything but that."

"But if there's anyone it's most painful for, then surely it's me," said Evgeny.

"That's obvious."

"What?"

"Nothing. I'm counting stitches."

Evgeny was standing by the bed just then, and Liza looked at him, and one of her moist hands, lying on top of the blanket, caught his and pressed it. "Bear with her for my sake. She won't keep us from loving each other," said her gaze.

"No more. You're right," he whispered and kissed her long, moist hand and then her dear eyes, which closed while he kissed them.

"Can it be the same thing again?" he said. "What's your feeling?"

"I'm afraid to say, for fear of being mistaken, but my feeling is that he's alive and will live," she said, looking at her stomach.

"Ah, it's frightening, frightening just to think of it."

Despite Liza's insistence that he leave, Evgeny spent the night with her, sleeping with one eye open and ready to serve her. But she spent the night well and, if they had not sent for the doctor, might even have got up.

By dinnertime the doctor arrived and, naturally, said that, though the repeated phenomenon might be cause for apprehension, strictly speaking there was no positive indication, but as there was no counter-indication either, one could on the one hand suppose, and on the other hand also suppose. And therefore she must stay in bed, and though I don't like prescribing things, take this all the same and stay in bed. Besides that, the doctor read Varvara Alexeevna a lecture on female anatomy, during which Varvara Alexeevna nodded her head significantly. Having received his fee, as usual, in the very back of his palm, the doctor left, and the patient stayed in bed for a week.

XV

EVGENY SPENT most of the time at his wife's bedside, waited on her, talked to her, read to her, and, what was hardest of all, endured without murmur Varvara Alexeevna's attacks, and was even able to make those attacks into a subject of jokes.

But he could not just sit at home. First, his wife kept sending him away, saying that he would fall ill if he stayed with her all the time, and second, the farming demanded his presence at every step. He could not sit at home, and was in the fields, the woods, the garden, at the threshing floor, and in all those places not only the thought but the living image of Stepanida pursued him, so that he only rarely forgot her. But that would have been nothing; he might have been able to overcome that feeling, but worst of all was that formerly he had lived for months without seeing her, while now he saw her and met her constantly. She obviously realized that he wanted to renew his relations with her and tried to cross his path. Neither he nor she said anything, and therefore neither he nor she went directly to the meeting place, but only tried to come together.

One place where they could come together was the woods, where the peasant women went with sacks to fetch grass for the cows. And Evgeny knew it, and therefore he went past those woods every day. Every day he said to himself that he would not go, and every day it ended with his heading towards the woods and, hearing the sound of voices, stopping behind a bush, looking with a sinking heart to see if it was she.

Why did he need to know if it was she? He did not know. If it was she and alone, he would not have gone to her—so he thought—he would have run away; but he needed to see her. Once he met her: as he was entering the woods, she was coming out of it with two other women and a heavy sack of grass on her back. A little earlier he might have run into her in the woods. Now, however, it was impossible, in the sight of the other women, for her to go back to him in the woods. But, despite his awareness of this impossibility, he stood for a long time behind a hazel bush, at the risk of attracting the attention of the other women. Of course, she did not turn back, but he stood there for a long time. And, my God, with such a lovely picture of her in his imagination! And this happened not once, but five or six times. And grew stronger and stronger. She had never seemed so attractive to him. And not merely attractive: she had never possessed him so fully.

He felt that he was losing his own will, was becoming almost insane. His severity towards himself did not diminish by a hair's breadth; on the contrary, he saw all the vileness of his desires, even of his actions, because his walking in the woods was an action. He knew that he needed only to run into her somewhere close, in the dark, where it was possible to touch her, and he would give way to his feeling. He knew that only shame before people, before her, and before himself held him back. And he knew that he was seeking conditions in which that shame would not be noticed—darkness, or a contact in which that shame would be stifled by animal passion. And therefore he knew that he was a vile criminal, and he despised and hated himself with all the powers of his soul. He hated himself because he still would not give up. Every day he prayed to God to strengthen him, to save him from perdition; every day he resolved that from then on he would not make a single step, would not look at her, would forget her. Every day he thought up ways to rid himself of this obsession, and every day he put those ways to use.

But it was all in vain.

One of those ways was to be constantly occupied; another was strenuous physical work and fasting; a third was to picture clearly the shame that would fall on his head when everyone knew of it—his wife, his mother-in-law, other people. He did it all, and it seemed to him that he was winning, but the time came, noonday, the time of their former meetings, and the time when he had met her with the grass, and he would go to the woods.

So five tormenting days went by. He saw her only from a distance, but never once came together with her.

XVI

LIZA WAS GRADUALLY RECOVERING, walked around, and worried about the change which had taken place in her husband and which she did not understand.

Varvara Alexeevna left for a while, and of outsiders only the uncle remained. Marya Pavlovna was at home as usual.

Evgeny was in that half-mad state when, as often happens after the June thunderstorms, the June downpours came, lasting for two days. The rain put a stop to all work. Wetness and mud even prevented the carting of dung. People sat at home. The herdsmen suffered with their cattle and finally drove them home. Cows and sheep walked about the common and strayed into yards. Village women, barefoot and wrapped in kerchiefs, splashing through the mud, rushed to look for the scattered cows. Everywhere streams ran down the roads, the leaves and grass were all waterlogged, streams, never still, poured from gutters into bubbling puddles. Evgeny sat at home with his wife, who was especially dull that day. She questioned Evgeny several times about the reason for his displeasure; he replied vexedly that it was nothing. And she stopped asking, but became upset.

They were sitting in the drawing room after breakfast. The uncle was telling for the hundredth time his fictions about his high-society acquaintances. Liza was knitting a little jacket and sighed, complaining about the weather and the pain in her back. The uncle advised her to lie down and asked for some wine for himself. Evgeny was terribly bored in the house. Everything was bland, boring. He was reading a book and smoking, but did not understand anything.

"Yes, I must go and look at the graters, they came yesterday," he said. He got up and went out.

"Take an umbrella."

"No, I'll wear a leather jacket. And it's only as far as the vats."

He put on his boots, his leather jacket, and went to the factory; but he had not gone twenty steps when he met her with her skirt tucked up high above her white calves. She was walking, her hands holding the shawl that was wrapped around her head and shoulders.

"What are you doing?" he asked, not recognizing her in the first moment. When he did, it was already too late. She stopped and, smiling, gazed at him for a long time.

"I'm looking for a calf. And where might you be going in such weather?" she said, as if she saw him every day.

"Come to the hut," he said suddenly, not knowing how himself. It was as if someone else inside him had said these words.

She bit at the kerchief, nodded with her eyes, and ran off where she had been going—to the hut in the garden—while he continued on his way, intending to turn behind the lilac bush and go to the same place.

"Master," a voice came from behind him. "The lady's calling you. She asks you to come back for a moment."

It was Misha, their servant.

"My God, this is the second time You have saved me," Evgeny thought and went back at once. His wife reminded him that he had promised to take medicine to a sick woman at dinnertime, and so she asked him to take it.

While the medicine was being prepared, some five minutes went by. Then, leaving with the medicine, he did not dare to go to the hut for fear of being seen from the house. But as soon as he was out of sight, he turned at once and went to the hut. In his imagination he already saw her in the middle of the hut, smiling gaily; but she was not there, and there was nothing in the hut to prove that she had been there. He was already thinking that she had not come, and had not heard or understood his words. He had muttered them under his breath, as if afraid she would hear him. "Or maybe she didn't want to come? What made me think she'd just rush to me? She has her own husband; only I alone am such a scoundrel that I have a wife, and a good one, and go running after another man's." So he thought, sitting in the hut, which had a leak in one place and dripped from its thatch. "And what happiness it would be if she came. Alone here in this rain. To embrace her again, if only once, and then let come what may. Ah, yes," he remembered, "if she was here, I can find her tracks." He looked at the dirt of the path beaten to the hut and not overgrown with grass, and on it there were the fresh tracks of bare, slipping feet. "Yes, she was here. That's it now. Wherever I see her, I'll go straight to her. I'll go to her at night." He sat in the hut for a long time and left it exhausted and crushed. He delivered the medicine, returned home, and lay down in his room, waiting for dinner.

XVII

BEFORE DINNER Liza came to him and, still wondering what could be the cause of his discontent, began telling him that she was afraid he did not like it that they wanted to take her to Moscow to give birth, and that she had decided to stay here. And wouldn't go to Moscow for anything. He knew how afraid she was both of the delivery itself and of giving birth to an unhealthy baby, and therefore he could not help being touched to see how easily she sacrificed everything out of love for him. Everything was so good, joyful, and pure in the house; but in his soul it was dirty, vile, terrible. Evgeny suffered the whole evening, because he knew that despite his sincere revulsion at his weakness, despite his firm intention to break it off, tomorrow would be the same.

"No, this is impossible," he said to himself as he paced up and down his room. "There must be some remedy for it. My God, what am I to do?"

Someone knocked on the door in a foreign manner. He knew it was the uncle.

"Come in," he said.

The uncle came as a self-appointed ambassador from his wife.

"You know, I do in fact notice a change in you," he said, "and I understand how it torments Liza. I understand that it's hard for you to leave all this excellent business you've got started, but what do you want, *que veux-tu?* I'd advise you to go away. It'll be easier for you and for her. And you know, my advice is to go to the Crimea. Climate is an excellent *accoucheur,* and you'll come right in the middle of the grape season."

"Uncle," Evgeny suddenly began, "can you keep my secret, a terrible secret for me, a shameful secret?"

"Good heavens, how can you doubt me?"

"Uncle, you can help me! Not so much help as save me," said Evgeny. And the thought of revealing his secret to the uncle, for whom he had no respect, the thought of appearing before him in the most unfavourable light, of humiliating himself before him, was pleasing to him. He felt himself vile, guilty, and he wanted to punish himself.

"Speak, my friend, you know how I've come to love you," said the uncle, clearly very content that there was a secret, and that the secret was shameful, and that this secret would be told to him, and that he might be useful.

"First of all, I must tell you that I'm a vile creature, and a villain, a scoundrel, precisely a scoundrel."

"No, really," the uncle began, puffing out his throat.

"How can I not be a scoundrel, when I, Liza's husband, Liza's!—you must know her purity, her love—when I, her husband, want to betray her with a peasant wench!"

"How do you mean you want to? So you haven't betrayed her?"

"No, but it's the same as if I've betrayed her, because it didn't depend on me. I was ready. Someone prevented me, otherwise now I . . . now I . . . I don't know what I'd have done."

"Excuse me, but can you explain . . ."

"Well, here's the thing. When I was a bachelor, I was foolish enough to have relations with a woman here, from our village. That is, I'd meet her in the woods, in the field . . ."

"A pretty little thing?" asked the uncle.

Evgeny winced at the question, but he was so much in need of outside help that he pretended not to hear and went on:

"Well, I thought it was just so, that I'd break it off and it would be over. And I did break it off before my marriage, and didn't see her or think of her for almost a year." Evgeny found it strange to hear himself, to hear the description of his own state. "Then suddenly, I don't know why—truly, one can sometimes believe in sorcery—I saw her and a worm got into my heart—it gnaws at me. I reproach myself, I under-stand all the horror of my action, that is, of what I might do at any moment, and I go to it myself, and if I haven't done it yet, only God has saved me. Yesterday I was going to her when Liza called me."

"What, in the rain?"

"Yes, I'm tormented, uncle, and I've decided to reveal it to you and ask for your help."

"Yes, of course, on your own estate it's not good. People will find out. I understand that Liza's weak, she must be spared, but why on your own estate?"

Again Evgeny tried not to hear what the uncle was saying and has-tened to get to the essence of the matter.

"Yes, save me from myself. That's what I ask you to do. Today some-one prevented me by chance, but tomorrow, some other time, no one will prevent me. And she knows now. Don't let me go out alone."

"Yes, I suppose," said the uncle. "But can you really be so in love?"

"Oh, it's not that at all. It's not that, it's some sort of force that has seized me and holds me. I don't know what to do. Maybe I'll get stronger, and then . . ."

"Well, so it turns out my way," said the uncle. "Let's go to the Crimea."

"Yes, yes, let's go, and meanwhile I'll be with you, I'll talk to you."

XVIII

THE FACT that Evgeny had confided his secret to his uncle and, above all, the pangs of conscience and shame he lived through after that rainy day, sobered him. It was decided to make the trip to Yalta in a week. During that week, Evgeny went to town to get money for the trip, gave orders about the farmwork from the house and the office, became cheerful and close to his wife again, and began to revive morally.

So, without having once seen Stepanida after that rainy day, he left with his wife for the Crimea. In the Crimea they spent two wonderful months. Evgeny had so many new impressions that all the former things seemed to have been erased completely from his memory. In the Crimea they met former acquaintances and became especially close with them; besides that, they made new acquaintances. Life in the Crimea was a permanent feast for Evgeny and, besides that, was also instructive and useful for him. They became close with the former provincial marshal[5] of their own province, an intelligent, liberal-minded man, who came to love Evgeny, and formed him, and drew him to his side. At the end of August, Liza gave birth to a beautiful, healthy girl, and the delivery was unexpectedly easy.

In September the Irtenevs went home, now four of them, with the baby and the wet nurse, because Liza was unable to nurse. Completely free of his former terrors, Evgeny returned home quite a new and happy man. Having lived through what a husband lives through during childbirth, he loved his wife still more strongly. His feeling for the baby, when he took her in his arms, was a funny, new, very pleasant, almost tickling feeling. Another new thing in his life was that, owing to his closeness with Dumchin (the former marshal), there emerged in his soul, besides farming, a new interest in zemstvo work,[6] partly out of ambition, partly out of an awareness of his own duty. In October an extraordinary meeting was to take place, at which he was to be elected. On returning home, he went to town once, and another time to see Dumchin.

He even forgot to think about his torments of temptation and struggle, and could hardly revive them in his imagination. It all appeared to him as some sort of fit of madness that he had been subjected to.

He now felt himself free to such an extent that he was even not afraid to make enquiries of the steward, at the first opportunity, when they were alone together. Since they had already talked about it, he was not ashamed to ask.

"Well, and is Sidor Pchelnikov still not living at home?" he asked.

"No, he's still in town."

"And his woman?"

"A frivolous wench! She's carrying on with Zinovy now. Completely on the loose."

"Well, splendid," thought Evgeny. "Amazing how little I care and how changed I am."

XIX

ALL THAT Evgeny wished for was accomplished. The estate remained his, the factory was running, the beet harvest was excellent, and a large profit was expected; his wife's delivery had gone well, and his mother-in-law had left, and he had been elected unanimously.

Evgeny was coming home from town after the election. He had been congratulated; he had had to return thanks. And he had had dinner and drunk five glasses of champagne. Quite new plans for life now presented themselves to him. He was driving home and thinking about them. It was an Indian summer. An excellent road, bright sun. Nearing the house, Evgeny was thinking of how, as the result of this election, he could occupy among the people precisely the position he had always dreamed of, that is, one in which he would be able to serve them not only by production, which provides work, but by direct influence. He imagined how his own and other peasants would regard him in three years. "And this one, too," he thought, driving through his village just then and looking at a muzhik and a woman who were crossing the road in front of him with a full tub. They stopped to let the tarantass go by. The man was old Pchelnikov, the woman was Stepanida. Evgeny looked at her, recognized her, and felt with joy that he remained perfectly calm. She was still as comely, but that did not touch him in the least. He drove home. His wife met him on the porch. It was a wonderful evening.

"Well, so can we congratulate you?" asked the uncle.

"Yes, I've been elected."

"Well, splendid. We must wet it."

The next morning Evgeny went to look over the farming, which he had been neglecting. At the farmstead a new thresher was at work. Looking it over as it worked, Evgeny moved among the women, trying not to notice them, but, try as he might, a couple of times he noticed the dark eyes and red kerchief of Stepanida, who was carrying straw. A couple of times he glanced sidelong at her and felt that there was again something, though he could not account for it to himself. Only the next day, when he again went to the threshing floor of the farmstead and spent two hours there, for which there was no need at all, never ceasing to caress with his eyes the familiar, beautiful form of the young woman, did he feel that he was lost, completely, irretrievably lost. Again those torments, again all that horror and fear. And no salvation.

. . .

WHAT HE EXPECTED did happen to him. The next evening, not knowing how, he found himself in her back-yard, across from her hay barn, where they had met once in the autumn. As if out for a stroll, he stopped there and lit a cigarette. A neighbour woman saw him and, as he was going back, he heard her say to someone:

"Go, he's waiting, strike me dead, he's standing there. Go, you fool!"

He saw a woman—her—run to the barn, but it was no longer possible for him to turn back, because he had met a muzhik, and so he went home.

XX

WHEN HE CAME to the drawing room, everything seemed wild and unnatural to him. In the morning he had got up still cheerful, with the decision to drop it, forget it, not let himself think. But, not noticing how himself, all morning he not only took no interest in his affairs, but tried to free himself of them. That which formerly had been important, had given him joy, was now worthless. He unconsciously tried to free himself from business. It seemed to him that he had to free himself from it in order to reason, to think. And he freed himself and was left alone. But as soon as he was left alone, he went to wander in the garden, in the woods. And all those places were befouled by memories, memories that gripped him. And he felt he was walking in the garden and saying to himself that he was thinking something over, but he was not thinking anything over, he was insanely, groundlessly waiting for her, waiting for her to understand, by some miracle, how he desired her and come there or somewhere where no one could see, or at night, when there would be no moon, and no one, not even herself, would see, on such a night she would come and he would touch her body . . .

"Yes, see how I broke it off when I wanted to," he said to himself. "Yes, see how for the sake of health I came together with a clean, healthy woman! No, clearly it was impossible to play with her like that. I thought I was taking her, but it was she who took me, took me and wouldn't let me go. I thought I was free, but I wasn't free. I was deceiving myself when I married. It was all nonsense, deceit. Once I came together with her, I experienced a new feeling, the real feeling of a husband. Yes, I should have lived with her.

"Yes, two lives are possible for me; one is the life I began with Liza: service, farming, the child, people's respect. If it's that life, then there must be no Stepanida. She must be sent away, as I said, or destroyed, so that she's no more. And the other life is right here. To take her from her husband, give him money, forget the shame and disgrace, and live with her. But then there must be no Liza and Mimi (the child). No, why, the child's no hindrance, but there must be no Liza, she must go away. Let her find out, curse me, and go away. Find out that I exchanged her for a peasant wench, that I'm a deceiver, a scoundrel. No, that's too terrible. That can't be done. Yes, but it might happen that Liza falls sick and dies. She dies, and then everything will be splendid.

"Splendid. Oh, villain! No, if anyone is to die, it's her. If she died, Stepanida, how good it would be.

"Yes, that's how men poison or murder their wives or mistresses. Take a revolver, go and call her out, and, instead of embraces—in the breast. Finished.

"She's a devil. An outright devil. She's taken possession of me against my will. Kill? yes. Only two ways out: kill my wife or her. Because to live like this is impossible.* Impossible. I must think and foresee. If it stays as it is, what will happen?

"It will happen that I again say to myself that I don't want it, that I'll drop it, but I'll only say it, and in the evening I'll be in her back-yard, and she knows it, and she'll come. Either people will find out and tell my wife, or I'll tell her myself, because I can't lie, I can't live like this, I can't. It will be known. Everybody will know, Parasha, and the blacksmith . . . Well, is it possible to live like this?

"No, it's not. Only two ways out: kill my wife or her. Or else . . .

"Ah, yes, there's a third way: myself," he said aloud, in a low voice, and a chill suddenly ran over him. "Yes, myself, then there's no need to kill them." He became frightened precisely because he felt that this was the only possible way out. "I have a revolver. Can it be that I'll kill myself? That's something I never thought of. How strange it will be."

He went back to his room and at once opened the cupboard where the revolver was. But he had only just opened it when his wife came in.

---

* What follows is the first version of the ending. The alternative ending begins on p. 206.

XXI

HE QUICKLY THREW a newspaper over the revolver.

"Again the same thing," she said in fear, looking at him.

"What same thing?"

"The same terrible expression as before, when you didn't want to tell me. Zhenya, darling, tell me. I can see you're suffering. Tell me, you'll feel better. Whatever it is, it will be better than this suffering. I know there's nothing bad."

"You know? Not yet."

"Tell me, tell me. I won't let you go."

He smiled a pathetic smile.

"Tell her? No, it's impossible. And there's nothing to tell."

Maybe he would have told her, but at that moment the wet nurse came in to ask if she could take the baby for a walk. Liza went to dress the baby.

"So you'll tell me. I'll be right back."

"Yes, maybe . . ."

She could never forget the suffering smile with which he said it. She left.

Hurriedly, stealthily, like a thief, he seized the revolver and took it out of the case. "It's loaded, yes, long ago, and there's one cartridge missing. Well, come what may."

He put it to his temple, hesitated, but as soon as he remembered Stepanida, his decision not to see her, the struggle, the temptation, the fall, the struggle again, he shuddered with horror. "No, better this." And he pulled the trigger.

When Liza came running into the room—she had only just had time to step down from the balcony—he was lying face down on the floor, dark, warm blood was gushing from the wound, and his body was still twitching.

There was an inquest. No one could understand or explain the cause of the suicide. It never even once occurred to the uncle that the cause had anything to do with the confession Evgeny had made to him two months earlier.

Varvara Alexeevna insisted that she had always predicted it. It was clear when he argued. Liza and Marya Pavlovna could never understand why it had happened, and all the same did not believe what the doctors said, that he was mentally ill. They simply could not agree with that, because they knew he was far more sound-minded than hundreds of people they knew.

And indeed, if Evgeny Irtenev was mentally ill, then all people are just as mentally ill, and the most mentally ill are undoubtedly those who see signs of madness in others that they do not see in themselves.

ALTERNATIVE ENDING TO *The Devil*

. . . he said to himself and, going to the table, he took out the revolver and, looking it over—one of the cartridges was missing—put it in his trouser pocket.

"My God! what am I doing?" he cried suddenly and, clasping his hands, he began to pray. "Lord, help me, deliver me. You know I do not want to do anything bad, but I am powerless alone. Help me," he said, crossing himself before an icon.

"But I can control myself. I'll go out for a walk and think it over."

He went to the front hall, put on a warm jacket, galoshes, and went out to the porch. Not noticing it, he directed his steps past the garden down the field road to the farmstead. There the noise of the thresher and the shouts of the driver lads were still heard. He went into the barn. She was there. He saw her at once. She was raking up the ears and, seeing him, laughing with her eyes, brisk, merry, she trotted over the scattered ears, deftly moving them together. Evgeny did not want to look at her, but could not help it. He came to his senses only when she went out of his sight. The steward told him that they were almost done threshing the compacted sheaves, and that took longer and yielded less. Evgeny went to the drum, which occasionally made a knock as it skipped over the poorly spread sheaves, and asked the steward if there were many such compacted sheaves.

"About five cartloads."

"So that's what . . ." Evgeny began and did not finish. She came up close to the drum to rake some ears from under it, and seared him with her laughing gaze.

That gaze spoke of the merry, carefree love between them, and of her knowing that he desired her, that he had come to her shed, and that she was ready, as always, to live and make merry with him, not thinking of any circumstances or consequences. Evgeny felt he was in her power, but he did not want to give in.

He remembered his prayer and tried to repeat it. He began to say it to himself, but felt at once that it was useless.

One thought now absorbed him entirely: how to set up a meeting with her unnoticed by the others?

"If we finish today, will you have us start on a new stack or wait until tomorrow?" asked the steward.

"Yes, yes," replied Evgeny, involuntarily making after her towards the heap of ears she was raking up along with another woman.

"Can I really not control myself?" he said to himself. "Can I really be lost? Lord! But there isn't any God. There is the devil. And it's she. The devil has possessed me. And I don't want it, I don't want it. The devil, yes, the devil."

He went up close to her, took the revolver from his pocket, and shot her once, twice, three times in the back. She ran and fell onto the heap.

"Saints alive! darling dears! what is it?" cried the women.

"No, it's not an accident. I killed her on purpose," cried Evgeny. "Send for the police."

He came home and, saying nothing to his wife, went to his room and locked himself in.

"Don't come to me," he cried to his wife through the door, "you'll learn everything."

An hour later he rang for the footman, and when he came, said:

"Go and find out if Stepanida's alive."

The footman already knew everything and said she had died about an hour ago.

"Well, splendid. Leave me now. When the police officer or the investigator comes, tell me."

The police officer and the investigator came the next morning, and Evgeny, after saying goodbye to his wife and baby, was taken to prison.

He was tried. This was in the early days of jury trials.[7] And he was found to have been temporarily insane and sentenced only to a church penance.

He spent nine months in prison and one month in a monastery.

He began to drink while still in prison, went on in the monastery, and returned home an enfeebled, irresponsible alcoholic.

Varvara Alexeevna insisted that she had always predicted it. It was clear when he argued. Liza and Marya Pavlovna simply could not understand why it had happened, and all the same did not believe what the doctors said, that he was mentally ill, a psychopath. They simply could not agree with that, because they knew he was far more sound-minded than hundreds of people they knew.

And indeed, if Evgeny Irtenev was mentally ill when he committed his crime, then all people are just as mentally ill, and the most mentally ill are undoubtedly those who see signs of madness in others that they do not see in themselves.

1889

Master and Man

I

THIS WAS in the seventies, on the day after the winter feast of St. Nicholas.[1] It was the parish feast day, and for the village inn-keeper, merchant of the second guild[2] Vassily Andreich Brekhunov, it was impossible to absent himself: he had to be in church—he was the church warden—and at home he had to receive and entertain his family and acquaintances. But now the last guests were gone, and Vassily Andreich started getting ready to go at once to a neighbouring landowner for the purchase of a wood he had long been negotiating. Vassily Andreich was in a hurry to leave, so that the town merchants would not outbid him on this profitable purchase. The young landowner was asking ten thousand for the woods only because Vassily Andreich had offered seven. Seven, however, was only one-third of the real value of the woods. Vassily Andreich might have bargained him down still more, because the lot was in his territory, and it was a long-standing rule between him and other village merchants of the district that one merchant would not run up the price in another's territory, but Vassily Andreich had found out that the timber dealers from the provincial capital wanted to come and negotiate for the Goryachkino woods, and he had decided to go at once and close the deal with the landowner. And therefore, as soon as the feast was over, he took his own seven hundred roubles from the coffer, added two thousand three hundred of church money he had at his disposal, so as to make three thousand roubles, and, having carefully counted them and put them in his wallet, got ready to go.

His man Nikita, the only one of his workmen who was not drunk that day, ran to harness up. Nikita was not drunk that day because he was a drunkard, and now, since the beginning of the fast,[3] when he had drunk up his coat and leather boots, he had sworn off drinking, and it was the second month that he hadn't drunk anything; nor did he drink now, despite the temptation of the vodka-drinking everywhere during the first two days of the feast.

Nikita was a fifty-year-old muzhik from a nearby village, an impractical fellow, as they said of him, who had spent most of his life not at home but with other people. He was valued everywhere for his industriousness, dexterity, and strength at work, and, above all, for his kind, pleasant character; but he never settled down anywhere, because twice a year, or even more often, he went on a drinking binge, and then, besides drinking up everything he had on, he became violent and quarrelsome. Vassily Andreich also fired him several times, but then took him back, valuing his honesty, his love of animals, and, above all, his cheapness. Vassily Andreich paid Nikita, not eighty roubles, which such a man was worth, but around forty, which he doled out to him without an accounting, and mostly not in money but in high-priced goods from the shop.

Nikita's wife Marfa, once a beautiful, sprightly woman, looked after the house with her adolescent son and two girls, and did not invite Nikita to live at home, first, because she had already been living for some twenty years with a cooper, a muzhik from another village, who lodged in their house; and, second, because, though she ordered her husband about as she liked when he was sober, she feared him like fire when he was drunk. Once, having got drunk at home, Nikita, probably to vent all his sober submissiveness on his wife, broke open her trunk, took out her most treasured clothes, put them on the chopping block, and, seizing an axe, chopped all her sarafans and dresses into little pieces. The wages Nikita earned were all handed over to his wife, and Nikita did not object to that. And so now, two days before the feast, Marfa had come to Vassily Andreich and collected white flour, tea, sugar, and a half-pint bottle of vodka, some three roubles' worth in all, plus five roubles in cash, and had thanked him profusely for it, as if for a special kindness, though at the cheapest rate Vassily Andreich owed them twenty roubles.

"Have there ever been any sort of conditions between us?" Vassily Andreich used to say to Nikita. "If you need anything, take it, you'll work it off. With me it's not like with others: delays, calculation, penalties. We go by honour. Serve me and I won't abandon you."

And in saying this, Vassily Andreich was sincerely convinced that he was Nikita's benefactor: so convincingly did he know how to speak, and so firmly did all those who depended on his money, beginning with Nikita, uphold him in the conviction that he was not deceiving them, but was indeed their benefactor.

"I understand, Vassily Andreich. Seems I do serve you, I try hard, like for my own father. I understand very well," Nikita replied, understanding very well that Vassily Andreich was cheating him, but feeling at the same time that there was no use even attempting to clear up his accounts with him, and one had to live, as long as there was no other work, and take what was given.

Now, having received his master's order to harness up, Nikita, as always, cheerfully and eagerly, with the brisk, light step of his pigeon-toed feet, went to the shed, took down a heavy leather bridle with a tassel from its nail, and, the rings of the curb bit jangling, went to the closed stable, where the horse that Vassily Andreich had told him to harness stood by itself.

"What, did you miss me, did you miss me, little fool?" said Nikita, responding to the faint whinny of greeting he was met with by the middle-sized, well-built, slightly low-rumped dark bay stallion standing alone in the little stable. "Now, now, don't rush, let me water you first," he said to the horse, just as one does to beings who understand words, and, having brushed with the skirt of his coat the chafed, dusty back, fat and with a groove down the middle, he put the bridle on the stallion's handsome young head, freed his ears and forelock, and, taking off the halter, led him out to water.

Carefully picking his way through the dung-heaped stable, Mukhorty frisked and bucked, pretending that he wanted to give a kick with his hind leg at Nikita, who was jogging beside him to the well.

"Go on, go on, you rascal!" muttered Nikita, who knew the care with which Mukhorty had thrown up his hind leg, just enough to touch his greasy sheepskin jacket but not to hit him, and who especially liked that trick.

After drinking the icy water, the horse sighed, moving his wet, firm lips, from the whiskers of which transparent drops dripped into the trough, and stood still as if in thought; then he suddenly gave a loud snort.

"If you don't want to, you don't have to, we'll remember that; don't go asking for more," Nikita said with perfect seriousness and thoroughness, explaining his behaviour to Mukhorty, and he ran back to the shed, tugging at the reins of the merry young horse, who went bucking and clattering all over the yard.

There were no workmen around; there was only one outsider, the cook's husband, who had come for the feast.

"Go, dear heart," Nikita said to him, "and ask which sleigh I should hitch up: the wide, low one or the wee one?"

The cook's husband went to the iron-roofed house on high foundations and soon returned with the report that he was ordered to hitch up the wee one. Nikita meanwhile had already put the collar on, strapped on the studded gig saddle, and, carrying a light, painted shaft-bow in one hand and leading the horse with the other, was going to the two sleighs standing under the shed roof.

"If it's the wee one, it's the wee one," he said and backed the intelligent horse, who kept pretending that he wanted to nip him, into the shafts, and with the help of the cook's husband began harnessing up.

When everything was almost done, and it only remained to attach the reins, Nikita sent the cook's husband to the shed for straw and to the barn for burlap.

"There, that's fine. Now, now, don't bristle up!" Nikita said as he packed the just-threshed oat straw brought by the cook's husband down into the sleigh. "And now let's spread the hop sacking this way and the burlap on top of it. There, like that, like that, and it'll be nice to sit on," he said, as he did what he was saying, tucking the burlap down over the straw on all sides around the seat.

"Thank you, dear heart," Nikita said to the cook's husband, "it's always better with two." And, sorting out the leather reins held together with a ring at the end, Nikita seated himself on the box and started the good horse, who was begging to go, across the frozen dung of the yard towards the gate.

"Uncle Nikita, uncle, hey, dear uncle!" a seven-year-old boy in a black coat, new white felt boots, and a warm hat cried behind him in a piping little voice, running hurriedly out of the front hall to the yard. "Let me get on," he begged, buttoning up his coat as he ran.

"Well, well, hurry up, little fellow," said Nikita and, stopping, he gave a seat to the master's little son, pale, thin, and beaming with joy, and drove out to the street.

It was past two. It was frosty—about ten degrees—grey and windy. Half the sky was covered by a low, dark cloud. But in the yard it was still. In the street the wind was more noticeable: snow was blowing from the roof of a neighbouring shed and swirling about at the corner by the bath-house. Nikita had barely driven through the gate and turned the horse to the porch when Vassily Andreich, with a cigarette in his mouth, wearing a fleece-lined coat, girdled low and tightly with a sash, came out of the front hall to the high porch covered with trampled snow, which squeaked under his leather-covered felt boots, and stopped. Dragging on what remained of his cigarette, he threw it down and stepped on it, and, exhaling smoke through his moustaches and giving a sidelong glance at the approaching horse, began tucking in the fur collar of his coat on both sides of his ruddy face, clean-shaven except for the moustaches, so that his breath would not wet the fur.

"See what a prankster, he's here already!" he said, seeing his son in the sleigh. Vassily Andreich was excited by the vodka he had drunk with his guests, and therefore was even more pleased than usual with everything that belonged to him and everything he did. The sight of his son, whom in his mind he always called his heir, afforded him great pleasure now; squinting and baring his long teeth, he looked at him.

Her head and shoulders wrapped in a woollen shawl so that only her eyes could be seen, Vassily Andreich's wife, pregnant, pale, and thin, stood behind him in the front hall, seeing him off.

"Really, you ought to take Nikita," she said, stepping timidly through the doorway.

Vassily Andreich said nothing and, in response to her words, which obviously displeased him, frowned angrily and spat.

"You've got money with you," his wife went on in the same plaintive voice. "And, by God, the weather really may blow up."

"What, don't I know the way, that I need a guide?" Vassily Andreich said, with that unnatural tension of the lips with which he usually talked with sellers and buyers, pronouncing each syllable with particular distinctness.

"Well, really, you ought to take him. In God's name I beg you!" his wife repeated, rewrapping her shawl on the other side.

"She sticks like a leaf in the bathhouse . . . Well, what should I take him for?"

"So then, Vassily Andreich, I'm ready," Nikita said gaily. "As long as somebody feeds the horses while I'm gone," he added, turning to the mistress.

"I'll see to it, Nikitushka, I'll tell Semyon," said the mistress.

"So, do I go or what, Vassily Andreich?" Nikita said, waiting.

"I guess we've got to humour the old girl. Only if you come, go put on some warmer gear," Vassily Andreich pronounced, smiling again and winking at Nikita's greasy and bedraggled jacket, torn under the arms and on the back, and with a frayed hem, which had seen it all.

"Hey, dear heart, come and hold the horse!" Nikita shouted to the cook's husband in the yard.

"I'll do it, I'll do it," piped the boy, taking his chilled red hands from his pockets and snatching at the cold leather reins.

"Only don't bother prettying up your gear. Step lively!" cried Vassily Andreich, giving Nikita a toothy smile.

"In a flash, dearest Vassily Andreich," said Nikita, and trotting quickly in his old felt boots with mended soles, he ran back to the yard and to the workers' cottage.

"Quick, Arinushka, give me my long coat from the stove[4]—I'm going with the master!" said Nikita, running into the cottage and taking his sash from a nail.

The cook, who had taken a nap after dinner and was now preparing the samovar for her husband, greeted Nikita cheerfully and, infected by his haste, got a move on like him, and took down from the stove a shabby, threadbare flannel kaftan that was drying there and hastily began shaking it and softening it up.

"Now you and your mister will have plenty of room for your fun," Nikita said to the cook, always finding something to say, out of good-natured politeness, when he was left alone with a person.

And, twining the narrow, bedraggled little sash around him, he drew in his belly, skinny to begin with, and pulled it around the jacket as tight as he could.

"There you go," he said after that, now addressing not the cook but the sash, as he tucked in its ends, "that way you won't come undone," and, raising and lowering his shoulders to make more room for his arms, he put his coat on over it and again arched his back so that his arms would be free, pulled it up under the armpits, and took his mittens from the shelf. "Well, there we are."

"Maybe you want to put something else on your feet, Stepanych," said the cook. "Your boots are no good."

Nikita paused as if recollecting.

"Ought to . . . Well, but it'll do like this, it's not far!"

And he ran out to the yard.

"Won't you be cold, Nikitushka?" said the mistress, when he came up to the sleigh.

"Why cold? I'm quite warm," replied Nikita, spreading the straw in the front of the sleigh so as to cover his feet and putting the whip, unnecessary for a good horse, under the straw.

Vassily Andreich was already sitting in the sleigh, his back, covered with two fur coats, filling almost the entire curved rear of the sleigh, and, taking the reins, at once touched up the horse. Nikita, in motion, found room for himself at the front on the left side and hung one leg out.

II

WITH A SLIGHT SCREECH of the runners, the good stallion got the sleigh moving and set off at a brisk pace down the trampled snow of the village road.

"What are you hanging on for? Give me the whip, Nikita!" cried Vassily Andreich, obviously rejoicing at his heir, who had found a place behind on the runners. "I'll give it to you! Run to your mother, you son of a bitch!"

The boy jumped off. Mukhorty speeded up his amble and, shifting feet, went into a trot.

Kresty, where Vassily Andreich's house stood, consisted of six houses. As soon as they passed the last, the blacksmith's, they noticed at once that the wind was much stronger than they had thought. The road could hardly be seen. The tracks of the runners were immediately blown over by snow, and the road could be made out only because it was higher than everything around. The fields were all in a whirl, and the limit where sky and earth met could not be seen. The Telyatino forest, usually quite visible, only occasionally showed faintly black through the snowy dust. The wind blew from the left, stubbornly throwing Mukhorty's mane to one side of his firm, well-fed neck and turning aside his fluffy tail tied in a simple knot. Nikita was sitting on the windy side, and his wide collar was pressed to his face and nose.

"He can't really run, too much snow," said Vassily Andreich, proud of his good horse. "I once drove with him to Pashutino, took him half an hour."

"Whazzat?" asked Nikita, not hearing well because of the collar.

"I say he made it to Pashutino in half an hour," shouted Vassily Andreich.

"What's there to talk about, he's a good horse!"

They fell silent. But Vassily Andreich wanted to talk.

"So, I s'pose you told your missus not to give the cooper any drink?" Vassily Andreich began in the same loud voice, so convinced that it should be flattering to Nikita to talk with such an important and intelligent man as himself, and so pleased with his joke, that it never even entered his head that this conversation might be unpleasant for Nikita.

Nikita again did not hear his master's words, which were carried away by the wind.

Vassily Andreich repeated his joke about the cooper in his loud, clear voice.

"God be with them, Vassily Andreich, I don't go into those things. So long as she doesn't mistreat the lad on me, God be with her."

"That's so," said Vassily Andreich. "Well, and are you going to buy a horse come spring?" he started a new subject of conversation.

"No way around it," replied Nikita, turning back the collar of his kaftan and leaning towards his master.

Now the conversation interested Nikita, and he wanted to hear everything.

"The lad's grown up, he's got to plough himself, and we keep hiring," he said.

"Why, then take the goose-rumped one, I won't ask a lot!" cried Vassily Andreich, feeling excited and as a result of that falling into his favourite occupation, which consumed all his mental powers—horse trading.

"Or else give me some fifteen roubles and I'll buy one at the horse market," said Nikita, knowing that a fair price for the goose-rumped one that Vassily Andreich was trying to foist on him was seven roubles, and that if Vassily Andreich sold him that horse, he would count it as twenty-five, and then he wouldn't see any money from him for half a year.

"He's a fine horse. I wish it for you as for myself. In all conscience. Brekhunov wouldn't wrong a man. Let it be my loss, it's not like with others. On my honour," he cried in that voice with which he fine-talked his sellers and buyers. "A real horse!"

"That's for sure," Nikita said with a sigh, and seeing that there was no point in listening further, he let go of the collar, which at once covered his ear and face.

For half an hour they drove in silence. The wind blew through Nikita's side and arm, where his coat was torn.

He hunched up and breathed into the collar, which covered his mouth, and was not cold all over.

"So, what do you think, shall we go through Karamyshevo or straight on?" asked Vassily Andreich.

The road to Karamyshevo was busier, marked by two rows of good stakes, but further. The straight way was closer, but the road was little used and had no stakes or else poor ones covered by the snow.

Nikita thought a little.

"To Karamyshevo's further, but better going," he said.

"But we've only got to go straight through the hollow without losing our way, and there the forest road's good," said Vassily Andreich, who wanted to go straight on.

"It's up to you," said Nikita, letting go of the collar again.

Vassily Andreich did just that and, having gone half a mile, at a tall oak branch swaying in the wind with dry leaves attached to it here and there, he turned left.

After the turn the wind was almost in their faces. And a light snow began to fall. Vassily Andreich drove on, puffing his cheeks and letting out his breath upwards through his moustaches. Nikita was dozing.

They rode silently like that for about ten minutes. Suddenly Vassily Andreich began to say something.

"Whazzat?" asked Nikita, opening his eyes.

Vassily Andreich did not answer and, twisting around, looked behind and then ahead over the horse. The horse, his coat curling from sweat in the groin and on the neck, went at a walk.

"Whazzat you said?" repeated Nikita.

"Whazzat, whazzat!" Vassily Andreich mimicked him angrily. "No stakes to be seen! We must have lost our way!"

"Stay here, I'll look for the road," said Nikita and, jumping lightly from the sleigh and taking the whip from under the straw, went to the left from the side he had been sitting on.

The snow was not deep that year, so that one could walk anywhere, but all the same it was knee-deep in some places and got into Nikita's boot. Nikita walked about, felt with his feet and the whip, but there was no road anywhere.

"Well?" said Vassily Andreich, when Nikita came back to the sleigh.

"There's no road on this side. I'll have to go and walk around on that side."

"Something looks black ahead there, go and have a look," said Vassily Andreich.

Nikita went there, came to what looked black—it was black soil that had spread over the snow from the bared winter wheat and turned it black. Nikita walked about to the right, came back to the sleigh, beat the snow from himself, shook it out of his boot, and got into the sleigh.

"We've got to go to the right," he said resolutely. "The wind was blowing on my left side and now it's straight in my mug. Go to the right!" he resolutely said.

Vassily Andreich obeyed and bore to the right. But there was still no road. They went on that way for some time. The wind did not slacken, and light snow was falling.

"Looks like we're quite lost, Vassily Andreich," Nikita said suddenly, as if with pleasure. "What's that?" he said, pointing to black potato tops sticking up from under the snow.

Vassily Andreich stopped the horse, who was already sweaty and heaving his steep flanks heavily.

"Well, what?" he asked.

"It means we're on the Zakharovka field. That's where we've got to!"

"Are you kidding?" Vassily Andreich shot back.

"I'm not kidding, Vassily Andreich, it's the truth I'm telling," said

Nikita, "and you can hear it from the sleigh—we're going over potatoes; and there's the heap where they gathered the tops. It's the Zakharovka factory field."

"See where we've strayed to!" said Vassily Andreich. "What now?"

"We've got to go straight, that's all, and we'll come out somewhere," said Nikita. "If not at Zakharovka, then at the manor farmstead."

Vassily Andreich obeyed and sent the horse off as Nikita told him to. They rode like that for a rather long time. At times they came upon bared winter growth, and the sleigh rumbled over ridges of frozen earth. At times they came upon stubble fields of winter or spring crops, with clumps of wormwood and straw sticking up from under the snow; at times they drove into deep, uniformly white, level snow with nothing showing above it.

Snow fell from above and at times rose up from below. The horse, obviously tired out, had his hide all curled up and frosted with sweat and went at a walk. Suddenly he lost his footing and sat down in a pothole or ditch. Vassily Andreich wanted to stop, but Nikita shouted at him:

"What are you stopping for! We got into it—we've got to get out of it. Hup, my little dear! Hup, hup, my darling!" he cried in a merry voice to the horse, jumping out of the sleigh and sinking into the ditch himself.

The horse pulled and at once got out onto the frozen bank. Obviously it was a man-made ditch.

"Where are we?" said Vassily Andreich.

"We'll soon find out!" replied Nikita. "Get going and we'll see where we come out."

"Oughtn't that to be the Goryachkino forest?" said Vassily Andreich, pointing to something black showing through the snow ahead of them.

"We'll come closer and see what sort of forest it is," said Nikita.

Nikita saw dry, elongated willow leaves flying from the direction of that blackish something, and therefore knew it was not a forest but a dwelling, but he did not want to say so. And indeed, when they had gone another twenty yards from the ditch, what were obviously trees appeared black before them, and a new, dismal sound was heard. Nikita had guessed right: it was not a forest, but a row of tall willows, with some leaves still fluttering on them here and there. The willows had obviously been planted along the ditch of a threshing floor. Having come up close to the willows, which droned dismally in the wind, the horse suddenly planted his forelegs higher than the sleigh, got his hind legs onto the high place as well, turned to the left, and stopped sinking knee-deep into the snow. It was the road.

"So we've arrived," said Nikita, "but there's no knowing where."

The horse went unerringly along the snow-covered road, and they had not gone a hundred yards when there appeared black before them the straight wattle strip of a threshing barn, under a roof thickly covered with snow, from which snow constantly sifted down. After passing the barn, the road turned into the wind, and they drove into a snowdrift. But ahead of them they could see the space between two houses, so that the snowdrift had obviously heaped up on the road, and they had to drive through it. And indeed, having driven through the snowdrift, they came out onto a street. By the first house, frozen laundry hung on a line, fluttering desperately in the wind: shirts, one red, one white, a pair of trousers, footcloths, and a skirt. The white shirt tore about especially desperately, waving its sleeves.

"See, the lazy wench didn't take her laundry down for the feast day—or else she's dying," said Nikita, looking at the dangling shirts.

III

AT THE HEAD of the street it was still windy, and the road was snow-covered, but in the middle of the village it became still, warm, and cheerful. In one yard a dog was barking, in another a woman, pulling her coat over her head, came running from somewhere and went through the door of a cottage, stopping on the threshold to look at the passers-by. From the middle of the village girls could be heard singing.

In the village it seemed there was less wind, snow, and cold.

"Why, this is Grishkino," said Vassily Andreich.

"So it is," replied Nikita.

And in fact it was Grishkino. It turned out that they had gone off to the left and driven some six miles not quite in the direction they wanted, but all the same heading towards their destination. It was about three miles from Goryachkino to Grishkino.

In the middle of the village they ran into a tall man walking down the middle of the road.

"Who's that driving?" cried the man, stopping the horse, and, recognizing Vassily Andreich at once, he took hold of the shaft and, feeling his way along it, reached the sleigh and sat himself on the box.

It was Vassily Andreich's acquaintance, the muzhik Isay, known in the neighbourhood as a first-class horse thief.

"Ah! Vassily Andreich! Where in God's name are you going?" said Isay, dousing Nikita with the smell of the vodka he had been drinking.

"We were going to Goryachkino."

"And look where you wound up! You had to go towards Malakhovo."

"Had to, maybe, but didn't manage to," said Vassily Andreich, stopping the horse.

"Nice little horse," said Isay, looking the horse over and, with a habitual movement, tightening the loosened knot of the thick tail right up to the root.

"So you'll spend the night, will you?"

"No, brother, we've absolutely got to go."

"Got to, clearly. And who's this? Ah, Nikita Stepanych!"

"Who else?" replied Nikita. "But tell us how, dear heart, so we don't go astray again."

"As if you could go astray! Turn back, go straight down the street, and, once out, keep on straight. Don't bear to the left. You come to the high road, and then—to the right."

"Where's the turn off the high road? Like in summer or like in winter?" asked Nikita.

"Like in winter. Right as you get there—bushes, and across from the bushes a big oak stake, standing with leaves on it—that's where."

Vassily Andreich turned the horse around and drove through the settlement.

"Or else spend the night!" Isay called out behind them.

But Vassily Andreich did not answer him and kept touching up the horse: three miles of level road, almost half of which went through the forest, seemed an easy drive, the more so as the wind had apparently died down and it was snowing less.

Having gone back down the trampled road with fresh dung lying black on it here and there, and passed the yard with the laundry, where the white shirt had already been torn off and was hanging by one frozen sleeve, they came again to the fearfully droning willows and again found themselves in the open field. The snowstorm not only had not died down, but seemed to have intensified. The road was completely covered with snow, and they could tell that they had not gone astray only by the stakes. But even the stakes ahead were hard to make out, because the wind was in their faces.

Vassily Andreich squinted, lowered his head, and looked out for the stakes, but for the most part he let the horse go, trusting in him. And in fact the horse did not lose the way, and went on, turning now right, now left, following the curves of the road, which he felt under his feet, so that even though the snowfall grew stronger and the wind grew stronger, the stakes continued to be visible now on the right, now on the left.

They went on like that for some ten minutes, when suddenly something black appeared right in front of the horse, moving in the slanting net of wind-driven snow. These were fellow travellers. Mukhorty caught up with them and knocked his legs against the seat of the sleigh ahead of him.

"Go around . . . aro-o-ound . . . pass us!" they shouted from the sleigh.

Vassily Andreich began to go around. In the sleigh sat three muzhiks and a woman. They were obviously guests coming from the feast. One muzhik kept whipping the snow-covered rump of the little nag with a switch. The other two, sitting in front, were waving their arms and shouting something. The woman, all wrapped up and covered with snow, sat hunched in the back and did not move.

"Where from?" cried Vassily Andreich.

"A-a-a . . . skoe!" was all he could hear.

"Where from, I say."

"A-a-a-skoe!" one of the muzhiks shouted with all his might, but it was still impossible to hear from where.

"Gee-up! Don't slacken!" shouted the other, constantly whipping the little nag with the switch.

"From the feast, must be?"

"Go on, go on! Gee-up, Semka! Go around! Gee-up!"

The sleighs bumped fenders, almost snagged, came unsnagged, and the muzhiks' sleigh began to drop behind.

The shaggy, fat-bellied little nag, all covered with snow, breathing heavily under the low shaft-bow, obviously using its last strength in a vain attempt to escape the switch that kept hitting it, hobbled over the deep snow on its short legs, kicking them under. Its muzzle, obviously young, the lower lip pulled up like a fish's, nostrils dilated and ears lying low from fear, remained for a few seconds beside Nikita's shoulder, then began to drop behind.

"That's what drink'll do," said Nikita. "Put the final touch to the poor little nag. Downright heathens!"

For a few minutes they could hear the puffing of the worn-out little nag's nostrils and the drunken shouting of the muzhiks, then the puffing died away, then the drunken shouting, too, fell silent. And again there was nothing to be heard around them except the wind whistling past their ears and, at times, the faint scraping of the runners over the bare spots in the road.

This meeting cheered and encouraged Vassily Andreich, and he drove his horse more boldly, not trying to make out the stakes, but relying on him.

There was nothing for Nikita to do, and, as always in such a situation, he dozed off, making up for much sleepless time. Suddenly the horse stopped, and Nikita nearly fell, nodding his nose forward.

"Again we're going wrong," said Vassily Andreich.

"What is it?"

"No stakes to be seen. Must have strayed from the road again."

"If we've strayed from it, we'll have to look for it," Nikita said shortly, got up, and again, stepping lightly on his pigeon-toed feet, began walking over the snow.

He walked for a long time, disappearing from sight, reappearing again, disappearing again, and finally came back.

"There's no road here, maybe somewhere ahead," he said, getting into the sleigh.

It was beginning to grow noticeably dark. The snowstorm had not increased, but neither had it slackened.

"If only we could hear those muzhiks," said Vassily Andreich.

"Yes, see, they haven't caught up with us, we must've gone pretty far astray. Or maybe they have," said Nikita.

"Where do we go now?" said Vassily Andreich.

"We must let the horse do it," said Nikita. "He'll bring us through. Give me the reins."

Vassily handed over the reins the more willingly in that his hands, in their warm gloves, were beginning to freeze.

Nikita took the reins and merely held them, trying not to move them, and rejoicing at the intelligence of his favourite. Indeed, the intelligent horse, turning one ear, then the other, to one side, then the other, began to swing about.

"Only don't tell him," Nikita kept murmuring. "See what he's doing! Go on, just go on. That's it, that's it."

The wind began blowing from behind, it became warmer.

"He's so smart," Nikita went on rejoicing over the horse. "Take Kirghizenok—he's strong, but stupid. But this one, look what he's doing with his ears. No need for any telegraph, he hears a mile off."

And half an hour had not gone by, when indeed something showed black ahead, either a forest or a village, and on the right side stakes appeared again. Evidently they had again come to the road.

"But this is Grishkino again," Nikita suddenly said.

Indeed, to the left of them now was the same threshing barn with snow blowing off it, and further on the same line with frozen laundry, shirts and trousers, which fluttered just as desperately in the wind.

Again they drove into the street, again it became quiet, warm, cheerful, again the dungy roadway could be seen, again voices and songs could be heard, again a dog barked. It was already so dark that lights shone in some of the windows.

Halfway down the street, Vassily Andreich turned the horse towards a big brick twin house and stopped him by the porch.

Nikita went to a snow-covered, lit-up window, in the light of which fluttering snowflakes sparkled, and knocked with the handle of the whip.

"Who's there?" a voice responded to Nikita's summons.

"Brekhunov, from Kresty, my dear man," Nikita replied. "Come out for a moment!"

The man inside left the window, and in a couple of minutes—it could be heard—the door to the front hall came unstuck, then the latch to the outside door clicked, and in the doorway, holding the door because of the wind, a tall old muzhik with a white beard thrust himself out, a sheepskin jacket thrown over his festive white shirt, and behind him a lad in a red shirt and leather boots.

"Is that you, Andreich?" said the old man.

"We've lost our way, brother," said Vassily Andreich. "We were going to Goryachkino and wound up here. We set off and lost our way again."

"See how you've strayed," said the old man. "Petrushka, go and open the gates!" he turned to the young man in the red shirt.

"Can do," the young man replied in a merry voice and ran to the front hall.

"We won't spend the night, brother," said Vassily Andreich.

"Why go anywhere—it's night-time, spend the night!"

"I'd be glad to spend the night, but I must go. Business, brother, no help for it."

"Well, at least warm up, the samovar's just ready," said the old man.

"Warm up—that we can do," said Vassily Andreich. "It won't get any darker, and once the moon rises, it'll be brighter. Shall we go in and warm up, Nikita?"

"Well, yes, that we can do," said Nikita, who was badly chilled and wished very much to get some warmth into his frozen limbs.

Vassily Andreich followed the old man into the cottage, and Nikita drove through the gates opened by Petrushka and, on his instructions, moved the horse under the shed of the barn. The shed was full of manure, and the high shaft-bow caught on the crossbeam. The hens and roosters already settled on the crossbeam cackled something in displeasure and scratched the beam with their feet. Disturbed sheep, stamping their hooves on the frozen dung, shied away. A dog, squealing desperately with fright and anger, dissolved in puppyish barking at the stranger.

Nikita talked with them all: apologized to the hens, assured them that he would not disturb them any more, reproached the sheep for being afraid for no reason, and admonished the little dog, all the while he was tying up the horse.

"There, that'll be just fine," he said, shaking the snow off himself. "Look at him barking away!" he added to the dog. "That'll do from you! Well, that'll do, stupid, that'll do. You're only worrying yourself," he said. "We're not thieves, we're friends . . ."

"The three domestic advisers, as they say," said the lad, with his strong arm shoving the sleigh, which had remained outside, under the shed roof.

"How do you mean, advisers?" said Nikita.

"That's what's printed in Poolson:⁵ a thief sneaks up to the house, the dog barks—meaning 'look sharp, watch out.' A rooster crows—meaning 'get up.' A cat licks itself—meaning 'a dear guest, get ready to welcome him,' " the lad said, smiling.

Petrukha could read and write and knew Paulson, the only book he owned, almost by heart, and, especially when he was a little tipsy, as now, he liked to quote sayings from it that seemed appropriate to the occasion.

"That's exactly right," said Nikita.

"I s'pose you're chilled through, uncle?" added Petrukha.

"And then some," said Nikita, and they went across the yard and through the front hall into the cottage.

IV

THE HOUSEHOLD where Vassily Andreich had stopped was one of the wealthiest in the village. The family owned five plots and also rented land elsewhere. They had six horses, three cows, two calves, and some twenty head of sheep. The family was made up of twenty-two souls in all: four married sons, six grandchildren, of whom one, Petrukha, was married, two great-grandchildren, three orphans, and four daughters-in-law with children. It was one of the rare houses that still remained undivided; but in it, too, an obscure inner work of dissension, begun as always among the women, was already going on, which inevitably would soon lead to division. Two of the sons were living in Moscow as water carriers; one was a soldier. At home now there were the old man, the old woman, the second son, who ran the farm, the eldest son, who had come from Moscow for the feast, and all the women and children; besides the family, there was a guest—a neighbour, godfather of one of the children.

In the cottage, a lamp with a shade above it hung over the table, brightly lighting up the tea things under it, a bottle of vodka, some food, and the brick walls hung with icons in the far right corner and some pictures on either side of them. At the table, in the place of honour, sat Vassily Andreich, in just his black sheepskin jacket, sucking on his frozen moustaches and looking at the people and the cottage around him with his prominent hawk's eyes. Sitting at the table along with Vassily Andreich were the bald, white-bearded old master of the house in a white homespun shirt; beside him the son who had come from Moscow for the feast, with a stout back and shoulders, wearing a thin cotton shirt, and yet another son, broad-shouldered, the one who ran the farm for the household, and a lean, red-haired muzhik—the neighbour.

The muzhiks, having drunk and eaten, were just about to have tea, and the samovar was already humming, standing on the floor by the stove. On planks between the wall and stove, and on the stove itself, children could be seen. A woman was sitting on a bunk bed over a cradle. The little old mistress of the house, her face covered with tiny wrinkles in all directions, which wrinkled even her lips, was tending to Vassily Andreich.

Just as Nikita came into the cottage, she was offering her guest vodka, which she had poured into a thick-sided shot glass.

"Don't begrudge us, Vassily Andreich, you mustn't, you've got to drink for the feast," she was saying. "Drink up, dearest."

The sight and smell of vodka, especially now, chilled and weary as he was, deeply perplexed Nikita. He frowned and, having shaken the snow from his hat and kaftan, stood facing the icons and, as if seeing no one, crossed himself three times and bowed three times before them; then, turning to the old host, he bowed first to him, then to all who were at the table, then to the women standing by the stove, and saying, "Happy feast day!" began to undress without looking at the table.

"Well, you're really frosted up, uncle," said the elder brother, looking at Nikita's face, eyes, and beard, all covered with snow.

Nikita took off his kaftan, shook it once more, hung it near the stove, and went to the table. He, too, was offered vodka. There was a moment of painful struggle: he almost took the little glass and tipped the fragrant, clear liquid into his mouth; but he glanced at Vassily Andreich, remembered his vow, remembered the drunk-up boots, remembered the cooper, remembered his lad, for whom he had promised to buy a horse by spring, sighed and refused.

"My humble thanks, I don't drink," he said, frowning, and sat down on a bench near the second window.

"Why's that?" asked the elder brother.

"If I don't drink, I don't drink," said Nikita, not raising his eyes and looking sidelong at his skimpy moustaches and beard as the icicles melted on them.

"It's not good for him," said Vassily Andreich, munching a pretzel after the glass he had drunk.

"Well, some tea, then," said the kindly old woman. "I s'pose you're chilled through, dear heart. Why are you women dawdling with the samovar?"

"It's ready," said a young woman, and she fanned the covered samovar, which was boiling over, with her apron, carried it with difficulty, lifted it, and banged it down on the table.

Meanwhile Vassily Andreich was telling how they had gone astray, how they had come back twice to the same village, how they had wandered about, how they had met some drunk people. The hosts were surprised, explained where and why they had lost their way, and who the drunk people they had met were, and taught them how to go.

"A little child could drive from here to Molchanovka, once you get to the turn from the high road—you'll see a bush there. You just didn't go far enough!" the neighbour said.

"Or else spend the night. The women will make up beds," the old woman urged.

"You can go in the wee hours, that'd be the most nicest thing," the old man agreed.

"Impossible, brother, it's business!" said Vassily Andreich. "Lose an hour, and you spend a year catching up," he added, remembering the woods and the merchants who might outbid him on the purchase. "Will we make it?" he turned to Nikita.

Nikita took a long time to answer, as if he was preoccupied with thawing out his beard and moustaches.

"If we don't go astray again," he said gloomily.

Nikita was gloomy because he passionately wanted vodka, and the one thing that could extinguish that desire was tea, but he had not yet been offered any.

"We only need to get to that turn, and from there on we won't get lost; it's a forest road all the way," said Vassily Andreich.

"It's your business, Vassily Andreich; if we go, we go," said Nikita, taking the offered glass of tea.

"We'll have tea and be off."

Nikita said nothing, but only shook his head and, carefully pouring tea into the saucer, began warming his hands, the fingers permanently swollen from work, over the steam. Then, having bitten off a tiny piece of sugar, he bowed to the hosts and said:

"To your health," and slurped up the warming liquid.

"If only somebody could take us to that turn," said Vassily Andreich.

"Why, that can be done," said the elder son. "Petrukha will hitch up and take you to the turn."

"Hitch up, then, brother. I'll thank you for it."

"Ah, none of that, dearest," said the kindly old woman. "We're heartily glad."

"Petrukha, go and hitch up the mare," said the elder brother.

"Can do," said Petrukha, smiling, and, snatching his hat from a nail, he ran at once to hitch up.

While the horse was being harnessed, the conversation returned to where it had stopped when Vassily Andreich drove up to the window. The old man was complaining to the neighbour, who was a headman, about the third son, who had sent him nothing for the feast, but had sent his wife a French kerchief.

"The young folk are getting out of hand," said the old man.

"And how," said the neighbour. "No managing 'em! Got too clever. Take Demochkin—broke his father's arm. All from such great cleverness, plainly."

Nikita listened, looked into their faces, and obviously also wished to take part in the conversation, but he was all engrossed in his tea and only nodded his head approvingly. He drank glass after glass and felt warmer and warmer, pleasanter and pleasanter. The conversation went on for a long time about the same thing, the harm of divisions; and the conversation was obviously not an abstract one, it had to do with the division of this household—a division demanded by the second son, who sat there and kept sullenly silent. Obviously, this was a sore spot, and the question concerned the whole family, but out of politeness they did not sort out their private affairs in front of strangers. But the old man finally could not hold himself back, and with tears in his voice he began talking about how he would not let them divide it up as long as he lived, that thank God he had such a house, and if they divided it up, they would all go begging through the world.

"Just like the Matveevs," said the neighbour. "They had a real household, but they divided it up—now nobody's got anything."

"And that's what you want," the old man said to his son.

The son did not reply and an awkward silence ensued. This silence was broken by Petrukha, who had already harnessed the horse and had come back to the cottage a few minutes before then and kept smiling all the while.

"There's a fable about that in Poolson," he said. "A father gives his sons a besom to break. They couldn't break it all at once, but twig by twig it was easy. It's the same here," he said with a broad smile. "Ready!" he added.

"If it's ready, let's go," said Vassily Andreich. "And as for dividing up, don't give in, grandpa. You earned it, you're the master. Turn it over to the justice of the peace. He'll show what's right."

"He's so ornery, so ornery," the old man kept repeating in his tearful voice, "there's no getting on with him. Just like the devil's got into him."

Nikita, meanwhile, having finished his fifth glass of tea, still did not turn it upside down but laid it on its side, hoping they would give him a sixth. But there was no more water in the samovar, and the hostess did not pour him more, and Vassily Andreich began to dress. There was nothing to be done. Nitika also got up, put his thoroughly nibbled piece of sugar back into the sugar bowl, wiped his sweaty face, and went to put on his coat.

Having dressed, he sighed deeply, and, after thanking his hosts and taking leave of them, went out of the warm, bright room into the dark, cold front hall, rumbling from the wind that wanted to tear its way inside, and with snow blowing in through the cracks in the shaking outer door, and from there to the dark yard.

Petrukha in his fur coat stood with his horse in the middle of the yard and, smiling, recited verses from Paulson. He said: "The storm in darkness hides the sky, sending snowy gusts awhirl, now like a wild beast it cries, now it weeps like a little girl."[6]

Nikita nodded his head approvingly and sorted out the reins.

The old man, seeing Vassily Andreich off, brought a lantern to the front hall to light the way, but the lantern was immediately blown out. Even in the yard one could see that the blizzard had picked up considerably.

"Well, what weather," thought Vassily Andreich. "Very likely we won't make it, but no help for it, it's business! And I'm all ready, and the host's horse is harnessed. We'll make it, God willing!"

The old host also thought they should not be going, but he had already urged them to stay, and they had not listened. There was no point in asking again. "Maybe it's old age that's got me so timid, and they'll make it all right," he thought. "And at least we'll get to bed on time. Without any fuss."

Petrukha was not even thinking of any danger: he knew the road and the whole area so well, and besides, the line "sending snowy gusts awhirl" stirred him by expressing perfectly what was happening outside. Nikita did not want to go at all, but he had long since grown used to not having his own will and serving others, and so no one held back the departing men.

V

VASSILY ANDREICH WENT to the sleigh, barely making out where they were in the darkness, got into it, and took the reins.

"Go in front!" he shouted.

Petrukha, kneeling in the low, wide sleigh, started his horse. Mukhorty, who had long been neighing, sensing a mare ahead of him, tore after her, and they drove out to the street. Again they drove through the settlement by the same road, past the same yard with frozen laundry on the line, which now could not be seen; past the same barn, which was now buried almost to the roof, and from which snow poured endlessly; past the same gloomily rustling, whistling, and swaying willows; and again drove into that snowy sea raging above and below. The wind was so strong that when it blew from the side and the riders sailed into it, it made the sleigh list and pushed the horse sideways. Ahead of them, Petrukha drove his good mare at a shambling trot and kept shouting cheerily. Mukhorty went tearing after her.

Having gone like that for some ten minutes, Petrukha turned around and shouted something. Neither Vassily Andreich nor Nikita could hear because of the wind, but they guessed that they had come to the turn. Indeed, Petrukha turned to the right, and the wind, previously from the side, was again in their faces, and something black could be seen through the snow to the right. It was the little bush at the turn.

"Well, Godspeed!"

"Thanks, Petrukha!"

"The storm in darkness hides the sky," Petrukha cried and vanished.

"See what a versifier," said Vassily Andreich, and he snapped the reins.

"Yes, a fine fellow, a real muzhik," said Nikita.

They drove on.

Nikita, wrapped up and drawing his head down into his shoulders so that his small beard lay on his neck, sat silently, trying not to lose the warmth he had accumulated in the cottage over tea. Ahead of him he saw the straight lines of the shafts, which kept deceiving him and appearing like a smooth road, the tossing rump of the horse with its knotted tail blown sideways, and further ahead the high shaft-bow and the horse's swaying head and neck with its flying mane. From time to time his eyes caught sight of stakes, and he knew that so far they had been following the road and there was nothing for him to do.

Vassily Andreich drove, letting the horse himself keep to the road. But Mukhorty, though he had had some rest in the village, ran reluctantly and seemed to get off the road, so that Vassily Andreich had to correct him several times.

"Here's one stake to the right, here's another, here's a third," Vassily Andreich counted, "and here's the forest ahead," he thought, peering at something that showed black ahead of him. But what had seemed like a forest to him was only a bush. They passed by the bush, went some fifty yards further—there was no fourth stake, nor any forest. "It should be the forest any minute now," thought Vassily Andreich and, excited by the drink and the tea, not stopping, he snapped the reins, and the good, submissive animal obeyed and, now at an amble, now at a brief trot, raced off where he had been sent, though he knew that where he had been sent was not at all where he ought to be going. Ten minutes went by, there was no forest.

"We've gone astray again!" said Vassily Andreich, stopping the horse.

Nikita silently got out of the sleigh and, holding his coat, which now clung to him with the wind, now flew open and wanted to tear itself off him, went to flounder about in the snow; he went to one side, he went to the other. Three times or so he completely disappeared from sight. At last he came back and took the reins from Vassily Andreich's hands.

"We must go to the right," he said sternly and resolutely, turning the horse.

"Well, to the right, so go to the right," said Vassily Andreich, surrendering the reins and tucking his chilled hands into his sleeves.

Nikita did not reply.

"Now, little friend, get to work!" he shouted to the horse; but, despite the snapping of the reins, the horse only went at a walk.

The snow was knee-deep in some places, and the sleigh jerked fitfully with each movement of the horse.

Nikita took the whip that hung in front and whipped the horse. The good horse, unaccustomed to whipping, plunged ahead, went into a trot, but at once changed back to an amble and then a walk. They went on like that for about five minutes. It was so dark and so smoky above and below that at times the shaft-bow could not be seen. The sleigh seemed at times to be standing in place and the fields rushing backwards. Suddenly the horse stopped abruptly, obviously feeling something wrong in front of him. Nikita again jumped out lightly, dropping the reins, and went ahead of the horse to see why he had stopped; but just as he tried to take a step in front of the horse, his feet slipped and he went sliding down some steep slope.

"Whoa, whoa, whoa," he said to himself, falling and trying to stop, but he could not, and stopped only when his feet met with the dense mass of snow heaped up at the bottom of the ravine.

A snowdrift hanging on the edge of the slope, dislodged by Nikita's fall, poured down on him and got behind his collar . . .

"So that's how you are!" Nikita said reproachfully, addressing the snowdrift and the ravine, and shaking the snow from behind his collar.

"Nikita! Hey, Nikita!" Vassily Andreich shouted from above.

But Nikita did not respond.

He had no time: he shook off the snow, then looked for the whip he had dropped when he slid down the slope. Having found the whip, he tried to climb straight back up the way he had slid down, but the ascent was impossible; he kept sliding back down, so that from the bottom he had to search for a way up. Some twenty feet from the place where he had slid down, he managed with difficulty to climb up the hill on all fours and went along the ridge of the ravine to the place where the horse should have been. He saw no horse or sleigh; but as he was walking against the wind, he heard, before he saw them, the cries of Vassily Andreich and the whinnies of Mukhorty, who were calling to him.

"I'm coming, I'm coming, what are you hooting about!" he said.

Only when he came quite close to the sleigh did he see the horse and Vassily Andreich standing beside it, looking enormous.

"Where the devil did you disappear to? We've got to go back. At least we'll get to Grishkino again," the master angrily began to reproach Nikita.

"I'd be glad to turn back, Vassily Andreich, but which way do we go? There's this big ravine here, fall into it and there's no getting out. I made such a fine job of it, I could barely drag myself out."

"But we're not just going to stand here, are we? We've got to go somewhere," said Vassily Andreich.

Nikita made no reply. He sat down in the sleigh with his back to the wind, took off his boots, shook out the snow that had got into them, and, picking up some straw, carefully plugged a hole in the left boot from inside.

Vassily Andreich was silent, as if leaving everything to Nikita now. After putting his boots back on, Nikita pulled his legs into the sleigh, put his mittens on again, took the reins, and turned the horse along the ravine. Before they had gone a hundred paces, the horse baulked again. In front of him there was again a ravine.

Nikita got out again and again went floundering through the snow. He walked about for a long time. At last he appeared on the opposite side from where he had started.

"Andreich, are you alive?" he cried.

"Here!" responded Vassily Andreich. "Well, what?"

"Can't make anything out. It's dark. Ravines of some kind. Got to drive into the wind again."

They drove on again, Nikita walked about again, floundering through the snow. Again he sat down, again he floundered about, and finally, out of breath, he stopped by the sleigh.

"Well, what?" asked Vassily Andreich.

"I'm all worn out! And the horse keeps stopping."

"So what are we to do?"

"Wait a bit."

Nikita left again and soon came back.

"Keep behind me," he said, getting in front of the horse.

Vassily Andreich no longer gave any orders, but obediently did what Nikita told him.

"This way, after me!" shouted Nikita, stepping quickly to the right and seizing Mukhorty by the reins and leading him down somewhere into a snowdrift.

The horse baulked at first, then plunged forward, hoping to jump over the drift, but could not make it and sank into it up to his collar.

"Get out!" Nikita shouted to Vassily Andreich, who went on sitting in the sleigh, and, taking hold of one shaft, he began to push the sleigh towards the horse. "It's a bit hard, brother," he said to Mukhorty, "but there's no help for it, just give a try! Hup, hup, a little more!" he cried.

The horse plunged forward once, twice, but still failed to get out, and sat down again, as if thinking something over.

"No, brother, that's no good," Nikita admonished Mukhorty. "Once more now."

Again Nikita pulled on the shaft on his side; Vassily Andreich did the same on the other side. The horse moved his head, then suddenly plunged on.

"Hup, now, don't worry, you won't sink," cried Nikita.

One leap, a second, a third, and the horse finally got out of the snow-drift and stopped, breathing heavily and shaking off snow. Nikita wanted to lead him further, but Vassily Andreich got so out of breath in his two fur coats that he could not walk and collapsed into the sleigh.

"Let me catch my breath," he said, loosening the kerchief he had tied around his coat collar in the village.

"Never mind, you lie there," said Nikita, "I'll lead him," and, with Vassily Andreich in the sleigh, he led the horse by the bridle down some ten paces and then slightly up and stopped.

The place where Nikita stopped was not in the hollow, where snow blowing off the hillocks and settling there could bury them completely, but was still partly shielded from snow by the edge of the ravine. There were moments when the wind seemed to drop a little, but that did not last long, and afterwards, as if to make up for this respite, the storm swooped down with ten times the force, and tore and whirled still more angrily. One such gust of wind struck just as Vassily Andreich, having caught his breath, got out of the sleigh and went up to Nikita, to talk over what to do. They both involuntarily ducked their heads and did not speak, waiting for the fury of the gust to pass. Mukhorty also laid his ears back in displeasure and shook his head. When the gust of wind had passed slightly, Nikita took off his mittens, tucked them under his sash, breathed on his hands, and began to remove the reins from the shaft-bow.

"What's that you're doing?" asked Vassily Andreich.

"Unharnessing, what else? I've got no strength left," Nikita said, as if apologizing.

"But won't we get somewhere?"

"No, we won't, we'll only exhaust the horse. Look at the dear heart, he's beside himself," said Nikita, pointing to the horse standing there submissively, ready for anything, his steep and wet flanks heaving heavily. "We'll have to spend the night," he said, as if he was preparing to spend the night at a roadside inn, and he started unfastening the hame straps.

The hames sprang open.

"But won't we freeze?" said Vassily Andreich.

"So? If you freeze, you can't say no," said Nikita.

VI

VASSILY ANDREICH WAS quite warm in his two fur coats, especially after the way he had floundered in the snowdrift, but a chill ran down his spine when he realized that they indeed had to spend the night there. To calm himself, he got into the sleigh and began taking out cigarettes and matches.

Nikita meanwhile was unharnessing the horse. He undid the girth, the saddle strap, removed the reins, took off the tugs, pulled out the shaft-bow, and never stopped speaking words of encouragement to the horse.

"Well, out you come, out you come," he said, leading him out of the shafts. "We'll tie you up here. I'll give you some straw and unbridle you," he said, while doing what he was saying. "You'll have a bite to eat, that'll cheer you up."

But Mukhorty obviously was not to be calmed down by Nikita's talk and felt anxious; he shifted from foot to foot, huddled up to the sleigh, standing with his rump to the wind, and rubbed his head against Nikita's sleeve.

As if only so as not to refuse Nikita's treat of straw, which Nikita put under his muzzle, Mukhorty impetuously snatched a wisp of straw from the sleigh, but at once decided that now was no time for straw, dropped it, and the wind immediately blew it about, carried it off, and covered it with snow.

"Now we'll set up a marker," said Nikita, turning the sleigh face to the wind, and, tying the shafts together with the saddle strap, he raised them up and pulled them towards the front of the sleigh. "If we get snowed in, good people will see the shafts and dig us out," said Nikita, slapping his mittens together and putting them on. "That's how the old folks taught us."

Meanwhile Vassily Andreich, spreading the skirts of his coat and using them as a shield, was striking one sulphur match after another against a steel box, but his hands were shaking and the matches were blown out by the wind, some before they flared up, some just as he put them to the cigarette. Finally one match began to burn and lit up for a moment the fur of his coat, his hand with a gold signet ring on the bent index finger, and the snow-covered oat straw sticking up from under the burlap, and the cigarette caught. He dragged on it eagerly a couple of times, inhaled, let the smoke out through his moustaches, was about to inhale again, but the burning tobacco was blown off and carried away to where the straw had gone.

But even those few puffs of tobacco smoke cheered Vassily Andreich up.

"If it's spend the night, it's spend the night!" he said resolutely. "Wait, now, I'll make us a flag, too," he said, picking up the kerchief he had thrown into the sleigh when he untied his collar, and, taking off his gloves, he stood in front of the sleigh and, stretching out to reach the saddle strap, tied the kerchief to it in a tight knot near the shaft.

The kerchief at once began to flutter desperately, now sticking to the shaft, now suddenly pulling away, stretching out, and flapping.

"See how clever," said Vassily Andreich, admiring his work, as he lowered himself into the sleigh. "It would be warmer together, but there's no room for two," he said.

"I'll find a place," replied Nikita, "only we've got to cover the horse, he's all in a sweat, the dear heart. Give it here," he added, and, going to the sleigh, he pulled the burlap from under Vassily Andreich.

And, having taken the burlap, he folded it in two and, first throwing off the girth and removing the gig saddle, covered Mukhorty with it.

"It'll be all the warmer for you, little fool," he said, putting the gig saddle and girth back on over the burlap. "And you won't be needing the sacking, will you? Give me some straw, too," said Nikita, finishing that task and going back to the sleigh.

And, having taken both from under Vassily Andreich, Nikita went behind the sleigh, dug a small hole for himself in the snow, put straw in it, and, pulling his hat down, wrapping himself in his kaftan, and covering himself with sacking, he sat on the spread straw, leaning against the back of the sleigh, which shielded him from the wind and snow.

Vassily Andreich shook his head disapprovingly at what Nikita was doing, as he generally did not approve of peasant ignorance and stupidity, and began to settle himself for the night.

He evened out the remaining straw in the sleigh, put a thicker layer under his side, and, tucking his hands into his sleeves, nestled his head in the corner of the sleigh, towards the front, to shelter himself from the wind.

He did not feel like sleeping. He lay there and thought: thought of ever the same thing, which constituted the sole aim, meaning, joy, and pride of his life—of how much money he had made and might still make; how much money other people he knew made and had, and how those other people had made and were making their money, and how he, like those others, might still make a great deal of money. The purchase of the Goryachkino woods constituted a matter of great importance to him. He hoped to make maybe ten thousand straight off on that woods. And mentally he began to evaluate the woods he had seen in the autumn, in which he had counted all the trees on five acres of land.

"The oaks will go for runners. For timber, too, needless to say. And there'll be some hundred cord of firewood per acre," he said to himself. "At the worst I'll end up with eighty-five roubles per acre. There are a hundred and fifty acres, so that means a hundred times eighty plus a hundred times five, plus fifty times eighty, plus fifty times five." He could see that it came to over twelve thousand, but without an abacus he could not work it out precisely. "All the same I won't give him ten thousand, but more like eight, and that minus the clearings. I'll grease the surveyor's palm—a hundred, a hundred and fifty. He'll measure me up some fifteen acres of clearings. He'll give it to me for eight. I'll give him three thousand in cash. He'll soften all right," he thought, feeling the wallet in his pocket with his forearm. "And how we went astray after the turn, God knows! There should be a forest and a watch-house here. We should hear the dogs. But the cursed things don't bark when they ought to." He took his collar away from his ear and began to listen; he could hear the same whistling of the wind, the fluttering and snapping of the kerchief in the shafts, and the lashing of the falling snow against the bast of the sleigh. He covered himself again.

"If I'd known, I would have spent the night. Well, it's all the same, we'll get there tomorrow. Only one extra day. In such weather they won't go there either." And he remembered that by the ninth he was to get money from the butcher for the wethers. "He was going to come himself; he won't find me—my wife won't be able to take the money. Very ignorant. No way with people," he went on thinking, recalling how she had not known how to behave with the police officer who had been their guest at yesterday's feast. "You know—a woman! Where has she ever seen anything? What was our house when my parents were alive? Nothing much, rich village peasants: a grist mill and an inn—that was the whole property. And what have I done in fifteen years? A shop, two pot-houses, a flouring mill, a granary, two rented estates, a house and barn with iron roofs," he recalled with pride. "A far cry from my father! Who makes noise in the district these days? Brekhunov.

"And why so? Because I stick to business, I try hard, not like others, who lie about or busy themselves with stupidities. I don't sleep nights. Blizzard or no blizzard—I go. So my business gets done. They think making money's just a joke. No, you've got to work at it, rack your brain. Spend the night in the fields like this and not sleep all night. So that the pillow whirls under your head from thinking," he reflected with pride. "They think people make it through luck. Look, the Mironovs are in the millions now. And why? Hard work. God will give. If only God gives you health."

And the thought that he, too, could be a millionaire like Mironov, who had started from nothing, so excited Vassily Andreich that he felt the need to talk with someone. But there was no one to talk with . . . If only he could get to Goryachkino, he would have a talk with the landowner, he would make him see straight.

"Look how it's blowing! It'll bury us so we'll never get out in the morning!" he thought, listening to the gusts of wind blowing at the front of the sleigh, bending it, and lashing its bast with snow. He raised himself slightly and looked around: in the white, undulating darkness he could see only the black shape of Mukhorty's head, and his back covered by the fluttering burlap, and his thick, knotted tail; but around on all sides, before, behind, there was one and the same uniform, white, undulating darkness, which sometimes seemed to grow a bit lighter, and sometimes thickened still more.

"And I was wrong to listen to Nikita," he thought. "We ought to have gone on, we'd have got somewhere anyway. At least we could have gone back to Grishkino and spent the night at Taras's. Now we've got to sit here all night. But what was it that was so nice? Ah, yes, that God gives to those who work hard, not to idlers, lie-abeds, or fools. And I must smoke!" He sat up, took out his cigarette case, lay on his stomach, shielding the fire from the wind with the skirt of his coat, but the wind found a way in and blew out one match after another. At last he managed to light one and began to smoke. The fact that he had brought it off gladdened him greatly. Though the wind smoked more of the cigarette than he did, he still took about three drags and began to feel cheerful again. He huddled against the back of the sleigh and again began to recall, to dream, and, quite unexpectedly, suddenly became oblivious and dozed off.

But suddenly it was if something nudged and roused him. Whether it was Mukhorty pulling straw from under him, or something inside him that stirred him, in any case he woke up, and his heart started pounding so rapidly and so hard that it seemed to him that the sled was shaking under him. He opened his eyes. Around him everything was the same, only it seemed brighter. "It's getting brighter," he thought, "it shouldn't be long till morning." But he remembered at once that it was brighter only because the moon had risen. He raised himself, looking first at the horse. Mukhorty still stood with his rump to the wind and was shaking all over. The snow-covered burlap was turned back on one side, the girth had also slipped sideways, and the snow-covered head with its wind-blown forelock and mane was now more visible. Vassily Andreich bent over and peered behind. Nikita was still sitting in the same position in which he had sat down. His legs and the sacking he had put over himself were thickly covered with snow. "The muzhik may well freeze; he's got such poor clothes on him. I'd have to answer for him. Muddleheaded folk. Real ignorance," thought Vassily Andreich, and he was going to take the burlap off the horse and cover Nikita, but it was too cold to get up and move, and he was afraid the horse, too, might freeze. "Why did I take him? It was all just her stupidity!" thought Vassily Andreich, remembering his unloved wife, and he rolled back again into his former place at the front of the sleigh. "My uncle once sat all night in the snow like this," he recalled, "and nothing happened. Well, but Sebastian got dug out," another case at once presented itself to him. "Dead he was, all stiff, like a frozen carcass.

"If I'd stayed overnight in Grishkino, nothing would have happened." And, wrapping himself up carefully, so that the warmth of the fur would not be wasted anywhere, but would keep him warm all over, at the neck, at the knees, at the soles of his feet—he closed his eyes, trying to fall asleep again. But no matter how he tried now, he could not become oblivious, but, on the contrary, felt completely alert and animated. Again he began counting his gains, the debts people owed him; again he began boasting to himself and rejoicing over himself and his situation—but now it was all constantly interrupted by a sneaking fear and the vexing thought of why he had not stayed for the night in Grishkino. "That would be just the thing: lying on a bench, nice and warm." He turned over several times, lay down, tried to find a position that was more comfortable and shielded from the wind, but it all seemed uncomfortable to him; again he would sit up, change position, wrap his legs, close his eyes, and lie still. But either his cramped feet in their stout felt boots began to ache, or it blew on him from somewhere, and having lain there for a short while, he would again remind himself with vexation of how he might now be lying peacefully in the warm cottage in Grishkino, and again he would sit up, turn over, wrap himself, and lie down again.

Once it seemed to Vassily Andreich that he heard a distant crowing of cocks. He was overjoyed, opened his coat, and began straining to hear, but no matter how he strained his hearing, he heard nothing except the sound of the wind whistling in the shafts and flapping the kerchief, and of snow lashing the bast of the sleigh.

Nikita sat all the while just as he had sat in the evening, not stirring and not even answering Vassily Andreich, who called to him a couple of times. "He couldn't care less. Must be asleep," Vassily Andreich thought vexedly, peering over the back of the sleigh at Nikita, who was thickly covered with snow.

Vassily Andreich got up and lay down some twenty times. It seemed to him that the night would never end. "It must be near morning by now," he thought once, sitting up and looking around. "Let's have a look at my watch. It'll be cold uncovering myself. Well, but if I know it's getting on towards morning, I'll be more cheerful. We'll start harnessing up." In the depths of his soul, Vassily Andreich knew that it could not be morning yet, but he was becoming more and more scared, and he wanted both to test and to deceive himself. He carefully undid the hooks of his fur coat and, putting his hand in his bosom, fumbled there for a long time before he got to his waistcoat. With great difficulty he took out his silver watch with enamel flowers and began to look. Without light, nothing could be seen. He lay down again, propping himself on his elbows and knees, as he had done when lighting a cigarette, took out his matches, and began to strike one. This time he set to work more precisely, and, feeling with his fingers for the match with the biggest amount of phosphorus, he lit it the first time. Putting the face of the watch to the light, he looked and could not believe his eyes . . . It was only ten minutes past midnight. The whole night was still ahead of him.

"Oh, it's a long night!" thought Vassily Andreich, feeling a chill run down his spine, and, hooking his coat and covering himself up again, he pressed himself into the corner of the sleigh, preparing to wait patiently. Suddenly, through the monotonous sound of the wind, he clearly heard some new, living sound. The sound increased regularly and, having reached perfect distinctness, began as regularly to diminish. There was no doubt that it was a wolf. And the wolf was so close that the changes in his voice as he moved his jaws could be clearly heard on the wind. Vassily Andreich opened his collar and listened attentively. Mukhorty also strained to listen, moving his ears, and when the wolf finished his part, he shifted his feet and snorted in warning. After that Vassily Andreich not only could not fall asleep, but could not even calm down. No matter how he tried to think of his accounts and affairs, and of his fame, and of his importance and wealth, fear took hold of him more and more, and all his thoughts were dominated by and mixed with the thought of why he had not stayed overnight in Grishkino.

"God keep it, the woods, there are enough deals without it, thank God. Ah, I should have spent the night!" he said to himself. "They say it's drunk ones that freeze to death," he thought. "And I drank." And paying heed to his sensations, he felt he was beginning to tremble, not knowing himself why he was trembling—from cold or from fear. He tried to cover himself and lie down as before, but he could no longer do it. He could not stay put, he wanted to get up, to undertake something, so as to stifle the fear that was rising in him, against which he felt powerless. He took out his cigarettes and matches again, but there were only three matches left, and all of them bad. All three fizzled without catching fire.

"Ah, devil take you, cursed thing, go to hell!" he swore, not knowing at whom himself, and flung away the crumpled cigarette. He was about to fling away the matchbox as well, but stopped the movement of his arm and put the box in his pocket. He was overcome with such anxiety that he could no longer stay put. He got out of the sleigh, turned his back to the wind, and began rewinding the sash around him tighter and lower down.

"Why lie there waiting for death! Mount up and be off," suddenly came to his head. "A mounted horse won't stop. As for him," he thought of Nikita, "it's all the same if he dies. What kind of life has he got! He won't feel sorry for his life, but for me, thank God, there's something to live for . . ."

And, having untethered the horse, he threw the bridle over his head and went to jump onto him, but his fur coats and boots were so heavy that he fell off. Then he stood on the sleigh and tried to get onto the horse from there. But the sleigh rocked under his weight and he fell again. Finally, the third time, he moved the horse up to the sleigh, and, standing carefully on its edge, managed to lie belly-down across the horse's back. After lying like that for a while, he shifted himself forward once, twice, and finally threw one leg over the horse's back and sat up, the soles of his feet resting on the horizontal straps of the girth. The lurch of the sleigh as it rocked awoke Nikita, and he sat up, and it seemed to Vassily Andreich that he said something.

"Listen to you fools! What, should I perish like this, for nothing?" cried Vassily Andreich, and, tucking the flying skirts of his fur coat under his knees, he turned the horse and urged him away from the sleigh in the direction in which he supposed the forest and the watch-house should be.

VII

NIKITA, ever since he sat down, covered with sacking, behind the rear of the sleigh, had been sitting motionlessly. He, like all people who live with nature and know want, was patient and could wait calmly for hours, even days, without feeling either alarm or vexation. He heard the master call him but did not reply, because he did not want to move and reply. Though he was still warm from the tea he had drunk, and because he had moved a lot, floundering through the snowdrifts, he knew that this warmth would not last long, and that he would no longer be able to warm himself by moving, because he felt as tired as a horse feels when it stops and cannot go further, despite any whipping, and the master sees that he must feed it so that it will be able to work again. One of his feet, in the torn boot, was cold, and he could no longer feel the big toe. And, besides that, his whole body was growing colder and colder. The thought that he could, and even in all probability would, die that night occurred to him, but this thought seemed neither especially unpleasant nor especially frightening to him. This thought did not seem especially unpleasant to him, because his whole life was not a continuous feast, but, on the contrary, a ceaseless servitude, which was beginning to weary him. And this thought was not especially frightening to him, because, besides masters like Vassily Andreich whom he had served here, he always felt himself dependent in this life on the chief master, the one who had sent him into this life, and he knew that, on dying, he would remain in the power of that same master, and that that master would not mistreat him. "It's a pity to abandon the accustomed, the usual? Well, no help for it, you'll have to get used to the new."

"Sins?" he thought and remembered his drunkenness, the drunk-up money, the mistreatment of his wife, the swearing, not going to church, not keeping the fasts, and all that the priest reprimanded him for at confession. "Sins, sure. But did I visit them on myself? It's clear God made me this way. Well, sins then! No getting away from them!"

So he thought at first about what might happen to him that night, and then he no longer went back to those thoughts, but gave himself to reflections that came to him of themselves. Now he remembered Marfa's visit, and the workers' drunkenness, and his refusal to drink, then the present journey and Taras's cottage, and the conversation about dividing up, then about his lad, and about Mukhorty, who would now get warm under the horse-cloth, then about his master, who made the sleigh creak turning over in it. "I don't suppose the dear heart's glad he went either. The kind of life he's got, you don't want to die. Not so the likes of us." And all these recollections began to overlap and mix up in his head, and he fell asleep.

When Vassily Andreich, getting onto the horse, rocked the sleigh, and the rear of it, against which Nikita leaned his back, was thrown sideways and its runner hit him in the back, he woke up and was forced willy-nilly to change his position. Straightening his legs with difficulty and throwing the snow off them, he got up, and at once an excruciating cold pierced his whole body. Realizing what was happening, he wanted Vassily Andreich to leave him the burlap, which the horse did not need now, so as to cover himself, and shouted that to him.

But Vassily Andreich did not stop and disappeared into the snowy dust.

Left alone, Nikita thought a moment about what he was to do. He did not feel strong enough to go in search of habitations. To sit in his old place was no longer possible—it was all buried in snow. And he felt he would not get warm in the sleigh, because he had nothing to cover himself with, and his kaftan and coat now did not warm him at all. He was as cold as if he were just in his shirt. It felt eerie to him. "Dear Father in heaven!" he said, and was reassured by the awareness that he was not alone, that someone heard him and would not abandon him. He sighed deeply and, without taking the sacking from his head, got into the sleigh and lay down in his master's place.

But in the sleigh, too, he could not get warm. At first he shivered all over, then the shivering went away and he gradually began to lose consciousness. Whether he was dying or falling asleep he did not know, but he felt equally prepared for the one and for the other.

VIII

MEANWHILE VASSILY ANDREICH, with his feet and with the ends of the reins, urged the horse on towards where he supposed for some reason that the forest and the watch-house would be. The snow blinded his eyes, and the wind seemed to want to stop him, but, leaning forward and constantly wrapping himself tighter in his fur coat and tucking it under him, which made it hard to sit on the cold gig saddle, he kept urging the horse on. The horse, with difficulty, but obediently, ambled on where he was sent.

For some five minutes he rode, as it seemed to him, straight ahead, seeing nothing except the horse's head and the white waste, and hearing nothing except the wind whistling past the horse's ears and the collar of his own coat.

Suddenly something loomed up black ahead of him. His heart began to beat joyfully, and he rode towards that black thing, already seeing in it the walls of village houses. But the black thing was not still, but all astir, and was not a village, but a tall clump of wormwood growing on a boundary, sticking up from the snow and desperately tossing about under the pressure of the wind bending it all to one side and whistling through it. And for some reason the sight of this clump of wormwood tormented by the merciless wind made Vassily Andreich shudder, and he hastened to urge the horse on, not noticing that as he rode up to the wormwood he changed his former direction completely and was now urging his horse in a totally different direction, still imagining he was going towards where the watch-house should be. But the horse kept bearing to the right, and therefore he kept on turning him to the left.

Again something loomed up black ahead of him. He rejoiced, confident that now it was certainly the village. But it was again a boundary overgrown with wormwood. Again the dry weeds tossed just as desperately, for some reason filling Vassily Andreich with fear. But not only were they the same weeds—beside them were hoofprints that the wind was covering over. Vassily Andreich stopped, bent down, looked closely: they were horse tracks, lightly covered with snow, and they could be no one else's but his. He was obviously going in a circle, and over a small space. "I'll perish like this!" he thought, and, not to give way to fear, he began urging his horse on still harder, peering into the white, snowy murk, in which points of light seemed to appear to him, disappearing at once as soon as he peered at them. Once he seemed to hear the barking dogs or the howling of wolves, but the sounds were so faint and indistinct that he did not know whether he heard them or only imagined them, and, stopping, he began to listen.

Suddenly some dreadful, deafening cry rang out by his ears, and everything shuddered and shook under him. Vassily Andreich clutched the horse by the neck, but the horse's neck was also shaking, and the dreadful cry became still more terrible. For a few seconds Vassily Andreich could not come to his senses and realize what had happened. What had happened was only that Mukhorty, either encouraging himself or calling for help, had neighed in his loud, ringing voice. "Pah, confound it, the damned beast scared me!" Vassily Andreich said to himself. But even having realized the true cause of his fear, he could no longer drive it away.

"I must think things over, steady myself," he said to himself, and at the same time he could not help himself and kept urging the horse on, not noticing that he was now riding with the wind, not against it. His body, especially between the legs, where it was uncovered and touched the gig saddle, was chilled and ached, his arms and legs trembled, and he gasped for breath. He sees he is perishing in the middle of this dreadful snowy waste, and sees no means of salvation.

Suddenly the horse crashed down under him and, sinking into a snowdrift, began to struggle and fell on his side. Vassily Andreich jumped off him, wrenching askew the girth on which his foot rested and the gig saddle, which he held to as he jumped off. As soon as Vassily Andreich jumped off, the horse righted himself, plunged forward, made a leap, another, and, neighing again, dragging the trailing burlap and girth, disappeared from sight, leaving Vassily Andreich alone in the snowdrift. Vassily Andreich rushed after him, but the snow was so deep and the coats on him were so heavy that each leg sank over the knee, and, having gone no more than twenty steps, he got out of breath and stopped. "The woods, the wethers, the rent, the shop, the pot-houses, the house and barn with the iron roofs, the heir," he thought, "what will become of it all? What is this? It can't be!" flashed in his head. And for some reason he recalled the wind-tossed wormwood, which he had passed twice, and such terror came over him that he did not believe in the reality of what was happening to him. He thought: "Isn't all this a dream?" and wanted to wake up, but there was nowhere to wake up in. This was real snow that lashed him in the face, and poured over him, and felt cold on his right hand, the glove for which he had lost, and this was a real waste, in which he now remained alone, like that wormwood, await-ing an inevitable, speedy, and senseless death.

"Queen of Heaven, holy father Nicholas, teacher of abstinence," he remembered yesterday's prayers, and the icon with its blackened face in the gilded casing, and the candles he had been selling to set before the icon, which had been brought back to him at once and he had put away, barely burnt, in a box. And he started asking that same Nicholas the Wonderworker to save him, promising him a prayer service and candles.

But he realized at once, clearly, unquestionably, that that face, the casing, the candles, the priest, the prayer services—all of it was very important and necessary there in church, but that here they could do nothing for him, that between those candles and prayer services and his wretched present position there was not and could not be any connection. "I mustn't be downcast," he thought. "I must follow the horse's tracks, or they, too, will get covered over" came to his head. "He'll lead me out, and I may even catch him. Only I mustn't hurry or I'll get winded and that will be the end of me." But despite his intention to go slowly, he rushed forward and ran, constantly falling, getting up, and falling again. The horse's tracks were already becoming barely visible in places where the snow was not deep. "It's the end of me," thought Vassily Andreich, "I'll lose the trail and not catch up with the horse." But at that same moment, looking ahead, he saw something black. It was Mukhorty, and not only Mukhorty, but the sleigh, and the shafts with the kerchief. Mukhorty, girth and burlap askew, now stood, not in his former place, but closer to the shafts, and bobbed his head, pulled down by the reins he had stepped over. It turned out that Vassily Andreich had sunk into the same hollow in which he and Nikita had sunk, that the horse had been carrying him back to the sleigh, and that he had jumped off him no more than fifty paces from where the sleigh was.

IX

WALLOWING UP to the sleigh, Vassily Andreich took hold of it and stood motionless like that for a long time, trying to calm down and catch his breath. Nikita was not in his former place, but something already covered with snow was lying in the sleigh, and Vassily Andreich guessed that this was Nikita. Vassily Andreich's fear was now gone completely, and if he was afraid of anything, it was that terrible state of fear he had experienced on the horse and especially when he was left alone in the snowdrift. He had at all costs to keep that fear away from him, and to keep it away he had to do something, to busy himself with something. And therefore the first thing he did was turn his back to the wind and untie his fur coat. Then, once he had caught his breath a little, he shook the snow out of his boots and out of his left glove, the right one being hopelessly lost and buried by now under a foot of snow; then he tied his sash again, tight and low down, as he used to do when coming out of the shop to buy grain that the muzhiks brought in carts, and prepared for action. The first task that presented itself to him was to free the horse's leg. Vassily Andreich did just that and, having released the rein, tied Mukhorty again to the cramp-iron at the front of the sleigh in his former place and started going behind the horse to straighten the girth, the gig saddle, and the burlap on him; but just then he saw something move in the sleigh, and Nikita's head rose from under the snow that covered it. Obviously with great effort, the already freezing Nikita raised himself, sat up, and waved his hand before his nose somehow strangely, as if driving flies away. He waved his hand and said something, calling Vassily Andreich, as it seemed to him. Vassily Andreich abandoned the burlap without having straightened it and went to the sleigh.

"What do you want?" he asked. "What are you saying?"

"I'm d-d-dying, that's what," Nikita said with difficulty, his voice faltering. "Give my pay to my lad or the woman, it's all the same."

"What, are you frozen?" asked Vassily Andreich.

"It's my death, I feel it . . . forgive me, for Christ's sake . . ." Nikita said in a tearful voice, while he went on waving his hands in front of his face as if driving flies away.

Vassily Andreich stood silent and motionless for half a minute, then suddenly, with the same resoluteness with which he used to strike a deal on a profitable purchase, he stepped back, pushed up his coat sleeves, and with both hands began scraping the snow from Nikita and out of the sleigh. Having scraped off the snow, Vassily Andreich hastily untied his sash, spread out his fur coat, and, pushing Nikita over, lay on top of him, covering him not only with his coat, but with his whole warm, flushed body. Tucking the sides of his coat between the bast of the sleigh and Nikita, and holding the skirt of it with his knees, Vassily Andreich lay face down like that, his head resting on the bast in front, and no longer heard either the movement of the horse or the whistling of the storm, but listened only to Nikita's breathing. At first Nikita lay motionless for a long time, then he sighed loudly and stirred.

"So there, and you said you were dying. Lie still, get warm, that's how we . . ." Vassily Andreich began.

But, to his great surprise, he could not go on, because tears came to his eyes and his lower jaw trembled rapidly. He stopped speaking and only swallowed what kept rising in his throat. "I had a scare, clearly, got all weak," he thought to himself. But this weakness not only was not unpleasant, but afforded him some peculiar, never yet experienced joy.

"That's how we are," he kept saying to himself, experiencing some peculiar, solemn tenderness. For quite a long time he lay silently like that, wiping his eyes against the fur of his coat and tucking under his knee the right coat skirt that the wind kept turning back.

But he so passionately wanted to tell someone about his joyful state.

"Nikita!" he said.

"Nice, warm," he was answered from below.

"You know, brother, I nearly perished. And you'd have frozen, and I'd . . ."

But here again his cheekbones quivered, and his eyes again filled with tears, and he could not go on.

"Well, never mind," he thought. "About myself I know what I know."

And he fell silent. He lay like that for a long time.

He was warm underneath from Nikita, and warm above from the fur coat; only his hands, with which he held the skirts of his coat in place around Nikita's sides, and his legs, which kept being uncovered by the wind, were beginning to suffer from the cold. His right hand without the glove suffered especially. But he did not think about his legs or hands, but only about warming up the muzhik who lay under him.

He glanced several times at the horse and saw that his back was uncovered and the burlap and girth were lying on the snow, that he ought to get up and cover the horse, but he could not resolve to leave Nikita and disturb the joyful state he was in even for a moment. He no longer felt any fear.

"No way he'll get out of it," he said to himself about keeping the muzhik warm, with the same boastfulness with which he talked about his buying and selling.

Vassily Andreich lay like that for an hour, two hours, three hours, but he did not notice the time passing. At first there raced through his imagination various impressions of the blizzard, of the shafts and the horse under the shaft-bow, jogging in front of his eyes, and then he remembered Nikita lying under him; then recollections of the feast began to mix in, of his wife, the police officer, the candle table, and again of Nikita lying under the candle table; then he began to picture muzhiks, sellers and buyers, and white walls, and houses with iron roofs, under which Nikita was lying; then it all mixed together, one thing going into another, and, as the colours of the rainbow combine into one white light, all these impressions came together into one nothing, and he fell asleep. He slept for a long time without dreaming, but before dawn dreams appeared again. He pictured himself as if he were standing by the candle table, and Tikhon's wife was asking him for a five-kopeck candle for the feast, and he wants to take a candle and give it to her, but his hands do not rise, they are stuck in his pockets. He wants to go around the table, but his feet will not move, his new, just-cleaned galoshes are rooted to the stone floor, and he cannot lift them or get his feet out of them. And suddenly the candle table is no longer a candle table, but a bed, and Vassily Andreich sees himself lying on his belly on the candle table, that is, on his bed, in his house. And he lies on his bed and cannot get up, and he must get up, because Ivan Matveich, the police officer, is about to come for him, and he must go with Ivan Matveich either to bargain for the woods or to straighten the girth on Mukhorty. And he asks his wife: "Well, Nikolavna, has he come?" "No," she says, "he hasn't." And he hears someone drive up to the porch. That must be him. No, it passed by. "Nikolavna, hey, Nikolavna, what, he's still not here?" "No." And he lies on his bed and still cannot get up, and he keeps waiting, and this waiting is both eerie and joyful. And suddenly his joy is fulfilled: the one he has been waiting for comes, and he is not Ivan Matveich, the police officer, he is someone else, but the very one he has been waiting for. He has come and is calling him, and this one who is calling him is the same one who called out to him and told him to lie on Nikita. And Vassily Andreich is glad that this someone has come for him. "I'm coming!" he cries joyfully, and this cry rouses him. And he wakes up, but wakes up not at all as he fell asleep. He wants to get up—and cannot, wants to move his arm—and cannot, his leg—and also cannot. He wants to turn his head—even that he cannot do. And he is surprised, but not in the least upset by it. He understands that this is death, and is not in the least upset by that either. And he remembers that Nikita is lying under him, and that he is warm and alive, and it seems to him that he is Nikita, and Nikita is he, and that his life is not in him, but in Nikita. He strains his hearing and hears Nikita breathing and even faintly snoring. "Nikita's alive, which means I'm alive, too," he says triumphantly to himself.

And he remembers about his money, about his shop, the house, the buying and selling, and the Mironovs' millions; it is hard for him to understand why this man called Vassily Brekhunov was busy with all he was busy with. "Well, he didn't know what it was about," he thinks of Vassily Brekhunov. "He didn't know, but now I know. Now there's no mistake. *Now I know.*" And again he hears the call of the one who already called out to him. "I'm coming, I'm coming!" his whole being says joyfully, tenderly. And he feels that he is free and nothing holds him any more.

And Vassily Andreich no longer saw or heard or felt anything in this world.

All around was the same smoky dimness. The same whirls of snow blew up, covering the dead Vassily Andreich's coat, and all of the shivering Mukhorty, and the barely visible sleigh, and deep inside it, lying under his now dead master, the warm Nikita.

X

NIKITA WOKE UP before morning. He was roused again by the cold that began to pierce his back. He dreamed he was coming from the mill with a cartload of flour for his master and, crossing a brook, missed the bridge and got the cart mired. And he saw himself crawling under the cart and lifting it, straightening his back. But, wondrous thing! The cart did not move and became stuck to his back, and he could neither lift the cart nor get out from under it. His whole lower back was crushed. And it was so cold! Clearly, he had to crawl out. "Enough of that," he says to whoever is pressing the cart down on his back. "Unload the sacks!" But the cart presses down colder and colder, and suddenly there is some peculiar knocking, and he wakes up completely and remembers everything. The cold cart is his dead, frozen master lying on him. And the knocking is Mukhorty, striking the sleigh twice with his hoof.

"Andreich, hey, Andreich!" Nikita, straining his back, calls out warily to his master, already sensing the truth.

But Andreich does not respond, and his belly and legs are hard, and cold, and heavy as weights.

"All over, must be. God rest his soul!" thinks Nikita.

He turns his head, digs through the snow in front of him, and opens his eyes. Daylight. The wind whistles in the shafts as before, the snow pours down as before, with the only difference that it does not lash against the bast of the sleigh, but noiselessly covers the sleigh and the horse more and more, and no movement or breathing of the horse can be heard any longer. "Must be he froze, too," Nikita thinks of Mukhorty. And indeed, those blows of the hoof on the sleigh that had awakened Nikita had been the dying attempts of the completely frozen Mukhorty to keep on his feet.

"Lord, dear Father, it's clear You're calling me, too," Nikita says to himself. "Thy holy will be done. But it's scary. Well, there's no dying twice, but once will suffice. Only let it be quicker . . ." And he hides his hand again, closes his eyes, and becomes oblivious, fully convinced that he is now dying for certain and for good.

It was not until dinnertime of the coming day that some muzhiks dug Vassily Andreich and Nikita out with shovels, about two hundred feet from the road and less than half a mile from the village.

The snow had heaped up higher than the sleigh, but the shafts with the kerchief tied to them were still visible. Mukhorty, up to his belly in snow, with the girth and burlap to one side, stood all white, pressing his dead head to his stiffened windpipe, his nostrils hung with icicles, his eyes all frosty and also hung with ice as if with tears. He had wasted away so much in one night that he was left only skin and bones. Vassily Andreich was stiff as a frozen carcass, and as his legs had been spread, so they detached him, bow legged, from Nikita. His protruding hawk's eyes were iced over and his open mouth under his trimmed moustaches was packed with snow. But Nikita was alive, though all frostbitten. When Nikita was roused, he was sure that he was already dead now, and that what was being done with him now came not from this but from the other world. But when he heard the shouts of the muzhiks digging him out and hauling the stiffened Vassily Andreich off him, he was surprised at first that in the other world muzhiks shouted in the same way and there was this same body, but when he realized that he was still here in this world, he was more upset than gladdened by it, especially when he felt that the toes of both his feet were frostbitten.

Nikita lay in the hospital for two months. He had three toes amputated, but the rest healed, so that he could work, and he went on living for another twenty years—first as a hired man, and then, in old age, as a watchman. He died only this year, at home, as he wished, under the icons and with a lighted candle in his hands. Before death, he asked forgiveness from his old wife and forgave her for the cooper; he took leave of his lad and grandchildren as well, and died, truly glad that by his death he was relieving his son and daughter-in-law of the burden of extra bread and was himself really passing from this life, which wearied him, to that other life, which with every year and hour had become more clear and enticing to him. Whether it is better or worse for him there, where he awakened after this real death, whether he was disappointed or found there the very thing he expected, we shall all soon learn.

1894–95

Father Sergius

I

*I*N PETERSBURG in the forties an event took place which astonished everyone: a handsome man, a prince, commander of the life squadron of a cuirassier regiment, who everyone predicted would be made an imperial adjutant and have a brilliant career around the emperor Nikolai I,[1] sent in his resignation a month before his wedding with a lady-in-waiting, a beauty who enjoyed the special favour of the empress, broke with his fiancée, gave his small estate to his sister, and went off to a monastery with the intention of becoming a monk. The event seemed extraordinary and inexplicable to people who did not know its inner causes; but for Prince Stepan Kasatsky himself it all happened so naturally that he could not even imagine how he could have acted otherwise.

Stepan Kasatsky's father, a retired colonel of the guards, had died when his son was twelve. Sorry as the mother was to send her son away from home, she did not dare not to carry out her late husband's will, which was that in case of his death his son should not be kept at home but should be sent to the Corps,[2] and so she sent him to the Corps. The widow herself, with her daughter Varvara, moved to Petersburg, so as to live where her son was and take him home on holidays.

The boy was distinguished by his brilliant abilities and enormous self-esteem, owing to which he was first both in sciences, especially mathematics, for which he had a special predilection, and in drill and horseback riding. Despite his more than usual height, he was handsome and adroit. In his conduct as well he would have been an exemplary cadet, had it not been for his hot temper. He did not drink, was not dissolute, and was remarkably truthful. The one thing that kept him from being exemplary was the fits of anger that used to come over him, during which he lost all self-control and turned into a beast. Once he nearly threw a cadet out the window when he began to make fun of his mineral collection. Another time it was nearly the end of him: he flung a whole platter of cutlets at the steward, fell upon the officer, and, it was said, struck him for going back on his word and lying right in his face. He would certainly have been reduced to the ranks if the director of the Corps had not concealed the whole affair and expelled the steward.

At the age of eighteen he was graduated as an officer in an aristocratic guards regiment. The emperor Nikolai Pavlovich had known him while still in the Corps and had singled him out later in the regiment, so that an imperial adjutantship was predicted for him. And Kasatsky strongly desired that, not only out of ambition, but chiefly because, ever since his time in the Corps, he had passionately, precisely passionately, loved Nikolai Pavlovich. Every time Nikolai Pavlovich visited the Corps—and he often came to them—when this tall figure in a military tunic, with his thrust-out chest, his hooked nose over his moustaches, and his trimmed side-whiskers, came in stepping briskly and greeted the cadets in a powerful voice, Kasatsky experienced the rapture of a lover, the same that he experienced later when he met the object of his love. Only his amorous rapture for Nikolai Pavlovich was stronger. He wanted to show him his boundless devotion, to sacrifice something to him, even his whole self. And Nikolai Pavlovich knew that he aroused this rapture and deliberately evoked it. He played with the cadets, surrounded himself with them, treating them now with childlike simplicity, now amicably, now with solemn majesty. After Kasatsky's last episode with the officer, Nikolai Pavlovich said nothing to him, but when Kasatsky came near him, he pushed him away theatrically and, frowning, shook his finger at him, and then, as he was leaving, said:

"Know that I am informed of everything, but there are certain things I do not want to know. But I have them here."

He pointed to his heart.

When the cadets appeared before him at graduation, he made no mention of it, said, as usual, that they could all turn to him directly, that they should be faithful servants to him and the fatherland, and that he would always remain their best friend. Everyone was moved, as always, and Kasatsky, recalling the past, wept real tears and vowed to serve his beloved tsar with all his powers.

When Kasatsky entered the regiment, his mother first moved to Moscow with her daughter, then to the country. Kasatsky gave up half his fortune to his sister. What remained to him was enough to maintain him in that magnificent regiment in which he served.

From the outside Kasatsky seemed like a most ordinary brilliant young guards officer making his career, but inside him complex and intense work was going on. The work that had been going on in him since childhood was, in appearance, most varied, but in essence was all one and the same, consisting in attaining perfection and success in every task that came his way, earning people's praise and astonishment. If it was learning, studies, he seized upon them and worked until he was praised and held up as an example to others. Having achieved one thing, he would seize upon another. Thus he achieved first place in his studies; thus, while still in the Corps, having noticed once an awkwardness in his spoken French, he worked until his command of French equalled his Russian; thus, later on, taking up chess, he worked until, while still in the Corps, he became an excellent player.

Besides his general vocation in life, which consisted in serving the tsar and the fatherland, he always set himself some sort of goal, and, however insignificant it was, he gave himself to it entirely and lived only for it until he achieved it. But as soon as he achieved the appointed goal, another at once emerged in his consciousness and replaced the previous one. This striving to distinguish himself, and to achieve a set goal in order to distinguish himself, filled his life. Thus, on becoming an officer, he set himself as a goal the greatest possible perfection in knowledge of the service and very soon became an exemplary officer, though again with that fault of an uncontrollable temper, which in the service as well involved him in bad actions harmful to his success. Then, having felt once in social conversation his deficiency of general education, he set his mind on making it up and sat down to his books, and achieved what he wanted. Then he set his mind on attaining a brilliant position in high society, learned to dance excellently, and very soon was invited to all high-society balls and to certain soirées. But that position did not satisfy him. He was used to being first, and in this case he was far from being so.

High society consisted then and, I think, has always and everywhere consisted of four sorts of people: (1) rich courtiers, (2) people who are not rich but were born and raised at court, (3) rich people who curry favour with courtiers, and (4) people who are neither rich nor courtiers, but curry favour with the first and the second. Kasatsky did not belong to the first. Kasatsky was willingly received in the last two circles. Even on entering society, he set himself the goal of a liaison with a woman of society—and unexpectedly for himself he soon attained it. But very soon he saw that the circles in which he turned were lower circles, and that there were higher circles, and that in those higher court circles, though he was received, he was an outsider; they were polite to him, but all their manners showed that some were their own and he was not one of them. And Kasatsky wanted to be one of them. For that he had either to be an imperial adjutant—and he was waiting for that—or to marry into that circle. And he resolved to do so. And he chose the girl, a beauty, of the court, not only at home in that society which he wanted to enter, but such as all the most highly and firmly established people in the highest circle strove to become close to. This was Countess Korotkov. It was not only for the sake of his career that Kasatsky began to court Countess Korotkov; she was extraordinarily attractive, and he soon fell in love with her. At first she was peculiarly cold towards him, but then everything suddenly changed, and she became affectionate, and her mother invited him to call with peculiar insistence.

Kasatsky proposed and was accepted. He was surprised by the ease with which he had attained such happiness, and by something peculiar, strange, in the manner of both mother and daughter. He was very much in love, and blinded, and therefore did not notice what almost everyone in town knew, that a year ago his fiancée had been Nikolai Pavlovich's mistress.

II

TWO WEEKS before the day appointed for the wedding, Kasatsky was staying at his fiancée's dacha in Tsarskoe Selo.[3] It was a hot May day.

The fiancés strolled through the garden and sat down on a bench in a shady linden alley. Mary[4] was especially beautiful in her white muslin dress. She seemed the embodiment of innocence and love. She sat, now with her head bent, now looking up at the enormous, handsome man, who talked to her with special tenderness and care, fearing with his every gesture or word to offend, to defile the angelic purity of his fiancée. Kasatsky was one of those men of the forties who no longer exist, men who, consciously allowing an impurity of sexual behaviour for themselves and not inwardly condemning it, demanded of a wife an ideal, heavenly purity, and saw that same heavenly purity in every girl of their circle, and treated them accordingly. In such a view and in the licentiousness that men allowed themselves there was much that was incorrect and harmful, but in relation to women such a view, sharply distinguished from that of present-day young men, who see every woman as a female looking for a mate—such a view was, I think, useful. Girls, seeing such deification, even tried more or less to be goddesses. Kasatsky also held such a view of women and looked at his fiancée in that way. He was especially in love that day and did not experience the slightest sensual feeling for his fiancée; on the contrary, he looked at her with tender emotion as something unattainable.

He rose to all his great height and stood before her, leaning with both hands on his sabre.

"Only now have I come to know all the happiness which a man can experience. And it is you, it is you, dearest," he said, smiling timidly, "who have given it to me!"

He was at that stage when endearments were not yet habitual, and, looking up to her morally, he felt frightened of saying "dearest" to this angel.

"I have come to know myself, thanks to you . . . dearest, to know that I am better than I thought."

"I have long known it. That is why I love you."

A nightingale trilled nearby, the fresh foliage rustled in the wafting breeze.

He took her hand and kissed it, and tears came to his eyes. She understood that he was thanking her for having said she loved him. He stepped away, fell silent, then came back and sat down.

"You know, miss, you know, my dearest—well, it's all the same. I was not disinterested when I sought your acquaintance, I wanted to establish connections with high society, but then . . . How insignificant that became in comparison with you, when I came to know you. You're not angry with me for that?"

She did not reply and only touched his hand with hers.

He understood that this meant "No, I'm not angry."

"Yes, you were just saying . . ." he hesitated, it seemed all too bold to him, "you were saying that you were in love with me, but, forgive me, I believe you, but, besides that, there's something that disturbs and inhibits you. What is it?"

"Yes, it's now or never," she thought. "He'll find out anyway. But now he won't leave. Oh, if he left, it would be terrible!"

And she took in his whole big, noble, powerful figure with a loving glance. She now loved him more than Nikolai and, were it not for his emperorship, would not have exchanged this one for that.

"Listen. I cannot be untruthful. I must tell all. You ask what it is? It's that I have loved."

She placed her hand on his in a pleading gesture.

He was silent.

"You want to know whom? Yes, him, the sovereign."

"We all love him. I imagine you, in girls' school . . ."

"No, afterwards. It was an infatuation, but then it passed. But I must tell you . . ."

"Well, so what?"

"No, it wasn't simply . . ."

She covered her face with her hands.

"What? You gave yourself to him?"

She was silent.

"As a mistress?"

She was silent.

He jumped up and, pale as death, with twitching cheekbones, stood before her. He remembered how Nikolai Pavlovich, meeting him on Nevsky Prospect, had congratulated him affectionately.

"My God, what have I done, Stiva?"

"Don't, don't touch me. Oh, how it hurts!"

He turned and walked to the house. In the house he met her mother.

"What's wrong, Prince? I . . ." She fell silent, seeing his face. The blood had suddenly rushed to his face.

"You knew it and wanted to use me to cover it up. If you weren't women," he cried, raising an enormous fist over her, and, turning, ran away.

If the one who had been his fiancée's lover had been a private person, he would have killed him, but it was his adored tsar.

The next day he applied for leave and his discharge, and, declaring himself sick so as to avoid seeing anyone, left for the country.

He spent the summer on his estate, settling his affairs. When summer was over, he did not return to Petersburg, but went to a monastery and entered it as a monk.

His mother wrote to him, trying to dissuade him from such a decisive step. He replied that the call of God was higher than any other consider-ations, and he felt it. Only his sister, as proud and ambitious as her brother, understood him.

She understood that he had become a monk in order to be higher than those who wanted to show him that they stood higher than he. And she understood him correctly. By becoming a monk, he showed that he scorned all that seemed so important to others and to himself at the time of his service, and that he had risen to a new height, from which he could look down on the people he had envied before. But it was not that feeling alone, as his sister thought, that guided him. There was in him another, genuinely religious feeling, which Varenka did not know about, and which, bound up with the feeling of pride and the desire for preemi-nence, guided him. His disappointment with Mary (his fiancée), whom he had imagined to be such an angel, and his feeling of offence were so strong that they led him to despair, and despair to what?—to God, to his childhood faith, which was still unbroken in him.

III

ON THE DAY of the Protection,[5] Kasatsky entered the monastery.

The abbot of the monastery was a nobleman, a learned writer, and an elder, that is, he belonged to that succession of monks, originating in Wallachia, who submit without murmur to a chosen guide and teacher. The abbot was a disciple of the famous elder Amvrosy, the disciple of Makary, the disciple of the elder Leonid, the disciple of Paissy Velich-kovsky.[6] Kasatsky submitted himself to this abbot as his elder.

Besides the sense of awareness of his superiority over others, which

Kasatsky experienced in the monastery, Kasatsky, as in all things he did, also found joy in the monastery in attaining to the greatest outer as well as inner perfection. As in the regiment he was not only an irreproachable officer, but such as would do more than was demanded and thus widen the boundaries of perfection, so as a monk he strove to be perfect: always hard-working, abstemious, humble, meek, pure not only in deed but in thought, and obedient. This last quality in particular made life easier for him. If many of the demands of monastic life in a monastery close to the capital and much visited displeased him and became temptations for him, that was all annulled by obedience: it is not my business to reason, my business is to bear the assigned obedience, whether it is standing by the relics, singing in the choir, or keeping the accounts for the guest house. Any possibility of doubting anything at all was removed by the same obedience to the elder. Had it not been for this obedience, he would have been burdened by the length and monotony of the church services, and the bustle of the visitors, and the bad qualities of the brothers, but now all this was not only joyfully endured, but constituted a comfort and support in life. "I don't know why one must hear the same prayers several times a day, but I know it's necessary. And knowing that it's necessary, I find joy in them." The elder told him that as material food is necessary to maintain life, so spiritual food—church prayer—is necessary to maintain spiritual life. He believed in that, and, indeed, church services, for which he sometimes had difficulty getting up in the morning, gave him an unquestionable tranquillity and joy. Joy was given by the consciousness of humility and the unquestionableness of his actions, which were all determined by the elder. Yet the interest of life did not consist only in an ever increasing submission of his will, in an ever increasing humility, but also in the attaining of all Christian virtues, which at first had seemed easily attainable to him. He gave all his property to the monastery and did not regret it. There was no sloth in him. Humility before his inferiors was not only easy for him, but gave him joy. Even the triumph over the sin of lust, both as greed and as lewdness, came easily to him. The elder warned him particularly about this sin, but Kasatsky rejoiced at being free of it.

The only thing that tormented him was the memory of his fiancée. And not only the memory, but the vivid picturing of what might have been. Involuntarily, he pictured to himself an acquaintance of his, one of the sovereign's favourites, who later married and became an excellent wife and mother of a family. Her husband occupied an important post, had power, respect, and a good, repentant wife.

In good moments, Kasatsky was not troubled by these thoughts. When he remembered these things in good moments, he rejoiced at having rid himself of those temptations. But there were moments when everything he lived by suddenly went dim before him; not that he ceased to believe in what he lived by, but he ceased to see it, could not call it up before him, and the memory of and—terrible to say—the regret for his conversion seized hold of him.

In this situation, salvation lay in obedience—work and prayer throughout the busy day. He prayed and made bows as usual, prayed even more than usual, but prayed with his body, his soul was not in it. And this would last for a day, sometimes two, and then go away of itself. But that day or two were terrible. Kasatsky felt that he was neither in his own nor in God's power, but in someone else's. And all he could do and did do at those times was what his elder advised—endure, undertake nothing during that time, and wait. In general Kasatsky lived all that time not by his own will, but by his elder's, and there was a special tranquillity in that obedience.

So Kasatsky spent seven years in the first monastery he entered. At the end of the third year he was tonsured a hieromonk[7] under the name of Sergius. The tonsuring was an important inner event for Sergius. Before, too, he had experienced a great comfort and spiritual uplift when he took communion; but now, when he happened to serve himself, the celebrating of the proskomedia[8] brought him to a state of rapturous tenderness. But then this feeling became more and more blunted, and once, when he happened to serve in that oppressed state of spirit which used to come over him, he sensed that this feeling, too, would pass. And indeed the feeling weakened, but the habit remained.

Generally, in the seventh year of his life in the monastery, Sergius became bored. All that he had had to learn, all that he had had to attain, he had attained, and there was nothing more to do.

Instead his state of apathy kept growing stronger. During that time he learned of his mother's death and Mary's marriage. He received both pieces of news with indifference. All his attention, all his interests were concentrated on his inner life.

In the fourth year after his tonsuring, the bishop showed him particular kindness, and the elder told him that he should not refuse if he were appointed to higher duties. And then monastic ambition, the very thing that is so repulsive in monks, arose in him. He was appointed to a monastery near the capital. He wanted to refuse, but the elder told him to accept the appointment. He accepted the appointment, took leave of the elder, and moved to the new monastery.

This transfer to the monastery near the capital was an important event in Sergius's life. There were many temptations of every sort, and all of Sergius's forces were directed at that.

In his former monastery Sergius had suffered little from the temptation of women, but here this temptation rose up with dreadful force and went so far that it even received a definite form. There was a lady known for her bad behaviour who began to ingratiate herself with Sergius. She struck up a conversation with him and asked him to visit her. Sergius sternly refused, but was horrified at the definiteness of his desire. He was so frightened that he wrote to his elder about it, and not only that but, in order to tether himself, he summoned a young novice and, overcoming his shame, confessed his weakness, asking him to keep watch on him and not let him go anywhere except to services and obediences.

Besides that, there was a great temptation for Sergius in the fact that the abbot of this monastery, a worldly, clever man embarked on a churchly career, was antipathetic to him in the highest degree. No matter how Sergius struggled with himself, he could not overcome this antipathy. He humbled himself, but in the depths of his soul he never ceased to judge him. And this bad feeling broke out.

This was during the second year of his residence in the new monastery. And here is how it happened. On the feast of the Protection, the all-night vigil was served in the big church. There were many visitors. The abbot himself celebrated. Father Sergius stood in his usual place and prayed, that is, was in that state of struggle which he was always in during services, especially in the big church, when he was not celebrating himself. The struggle was against the irritation caused by the visitors, the gentlemen and especially the ladies. He tried not to see them, not to notice all that was going on: not to see how the soldier escorting them pushed his way through the people, or how the ladies pointed out monks to each other—often even himself and another monk known for being handsome. He tried, as if putting blinkers on his attention, to see nothing except the shining of candles by the iconostasis, the icons, and the celebrants; to hear nothing except the words of the prayers, spoken or sung, and to experience no other feelings except that self-forgetfulness in the consciousness of the fulfilment of his duty which he always experienced when listening to and repeating prayers heard so many times before.

So he stood, bowing, crossing himself where necessary, and struggled, giving himself now to cold condemnation, now to a consciously evoked suspension of thoughts and feelings, when the sacristan, Father Nicodemus—also a great temptation for Father Sergius—Nicodemus, whom he involuntarily reproached for currying favour and flattering the abbot—came over to him and, bending double as he bowed, said that the abbot was summoning him to the altar. Father Sergius straightened his mantle, put on his cowl, and walked warily through the crowd.

"*Lise, regardez à droite, c'est lui,*"* he heard a woman's voice say.

"*Où, où? Il n'est pas tellement beau.*"†

He knew they were talking about him. He heard it and, as always in moments of temptation, repeated the words: "And lead us not into temptation," and, lowering his head and eyes, walked past the ambo and, going around the choir leaders in their cassocks, who were just then passing in front of the iconostasis, entered through the north door. Going into the sanctuary, he crossed himself and bowed as was customary, bending double before the icon, then raised his head and glanced at the abbot, whose figure he saw out of the corner of his eye, standing next to another figure in something glittering, without turning to them.

The abbot stood in his vestments by the wall and, having freed his short, plump arms from under the chasuble that covered his fat body and stomach, was fingering the gold trimming, smiling and saying something to a military man in the uniform of a general of the imperial suite with a monogram and aglets, which Father Sergius noticed at once with his practised military eye. This general was his former regimental commander. He now obviously occupied an important position, and Father Sergius noticed at once that the abbot knew it and was glad of it, and that was why his fat, red face with its bald brow was beaming so. This offended and distressed Father Sergius, and this feeling increased still

---

* Lise, look to the right, it's him.
† Where, where? He's not so handsome.

more when he heard from the abbot that he had summoned him, Father
Sergius, out of no other need than to satisfy the general's curiosity to see
his former colleague, as he put it.

"Very glad to see you in angelic guise,"9 said the general, holding out
his hand. "I hope you haven't forgotten your old comrade."

The abbot's whole face, red and smiling amidst its white hair, as if
approving of what the general had said, the general's pampered face with
its self-satisfied smile, the smell of wine from the general's mouth and of
cigars from his side-whiskers—all this made Father Sergius explode. He
bowed once more to his superior and said:

"Your Reverence was pleased to summon me?" And he stopped, the
whole expression of his face and posture asking: Why?

The abbot said:

"Yes, to meet the general."

"Your Reverence, I left the world to save myself from temptations,"
he said, turning pale and with trembling lips. "Why do you subject me to
them here? In a time of prayer and in God's church?"

"Go, go," the abbot said, flaring up and frowning.

The next day Father Sergius asked forgiveness of the abbot and the
brothers for his pride, but along with that, after a night spent in prayer,
decided that he had to leave that monastery, and wrote a letter about it to
his elder, begging to be allowed to go back to the elder's monastery. He
wrote that he felt his weakness and inability to fight against temptations
alone, without the elder's help. And he confessed to his sin of pride. With
the next mail came a letter from the elder, in which he wrote that the
cause of it all was his pride. The elder explained to him that his fit of
anger came from the fact that his humility in refusing churchly honours
was not for the sake of God but for the sake of his own pride: just see how
I am, I don't need anything. Because of that, he could not bear what the
abbot had done. I spurned everything for God, and they exhibit me like a
wild beast. "If you had spurned glory for God, you would have borne it.
Worldly pride has not yet been extinguished in you. I have thought about
you, Sergius my child, and prayed, and this is what God has inspired me
with concerning you: live as before and submit. Just now it has become
known that Hilarion, a recluse of holy life, has died in his cell. He lived in
it for eighteen years. The abbot of Tambino is asking if there is a monk
who would like to live there. And here your letter comes. Go to Father

Paissy in the monastery of Tambino, I will write to him, and ask to occupy Hilarion's cell. Not so that you can replace Hilarion, but you need solitude in order to humble your pride. May God bless you."

Sergius obeyed the elder, showed his letter to the abbot, and, having obtained his permission, gave up his cell and all his possessions to the monastery and left for the Tambino hermitage.

In the Tambino hermitage the superior, an excellent manager, of merchant stock, received Sergius simply and calmly and placed him in Hilarion's cell, at first giving him an attendant, but later, at Sergius's request, leaving him by himself. The cell was a cave dug into a hillside. Hilarion was buried in it. In the back part of it Hilarion was buried, and in the front part was a niche for sleeping, with a straw mattress, a little table, and a shelf with icons and books. Outside the door, which could be locked, there was a shelf; on this shelf once a day a monk placed food from the monastery.

And so Father Sergius became a recluse.

IV

DURING MEATFARE WEEK in the sixth year of Sergius's life in reclusion, a merry company of rich people, men and women, from the neighbouring town, after pancakes and drink, went for a troika ride.[10] The company consisted of two lawyers, a rich landowner, an officer, and four women. One was the officer's wife, another the landowner's wife, the third was a young lady, the landowner's sister, and the fourth was a divorced woman, a beauty, rich and whimsical, who astonished and stirred up the town with her escapades.

The weather was beautiful, the road like a smooth floor. They drove some seven miles out of town, stopped, and began to discuss where to go: back or further on.

"Where does this road lead to?" asked Mrs. Makovkin, the divorced lady, the beauty.

"To Tambino, eight miles from here," said the lawyer, who was courting Mrs. Makovkin.

"Well, and then?"

"And then to L——, past the monastery."

"The one where this Father Sergius lives?"

"Yes."

"Kasatsky? The handsome hermit?"

"Yes."

"*Mesdames!* Gentlemen! Let's go to see Kasatsky. We can rest and have something to eat in Tambino."

"But we won't make it home before nightfall."

"Never mind, we'll spend the night at Kasatsky's."

"We could, there's a guest house at the monastery, and a very good one. I stayed there when I defended Makhin."

"No, I'll spend the night at Kasatsky's."

"Well, that's impossible, even with your almightiness."

"Impossible? Let's bet."

"You're on. If you spend the night at his place, ask whatever you like."

"*À discrétion.*"*

"And you, too!"

"Of course. Let's go."

The drivers were offered drink. The travellers themselves took out the box with pirozhki, wine, sweets. The ladies wrapped themselves in white dog-fur coats. The drivers argued over who would go first, and one of them, a young fellow, turned dashingly sideways, brandished the long whip handle, shouted—and the bells rang out and the runners squealed.

The sleigh shook and swayed slightly, the outrunner galloped steadily and merrily with his tail tied up tightly over the laminated breeching, the smooth, buttery road raced quickly past, the driver dashingly flourished the reins, the lawyer and the officer, sitting opposite, babbled something to Mrs. Makovkin's neighbour, and she herself, wrapped tightly in her fur coat, sat motionless and thought: "It's all the same, and all vile: shiny red faces with a smell of drink and tobacco, the same talk, the same thoughts, and it all turns around that very vileness. And they're all satisfied and convinced that it has to be so, and can go on living like that till they die. But I can't. I'm bored. I want something to upset it all, overturn it. Well, even if it's like those people in Saratov, was it, who went off and froze to death. Well, what would ours do? How would they behave? Meanly, I'm

---

* As much as I want.

sure. Every man for himself. And I'd also behave meanly myself. But, anyhow, I'm a good one. They know it. Well, and this monk? Can it be he no longer understands such things? Not true. It's the one thing they do understand. Like with that cadet last autumn. And what a fool he was . . ."

"Ivan Nikolaich!" she said.

"What can I do for you?"

"How old is he?"

"Who?"

"This Kasatsky."

"Over forty, I think."

"And what, does he receive everybody?"

"Everybody, but not always."

"Cover my legs. Not like that. How clumsy you are! No, more, more, like that. And there's no need to squeeze my legs."

So they reached the forest where the cell was.

She got out and told them to go on. They tried to talk her out of it, but she became angry and told them to keep going. Then the sleigh drove off, and she, in her white dog-fur coat, went down the path. The lawyer got out and stayed to watch.

V

FATHER SERGIUS WAS SPENDING his sixth year as a recluse. He was forty-nine. His life was difficult. Not the work of fasting and prayer, that was not difficult, but the inner struggle, which he had not expected. The sources of the struggle were two: doubt and fleshly lust. These two enemies always rose up together. It seemed to him that they were two different enemies, whereas they were one and the same. As soon as doubt was crushed, lust was crushed. But he thought they were two different devils and struggled with them separately.

"My God! My God!" he thought. "Why do you not give me faith? Lust, yes, St. Anthony[11] and others struggled with it—but faith. They had it, while for me there are moments, hours, days when I don't have it. Why the whole world, all its delight, if it is sinful and one must renounce it? Why did you create this temptation? Temptation? But isn't it a temptation that I want to leave the world's joys and prepare something there where there may be nothing?" he said to himself and felt horror and loathing for his own self. "Vile creature! Vile creature! And you want to be a saint," he began to denounce himself. And he stood up to pray. But as soon as he began to pray, he vividly imagined himself as he had been in the monastery: in a cowl, a mantle, looking majestic. And he shook his head. "No, that's not it. That's a deception. I can deceive others, but not myself or God. I'm not a majestic man, but pathetic, ridiculous." And he opened the skirts of his cassock and looked at his pathetic legs in their drawers. And smiled.

Then he lowered the skirts and started to recite prayers, cross himself, and bow. "Shall this bed be to me a coffin?" he recited. And it was as if some devil whispered to him: "A solitary bed, too, is a coffin. Lies!" And he saw in imagination the shoulders of the widow with whom he used to live. He shook himself and went on reciting. Having recited the rule,[12] he picked up the Gospel, opened it, and came upon a place which he often repeated and knew by heart: "Lord, I believe; help thou my unbelief."[13] He drove back all his emerging doubts. As one steadies a poorly balanced object, he steadied his faith again on its shaky pedestal and carefully stepped back so as not to knock it over. The blinkers were put in place again, and he calmed down. He repeated his childhood prayer: "Lord, take me, take me"—and felt not only lightness but a joyful tenderness. He crossed himself and lay down on his pallet on its narrow bench, putting his summer cassock under his head. And he fell asleep. In his light sleep he seemed to hear harness bells. He did not know whether it was in reality or in dream. But a knock on the door awakened him. He got up, not believing his ears. But the knock was repeated. Yes, there was a knock close by, on his door, and a woman's voice.

"My God, is it really true what I've read in the *Lives*,[14] that the devil takes the form of a woman . . . Yes, that's a woman's voice. And a gentle, timid, and sweet voice! Pah!" he spat. "No, I'm imagining it," he said and went to the corner, where a little lectern stood, and lowered himself to his knees in that habitual, regular movement, in which, in the movement itself, he found comfort and pleasure. He lowered himself, his hair hanging over his face, and pressed his already balding brow to the damp, cold matting. (There was a draught through the floor.)

. . . he was reading a psalm which old Father Pimen had told him would help against hauntings. He lightly raised his emaciated, light body on his strong, nervous legs and wanted to go on reading, but he did not read, but involuntarily strained his ears in order to hear. He wanted to hear. It was perfectly quiet. The same drops from the roof fell into the tub placed under the corner. Outside there was murk, fog, which ate up the snow. It was quiet, quiet. And suddenly there was a rustling by the window, and what was clearly a voice—the same gentle, timid voice, a voice that could belong only to an attractive woman—said:

"Let me in. For Christ's sake . . ."

All his blood seemed to rush to his heart and stop there. He could not breathe. "Let God arise, let his enemies be scattered . . ."[15]

"I'm not a devil . . ." and he could hear that the lips pronouncing it were smiling. "I'm not a devil, I'm simply a sinful woman, lost, not figuratively but literally" (she laughed), "freezing, and asking for shelter . . ."

He put his face to the windowpane. The reflection of the icon lamp shone all over the pane. He put his palms to both sides of his face and peered out. Fog, murk, a tree, and there to the right. She. Yes, she, a woman in a coat with long white fur, in a hat, with a sweet, sweet, kind, frightened face, there, three inches from his face, leaning towards him. Their eyes met and they recognized each other. Not that they had ever seen each other: they never had, but in the glance they exchanged, they (he especially) felt that they knew each other, understood each other. To suspect, after that glance, that this was a devil and not a simple, kind, sweet, timid woman was impossible.

"Who are you? What are you doing here?" he asked.

"Open up," she said with capricious imperiousness. "I'm freezing. I've lost my way, I tell you."

"But I'm a monk, a hermit."

"Well, open up anyway. Or do you want me to freeze to death under your window while you pray."

"But how did you . . ."

"I won't eat you. For God's sake, let me in. I'm just plain cold."

She was getting scared herself. She said it in an almost tearful voice.

He left the window, glanced at the icon of Christ in a crown of thorns. "Lord, help me, Lord, help me," he said, crossing himself and bowing to the ground, and he went to the door and opened it to the little front hall. In the hall he felt for the hook and began to lift it. He heard footsteps outside. She was moving from the window to the door. "Aie!" she suddenly cried. He realized that her foot had landed in the puddle that had formed by the doorway. His hands trembled, and he could not lift the tight hook that held the door shut.

"What's the matter? Let me in. I'm all wet. I'm freezing to death. You think about saving your soul, while I'm freezing."

He pulled the door towards him, lifted the hook, and, without intending it, shoved the door outwards so that it pushed her.

"Ah, I beg your pardon!" he said, suddenly shifting over completely to his old, habitual way with ladies.

She smiled, hearing this "I beg your pardon." "Well, he's not all that frightening," she thought.

"It's nothing, it's nothing. Forgive me," she said, stepping past him. "I'd never have dared. But this is such a special case."

"Come in, please," he said, letting her pass. The strong scent of fine perfume, which he had not smelled for a long time, struck him. She passed through the front hall into the room. He slammed the outside door without hooking it, crossed the hall, and went into the room.

"Lord Jesus Christ, Son of God, have mercy on me a sinner, Lord, have mercy on me a sinner,"[16] he prayed without ceasing, not only inwardly, but even outwardly, moving his lips involuntarily.

"Please come in," he said.

She stood in the middle of the room, dripping water on the floor, and studied him. Her eyes were laughing.

"Forgive me for trespassing on your solitude. But you see what situation I'm in. It came about because we went for a sleigh ride out of town, and I made a bet that I could walk back alone from Vorobyevka, but I lost my way here, and now, if I hadn't happened upon your cell . . ." she began to lie. But his face confused her, so that she could not go on and fell silent. She had expected him to be quite different. He was not such a handsome man as she had imagined him, but he was beautiful in her eyes. His curly hair and beard shot with grey, his thin, fine nose, and his eyes burning like coals when he looked at her directly, struck her.

He saw that she was lying.

"Well, so," he said, glancing at her and lowering his eyes again. "I'll go there, and you make yourself comfortable."

And, taking down a little lamp, he lit the candle and, bowing low to her, went to a tiny room behind a partition, and she heard him start moving something there. "Probably barricading himself from me with something," she thought, smiling, and, throwing off her white dog-fur rotonde, she began to remove her hat, which got caught in her hair, and the knitted kerchief that was under it. She had not been soaking wet at all when she was standing at the window and had only said it as a pretext, so that he would let her in. But at the door she had in fact stepped in a puddle, and her left leg was wet to the calf, and her shoe and overshoe were full of water. She sat on his cot—a plank covered only with a rug—and began to take her shoes off. This little cell seemed charming to her. The narrow room, some seven feet wide by nine feet long, was clean as a whistle. There was nothing in it but the cot she was sitting on and a shelf of books above it. In the corner a little lectern. On nails by the door a fur coat and a cassock. Above the lectern an icon of Christ with the crown of thorns and an icon lamp. There was a strange smell of oil, sweat, and earth. She liked everything. Even that smell.

Her wet feet, one especially, worried her, and she hurriedly began taking her shoes off, not ceasing to smile, glad not so much of having attained her goal as of seeing that she embarrassed him—this charming, striking, strange, attractive man. "Well, he didn't respond, but there's no harm in that," she said to herself.

"Father Sergius! Father Sergius! That's your name, isn't it?"

"What do you want?" a soft voice responded.

"Forgive me, please, for trespassing on your solitude. But, truly, I couldn't do anything else. I'd have fallen ill straight off. Even now I don't know. I'm all wet, my feet are like ice."

"Forgive me," the soft voice replied, "I cannot be of any service to you."

"I wouldn't have troubled you for anything. I'll only stay till daybreak."

He did not respond. And she heard him whispering something—he was evidently praying.

"You won't come in here?" she asked, smiling. "Because I'll have to undress in order to get dry."

He did not respond, but went on reciting prayers in an even voice behind the wall.

"Yes, there's a man," she thought, pulling off her squelching overshoe with effort. She tugged at it and could not get it off, and that became funny to her. And she laughed barely audibly, but, knowing that he could hear her laughter and that this laughter would affect him in precisely the way she wanted, she laughed louder, and this merry, natural, kindly laughter indeed affected him, and in precisely the way she wanted.

"Yes, one could fall in love with such a man. Those eyes. And that simple, noble, and—no matter how he murmurs prayers—and passionate face!" she thought. "We women can't be fooled. Already then, when he put his face to the windowpane and looked at me, and understood, and recognized me. There was a flash in his eyes, and that sealed it. He loved, he desired me. Yes, desired," she said, having finally taken off her overshoe and shoe and setting to work on her stockings. To take them off, those long stockings on elastics, she had to lift her skirts. She felt ashamed and said:

"Don't come in."

But there was no reply from behind the wall. The even murmuring went on and sounds of movement as well. "He's probably bowing to the ground," she thought. "But he won't bow out," she said. "He's thinking about me. Just as I am about him. He's thinking with the same feeling about these legs," she said, as she pulled off her wet stockings, stepping onto the cot with her bare feet and tucking them under her. She sat like that for a short time, clasping her knees with her arms and looking pensively before her. "Yes, this solitude, this silence. And nobody would ever know . . ."

She got up, took her stockings to the stove, and hung them on the damper. It was some special kind of damper. She turned it and then, stepping lightly on her bare feet, went back to the cot and again sat on it with her feet up. Behind the wall there was total silence. She looked at the tiny watch that hung on her neck. It was two o'clock. "Our people should be here around three." There was no more than an hour left.

"What is it, me sitting here alone like this. What nonsense! I don't want to. I'll call him right now."

"Father Sergius! Father Sergius! Sergei Dmitrich, Prince Kasatsky!"

There was silence behind the door.

"Listen, this is cruel. I wouldn't be calling you if I didn't need to. I'm sick. I don't know what's the matter with me," she said in a suffering voice. "Ohh, ohh!" she moaned, falling on the cot. And, strangely enough, she really felt that she was faint, quite faint, that she ached all over and was trembling with fever.

"Listen, help me! I don't know what's the matter with me. Ohh!

Ohh!" She unbuttoned her dress, exposed her breast, and threw back her arms, which were bared to the elbow. "Ohh! Ohh!"

All this time he stood in his closet and prayed. Having recited all the evening prayers, he now stood motionless, his eyes fixed on the tip of his nose, mentally repeating the prayer: "Lord Jesus Christ, Son of God, have mercy on me."

But he heard everything. He heard how she rustled the silk fabric, taking off her dress, how she stepped barefoot across the floor; he heard her rub her feet with her hand. He felt that he was weak and might perish at any moment, and therefore he prayed without ceasing. He experienced something like what a folktale hero must experience, having to walk on without looking back.[17] So, too, Sergius heard, felt, that danger, perdition, was here, over him, around him, and he could save himself only by not turning to look at her even for a minute. But suddenly the desire to look came over him. At that moment she said:

"Listen, this is inhuman. I may die."

"Yes, I'll go, but the way that elder did, who laid one hand on the harlot and put the other into a brazier. But there's no brazier." He looked around. The icon lamp. He put his finger over the flame and frowned, preparing to endure, and for quite a long time he seemed not to feel it, but suddenly—he had not yet decided whether it was painful and how much—he winced all over and pulled his hand back, waving it. "No, I can't do it."

"For God's sake! Ohh, come to me! I'm dying! Ohh!"

"So, what, am I to perish? No, I won't!"

"I'll come to you at once," he said, and, opening his door, not looking at her, he went past her to the door of the front hall, where he usually chopped wood, felt for the block on which he chopped wood, and for the axe leaning against the wall.

"At once," he said, and, taking the axe in his right hand, he put the index finger of his left hand on the block, swung the axe, and struck it below the second joint. The finger bounced off more easily than a stick of the same thickness, spun in the air, and plopped onto the edge of the block and then onto the floor.

He heard that sound before he felt any pain. But he had no time to be surprised that there was no pain before he felt a sharp pain and the warmth of flowing blood. He quickly covered the cut joint with the skirt of his cassock and, pressing it to his hip, came back through the door, and, stopping before the woman, his eyes lowered, quietly asked:

"What is it?"

She looked at his pale face with its twitching left cheek and suddenly felt ashamed. She jumped up, seized her fur coat, and, throwing it on, wrapped herself in it.

"Yes, I was in pain . . . I've caught cold . . . I . . . Father Sergius . . . I . . ."

He raised his eyes, shining with a quiet, joyful light, to her and said:

"Dear sister, why did you want to destroy your immortal soul? It is necessary that temptations come into the world, but woe to the man by whom the temptation comes . . .[18] Pray that God may forgive us."

She listened to him and looked at him. Suddenly she heard drops of liquid falling. She glanced and saw that blood was flowing down his cassock from his hand.

"What have you done to your hand?" She remembered the sound she had heard and, seizing the lamp, ran to the front hall, where she saw a bloody finger on the floor. She came back paler than he was and wanted to say something to him; but he quietly went to the closet and shut the door behind him.

"Forgive me," she said. "How can I redeem my sin?"

"Go."

"Let me bandage your wound."

"Go away."

She dressed hurriedly and silently. And sat ready, in her fur coat, waiting. The sound of bells came from outside.

"Father Sergius. Forgive me."

"Go. God will forgive."

"Father Sergius. I'll change my life. Don't abandon me."

"Go."

"Forgive me and bless me."

"In the name of the Father, and of the Son, and of the Holy Spirit," came from behind the partition. "Go."

She burst into sobs and left the cell. The lawyer was coming to meet her.

"Well, I lost, no help for it. Where are you going to sit?"

"It makes no difference."

She got into the sleigh and did not say a word all the way home.

. . .

A YEAR LATER she was tonsured a nun and lived a strict life in a convent under the guidance of the recluse Arseny, who occasionally wrote her letters.

VI

FATHER SERGIUS LIVED as a recluse for another seven years. At first he accepted much of what people brought him: tea, and sugar, and white bread, and milk, and clothing, and firewood. But as more and more time passed, he made his life stricter and stricter, renouncing all that was superfluous, and finally reached the point of not accepting anything except black bread once a week. All that was brought to him he gave to the poor who came to see him.

Father Sergius spent all his time in his cell at prayer or in conversation with visitors, who became more and more numerous. He went out only three times a year to church, and for water and firewood when they were needed.

After five years of such life, the event with Mrs. Makovkin took place—known soon enough everywhere—her night visit, the change that came over her after that, and her entering the convent. After that the fame of Father Sergius began to grow. More and more visitors began to come, and monks settled around his cell, a church and a guest house were built. Father Sergius's fame, exaggerating his deeds, as usual, spread further and further. People began flocking to him from far away, and began bringing sick people to him, declaring that he could heal the sick.

The first healing took place in the eighth year of his life as a recluse. It was the healing of a fourteen-year-old boy, whose mother brought him to Father Sergius, asking that he lay his hands on him. The thought that he could heal the sick had never occurred to Father Sergius. He would have considered such a thought a great sin of pride; but the mother who brought the boy entreated him insistently, lying at his feet, saying why, when he healed others, did he not want to help her son, begging him for Christ's sake. To Father Sergius's assertion that only God heals, she said that she asked him only to lay his hand on him and pray. Father Sergius refused and went to his cell. But the next day (it was autumn and the nights were already cold) he left his cell to fetch water and saw the mother with her son, a pale, emaciated fourteen-year-old boy, and heard the same pleas. Father Sergius remembered the parable of the unrighteous judge[19] and, while previously he had felt no doubts that he should refuse, he now felt some doubts, and, feeling those doubts, he began to pray and prayed until a decision formed in his soul. The decision was that he must fulfil what the woman asked, that her faith would save her son; he himself, Father Sergius, would in that case be nothing but an insignificant instrument chosen by God.

And, going out to the mother, Father Sergius fulfilled her wish, laid his hand on the boy's head, and began to pray.

The mother and son left, and a month later the boy recovered, and the rumour spread throughout the district about the holy healing power of the elder Sergius, as they now called him. Since then a week did not pass without sick people coming on foot or in carriages to see Father Sergius. And, having not refused one, he could not refuse others, and so he laid his hand on them and prayed, and many were healed, and the fame of Father Sergius spread further and further.

Thus he spent nine years in the monastery and thirteen in solitude. Father Sergius had the look of an elder: his beard was long and grey, but his hair, though sparse, was still black and curly.

VII

FOR SOME WEEKS now Father Sergius had been living with one persistent thought: whether he had done well in submitting to the position in which he had been placed not so much by himself as by the archimandrite and the abbot.[20] It had begun after the recovery of the fourteen-year-old boy, and since then with every month, week, and day Sergius had felt that his inner life was being destroyed and replaced by external life. As if he were being turned inside out.

Sergius saw that he was a means of attracting visitors and donors to the monastery, and that the monastery authorities therefore surrounded him with conditions in which he could be of greatest use. For instance, they no longer gave him any opportunity to work. They supplied him with everything he might need and asked of him only that he not deny his blessing to the visitors who came to him. For his convenience, they arranged the days when he would receive. They arranged an anteroom for men and a place surrounded by railings so that he would not be knocked off his feet by the visiting ladies who rushed to him—a place where he could bless those who came to him. If they said that people needed him, that, fulfilling Christ's law of love, he could not refuse people who asked to see him, that to withdraw from these people would be cruel, he could not help agreeing with them, but insofar as he gave himself to that life, he felt that the internal was turning into the external, that the source of living water was drying up in him, that everything he did was done more and more for people and not for God.

Whether he admonished people, or simply gave them a blessing, or prayed for the sick, or gave people advice about directing their lives, or listened to the thanks of people he had helped either by healing them, as they said, or by instruction, he could not help rejoicing over it, could not help being concerned with the consequences of his activity, with the way it affected people. He thought of himself as a shining light, and the more he felt that, the more he felt the weakening, the dying out of the divine light of truth burning in him. "How much of what I do is for God and how much for people?" was the question which constantly tormented him and to which he never not so much could as dared to give himself an answer. He felt in the depths of his soul that the devil had changed all his activity for God into activity for people. He felt it because, as he had been oppressed before when his solitude was disturbed, so now he was oppressed by his solitude. He was burdened by his visitors, wearied by them, but in the depths of his soul he was glad of them, glad of the praise with which they surrounded him.

There was even a time when he decided to go away, to hide himself. He even kept thinking over how to do it. He prepared a peasant shirt for himself, breeches, a kaftan, and a hat. He explained that he wanted them so as to give them to the needy. And he kept these clothes with him, planning how he would put them on, cut his hair, and leave. First he would take a train, go two hundred miles, get off, and go about the villages. He asked an old soldier how he went about, how people gave to him and took him in. The soldier told him how and where it was best for giving and taking in, and that was what Father Sergius wanted to do. One night he even got dressed and was about to go, but he did not know which was good: to stay or to flee. At first he was undecided, then the indecision went away, he got used to the devil and submitted to him, and the peasant clothes only reminded him of his thoughts and feelings.

With every day more and more people came to him and less and less time remained for spiritual fortification and prayer. Occasionally, in his brighter moments, he thought he had become like a place where there used to be a spring. "There was a slender spring of living water that quietly flowed from me, through me. That was true life, when 'she' " (he always remembered with rapture that night and her—now Mother Agnia) "tempted me. She tasted that pure water. But since then, before the water can gather, the thirsty ones have come, crowding and jostling each other. And they've churned it up, so that only mud is left." So he thought in his rare brighter moments; but his most usual state was weariness and a tender feeling for himself on account of that weariness.

IT WAS SPRING, the eve of the feast of Mid-Pentecost.[21] Father Sergius served the vigil in his cave church. There were as many people as could find room, around twenty. They were all gentry and merchants—rich people. Father Sergius admitted everyone, but the selection was made by the monk attached to him and by the attendant sent daily to his hermitage from the monastery. A crowd of people, some eighty pilgrims, peasant women in particular, crowded outside, waiting for Father Sergius to come out and give them his blessing. Father Sergius served, and when he came out, singing praises, to the tomb of his predecessor, he staggered and would have fallen, if a merchant standing behind him and the monk who served as deacon had not supported him.

"What's the matter? Little father! Father Sergius! Dearest! Lord!" women's voices said. "You're white as a sheet!"

But Father Sergius recovered at once and, though very pale, pushed the merchant and the deacon away and went on singing. Father Serapion, the deacon, and the attendants, and Sofya Ivanovna, a lady who lived permanently near the hermitage and took care of Father Sergius, began begging him to stop serving.

"It's nothing, it's nothing," said Father Sergius, smiling almost imperceptibly under his moustaches, "don't disrupt the service."

"Yes," he thought, "this is how saints do it."

"A saint! God's angel!" he at once heard behind him the voice of Sofya Ivanovna and also of the merchant who had supported him. He did not heed their entreaties and went on serving. Pressing together again, they all went back down the narrow corridors to the small church, and there, abbreviating it a little, Father Sergius finished serving the vigil.

Immediately after the service Father Sergius blessed those who were present and went out to sit on the bench under the elm tree by the entrance to the cave. He wanted to rest, to breathe the fresh air, he felt it was necessary for him, but as soon as he came out, the crowd of people rushed to him, asking for his blessing and seeking advice and help. There were pilgrim women there, who always go from holy place to holy place, from elder to elder, and always feel a tender emotion before every relic and every elder—Father Sergius knew this ordinary, most unreligious, cold, conventional type; there were pilgrim men, for the most part retired soldiers, unaccustomed to sedentary life, poverty-stricken and for the most part tippling old men, who dragged themselves from monastery to monastery only in order to be fed; there were also coarse peasant men and women with their egocentric demands for healing or the resolving of their doubts concerning the most practical matters: getting a daughter married, renting a shop, buying a plot of land, or taking away the sin of overlying a baby or begetting one out of wedlock. All this was long familiar to Father Sergius and did not interest him. He knew that he would learn nothing new from these persons, that they would not call up any religious feeling in him, but he liked to see them as a crowd who needed and cherished him, his blessing, his words, and therefore he was burdened by this crowd and at the same time found it pleasing. Father Serapion started driving them away, saying that Father Sergius was tired, but he, recalling the words of the Gospel, "Suffer them [the children] to come unto me,"[22] and waxing tender towards himself at this recollection, told him to let them stay.

He stood up, went to the railing where they crowded, and began to bless them and to answer their questions in a weak voice, feeling a tenderness for the weakness of its sound. But, despite his wish to receive them all, he could not do it: again there was darkness in his eyes, he staggered and grasped the railing. Again he felt the blood rush to his head, and at first he turned pale and then suddenly flushed.

"Yes, it will have to be tomorrow. I cannot now," he said and, giving them all a general blessing, went to the bench. The merchant again supported him, led him by the arm, and sat him down.

"Father!" came from the crowd. "Father! Dearest! Don't abandon us! We'll perish without you!"

The merchant, having sat Father Sergius down on the bench under the elm, took upon himself the duty of a policeman and resolutely undertook to drive the people away. True, he spoke very softly, so that Father Sergius could not hear him, but he spoke resolutely and angrily:

"Get out, get out. He blessed you, well, what more do you want? Off with you. Or else you'll really get it in the neck. Well? Well? You, auntie, in the black leggings, clear off, clear off! Where do you think you're going? That's it, I told you. Tomorrow as God wills, but it's finished for today."

"Dearie, just let me have a peek at his sweet face," said a little old woman.

"I'll give you a peek! Where are you going?"

Father Sergius noticed that the merchant was being rather severe and told his cell attendant in a weak voice that the people should not be driven away. Father Sergius knew that he would drive them away in any case, and he wished very much to be left alone and rest, but he sent the attendant so as to make an impression.

"All right, all right. I'm not driving them away, I'm admonishing them," the merchant replied. "Oh, they're glad to finish a man off. They have no pity, they're only mindful of themselves. Impossible, I said. Go away. Come tomorrow."

And the merchant drove them all away.

The merchant was so zealous both because he liked order and liked shoving people around, making them obey, and, above all, because he had need of Father Sergius. He was a widower, and he had an only daughter, sick, unmarried, and he had brought her to Father Sergius from a thousand miles away so that Father Sergius could heal her. In the two years of her illness, he had had this daughter treated in various places. First in a clinic in a provincial university town—no help; then he had taken her to a muzhik in Samara province—she got slightly better; then he had taken her to a doctor in Moscow, paid him a lot of money— no help at all. Now he had been told that Father Sergius could heal people, and he had brought her. So, once the merchant had driven all the people away, he went up to Father Sergius and, without any preliminaries, going on his knees, said in a loud voice:

"Holy father, bestow your blessing upon my ailing daughter, that she be healed of the pain of illness. I make so bold as to seek refuge at your holy feet." And he held out his cupped hands. He did and said all this as if he was doing something clearly and firmly defined by law and custom, as if it was precisely in this way and not in any other that one had to ask for the healing of one's daughter. He did it with such assurance that it even seemed to Father Sergius that it all had to be said and done in precisely that way. But even so he ordered him to stand up and tell him what was the matter. The merchant told him that his daughter, a girl of twenty-two, had fallen ill two years ago, after her mother's sudden death, had gasped, as he put it, and since then had not been right. And so he had brought her from a thousand miles away, and she was waiting at the guest house until Father Sergius ordered her brought to him. She did not go out in the daytime, she was afraid of the light, and could only go out after sunset.

"What, is she very weak?" asked Father Sergius.

"No, she has no special weakness, and she's got flesh on her, only she's a neerastheniac, as the doctor said. If you ordered her brought now, Father Sergius, I'd fly there in no time. Holy father, revive a parent's heart, restore his generation—save his ailing daughter with your prayers."

And the merchant again dropped to his knees and, bowing his head sideways over his two cupped hands, froze. Father Sergius again ordered him to stand up and, reflecting on how difficult his activity was and how, despite that, he humbly endured it, sighed deeply and, after a few seconds of silence, said:

"Very well, bring her in the evening. I will pray for her, but now I'm tired." And he closed his eyes. "I'll send for you then."

The merchant withdrew, tiptoeing over the sand in his boots, which made them creak even more loudly, and Father Sergius remained alone.

Father Sergius's whole life was filled with services and visitors, but that day had been especially difficult. In the morning there had been a visit from an important dignitary, who had had a long conversation with him. After that a lady had come with her son. This son was a young professor, an unbeliever, whom his mother, an ardent believer and devoted to Father Sergius, had brought to him, begging him to have a talk with him. The conversation had been very difficult. The young man, obviously not wishing to get into an argument with a monk, had agreed with him in everything, as with a weak person, but Father Sergius had seen that the young man did not believe and, in spite of that, was quite well, calm, and at ease. Father Sergius now recalled that conversation with displeasure.

"Would you care to eat, dear father?" asked the cell attendant.

"Yes, bring me something."

The attendant went to his cell, built some ten paces from the entrance to the cave, and Father Sergius remained alone.

The time was long past when Father Sergius lived alone and did everything for himself and ate only prosphora[23] and bread. It had long since been demonstrated to him that he had no right to neglect his health, and he was given lenten but healthful things to eat. He consumed little, but much more than before, and often with great pleasure, and not, as before, with revulsion and an awareness of sin. And so it was now. He had some gruel, drank a cup of tea, and ate half a loaf of white bread.

The cell attendant left, and he remained alone on the bench under the elm tree.

It was a wonderful May day; the leaves were just barely unfurling on the birches, aspens, elms, bird cherries, and oaks. The bird-cherry bushes behind the elm were in full bloom and had not yet begun to lose their petals. Nightingales, one quite near, another two or three below in the bushes by the river, twittered and trilled. From far down the river one could hear the songs of workmen, probably coming back from work; the sun was setting behind the forest, and its broken rays sprayed through the greenery. This whole side was pale green, the other, with the elm, was dark. Beetles flew about and bumped and fell.

After supper Father Sergius began to repeat the mental prayer: "Lord Jesus Christ, Son of God, have mercy on us," and then began to recite a psalm, and suddenly, in the middle of the psalm, out of nowhere, a sparrow flew down from a bush onto the ground and, chirping and hopping, jumped up to him, became frightened at something, and flew away. He recited a prayer which spoke of his renouncing the world, and hastened to finish reciting it, so as to send for the merchant and his sick daughter: she interested him. She interested him in that she was a new person, a diversion, and also in that she and her father considered him a saintly man, one whose prayers were fulfilled. He denied it, but in the depths of his soul he considered himself such.

He was often surprised at how it happened that he, Stepan Kasatsky, had come to be such an extraordinarily saintly man and an outright miracle worker, but there could be no doubt that he was that: he could not help believing in the miracles he had seen himself, beginning with the paralysed boy and down to the latest old woman, who had recovered her sight through his prayers.

Strange as it was, it was so. And so the merchant's daughter interested him in that she was a new person, that she had faith in him, and also in that he was about to confirm once again on her his power of healing and his fame. "They come from thousands of miles away, it is written up in newspapers, the sovereign knows, in Europe, in unbelieving Europe, they know," he thought. And suddenly he became ashamed of his vanity, and he started praying to God again. "Lord, heavenly king, the comforter, the spirit of truth, come and abide in us, cleanse us of every impurity, and save our souls, O good one.[24] Cleanse me of the defilement of human fame that afflicts me," he repeated and recalled how many times he had prayed for that and how useless his prayers had so far been in this regard: his prayer performed miracles for others, but for himself he could not obtain God's deliverance from this paltry passion.

He recalled his prayers in the early time of his life as a recluse, when he had prayed to be granted purity, humility, and love, and how it had seemed to him then that God had heard his prayers, that he had been pure and had chopped off his finger, and he raised the wrinkled stub of the cut-off finger and kissed it; it seemed to him that he had been humble then, when he had constantly considered himself vile in his sinfulness, and it seemed to him that he had also had love then, when he recalled with what tender emotion he had received an old man who had come to him, a drunken soldier, asking for money, and also her. But now? And he asked himself: did he love anyone? Did he love Sofya Ivanovna, Father Serapion, had he experienced a feeling of love for all those persons who had come to him that day, for that learned young man with whom he had discoursed so instructively, anxious only to show his own intelligence and up-to-date education? Their love was pleasant and necessary for him, but he felt no love for them. There was no love in him now, nor humility, nor purity.

He had been pleased to learn that the merchant's daughter was twenty-two, and he would have liked to know if she was beautiful. And, in asking about her weakness, he had precisely wanted to know whether she had feminine charm or not.

"Can it be that I've fallen so low?" he thought. "Lord, help me, restore me, my Lord and my God." And he put his hands together and began to pray. The nightingales trilled. A beetle flew at him and crawled on the back of his neck. He brushed it off. "But does He exist? What if I'm knocking at a house locked from outside . . . There's a padlock on the door, and I could see it. That padlock is the nightingales, the beetles, nature. Maybe the young man was right." And he started praying aloud and prayed for a long time, until these thoughts disappeared and he again felt calm and assured. He rang the bell, and when the cell attendant appeared, told him to let the merchant and his daughter come now.

The merchant came, holding his daughter under the arm, led her into the cell, and left at once.

The daughter was a blonde, extremely white, pale, plump, and extremely short girl, with a frightened, childish face and very developed feminine forms. Father Sergius remained on the bench by the door. As the girl passed and stopped near him, and he blessed her, he was horrified at himself for the way he looked her body over. She passed by, and he felt stung. He saw by her face that she was sensual and feeble-minded. He got up and went into the cell. She was sitting on a stool waiting for him.

When he came in, she stood up.

"I want to go to papa," she said.

"Don't be afraid," he said. "What is it that ails you?"

"Everything ails me," she said, and her face suddenly lit up with a smile.

"You'll get well," he said. "Pray."

"What use is praying? I prayed, and it didn't help at all." And she went on smiling. "You should pray and lay your hands on me. I had a dream about you."

"What did you dream?"

"I dreamed that you put your hand on my breast like this." She took his hand and pressed it to her breast. "Just here."

He let her have his right hand.

"What is your name?" he asked, trembling all over and feeling that he was defeated, that his lust had already gone beyond his control.

"Marya. Why?"

She took his hand and kissed it, then put one arm around his waist and pressed herself to him.

"What are you doing?" he said. "Marya. You're the devil."

"Well, maybe it's no matter."

And, embracing him, she sat with him on the bed.

AT DAWN he went out to the porch.

"Can all this really have happened? Her father will come. She'll tell him. She's the devil. What am I to do? Here's the axe with which I cut off my finger." He seized the axe and went into the cell.

His cell attendant met him.

"Do you want me to cut some wood? Give me the axe."

He gave him the axe. Went into the cell. She lay there asleep. He glanced at her with horror. Went on into the cell, took down his peasant clothes, put them on, picked up the scissors, cut his hair, and went by a path down to the river, where he had not been for four years.

A road went along the river. He followed it and walked until dinnertime. At dinnertime he went into a rye field and lay down there. Towards evening he came to a village on the river. He did not go into the village, but to the river, to the steep bank.

It was early morning, about half an hour before sunrise. Everything was grey and bleak, and the cold pre-dawn wind blew from the west. "Yes, I must put an end to it. There is no God. End it how? Throw myself down? I can swim, I won't drown. Hang myself? Yes, my sash there, on that branch." This seemed so possible and close at hand that he was horrified. He wanted to pray, as usual in moments of despair. But there was no one to pray to. There was no God. He lay with his head propped on his hand. And suddenly he felt such a need for sleep that he could no longer support his head with his hand, straightened his arm, lay his head on it, and fell asleep at once. But this sleep lasted only a moment; he wakes up at once and begins not quite to daydream, not quite to recall.

And here he sees himself almost a child, in his mother's home in the country. And a carriage drives up to them, and out of this carriage steps Uncle Nikolai Sergeevich with his enormous, black spade beard, and with him the thin little girl Pashenka, with large, meek eyes and a pathetic, timid face. And here to them, to their company of boys, this Pashenka is brought. And they have to play with her, but it's boring. She's stupid. It ends with them making fun of her, forcing her to show that she knows how to swim. She lies on the floor and gives a dry demonstration. And they all guffaw and make a fool of her. And she sees it and turns a blotchy red and becomes pathetic, so pathetic that it is shameful and it is impossible ever to forget that crooked, kindly, submissive smile. And Sergius remembers seeing her again after that. He had seen her long afterwards, just before he became a monk. She was married to some landowner who squandered all her fortune and beat her. She had two children: a son and a daughter. The son died young.

Sergius remembered seeing her unhappy. Then he saw her in the monastery as a widow. She was the same—not to say stupid, but insipid, insignificant, and pathetic. She came with her daughter and the daughter's fiancé. And they were already poor. Then he heard that she was living somewhere in a district capital and was very poor. "Why am I thinking about her?" he kept asking himself. But he could not stop thinking about her. "Where is she? How is it with her? Is she still as unhappy as she was when she showed us how to swim on the floor? But why am I thinking about her? What am I doing? I must put an end to it."

And again he felt frightened, and again, to save himself from this thought, he began to think about Pashenka.

He lay like that for a long time, thinking now about his necessary end, now about Pashenka. Pashenka appeared to him as his salvation. Finally he fell asleep. And in his sleep he saw an angel, who came to him and said: "Go to Pashenka and find out from her what you should do, and where your sin lies, and where lies your salvation."

He woke up and, deciding that this had been a vision from God, rejoiced and decided to do as he had been told. He knew the town she lived in—it was two hundred miles away—and he went there.

VIII

PASHENKA HAD long since been not Pashenka, but old, withered, wrinkled Praskovya Mikhailovna, the mother-in-law of a failed official, the drunkard Mavrikyev. She lived in a district town where her son-in-law had had his last post, and there she fed the family: her daughter, and her ailing, neurasthenic son-in-law, and five grandchildren. She fed them by giving music lessons to merchants' daughters at fifty kopecks an hour. She had sometimes four, sometimes five lessons a day, so that she made about sixty roubles a month. They lived on that, while waiting for a post. Praskovya Mikhailovna had sent letters soliciting a post to all her relations and acquaintances, including Sergius. But the letter had not found him there.

It was Saturday, and Praskovya Mikhailovna herself was mixing short dough with raisins, which her father's serf cook used to do so well. Praskovya Mikhailovna wanted to give her grandchildren a treat on Sunday.

Masha, her daughter, was dandling her youngest; the eldest, a boy and a girl, were at school. The son-in-law had not slept all night and was now asleep. Praskovya Mikhailovna had gone to sleep late that night, after trying to soften her daughter's anger against her husband.

She saw that her son-in-law—a weak being—could not speak or live any other way, and she saw that her daughter's reproaches would not help, and she tried all she could to soften them, so that there would be no reproaches, no ill will. She was almost physically unable to endure unkindly relations between people. It was so clear to her that nothing could be improved by it, but everything would be made worse. She did not even think of it, she simply suffered from the sight of anger, as from a bad smell, a sharp noise, blows to the body.

She was just self-contentedly teaching Lukerya how to mix the leavened dough, when Misha, her six-year-old grandson, in a pinafore, bandy-legged, in darned stockings, ran into the kitchen with a frightened face.

"Grandma, a scary old man is looking for you."

Lukerya peeked outside.

"That's right, ma'am, it's some pilgrim."

Praskovya Mikhailovna wiped her skinny elbows against each other and her hands on her apron and went inside to fetch her purse and give five kopecks in alms, but then remembered that she had nothing smaller than ten-kopeck pieces, and decided to give bread and went back to the cupboard, but suddenly blushed at the thought that she had grudged the money, and, telling Lukerya to cut a chunk of bread, went back to fetch a ten-kopeck piece on top of it. "There's a punishment for you," she said to herself, "giving twice as much."

She gave both to the pilgrim, with an apology, and, as she was giving it, no longer felt proud, but, on the contrary, was ashamed to be giving so little. Such an imposing look the pilgrim had.

Though he had walked two hundred miles begging in the name of Christ, and was ragged, and thin, and wind-burnt, had cropped hair, a peasant's hat and boots to match, and though he bowed humbly, Sergius had that imposing look that so attracted people to him. But Praskovya Mikhailovna did not recognize him. Nor could she have recognized him, not having seen him in almost thirty years.

"Don't scorn it, dear man. Maybe you'd like to eat something?"

He took the bread and the money. And Praskovya Mikhailovna was surprised that he did not go away, but went on looking at her.

"Pashenka. I've come to you. Take me in."

And dark, beautiful eyes looked at her attentively and entreatingly, glistening with the tears that welled up in them. And the lips twitched pathetically under greying moustaches.

Praskovya Mikhailovna clutched her withered breast, opened her mouth, and fixed her staring eyes on the pilgrim's face.

"It can't be! Styopa! Sergius! Father Sergius!"

"Yes, himself," Sergius said softly. "Only not Sergius, not Father Sergius, but the great sinner Stepan Kasatsky, a lost man, a great sinner. Take me in, help me."

"No, it can't be, how is it you've humbled yourself so? Come in, then."

She held out her hand; but he did not take it and walked behind her.

But where was she to take him? The apartment was small. There had been a tiny room, almost a closet, set apart for her, but then she had given up even that closet to her daughter. And now Masha was sitting there rocking the nursling to sleep.

"Sit down here, one moment," she said to Sergius, pointing to a bench in the kitchen.

Sergius sat down at once and took off his sack, with what was obviously an already habitual gesture, first from one shoulder, then from the other.

"My God, my God, how you've humbled yourself, dear father! Such fame, and suddenly so . . ."

Sergius did not reply and only smiled meekly, setting his sack down next to him.

"Masha, do you know who this is?"

And Praskovya Mikhailovna told her daughter in a whisper who Sergius was, and together they carried the bedding and cradle out of the closet, vacating it for Sergius.

Praskovya Mikhailovna brought Sergius to the closet.

"Here, get some rest. Don't scorn it. And I must go out."

"Where to?"

"I give lessons here, I'm ashamed to say—I teach music."

"Music—that's good. There's just one thing, Praskovya Mikhailovna, you see, I've come to you on business. When can I speak with you?"

"I shall account it my good fortune. Can it be this evening?"

"Yes, only I have another request: don't talk about me, about who I am. I've revealed myself only to you. No one knows where I've gone. It has to be that way."

"Ah, but I told my daughter."

"Well, ask her not to speak of it."

Sergius took off his boots, lay down, and fell asleep at once after a sleepless night and walking twenty-five miles.

WHEN PRASKOVYA MIKHAILOVNA CAME BACK, Sergius was sitting in his closet waiting for her. He did not come out for dinner, but ate the soup and kasha that Lukerya brought him there.

"Why is it you came earlier than you promised?" said Sergius. "Can we talk now?"

"And how is it I'm so fortunate as to have such a visitor? I skipped the lesson. After . . . I was dreaming all the time of going to you, I wrote to you, and suddenly such good fortune."

"Pashenka! Please take the words I say to you now as a confession, as the words I shall speak before God in the hour of death. Pashenka! I'm not a holy man, not even a simple, ordinary man: I'm a sinner, a dirty, vile, lost, proud sinner, whether worse than all, I don't know, but worse than the worst people."

Pashenka first stared wide-eyed at him. She believed him. Then, when she fully believed him, she touched his hand with hers and, smiling pityingly, said:

"Stiva, maybe you're exaggerating?"

"No, Pashenka. I'm a fornicator, I'm a murderer, I'm a blasphemer and deceiver."

"My God! What is this?" said Praskovya Mikhailovna.

"But one must live. And I, who thought I knew everything, who taught others how to live—I know nothing, and I ask you to teach me."

"What are you saying, Stiva? You're making fun of me. Why must people always make fun of me?"

"Well, all right, I'm making fun: only tell me, how do you live and how have you lived your life?"

"Me? Oh, I've lived the most vile, nasty life, and now God is punishing me, and it serves me right. I live so badly, so badly . . ."

"How did you get married? How did you live with your husband?"

"It was all bad. I married—I fell in love in the most vile way. Papa didn't want it. I disregarded everything and got married anyway. And, once I was married, instead of helping my husband, I tormented him with jealousy, which I couldn't overcome in myself."

"He drank, I heard."

"Yes, but I was unable to give him peace. I reproached him. But it's an illness, he couldn't control himself, and I remember how I wouldn't let him. And we had terrible scenes."

And she looked at Kasatsky with her beautiful eyes, suffering from the memory.

Kasatsky remembered being told that Pashenka's husband beat her. And now, looking at her thin, withered neck with the veins bulging behind her ears, and at her knot of scanty hair, half grey, half blonde, it was as if he could see how it had happened.

"Then I was left alone with two children and without any means."

"But you had an estate."

"We sold it while Vasya was still alive and . . . spent it all. We had to live, and I couldn't do anything—like all of us young ladies. But I was especially bad, quite helpless. So we lived through the last we had, I taught the children—and learned a little myself. And then Mitya fell ill when he was in the fourth form, and God took him. Manechka fell in love with Vanya—my son-in-law. And why not, he's a good man, only unfortunate. He's ill."

"Mother," her daughter interrupted. "Take Misha, I can't do everything at once."

Praskovya Mikhailovna gave a start, got up, and, stepping quickly in her down-at-heel shoes, went out and came back at once with a two-year-old boy in her arms, who threw himself back and snatched at her shawl with his little hands.

"Now, where did I leave off? Ah, yes, so he had a good post here—and his superior was so nice, but Vanya couldn't do it and resigned."

"What is he sick with?"

"Neurasthenia, it's a terrible illness. We got advice, but it meant having to travel, and we have no means. But I keep hoping it will just go away. He has no particular pains, but . . ."

"Lukerya!" came a man's voice, angry and weak. "They always send her somewhere when she's needed. Mother!"

"Coming," Praskovya Mikhailovna interrupted herself again. "He hasn't had dinner yet. He can't eat with us."

She stepped out, took care of something there, and came back wiping her thin, sunburnt hands.

"That's how I live. And we keep complaining, we keep being displeased, but, thank God, our grandchildren are all fine, healthy, and we can still live. But why talk about me?"

"And what do you live on?"

"I earn a little. I used to get bored with music, but how useful it is to me now."

She placed her small hand on the chest she was sitting next to and moved her thin fingers, as if playing an exercise.

"How much are you paid for your lessons?"

"Sometimes a rouble, or fifty kopecks, or else thirty. They're all so kind to me."

"And do they make any progress?" Kasatsky asked, his eyes smiling slightly.

Praskovya Mikhailovna did not believe at first that the question was serious and looked enquiringly into his eyes.

"Some make progress. There's one nice girl, the butcher's daughter. A kind, good girl. If I'd been a proper woman, then, of course, I could have used my father's connections to find my son-in-law a post. But I never knew how to do anything and so I've brought them all to this."

"Yes, yes," said Kasatsky, bowing his head. "Well, Pashenka, and do you take any part in church life?" he asked.

"Oh, don't speak of it. I'm so bad, I've let it all go. I do prepare for communion[25] and go to church with the children, but then for months I don't go. I send the children."

"And why don't you go yourself?"

"To tell the truth," she blushed, "I'm ashamed to go in tatters in front of my daughter and grandchildren, and I haven't anything new. I'm also lazy."

"Well, and do you pray at home?"

"I do, but what sort of prayer is it—just mechanical. I know it shouldn't be like that, but I have no real feeling, the only thing is that I know all my vileness . . ."

"Yes, yes, so, so," Kasatsky murmured as if in approval.

"Coming, coming," she responded to her son-in-law's call and, straightening the little braid on her head, she left the room.

This time it was long before she returned. When she did, Kasatsky was sitting in the same position, his elbows resting on his knees, his head bowed. But his sack was on his back.

When she came in carrying a tin lamp without a shade, he raised his beautiful, weary eyes to her and sighed very deeply.

"I didn't tell them who you were," she began timidly, "I only said you were a pilgrim, a nobleman, and that I used to know you. Let's go to the dining room and have tea."

"No . . ."

"Then I'll bring it here."

"No, I don't need anything. God save you, Pashenka. I'm leaving. If you have pity, don't tell anyone you saw me. As God lives, I adjure you, don't tell anyone. I thank you. I would bow to your feet, but I know it would embarrass you. Thank you, and forgive me for Christ's sake."

"Bless me."

"God will bless you. Forgive me for Christ's sake."

And he was about to leave, but she would not let him and brought him some bread, hard rolls, and butter. He took it all and left.

It was dark, and before he had passed two houses she lost sight of him and knew he was walking on only because the archpriest's dog barked at him.

.   .   .   .

"So THAT'S WHAT my dream meant. Pashenka is precisely what I should have been and was not. I lived for people under the pretext of God, she lives for God, fancying she's living for people. Yes, one good deed, a cup of water given without thought of reward, is worth more than all my benefactions for people. But wasn't there a portion of sincere desire to serve God?" he asked himself, and the answer was: "Yes, but it was all soiled, overgrown by human glory. Yes, there is no God for someone who lives, as I did, for human glory. I will seek Him."

And he walked from village to village, as he had done before Pashenka, meeting and parting with pilgrims, men and women, and begging for bread and a night's lodging for Christ's sake. Occasionally an angry housewife would scold him, a drunken muzhik would abuse him, but for the most part he was given food and drink and even more for the road. His gentlemanly looks disposed some in his favour. Some, on the contrary, were as if glad to see a gentleman reduced to such poverty. But his meekness won them all over.

Often, finding the Gospels in a house, he would read from them, and everywhere people were moved and surprised, as if they were listening to something new and at the same time long familiar.

If he succeeded in serving people by advice, or by his being literate, or by settling a quarrel, he did not see their gratitude, because he was gone. And gradually God began to be revealed in him.

Once he was walking with two old women and a soldier. A gentleman and lady in a charabanc drawn by a trotter and a man and woman on horseback stopped him. The lady's husband and daughter were on horseback; the lady herself rode in the charabanc with, obviously, a travelling Frenchman.

They stopped to show him *les pélérins*,* who, following Russian superstition, go from place to place instead of working.

They spoke in French, thinking they would not be understood.

"Demandez-leur," said the Frenchman, *"s'ils sont bien sûrs de ce que leur pélérinage est agréable à Dieu."*†

They were asked. One old woman said:

"As God takes it. Our feet have been there, but what of our hearts?"

---

* The pilgrims.
† Ask them . . . if they are quite sure their pilgrimage is pleasing to God.

They asked the soldier. He said he was alone and had nowhere to go. They asked Kasatsky who he was.

"A servant of God."

"Qu'est-ce qu'il dit? Il ne répond pas." *

"Il dit qu'il est un serviteur de Dieu."†

"Cela doit être un fils de prêtre. Il a de la race. Avez-vous de la petite monnaie?"‡

The Frenchman happened to have some small change. And he gave them twenty kopecks each.

*"Mais dites-leur que ce n'est pas pour des cierges que je leur donne, mais pour qu'ils se régalent de thé—*tea, tea," he smiled, *"pour vous, mon vieux,"* he said, patting Kasatsky on the shoulder with his gloved hand.§

"Christ save you," replied Kasatsky, not putting his hat back on and bowing his bald head.

And this meeting gave Kasatsky special joy, because he disdained people's opinion and did the most trifling and easy thing—humbly took the twenty kopecks and gave it to his companion, a blind beggar. The less significance people's opinion had, the stronger was the feeling of God.

Kasatsky walked about like this for eight months; in the ninth month he was arrested in a provincial capital, in a shelter where he was spending the night with other pilgrims, and, as he had no passport,[26] he was taken to the police. To the questions of where his papers were and who he was, he replied that he had no papers and that he was a servant of God. He was reckoned a vagabond, tried, and sent to Siberia.

In Siberia he settled on a rich muzhik's farmstead, and is living there now. He works in the owner's kitchen garden, teaches the children, and looks after the sick.

1890–98

---

* What does he say? He doesn't answer.
† He says he is a servant of God.
‡ That one must be a priest's son. He has some breeding. Do you have any small change?
§ But tell them I'm not giving it to them for candles, but so that they can treat themselves to tea . . . for you, old fellow.

After the Ball

"So you say that man cannot understand what's good and what's bad on his own, that it's all a matter of the environment, that he's a prey to the environment. But I think it's all a matter of chance. Here, I'll tell you about myself."

So began the universally esteemed Ivan Vassilievich, after the conversation that had gone on among us about the necessity, for personal perfection, of first changing the conditions in which people live. No one, as a matter of fact, had said it was impossible to understand for oneself what is good and what is bad, but Ivan Vassilievich had that way of responding to his own thoughts as they emerged during a conversation, and of using those thoughts as an occasion for recounting episodes from his life. Often he completely forgot the pretext for his telling the story, being carried away by the telling itself, the more so as he did it very candidly and truthfully.

And so he did now.

"I'll tell you about myself. My whole life has turned out thus and not otherwise, not from the environment, but from something else entirely."

"From what, then?" we asked.

"That's a long story. It will take a lot of telling to understand it."

"Well, so tell us."

Ivan Vassilievich fell to thinking and shook his head.

"Yes," he said. "My whole life was changed by one night, or rather one morning."

"What on earth happened?"

"What happened was that I was deeply in love. I had been in love many times before, but never so deeply as that. It's a thing of the past; she already has married daughters. It was B . . . , yes, Varenka B. . . ." Ivan Vassilievich gave her name. "She was a remarkable beauty even at the age of fifty. But in her youth, at eighteen, she was enchanting: tall, slender, graceful, majestic, precisely majestic. She always held herself extraordinarily erect, as if she could not do otherwise, throwing her head back slightly, and this, along with her beauty and her height, despite her thinness, even boniness, gave her a sort of regal look, which would have frightened people off, if it hadn't been for the gracious, always cheerful smile of her mouth, and of her enchanting, shining eyes, and of the whole of her sweet, young being."

"How well Ivan Vassilievich describes her!"

"No matter how I describe her, it's impossible to describe her so that you understand how she was. But that's not the point: what I want to tell you about happened back in the forties. I was then a student at a provincial university. I don't know whether this was good or bad, but at that time there were no circles, no theories in our university; we were simply young and lived the way young people do: studied and had fun. I was a very pert and merry lad, and rich besides. I owned a dashing ambler, I went sledding with girls (skating wasn't in fashion yet), and caroused with my comrades (at that time we drank nothing but champagne; if we had no money, we drank nothing, but we did not drink vodka as they do now). But my chief pleasure consisted in soirées and balls. I was a good dancer and not ugly to look at."

"Now, don't be modest," one of his lady listeners interrupted him. "We know your daguerreotype portrait. Not only were you not ugly, you were a handsome man."

"Handsome if you like, that's not the point. The point is that at the time of this deepest love of mine for her, on the last day before Lent, I was at a ball at the provincial marshal's,[1] a good-natured old man, rich and hospitable, and a gentleman of the chamber. The hostess was his equally good-natured wife, in a puce-coloured velvet dress, with a diamond frontlet on her head, and with her old, plump, white shoulders and bosom exposed, as in the portraits of Elizaveta Petrovna.[2] The ball was wonderful: an excellent ballroom, with a choir loft, musicians—the then-famous serfs of a music-loving landowner, a magnificent buffet, and an endless sea of champagne. Though I was a fancier of champagne, I did not drink, because, without any wine, I was drunk with love, but to make up for it I danced till I dropped, danced quadrilles, and waltzes, and polkas—naturally, as much as possible, with Varenka. She was wearing a white gown with a pink sash and white kid gloves that reached almost to her thin, sharp elbows, and white satin slippers. The mazurka was taken from me: a most disgusting engineer, Anisimov—to this day I can't forgive him for it—invited her as soon as she came in, while I had stopped at the barber's and for gloves and was late. So I danced the mazurka not with her, but with a little German girl whom I had once courted a bit. But I'm afraid I was very impolite to her that evening, did not talk to her, did not look at her, but saw only the tall, slender figure in a white gown with a pink sash, her radiant, flushed face with its dimples, and her tender, sweet eyes. Not just I, everyone looked at her and admired her, both men and women admired her, even though she outshone them all. It was impossible not to admire her.

"By the rules, so to speak, I did not dance the mazurka with her, but in fact I danced it with her almost all the time. She, quite unembarrassed, would come straight to me across the entire ballroom, and I would jump up without waiting for an invitation, and she would thank me with her smile for my perceptiveness. When we were brought to her and she failed to guess my quality,[3] she, not giving me her hand, would shrug her thin shoulders and smile at me, as a sign of regret and consolation. When the figure of the mazurka was a waltz, I would waltz with her for a long time, and she, breathing quickly, would smile at me and say, *'Encore.'*

"And I would waltz more and more and was not even aware of my own body."

"Well, how could you not be aware of it? I suppose, when you put your arm around her waist, you were quite aware not only of your own body, but of hers as well," said one of the guests.

Ivan Vassilievich suddenly turned red and almost shouted angrily:

"Yes, that's you, today's young people. You see nothing but the body. In our time it wasn't so. The more deeply in love I was, the more bodiless she became for me. You now see feet, ankles, and what-not else, you undress the women you're in love with, but for me, as Alphonse Karr[4]— he was a good writer—said: 'The object of my love always wore bronze clothing.' We not only did not undress, we tried to cover up nakedness, like Noah's good son.⁵ Well, you won't understand . . ."

"Don't listen to him. What happened next?" said one of us.

"Yes. So I danced mostly with her and did not notice how the time passed. The musicians now kept repeating the same tune of the mazurka with a sort of weary despair, you know, as it happens at the end of a ball; the papas and mamas had already got up from their card tables in the drawing rooms in anticipation of supper; servants scurried about more frequently, carrying things. It was past two o'clock. We had to take advantage of the last minutes. I chose her once more, and for the hundredth time we went the length of the ballroom.

" 'So the quadrille is mine after supper?' I said to her, escorting her to her place.

" 'Certainly, if I'm not taken away,' she said, smiling.

" 'I won't let them,' I said.

" 'Give me back my fan,' she said.

" 'I'm sorry to give it up,' I said, handing her the inexpensive white fan.

" 'Take this, then, so that you won't be sorry,' she said, plucking a little feather from the fan and giving it to me.

"I took the little feather and only with my glance could I express all my rapture and gratitude. I was not only cheerful and content, I was happy, blissful, I was good, I was not I but some unearthly being, knowing no evil and capable only of good. I put the feather into my glove and stood, unable to part from her.

" 'Look, papà has been asked to dance,' she said, pointing to the tall, stately figure of her father, a colonel, with silver epaulettes, standing in the doorway with the hostess and other ladies.

" 'Varenka, come here,' we heard the loud voice of the hostess in the diamond frontlet and with Elizavetan shoulders.

"Varenka went to the door, and I followed.

" 'Persuade your father to take a turn with you, *ma chère*.* Please, Pyotr Vladislavich,' the hostess turned to the colonel.

"Varenka's father was a very handsome, stately, tall, and fresh old man. His face was very ruddy, with white moustaches twirled up à la

* My dear.

Nicolas I,[6] side-whiskers, also white and meeting the moustaches, and the hair brushed forward on his temples, and there was the same gracious, joyful smile as his daughter's in his shining eyes and his lips. He was splendidly built, with a broad, thrust-out martial chest, not overly adorned by medals, with strong shoulders and long, slim legs. He was a military commander with the typical bearing of an old campaigner of Nicolas's time.

"As we approached the door, the colonel was refusing, saying that he had forgotten how to dance, but all the same, smiling, he reached his hand to his left side, took the sword from his sword belt, handed it to an obliging young man, and, drawing a kid glove onto his right hand, said with a smile, 'Everything according to the rules,' took his daughter's hand, and stood in quarter profile waiting for the beat.

"Having waited for the start of the mazurka tune, he pertly stamped one foot, kicked up the other, and his tall, heavy figure began to move about the room, now slowly and smoothly, now noisily and stormily, with a tapping of soles and of foot against foot. Varenka's graceful figure floated beside him inconspicuously, shortening or lengthening the steps of her small white satin feet in time with the music. The whole ballroom followed every movement of the pair. I not only admired them, but watched them with rapturous tenderness. I was especially moved by his boots with their tight foot-straps—good calfskin boots, not with fashionable pointed toes, but with old-fashioned square toes and no heels. The boots had obviously been constructed by a battalion bootmaker. 'He doesn't buy fashionable boots, but wears home-made ones, so as to dress his beloved daughter and take her out,' I thought, and those square-toed boots especially moved me. It was clear that he had once been an excellent dancer, but was now heavy, and his legs were not sufficiently supple for all those beautiful and quick steps he was trying to perform. But all the same he adroitly made two circles. When, quickly spreading his legs, he brought them together again and dropped, if somewhat heavily, to one knee, and she, smiling and straightening her skirt, which he had snagged on, walked smoothly around him, everyone applauded loudly. Getting to his feet with some effort, he took his daughter tenderly and sweetly by the ears with his hands and, having kissed her on the forehead, led her over to me, thinking I was going to dance with her. I said that I was not her partner.

" 'Well, all the same, take a turn with her now,' he said, smiling graciously and putting his sword through the sword belt.

"As it happens that after one drop is poured from a bottle, its contents pour out in great streams, so in my soul my love for Varenka released all the capacity for love concealed in it. At that moment I embraced the whole world with my love. I loved the hostess in the frontlet, with her Elizavetan bosom, and her husband, and her guests, and her servants, and even the engineer Anisimov, who was pouting at me. As for her father, with his home-made boots and gracious smile, just like his daughter's, at that moment I felt for him a sort of rapturously tender feeling.

"'The mazurka ended, the hosts asked their guests to supper, but Colonel B. declined, saying that he had to get up early the next day, and took leave of them. I was afraid that he would take her away, too, but she stayed with her mother.

"After supper I danced the promised quadrille with her and, though it seemed I was infinitely happy, my happiness kept growing and growing. We said nothing about love. I did not ask her or even myself if she loved me. It was enough for me that I loved her. And I feared only that something would spoil my happiness.

"When I came home, undressed, and thought of sleeping, I saw that it was completely impossible. In my hand was the little feather from her fan and the whole glove she had given me as she was leaving and getting into the carriage, and I was helping her mother in and then her. I looked at these things and, without closing my eyes, saw her before me at the moment when, choosing one of two partners, she had guessed my quality, and heard her dear voice as she said: '*Pride?* Yes?' and joyfully gave me her hand, or when, at dinner, she put her lips to the glass of champagne and looked at me from under her eyebrows with caressing eyes. But most of all I saw her dancing with her father, when she moved smoothly around him and glanced, with pride and joy for herself and for him, at the admiring spectators. And I involuntarily united him and her in one feeling of tender emotion.

"My late brother and I were then living on our own. My brother generally did not like society and did not go to balls, and now he was preparing for his qualifying examinations and was leading a most regular life. He was asleep. I looked at his head buried in the pillow and half covered with a flannel blanket, and felt a loving pity for him, a pity that he did not know or share the happiness I was experiencing. Our serf valet Petrusha met me with a candle and wanted to help me undress, but I dismissed him. The look of his sleepy face with tousled hair seemed sweetly touching to me. Trying to make no noise, I tiptoed to my room and sat on the bed. No, I was too happy, I couldn't sleep. Besides, I felt hot in the overheated rooms, and, without taking off my uniform, I went quietly to the hall, put on my overcoat, opened the front door, and stepped outside.

"I had left the ball after four o'clock; while I was going home and then sitting at home, two more hours went by, so that when I went out it was already light. It was perfect pre-Lenten weather, there was a mist, the waterlogged snow melted on the roads, and all the roofs were dripping. The B.s were living then on the edge of town, next to a big field, at one end of which was a promenade, at the other a girls' boarding school. I walked through our deserted lane and came out on the main street, where I began to meet passers-by and sledges loaded with firewood, their runners scraping the pavement. The horses rhythmically tossing their wet heads under the glistening shaft-bows, and the draymen, covered with bast mats, splashing through the water in their enormous boots beside their sledges, and the houses on the street, looking very tall in the mist— everything was especially dear and significant to me.

"When I came out to the field where their house was, I saw something big and black at the end of it, in the direction of the promenade, and heard the sounds of a fife and drum coming from there. There had been a singing in my soul all the while, and occasionally I had heard the tune of the mazurka. But this was a different, a harsh, bad music.

" 'What's this?' I thought and went in the direction of the sounds down the slippery road across the field. Having gone some hundred paces, I began to make out the black figures of many people through the mist. Soldiers, obviously. 'It must be a drill,' I thought, and along with a blacksmith in a greasy jacket and apron, who was carrying something and walked ahead of me, I went closer. The soldiers in black uniforms were standing in two rows facing each other, holding their guns at their sides and not moving. Behind them stood the drummer and fifer, ceaselessly repeating the same unpleasant, shrill melody.

" 'What are they doing?' I asked the blacksmith, who stopped beside me.

" 'A Tartar's running the gauntlet for desertion,' the blacksmith said angrily, looking at the far end of the rows.

"I began to look there, too, and saw something dreadful approaching me between the rows. What was approaching me was a man stripped to the waist, tied to the guns of two soldiers, who were leading him. Beside him walked a tall officer in a greatcoat and a peaked cap, whose figure seemed familiar to me. His whole body jerking, his feet splashing through the melting snow, the punished man moved towards me under a shower of blows from both sides, now lurching backwards—and then the corporals leading him by the guns shoved him ahead—now falling forward—and then the corporals pulled him back to keep him from falling. And the tall officer, not lagging behind him, walked along with a firm, springing gait. It was her father, with his ruddy face and white moustaches and side-whiskers.

"At each blow, the punished man, as if astonished, turned his face twisted with suffering in the direction from which the blow had fallen and, baring his white teeth, repeated the same words. Only when they were quite near could I hear those words. He did not say, but sobbed: 'Have mercy, brothers. Have mercy, brothers.' But his brothers had no mercy, and when the procession came even with me, I saw the soldier standing opposite me step forward resolutely and, swinging his rod with a whistle, give a strong blow to the Tartar's back. The Tartar jerked foward, but the corporals held him, and the same blow fell on him from the other side, and again from this side, and again from that. The colonel walked next to him and, glancing now at his feet, now at the punished man, breathed in air and, puffing his cheeks, let it out slowly through his protruding lips. When the procession had passed the place where I was standing, I caught a glimpse of the punished man's back between the rows. It was something so mottled, wet, red, unnatural, that I could not believe it was a man's body.

" 'Oh Lord,' said the blacksmith next to me.

"The procession moved further on, the blows falling in the same way from both sides on the stumbling, writhing man, the drum beating and the fife whistling in the same way, and the tall, stately figure of the colonel stepping firmly in the same way beside the punished man. Suddenly the colonel stopped and quickly went up to one of the soldiers.

" 'I'll go easy for you,' I heard his wrathful voice. 'So you want to go easy, do you?'

"And I saw how, with his strong hand in its kid glove, he beat the frightened, puny, weak soldier on the face for having brought his rod down on the Tartar's red back without enough force.

" 'Bring fresh rods!' he shouted, looking around, and he saw me. Pretending he didn't know me, he quickly turned away, frowning menacingly and angrily. I was so ashamed that, not knowing where to look, as if I'd been caught in a most shameful act, I lowered my eyes and hurriedly went home. All the way home the beating of the drum and whistling of the fife rang in my ears, then I heard the words 'Have mercy, brothers,' then I heard the self-assured, wrathful voice of the colonel shouting: 'So you want to go easy, do you?' And meanwhile in my heart there was an almost physical, nauseating anguish, so intense that I stopped several times, and it seemed to me that I was about to vomit up the whole horror that had entered into me from that spectacle. I don't remember how I reached home and lay down. But as soon as I began to fall asleep, I heard and saw it all again and jumped up.

" 'He obviously knows something that I don't know,' I thought about the colonel. 'If I knew what he knows, I'd understand what I saw, and it wouldn't torment me.' But however much I thought, I could not understand what the colonel knew, and I fell asleep only towards evening, and then only after going to see a friend and getting quite drunk with him.

"So, do you think I decided then that what I had seen was a bad thing? Not a bit of it. 'If it was done with such assurance and was acknowledged by everyone as necessary, it means they know something that I don't know,' I thought and tried to find it out. But however much I tried, even afterwards I could not find it out. And not having found it out, I could not enter military service, as I had wanted to before, and not only did not serve in the military, but did not serve anywhere and, as you see, have been good for nothing."

"Well, we know how good for nothing you've been," one of us said. "Better tell us how many people would have been good for nothing if it hadn't been for you."

"Well, now that's sheer nonsense," Ivan Vassilievich said with sincere vexation.

"Well, and what about your love?" we asked.

"My love? My love began to wane from that day on. When, as often happened with her, she would lapse into thought, with a smile on her face, I would at once recall the colonel on the square, and it somehow became awkward and unpleasant for me, and I began to see her more rarely. And so love dwindled away. There you see what sort of things can happen and how they can change and redirect a man's whole life. And you say . . ." he concluded.

1903

The Forged Coupon

I

FYODOR MIKHAILOVICH SMOKOVNIKOV, chairman of the tax board, a man of incorruptible honesty, and proud of it, and a gloomy liberal, and not only a freethinker but one who hated every manifestation of religiosity, which he considered a leftover of superstition, came back from the board in the worst of moods. The governor had written him the stupidest of notes, from which it could be inferred that Fyodor Mikhailovich had acted dishonestly. Fyodor Mikhailovich had become very angry and had at once written a pert and stinging reply.

At home it seemed to Fyodor Mikhailovich that everything was being done against him.

It was five minutes to five. He thought dinner would be served at once, but dinner was not ready yet. Fyodor Mikhailovich slammed the door and went to his room. Someone knocked on the door. "Who the devil is that," he thought and shouted:

"Who's there?"

A fifteen-year-old boy, in the fifth class at school, Fyodor Mikhailovich's son, came in.

"What brings you here?"

"Today's the first."

"What? Money?"

The custom was that on the first of each month the father gave his son an allowance of three roubles for entertainment. Fyodor Mikhailovich frowned, took out his wallet, rummaged in it, and pulled out a coupon[1] worth two and a half roubles, then took out his change purse and counted out another fifty kopecks. His son was silent and did not take it.

"Papa, please advance me some."

"What?"

"I wouldn't be asking, but I borrowed on my word of honour, I promised. As an honest man, I can't . . . I need another three roubles, really, I wouldn't ask . . . or not that I wouldn't ask, but just . . . please, papa."

"You've been told . . ."

"Yes, papa, but just this once . . ."

"You get a three-rouble allowance and it's not enough. At your age I didn't get even fifty kopecks."

"All my friends get more now. Petrov and Ivanitsky get fifty roubles."

"And I tell you that if you behave like this you'll turn into a swindler. I have spoken."

"So you've spoken. You never enter into my situation, I'll have to become a scoundrel. It's all very well for you."

"Get out, scapegrace! Out!"

Fyodor Mikhailovich jumped up and rushed at his son.

"Out! Your kind want whipping!"

His son was frightened and angry, but more angry than frightened, and, bowing his head, he walked with quick steps to the door. Fyodor Mikhailovich had no intention of beating him, but he was glad of his wrath and went on shouting abusive words for a long time at his son's back.

When the maid came and said that dinner was ready, Fyodor Mikhailovich stood up.

"At last," he said. "I don't even want to eat any more."

And, scowling, he went to dinner.

At the table his wife started talking with him, but he barked so angrily and curtly in reply that she fell silent. His son also did not raise his eyes from his plate and kept silent. They ate in silence and in silence got up and went their separate ways.

After dinner the student went to his room, took the coupon and change from his pocket and flung them on the table, then took off his uniform and put on a jacket. First the student picked up a tattered Latin grammar, then he put the hook on the door, swept the money from the table into the drawer with his hand, took cigarette papers from the drawer, rolled a cigarette, and began to smoke.

He sat over his grammar and notebooks for some two hours, not understanding a thing, then got up and began to pace the room, stamping his heels, recalling all that had gone on between him and his father. All his father's abusive words, his angry face especially, came back to him as if he had just heard and seen him. "Scapegrace. You want whipping." And the more he remembered, the angrier he became with his father. He remembered his father saying, "I see what will become of you—a swindler. Be it known to you." "And so I'll become a swindler. It's all very well for him. He's forgotten what it's like to be young. Well, what crime have I committed? I simply went to the theatre, had no money, and borrowed from Petya Grushetsky. What's so bad about that? Another father would feel sorry, ask questions, but this one only abuses me and thinks of himself. When there's something he hasn't got, there's shouting all over the house, but I'm a swindler. No, he may be my father, but I don't like him. I don't know about anybody else, but I don't like him."

A maid knocked on his door. She brought him a note.

"Answer expected without fail."

The note read:

For the third time now I ask you to return the six roubles you borrowed from me, but you try to get out of it. Honest people do not act that way. I ask you to send the money immediately with the bearer. I need it badly myself. Can't you get hold of it somewhere?

Your (depending on whether you pay it back or not) disdainful or respectful comrade,

Grushetsky.

"Think of that. What a swine. He can't wait. I'll try once more."

Mitya went to his mother. This was his last hope. His mother was kind and could not say no, and she probably would have helped him, but that day she was upset by the illness of her younger son, the two-year-old Petya. She became angry with Mitya for coming and making noise and refused him at once.

He muttered something under his breath and started out the door. She felt sorry for her son and called him back.

"Wait, Mitya," she said. "I don't have it now, but I'll get it by tomorrow."

But Mitya was still seething with rage against his father.

"What's tomorrow to me, when I need it today? Be it known to you that I'm going to a schoolmate."

And he left, slamming the door.

"There's nothing else to do. He'll let me know where to pawn my watch," he thought, feeling for his watch in his pocket.

Mitya took the coupon and change from the drawer, put his coat on, and went to see Makhin.

II

MAKHIN WAS a student with a moustache. He played cards, knew women, and always had money. He lived with his aunt. Mitya knew that Makhin was a bad sort, but when he was with him, he involuntarily submitted to him. Makhin was at home and was getting ready to go to the theatre: his dirty little room smelled of scented soap and cologne.

"That, brother, is the last resort," Makhin said, when Mitya told him of his trouble, showed the coupon and the fifty kopecks, and said he needed nine roubles. "You can pawn your watch, but you can also do better," said Makhin, winking his eye.

"How's that?"

"Very simple." Makhin took the coupon. "Put a one in front of the 2.50 and it'll be 12.50."

"But are there any like that?"

"Why not, on thousand-rouble notes. I cashed one like that."

"Can it be?"

"Well, shall I go ahead?" said Makhin, taking a pen and smoothing the coupon out with one finger of his left hand.

"But it's not right."

"What nonsense."

"True," thought Mitya, and again he recalled his father's abusive term: swindler. "So I'll be a swindler." He looked into Makhin's face. Makhin looked at him, smiling calmly.

"Shall I go ahead?"

"Yes."

Makhin carefully traced a one.

"Well, now let's go to the shop. Here at the corner: photography accessories. I happen to need a frame, for this person here."

He took out a photograph of a big-eyed girl with an enormous head of hair and a magnificent bust.

"Isn't she a sweetheart, eh?"

"Yes, yes. But how . . ."

"Very simple. Come on."

Makhin got dressed, and they left together.

III

AT THE FRONT DOOR to the photography shop a little bell rang. The students went in, looking around the empty shop, its shelves laden with photography accessories, and with display cases on the counters. From the rear door a homely woman with a kind face came out and, standing behind the counter, asked them what they wanted.

"A pretty little frame, madam."

"At what price?" the lady asked, her hands in half-gloves, their joints swollen, moving quickly and deftly over frames of different designs. "These are fifty kopecks, and these are a bit more. And here's a very sweet one, a new design, for a rouble twenty."

"Well, give me that one. But couldn't you come down a little? Make it a rouble."

"We don't bargain," the lady said with dignity.

"Well, have it your way," said Makhin, placing the coupon on the display case. "Give us the frame and the change, and be quick about it. We'll be late for the theatre."

"There's still time," the lady said, and she began to scrutinize the coupon with her nearsighted eyes.

"It'll go nicely in this frame, eh?" said Makhin, turning to Mitya.

"Don't you have some other money?" asked the saleswoman.

"The trouble is that I don't. My father gave it to me, it's got to be broken."

"You don't have a rouble twenty?"

"I've got fifty kopecks. What, are you afraid we're cheating you with forged money?"

"No, never mind."

"Give it back, then. We'll get it changed."

"So how much do I owe you?"

"Oh, it should be eleven and something."

The saleswoman clicked her abacus, opened the cash box, took out a ten-rouble bill and, fishing around in the change, came up with six twenty-kopeck and two five-kopeck pieces.

"Can I trouble you to wrap it?" asked Makhin, taking the money unhurriedly.

"Just a moment."

The saleswoman wrapped the frame and tied it with string.

Mitya breathed again only when the little bell at the front door rang behind him and they were outside.

"Here's ten roubles for you, and let me keep the rest. I'll pay it back."

And Makhin went to the theatre, while Mitya went to Grushetsky and settled accounts with him.

IV

AN HOUR after the students left, the owner of the shop came home and began to count the receipts.

"Ah, you lopsided fool! What a fool you are!" he shouted at his wife, seeing the coupon and noticing the forgery at once. "And what are you taking coupons for?"

"But, Zhenya, you yourself took some in front of me, and precisely twelve-rouble ones," said his wife, embarrassed, upset, and ready to cry. "I don't understand how they fooled me," she said, "they're students. A handsome young man, seemed so *comme il faut*."

"*Comme il faut* fool," her husband went on scolding while he counted the money. "If I take a coupon, it's that I know and can see what's written on it. But you, I bet you just stared at the students' mugs in your old age."

That his wife could not bear and she became angry herself.

"A real man! You only judge others, but when you gamble away fifty-four roubles at cards, it's nothing."

"I'm another matter."

"I don't want to talk to you," his wife said and went to her room and started remembering how her family had opposed her marriage, considering her husband much beneath her socially, and how she alone had insisted on the marriage; she remembered her dead child and her husband's indifference to that loss, and she hated her husband so much that she thought how good it would be if he died. But, having thought that, she became frightened of her own feelings and hastened to get dressed and leave. When her husband came home, his wife was not there. Without waiting for him, she had dressed and gone alone to visit an acquaintance, a French teacher, who had invited them to a soirée that evening.

V

THE FRENCH TEACHER, a Russian Pole, gave a formal tea party with sweet pastry, and then they sat down to several tables of vint.[2] The wife of the dealer in photography accessories sat with the host, an officer, and a deaf old lady in a wig, the widow of the owner of a music shop, a great enthusiast and skilful player of cards. The wife of the dealer in photographic accessories kept getting lucky cards. She twice bid a grand slam. Next to her was a little plate with grapes and a pear, and she was in merry spirits.

"Why doesn't Evgeny Mikhailovich come?" asked the hostess from another table. "We wrote him down as a fifth."

"He probably got carried away with the accounts," said Evgeny Mikhailovich's wife. "Today we have to pay up for food and firewood."

And, recalling the scene with her husband, she frowned, and her hands in their half-gloves trembled with anger against him.

"Well, speak of the devil," said the host, addressing the entering Evgeny Mikhailovich. "Why so late?"

"Oh, various things," Evgeny Mikhailovich replied in a merry voice, rubbing his hands. And, to his wife's surprise, he went over to her and said:

"You know, I passed off that coupon."

"Really?"

"Yes, on a muzhik for firewood."

And Evgeny Mikhailovich told them all in great indignation—with his wife adding details to the story—how some shameless students had cheated his wife.

"Well, sirs, now to business," he said, sitting down at the table when his turn came and shuffling the cards.

VI

INDEED, Evgeny Mikhailovich had passed off the coupon on the peasant Ivan Mironov for firewood.

Ivan Mironov's business consisted in buying a cord of firewood from the wood depot, taking it around the city, and dividing it into five parts, which he sold for the price of a quarter cord at the wood yard. On that unlucky day for Ivan Mironov he had taken a load early in the morning and, having quickly sold it, had taken another load and hoped to sell it, but had driven around until evening looking for buyers but not finding any. He kept running into experienced city-dwellers, who knew the usual tricks of muzhiks who sold firewood and did not believe that he, as he assured them, had brought the wood from the country. He was hungry, chilled through in his worn sheepskin jacket and tattered smock; it went down to twenty degrees of frost towards evening; his nag, which he did not spare because he intended to sell it for slaughter, refused to budge. So Ivan Mironov was even ready to sell the wood at a loss when he met Evgeny Mikhailovich, who had gone out to buy tobacco and was on his way home.

"Take it, master, I'll sell it cheap. My nag refuses to budge."

"Where are you from?"

"The country. It's my own wood, good and dry."

"We know all that. Well, what's your price?"

Ivan Mironov told him, then lowered it, and finally let it go for cost.

"Just for you, master, because it's nearby," he said.

Evgeny Mikhailovich did not bargain much, glad at the thought of passing off the coupon. Pulling at the shafts himself, Ivan Mironov somehow managed to bring the wood into the yard and unloaded it in the shed. The yard porter was not there. Ivan Mironov hesitated at first to take the coupon, but Evgeny Mikhailovich was so persuasive and seemed like such an imposing gentleman that he agreed to take it.

Going into the servants' quarters by the back door, Ivan Mironov crossed himself, wiped the icicles from his beard, and, raising the skirt of his kaftan, took out a leather purse and from it eight roubles and fifty kopecks and handed over the change, then wrapped the coupon in paper and put it in the purse.

Having thanked the gentleman properly, Ivan Mironov, urging on his frost-covered nag, condemned to death and barely moving its legs, not with the whip but with its handle, drove the empty sled to the tavern.

In the tavern, Ivan Mironov asked for eight kopecks' worth of vodka and tea, and, warmed up and even sweaty, in the merriest mood, conversed with a yard porter who was sitting at his table. He got to talking with him, told him all his circumstances. He told him he was from the village of Vassilievskoe, eight miles away, that he lived apart from his father and brothers, with his wife and two boys, the elder of whom only went to school but was not of any help yet. He told him that he was staying in somebody's apartment and would go to the horse fair tomorrow and sell his nag, and find, and maybe even buy, another horse. He told him that he had now saved up one rouble short of twenty-five, and that half his money was in a coupon. He took out the coupon and showed it to the yard porter. The yard porter was illiterate, but said he did exchange such money for tenants, that it was good money, but sometimes it was forged, and therefore his advice was to exchange it here at the counter, to be on the safe side. Ivan Mironov gave the coupon to the waiter and told him to bring the change, but the waiter did not bring the change, instead the bald-headed, glossy-faced tavernkeeper came with the coupon in his plump hand.

"Your money's no good," he said, pointing to the coupon, but not giving it back.

"It's good money, a gentleman gave it to me."

"Even so it's no good, it's forged."

"If it's forged, give it here."

"No, brother, your kind need a lesson. You forged it with some swindlers."

"Give me the money, what right have you got?"

"Sidor, call the police!" the barman turned to the waiter.

Ivan Mironov was tipsy. When tipsy, he could be rowdy. He seized the tavernkeeper by the collar and shouted:

"Give it back, I'll go to the gentleman. I know where he is."

The tavernkeeper tore free of Ivan Mironov, and his shirt made a ripping sound.

"Ah, so that's how you are. Hold him."

The waiter seized Ivan Mironov, and just then a police officer appeared. Having listened to the whole matter as an authority, he decided it at once:

"To the police station."

The officer put the coupon in his wallet and took Ivan Mironov, along with his horse, to the police station.

VII

IVAN MIRONOV SPENT the night in the police station with drunks and thieves. Only towards noon was he summoned to the police chief. The police chief questioned him and sent him with an officer to the dealer in photography accessories. Ivan Mironov remembered the street and house.

When the officer called out the gentleman and presented him with the coupon and with Ivan Mironov, who insisted that this same gentleman had given him the coupon, Evgeny Mikhailovich made an astonished and then stern face.

"You're clearly out of your mind. This is the first I've seen of him."

"Master, that's a sin, we'll all die," said Ivan Mironov.

"What's to be done with him? You're dreaming, surely. You sold it to somebody else," said Evgeny Mikhailovich. "Wait a minute, though. I'll go and ask my wife if she bought firewood yesterday."

Evgeny Mikhailovich went out and at once summoned the yard porter, a handsome, extraordinarily strong and deft fellow, the merry young fop Vassily, and told him that if he was asked where the last batch of firewood came from, he should say from the wood depot, and that no wood was bought from muzhiks.

"Because there's this muzhik who is testifying that I gave him a forged coupon. A muddle-headed muzhik, says God knows what, but you're a man of sense. So tell them we buy firewood only at the depot. And I've long been meaning to give you this so you can buy yourself a jacket," Evgeny Mikhailovich added, giving the porter five roubles.

Vassily took the money, his eyes flashed at the note, then at Evgeny Mikhailovich's face, he shook his mop of hair and smiled slightly.

"It's a known fact, they're muddle-headed folk. Uneducated. Please don't worry, sir. I know what to say."

No matter how much and how tearfully Ivan Mironov begged Evgeny Mikhailovich to recognize the coupon as his, and with the yard porter to confirm his words, both Evgeny Mikhailovich and the porter stood firm: they never bought firewood from carts. And the police officer took Ivan Mironov, accused of forging the coupon, back to the station.

Only on the advice of a drunken scrivener who was locked up with him did Ivan Mironov, having given the police chief a fiver, get out of jail, without the coupon and with seven roubles instead of the twenty-five he had had the day before. Of those seven roubles, Ivan Mironov drank up three and, with a bruised face, dead drunk, went home to his wife.

His wife was in the last days of pregnancy and feeling ill. She began to scold her husband, he shoved her aside, she started beating him. He, without responding, lay belly-down on the plank bed and sobbed loudly.

Only the next morning did his wife understand what it was all about, and, believing her husband, she spent a long time cursing the robber gentleman who had cheated her Ivan. And Ivan, sobering up, remembered what an artisan with whom he had been drinking the day before had told him and decided to go to an attorneyer to lodge a complaint.

VIII

THE LAWYER TOOK the case, not because of the money he might earn, but because he believed Ivan and was indignant that a muzhik had been so shamelessly deceived.

Both sides appeared in court, and the yard porter Vassily was the witness. The same thing was repeated in court. Ivan Mironov mentioned God and the fact that we will all die. Evgeny Mikhailovich, though suffering from the awareness of the vileness and riskiness of what he was doing, could not change his testimony now and with an externally calm air went on denying everything.

The yard porter Vassily got another ten roubles and with a smile calmly maintained that he had never set eyes on Ivan Mironov. And when he was taken to swear an oath, though cowering inwardly, outwardly he calmly repeated the words of the oath after the old priest who had been called in, swearing upon the Cross and the Holy Gospel that he would tell the whole truth.

The affair ended with the judge rejecting Ivan Mironov's suit and sentencing him to pay five roubles in court costs, which Evgeny Mikhailovich magnanimously forgave him. In dismissing Ivan Mironov, the judge admonished him, saying that henceforth he should be more careful about bringing charges against respectable people and should be grateful that he had been forgiven the court costs and not pursued for slander, for which he could have spent three months in prison.

"I humbly thank you," said Ivan Mironov and, shaking his head and sighing, he left his cell.

All this seemed to have ended well for Evgeny Mikhailovich and the yard porter Vassily. But it only seemed so. Things happened which no one saw but which were more important than all that people did see.

It was the third year now since Vassily had left his village and gone to live in the city. With each year he sent his father less and less, and he did not invite his wife, having no need of her. Here in the city he had as many such wives as he wanted, and better than that slut of his. With each year Vassily forgot village rules more and more and acquired city ways. There everything was crude, grey, poor, muddled; here everything was refined, nice, clean, rich, everything was in order. And he was becoming more and more convinced that village folk lived without sense, like beasts in the forest, while here there were real people. He read books by good writers, novels, went to performances at People's House.[3] In the village you could not even dream of anything like that. In the village the old folk say: Live with your lawful wife, work hard, do not eat more than you need, do not show off; but here intelligent, educated people— meaning, who know the real rules—live for their own good pleasure. And all goes well. Before the affair of the coupon, Vassily had never believed that the masters have no law regarding how to live. It had always seemed to him that he did not know that law, but there was a law. But this latest affair with the coupon and, above all, his false oath, from which, despite his fear, nothing bad came, but, on the contrary, there came another ten roubles, convinced him completely that there were no laws and one should live for one's own good pleasure. So he lived, and so he went on living. At first he profited only on purchases for the tenants, but that was too little for all his expenses, and, wherever he could, he began to pilfer money and valuables from the tenants' apartments, and stole a purse from Evgeny Mikhailovich. Evgeny Mikhailovich caught him, but, instead of taking him to court, dismissed him.

Vassily did not want to go home, and he went on living in Moscow with his sweetheart, looking for a job. A low-paying job was found as a shopkeeper's yard porter. Vassily took it, but the very next month was caught stealing sacks. The owner did not lodge a complaint, but gave Vassily a beating and threw him out. After that occurrence no job could be found, his money went, then his clothes went, and in the end all he had left was one torn jacket, a pair of trousers, and worn-out boots. His sweetheart left him. But Vassily did not lose his cheerful, merry disposition and, waiting till spring, went home on foot.

IX

PYOTR NIKOLAEVICH SVENTITSKY, a short, stocky man in dark spectacles (he had failing eyes and was threatened with total blindness), got up, as usual, before dawn and, after drinking a glass of tea, put on a short lambskin coat and made the rounds of his estate.

Pyotr Nikolaevich had been a customs official and had saved up eighteen thousand roubles on the job. Some twelve years ago he had resigned, not entirely of his own will, and had bought a little estate from a young landowner who had squandered his fortune. Pyotr Nikolaevich had married while still in the service. His wife was a poor orphan of old noble stock, a large, plump, beautiful woman, who did not give him any children. Pyotr Nikolaevich was a solid and persistent man in all his doings. Knowing nothing of farming (he was the son of a minor Polish nobleman), he took it up so well that in ten years the ruined thousand-acre estate became exemplary. All his constructions, from the house, to the barn, to the canopy over the fire pump, were solid, well-built, roofed with sheet iron, and painted regularly. In the toolshed, carts, wooden and metal ploughs, a harrow stood in order. The harness was oiled. The horses, almost all from his own stud, were not very big, of a greyish colour, well-fed, sturdy, all alike. The threshing machine operated in a covered threshing barn, fodder was stored in a special shed, dung wash was collected in a stone-lined pit. The cows were also from his own stock, not large, but milky. The pigs were English. There was a hen-house with a breed of especially good layers. The fruit trees were white-washed and regularly renewed. Everything everywhere was well managed, solid, clean, correct. Pyotr Nikolaich rejoiced over his management and took pride in having achieved it all not by oppressing his peasants, but, on the contrary, by being strictly fair towards them. Even among the nobility he held moderate views, sooner liberal than conservative, and before advocates of serfdom always defended the people. Be good to them and they will be good to you. True, he was not lenient towards the blunders and mistakes of workers, and sometimes gave them a push himself, demanding work from them, but then, too, their lodgings and food were of the best, their wages were always paid punctually, and on feast days he gave them vodka.

Stepping cautiously over the melting snow—it was the end of February—Pyotr Nikolaich headed past the workhorse stable to the cottage where the farmhands lived. It was still dark, and even darker because of the fog, but he could see light in the windows of the farmhands' cottage. They were getting up. He intended to hurry them: the plan was to take a sledge and six and go to the grove for the rest of the firewood.

"What's this?" he thought, seeing the door to the stable open.

"Hey, who's there?"

No one answered. Pyotr Nikolaich went into the stable.

"Hey, who's there?"

No one answered. It was dark, soft underfoot, and smelled of dung. To the right of the door was the stall of two young grey horses. Pyotr Nikolaich reached out—it was empty. He felt with his foot. Maybe he was lying down? His foot encountered nothing. "Where have they taken him?" Pyotr Nikolaich went back outside and shouted loudly:

"Hey, Stepan!"

Stepan was the senior farmhand. He was just coming out of the cottage.

"Ho-ho!" Stepan responded cheerfully. "Is that you, Pyotr Nikolaich? The lads are coming right now."

"Why's the stable open?"

"The stable? I wouldn't know. Hey, Proshka, give me a lantern."

Proshka came running with a lantern. They went into the stable. Stepan understood at once.

"It was thieves, Pyotr Nikolaich. The lock's broken."

"Are you kidding?"

"They took 'em, the robbers. Mashka's gone, Hawk's gone. No, Hawk's here. Pepper's gone. Prettyboy's gone."

Three horses were missing. Pyotr Nikolaich said nothing.

He frowned and breathed deeply.

"Oh, let me get my hands on them! Who was on watch?"

"Petka. Petka slept through it."

Pyotr Nikolaich informed the police, the district chief, the local authorities, sent his own people around. The horses were not found.

"Filthy folk!" said Pyotr Nikolaich. "To do that! Wasn't I good to them? Just you wait. Robbers, you're all robbers. Now I'll deal differently with you."

X

THE HORSES, the three greys, were already disposed of. One, Mashka, was sold to some gypsies for eighteen roubles; another, Pepper, was traded to a muzhik thirty miles away, and Prettyboy got overdriven and was slaughtered. The hide was sold for three roubles. The whole affair was directed by Ivan Mironov. He had worked for Pyotr Nikolaich and knew the layout of things at Pyotr Nikolaich's and decided to get his money back. He set it up.

After his bad luck with the forged coupon, Ivan Mironov went drinking for a long time and would have drunk up everything, if his wife had not hidden the yokes, his clothes, and whatever else he might have drunk up. During his drunkenness, Ivan Mironov thought ceaselessly not only about his offender, but about all the masters, great and small, who only live by fleecing our kind. Once Ivan Mironov was drinking with some muzhiks from near Podolsk. And the muzhiks, driving along, drunk, told him how they had stolen a horse from a muzhik. Ivan Mironov began to scold the horse thieves for doing harm to a muzhik. "It's a sin," he said, "a muzhik's horse is like a brother to him, and you deprived him of it. If you're going to steal, steal from the masters. Those dogs deserve it." They talked more and longer, and the Podolsk muzhiks said it was tricky to steal horses from the masters. You've got to know the ins and outs, and it's impossible without one of their own people. Then Ivan Mironov remembered Sventitsky and that he had lived on his estate as a farmhand, remembered that in the final reckoning Sventitsky had withheld a rouble fifty from him for a broken pintle, and remembered the little grey horses he used to work with.

Ivan Mironov went to Sventitsky as if to be hired, but only in order to spy out and learn everything. And having learned everything—that there was no watchman, that the horses were kept in stalls in the stable— he hooked up with the thieves and carried out the whole thing.

Having divided the profits with the Podolsk muzhiks, Ivan Mironov came home with five roubles. At home there was nothing to do: he had no horse. And from then on Ivan Mironov began keeping company with horse thieves and gypsies.

XI

PYOTR NIKOLAICH SVENTITSKY TRIED as hard as he could to find the thief. The thing could not have been done without one of his own people. And therefore he began to suspect his people, and, enquiring among his farmhands if anyone had not spent the night at home, learned that Proshka Nikolaev had not. He was a young lad who had just come back from military service, a handsome, adroit lad, whom Pyotr Nikolaich employed as a driver in place of a coachman. The district police chief was Pyotr Nikolaich's friend, and he knew the local constable, and the marshal of nobility, and the head of the zemstvo,[4] and the prosecutor. These persons all came to his name-day parties and were acquainted with his tasty liqueurs and pickled mushrooms of various sorts. They all felt sorry for him and tried to help him.

"See, and you defend the muzhiks," said the district police chief. "It was true what I said, that they're worse than beasts. Without the knout and the stick you can't do anything with them. So you say it's Proshka, who drives around as your coachman?"

"Yes, him."

"Bring him here."

Proshka was summoned and they started questioning him:

"Where were you?"

Proshka tossed his hair and flashed his eyes.

"At home."

"How do you mean, at home? All the farmhands testify that you weren't."

"As you will."

"My will has nothing to do with it. Where were you?"

"At home."

"Well, all right. Officer, take him to jail."

"As you will."

And so Proshka did not tell where he had been, and he did not tell because he had spent the night with his girlfriend Parasha and had promised not to give her away, and did not. There was no evidence. And so Proshka was released. But Pyotr Nikolaich was sure it had been done by him, and he hated him. Once Pyotr Nikolaich, using Proshka as a driver, sent him to the posting station. Proshka, as he always did, bought two measures of oats at the inn yard. One and a half went for feed, one half he drank up. Pyotr Nikolaich found it out and lodged a complaint with the justice of the peace. The justice of the peace sentenced Proshka to three months in jail. Proshka had great self-esteem. He considered himself above other people and was proud of himself. Jail humiliated him. It was impossible for him to be proud before people, and all at once his spirits fell.

Proshka came home from jail embittered not so much against Pyotr Nikolaich as against the whole world.

After jail, as everybody said, Proshka let himself go, became lazy, started drinking, and was soon caught stealing clothes from a town woman and landed in jail again.

The only thing Pyotr Nikolaich learned about his horses was that the hide of a grey gelding had been found, which Pyotr Nikolaich recognized as Prettyboy's hide. And the fact that the thieves went unpunished vexed Pyotr Nikolaich still more. He was now unable to see or speak of muzhiks without anger, and he tried to put the squeeze on them wherever he could.

XII

ALTHOUGH EVGENY MIKHAILOVICH stopped thinking about the coupon once he had disposed of it, his wife, Marya Vassilievna, was unable to forgive either herself for falling for the deception, or her husband for the cruel words he had said to her, or, above all, the two scoundrelly boys who had so skilfully deceived her.

From the very day she was deceived, she began keeping an eye on all the students. She met Makhin once, but did not recognize him, because, on seeing her, he made such a mug that it completely altered his looks. But when she came face-to-face with Mitya Smokovnikov on the pavement two weeks after the event, she recognized him at once. She let him pass, turned, and followed after him. Having reached his apartment and learned whose son he was, she went to school the next day and in the front hall met the catechism teacher, Mikhail Vvedensky. He asked what she wanted. She said she wished to see the director.

"The director's not here, he's unwell. Maybe I can do something, or give him a message?"

Marya Vassilievna decided to tell the catechism teacher everything.

The catechism teacher Vvedensky was a widower, an academician, and a man of great self-esteem. A year ago he had met Smokovnikov's father socially and, confronting him in a conversation about faith, in which Smokovnikov had beaten him on all points and held him up to mockery, had decided to pay special attention to the son and, finding in him the same indifference to religion as in his unbelieving father, had begun to persecute him and had even failed him in an examination.

Having learned of young Smokovnikov's act from Marya Vassilievna, Vvedensky could not help feeling satisfaction, finding in this occasion a confirmation of his assumptions about the immorality of people deprived of the Church's guidance, and decided to use the occasion, as he tried to persuade himself, to demonstrate the danger that threatens all those who fall away from the Church—but in the depths of his soul it was to take revenge on the proud and self-assured atheist.

"Yes, that's very sad, very sad," Father Mikhail Vvedensky said, stroking the smooth side of his pectoral cross with his hand. "I'm very glad that you have entrusted the matter to me; as a servant of the Church, I shall be at pains not to let the young man go without admonition, but shall also be at pains if possible to soften the edification."

"Yes, I shall do as befits my station in life," Father Mikhail said to himself, completely forgetting the father's hostility towards him, and thinking that he had in mind only the young man's own good and salvation.

The next day in catechism class, Father Mikhail told the students the whole episode of the forged coupon and said that a student had done it.

"A bad, shameful act," he said, "but to deny it is still worse. If, which I don't believe, it was done by one of you, it would be better for him to confess than to conceal it."

As he said that, Father Mikhail looked fixedly at Mitya Smokovnikov. The boys, following his gaze, also turned to look at Smokovnikov. Mitya turned red, sweated, finally burst into tears, and ran out of the room.

Mitya's mother, on learning of it, coaxed the whole truth from her son and went running to the photography accessories shop. She gave the owner's wife twelve roubles and fifty kopecks, and persuaded her to conceal the student's name. She told her son to deny everything and by no means confess to his father.

And indeed, when Fyodor Mikhailovich learned about what had happened at school, and when his son, summoned, denied everything, he went to the director and, having recounted the whole affair, said that the behaviour of the catechism teacher was in the highest degree reprehensible, and he would not leave it at that. The director summoned the priest, and a heated conversation took place between him and Fyodor Mikhailovich.

"The foolish woman mistook my son's identity, then took back her testimony herself, and you found nothing better to do than to slander an honest, truthful boy."

"I didn't slander him, and I will not allow you to talk to me like that. You forget my office."

"I spit on your office."

"Your wrong notions," the catechism teacher said, his chin trembling, making his sparse little beard shake, "are known to the whole town."

"Gentlemen . . . Father . . ." the director attempted to calm the arguing men. But it was impossible to calm them.

"By the duty of my office, I must concern myself with religious and moral upbringing."

"Enough pretending. As if I don't know that you don't believe in a blessed thing."

"I consider it unworthy of me to speak with such a gentleman as you," said Father Mikhail, insulted by Smokovnikov's last words, especially since he knew they were true. He had gone through the entire course of divinity school and therefore had long ceased to believe in what he confessed and professed, but believed only that people should force themselves to believe what he forced himself to believe.

Smokovnikov was not so much indignant at the catechism teacher's action as he found it a good illustration of the clerical influence that was beginning to manifest itself among us, and he told everybody about this occurrence.

Father Vvedensky, however, seeing the manifestation of established nihilism and atheism not only in the younger, but in the older generation, became more and more convinced of the necessity of combating it. The more he condemned the disbelief of Smokovnikov and his like, the more convinced he became of the firmness and stability of his faith, and the less need he felt to test it or to accord it with his life. His faith, recognized by all the world around him, was for him the main instrument for combating its adversaries.

These thoughts, called up in him by his confrontation with Smokovnikov, along with the unpleasantnesses in the school caused by that confrontation—more precisely, the reprimand, the reproach he received from his superior—forced him to make a decision that had been beckoning to him for a long time, ever since his wife's death: to become a monk and choose the same career as that followed by some of his classmates in divinity school, one of whom was already a bishop and another an archimandrite waiting to fill the vacancy of a bishop.

At the end of the academic year Vvedensky left the school, was tonsured a monk under the name of Misaïl, and very soon obtained the post of rector of a seminary in a town in the Volga region.

XIII

MEANWHILE THE YARD PORTER Vassily was heading south along the high road.

During the day he walked, and at night a local constable would lead him to his next quarters. Everywhere he was given bread, and sometimes he was given a place at the supper table. In one village of Orel province where he spent the night, he was told that a merchant had rented an orchard from a landowner and was now looking for some stalwart watchmen. Vassily was sick of begging, but he did not want to go home, and so he went to the merchant fruit-grower and got hired as a watchman for five roubles a month.

Life in a hut, especially once the early apples began to ripen and the overseers from the landowner's threshing floor brought huge bundles of fresh straw straight from the thresher, was very pleasing for Vassily. You lie all day on fresh, fragrant straw, next to heaps of fallen spring and winter apples, still more fragrant than the straw, watching out that children do not sneak in somewhere to take apples, whistling away and singing songs. At singing songs Vassily was a master. And he had a good voice. Women and girls came from the village for apples. Vassily would banter with them, would exchange more or fewer apples, depending on how much he liked the girl, for eggs or a few kopecks—and then would lie there again. The only thing to do was have breakfast, lunch, and dinner.

The shirt on Vassily was a pink cotton one, and all torn at that, his feet were bare, but his body was strong, healthy, and when the pot of kasha was taken from the fire, Vassily ate enough for three, so that the old watchman only marvelled at him. At night Vassily did not sleep, but either whistled or shouted, and, like a cat, he could see far into the darkness. Once some big lads from the village got into the orchard to shake down apples. Vassily crept up and fell on them; they tried to fight, but he scattered them all, and took one to the hut and turned him over to the owner.

Vassily's first hut was far away in the orchard, but the second, once the early apples were over, was forty paces from the manor house. And in this hut it was even merrier for Vassily. All day Vassily saw how gentlemen and young ladies played, went for rides, strolled, and in the evening and at night played the pianoforte, the violin, sang, danced. He saw how young ladies and students sat on the windowsills and caressed each other and then went by themselves to stroll in the dark linden alleys, where moonlight broke through only in stripes and spots. He saw how servants ran about with food and drink and how cooks, laundresses, clerks, gardeners, coachmen—all worked only so that the masters could eat, drink, and make merry. Young people occasionally came to his hut, and he would choose and offer them the best, ripest, and reddest apples, and the young ladies would take crunching bites at once, and praise them, and say something—he knew it was about him—in French, and get him to sing.

And Vassily admired that life, remembering his Moscow life, and the thought that it was all a matter of money sank more and more deeply into his head.

And Vassily began to think more and more about what to do in order to get hold of a great deal of money all at once. He began to recall how he had profited from things before, and decided that it should not be done that way, that he should not, as before, just grab something that was lying around, but should think ahead, find things out, and do it neatly, so that there are no loose ends. By the Nativity of the Mother of God,⁵ the last winter apples were picked. The owner made a good profit and paid and thanked all the watchmen, including Vassily.

Vassily got dressed—the young master had given him a jacket and a hat—and did not go home—the thought of coarse, peasant life quite sickened him—but went back to town with some drunken soldiers who had kept watch on the orchard with him. In town he decided to go by night, break into and rob the shop where he used to live, the owner of which had beaten him and thrown him out without any pay. He knew all the ins and outs and where the money was, left a soldier on watch, and himself broke a window onto the yard, climbed in, and took all the money. The thing was done artfully, and no traces were found. The money amounted to three hundred and seventy roubles. Vassily gave a hundred roubles to his comrade, and with the rest went to another town and caroused there with some men and women he knew.

XIV

MEANWHILE, Ivan Mironov had become a deft, bold, and successful horse thief. Afimya, his wife, who formerly had scolded him for his bad dealings, as she put it, was now pleased and felt proud of her husband, in that he had a fleece-lined coat and she herself had a shawl and a new fur coat.

In the village and the countryside around everybody knew that not a single horse theft was brought off without him, but people were afraid to give evidence against him, and whenever there was a suspicion, he came out clean and right. His last theft had been from a night pasture in Kolotovka. When he could, Ivan Mironov sorted out who he stole from and liked best to steal from landowners and merchants. But from landowners and merchants it was also more difficult. And therefore, when there was nothing forthcoming from landowners and merchants, he also stole from peasants. So he laid hands on whatever horses were found in the night pasture at Kolotovka. He did not do it himself, but put the adroit young fellow Gerasim up to it. The muzhiks found the horses missing only at dawn and went rushing to look for them along the roads. The horses were standing in a ravine, in a state forest. Ivan Mironov intended to keep them there until the next night, and then make off by night thirty miles away to an innkeeper he knew. Ivan Mironov visited Gerasim in the forest, brought him some pie and vodka, and went home along a forest path, where he hoped to meet no one. As ill luck would have it, he ran into the soldier on watch.

"Out for mushrooms, eh?" said the soldier.

"There aren't any today," replied Ivan Mironov, pointing to the basket he had taken along just in case.

"Yes, it's not a mushroom summer," said the soldier, "maybe there'll be some during the fast,"[6] and he walked on.

The soldier realized that something was wrong here. Ivan Mironov had no business walking about in the state forest early in the morning. The soldier went back and began searching through the forest. Nearby the ravine he heard the snort of horses and went quietly to the place where the sound came from. There was trampled earth and horse dung in the ravine. Further on, Gerasim sat eating something, and two horses stood tethered to a tree.

The soldier ran to the village and fetched the headman, the village constable, and two witnesses. From three sides they approached the place where Gerasim was and seized him. Geraska made no denials and at once drunkenly admitted everything. He told them how Ivan Mironov had got him drunk and put him up to it, and how he had promised to come to the forest that night for the horses. The muzhiks left the horses and Gerasim in the forest and set up an ambush, waiting for Ivan Mironov. When dusk came, a whistle was heard. Gerasim responded. As soon as Ivan Mironov started down the hill, they fell on him and took him to the village. The next morning a crowd gathered in front of the headman's cottage.

Ivan Mironov was brought out and questioned. Stepan Pelageyushkin, a tall, stoop-shouldered man with an eagle's nose and a gloomy expression on his face, was the first to ask questions. Stepan was a lone muzhik, who had gone through military service. He had just separated from his father and was beginning to manage on his own when his horse was stolen. After working for a year in the mines, Stepan again bought two horses. Both were stolen.

"Speak, where are my horses?" Stepan began, glancing gloomily now at the ground, now into Ivan's face, and turning pale with anger.

Ivan Mironov said he knew nothing. Then Stepan hit him in the face and smashed his nose, which began to bleed.

"Speak or I'll kill you!"

Ivan Mironov was silent, his head bent. Stepan struck him with his long arm once, twice. Ivan kept silent, only tossing his head now this way, now that.

"Everybody beat him!" cried the headman.

And everybody began to beat him. Ivan Mironov silently fell down and cried out:

"Barbarians, devils, beat me to death! I'm not afraid of you!"

Then Stepan seized a stone from a ready pile and smashed Ivan Mironov's head.

XV

IVAN MIRONOV'S KILLERS WERE TRIED. Among the killers was Stepan Pelageyushkin. He was charged more severely than the others, because everyone testified that he had smashed Ivan Mironov's head with a stone.

Stepan did not conceal anything at the trial, explaining that when his last pair of horses were stolen he had reported it to the police, and traces could have been found through the gypsies, but the police had refused to see him and had made no search at all.

"What were we to do with such a man? He was ruining us."

"Then why was it you who beat him and not the others?" asked the prosecutor.

"Not true, we all beat him, the whole village decided to kill him. I just finished him off. Why torture a man uselessly?"

The judges were struck by the perfectly calm expression with which Stepan told about his act, and how they had beaten Ivan Mironov, and how he had finished him off.

Stepan actually saw nothing terrible in this killing. In the service he happened to have executed a soldier, and, as then, so in the killing of Ivan Mironov he saw nothing terrible. Killed is killed. Today him, tomorrow me.

Stepan was given a light sentence, one year in prison. His peasant clothes were taken off and put away under a number in the storehouse, and he was dressed in a prisoner's smock and overshoes.

Stepan had never had any respect for the authorities, but now he was fully convinced that all the authorities, all the masters, everybody except the tsar, who alone was just and pitied the people, all were robbers who sucked the people's blood. The accounts of men he met in prison, who had been sent to exile or hard labour, confirmed such a view. One had been sent to hard labour because he had exposed the authorities for thievery, another because he had struck a superior when he began to confiscate peasant property for no reason, a third because he had forged banknotes. The masters, the merchants got away with whatever they did, but the poor muzhik, for anything at all, was sent to jail to feed lice.

His wife visited him in jail. Without him her life was wretched enough, but then their house burned down and, being utterly destitute, she went begging with the children. His wife's misery embittered Stepan still more. In jail he was angry with everyone and once nearly killed the mess cook with an axe, for which he was given another year. During that year he learned that his wife had died and he no longer had a home . . .

When Stepan had served his term, he was summoned to the storehouse, the clothes in which he had come were taken from the shelf and given to him.

"Where will I go now?" he said, while dressing, to the quartermaster-sergeant.

"Home, surely."

"I've got no home. Means I'll have to take to the highway. Rob people."

"If you rob people, you'll end up with us again."

"Well, that's as it may be."

And Stepan left. He headed for home anyway. He had nowhere else to go.

Before he reached home, he stopped for the night at an inn he knew with a pot-house.

The inn was kept by a fat tradesman from Vladimir. He knew Stepan. And he knew that he had landed in jail by ill luck. And he let Stepan stay the night with him.

This rich tradesman had won away the wife of a neighbouring muzhik, and she lived with him as a worker and wife.

Stepan knew the whole affair—how the tradesman had offended the muzhik, how this nasty wench had left her husband and had now grown fat and sat sweating over her tea and also treated Stepan to tea out of charity. There were no other travellers. Stepan was left to spend the night in the kitchen. Matriona put everything away and went to her bedroom. Stepan lay on the stove[7] but could not sleep and kept tossing and crackling the splinters of wood that were drying on the stove. He could not get out of his head the tradesman's fat belly, protruding from under the belt of his much-laundered and faded cotton shirt. The idea kept going through his head of slashing that belly with a knife and letting the fat out. And the same for the wench. First he would say to himself: "Well, devil take them, I'm leaving tomorrow," then he would remember Ivan Mironov and again think of the tradesman's belly and Matriona's white, sweaty throat. If it's kill, then it's both. The cock crowed for the second time. If it's do it, then it's now, or else dawn will come. He had spotted the knife that evening, and the axe. He slipped down from the stove, took the axe and the knife, and left the kitchen. Just as he left, he heard the latch click outside a door. The tradesman came through the door. He did not do it the way he wanted. The knife did not come into it, but he swung the axe and split his skull. The tradesman fell against the doorpost and then to the ground.

Stepan went into the bedroom. Matriona jumped up and stood by the bed in nothing but her nightshirt. Stepan killed her in the same way with the axe.

Then he lit a candle, took the money from the desk, and left.

XVI

IN A DISTRICT TOWN, in his own house, set apart from other buildings, lived an old man, a former official, a drunkard, with two daughters and a son-in-law. The married daughter also drank and led a bad life, while the older one, the widow Marya Semyonovna, a wrinkled, thin, fifty-year-old woman, supported them all by herself: she had a pension of two hundred and fifty roubles. This money fed the entire family. Marya Semyonovna was the only one who did any work in the house. She looked after her weak, drunken old father and her sister's child, and cooked and did the laundry. And, as always happens, everything that needed doing was piled on her, and the other three abused her, and the brother-in-law even beat her when he was drunk. She endured it all silently and with meekness, and, also as always happens, the more she had to do, the more she managed to do. She helped the poor as well, going without herself, giving away her clothes, and also helped to look after the sick.

Once a lame, crippled village tailor was working at Marya Semyonovna's. He was altering a jacket for the old man and putting broadcloth on Marya Semyonovna's lambskin coat—for going to the market in winter.

The lame tailor was an intelligent and observant man, who in his line of work had seen many different people and, as a result of his lameness, was always sitting down and was therefore inclined to think. Having spent a week at Marya Semyonovna's, he could not marvel enough at her life. Once she came to him in the kitchen, where he did his sewing, to wash some towels, and fell to talking with him about his life, how his brother had mistreated him, and how he had separated from him.

"I thought it would be better, but it's all the same—want."

"It's better not to change anything, but just live the way you live," said Marya Semyonovna.

"Yes, and then again I marvel at you, Marya Semyonovna, seeing how you go bustling every which way for people, all on your own. And there's little kindness from them that I can see."

Marya Semyonovna said nothing.

"Must be you got it from books, that there'll be a reward for it in the next world."

"Of that we know nothing," said Marya Semyonovna, "only it's better to live this way."

"And is that in the books?"

"It's in the books, too," she said, and she read him the Sermon on the Mount from the Gospels.[8] The tailor fell to thinking. And when he got paid and went home, he kept thinking about what he had seen at Marya Semyonovna's and what she had said and read to him.

XVII

PYOTR NIKOLAICH HAD CHANGED towards the people, and the people had changed towards him. Before the year was out, they had cut down twenty-seven oaks and burned an uninsured threshing barn and threshing floor. Pyotr Nikolaich decided that it was impossible to get along with the local people.

At that same time, the Liventsovs were looking for a steward for their estates, and the marshal of nobility recommended Pyotr Nikolaich as the best farmer in the district. The Liventsovs' estates, enormous as they were, did not produce any income, and the peasants availed themselves of everything. Pyotr Nikolaich undertook to restore it all to order and, putting his own estate up for rent, moved with his wife to a distant Volga province.

Pyotr Nikolaich had always liked order and lawfulness, and now it was all the more impossible for him to allow these wild, crude people, against the law, to appropriate what did not belong to them. He was glad of the chance to teach them a lesson and sternly set to work. He had one peasant sent to jail for stealing wood, another he beat with his own hands for not making way and taking off his hat. Of some pastures which had come into dispute and which the peasants considered theirs, Pyotr Nikolaich made it known to the peasants that if any cattle were let into them, he would arrest them.

Spring came, and the peasants, as they had done in previous years, let their cattle into the landowner's pastures. Pyotr Nikolaich gathered all the farmhands and told them to round up the cattle in the master's barnyard. The muzhiks were at the ploughing, and therefore the farmhands, in spite of the women's shouting, rounded up the cattle. When they returned from work, the muzhiks, gathering together, went to the master's yard to demand the cattle. Pyotr Nikolaich came out to them with a gun on his shoulder (he had just finished making the rounds) and informed them that he would give back the cattle not otherwise than on a payment of fifty kopecks for each cow and ten for each sheep. The muzhiks started shouting that the pastures were theirs, that their fathers and grandfathers had owned them, and that no one had the right to take other people's cattle.

"Give us back the cattle, or it'll go badly," said one old man, stepping towards Pyotr Nikolaich.

"What will go badly?" shouted Pyotr Nikolaich, all pale, moving towards the old man.

"Give them back for fear of sin. Sneak thief."

"What?" cried Pyotr Nikolaich, and he struck the old man in the face.

"You don't dare fight. Lads, take the cattle by force."

The crowd moved closer. Pyotr Nikolaich wanted to leave, but they would not let him. He began to push his way through. His gun went off and killed one of the peasants. There was a violent scuffle. Pyotr Nikolaich was trampled. And five minutes later his mutilated body was thrown into a ravine.

The killers were tried by court-martial, and two were sentenced to be hanged.

XVIII

IN THE VILLAGE the tailor came from, five rich peasants leased from a landowner, for one thousand one hundred roubles, three hundred acres of land, arable, rich, black as tar, and let it out to muzhiks, some for six roubles an acre, some for five. None went for less than four. So it made a good profit. The leaseholders themselves took fifteen acres each, and this land they got free. One of these muzhik associates died, and they invited the lame tailor to come and join them.

When the leaseholders began to divide up the land, the tailor did not drink vodka with them, and when the talk turned to who should get how much land, the tailor said the assessment ought to be the same for all, that the leaseholders ought not to take more than they paid.

"How's that?"

"We're not heathens. It's all very well for the masters, but we're peasants.[9] We must do it God's way. That's the law of Christ."

"And where is this law?"

"In the book, in the Gospels. Come on Sunday, I'll read it and we can talk."

And on Sunday, not all, but three of them came to the tailor, and he started reading to them.

He read five chapters from Matthew, and they began to talk. They all listened, but only Ivan Chuyev took it to heart. He took it so much to heart that he began to live in God's way in all things. And his family, too, began to live that way. He refused the extra land and took only his share.

And people began coming to the tailor and to Ivan, and began to understand, and understood, and gave up smoking, drinking, and using foul language, and began helping each other. And they stopped going to church and brought their icons to the priest. And there were seventeen such families. Sixty-five souls in all. And the priest became frightened and informed the bishop. The bishop pondered what to do, and decided to send the archimandrite Misaïl, the former high-school catechism teacher, to the village.

XIX

THE BISHOP SAT Misaïl down with him and began talking about what new things had appeared in his diocese.

"It's all from spiritual weakness and ignorance. You're a learned man. I put my hopes in you. Go, call the people together, and explain to them."

"If Your Grace gives me his blessing, I will try my best," said Father Misaïl. He was glad to be entrusted with it. He rejoiced at every situation where he could show that he believed. And in converting others, he persuaded himself most strongly that he believed.

"Try your best, I suffer very much for my flock," said the bishop, unhurriedly receiving into his plump white hands the glass of tea his attendant offered him.

"Why just one preserve? Bring another," he turned to the attendant. "It pains me very, very much," he continued his speech to Misaïl.

Misaïl was glad to declare himself. But, being a man of modest means, he asked for money for the expenses of the trip, and, fearing the opposition of the coarse people, he also asked for an order from the governor that, in case of need, the local police could come to his assistance.

The bishop arranged everything for him, and Misaïl, having packed, with the help of his attendant and a kitchen maid, a cellaret and some provisions it was necessary to lay up in setting out for a remote place, went off to his appointed destination. In setting out on this special mission, Misaïl experienced the pleasant feeling of a consciousness of his own importance and with that the cessation of any doubts about his faith, and, on the contrary, a perfect certainty of its truth.

His thoughts were directed not at the essence of faith—that was taken for an axiom—but at a refutation of objections made in relation to its external form.

XX

THE VILLAGE PRIEST and his wife received Misaïl with great honour and the day after his arrival assembled the people in the church. Misaïl, in a new silk cassock, with a pectoral cross and his hair combed long, came out to the ambo; next to him stood the priest, a little further away the deacons, the choir, and by the side doors policemen. The sectarians also came—in greasy, coarse sheepskin jackets.

After the prayer service, Misaïl delivered a sermon, admonishing those who had fallen away to return to the bosom of the Mother Church, threatening them with the torments of hell and promising full forgiveness to those who repented.

The sectarians said nothing. When asked questions, they answered.

To the question of why they had fallen away, they answered that in church wooden and man-made gods were worshipped, and in the Scriptures not only was that not shown, but in the prophecies[10] the opposite was shown. When Misaïl asked Chuyev if it was true that they called the holy icons "boards," Chuyev answered: "Go turn over any icon you like, you'll see for yourself." When asked why they did not recognize the priesthood, they answered that the Scriptures said: "Freely ye have received, freely give,"[11] but priests only hand out their blessings for money. To all Misaïl's attempts to support himself by Holy Scripture, the tailor and Ivan calmly but firmly retorted by themselves pointing to the Scriptures, of which they had firm knowledge. Misaïl became angry and threatened them with the secular authorities. To this the sectarians said that it was said: "If they have persecuted me, they will also persecute you."[12]

It came to nothing, and all would have gone well, but the next day at the liturgy Misaïl delivered a sermon about the perniciousness of seducers and that they deserved every punishment, and among the people leaving church talk arose about the godless fellows needing to be taught a lesson, so that they would not confuse people. And that day, while Misaïl was snacking on smoked salmon and whitefish with the provost and an inspector come from town, in the village a scuffle took place. The Orthodox crowded by Chuyev's cottage and waited for them to come out in order to give them a beating. There were twenty sectarians, men and women. Misaïl's sermon and now this gathering of the Orthodox and their menacing talk aroused an angry feeling in the sectarians which had not been there before. Evening was coming, it was time for the women to milk the cows, and the Orthodox still stood and waited, and when a young lad came out, they beat him and drove him back into the cottage. They talked over what to do and could not agree.

The tailor said they must bear it and not defend themselves. Chuyev, however, said that if they bore it like that, they would all be beaten and, seizing an iron poker, he went outside. The Orthodox fell upon him.

"Well, then, by the law of Moses,"[13] he cried and began beating the Orthodox and knocked out one man's eye. The rest slipped out of the cottage and went home.

Chuyev was tried for seduction and blasphemy and sentenced to exile.[14]

Father Misaïl, however, was given a reward and made an archimandrite.

XXI

Two years earlier, a beautiful, healthy girl of the eastern type, a Miss Turchaninov, had come from the Don army territory[15] to study in Petersburg. In Petersburg this girl had met the student Tyurin, the son of a zemstvo official in Simbirsk province, and had fallen in love with him, but this love was not an ordinary woman's love, with the wish to become his wife and the mother of his children, but a comradely love, nourished primarily by the same indignation and hatred not only for the existing system, but also for the people who represented it, and the consciousness of her intellectual, educational, and moral superiority to them.

She was a capable student and remembered lectures and passed examinations easily, and, besides that, devoured the newest books in enormous quantities. She was convinced that her calling was not in bearing and bringing up children—she even looked upon such a calling with squeamishness and scorn—but in destroying the existing system, which fettered the best forces of the people, and pointing out to the people that new path of life which for her was pointed out by the new European writers. Full-bodied, white-skinned, red-cheeked, beautiful, with shining black eyes and a big black braid, she aroused feelings in men that she could not and did not wish to share—so absorbed she was in her agitational, oratorical activity. But all the same it pleased her that she aroused these feelings, and therefore, though she did not dress up, she did not neglect her appearance. It pleased her that she was admired, and that she could show in reality how she scorned that which other women valued so highly. In her views of the means of struggle with the existing order she went further than the majority of her comrades and her friend Tyurin and allowed that all means are good and can be made use of in the struggle, including murder. And yet this same revolutionary, Katya Turchaninov, was in the depths of her soul a very kind and self-denying woman, always ready to put another person's profit, pleasure, well-being before her own profit, pleasure, and well-being, and always sincerely glad of the opportunity to do something nice—for a child, an old man, an animal.

Miss Turchaninov spent the summer in a provincial town on the Volga with a friend of hers, a village schoolteacher. Tyurin, too, lived in that district, at his father's. The three of them, together with the district doctor, saw each other frequently, exchanged books, argued, became indignant. The estate of the Tyurins was next to the estate of the

Liventsovs, where Pyotr Nikolaich came as a steward. As soon as Pyotr Nikolaich came and began to put things in order, the young Tyurin, seeing an independent spirit in the Liventsovs' peasants and the firm intention of defending their rights, became interested in them and went frequently to the village and talked with the peasants, developing among them the theory of socialism in general and of the nationalization of the land in particular.

When the killing of Pyotr Nikolaich took place and the court arrived,[16] the circle of revolutionaries in the town had a strong pretext for being indignant at the trial and boldly voiced it. The fact that Tyurin went to the village and talked with the peasants came out at the trial. A search was made at Tyurin's, several revolutionary pamphlets were found, and the student was arrested and taken to Petersburg.

Miss Turchaninov followed him and went to prison to visit him, but they would not let her in on an ordinary day, but only on the day for general visits, when she looked at him through two gratings. This meeting increased her indignation still more. What drove her indignation to the utmost limit was her exchange with a handsome gendarme officer, who was obviously ready for leniency in case she accepted his propositions. This drove her to the last degree of indignation and anger at all persons in authority. She went to the police chief to complain. The police chief said the same thing as the gendarme, that they could do nothing, that there was an order for it from a minister. She sent a report to the minister, asking for a meeting; she was refused. Then she resolved upon a desperate act and bought a revolver.

XXII

THE MINISTER WAS RECEIVING at his usual hour. The minister went through three petitioners, received a governor, and then went up to a beautiful, dark-eyed young woman in black, who was standing with a paper in her left hand. A tenderly lustful little light lit up in the minister's eyes at the sight of the beautiful petitioner, but, remembering his position, the minister made a serious face.

"What can I do for you?" he said, going up to her.

Without replying, she quickly pulled a revolver from under her cape, aimed it at the minister's chest, fired, but missed.

The minister went to seize her hand; she backed away and fired a second time. The minister fled. They seized her. She was trembling and could not speak. And suddenly she burst into hysterical laughter. The minister was not even wounded.

It was Miss Turchaninov. She was put in preliminary detention. The minister, having received congratulations and condolences from very highly placed persons and even from the sovereign himself, appointed a commission to investigate the conspiracy of which this attempt had been the result.

There was, of course, no conspiracy; but members of the secret and the overt police diligently took up the search for all the threads of the non-existent conspiracy and conscientiously earned their salaries and keep: got up early in the morning, in the dark; carried out search after search; copied papers and books; read diaries, private letters, and made summaries of them on beautiful paper, in beautiful handwriting; and interrogated Miss Turchaninov many times and set up confrontations, wishing to wheedle out of her the names of her accomplices.

The minister was a kind man at heart and felt very sorry for this robust, beautiful Cossack woman, but he said to himself that upon him lay heavy state obligations, which he fulfilled, however hard it was for him. And when his former colleague, a gentleman-in-waiting, an acquaintance of the Tyurins, met him at a court ball and began to solicit for Tyurin and Miss Turchaninov, the minister shrugged his shoulders, wrinkling the red sash on his white waistcoat, and said:

*"Je ne demanderais pas mieux que de lâcher cette pauvre fillette, mais vous savez—le devoir."**

And meanwhile Miss Turchaninov sat in preliminary detention and sometimes calmly exchanged knocks with her neighbours or read the books she was given, and sometimes suddenly lapsed into despair and rage, threw herself against the walls, shrieked and roared with laughter.

XXIII

ONCE MARYA SEMYONOVNA GOT her pension from the treasury and on her way home met a teacher she knew.

* I would ask nothing better than to let that poor little girl go, but you know—duty.

"So, Marya Semyonovna, did you get something from the coffers?" he called out to her from the other side of the street.

"I did," replied Marya Semyonovna, "just enough to plug the holes."

"Well, it's a lot of money, it'll plug the holes and then some," said the teacher and, with a goodbye, he went on.

"Goodbye," said Marya Semyonovna and, looking at the teacher, she ran straight into a tall man with very long arms and a stern face.

Nearing home, she was surprised to see this long-armed man again. Seeing her go into the house, he stood there for a while, turned, and left.

Marya Semyonovna felt eerie at first, then sad. But once she was in the house, and had given little treats to the old man, and the scrofulous little nephew Fedya, and had patted the joyfully squealing Tresorka, she felt good again, and, handing the money over to her father, she got down to work, which for her was never lacking.

The man she had run into was Stepan.

From the inn, where he had killed the innkeeper, Stepan went to town. And, surprisingly enough, the memory of killing the innkeeper not only was not unpleasant to him, but he recalled it several times a day. It pleased him to think that he could do it so cleanly and deftly, that no one would find out and keep him from doing it further on and to others. Sitting in a tavern over tea and vodka, he kept looking at people from the same angle: how he could kill them. He went to spend the night with a fellow countryman, a carter. The carter was not at home. He said he would wait and sat talking with his wife. Then, when she turned to the stove, it came into his head to kill her. He was surprised, shook his head at himself, then took the knife from his boot top and, having thrown her down, cut her throat. The children began to scream, he killed them as well, and, without spending the night, left town. Outside town, in a village, he went to an inn and there had a good sleep.

The next day he went back to the district town and in the street heard the conversation between Marya Semyonovna and the teacher. Her look frightened him, but all the same he decided to get into her house and take the money she had received. That night he broke the lock and went into the bedroom. The first to hear him was the younger, married daughter. She cried out. Stepan immediately put the knife to her. The son-in-law woke up and grappled with him. He seized Stepan by the throat and struggled with him for a long time, but Stepan was stronger. And, having finished off the son-in-law, Stepan, excited, agitated by the struggle, went behind the partition. Behind the partition Marya Semyonovna was in bed and, sitting up, looked at Stepan with frightened, meek eyes, crossing herself. Her look again frightened Stepan. He lowered his eyes.

"Where's the money?" he said, not raising his eyes.

She was silent.

"Where's the money?" said Stepan, showing her the knife.

"What are you doing? Can it be?" she said.

"It can all right."

Stepan went up to her, preparing to seize her by the hands so that she would not hinder him, but she did not raise her hands, did not resist, and only pressed them to her breast and sighed deeply and repeated:

"Oh, it's a great sin. What are you doing? Take pity on yourself. You destroy other people's souls, but your own most of all . . . Ohh!" she cried out.

Stepan could not stand her voice and look any more and slashed her throat with the knife. "Enough of your talk." She sank back on the pillows and wheezed, blood flowing onto her pillow. He turned away and went around the rooms collecting things. Having picked up what he wanted, Stepan lit a cigarette, sat for a while, cleaned off his clothes, and left. He thought he would get away with this murder as he had with the previous ones, but before he reached his night's lodgings, he suddenly felt such weariness that he could not move a limb. He lay down in a ditch and went on lying in it for the rest of the night, the whole day, and the following night.

PART TWO

I

LYING IN THE DITCH, Stepan constantly saw before him the meek, thin, frightened face of Marya Semyonovna and heard her voice: "Can it be?"—she said in her peculiar, her lisping, pitiful voice. And Stepan would again live through all he had done to her. And he became frightened, and closed his eyes and wagged his hairy head, so as to shake these thoughts and memories out of it. And he would free himself of memories for a moment, but in their place there appeared to him first one, then another black one, and after that other came yet another black one with red eyes, and they pulled faces and all said one thing: "You finished her off—finish yourself off, too, or we won't give you any peace." And he would open his eyes and see her again and hear her voice, and feel pity for her and loathing and fear for himself. And he would close his eyes again, and again—the black ones.

Towards evening of the second day he got up and went to a pot-house. He barely dragged himself to the pot-house and started drinking. But no matter how much he drank, he could not get drunk. He sat silently at the table and drank glass after glass. A local constable came into the pot-house.

"Where from?" the constable asked him.

"I'm the one who put the knife to them all at Dobrotvorov's last night."

He was bound and, after being kept for a day at police headquarters, was sent to the provincial capital. The prison warden, recognizing him as his former rowdy inmate and now a great evildoer, received him sternly.

"Watch out, don't try any mischief," the warden rasped, frowning and thrusting out his lower jaw. "If I notice anything, I'll flog you to death. You won't escape me."

"What's escaping to me," said Stepan, lowering his eyes. "I gave myself up."

"No backtalk with me. And when your superior is talking, look him in the eye," the warden shouted and hit him in the jaw with his fist.

At that moment Stepan was picturing her again and hearing her voice. He did not hear what the warden said to him.

"Wha—?" he asked, coming to his senses when he felt the blow to his face.

"Well, well—off with you, there's no point pretending."

The warden expected violence, communications with other inmates, attempts to escape. But there was none of it. Whenever the guard or the warden himself looked through the peephole in his door, Stepan was sitting on the straw-stuffed sack, his head propped in his hands, whispering something. At the investigator's interrogations, he was also not like the other inmates: he was absent-minded, did not listen to the questions;

when he did understand them, he was so truthful that the investigator, who was used to struggling with the accused by cleverness and cunning, here experienced a feeling similar to that of coming to the top of a stairway in the darkness and lifting your foot onto a step that is not there. Stepan recounted all his murders, frowning and fixing his eyes on a single point, in the most simple, businesslike tone, trying to remember all the details: "He came out barefoot," Stepan recounted his first murder, "stood in the doorway, so I clobbered him once, he began to wheeze, then I got straight to work on the woman . . ." and so on. During the prosecutor's rounds of the prison cells Stepan was asked if he had any complaints or needed anything. He replied that he did not need anything and that no one mistreated him. The prosecutor, having gone a few steps down the stinking corridor, stopped and asked the warden accompanying him how this inmate was behaving himself.

"I keep marvelling at him," said the warden, pleased that Stepan had praised his treatment. "It's the second month he's with us, his behaviour is exemplary. My only fear is that he may be plotting something. He's a courageous man and immensely strong."

II

DURING HIS FIRST MONTH in prison, Stepan had been constantly tormented by the same thing: he saw the grey walls of his cell, heard the prison sounds—the noise of the common cell below, the steps of the sentry in the corridor, the striking of the clock—and at the same time saw her, with her meek look, which had already vanquished him when he met her in the street, and her thin, wrinkled neck, which he had cut, and heard her touching, pitiful, lisping voice: "You destroy other people's souls and your own. Can it be?" Then the voice would die away and those three would appear—the black ones. And they appeared all the same, whether his eyes were open or shut. When his eyes were shut, they appeared more clearly. When Stepan opened his eyes, they became confused with the doors, the walls, and gradually vanished, but then emerged again and came from three sides, pulling faces and repeating: "Finish it, finish it. Make a noose, set a fire." And here Stepan would start shaking all over, and he would begin to recite the prayers he knew—the Hail Mary, the Our Father—and at first that seemed to help. As he recited the prayers, he would begin to remember his life: he remembered his father, his mother, his dog Volchok, his grandfather on the stove, the benches he rode on with the other children; then he remembered the village girls with their songs, then the horses, how they got stolen, how the horse thief got caught, how he finished him off with a stone. Remembered his first jail, how he came out, and remembered the fat innkeeper, the carter's wife, the children, and then again remembered her. And he felt hot, and freeing his shoulders from the robe, he jumped up from the bunk and, like a beast, began pacing with rapid steps up and down the short cell, turning quickly at the damp, sweaty walls. And again he recited prayers, but the prayers no longer helped.

On one of the long autumn evenings, when the wind whistled and droned in the chimneys, after rushing about his cell, he sat down on his cot and felt that he could not struggle any more, that the black ones had overpowered him, and he submitted to them. He had long been eyeing the air vent of the stove. If thin ropes or narrow strips of cloth were fastened to it, they would not slip off. But it had to be arranged intelligently. And he got down to work and spent two days preparing strips of cloth from the sack he slept on (when the guard came in, he covered the cot with his robe). He tied the strips together and made double knots so that they would not come apart, but would bear his body. While he was preparing it all, he did not suffer. When it was all prepared, he made a noose, put it around his neck, climbed onto the bed, and hanged himself. But just as his tongue began to protrude, the strips came apart and he fell. The guard heard the noise and came in. A medic was called, and he was taken to the hospital. The next day he recovered completely and was taken from the hospital and placed not in an individual, but in a common cell.

In the common cell he lived among twenty people as if he were alone, saw no one, spoke with no one, and suffered in the same way. It was especially hard for him when they all slept, while he did not sleep, but saw her as before, heard her voice, then the black ones appeared again with their frightening eyes and taunted him.

Again, as before, he recited prayers, and, as before, they did not help.

Once, when, after his prayers, she appeared to him again, he began to pray to her, to her dear soul, so that she would release him, forgive him. And when he collapsed on his crumpled sack towards morning, he fell fast asleep, and in his sleep she, with her thin, wrinkled, slashed neck, came to him.

"So, will you forgive me?"

She looked at him with her meek eyes and said nothing.

"Will you?"

And he asked her three times like that. But she still said nothing. And he woke up. After that it became easier for him, and it was as if he recovered his senses, looked around himself, and for the first time began to make friends and speak with his cell mates.

III

IN THE SAME CELL with Stepan was Vassily, who had again been caught thieving and been sentenced to exile, and Chuyev, also sentenced to deportation. Vassily either sang songs all the time with his beautiful voice or told his cell mates about his adventures. Chuyev either worked, sewing some clothing or shirts, or read the Gospels and the Psalter.

To Stepan's question why he had been exiled, Chuyev explained that he had been exiled because of his true Christian faith, because the deceitful priests could not stand the sight of those who lived by the Gospels and who denounced them. When Stepan asked Chuyev what made up the Gospel law, Chuyev explained to him that the Gospel law was not to pray to man-made gods, but to worship in spirit and in truth. And he told him how they had learned this true faith from the crippled tailor while dividing up the land.

"Well, and what do you get for bad deeds?" asked Stepan.

"It's all said here."

And Chuyev read to him:

" 'When the Son of man shall come in his glory, and all the holy angels with him, then shall he sit upon the throne of his glory. And before him shall be gathered all nations: and he shall separate them one from another, as a shepherd divideth his sheep from the goats. And he shall set the sheep on his right hand, but the goats on the left. Then shall the King say unto them on his right hand, "Come, ye blessed of my Father, inherit the kingdom prepared for you from the foundation of the world: For I was an hungred, and ye gave me meat; I was thirsty, and ye gave me drink; I was a stranger, and ye took me in; naked, and ye clothed me; I was sick, and ye visited me; I was in prison, and ye came unto me." Then shall the righteous answer him, saying, "Lord, when saw we thee an hungred, and fed thee? or thirsty, and gave thee drink? When saw we thee a stranger, and took thee in? or naked, and clothed thee? Or when saw we thee sick, or in prison, and came unto thee?" And the King shall answer and say unto them, "Verily I say unto you, inasmuch as ye have done it unto one of the least of these my brethren, ye have done it unto me." Then shall he say also unto them on his left hand, "Depart from me, ye cursed, into everlasting fire, prepared for the devil and his angels: For I was an hungred, and ye gave me no meat; I was thirsty, and ye gave me no drink; I was a stranger, and ye took me not in; naked, and ye clothed me not; sick, and in prison, and ye visited me not." Then shall they also answer him, saying, "Lord, when saw we thee an hungred, or athirst, or a stranger, or naked, or sick, or in prison, and did not minister unto thee?" Then shall he answer them, saying, "Verily I say unto you, inasmuch as ye did it not to one of the least of these, ye did it not to me." And these shall go away into everlasting punishment, but the righteous into life eternal' " (Matthew 25:31–46).

Vassily, who came out and sat on the floor facing Chuyev and listened to the reading, nodded his handsome head approvingly.

"Right," he said resolutely, "go, you cursed, into everlasting punishment, you didn't feed anybody, but stuffed yourselves. Serves them right. Give it here, I'll read from it," he added, wishing to show off his reading.

"Well, and won't there be any forgiveness?" asked Stepan, who had been listening to the reading silently, hanging his shaggy head.

"Hold on, keep still," Chuyev said to Vassily, who kept mumbling about the rich not feeding the stranger or visiting the prisoner. "Hold on, I said," Chuyev repeated, leafing through the Gospels. Finding what he was looking for, Chuyev spread the pages with his big, strong hand, gone white in jail.

" 'And there were also two other, malefactors, led with him'— meaning with Christ," Chuyev began, " 'to be put to death. And when they were come to the place, which is called Calvary, there they crucified him, and the malefactors, one on the right hand, and the other on the left.

" 'Then said Jesus, "Father, forgive them; for they know not what they do . . ." And the people stood beholding. And the rulers also with them derided him, saying, "He saved others; let him save himself, if he be Christ, the chosen of God." And the soldiers also mocked him, coming to him, and offering him vinegar, and saying, "If thou be the king of the Jews, save thyself." And a superscription also was written over him in letters of Greek, and Latin, and Hebrew, THIS IS THE KING OF THE JEWS. And one of the malefactors which were hanged railed on him, saying, "If thou be Christ, save thyself and us." But the other answering rebuked him, saying, "Dost not thou fear God, seeing thou art in the same condemnation? And we indeed justly; for we receive the due reward of our deeds: but this man hath done nothing amiss." And he said unto Jesus, "Lord, remember me when thou comest into thy kingdom." And Jesus said unto him, "Verily I say unto thee, today shalt thou be with me in paradise" ' " (Luke 23:32–43).

Stepan said nothing and sat deep in thought, as if listening, but he no longer heard anything of what Chuyev read further.

"So that's what makes up the true faith," he thought. "Only those will be saved who gave food and drink to the poor, visited the prisoners, and those who didn't will go to hell. Yet the robber only repented on the cross, and all the same he went to paradise." He saw no contradiction here, but, on the contrary, the one confirmed the other: that the merciful will go to paradise and the unmerciful to hell, meant that everybody should be merciful, and that Christ forgave the robber meant that Christ, too, was merciful. All this was completely new to Stepan; he only wondered why it had been hidden from him up to then. And he spent all his free time with Chuyev, asking and listening. And, listening, he understood. The general meaning was revealed to him of the whole teaching about men being brothers and having to love and pity one another, and then it would be good for them all. And when he listened, he took in, as something forgotten and familiar, everything that confirmed the general meaning of this teaching, and let pass by whatever did not confirm it, ascribing it to his own incomprehension.

And from then on Stepan became a different person.

IV

STEPAN PELAGEYUSHKIN HAD BEEN peaceable even before, but of late he had astounded the warden and the guards and the inmates by the change that had taken place in him. Without orders, out of turn, he performed all the hardest work, even including the cleaning of the latrine buckets. But, in spite of his submissiveness, his fellows respected and feared him, knowing his firmness and great physical strength, especially after an incident with two tramps who attacked him, but whom he fought off, breaking the arm of one. These tramps had started gambling with a young and rich inmate, and had taken everything he had from him. Stepan interceded for him and took from them the money they had won. The tramps began to abuse him, then to beat him, but he overcame them both. When the warden enquired into the cause of the quarrel, the tramps declared that Pelageyushkin had started beating them. Stepan did not try to justify himself and submissively accepted the penalty, which consisted of three days in the punishment cell and being moved to solitary confinement.

Solitary confinement was hard for him, in that it separated him from Chuyev and the Gospels, and, besides that, he was afraid that his visions of her and of the black ones would come back. But there were no visions. His whole soul was filled with new, joyful content. He would have been glad of his solitude, if he could read and had had the Gospels. They would have given him the Gospels, but he could not read.

As a boy he had begun to learn the letters of the old alphabet—*az*, *buki*, *vedi*[17]—but out of slow-wittedness he never went further than the alphabet and could not understand the making of syllables and so remained illiterate. But now he decided to learn to read and asked a guard to bring him the Gospels. The guard brought the book, and he got down to work. The letters he recognized, but he could not join anything together. However much he struggled to understand how letters join together into words, nothing came of it. He did not sleep nights, kept thinking, did not want to eat, and the louse of anguish attacked him so fiercely that he could not scrape it off.

"What, you still haven't got there?" the guard asked him once.

"No."

"Do you know the Our Father?"

"Yes."

"Well, read it then. Here it is," and the guard showed him the Our Father in the Gospels.

Stepan started reading the Our Father, comparing the familiar letters with the familiar sounds. And suddenly the mystery of joining letters together was revealed to him, and he started to read. This was a great joy. And from then on he started reading, and the meaning that gradually emerged from the words he put together with such effort acquired still greater significance.

Now solitude no longer burdened, but gladdened Stepan. He was all filled with his work, and was not glad when, in order to free the cell for newly arrived political prisoners, he was sent back to the common cell.

V

Now it was not just Chuyev, but Stepan who often read the Gospels in the cell, and while some of the inmates sang obscene songs, others listened to his reading and his talking about what he had read. Two always listened to him silently and attentively: the murderer-hangman Makhorkin, sentenced to hard labour, and Vassily, who had been caught thieving and, while awaiting trial, was kept in the same cell. Makhorkin had performed his duties twice during the time he was kept in prison, both times away, because no one could be found to carry out the sentence of the judges. The peasants who had killed Pyotr Nikolaich were court-martialed and two of them were sentenced to death by hanging.

Now Makhorkin was summoned to Penza to perform his duties. Previously, on such occasions, he would at once write—he was quite literate—a note to the governor explaining that he was being dispatched to perform his duties in Penza, and therefore asked the chief of the province to allocate him the money for food and daily expenses; but now, to the astonishment of the prison superintendent, he announced that he would not go and would no longer perform the duties of a hangman.

"Forgotten the lash?" shouted the prison superintendent.

"Well, if it's the lash, it's the lash, but there's no law that says kill."

"What's that? Did you get it from Pelageyushkin? Found ourselves a jailhouse prophet! Just you wait!"

VI

Meanwhile Makhin, the student at whose prompting the coupon was forged, had finished high school and his university studies in the faculty of law. Thanks to his success with women, with the former mistress of an elderly deputy minister, he was appointed an examining magistrate while quite young. He was a dishonest man in his debts, a seducer of women, a gambler, but he was a clever, shrewd man, with an excellent memory, and well able to conduct a case.

He was examining magistrate in the district where Stepan Pelageyushkin was tried. From the very first interrogation, Stepan astonished him by his simple, truthful, and calm answers. Makhin felt unconsciously that this man who stood before him in chains and with a shaved head, who had been brought in guarded and would be led back to be locked up by two soldiers, that this man was totally free, and morally stood inaccessibly higher than himself. And therefore, while interrogating him, he ceaselessly encouraged and prodded himself, so as not to get thrown off and confused. What struck him was that Stepan spoke of his deeds as of something long past, performed not by himself, but by some other person.

"And you had no pity for them?" asked Makhin.

"No. I didn't understand then."

"Well, and now?"

Stepan smiled sadly.

"Now you could burn me at the stake, but I wouldn't do it."

"Why's that?"

"Because I understood that all men are brothers."

"Well, and am I your brother, too?"

"What else?"

"How is it I'm your brother, and I send you to hard labour?"

"From not understanding."

"You mean I don't understand?"

"You don't, since you judge me."

"Well, let's continue. Where did you go then? . . ."

Makhin was struck most of all by what he learned about Pelageyushkin's influence on the hangman Makhorkin, who, at the risk of being punished, had refused to perform his duties.

VII

AT A SOIRÉE at the Eropkins', where there were two rich, eligible young ladies whom Makhin was courting at the same time, after singing romances, which the very musical Makhin was especially good at—he sang duets excellently and played the accompaniment—he told very precisely and in detail—he had an excellent memory—and with perfect indifference, about the strange criminal who had converted the hangman. Makhin could remember and recount it all so well, because he was always perfectly indifferent to the people he dealt with. He did not enter and was unable to enter the inner state of other people, and therefore could remember so well everything that went on with people, what they did and said. But Pelageyushkin interested him. He did not enter Stepan's soul, but he involuntarily asked himself what was in his soul, and, finding no answer, but feeling that this was something interesting, he told about the whole case at the soirée: the seduction of the hangman, and the warden's stories of how strangely Pelageyushkin behaved himself, and how he read the Gospels, and what a strong influence he had on his fellow inmates.

Everyone became interested in Makhin's story, but most of all the youngest—Liza Eropkin, an eighteen-year-old girl just out of boarding school and just recovering from the darkness and narrowness of the false conditions in which she had grown up, and, like someone emerging from the water, passionately breathing in the fresh air of life. She started asking Makhin about the details and about how and why such a change had taken place in Pelageyushkin, and Makhin told her what he had heard from Stepan about his last murder, and how the meekness, submissiveness, and fearlessness of death of this very good woman, whom he had murdered last, had vanquished him, had opened his eyes, and how the reading of the Gospels had then finished the task.

For a long time that night Liza Eropkin could not fall asleep. For several months already a struggle had been going on in her between social life, to which her sister was drawing her, and her attraction to Makhin, combined with the desire to reform him. And now the latter prevailed. She had heard about the murdered woman before. But now, after this terrible death and Makhin's account in Pelageyushkin's words, she had learned the story of Marya Semyonovna in detail and was struck by all she had learned about her.

Liza passionately wished to become such a Marya Semyonovna. She was rich and feared that Makhin was courting her for the sake of money. And she decided to give away her property and told this to Makhin.

Makhin was glad of the chance to show his disinterestedness and told

Liza that he did not love her for the sake of money, and he himself was touched by this, as it seemed to him, magnanimous decision. On Liza's side, meanwhile, a struggle began with her mother (the property was her father's), who would not allow her to give her property away. And Makhin supported Liza. And the more he did so, the more he understood the totally different world of spiritual aspiration, foreign to him until then, which he saw in Liza.

VIII

EVERYTHING BECAME quiet in the cell. Stepan lay in his place on the bunk and was not yet asleep. Vassily went up to him and, pulling him by the leg, winked at him to get up and come over to him. Stepan slipped off the bunk and went over to Vassily.

"Well, brother," said Vassily, "take the trouble now to help me."

"Help you in what?"

"You see, I want to escape."

And Vassily revealed to Stepan that he had prepared everything for an escape.

"Tomorrow I'll stir them all up," he pointed to the men lying down. "They'll tell on me. I'll be transferred upstairs, and there I already know what to do. Only you must unscrew the lock on the mortuary door for me."

"That's possible. Where will you go?"

"Wherever my feet take me. Is there any lack of bad people?"

"That's so, brother, only it's not for us to judge them."

"Well, I'm no murderer. I never murdered a single soul—and what's thieving? What's so wrong with it? Don't they rob our kind?"

"That's their business. They'll answer for it."

"Why should I look them in the teeth? So I rob a church. What's the harm in that? Now I want to do it so that it's not some little shops, but I grab a whole treasure chest and give it away. Give it away to good people."

Just then one of the inmates sat up on his bunk and started listening. Stepan and Vassily parted.

The next day Vassily did as he wanted. He started complaining about the bread being soggy, incited all the inmates to call the warden and lodge a complaint. The warden came, yelled at them all, and, learning that the instigator of the whole thing was Vassily, ordered him to be put separately in solitary confinement on the upper floor.

That was just what Vassily wanted.

IX

VASSILY KNEW that upstairs cell he was put in. He knew the floor of it, and as soon as he got there, he started taking the floor up. When it was possible to wriggle through, he took apart the laths and jumped to the lower floor, into the mortuary. On that day one dead man lay on a table in the mortuary. In that same mortuary they stored the sacks for making straw mattresses. Vassily knew that and was counting on that cell. The lock on the door had been unscrewed and put back. Vassily went out the door and down to the latrine being built at the end of the corridor. In this latrine there was a hole all the way through from the third floor to the basement. Having felt for the door, Vassily went back to the mortuary, took the sheet off the ice-cold dead man (he touched his hand as he took it off), then took some sacks, tied them together so as to make a rope, and took this rope of sacks to the latrine; there he tied the rope to a crossbeam and began to climb down it. The rope did not reach to the floor. Whether it was a lot or a little too short he did not know, but there was nothing to do, he hung from the end and jumped. His feet were hurt, but he could walk. There were two windows in the basement. He could wriggle through them, but they were fitted with iron grates. These had to be broken out. With what? Vassily started rummaging around. There were broken boards lying about the basement. He found one with a sharp end and began to prise out the bricks that held the grate. He worked for a long time. The cocks had crowed twice, but the grate still held. Finally one side came loose. Vassily put the board underneath and leaned on it, the grate came out whole, but a brick fell and made a noise. The sentry might have heard it. Vassily froze. All was quiet. He climbed through the window. Climbed out. His escape had to be over the wall. In the corner of the yard there was an outbuilding. He had to climb onto the outbuilding and from it over the wall. He should have taken that board with him.

Without it he could not climb up. Vassily went back. He returned with the board and froze, listening for where the sentry was. The sentry, as he had calculated, was pacing along the other side of the square yard. Vassily went up to the outbuilding, leaned the board against it, climbed. The board slipped and fell. Vassily was wearing socks. He took off the socks to have a better grip with his feet, put the board in place again, climbed up it, and seized the gutter with his hand. "Dear God, don't tear off, stay put." He clung to the gutter, and now his knee is on the roof. The sentry is coming. Vassily lies down, freezes. The sentry does not see him and walks away again. Vassily jumps up. The sheet iron crackles under his feet. Another step, two, here is the wall. It is easy to reach the top of the wall with his hand. One hand, the other, he stretches out all the way, and now he is on top of the wall. If only he does not break anything jumping down. Vassily shifts his position, hangs down, holding on with his hands, stretches out, lets one hand go, the other—Lord bless us!—he is on the ground. And the ground is soft. His feet are unhurt, and he runs off.

On the outskirts Malanya opens the door, and he gets in under the warm patchwork quilt impregnated with the smell of sweat.

X

BIG, BEAUTIFUL, always calm, childless, full-bodied, like a barren cow, Pyotr Nikolaich's wife saw from the window how her husband was killed and dragged somewhere into the fields. The feeling of horror that Natalya Ivanovna (that was the name of Pyotr Nikolaich's widow) experienced at the sight of this slaughter was, as always happens, so strong that it stifled all other feelings in her. But when the whole crowd disappeared beyond the garden fence, and the hubbub of voices died down, and barefoot Malanya, the wench who did chores for them, with her eyes popping out, came running with the news, as if it was something joyful, that Pyotr Nikolaich had been killed and thrown into the ravine, another feeling began to emerge from behind the first feeling of horror: a feeling of the joy of liberation from the despot with his eyes hidden behind dark glasses, eyes which for nineteen years had kept her in slavery. She was horrified at this feeling and did not admit it to herself, still less tell anyone about it. When the mangled, yellow, hairy body was being washed and dressed and put in the coffin, she was horrified, wept and sobbed. When the investigator of high crimes came and questioned her as a witness, she saw there in the investigator's quarters two peasants in chains, recognized as the chief culprits. One was an old man with a long, curly, flaxen beard and a calm, stern, and handsome face; the other was of a gypsy type, not yet old, with shining black eyes and curly, dishevelled hair. She told what she knew, recognized these people as the ones who had been first to seize Pyotr Nikolaich by the arms, and though the gypsy-like muzhik, his eyes shining and wandering under his moving eyebrows, said reproachfully, "It's a sin, mistress! Oh, we'll all die one day," even so she did not feel the least bit sorry for them. On the contrary, during the investigation a feeling of hostility arose in her and a wish to take revenge on her husband's killers.

But when the case, transferred to court-martial, was decided a month later, eight men being sentenced to hard labour and two, the white-bearded old man and the black gypsy, as they called him, to hanging, it gave her an unpleasant feeling. But, under the influence of court solemnity, this unpleasant doubt soon passed. If the higher authorities owned that it must be so, that meant it was right.

The execution was to be performed in the village. And, returning from the liturgy on Sunday, Malanya, in a new dress and new shoes, reported to her mistress that the gallows was being set up and a hangman from Moscow was expected by Wednesday and that the families were howling incessantly for the whole village to hear.

Natalya Ivanovna did not leave her house, so as not to see the gallows or the people, and had only one wish: that what had to be done should be over quickly. She thought only of herself, and not of the condemned and their families.

XI

ON TUESDAY her acquaintance, the local constable, came calling, and Natalya Ivanovna treated him to vodka and pickled mushrooms of her own making. The constable, having drunk the vodka and eaten a bit, informed her that there would be no execution the next day.

"What? Why's that?"

"An amazing story. They couldn't find a hangman. There was one in Moscow, but he, as my son tells me, read himself up on the Gospels and says: 'I cannot kill.' Got himself sentenced to hard labour for murder, and now suddenly he can't kill according to the law. They told him he'd be whipped. 'Whip me,' he says, 'I just can't do it.' "

Natalya Ivanovna suddenly blushed and even broke into a sweat from her thoughts.

"But can't they be pardoned now?"

"How can they be pardoned, if they've been sentenced by the court? The tsar alone can pardon them."

"How will the tsar find out?"

"They have the right to ask for a pardon."

"But they're being punished on account of me," said the stupid Natalya Ivanovna. "And I forgive them."

The constable laughed.

"Ask, then."

"Can I?"

"Of course you can."

"Is there still enough time?"

"You can send a telegram."

"To the tsar?"

"Yes, even to the tsar."

The news that the hangman had refused and was prepared to suffer rather than kill had suddenly overturned Natalya Ivanovna's soul, and that feeling of compassion and horror, which had asked several times to be let out, broke through and took possession of her.

"Dearest Filipp Vassilievich, write a telegram for me. I want to ask the tsar to pardon them."

The constable shook his head.

"What if we get in trouble for it?"

"I'll be the one to answer. I won't tell on you."

"Such a kind woman," thought the policeman, "a good woman. If mine were like that, it would be paradise, and not what it is now."

And the policeman wrote a telegram to the tsar: "To His Imperial Majesty the Sovereign Emperor. A faithful subject of Your Imperial Majesty, the widow of the collegiate assessor Pyotr Nikolaevich Sventitsky, murdered by his peasants, falling at the sacred feet" (this place in the telegram was especially pleasing to the constable who composed it) "of Your Imperial Majesty, beseeches you to pardon the peasants so-and-so, of such-and-such province, district, department, village, who have been sentenced to death."

The telegram was sent by the constable himself, and in Natalya Ivanovna's soul all was well, joyful. It seemed to her that if she, the murdered man's widow, could forgive and ask for pardon, the tsar could not but grant it.

XII

LIZA EROPKIN LIVED in a ceaselessly rapturous state. The further she went along the path of Christian life that had been revealed to her, the more certain she was that it was the true path and the more joyful her soul became.

She had two immediate goals now: the first was to convert Makhin, or, rather, as she put it inwardly, to bring him back to himself, to his kind, beautiful nature. She loved him, and the light of her love revealed to her the divine in his soul, common to all people, though she saw in this principle of life, common to all people, a kindness, a tenderness, a loftiness proper to him alone. Her other goal was to stop being rich. She wanted to free herself from her property, first in order to test Makhin, and then for herself, for her own soul—according to the word of the Gospels. At first she began giving it away, but was stopped by her father and, still more than by her father, by the mass of petitions, personal or in writing, that came pouring in. Then she decided to address an elder known for his holy life and ask him to take her money and do with it as he found necessary. Learning of this, her father became angry and in a heated conversation with her called her mad, psychopathic, and said he would take measures to protect her, as a mad person, from her own self.

Her father's irate, vexed tone communicated itself to her, and before she knew it, she burst into angry tears and said all sorts of rude things to him, calling him a despot and even a money-lover.

She asked her father to forgive her. He said he was not angry, but she saw that he was offended and in his soul did not forgive her. She did not want to tell Makhin about it. Her sister, who was jealous of her over

Makhin, withdrew from her completely. She had no one to share her feelings with, no one to confess to.

"I must confess to God," she said to herself, and as it was the Great Lent,[18] she decided to fast and pray and tell everything to a priest at confession and ask his advice about how she should act in the future.

Not far from town there was a monastery in which an elder lived who was famous for his life, his teachings and prophecies, and for the healings ascribed to him.

The elder received a letter from the old Eropkin warning him of his daughter's coming and of her abnormal, agitated state, and expressing confidence that the elder would guide her onto the right path—of the golden mean, of a good Christian life, without violating existing conditions.

Weary from receiving, the elder received Liza and calmly began to admonish her about moderation, submission to existing conditions and to parents. Liza was silent, kept blushing, broke into a sweat, but when he finished, she, with tears brimming her eyes, began to speak, timidly at first, about Christ saying, "Leave thy father and mother, and follow me,"[19] then, growing more and more animated, she spoke out the whole notion of how she understood Christianity. The elder smiled at first and objected with the usual admonitions, but then fell silent and began to sigh, only repeating: "Oh, Lord."

"Well, all right, come tomorrow to confess," he said and blessed her with his wrinkled hand.

The next day he heard her confession and dismissed her, bluntly refusing to take upon himself the management of her fortune.

The purity, the total surrender to the will of God, and the ardour of this girl struck the elder. He had long wanted to renounce the world, but the monastery demanded his activity from him. His activity provided income for the monastery. And he consented, though with a vague sense of all the falsity of his position. He was made into a saint, a miracle worker, but he was a weak man carried away by success. And this girl's opening of her soul to him opened his own soul as well. And he saw how far he was from what he wanted to be, from what he was drawn to in his heart.

Soon after Liza's visit, he shut himself away and came to church only after three weeks, served the liturgy, and after the liturgy delivered a sermon in which he denounced himself and accused the world of sin and called it to repentance.

He delivered sermons every two weeks. And more and more people gathered to hear his sermons. And his fame as a preacher spread more and more. There was something special, bold, sincere in his sermons. And that was why he affected people so strongly.

XIII

MEANWHILE VASSILY DID everything as he had wanted. At night, with some cronies, he broke into the house of the rich Krasnopuzov. He knew how stingy and depraved the man was, and got into his desk and made off with some thirty thousand in cash. And Vassily did as he had wanted. He even stopped drinking, and gave money to poor brides. He got them married, paid off debts, and disappeared. His only concern was to distribute the money well. He gave some to the police, too. And they did not go looking for him.

His heart was joyful. And when he was finally taken, he laughed during the trial and boasted that with the fat-belly the money lay stagnant, he didn't even know how much there was, but I got it moving and helped good people with it.

And his defence was so cheerful and kind that the jury almost acquitted him. He was sentenced to exile.

He thanked them and told them beforehand that he would escape.

XIV

MRS. SVENTITSKY'S TELEGRAM to the tsar did not produce any effect. In the appeals commission, they first decided not even to report it to the tsar, but then, when at the sovereign's lunch the talk got on to the Sventitsky case, the director lunching with the sovereign made mention of the telegram from the murdered man's wife.

"*C'est très gentil de sa part,* "* said one of the ladies in the tsar's family.

* That's very nice of her.

The sovereign merely sighed, shrugged his epauletted shoulders, and said: "Law"—and held out a glass, into which the court lackey poured sparkling Moselle wine. Everyone made as if they were surprised at the wisdom of the word uttered by the sovereign. And there was no more talk of the telegram. And the two muzhiks—the old one and the young one—were hanged with the help of a Tartar hangman invited from Kazan, a cruel murderer and bestialist.

The old woman wanted to dress the body of her old man in a white shirt, white leg cloths, and new burial shoes, but they did not allow her to, and both men were buried in a single pit outside the cemetery pale.

"PRINCESS SOFYA VLADIMIROVNA MENTIONED to me that he was a wonderful preacher," the old empress, the sovereign's mother, once told her son. *"Faites-le venir. Il peut prêcher à la cathédrale."**

"No, better with us," said the sovereign, and he ordered the elder Isidor to be invited.

The entire generalship assembled in the palace church. A new, extraordinary preacher was an event.

A little old man came out, grey-haired, skinny, and looked around at them all: "In the name of the Father, and of the Son, and of the Holy Spirit," and began.

At first it went well, but the longer it lasted, the worse it became. *"Il devenait de plus en plus agressif,"†* as the empress said afterwards. He thundered against everybody. He spoke of execution. And ascribed the necessity of execution to bad government. How can people be killed in a Christian country?

Everyone exchanged glances, and everyone was concerned only with the impropriety and unpleasantness of it all for the sovereign, but no one said anything. When Isidor said, "Amen," the metropolitan went up to him and invited him to his office.

After conversations with the metropolitan and the ober-procurator,[20] the old man was at once sent back to the monastery—not to his own, but to one in Suzdal, where the superior and commandant was Father Misaïl.

* Have him come. He can preach in the cathedral.
† He became more and more aggressive.

XV

EVERYONE MADE it look as if there had been nothing unpleasant in Isidor's sermon, and no one mentioned it. And it seemed to the tsar that the elder's words had left no trace in him, but twice during the day he recalled the execution of the peasants, for whose pardon Mrs. Sventitsky's telegram had pleaded. In the afternoon there was a review, then a promenade, then a reception of ministers, then dinner, and theatre in the evening. As usual, the tsar fell asleep as soon as his head touched the pillow. In the night he was awakened by a frightful dream: gallows stood in a field, corpses swung from them, and the corpses stuck their tongues out, and the tongues protruded further and further. And someone cried: "It's your work, your work." The tsar woke up in a sweat and began to think. For the first time he began to think about the responsibility that lay upon him, and all the old man's words came back to him . . .

But he saw the man in himself only from a distance, and could not yield to simple human demands, owing to the demands that press upon a tsar from all sides; to acknowledge human demands as more obligatory than the demands of a tsar was beyond his strength.

XVI

HAVING FINISHED his second term in jail, Proshka, that cocky, vain young fop, came out a totally destroyed man. When he was sober, he sat and did nothing, and however much his father scolded him, he ate, did not work, and, moreover, kept an eye out for things he could smuggle to the pot-house for drink. He sat, coughed, hawked, and spat. The doctor he went to listened to his chest and shook his head.

"What you need, brother, is what you haven't got."

"Sure enough, that's always needed."

"Drink milk, don't smoke."

"It's Lent, and anyway there's no cow."

Once in the spring he did not sleep all night, suffered anguish, wanted to drink. There was nothing to snatch at home. He put his hat on and left. He went down the street to where the clergy lived. At the beadle's a harrow stood leaning against the wattle fence. Proshka went over, hoisted the harrow on his back, and carried it to Petrovna's tavern. "Maybe she'll give me a little bottle." He had no time to get away before the beadle came out on the porch. It was full daylight—he saw Proshka carrying off the harrow.

"Hey, what are you doing?"

People came out, seized Proshka, put him in the lock-up. The justice of the peace sentenced him to eleven months in prison.

It was autumn. Proshka was transferred to the hospital. He coughed and racked his whole chest. And he could no longer get warm. Those who were stronger did not shiver yet. But Proshka shivered day and night. The warden was on a drive to save firewood and did not heat the hospital until November. Proshka suffered painfully in his body, but worst of all in his soul. He was disgusted by everything and hated everyone: the beadle, and the warden, because he did not heat the place, and the guard, and his neighbour on the cot with his red, swollen lip. He also came to hate the new convict who was brought to them. This convict was Stepan. He had contracted erysipelas on his head and was transferred to the hospital and put next to Proshka. At first Proshka hated him, but then he came to love him so much that he only waited for when he could talk with him. Only after talking with him would the anguish quieten down in Proshka's heart.

Stepan always told everyone about his last murder and how it had affected him.

"It's not only that she didn't scream or anything," he said, "but just—here, stab me. Pity yourself, she said, not me."

"Well, sure, it's awful to kill a person. I once undertook to butcher a sheep and wasn't glad I did. But I never killed anybody, and what did those villains destroy me for? I never did anybody harm . . ."

"Then it will all be counted to your credit."

"Where's that?"

"How do you mean, where? What about God?"

"Never set eyes on him. I'm not a believer, brother. I think—you die, the grass grows over you. That's all."

"How can you think that way? I killed a lot of people, and she, the dear heart, only helped everybody. And what, you think it'll be the same for her and me? No, hold on a minute . . ."

"So you think you die and your soul is left?"

"What else. It's a sure thing."

Dying was hard for Proshka, he was suffocating. But in his last hour it suddenly became easy. He called for Stepan.

"So, farewell, brother. It's clear my death has come. And here I was afraid, but now it's all right. I'd only like it to be soon."

And Proshka died in the hospital.

XVII

MEANWHILE Evgeny Mikhailovich's affairs were going from bad to worse. The shop was mortgaged. Trade fell off. Another shop opened in town, yet the interest had to be paid. It was necessary to borrow on interest again. And it ended with the shop and all its stock being put up for sale. Evgeny Mikhailovich and his wife rushed all over and nowhere could get hold of the four hundred roubles that were needed to save the business.

A small hope rested on the merchant Krasnopuzov, whose mistress was acquainted with Evgeny Mikhailovich's wife. But by now the whole town was informed that Krasnopuzov had been robbed of an enormous sum of money. Half a million, the story went.

"And who stole it?" said Evgeny Mikhailovich's wife. "Vassily, our former yard porter. They say he's throwing the money around now and has bought off the police."

"He was a scoundrel," said Evgeny Mikhailovich. "He agreed so easily to perjury then. I never thought he would."

"They say he came to us here. The cook said it was him. She says he got fourteen poor brides married off."

"Well, they're making it up."

Just then some strange elderly man in a twill jacket came into the shop.

"What do you want?"

"A letter for you."

"From whom?"

"It says inside."

"What, no need for an answer? Wait a minute."

"I can't."

And the strange man, having handed over the envelope, hurriedly left.

"That's odd!"

Evgeny Mikhailovich tore open the fat envelope and could not believe his eyes: hundred-rouble bills. Four of them. What was this? And there was an illiterate letter to Evgeny Mikhailovich: "According to the Gospels it says, do good for evil. You did me much evil with the coupon, and I did mighty wrong to that muzhik, and yet I pity you. Here, take four big ones and remember your yard porter Vassily."

"No, it's amazing," said Evgeny Mikhailovich, both to his wife and to himself. And whenever he remembered it or spoke of it to his wife, tears came to his eyes and his soul was joyful.

XVIII

FOURTEEN CLERGYMEN WERE KEPT in the Suzdal prison, all chiefly for deviating from Orthodoxy. Isidor, too, had been sent there. Father Misaïl had received Isidor according to instructions and, without talking with him, had ordered him put in a separate cell as a serious criminal. In the third week of Isidor's stay in prison, Father Misaïl made the rounds of the prisoners. Going into Isidor's cell he asked if he needed anything.

"I need many things, but I cannot say it in front of people. Give me a chance to talk with you alone."

They looked at each other, and Misaïl realized that he had nothing to fear. He ordered Isidor brought to his cell and, when they were alone, he said:

"Well, speak."

Isidor fell on his knees.

"Brother!" said Isidor. "What are you doing? Have pity on yourself. There's no villain worse than you, you've profaned all that's holy . . ."

A MONTH LATER Misaïl handed in documents for the release, on grounds of repentance, not only of Isidor but of seven others, and asked to be retired to a monastery.

XIX

Ten years passed.

Mitya Smokovnikov had finished his studies in technical school and was an engineer with a big salary in the gold mines of Siberia. He had to travel over his sector. The director suggested that he take the convict Stepan Pelageyushkin.

"A convict? Isn't that dangerous?"

"With him it's not. He's a holy man. Ask anyone you like."

"What did he do?"

The director smiled.

"He killed six people, but he's a holy man. I'll vouch for him."

And so Mitya Smokovnikov received Stepan, a bald, thin, sunburnt man, and travelled with him.

On the road, Stepan looked after Smokovnikov like one of his own children, as he attended to everyone wherever he could, and told him his whole story. And then how, and why, and by what he lived now.

And, astonishing thing! Mitya Smokovnikov, who up to then had lived only by drink, food, cards, wine, and women, fell to thinking about life for the first time. And these thoughts did not abandon him, but turned his soul around more and more. He was offered a post where there were great profits to be made. He refused and decided to use what he had, buy an estate, marry, and serve people as he could.

XX

And so he did. But before that he went to see his father, with whom his relations had become unpleasant on account of the new family his father had started. Now, however, he resolved to become closer with his father. And so he did. And his father was astonished, laughed at him, but then stopped attacking him and recalled many, many occasions when he had been to blame before him.

CA. 1880, 1902–04

Alyosha the Pot

ALYOSHA WAS the younger brother. He was nicknamed "the Pot" because his mother sent him to the deacon's wife with a pot of milk, and he tripped and broke the pot. His mother gave him a beating, and the children began to tease him with "the Pot." Alyosha the Pot—so he got his nickname.

Alyosha was a skinny, lop-eared lad (his ears stuck out like wings), and his nose was big. The children teased him: "Alyosha has a nose like a hound on a hill." There was a school in the village, but reading and writing did not come easy to Alyosha, nor did he have time to study. His older brother lived at a merchant's in town, and from childhood Alyosha began to help his father. When he was six, he already went with his older sister to watch the sheep and a cow on the village green, and when he grew up a little, he began to watch the horses during the day and at night pasture. By the age of twelve he was already ploughing and carting. He was not strong, but he had a knack for things. He was always cheerful. The boys laughed at him; he said nothing or else laughed. If his father scolded him, he said nothing and listened. And as soon as the scolding was over, he smiled and set about whatever work was before him.

Alyosha was nineteen when his brother was taken as a soldier. And his father sent Alyosha to the merchant's to replace his brother as a yard porter. Alyosha was given his brother's old boots, his father's hat and jerkin, and taken to town. Alyosha could not have been more glad of his clothes, but the merchant was left displeased with Alyosha's appearance.

"I thought you'd put a real man in Semyon's place," the merchant said, looking Alyosha over. "But you've brought me a milksop. What's he good for?"

"He can do everything—hitch up, and drive anywhere, and work like a fury. He only looks wispy. In fact, he's tough."

"Well, we'll see about that."

"And, above all, he's uncomplaining. Greedy for work."

"Well, what can I do with you? Let him stay."

And Alyosha started living at the merchant's.

The merchant's family was not large: his wife, his old mother, the older married son, of simple education, who was in business with his father, and another son, a studious one, who had finished high school and gone to university, but had been expelled and lived at home, and also a daughter, a schoolgirl.

At first they did not like Alyosha—he was much too peasantlike, and poorly dressed, and had no manners, addressing everyone informally—but they soon got used to him. He served them better than his brother. He was indeed uncomplaining, was sent to do all kinds of things, and did them all eagerly and quickly, going without pause from one thing to another. And, as at home, so at the merchant's, all the work was heaped on Alyosha. The more he did, the more work they heaped on him. The master's wife, and the master's mother, and the master's daughter, and the master's son, and the clerk, and the cook all sent him now here, now there, making him do now this, now that. All one heard was "Off you run, brother," or "Alyosha, take care of this." "What's the matter, Alyosha, did you forget or something?" "Look out you don't forget, Alyosha." And Alyosha ran, took care, looked out, and did not forget, and had time for it all, and smiled through it all.

He soon wore out his brother's boots, and the master gave him a good scolding for going around with torn boots and bare toes, and had new boots bought for him at the market. The boots were new, and Alyosha was glad of them, but his feet were still the old ones, and by evening they ached from running around, and he was angry with them. Alyosha was afraid that his father, when he came to take the money for him, might be upset that the merchant had deducted the cost of the boots from his pay.

In winter Alyosha got up before dawn, split wood, then swept the yard, fed the cow, the horse, and watered them. Then he stoked the stove, cleaned the master's boots and clothes, prepared samovars, cleaned them, then either the clerk called him to take out the wares or the cook ordered him to knead dough or scrub pots. Then they sent him to town now with a message, now for the master's daughter at school, now for lamp oil for the old woman. "Where'd you disappear to, curse you," now one, now another said to him. "Why should you go—Alyosha'll run over. Alyosha! Hey, Alyosha!" And off Alyosha ran.

He ate breakfast on the move, and he rarely managed to eat dinner with the rest of them. The cook scolded him for not coming with the rest, but took pity on him all the same and left him some hot food for dinner and supper. There was especially much work before and during holidays. And Alyosha was especially glad of the holidays, because on holidays they gave him tips—small ones, but they added up to some sixty kopecks, and after all it was his own money. He could spend it as he liked. As for his pay, he never set eyes on it. His father came, took it from the merchant, and only reprimanded Alyosha for having worn out his boots so quickly.

When he had saved up two roubles of this "tip" money, he bought, on the cook's advice, a red knitted jacket, and when he put it on, he could not keep his lips shut from satisfaction.

Alyosha spoke little, and when he did, it was always abruptly and briefly. And when he was told to do or was asked whether he could do this or that, he always said without the slightest hesitation, "It can all be done," and at once rushed to do it and did it.

He did not know any prayers. What his mother had taught him, he had forgotten; but he still prayed in the morning and in the evening—prayed with his hands, crossing himself.

So Alyosha lived for a year and a half, and then, in the second half of the second year, the most extraordinary event of his life happened to him. This event consisted in his learning, to his own amazement, that besides the relations between people that come from their need of each other, there are also quite special relations: not that a person needs to have his boots polished, or a purchase delivered, or a horse harnessed, but that a person just needs another person for no reason, so as to do something for him, to be nice to him, and that he, Alyosha, was that very person. He learned it through the cook, Ustinya. Ustyusha was an orphan, young, as hard-working as Alyosha. She began to pity Alyosha, and Alyosha felt for the first time that another person needed him, not his work, but him himself. When his mother pitied him, he did not notice it, it seemed to him that it had to be so, that it was as if he were pitying himself. But here he suddenly saw that Ustinya, a perfect stranger, pitied him, left him a pot of kasha with butter, and watched him while he ate, her head propped on her hand with her sleeve rolled up. And he glanced at her, and she laughed, and he laughed.

This was so new and strange that Alyosha was frightened at first. He sensed that it would hinder him from working as he used to work. But even so he was glad, and when he looked at his trousers, mended by Ustinya, he shook his head and smiled. Often while working or going somewhere, he would remember Ustinya and say: "Ah, that Ustinya!" Ustinya helped him where she could, and he helped her. She told him her life, how she became an orphan, how she was taken by her aunt, how they sent her to town, how the merchant's son tried to talk her into some foolishness, and how she brought him up short. She liked to talk, and he found it pleasant to listen to her. He heard that it often happens in towns: some muzhik workman marries the cook. And once she asked him if he would soon be married off. He said he did not know and had no wish to marry in his village.

"Why, have you got your eye on somebody?" she asked.

"I'd take you. Would you accept?"

"See, the pot, the pot, but what a catchy way he says it," she said, slapping him in the back with a towel. "And why shouldn't I?"

At Shrovetide the old man came to town for the money. The merchant's wife had found out that Alexei was of a mind to marry Ustinya, and she did not like it. "She'll get pregnant, and what good will she be with a baby?" She told her husband.

The merchant gave Alexei's father the money.

"So, then, is my boy doing all right?" asked the muzhik. "Like I said—he's uncomplaining."

"Uncomplaining he is, but he's got his mind on some foolishness. He's thinking about marrying the cook. And I won't keep a married couple. It doesn't suit us."

"A fool, a fool, but he's got his notions," said the father. "But never you mind. I'll order him to drop it."

Going to the kitchen, the father sat down at the table to wait for his son. Alyosha was running errands and came back out of breath.

"I thought you were sensible. But what's this you've taken into your head?" said the father.

"Nothing, really."

"How, nothing? You're meaning to get married. I'll marry you off when the time comes, and marry you as you ought, not to some town slut."

The father spoke a lot. Alyosha stood and sighed. When the father finished, Alyosha smiled.

"Well, it can be given up."

"That's the way."

When his father left and he remained alone with Ustinya, he said to her (she had been standing behind the door and listening while the father and son talked):

"Our plan's no good, it won't work. Did you hear? He's angry, he forbids it."

She wept silently into her apron.

Alyosha clucked his tongue.

"How can I disobey him? Seems we'll have to drop it."

In the evening, when the merchant's wife called him to close the blinds, she said to him:

"So you've obeyed your father, you've dropped this foolishness of yours?"

"Seems I have," said Alyosha, and he laughed and all at once wept.

FROM THEN ON Alyosha and Ustinya said no more about marriage and lived as before.

During Lent the clerk sent him to clear the snow off the roof. He climbed up on the roof, cleared it all off, started chipping away the snow that was frozen to the gutters, his feet slipped, and he fell with his shovel. The trouble was that he fell not on the snow but on the iron roof of the porch. Ustinya ran to him and so did the merchant's daughter.

"Are you hurt, Alyosha?"

"I guess so. Never mind."

He wanted to stand up but could not and began to smile. They carried him to the yard porter's room. A doctor's aide came. He examined him and asked where it hurt.

"It hurts everywhere, but never mind. Only the master will be cross. We must send word to my father."

Alyosha lay there for two days; on the third they sent for a priest.

"So, what, you mean you're going to die?" asked Ustinya.

"And why not? Can we just keep on living? Someday it's got to be," Alyosha said, quickly, as always. "Thank you, Ustyusha, for pitying me. You see, it's better that they told us not to get married, otherwise it would have come to nothing. Now it's all for the best."

He prayed with the priest only with his hands and heart. And in his heart was this: that, as it is good here, provided you obey and do not hurt anyone, so it will be good there.

He spoke little. Only asked to drink and kept being surprised at something.

He got surprised at something, stretched out, and died.

1905

Hadji Murat

I WAS RETURNING home through the fields. It was the very middle of summer. The meadows had been mowed, and they were just
about to reap the rye.

There is a delightful assortment of flowers at that time of year: red,
white, pink, fragrant, fluffy clover; impudent marguerites; milk-white
"love-me-love-me-nots" with bright yellow centres and a fusty, spicy
stink; yellow wild rape with its honey smell; tall-standing, tulip-shaped
campanulas, lilac and white; creeping vetch; neat scabious, yellow, red,
pink, and lilac; plantain with its faintly pink down and faintly perceptible, pleasant smell; cornflowers, bright blue in the sun and in youth, and
pale blue and reddish in the evening and when old; and the tender,
almond-scented, instantly wilting flowers of the bindweed.

I had gathered a big bouquet of various flowers and was walking
home, when I noticed in a ditch, in full bloom, a wonderful crimson thistle of the kind which is known among us as a "Tartar" and is carefully
mowed around, and, when accidentally mowed down, is removed from
the hay by the mowers, so that it will not prick their hands. I took it into
my head to pick this thistle and put it in the centre of the bouquet. I got
down into the ditch and, having chased away a hairy bumblebee that had
stuck itself into the centre of the flower and sweetly and lazily fallen
asleep there, I set about picking the flower. But it was very difficult: not
only was the stem prickly on all sides, even through the handkerchief I

had wrapped around my hand, but it was so terribly tough that I struggled with it for some five minutes, tearing the fibres one by one. When I finally tore off the flower, the stem was all ragged, and the flower no longer seemed so fresh and beautiful. Besides, in its coarseness and gaudiness it did not fit in with the delicate flowers of the bouquet. I was sorry that I had vainly destroyed and thrown away a flower that had been beautiful in its place. "But what energy and life force," I thought, remembering the effort it had cost me to tear off the flower. "How staunchly it defended itself, and how dearly it sold its life."

The way home went across a fallow, just-ploughed field of black earth. I walked up a gentle slope along a dusty, black-earth road. The ploughed field was a landowner's, a very large one, so that to both sides of the road and up the hill ahead nothing could be seen except the black, evenly furrowed, not yet scarified soil. The ploughing had been well done; nowhere on the field was there a single plant or blade of grass to be seen—it was all black. "What a destructive, cruel being man is, how many living beings and plants he annihilates to maintain his own life," I thought, involuntarily looking for something alive amidst this dead, black field. Ahead of me, to the right of the road, I spied a little bush. When I came closer, I recognized in this bush that same "Tartar" whose flower I had vainly picked and thrown away.

The "Tartar" bush consisted of three shoots. One had been broken off, and the remainder of the branch stuck out like a cut-off arm. On each of the other two there was a flower. These flowers had once been red, but now they were black. One stem was broken and half of it hung down, with the dirty flower at the end; the other, though all covered with black dirt, still stuck up. It was clear that the whole bush had been run over by a wheel, and afterwards had straightened up and therefore stood tilted, but stood all the same. As if a piece of its flesh had been ripped away, its guts turned inside out, an arm torn off, an eye blinded. But it still stands and does not surrender to man, who has annihilated all its brothers around it.

"What energy!" I thought. "Man has conquered everything, destroyed millions of plants, but this one still does not surrender."

And I remembered an old story from the Caucasus, part of which I saw, part of which I heard from witnesses, and part of which I imagined to myself. The story, as it shaped itself in my memory and imagination, goes like this.

I

IT WAS the end of 1851.

On a cold November evening Hadji Murat rode into the hostile Chechen aoul of Makhket, filled with the fragrant smoke of kizyak.*

The strained chanting of the muezzin had just died down, and in the clear mountain air, saturated with the smell of kizyak smoke, one could hear distinctly, through the lowing of cows and the bleating of sheep dispersing among the saklyas, stuck tightly together like a honeycomb, the guttural sounds of arguing male voices and women's and children's voices coming from the spring below.

This Hadji Murat was Shamil's[1] naïb, famous for his exploits, who never rode out otherwise than with his guidon and an escort of dozens of murids caracoling around him. Now, wrapped in a bashlyk and a burka, from under which a rifle stuck out, he rode with one murid, trying to be as little noticed as possible, warily peering with his quick, black eyes into the faces of the villagers he met on the way.

Coming to the centre of the aoul, Hadji Murat did not ride along the street that led to the square, but turned to the left, into a narrow lane. Riding up to the second saklya in the lane, dug into the hillside, he stopped and looked around. There was no one on the porch in front of the saklya, but on the roof, behind the freshly whitewashed clay chimney, a man lay covered with a sheepskin coat. Hadji Murat touched the man lying on the roof lightly with the handle of his whip and clucked his tongue. An old man rose from under the sheepskin coat, in a nightcap and a shiny, tattered beshmet. The old man's lashless eyes were red and moist, and he blinked in order to unstick them. Hadji Murat spoke the usual *"Salaam aleikum, "* and uncovered his face.

"Aleikum salaam, " said the old man, smiling with his toothless mouth, recognizing Hadji Murat, and, getting up on his skinny legs, he started putting his feet into the wooden-heeled shoes that stood by the chimney. Once shod, he unhurriedly put his arms into the sleeves of the wrinkled, raw sheepskin coat and climbed backwards down the ladder that leaned against the roof. While dressing and climbing down, the old man kept shaking his head on its thin, wrinkled, sunburnt neck and

* See glossary of Caucasian mountaineer words following text.

constantly munched his toothless gums. Having reached the ground, he hospitably took hold of the bridle and right stirrup of Hadji Murat's horse. But Hadji Murat's nimble, strong murid quickly got off his horse and, moving the old man aside, replaced him.

Hadji Murat got off his horse and, limping slightly, went up to the porch. He was met by a boy of about fifteen, who quickly came out of the door and fixed his shining eyes, black as ripe currants, on the arrivals.

"Run to the mosque, call your father," the old man ordered him, and, going ahead of Hadji Murat, he opened for him the light, creaking door of the saklya. As Hadji Murat went in, a slight, thin, middle-aged woman in a red beshmet over a yellow shirt and blue sharovary came from an inner door carrying pillows.

"Your coming bodes good fortune," she said and, bending double, she began to arrange the pillows by the front wall for the guest to sit on.

"May your sons live long," replied Hadji Murat, taking off his burka, rifle, and sabre, and handing them to the old man.

The old man carefully hung the rifle and sabre on nails next to the hung-up weapons of the master, between two large basins shining on the smoothly plastered and clean whitewashed wall.

Hadji Murat, straightening the pistol at his back, went to the pillows the woman had laid out and, wrapping the skirts of his cherkeska around him, sat down. The old man sat down on his bare heels facing him and, closing his eyes, raised his hands palms up. Hadji Murat did the same. Then the two of them, having recited a prayer, stroked their faces with their hands, bringing them together at the tip of the beard.

"*Ne khabar?*" Hadji Murat asked the old man—that is, "Any news?"

"*Khabar yok*"—"No news," the old man replied, looking not at the face but at the chest of Hadji Murat with his red, lifeless eyes. "I live at the apiary, I've just come today to see my son. He knows."

Hadji Murat understood that the old man did not want to tell what he knew and what Hadji Murat wanted to know, and nodding his head slightly, he asked nothing more.

"There's no good news," the old man began. "The only news is that the hares keep discussing how to drive away the eagles. And the eagles keep rending first one, then another. Last week the Russian dogs burned up the hay in Michitsky—tear their faces!" the old man croaked spitefully.

Hadji Murat's murid came in and, stepping softly over the earthen floor with the big strides of his strong legs, he took off his burka, rifle, and sabre, as Hadji Murat had done, and hung them on the same nails on which Hadji Murat's weapons hung, leaving himself with only a dagger and a pistol.

"Who is he?" the old man asked Hadji Murat, pointing to the man who had come in.

"My murid. His name is Eldar," said Hadji Murat.

"Very well," said the old man, and he pointed Eldar to a place on the felt next to Hadji Murat.

Eldar sat down, crossing his legs, and silently fixed his beautiful sheep's eyes on the face of the now talkative old man. The old man was telling how their brave lads had caught two Russian soldiers the week before: they had killed one and sent the other to Shamil in Vedeno. Hadji Murat listened distractedly, glancing at the door and giving ear to the sounds outside. Steps were heard on the porch in front of the saklya, the door creaked, and the master came in.

The master of the saklya, Sado, was a man of about forty, with a small beard, a long nose, and the same black eyes, though not as shining, as the fifteen-year-old boy, his son, who ran for him and together with his father came into the saklya and sat down by the door. Having taken off his wooden shoes by the door, the master pushed his old, shabby papakha to the back of his long-unshaven head, overgrowing with black hair, and at once squatted down facing Hadji Murat.

He closed his eyes just as the old man had, raised his hands palms up, recited a prayer, wiped his face with his hands, and only then began to talk. He said there was an order from Shamil to take Hadji Murat dead or alive, that Shamil's envoys had left only yesterday, and that the people were afraid to disobey Shamil, and therefore he had to be careful.

"In my house," said Sado, "no one will do anything to my kunak while I live. But what about in the field? We must think."

Hadji Murat listened attentively and nodded his head approvingly. When Sado finished, he said:

"Very well. Now a man must be sent to the Russians with a letter. My murid will go, only he needs a guide."

"I'll send brother Bata," said Sado. "Call Bata," he turned to his son.

The boy, as if on springs, jumped up on his nimble legs and, swinging his arms, quickly left the saklya. Ten minutes later he came back with a deeply tanned, sinewy, short-legged Chechen man wearing a tattered yellow cherkeska with ragged cuffs and baggy black leggings. Hadji Murat greeted the new arrival and at once, also not wasting words, said briefly:

"Can you take my murid to the Russians?"

"It's possible," Bata said quickly, merrily. "Everything's possible. No Chechen could get through better than me. Another man would go, promise everything, and do nothing. But I can do it."

"Good," said Hadji Murat. "You'll get three for your trouble," he said, holding up three fingers.

Bata nodded his head to indicate that he understood, but added that he did not value money, but was ready to serve Hadji Murat for the honour of it. Everyone in the mountains knew Hadji Murat, how he had beaten the Russian swine . . .

"Very well," said Hadji Murat. "Rope is good when it's long, speech when it's short."

"Then I'll be silent," said Bata.

"Where the Argun bends, across from the steep bank, there is a clearing in the forest, two haystacks stand there. You know it?"

"I do."

"My three horsemen are waiting for me there," said Hadji Murat.

"Aya!" said Bata, nodding his head.

"Ask for Khan Mahoma. Khan Mahoma knows what to do and what to say. Take him to the Russian chief, to Vorontsov, the prince.[2] Can you do that?"

"I'll take him."

"Take him and bring him back. Can you do that?"

"I can."

"Take him, and return with him to the forest. I will be there, too."

"I will do it all," Bata said, stood up and, putting his hands to his chest, went out.

"Another man must be sent to Gekhi," said Hadji Murat, when Bata had gone. "In Gekhi here is what must be done," he began, taking hold of one of the cartridge bands on his cherkeska, but he dropped his hand at once and fell silent, seeing two women come into the saklya.

One was Sado's wife, the same thin, middle-aged woman who had arranged the pillows. The other was a very young girl in red sharovary and a green beshmet, with a curtain of silver coins covering her whole breast. At the end of her black braid, not long but stiff, thick, which lay between the shoulder blades on her thin back, hung a silver rouble; the same black-currant eyes as her father and brother shone merrily on her young face, which was trying to look stern. She did not glance at the guests, but was obviously aware of their presence.

Sado's wife carried a low, round table on which there were tea, dumplings, pancakes with butter, cheese, churek—a thinly rolled-out bread—and honey. The girl carried a basin, a kumgan, and a towel.

Sado and Hadji Murat were silent all the while the women, moving quietly in their soleless red chuviaki, were setting what they had brought before the guests. Eldar, his sheep's eyes directed at his crossed legs, was immobile as a statue all the while the women were in the saklya. Only when they left and their soft steps had died away completely behind the door, did Eldar sigh with relief and Hadji Murat take out one of the cartridges of his cherkeska, remove the bullet that stopped it up, and, from under the bullet, a note rolled into a tube.

"To my son," he said, pointing to the note.

"Where to reply?" asked Sado.

"To you, and you deliver it to me."

"It will be done," said Sado, and he put the note into a cartridge of his cherkeska. Then, taking the kumgan, he moved the basin towards Hadji Murat. Hadji Murat rolled up the sleeves of his beshmet on his muscular arms, white above the hands, and held them under the stream of cold, transparent water that Sado was pouring from the kumgan. Having wiped his hands on a clean, rough towel, Hadji Murat turned to the food. Eldar did the same. While the guests were eating, Sado sat facing them and thanked them several times for coming. The boy, sitting by the door, not taking his shining black eyes from Hadji Murat, was smiling, as if to confirm his father's words by his smile.

Though Hadji Murat had eaten nothing for more than twenty-four hours, he ate only a little bread and cheese, and, taking a small knife from under his dagger, gathered up some honey and spread it on bread.

"Our honey is good. This year of all years the honey is both plentiful and good," said the old man, obviously pleased that Hadji Murat was eating his honey.

"Thank you," said Hadji Murat and drew back from the food.

Eldar would have liked to eat more, but, like his murshid, he moved away from the table and gave Hadji Murat the basin and the kumgan.

Sado knew that in receiving Hadji Murat he was risking his life, because after the quarrel between Shamil and Hadji Murat, it had been announced to all the inhabitants of Chechnya that, on pain of death, they were not to receive Hadji Murat. He knew that the inhabitants of the aoul might learn of Hadji Murat's presence at any moment and might demand that he be handed over. But that not only did not trouble Sado, it even gladdened him. Sado considered it his duty to defend his guest—his kunak—even if it cost him his life, and he was glad in himself and proud of himself that he was acting as one should.

"While you are in my house and my head is on my shoulders, no one will do anything to you," he repeated to Hadji Murat.

Hadji Murat looked attentively into his shining eyes and, understanding that this was true, said with a certain solemnity:

"May you be granted joy and life."

Sado silently pressed his hand to his chest in a sign of gratitude for the kind words.

Having closed the shutters of the saklya and kindled the wood in the fireplace, Sado, in a particularly merry and excited state, left the guest room and went to the part of the saklya where his whole family lived. The women were not asleep yet and were talking about the dangerous guests who were spending the night in their guest room.

II

THAT SAME NIGHT, at the frontier fortress of Vozdvizhenskoe, some ten miles from the aoul where Hadji Murat was spending the night, three soldiers and a corporal left the stronghold by the Chakhgirinsky gate. The soldiers were wearing sheepskin jackets and papakhas, with rolled-up greatcoats on their shoulders, and big boots above the knee, as soldiers in the Caucasus went around then. The soldiers, with muskets on their shoulders, first went along the road, then, having gone some five hundred paces, turned off and, their boots rustling over dry leaves, went some twenty paces to the right and stopped by a broken chinara, whose black trunk was visible even in the darkness. The listening post was usually sent to this chinara.

The bright stars that had seemed to race over the treetops while the soldiers walked through the forest now stopped, shining brightly between the bare branches of the trees.

"It's dry—thanks be for that," said Corporal Panov, taking his long musket with its bayonet from his shoulder and leaning it with a clank against the trunk of a tree. The three soldiers did the same.

"That's it—I've lost it," Panov grumbled crossly. "Either I forgot it, or it fell out on the way."

"What are you looking for?" asked one of the soldiers in a lively, cheerful voice.

"My pipe. Devil knows what's become of it!"

"Is the stem still there?" asked the lively voice.

"Yes, here it is."

"Then why not right in the ground?"

"Ah, come on."

"I'll set it up in a flash."

Smoking at a listening post was forbidden, but this was not really a listening post, but more of an advance patrol, which was sent out so that the mountaineers could not bring a cannon up surreptitiously, as they used to do, and fire at the stronghold, and Panov did not consider it necessary to deprive himself of smoking and therefore agreed to the cheerful soldier's suggestion. The cheerful soldier took a knife from his pocket and began digging in the ground. Having dug out a little hole, he smoothed it all around, pressed the pipe stem into it, then filled the hole with tobacco, tamped it down, and the pipe was ready. The sulphur match flame lit up for a moment the high-cheekboned face of the soldier lying on his belly. There was a whistling in the stem, and Panov caught the pleasant smell of burning shag.

"All set up?" he said, getting to his feet.

"That it is."

"Fine lad you are, Avdeev! A foxy fellow. Well, then?"

Avdeev rolled aside, giving his place to Panov and letting smoke out of his mouth.

Having had their smoke, the soldiers started a conversation among themselves.

"They say the company commander got into the cash box again. Seems he lost at cards," one of the soldiers said in a lazy voice.

"He'll pay it back," said Panov.

"Sure, he's a good officer," Avdeev confirmed.

"Good, yes, good," the one who had started the conversation went on gloomily, "but my advice is that the company should have a talk with him: if you've taken, tell us how much, and when you'll pay it back."

"That's as the company decides," said Panov, tearing himself away from the pipe.

"Sure thing—we're all one big man," Avdeev agreed.

"We've got to buy oats and get boots by spring, we need cash, and if he's taken it . . ." the disgruntled man insisted.

"I said, it's as the company wants," repeated Panov. "It's not the first time: he takes and pays it back."

At that time in the Caucasus every company administered all its practical affairs through its own chosen people. They received cash from the treasury to the amount of six roubles fifty kopecks per man and supported themselves on it: planted cabbage, made hay, kept their own carts, pranced about on well-fed company horses. The company money was kept in a cash box, the key to which was kept by the company commander, and it often happened that the company commander borrowed from the company cash box. So it was now, and it was this that the soldiers were talking about. The gloomy soldier Nikitin wanted to demand an accounting from the commander, but Panov and Avdeev considered that there was no need for that.

After Panov, Nikitin also had a smoke and, spreading his greatcoat under him, sat leaning against a tree. The soldiers quietened down. Only the wind could be heard rustling in the treetops high above their heads. Suddenly the howling, shrieking, wailing, and laughing of jackals came through that ceaseless, quiet rustling.

"Hear how the cursed things pour it out!" said Avdeev.

"It's you they're laughing at, because your mug's all askew," said the high Ukrainian voice of the fourth soldier.

Again everything was quiet, only the wind rustled in the branches, now covering, now uncovering the stars.

"Say, Antonych," the cheerful Avdeev suddenly asked Panov, "do you ever feel heartsick?"

"What do you mean, heartsick?" Panov answered reluctantly.

"I sometimes feel so heartsick, so heartsick, it's like I don't know what I may do to myself."

"Ah, you!" said Panov.

"That time when I drank up the money, it was all from feeling heartsick. It came over me, just came over me. I thought: why don't I get crocked?"

"Drink can make it worse."

"And did. But how can you get away from it?"

"What are you heartsick for?"

"Me? For home."

"So, it was a rich life there?"

"Not rich, but a right life. A good life."

And Avdeev started telling what he had already told many times to the same Panov.

"I volunteered to go for my brother," Avdeev told them. "He had four children! And they'd only just married me off. Mother started pleading. I think: what's it to me? Maybe they'll remember my kindness. I went to the master. Our master was nice, he said: 'Good boy! Off you go!' And so I went for my brother."

"Well, that's a good thing," said Panov.

"But would you believe it, Antonych, I'm heartsick now. And I'm heartsick most of all because, I say, why did you go for your brother? He lives like a king now, I say, and you suffer. And the more I think, the worse it gets. Some kind of sin, surely."

Avdeev fell silent.

"Maybe we'll have another smoke?" asked Avdeev.

"Well, set it up, then!"

But the soldiers were not to have their smoke. Avdeev had just stood up and begun setting up the pipe, when they heard through the rustling of the wind the sound of footsteps coming down the road. Panov took his musket and shoved Nikitin with his foot. Nikitin got to his feet and picked up his greatcoat. The third man—Bondarenko—also stood up.

"And I had such a dream, brothers . . ."

Avdeev hissed at Bondarenko, and the soldiers froze, listening. The soft footsteps of people not shod in boots were coming near. The crunch of twigs and dry leaves could be heard more and more clearly in the darkness. Then talk was heard in that special guttural tongue spoken by the Chechens. The soldiers now not only heard but saw two shadows passing in the spaces between the trees. One shadow was shorter, the other taller. When the shadows came even with the soldiers, Panov, gun in hand, stepped out on the road with two of his comrades.

"Who goes there?" he called out.

"Peaceful Chechen," said the shorter one. It was Bata. "Gun *yok*, sabre *yok*," he said, pointing to himself. "Want preenze."

The taller one stood silently beside his comrade. He also wore no weapons.

"An emissary. That means—to the regimental commander," Panov said, explaining to his comrades.

"Much want Preenze Vorontsov, want big business," said Bata.

"All right, all right, we'll take you," said Panov. "Well, so take them, you and Bondarenko," he turned to Avdeev, "and once you've handed them over to the officer of the day, come back. Watch out," said Panov, "be careful, tell them to walk ahead of you. These shave-heads can be tricky."

"And what about this?" said Avdeev, making a stabbing movement with his bayonet. "One little poke, and he's out of steam."

"What's he good for if you stab him?" said Bondarenko. "Well, off with you!"

When the footsteps of the two soldiers and the emissaries died away, Panov and Nikitin went back to their place.

"Why the devil do they go around at night!" said Nikitin.

"Must mean they've got to," said Panov. "It's turning chilly," he added and, unrolling his greatcoat, he put it on and sat down by the tree.

About two hours later Avdeev and Bondarenko came back.

"So you handed them over?" asked Panov.

"Yes. They're not asleep yet at the regimental commander's. We took them straight to him. And what nice lads these shave-heads are," Avdeev went on. "By God! I got to talking with them."

"You'd be sure to," Nikitin said with displeasure.

"Really, they're just like Russians. One's married. *'Marushka bar?'* I say. *'Bar,'* he says. *'Baranchuk bar?'* I say. *'Bar.'* 'Many?' 'A couple,' he says. Such a nice talk we had! Nice lads."

"Nice, yes," said Nikitin, "just meet him face-to-face, he'll spill your guts for you."

"Should be dawn soon," said Panov.

"Yes, the stars are already going out," said Avdeev, sitting down.

And the soldiers became quiet again.

III

THE WINDOWS of the barracks and the soldiers' houses had long been dark, but in one of the best houses of the fortress the windows were all still lit up. This house was occupied by the commander of the Kurinsky regiment, the son of the commander in chief, the imperial adjutant Prince Semyon Mikhailovich Vorontsov. Vorontsov lived with his wife, Marya Vassilievna, a famous Petersburg beauty, and lived in such luxury in the small Caucasian fortress as no one had ever lived there before. To Vorontsov, and especially to his wife, it seemed that they lived not only a modest life, but one filled with privation; but this life astonished the local people by its extraordinary luxury.

Now, at twelve midnight, in a large drawing room with a wall-to-wall carpet, with the heavy curtains drawn, at a card table lighted by four candles, the host and hostess sat with their guests and played cards. One of the players was the host himself, a long-faced, fair-haired colonel with an imperial adjutant's insignia and aglets, Vorontsov; his partner was a graduate of Petersburg University, a dishevelled young man of sullen appearance, recently invited by Princess Vorontsov as a tutor for her little son by her first marriage. Against them played two officers: one the broad-faced, red-cheeked company commander, Poltoratsky,[3] transferred from the guards; the other a regimental adjutant, who sat very straight, with a cold expression on his handsome face. Princess Marya Vassilievna herself, an ample, big-eyed, dark-browed beauty, sat next to Poltoratsky, touching his legs with her crinoline and peeking at his cards. In her words, and in her glances, and in her smile, and in all the movements of her body, and in the scent that wafted from her, there was something that drove Poltoratsky to obliviousness of everything except the awareness of her proximity, and he made mistake after mistake, annoying his partner more and more.

"No, this is impossible! You've squandered your ace again!" said the adjutant, turning all red, when Poltoratsky discarded an ace.

Poltoratsky, as if waking up, gazed without understanding at the displeased adjutant with his kind, wide-set, dark eyes.

"Well, forgive him!" Marya Vassilievna said, smiling. "You see, I told you," she said to Poltoratsky.

"But you said something else entirely," Poltoratsky said, smiling.

"Did I really?" she said and also smiled. And this returned smile flustered and delighted Poltoratsky so terribly that he turned a deep red and, seizing the cards, began to shuffle them.

"It's not your turn to shuffle," the adjutant said sternly, and his white hand with its signet ring began dealing the cards as if he only wanted to get rid of them as quickly as possible.

The prince's valet came into the drawing room and announced that the officer of the day was asking to see the prince.

"Excuse me, gentlemen," Vorontsov said, speaking Russian with an English accent. "Will you sit in for me, Marie?"

"Do you agree?" the princess asked, quickly and lightly rising to her full, tall height, rustling her silks, and smiling her radiant smile of a happy woman.

"I always agree to everything," said the adjutant, very pleased that the princess, who was quite unable to play, would now be playing against him. Poltoratsky only spread his arms, smiling.

The rubber was nearing its end when the prince returned to the drawing room. He was especially cheerful and excited.

"Do you know what I propose?"

"Well?"

"That we drink some champagne."

"I'm always ready for that," said Poltoratsky.

"Say, that's a very nice idea," said the adjutant.

"Serve it, Vassily!" said the prince.

"Why did they send for you?" asked Marya Vassilievna.

"It was the officer of the day and another man."

"Who? For what?" Marya Vassilievna asked hastily.

"I can't tell you," said Vorontsov, shrugging his shoulders.

"Can't tell me?" Marya Vassilievna repeated. "We'll see about that."

Champagne was brought. The guests drank a glass and, having finished the game and settled accounts, began taking their leave.

"Is it your company that's assigned to the forest tomorrow?" the prince asked Poltoratsky.

"Yes, mine. Why?"

"Then we'll see each other tomorrow," said the prince, smiling slightly.

"Very glad," said Poltoratsky, without quite understanding what

Vorontsov was telling him and preoccupied only with the fact that he was about to press Marya Vassilievna's big white hand.

Marya Vassilievna, as always, not only pressed Poltoratsky's hand firmly but even shook it hard. And, reminding him once more of his mistake in leading diamonds, she smiled at him, as it seemed to Poltoratsky, with a lovely, tender, and significant smile.

POLTORATSKY WENT HOME in that rapturous state which can be understood only by people like himself, who grew up and were educated in society, when, after months of isolated military life, they again meet a woman from their former circle. And, moreover, such a woman as Princess Vorontsov.

On reaching the little house where he lived with a comrade, he pushed the front door, but it was locked. He knocked. The door did not open. He became vexed and started beating on the locked door with his foot and his sabre. Footsteps were heard behind the door, and Vavilo, Poltoratsky's domestic serf, lifted the hook.

"What made you think of locking it!? Blockhead!"

"Ah, how can you, Alexei Vladimir. . ."

"Drunk again! I'll show you how I can . . ."

Poltoratsky was about to hit Vavilo, but changed his mind.

"Well, devil take you. Light a candle."

"This minute."

Vavilo was indeed tipsy, and he had been drinking because he had been to a name-day party at the quartermaster's. On coming home, he fell to thinking about his life in comparison with the life of Ivan Makeich, the quartermaster. Ivan Makeich had income, was married, and hoped for a full discharge in a year. As a boy, Vavilo had been "taken upstairs," that is, to wait on his masters, and now he was already past forty, but was still not married and lived a campaign life with his desultory master. He was a good master, beat him little, but what sort of life was it! "He's promised to give me my freedom when he returns from the Caucasus. But where am I to go with my freedom? It's a dog's life!" thought Vavilo. And he became so sleepy that, fearing lest someone come in and steal something, he hooked the door and fell asleep.

Poltoratsky went into the room where he slept with his comrade Tikhonov.

"Well, what, did you lose?" said Tikhonov, waking up.

"Oh, no, I won seventeen roubles, and we drank a bottle of Cliquot."

"And looked at Marya Vassilievna?"

"And looked at Marya Vassilievna," Poltoratsky repeated.

"It'll be time to get up soon," said Tikhonov, "and we must set out at six."

"Vavilo," cried Poltoratsky. "See that you wake me up properly at five in the morning."

"How can I wake you up if you hit me?"

"I said wake me up. Do you hear?"

"Yes, sir."

Vavilo left, taking away the boots and clothes.

And Poltoratsky got into bed and, smiling, lit a cigarette and put out the candle. In the darkness he saw before him the smiling face of Marya Vassilievna.

AT THE VORONTSOVS' they also did not go to sleep at once. When the guests left, Marya Vassilievna went up to her husband and, standing in front of him, said sternly:

"*Eh bien, vous allez me dire ce que c'est?*"

"*Mais, ma chère . . .*"

"*Pas de 'ma chère'! C'est un émissaire, n'est-ce pas?*"

"*Quand même je ne puis pas vous le dire.*"

"*Vous ne pouvez pas? Alors c'est moi qui vais vous le dire!*"

"*Vous?*"*

"Hadji Murat? Yes?" said the princess, who had been hearing for several days already about the negotiations with Hadji Murat and supposed that Hadji Murat himself had come to see her husband.

Vorontsov could not deny it, but disappointed his wife in that it was not Hadji Murat himself, but only his emissary, who had announced that Hadji Murat would come over to him the next day at the place appointed for woodcutting.

* "Well, are you going to tell me what it is?"
   "But, my dear . . ."
   "No 'my dear'! It's an emissary, isn't it?"
   "Even so I can't tell you."
   "You can't? Then it's I who will tell you!"
   "You?"

Amidst the monotony of their life in the fortress, the Vorontsovs—husband and wife—were very glad of this event. Having talked about how pleased his father would be with this news, the husband and wife went to bed past two o'clock.

IV

AFTER THE THREE SLEEPLESS NIGHTS he had spent fleeing from the murids Shamil sent against him, Hadji Murat fell asleep as soon as Sado left the saklya, wishing him a good night. He slept without undressing, his head resting on his arm, the elbow sunk deep in the red down pillows his host had laid out for him. Not far from him, near the wall, slept Eldar. Eldar lay on his back, his strong young limbs spread wide, so that his high chest, with black cartridges on a white cherkeska, was higher than his freshly shaven blue head thrown back and fallen from the pillow. Pouting slightly like a child's, his upper lip, barely covered with down, contracted and then relaxed as if sipping something. He slept as did Hadji Murat: dressed, with a pistol and dagger in his belt. In the fireplace of the saklya, the logs were burning down, and a night lamp shone faintly from a niche in the small stove.

In the middle of the night the door of the guest room creaked, and Hadji Murat instantly sat up and put his hand to his pistol. Sado came into the room, stepping softly over the earthen floor.

"What is it?" Hadji Murat asked briskly, as if he had never been asleep.

"We must think," said Sado, squatting in front of Hadji Murat. "A woman on the roof saw you ride in," he said, "and told her husband, and now the whole aoul knows. A neighbour just ran by and told my wife that the old men have gathered by the mosque and want to detain you."

"We must go," said Hadji Murat.

"The horses are ready," Sado said and quickly left the room.

"Eldar," Hadji Murat whispered, and Eldar, hearing his name and, above all, the voice of his murshid, jumped up on his strong legs, straightening his papakha. Hadji Murat put on his weapons over his burka. Eldar did the same. And the two men silently went out of the saklya onto the porch. The black-eyed boy brought the horses. At the clatter of hoofs on the beaten earth of the street, some head stuck out the door of a neighbouring saklya, and, with a clatter of wooden shoes, someone went running up the hill towards the mosque.

There was no moon, but the stars shone brightly in the black sky, and the outlines of the roofs of saklyas could be seen in the darkness and, larger than the others, the edifice of the mosque with its minaret in the upper part of the aoul. A hum of voices came from the mosque.

Hadji Murat, quickly seizing his gun, put his foot into the narrow stirrup and, noiselessly, inconspicuously throwing his body over, inaudibly seated himself on the high cushion of the saddle.

"May God reward you!" he said, addressing his host, feeling for the other stirrup with a habitual movement of the right foot, and he lightly touched the boy who was holding the horse with his whip, as a sign that he should step aside. The boy stepped aside, and the horse, as if knowing himself what had to be done, set off at a brisk pace down the lane towards the main road. Eldar rode behind; Sado, in a fur coat, swinging his arms rapidly, almost ran after them, crossing from one side of the narrow street to the other. At the end, across the road, a moving shadow appeared, then another.

"Stop! Who goes there? Halt!" a voice cried, and several men barred the road.

Instead of stopping, Hadji Murat snatched the pistol from his belt and, putting on speed, aimed his horse straight at the men barring the road. The men standing in the road parted, and Hadji Murat, without looking back, set off down the road at a long amble. Eldar followed him at a long trot. Behind them two shots cracked, two bullets whistled by, hitting neither him nor Eldar. Hadji Murat went on riding at the same pace. Having gone some three hundred paces, he stopped the slightly panting horse and began to listen. Ahead, below, was the noise of swift water. Behind, in the aoul, came the roll call of the cocks. Above these sounds, voices and the tramp of approaching horses could be heard from behind Hadji Murat. Hadji Murat touched up his horse and rode on at the same steady pace.

Those riding behind galloped and soon caught up with Hadji Murat. They were some twenty mounted men. They were inhabitants of the aoul, who had decided to detain Hadji Murat, or at least to pretend that they wanted to detain him, so as to clear themselves before Shamil.

When they came close enough to be seen in the darkness, Hadji Murat stopped, dropped the reins, and, unbuttoning the cover of his rifle with an accustomed movement of his left hand, drew it out with his right. Eldar did the same.

"What do you want?" cried Hadji Murat. "To take me? So, take me!" and he raised his rifle. The inhabitants of the aoul stopped.

Hadji Murat, holding the rifle in his hand, began to descend into the hollow. The riders, without coming closer, went after him. When Hadji Murat crossed to the other side of the hollow, the mounted men following him called out that he should listen to what they wanted to say. In response to that, Hadji Murat fired his rifle and sent his horse into a gallop. When he stopped, the pursuit behind him could no longer be heard; nor could the cocks be heard; only the murmur of water could be heard more clearly in the forest, and the occasional lament of an owl. The black wall of the forest was quite close. This was the same forest where his murids were waiting for him. Having ridden up close to it, Hadji Murat stopped and, drawing a quantity of air into his lungs, whistled and then fell silent, listening. After a moment, the same whistle was heard from the forest. Hadji Murat turned off the road and went into the forest. Having gone about a hundred paces, Hadji Murat saw a campfire between the trunks of the trees, the shadows of men sitting by it, and, half lit by the fire, a hobbled horse with a saddle.

One of the men sitting by the fire rose quickly and went to Hadji Murat, taking hold of his bridle and stirrup. It was the Avar[4] Hanefi, Hadji Murat's adopted brother, who managed his household.

"Put out the fire," said Hadji Murat, getting off his horse. The men started scattering the campfire and stamping on the burning branches.

"Was Bata here?" asked Hadji Murat, going over to the spread-out burka.

"He was. He left long ago with Khan Mahoma."

"What road did they take?"

"That one," replied Hanefi, pointing the opposite way from that by which Hadji Murat had come.

"All right," said Hadji Murat and, taking off his rifle, he began to load it. "We must be careful, they pursued me," he said, addressing the man who was putting out the fire.

This was the Chechen Gamzalo. Gamzalo went to the burka, picked up a rifle lying there in its cover, and silently went to the edge of the clearing, to the place Hadji Murat had come from. Eldar, getting off his horse, took Hadji Murat's horse and, pulling the heads of both up high, tied them to trees, then, like Gamzalo, stood at the other edge of the clearing, his rifle behind his shoulders. The campfire was extinguished, and the forest no longer seemed as dark as before, and stars still shone, though faintly, in the sky.

Looking at the stars, at the Pleiades already risen halfway up the sky, Hadji Murat calculated that it was already long past midnight and that it had long been time for the night's prayer. He asked Hanefi for the kumgan that they always carried with them in their baggage, and, putting on his burka, went towards the water.

After taking off his shoes and performing the ablution, Hadji Murat stood barefoot on the burka, then squatted on his calves and, first stopping his ears with his fingers and closing his eyes, turned to the east and said his usual prayers.

Having finished his prayers, he went back to his place, where his saddlebags were, and, sitting on his burka, rested his hands on his knees, bowed his head, and fell to pondering.

Hadji Murat had always believed in his luck. When he undertook something, he was firmly convinced beforehand of success—and everything succeeded for him. That had been so, with rare exceptions, in the whole course of his stormy military life. So he hoped it would be now as well. He imagined himself, with the army Vorontsov would give him, going against Shamil and taking him prisoner, and avenging himself, and how the Russian tsar would reward him, and he again would rule not only Avaria, but also the whole of Chechnya, which would submit to him. With these thoughts he did not notice how he fell asleep.

He dreamed of how he and his brave men, singing and shouting "Hadji Murat is coming," swoop down on Shamil and take him and his wives, and hear his wives weeping and wailing. He woke up. The song *"La ilaha,"*³ and the shouts of "Hadji Murat is coming," and the weeping of Shamil's wives—these were the howling, weeping, and laughter of the jackals, which woke him up. Hadji Murat raised his head, looked through the tree trunks at the sky already brightening in the east, and asked the murid sitting some distance from him about Khan Mahoma. Learning that Khan Mahoma had not come back yet, Hadji Murat lowered his head and at once dozed off again.

He was awakened by the merry voice of Khan Mahoma, coming back with Bata from his embassy. Khan Mahoma sat down at once by Hadji Murat and began telling about how the soldiers had met them and taken them to the prince himself, how the prince was glad and promised to meet them tomorrow where the Russians would be cutting wood, across the Michik, at the Shalinskoe clearing. Bata interrupted his comrade's speech, putting in his own details.

Hadji Murat asked in detail about the precise words in which Vorontsov had responded to the proposal of Hadji Murat going over to the Russians. And Khan Mahoma and Bata said with one voice that the prince had promised to receive Hadji Murat as his guest and make it so that all would be well for him. Hadji Murat also asked about the road, and when Khan Mahoma assured him that he knew the road well and would bring him straight there, Hadji Murat took out some money and gave Bata the promised three roubles; and he told his own men to take his gold-inlaid arms and the papakha with a turban from the saddlebags, and to clean themselves up, so as to come to the Russians looking well. While the weapons, saddles, bridles, and horses were being cleaned, the stars grew pale, it became quite light, and a pre-dawn breeze sprang up.

V

EARLY IN THE MORNING, while it was still dark, two companies with axes, under the command of Poltoratsky, went out seven miles from the Chakhgirinsky gate and, posting a line of riflemen, set about cutting wood as soon as it became light. By eight o'clock the mist, which had merged with the fragrant smoke of damp branches hissing and crackling on the bonfires, began to lift, and the woodcutters, who earlier, from five paces away, could not see but could only hear each other, began to see both the bonfires and the forest road choked with trees; the sun now appeared as a bright spot in the mist, now disappeared again. In a small clearing off the road, Poltoratsky, his subaltern Tikhonov, two officers of the third company, and Poltoratsky's comrade from the Corps of Pages, Baron Freze, a former horse guard demoted to the ranks for duelling, were sitting on drums. Around the drums lay food wrappings, cigarette butts, and empty bottles. The officers had drunk vodka, eaten a bit, and were drinking porter. The drummer was uncorking the eighth bottle.

Poltoratsky, though he had not had enough sleep, was in that special state of high spirits and kindly, carefree merriment, which he always felt among his soldiers and comrades where there might be danger.

The officers were having a lively conversation about the latest news, the death of General Sleptsov. No one saw in that death the most important moment of that life—its ending and returning to the source from which it had come—but saw only the gallantry of a dashing officer falling upon the mountaineers with his sabre and desperately cutting them down.

Though everyone, especially officers who had been in action, could and did know that neither in the war then in the Caucasus nor anywhere else could there ever be that hand-to-hand cutting down with sabres which is always surmised and described (and if there is such hand-to-hand combat with sabres and bayonets, it is only those running away who are cut down and stabbed), this fiction of hand-to-hand combat was recognized by the officers and lent them that calm pride and gaiety with which they were sitting on the drums, some in dashing, others, on the contrary, in the most modest poses, smoking, drinking, and joking, not troubling about death, which, as it had Sleptsov, might overtake each of them at any moment. And indeed, as if to confirm their expectations, in the midst of their talk they heard, to the left of the road, the bracing, beautiful sound of a sharp, cracking rifle shot, and with a merry whistle a little bullet flew by somewhere in the foggy air and smacked into a tree. A few ponderously loud booms of the soldiers' muskets answered the enemy shot.

"Aha!" Poltoratsky cried in a merry voice, "that's from the line! Well, brother Kostya," he turned to Freze, "here's your chance. Go to your company. We'll arrange a lovely battle for them! And put you up for a promotion."

The demoted baron jumped to his feet and went at a quick pace to the smoky area where his company was. A small, dark bay Kabarda horse was brought to Poltoratsky, he mounted it, and, forming up his company, led it towards the line in the direction of the shooting. The line stood at the edge of the forest before the bare slope of a gully. The wind was blowing towards the forest, and not only the slope, but the far side of the gully was clearly visible.

As Poltoratsky rode up to the line, the sun emerged from the fog, and on the opposite side of the gully, by the sparse young forest that began there, some two hundred yards away, several horsemen could be seen. These Chechens were the ones who had pursued Hadji Murat and wanted to see his coming to the Russians. One of them shot at the line. Several soldiers from the line answered. The Chechens pulled back and the shooting stopped. But when Poltoratsky arrived with his company, he gave the order to fire, and as soon as the command was passed on, the merry, bracing crackle of muskets was heard all along the line, accompanied by prettily dispersing puffs of smoke. The soldiers, glad of a diversion, hurriedly reloaded and fired off round after round. The Chechens obviously took up the challenge and, leaping forward one after another, fired off several shots at the soldiers. One of their shots wounded a soldier. This soldier was that same Avdeev who had been at the listening post. When his comrades went over to him, he was lying face down, holding the wound in his stomach with both hands and rocking rhythmically.

"I was just starting to load my musket, and I heard a thwack," the soldier paired with him was saying. "I looked: he let his musket drop."

Avdeev was from Poltoratsky's company. Seeing a bunch of soldiers gathered, Poltoratsky rode up to them.

"What, brother, been hit?" he said. "Where?"

Avdeev did not reply.

"I was just starting to load, Your Honour," the soldier paired with Avdeev began to say, "I heard a thwack, I looked—he let his musket drop."

"Tsk, tsk," Poltoratsky clucked his tongue. "Does it hurt, Avdeev?"

"It doesn't hurt, but it won't let me walk. I could use a drink, Your Honour."

They found some vodka, that is, the alcohol the soldiers used to drink in the Caucasus, and Panov, frowning sternly, offered it to Avdeev in the bottle cap. Avdeev began to drink, but pushed the cap away at once with his hand.

"My soul won't take it," he said. "You drink it."

Panov finished the alcohol. Avdeev again tried to get up and again sat down. They spread out a greatcoat and laid Avdeev on it.

"Your Honour, the colonel's coming," the sergeant major said to Poltoratsky.

"Well, all right, you see to it," said Poltoratsky and, brandishing his whip, he rode at a long trot to meet Vorontsov.

Vorontsov was riding his English thoroughbred bay stallion, accompanied by the regimental adjutant, a Cossack, and a Chechen interpreter.

"What's going on here?" he asked Poltoratsky.

"A party of them came and attacked the line," Poltoratsky answered him.

"Well, well, so you started it all."

"Not me, Prince," said Poltoratsky, smiling. "They were spoiling for it."

"I heard a soldier's been wounded?"

"Yes, very sad. A good soldier."

"Seriously?"

"Seems so—in the stomach."

"And do you know where I'm going?" asked Vorontsov.

"No, I don't."

"You really can't guess?"

"No."

"Hadji Murat has come over and is going to meet us right now."

"It can't be!"

"Yesterday an emissary came from him," said Vorontsov, barely suppressing a smile of joy. "He's supposed to be waiting for me right now at the Shalinskoe clearing. Post your riflemen as far as the clearing and then come to me."

"Yes, sir," said Poltoratsky, putting his hand to his papakha, and he rode to his company. He himself led the line along the right side and ordered the sergeant major to do the same on the left side. Meanwhile four soldiers carried the wounded man to the fortress.

Poltoratsky was already on his way back to Vorontsov when he saw some horsemen overtaking him from behind. Poltoratsky stopped and waited for them.

At the head of them all, on a white-maned horse, in a white cherkeska, in a papakha with a turban, and with gold-inlaid arms, rode a man of imposing appearance. This man was Hadji Murat. He rode up to Poltoratsky and said something to him in Tartar. Poltoratsky raised his eyebrows, spread his arms in a sign that he did not understand, and smiled. Hadji Murat answered his smile with a smile, and that smile struck Poltoratsky by its childlike good nature. Poltoratsky had never expected this fearsome mountaineer to be like that. He had expected to see a gloomy, dry, alien man, and before him was a most simple man, who smiled such a kindly smile that he seemed not alien, but a long-familiar friend. Only one thing was peculiar about him: this was his wide-set eyes, which looked attentively, keenly, and calmly into the eyes of other people.

Hadji Murat's suite consisted of four men. In that suite was Khan Mahoma, the one who had gone to Vorontsov the night before. He was a red-cheeked, round-faced man with bright, black, lidless eyes, radiant with an expression of the joy of life. There was also a stocky, hairy man with joined eyebrows. This was the Tavlin Hanefi, who managed all of Hadji Murat's belongings. He was leading a spare horse with tightly packed saddlebags. Two men especially stood out among the suite: one young, slender as a woman in the waist and broad in the shoulders, with a barely sprouting blond beard, a handsome man with sheep's eyes—this was Eldar; and the other, blind in one eye, with no eyebrows or lashes, with a trimmed red beard and a scar across his nose and face—the Chechen Gamzalo.

Poltoratsky pointed out Vorontsov for Hadji Murat as he appeared down the road. Hadji Murat headed towards him and, coming close, put his right hand to his chest, said something in Tartar, and stopped. The Chechen interpreter translated:

" 'I surrender myself,' he says, 'to the will of the Russian tsar. I wish to serve him,' he says. 'I have long wished it,' he says. 'Shamil would not let me.' "

Having heard out the interpreter, Vorontsov offered his suede-gloved hand to Hadji Murat. Hadji Murat looked at this hand, paused for a second, but then pressed it firmly and said something more, looking now at the interpreter, now at Vorontsov.

"He says he did not want to come over to anyone but you, because you are the sardar's son. He respects you firmly."

Vorontsov nodded as a sign that he thanked him. Hadji Murat said something more, pointing to his suite.

"He says these people, his murids, will serve the Russians just as he will."

Vorontsov turned to look and nodded to them, too.

The merry, black-eyed, lidless Khan Mahoma, nodding in the same way, said something to Vorontsov that must have been funny, because the hairy Avar bared his bright white teeth in a smile. The red-haired Gamzalo only flashed his one red eye for an instant at Vorontsov and again fixed it on his horse's ears.

As Vorontsov and Hadji Murat, accompanied by the suite, rode back to the fortress, the soldiers taken from the line, gathering in a bunch, made their observations:

"He's been the ruin of so many souls, curse him, and now just think how they'll oblige him," said one.

"And what else? He was Shammel's top lootnant. Now, I bet . . ."

"He's a brave dzhigit, there's no denying."

"And the redhead, the redhead, now—looks sideways, like a beast."

"Ugh! Must be a real dog."

They all took special notice of the redhead.

WHERE THE WOODCUTTING WAS going on, the soldiers who were closer to the road ran out to have a look. An officer yelled at them, but Vorontsov told him to stop.

"Let them look at their old acquaintance. Do you know who this is?" Vorontsov asked a soldier standing closer by, articulating the words slowly with his English accent.

"No, Your Excellency."

"Hadji Murat—heard of him?"

"How could I not, Your Excellency, we beat him many times."

"Well, well, and you got it from him, too."

"That we did, Your Excellency," the soldier replied, pleased that he had managed to talk with his commander.

Hadji Murat understood that they were talking about him, and a merry smile lit up in his eyes. Vorontsov returned to the fortress in the most cheerful spirits.

VI

VORONTSOV WAS very pleased that he, precisely he, had managed to lure out and receive the chief, the most powerful enemy of Russia, after Shamil. There was only one unpleasant thing: the commander of the army in Vozdvizhenskoe was General Meller-Zakomelsky, and in fact the whole affair should have been conducted through him. But Vorontsov had done everything himself, without reporting to him, which might lead to unpleasantness. And this thought poisoned Vorontsov's pleasure a little.

On reaching his house, Vorontsov entrusted the murids to the regimental adjutant and led Hadji Murat into the house himself.

Princess Marya Vassilievna, dressed up, smiling, together with her son, a handsome, curly-headed, six-year-old boy, met Hadji Murat in the drawing room, and Hadji Murat, pressing his hands to his chest, said somewhat solemnly, through the interpreter who accompanied him, that he considered himself the prince's kunak, since the prince had received him into his house, and a kunak's whole family was as sacred for a kunak as he himself. Marya Vassilievna liked both the appearance and the manners of Hadji Murat. That he blushed when she gave him her big white hand disposed her still more in his favour. She invited him to sit down and, having asked him whether he drank coffee, ordered it served. However, Hadji Murat declined coffee when it was served to him. He had a little understanding of Russian, but could not speak it, and, when he did not understand, he smiled, and Marya Vassilievna liked his smile, just as Poltoratsky had. And Marya Vassilievna's curly-headed, sharp-eyed little son, whom she called Bulka, standing by his mother, did not take his eyes from Hadji Murat, whom he had heard of as an extraordinary warrior.

Leaving Hadji Murat with his wife, Vorontsov went to his office to make arrangements for informing his superiors about Hadji Murat's coming over. Having written a report to the commander of the left flank, General Kozlovsky, in Grozny, and a letter to his father, Vorontsov hurried home, fearing his wife's displeasure at having a strange, frightening man foisted on her, who had to be treated so that he was neither offended nor overly encouraged. But his fear was needless. Hadji Murat was sitting in an armchair holding Bulka, Vorontsov's stepson, on his knee, and, inclining his head, was listening attentively to what the interpreter was saying to him, conveying the words of the laughing Marya Vassilievna. Marya Vassilievna was telling him that if he were to give every kunak whatever thing of his the kunak praised, he would soon be going around like Adam . . .

When the prince came in, Hadji Murat took Bulka, who was surprised and offended by it, from his knee, and stood up, immediately changing the playful expression on his face to a stern and serious one. He sat down only when Vorontsov sat down. Continuing the conversation, he replied to Marya Vassilievna's words by saying that it was their law, that whatever a kunak likes must be given to the kunak.

"Your son—my kunak," he said in Russian, stroking the curly head of Bulka, who again climbed on his knee.

"He's charming, your brigand," Marya Vassilievna said to her husband in French. "Bulka admired his dagger, and he gave it to him."

Bulka showed his stepfather the dagger.

"C'est un objet de prix," said Marya Vassilievna.

*"Il faudra trouver l'occasion pour lui faire cadeau,"** said Vorontsov.

Hadji Murat sat with lowered eyes and, stroking the boy's curly head, repeated:

"Dzhigit, dzhigit."

"A beautiful dagger, beautiful," said Vorontsov, half drawing the sharp steel dagger with a groove down the middle. "Thank you."

"Ask him whether I can be of service to him," Vorontsov said to the interpreter.

The interpreter translated, and Hadji Murat replied at once that he did not need anything, but asked that he now be taken to a place where he could pray. Vorontsov called a valet and told him to carry out Hadji Murat's wish.

As soon as Hadji Murat was left alone in the room he was taken to, his face changed: the expression of pleasure and of alternating affection and solemnity vanished, and a preoccupied expression appeared.

The reception Vorontsov had given him was far better than he had expected. But the better that reception was, the less Hadji Murat trusted Vorontsov and his officers. He feared everything: that he would be seized, put in chains, and sent to Siberia, or simply killed; and therefore he was on his guard.

Eldar came, and he asked him where the murids were quartered, where the horses were, and whether their weapons had been taken from them.

Eldar reported that the horses were in the prince's stable, the men had

* "It's a valuable thing."
  "We'll have to find the occasion to make him a gift."

been quartered in a shed, their weapons had remained with them, and the interpreter had treated them to food and tea.

Perplexed, Hadji Murat shook his head and, having undressed, stood in prayer. When he finished, he ordered his silver dagger brought to him and, dressed and girded, sat cross-legged on the divan, waiting for what would happen.

At four o'clock he was called to the prince's for dinner.

Hadji Murat ate nothing at dinner except pilaf, which he served himself from the same place on the dish from which Marya Vassilievna had taken for herself.

"He's afraid we may poison him," Marya Vassilievna said to her husband. "He took from where I did." And she at once addressed Hadji Murat through the interpreter, asking when he would now pray again. Hadji Murat held up five fingers and pointed to the sun.

"Soon, in other words."

Vorontsov took out his Breguet[6] and pressed the release. The watch struck four and one quarter. Hadji Murat was obviously surprised by this chiming, and he asked to hear it chime again and to look at the watch.

*"Voilà l'occasion. Donnez-lui la montre,"** Marya Vassilievna said to her husband.

Vorontsov at once offered Hadji Murat the watch. Hadji Murat put his hand to his chest and took the watch. He pressed the release several times, listened, and shook his head approvingly.

After dinner Meller-Zakomelsky's adjutant was announced to the prince.

The adjutant informed the prince that when the general learned of Hadji Murat's coming over, he was very displeased that it had not been reported to him, and he requested that Hadji Murat be brought to him immediately. Vorontsov said that the general's order would be carried out, and, informing Hadji Murat through the interpreter of the general's request, asked him to go with him to Meller.

Marya Vassilievna, learning why the adjutant had come, understood at once that there might be trouble between her husband and the general, and, despite all her husband's protests, made ready to go to the general with her husband and Hadji Murat.

* "Here's the occasion. Give him the watch."

"Vous feriez beaucoup mieux de rester; c'est mon affaire, mais pas la vôtre."

*"Vous ne pouvez pas m'empêcher d'aller voir madame la générale."**

"You could do it some other time."

"I want to do it now."

There was no help for it. Vorontsov agreed, and all three of them went.

When they came in, Meller, with glum courtesy, conducted Marya Vassilievna to his wife, and told the adjutant to take Hadji Murat to the reception room and not let him go anywhere until he was ordered to.

"If you please," he said to Vorontsov, opening the door of his study and allowing the prince to go in ahead of him.

On entering the study, he stopped before the prince and, without inviting him to sit down, said:

"I am the military commander here, and therefore all negotiations with the enemy must be conducted through me. Why did you not inform me of Hadji Murat's coming over?"

"An emissary came to see me and announced Hadji Murat's wish to give himself up to me," Vorontsov replied, turning pale with agitation, expecting a rude outburst from the wrathful general and at the same time becoming infected by his wrath.

"I ask you, why did you not report it to me?"

"I intended to, Baron, but . . ."

"I am not 'Baron' to you, I am 'Your Excellency.' "

And here the baron's long-restrained irritation suddenly burst out. He voiced all that for a long time had been seething in his soul.

"I have not served my sovereign for twenty-seven years in order to have men who began their service yesterday, availing themselves of their family connections, make arrangements under my very nose about things that do not concern them."

"Your Excellency! I beg you not to speak unfairly," Vorontsov interrupted him.

"I am speaking fairly and will not allow . . ." the general spoke even more irritably.

* "You would do much better to stay here; this is my affair, not yours."
"You can't stop me from going to see the general's wife."

Just then Marya Vassilievna came in, rustling her skirts, followed by a rather small, modest lady, Meller-Zakomelsky's wife.

"Well, enough, Baron. Simon didn't mean to cause any unpleasantness," Marya Vassilievna began.

"I was not speaking of that, Princess . . ."

"Well, you know, we'd better just drop it. You know: a bad spat is better than a good quarrel. Oh, what am I saying! . . ." She laughed.

And the irate general gave in to the bewitching smile of the beauty. A smile flashed under his moustache.

"I admit I was wrong," said Vorontsov, "but . . ."

"Well, I got a bit heated myself," said Meller, and he offered the prince his hand.

Peace was established, and it was decided to leave Hadji Murat with Meller temporarily and then send him to the commander of the left flank.

Hadji Murat was sitting in the next room, and though he did not understand what they were saying, he understood what he needed to understand: that the argument was about him, that his coming over from Shamil was a matter of great importance for the Russians, and that therefore, if only they did not exile or kill him, he could demand much from them. Besides that, he understood that Meller-Zakomelsky, though he was superior in rank, did not have the significance that Vorontsov, his subordinate, had, and that Vorontsov was important, while Meller-Zakomelsky was not; and therefore, when Meller-Zakomelsky summoned Hadji Murat and began to question him, Hadji Murat bore himself proudly and solemnly, saying that he had come from the mountains to serve the white tsar, and that he would give an accounting of everything only to his sardar, that is, commander in chief, Prince Vorontsov, in Tiflis.

VII

THE WOUNDED AVDEEV WAS CARRIED to the hospital, housed in a small building with a plank roof at the exit from the fortress, and put on one of the empty beds in the common ward. There were four patients in the ward: one thrashing in typhoid fever; another pale, with blue under his eyes, sick with the ague, waiting for a paroxysm and yawning constantly; and another two wounded in a raid some three weeks earlier—one in the hand (he was walking about), the other in the shoulder (he was sitting on the bed). All of them, except for the one with typhoid, surrounded the new arrival and questioned those who brought him.

"Sometimes they shoot like spilling peas and nothing happens, but here they fired maybe five shots in all," one of the bearers was telling them.

"His time had come!"

"Oh," Avdeev grunted loudly, struggling against the pain, when they began to put him on the bed. Once he was laid out, he frowned and did not groan any more, but only kept moving his feet. He held his wound with his hands and stared straight ahead fixedly.

A doctor came and ordered the wounded man turned over to see whether the bullet had come out the other side.

"What's this?" the doctor asked, pointing to the criss-crossed white scars on his back and behind.

"That's an old thing, Your Honour," Avdeev said, groaning.

These were the traces of his punishment for the money he drank up.

Avdeev was turned back over, and the doctor picked in his stomach with the probe for a long time and found the bullet, but could remove it. Having bandaged the wound and pasted a sticking plaster over it, the doctor left. All through the picking in the wound and the bandaging of it, Avdeev lay with clenched teeth and closed eyes. When the doctor left, he opened his eyes and looked around him in surprise. His eyes were directed at the patients and the orderly, but it was as if he did not see them, but saw something else that surprised him very much.

Avdeev's comrades came—Panov and Seryogin. Avdeev went on lying in the same way, gazing straight ahead in surprise. For a long time he could not recognize his comrades, though his eyes were looking straight at them.

"Don't you want to have somebody write home, Pyotr?" said Panov.

Avdeev did not answer, though he was looking at Panov's face.

"I said, don't you want to have somebody write home?" Panov asked again, touching his cold, broad-boned hand.

It was as if Avdeev came to.

"Ah, Antonych has come!"

"Yes, here I am. Don't you want to have somebody write home? Seryogin will write for you."

"Seryogin," said Avdeev, shifting his gaze with difficulty to Seryogin, "will you write? . . . Write this, then: 'Your son, Petrukha, wishes you long life.' I envied my brother. I told you today. But now I'm glad. I mean, let him live on and on. God grant it, I'm glad. Write that."

Having said that, he fell silent for a long time, his eyes fixed on Panov.

"Well, and did you find your pipe?" he suddenly asked.

Panov shook his head and did not answer.

"Your pipe, your pipe, I'm saying, did you find it?" Avdeev repeated.

"It was in my bag."

"So there. Well, and now give me a candle, I'll be dying," said Avdeev.

Just then Poltoratsky came to visit his soldier.

"What, brother, is it bad?" he said.

Avdeev closed his eyes and shook his head negatively. His high-cheekboned face was pale and stern. He said nothing in reply and only repeated again, addressing Panov:

"Give me a candle. I'll be dying."

They put a candle in his hand, but his fingers would not bend, so they stuck it between his fingers and held it there. Poltoratsky left, and five minutes after he left, the orderly put his ear to Avdeev's heart and said it was all over.

In the report sent to Tiflis, Avdeev's death was described in the following way: "On the 23rd of November two companies of the Kurinsky regiment went out of the fortress to cut wood. In the middle of the day, a considerable body of mountaineers suddenly attacked the woodcutters. The picket line began to drop back, and at that moment the second company fell upon the mountaineers with bayonets and overcame them. Two privates were lightly wounded in the action and one was killed. The mountaineers lost around a hundred men killed and wounded."

VIII

ON THE SAME DAY that Petrukha Avdeev was dying in the Vozdvizhen-skoe hospital, his old father, the wife of his brother, for whom he had gone as a soldier, and the older brother's daughter, a girl of marriageable age, were threshing oats on the frozen threshing floor. Deep snow had fallen the day before, and towards morning it had become freezing cold. The old man woke up at the third cockcrow and, seeing bright moonlight in the frosted window, got down from the stove,7 put on his boots, his winter coat, his hat, and went to the threshing floor. After working there for some two hours, the old man went back to the cottage and woke up his son and the women. When the women and the girl came to the threshing floor, it had been cleared, a wooden shovel was stuck into the dry white snow and next to it a besom, twigs up, and the oat sheaves were laid out in two rows, ears to ears, in a long line across the clean floor. They sorted out the flails and began to beat in a measured rhythm of three strokes. The old man beat hard with his heavy flail, breaking up the straw, the girl beat steadily from above, the daughter-in-law knocked it aside.

The moon set, and it began to grow light; and they were already finishing the line when the elder son, Akim, in a short coat and hat, came out to the workers.

"What are you loafing about for?" the father shouted at him, interrupting the threshing and leaning on his flail.

"Somebody's got to tend to the horses."

"Tend to the horses," the father mimicked him. "The old woman'll tend to them. Take a flail. You've grown too fat. Drunkard!"

"Wasn't your drink, was it?" the son grumbled.

"What's that?" the old man asked menacingly, frowning and skipping a stroke.

The son silently took a flail, and the work went on with four flails: trap, tra-ta-tap, trap, tra-ta-tap . . . trap! The old man's heavy flail struck every fourth time.

"Just look at the nape on him, like some real, good squire. And I can't keep my pants up," the old man said, skipping a stroke and swinging the flail in the air so as not to lose the rhythm.

The line was finished, and the women started removing the straw with rakes.

"Petrukha's a fool to have gone for you. They'd have beaten the nonsense out of you in the army, and at home he was worth five the likes of you."

"Well, enough, father," the daughter-in-law said, throwing aside the broken sheaf binders.

"Yes, feed the five of you and there's not even one man's work from you. Petrukha used to work like two men by himself, not like . . ."

Down the beaten path from the yard, creaking over the snow in new bast shoes with tightly wrapped woollen footcloths under them, came the old woman. The men were raking the unwinnowed grain into a pile, the women and the girl were sweeping up.

"The headman came by. Everybody's got to go and transport bricks for the master," said the old woman. "I've made breakfast. Come along now."

"All right. Hitch up the roan and go," the old man said to Akim. "And see that I don't have to answer for you like the other day. Mind you of Petrukha."

"When he was at home, you yelled at him," Akim now snarled at his father, "but he's not, so you nag me."

"Means you deserve it," his mother said just as crossly. "You can't take Petrukha's place."

"Well, all right!" said the son.

"Oh, yes, all right. You drank up the flour, and now you say 'all right.'"

"Don't open old wounds," said the daughter-in-law, and they all laid down their flails and went to the house.

The friction between the father and the son had begun long ago, almost from the time when Pyotr was sent as a soldier. Even then the old man already sensed that he had exchanged a hawk for a cuckoo bird. True, according to the law, as the old man understood it, the childless son had to go in place of the family man. Akim had four children, Pyotr had none, but Pyotr was the same kind of worker as his father: skilful, keen-witted, strong, enduring, and, above all, industrious. He was always working. When he passed by people at work, just as his father used to do, he at once offered to help—to go a row or two with the scythe, or to load a cart, or to fell a tree, or to chop wood. The old man was sorry about him, but there was nothing to be done. Soldiering was like death. A soldier was a cut-off limb, and to remember him—to chafe your soul—was useless. Only rarely did the old man remember him, like today, in order to needle the elder son. But the mother often remembered her younger son, and for two years now she had been asking the old man to send Petrukha some money. But the old man kept silent.

The Avdeevs' farmstead was rich, and the old man had a bit of cash tucked away, but he would not venture to touch what he had saved for anything. Now, when the old woman heard him mention the younger son, she decided to ask him again to send their son at least one little rouble once the oats were sold. And so she did. Left alone with the old man once the younger people went to work for the master, she persuaded him to send one rouble of the oat money to Petrukha. So that, when the piles had been winnowed and twelve quarters of oats had been poured on sheets of burlap in three sledges, and the sheets had been neatly pinned with wooden pins, she gave her old man a letter written in her words by the village clerk, and the old man promised that in town he would put a rouble into the letter and send it.

The old man, dressed in a new fur coat and a kaftan, and in clean white woollen leggings, took the letter, put it in his pouch, and, having prayed to God, got into the front sledge and went to town. His grandson rode in the rear sledge. In town the old man told the innkeeper to read him the letter and listened to it attentively and approvingly.

In her letter Petrukha's mother sent, first, her blessing, second, greetings from them all, the news of his godfather's death, and at the end the news that Aksinya (Pyotr's wife) "did not want to live with us and went off on her own. We hear that she lives a good and honourable life." There was mention of the present, the rouble, and added to that, word for word, was what the rueful old woman, with tears in her eyes, had told the clerk to write straight from her heart:

"And so, dear little child of mine, my little dove Petrushenka, I've wept my eyes out grieving over you. My beloved little sun, why did you leave me . . ." At this point the old woman had begun to wail and weep, and said:

"Leave it like that."

It remained like that in the letter, but Petrukha was not fated to receive either the news that his wife had left home, or the rouble, or his mother's last words. The letter and the money came back with the news that Petrukha had been killed in the war, "defending the tsar, the fatherland, and the Orthodox faith." So wrote the army scribe.

The old woman, on receiving this news, wailed for as long as she had time, and then got back to work. On the first Sunday she went to church and handed out little pieces of communion bread "to the good people in memory of the servant of God Pyotr."

The soldier's wife Aksinya also wailed on learning of the death of her "beloved husband" with whom she had "lived only one little year." She pitied both her husband and all her own ruined life. And in her wailing she mentioned "Pyotr Mikhailovich's light-brown curls, and his love, and her wretched life with the orphan Vanka," and bitterly reproached "Petrusha for pitying his brother and not pitying wretched her, a wanderer among strangers."

But deep in her heart Aksinya was glad of Pyotr's death. She was pregnant again by the sales clerk she lived with, and now no one could reproach her any more, and the sales clerk could marry her, as he had said he would when he was persuading her to love him.

IX

MIKHAIL SEMYONOVICH VORONTSOV,[8] brought up in England, the son of the Russian ambassador, was a man of European education rare at that time among highly placed Russian officials, ambitious, mild and gentle in his dealings with his inferiors, and a subtle courtier in his relations with his superiors. He could not understand life without power and obedience. He had all the highest ranks and decorations and was considered a skilful military man, even as the vanquisher of Napoleon at Craonne.[9] In the year 1851 he was over seventy, but he was still quite fresh, moved briskly, and above all was in full possession of all the adroitness of a fine and pleasant intelligence, directed at the maintaining of his power and the strengthening and spreading of his popularity. He possessed great wealth—both his own and that of his wife, Countess Branitsky—and received an enormous maintenance in his quality as vicegerent, and spent the greater part of his means on the construction of a palace and garden on the southern coast of the Crimea.

On the evening of 7 December 1851, a courier's troika drove up to his palace in Tiflis. A weary officer, all black with dust, bringing news from General Kozlovsky that Hadji Murat had come over to the Russians, stretching his legs, walked past the sentries onto the wide porch of the vicegerent's palace. It was six o'clock in the evening, and Vorontsov was about to go to dinner when the courier's arrival was announced to him. Vorontsov received the courier without delay and was therefore several minutes late for dinner. When he entered the dining room, the dinner guests, some thirty of them, sitting around Princess Elizaveta Ksaverievna or standing in groups by the windows, rose and turned their faces towards him. Vorontsov was in his usual black military tunic without epaulettes, with narrow shoulder straps and a white cross on his neck. His clean-shaven, foxy face smiled pleasantly, and his eyes narrowed as he looked over the whole gathering.

Having entered the dining room with soft, hurrying steps, he apologized to the ladies for being late, greeted the men, and went up to the Georgian princess Manana Orbeliani, a full-bodied, tall, forty-five-year-old beauty of the Oriental type, and gave her his arm to lead her to the table. Princess Elizaveta Ksaverievna herself took the arm of a visiting reddish-haired general with bristling moustaches. The Georgian prince gave his arm to Countess Choiseul, the princess's friend. Doctor Andreevsky, the adjutants, and others, some with, some without ladies, followed the three couples. Footmen in kaftans, stockings, and shoes pulled out and pushed back the chairs, seating them; the head waiter solemnly ladled steaming soup from a silver tureen.

Vorontsov sat at the middle of the long table. Across from him sat his wife, with the general. To his right was his lady, the beautiful Orbeliani; to his left, a slender, dark-haired, red-cheeked young Georgian princess in glittering jewellery, who never stopped smiling.

"*Excellentes, chère amie,*" Vorontsov replied to the princess's question of what news he had received from the courier. "*Simon a eu de la chance.*"*

And he began to tell, so that all those sitting at the table could hear, the astounding news—for him alone it was not entirely news, because the negotiations had long been going on—that the famous Hadji Murat, the bravest of Shamil's lieutenants, had come over to the Russians and would be brought to Tiflis today or tomorrow.

All the dinner guests, even the young men, adjutants and clerks, who sat at the far ends of the table and had been quietly laughing about something just before, became silent and listened.

"And you, General, have you met this Hadji Murat?" the princess asked her neighbour, the red-haired general with bristling moustaches, when the prince finished speaking.

"More than once, Princess."

* Excellent, my dear friend. . . Simon has been lucky.

And the general told how, in the year forty-three, after the mountaineers had taken Gergebil, Hadji Murat had happened upon General Passek's detachment, and how he had killed Colonel Zolotukhin almost before their eyes.

Vorontsov listened to the general with an agreeable smile, obviously pleased that the general was talking. But suddenly Vorontsov's face assumed a distracted and glum expression.

The talkative general began to tell about where he had met Hadji Murat the second time.

"It was he," the general was saying, "kindly remember, Your Excellency, who set up an ambush on the rescue during the biscuit expedition."

"Where?" Vorontsov asked, narrowing his eyes.

The thing was that what the brave general referred to as the "rescue" was that action during the unfortunate Dargo campaign, in which an entire detachment, with its commander, Prince Vorontsov, would indeed have perished, if fresh troops had not come to their rescue. It was known to everyone that the entire Dargo campaign, under Vorontsov's command, in which the Russians suffered great losses in killed and wounded and several cannon, was a shameful event, and therefore if anyone did talk about that campaign in front of Vorontsov, it was only in the sense in which Vorontsov had written his report to the tsar, that is, that it had been a brilliant exploit of the Russian army. But the word "rescue" pointed directly to the fact that it had been, not a brilliant exploit, but a mistake that had destroyed many men. Everyone understood that, and some pretended that they had not caught the meaning of the general's words, others waited fearfully for what would happen next; a few smiled and exchanged glances.

Only the red-haired general with the bristling moustaches noticed nothing and, carried away by his story, calmly replied:

"On the rescue, Your Excellency."

And once launched upon his favourite theme, the general told in detail how "this Hadji Murat had so deftly cut the detachment in two that, if it hadn't been for the 'rescue' "—he seemed to repeat the word "rescue" with a special fondness—"we'd all have stayed there, because . . ."

The general did not manage to finish, because Manana Orbeliani, realizing what was the matter, interrupted the general's speech, asking him about the comforts of his accommodations in Tiflis. The general was surprised, looked around at them all and at his adjutant at the end of the table, who was looking at him with a fixed and meaningful gaze—and suddenly understood. Without answering the princess, he frowned, fell silent, and hurriedly started eating, without chewing, the delicacy that lay on his plate, incomprehensible in look and even in taste.

Everyone felt awkward, but the awkwardness of the situation was remedied by the Georgian prince, very stupid, but a remarkably subtle and skilful flatterer and courtier, who was sitting on the other side of Princess Vorontsov. As if he had not noticed anything, he began telling in a loud voice about Hadji Murat's abduction of the widow of Akhmet Khan of Mekhtulin.

"He came into the village at night, seized what he wanted, and rode off with his entire party."

"Why did he want precisely that woman?" asked the princess.

"He was her husband's enemy, pursued him, but was never able to confront the khan before his death, so he took revenge on the widow."

The princess translated this into French for her old friend, Countess Choiseul, who was sitting next to the Georgian prince.

*"Quelle horreur!"** said the countess, closing her eyes and shaking her head.

"Oh, no," Vorontsov said, smiling, "I was told that he treated his prisoner with chivalrous respect and then released her."

"Yes, for a ransom."

"Well, of course, but even so he acted nobly."

The prince's words set the tone for the further stories told about Hadji Murat. The courtiers understood that the more importance they ascribed to Hadji Murat, the more pleased Prince Vorontsov would be.

"Amazing boldness the man has. A remarkable man."

"Why, in the year forty-nine he burst into Temir Khan Shura in broad daylight and looted the shops."

An Armenian man sitting at the end of the table, who had been in Temir Khan Shura at the time, told in detail about this exploit of Hadji Murat's.

Generally, the whole dinner passed in telling stories about Hadji Murat. They all vied with each other in praising his courage, intelli-

* How horrible!

gence, magnanimity. Someone told how he had ordered twenty-six prisoners killed; but to this there was the usual objection:

"No help for it! *À la guerre comme à la guerre.*"*

"He's a great man."

"If he'd been born in Europe, he might have been a new Napoleon,"
said the stupid Georgian prince with the gift for flattery.

He knew that every mention of Napoleon, for the victory over whom
Vorontsov wore a white cross on his neck, was pleasing to the prince.

"Well, maybe not Napoleon, but a dashing cavalry general—yes,"
said Vorontsov.

"If not Napoleon, then Murat."[10]

"And his name is Hadji Murat."

"Hadji Murat has come over, now it's the end of Shamil," someone
said.

"They feel that now" (this "now" meant under Vorontsov) "they
won't hold out," said someone else.

"Tout cela est grâce à vous, "† said Manana Orbeliani.

Prince Vorontsov tried to keep down the waves of flattery that were
already beginning to inundate him. But it was pleasant for him, and he
escorted his lady to the drawing room in the best of spirits.

After dinner, when coffee was served in the drawing room, the prince
was especially amiable with everyone and, going up to the general with
red, bristling moustaches, tried to show him that he had not noticed his
awkwardness.

Having made the round of all his guests, the prince sat down to cards.
He played only the old-fashioned game of ombre. The prince's partners
were the Georgian prince, then the Armenian general, who had learned
to play ombre from the prince's valet, and the fourth—famous for his
power—Dr. Andreevsky.

Placing a gold snuffbox with a portrait of Alexander I beside him,
Vorontsov cracked the deck of satiny cards and was about to deal them
when his valet, the Italian Giovanni, came in with a letter on a silver
salver.

"Another courier, Your Excellency."

* War is war.
† All that is thanks to you.

Vorontsov put down the cards and, apologizing, unsealed the letter and began to read.

The letter was from his son. He described Hadji Murat's coming over and his own confrontation with Meller-Zakomelsky.

The princess came over and asked what their son wrote.

"The same thing. *Il a eu quelques désagréments avec le commandant de la place. Simon a eu tort.** But all is well that ends well," he said in English, and, turning to his respectfully waiting partners, he asked them to take their cards.

When the first hand had been dealt, Vorontsov opened the snuffbox and did what he always did when he was in especially good spirits: he took a pinch of French tobacco with his old man's wrinkled white hand, put it to his nose, and snuffed it in.

X

WHEN HADJI MURAT PRESENTED himself to Vorontsov the next day, the prince's anteroom was full of people. There was yesterday's general with the bristling moustaches, in full-dress uniform and decorations, come to take his leave; there was a regimental commander who was threatened with court action for abuses to do with regimental provisions; there was a rich Armenian, patronized by Dr. Andreevsky, who held the monopoly on vodka and was now soliciting for the renewal of his contract; there, all in black, was the widow of an officer who had been killed, come to ask for a pension or for child support from the state treasury; there was a ruined Georgian prince in magnificent Georgian dress, soliciting for some abandoned Church property; there was a district police commissioner with a big packet containing plans for a new way of subjugating the Caucasus; there was a khan who came only so as to be able to tell them at home that he had called upon the prince.

They all waited their turn and one after another were shown into the prince's office by a handsome, fair-haired young adjutant.

When Hadji Murat, at a brisk stride, limping slightly, came into the

* He had some unpleasantness with the local commandant. Simon was in the wrong.

anteroom, all eyes turned to him, and from various sides he heard his name spoken in a whisper.

Hadji Murat was dressed in a long white cherkeska over a brown beshmet with fine silver piping on its collar. On his legs there were black leggings and on his feet matching chuviaki that fitted them like a glove, on his shaven head a papakha with a turban—the same for which, on the denunciation of Akhmet Khan, he had been arrested by General Klüge-nau,[11] and which had been the reason for his going over to Shamil. Hadji Murat walked in, stepping briskly over the parquet of the anteroom, his whole slender body swaying from the slight lameness of one leg, which was shorter than the other. His wide-set eyes looked calmly before him and seemed not to notice anyone.

The handsome adjutant, having greeted him, asked Hadji Murat to sit down while he announced him to the prince. But Hadji Murat declined to sit down and, putting his hand behind his dagger and advancing one foot, went on standing, scornfully looking around at those present.

The interpreter, Prince Tarkhanov, came up to Hadji Murat and began speaking to him. Hadji Murat replied reluctantly, curtly. A Kumyk prince, who had a complaint against a police commissioner, came out of the office, and after him the adjutant called Hadji Murat, led him to the door of the office, and showed him in.

Vorontsov received Hadji Murat standing by the edge of his desk. The old white face of the commander in chief was not smiling, as the day before, but rather stern and solemn.

On entering the big room, with its enormous desk and big windows with green jalousies, Hadji Murat put his small, sunburnt hands to the place on his chest where the edges of his white cherkeska overlapped and, unhurriedly, clearly, and respectfully, in the Kumyk dialect, which he spoke well, lowering his eyes, said:

"I place myself under the great tsar's high protection and your own. I promise to serve the white tsar faithfully, to the last drop of my blood, and I hope to be of use in the war with Shamil, my enemy and yours."

Having listened to the interpreter, Vorontsov glanced at Hadji Murat, and Hadji Murat glanced into Vorontsov's face.

The eyes of these two men, as they met, said much to each other that could not be expressed in words and that certainly was not what the interpreter was saying. They spoke the whole truth about each other directly, without words. Vorontsov's eyes said that he did not believe a single word of all that Hadji Murat had said, that he knew he was the enemy of all things Russian, would always remain so, and was submitting now only because he had been forced to do so. And Hadji Murat understood that and all the same assured him of his fidelity. Hadji Murat's eyes said that this old man ought to be thinking about death, and not about war, but though he was old, he was cunning, and one had to be careful with him. And Vorontsov understood that and all the same said to Hadji Murat what he considered necessary for the success of the war.

"Tell him," Vorontsov said to the interpreter (he spoke informally to the young officer), "that our sovereign is as merciful as he is mighty, and probably, at my request, will pardon him and take him into his service. Did you tell him?" he asked, looking at Hadji Murat. "Tell him that, until I receive the merciful decision of my ruler, I take it upon myself to receive him and make his stay with us agreeable."

Hadji Murat once more put his hands to the middle of his chest and began to say something animatedly.

He said, as conveyed by the interpreter, that formerly, when he ruled Avaria, in the year thirty-nine, he served the Russians faithfully and would never have betrayed them if it had not been for his enemy Akhmet Khan, who wanted to ruin him and slandered him before General Klügenau.

"I know, I know," said Vorontsov (though if he had known, he had long forgotten it all). "I know," he said, sitting down and pointing Hadji Murat to the divan that stood by the wall. But Hadji Murat did not sit down, shrugging his strong shoulders as a sign that he would not venture to sit in the presence of such an important man.

"Akhmet Khan and Shamil are both my enemies," he went on, turning to the interpreter. "Tell the prince: Akhmet Khan died, I could not be revenged on him, but Shamil is still alive, and I will not die before I have repaid him," he said, frowning and tightly clenching his jaws.

"Yes, yes," Vorontsov said calmly. "But how does he want to repay Shamil?" he said to the interpreter. "And tell him that he may sit down."

Hadji Murat again declined to sit down and, to the question conveyed to him, replied that he had come over to the Russians in order to help them to destroy Shamil.

"Fine, fine," said Vorontsov. "But precisely what does he want to do? Sit down, sit down . . ."

Hadji Murat sat down and said that, if they would only send him to the Lezghian line and give him an army, he guaranteed that he would raise the whole of Daghestan, and Shamil would be unable to hold out.

"That's fine. That's possible," said Vorontsov. "I'll think about it."

The interpreter conveyed Vorontsov's words to Hadji Murat. Hadji Murat fell to thinking.

"Tell the sardar," he said further, "that my family is in my enemy's hands; and as long as my family is in the mountains, my hands are tied and I cannot serve him. He will kill my wife, kill my mother, kill my children, if I go against him directly. Let the prince only rescue my family, exchange them for prisoners, and then I will either die or destroy Shamil."

"Fine, fine," said Vorontsov. "We'll think about that. And now let him go to the chief of staff and explain to him in detail his situation, his intentions and wishes."

So ended Hadji Murat's first meeting with Vorontsov.

In the evening of that same day, in the new theatre decorated in Oriental taste, an Italian opera was playing. Vorontsov was in his box, and in the parterre appeared the conspicuous figure of the lame Hadji Murat in his turban. He came in with Vorontsov's adjutant, Loris-Melikov,[12] who had been attached to him, and took a seat in the front row. With Oriental, Muslim dignity, not only with no expression of surprise, but with an air of indifference, having sat through the first act, Hadji Murat stood up and, calmly looking around at the spectators, went out, drawing the attention of all the spectators to himself.

The next day was Monday, the habitual soirée at the Vorontsovs'. In the big, brightly lit hall an orchestra, hidden in the winter garden, was playing. Young and not-so-young women, in dresses baring their necks, their arms, and almost their breasts, turned in the arms of men in bright uniforms. By the mountains of snacks, valets in red tailcoats, stockings, and shoes poured champagne and went about offering sweets to the ladies. The wife of the "sardar," also just as half-bared, despite her no longer young years, walked among the guests, smiling affably, and, through the interpreter, said a few amiable words to Hadji Murat, who, with the same indifference as the day before in the theatre, was looking the guests over. After the hostess, other bared women came up to Hadji Murat, and all of them, unashamed, stood before him and, smiling, asked one and the same thing: how did he like what he saw. Vorontsov himself, in gold epaulettes and aglets, with the white cross on his neck and a ribbon, came up to him and asked the same thing, obviously convinced, like all the questioners, that Hadji Murat could not help liking all he saw. And Hadji Murat gave Vorontsov the same answer he gave them all: that his people did not have it—without saying whether it was good or bad that they did not have it.

Hadji Murat tried to talk with Vorontsov even here, at the ball, about the matter of ransoming his family, but Vorontsov, pretending that he had not heard his words, walked away from him. Loris-Melikov said later to Hadji Murat that this was not the place to talk business.

When it struck eleven and Hadji Murat verified the time on his watch, given to him by Marya Vassilievna, he asked Loris-Melikov whether he could leave. Loris-Melikov said he could, but it would be better to stay. In spite of that, Hadji Murat did not stay and drove off in the phaeton put at his disposal to the quarters assigned to him.

XI

ON THE FIFTH DAY of Hadji Murat's stay in Tiflis, Loris-Melikov, the vicegerent's adjutant, came to him on orders from the commander in chief.

"My head and my hands are glad to serve the sardar," said Hadji Murat with his usual diplomatic expression, bowing his head and putting his hands to his chest. "Order me," he said, glancing amiably into Loris-Melikov's eyes.

Loris-Melikov sat in an armchair that stood by the table. Hadji Murat seated himself on a low divan facing him and, his hands propped on his knees, bowed his head and began listening attentively to what Loris-Melikov said to him. Loris-Melikov, who spoke Tartar fluently, said that the prince, though he knew Hadji Murat's past, wished to learn his whole story from him.

"You tell it to me," said Loris-Melikov, "and I will write it down, then translate it into Russian, and the prince will send it to the sovereign."

Hadji Murat paused (he not only never interrupted anyone's speech, but always waited to see if his interlocutor was going to say something more), then raised his head, shook back his papakha, and smiled that special childlike smile that had already captivated Marya Vassilievna.

"That is possible," he said, obviously flattered by the thought that his story would be read by the sovereign.

"Tell it to me," Loris-Melikov said to him informally (in Tartar there is no formal address), "right from the beginning, and don't hurry." And he took a notebook from his pocket.

"That is possible, only there is much, very much to tell. Many things happened," said Hadji Murat.

"If you don't manage in one day, you can finish the next," said Loris-Melikov.

"Begin from the beginning?"

"Yes, from the very beginning: where you were born, where you lived."

Hadji Murat lowered his head and sat like that for a long time; then he picked up a little stick that lay by the divan, took from under his dagger with its gold-mounted ivory hilt a razor-sharp steel knife and began to whittle the stick with it and at the same time to tell his story:

"Write: Born in Tselmes, a small aoul, the size of an ass's head, as we say in the mountains," he began. "Not far from us, a couple of shots away, was Khunzakh, where the khans lived. And our family was close to them. My mother nursed the eldest khan, Abununtsal Khan, which is why I became close to the khans. There were three khans: Abununtsal Khan, the foster brother of my brother Osman, Umma Khan, my sworn brother, and Bulatch Khan, the youngest, the one Shamil threw from the cliff. But of that later. I was about fifteen years old when the murids started going around the aouls. They struck the stones with wooden sabres and cried: 'Muslims, ghazavat!' All the Chechens went over to the murids, and the Avars began to go over. I lived in the palace then. I was like a brother to the khans: I did as I liked and became rich. I had horses, and weapons, and I had money. I lived for my own pleasure, not thinking about anything. And I lived like that till the time when Kazi Mullah was killed and Hamzat stood in his place.[13] Hamzat sent envoys to the khans to tell them that, if they did not take up the ghazavat, he would lay waste to Khunzakh. This needed thought. The khans were afraid of the Russians, afraid to take up the ghazavat, and the khansha sent me with her son, the second one, Umma Khan, to Tiflis, to ask the chief Russian commander for help against Hamzat. The chief commander was Rosen, the baron. He did not receive me or Umma Khan. He sent to tell us he would help and did nothing. Only his officers began coming to us and playing cards with Umma Khan. They got him drunk and took him to bad places, and he lost all he had to them at cards. He was strong as a bull in body, and brave as a lion, but his soul was weak as water. He would have gambled away his last horses and weapons, if I hadn't taken him away. After Tiflis my thinking changed, and I began to persuade the khansha and the young khans to take up the ghazavat."

"Why did your thinking change?" asked Loris-Melikov. "You didn't like the Russians?"

Hadji Murat paused.

"No, I didn't," he said resolutely and closed his eyes. "And there was something else that made me want to take up the ghazavat."

"What was that?"

"Near Tselmes the khan and I ran into three murids: two got away, but the third I killed with my pistol. When I went up to him to take his weapons, he was still alive. He looked at me. 'You have killed me,' he said. 'That is well with me. But you are a Muslim, and young and strong. Take up the ghazavat. God orders it.' "

"Well, and did you take it up?"

"I didn't, but I started thinking," said Hadji Murat, and he went on with his story. "When Hamzat approached Khunzakh, we sent some old men and told them to say that we were ready to take up the ghazavat, if only he would send a learned man to explain how we were to keep it. Hamzat ordered the old men's moustaches shaved, their nostrils pierced, and flat cakes hung from their noses, and sent them back. The old men said that Hamzat was ready to send a sheikh to teach us the ghazavat, but only if the khansha sent her youngest son to him as an amanat. The khansha trusted Hamzat and sent Bulatch Khan to him. Hamzat received Bulatch Khan well, and sent to us to invite the older brothers, too. He told the messenger to say that he wanted to serve the khans just as his father had served their father. The khansha was a weak woman, foolish and bold, as all women are when they live by their own will. She was afraid to send both her sons, and sent only Umma Khan. I went with him. The murids rode out a mile ahead to meet us, and sang, and fired their guns, and caracoled around us. And when we rode up, Hamzat came out of his tent, went to the stirrup of Umma Khan, and received him as befits a khan. He said: 'I have done no harm to your house and do not want to. Only do not kill me and do not hinder me from bringing people over to the ghazavat. And I will serve you with my whole army as my father served your father. Let me live in your house. I will help you with my advice, and you do what you want.' Umma Khan was dull of speech. He did not know what to say, and was silent. Then I said, if it was so, let Hamzat go to Khunzakh. The khansha and the khan would receive him with honour. But they did not let me finish, and here for the first time I encountered Shamil. He was right there by the imam. 'It was not you who were asked, but the khan,' he said to me. I fell silent, and Hamzat took Umma Khan to the tent. Then Hamzat called me and told me to go to Khunzakh with his envoys. I went. The envoys started persuading the khansha to let the oldest khan go to Hamzat as well. I saw the treachery and told the khansha not to send her son. But a woman has as much sense in her head as there are hairs on an egg. She trusted them and told her son to go. Abununtsal did not want to. Then she said, 'It's clear you're afraid.' Like a bee, she knew where to sting him most painfully. Abununtsal flared up, did not speak any more with her, and ordered his horse saddled. I went with him. Hamzat met us still better than Umma Khan. He himself rode out two shots' distance down the hill. After him rode horsemen with standards, singing *'La ilaha il Allah,'* shooting off their guns, and caracoling. When we came to the camp, Hamzat led the khan into the tent. And I stayed with the horses. I was at the foot of the hill when shooting began in Hamzat's tent. I ran to the tent. Umma Khan lay face down in a pool of blood, and Abununtsal was fighting with the murids. Half his face had been cut off and hung down. He held it with one hand and held a dagger in the other, with which he cut down everyone who came near him. In front of me he cut down Hamzat's brother and turned against another man, but here the murids started shooting at him and he fell."

Hadji Murat stopped, his tanned face turned reddish brown, and his eyes became bloodshot.

"Fear came over me, and I ran away."

"Really?" said Loris-Melikov. "I thought you were never afraid of anything."

"Never afterwards. Since then I always remembered that shame, and when I remembered it, I was no longer afraid of anything."

XII

"ENOUGH FOR NOW. I must pray," said Hadji Murat, and he took Vorontsov's Breguet from the inside breast pocket of his cherkeska, carefully pressed the release, and, inclining his head to one side and repressing a childlike smile, listened. The watch rang twelve and a quarter.

"Kunak Vorontsov peshkesh," he said, smiling. "A good man."

"Yes, a good man," said Loris-Melikov. "And a good watch. You go and pray, then, and I'll wait."

"*Yakshi*, good," said Hadji Murat, and he went to the bedroom.

Left alone, Loris-Melikov wrote down in his notebook the main things from what Hadji Murat had told him, then lit a cigarette and began pacing up and down the room. Coming to the door opposite the bedroom, Loris-Melikov heard the animated voices of people speaking about something rapidly in Tartar. He realized that these were Hadji Murat's murids and, opening the door, went in.

In the room there was that special sour, leathery smell that mountaineers usually have. On the floor, on a burka by the window, sat one-eyed, red-haired Gamzalo, in a ragged, greasy beshmet, plaiting a bridle. He was saying something heatedly in his hoarse voice, but when Loris-Melikov came in, he fell silent at once and, paying no attention to him, went on with what he was doing. Facing him stood the merry Khan Mahoma, baring his white teeth and flashing his black, lashless eyes, and repeating one and the same thing. The handsome Eldar, the sleeves rolled up on his strong arms, was rubbing the girth of a saddle that hung from a nail. Hanefi, the chief worker and household manager, was not in the room. He was in the kitchen cooking dinner.

"What were you arguing about?" Loris-Melikov asked Khan Mahoma, having greeted him.

"He keeps praising Shamil," said Khan Mahoma, giving Loris his hand. "He says Shamil is a great man. A scholar, and a holy man, and a dzhigit."

"But how is it that he left him and keeps praising him?"

"He left him, and he praises him," said Khan Mahoma, baring his teeth and flashing his eyes.

"And do you, too, regard him as a holy man?" asked Loris-Melikov.

"If he weren't a holy man, people wouldn't listen to him," said Gamzalo.

"The holy man was not Shamil, but Mansur,"[14] said Khan Mahoma. "That was a real holy man. When he was imam, all the people were different. He went around the aouls, and the people came out to him, kissed the skirts of his cherkeska, and repented of their sins, and swore not to do bad things. The old men said: Back then all the people lived like holy men—didn't smoke, didn't drink, didn't miss prayers, forgave each other's offences, even blood offences. Back then, if they found money or things, they tied them to poles and set them up on the roads. Back then God granted the people success in all things, and it wasn't like now," said Khan Mahoma.

"Now, too, they don't drink or smoke in the mountains," said Gamzalo.

"Your Shamil is a lamoroi," said Khan Mahoma, winking at Loris-Melikov.

"Lamoroi" was a contemptuous name for the mountaineers.

"A lamoroi is a mountaineer. It's in the mountains that eagles live," replied Gamzalo.

"Good boy! A neat cut," said Khan Mahoma, baring his teeth, glad of his opponent's neat reply.

Seeing the silver cigarette case in Loris-Melikov's hand, he asked for a cigarette. And when Loris-Melikov said that they were forbidden to smoke, he winked one eye, nodding his head towards Hadji Murat's bedroom, and said that he could as long as nobody saw it. And he at once began to smoke, not inhaling and putting his red lips together awkwardly as he blew the smoke out.

"That's not good," Gamzalo said sternly, and he left the room. Khan Mahoma winked at him, too, and, while smoking, began questioning Loris-Melikov about where it was best to buy a silk beshmet and a white papakha.

"What, have you got so much money?"

"Enough," Khan Mahoma replied, winking.

"Ask him where he got his money," said Eldar, turning his handsome, smiling head to Loris.

"I won it," Khan Mahoma said quickly, and he told how, the day before, strolling about Tiflis, he had come upon a bunch of men, Russian orderlies and Armenians, playing at pitch-and-toss. The stake was big: three gold coins and many silver ones. Khan Mahoma understood at once what the game involved, and, clinking the coppers he had in his pocket, entered the circle and said he staked for all that was there.

"How could you do that? Did you have it on you?" asked Loris-Melikov.

"All I had was twelve kopecks," said Khan Mahoma, baring his teeth.

"Well, but if you'd lost?"

"There's this."

And Khan Mahoma pointed to his pistol.

"What, you'd give it to them?"

"Why give it to them? I'd have run away, and if anybody had tried to stop me, I'd have killed him. And that's that."

"And, what, you won?"

"Aya, I gathered it all up and left."

Loris-Melikov fully understood Khan Mahoma and Eldar. Khan Mahoma was a merrymaker, a carouser, who did not know what to do with his surplus of life, always cheerful, light-minded, playing with his own and other people's lives, who from that playing with life had now come over to the Russians and from that playing might in just the same way go back to Shamil tomorrow. Eldar was also fully understandable: this was a man fully devoted to his murshid, calm, strong, and firm. The only one Loris-Melikov did not understand was the red-haired Gamzalo. Loris-Melikov saw that this man was not only devoted to Shamil, but felt an insuperable loathing, scorn, disgust, and hatred for all Russians; and therefore Loris-Melikov could not understand why he had come over to the Russians. The thought sometimes occurred to Loris-Melikov, and it was shared by certain of the authorities, that Hadji Murat's coming over and his stories of enmity with Shamil were a deception, that he had come over only so as to spy out the weak spots of the Russians and, fleeing to the mountains again, to direct his forces to where the Russians were weak. And Gamzalo, with his whole being, confirmed that supposition. "The other two, and Hadji Murat himself," thought Loris-Melikov, "are able to conceal their intentions, but this one gives himself away by his unconcealed hatred."

Loris-Melikov tried to talk to him. He asked whether it was boring for him here. But, without leaving off his work, giving Loris-Melikov a side-long glance with his one eye, he produced a hoarse and abrupt growl:

"No, it's not."

And he answered all other questions in the same way.

While Loris-Melikov was in the nukers' room, Hadji Murat's fourth murid came in, the Avar Hanefi, with his hairy face and neck and shaggy, protruding chest, as if overgrown with fur. He was an unreflecting, stalwart worker, always absorbed in what he was doing and, like Eldar, obeyed his master without argument.

When he came into the nukers' room to get rice, Loris-Melikov stopped him and asked where he was from and how long he had been with Hadji Murat.

"Five years," Hanefi replied to Loris-Melikov's question. "We're from the same aoul. My father killed his uncle, and they wanted to kill me," he said, looking calmly from under his joined eyebrows into Loris-Melikov's face. "Then I asked to be received as a brother."

"What does it mean, to be received as a brother?"

"I didn't shave my head or cut my fingernails for two months, and I came to them. They let me see Patimat, his mother. Patimat gave me her breast, and I became his brother."

In the next room the voice of Hadji Murat was heard. Eldar at once recognized his master's call and, wiping his hands, went hastily, with big strides, to the drawing room.

"He's calling you," he said, coming back. And, having given one more cigarette to the merry Khan Mahoma, Loris-Melikov went to the drawing room.

XIII

WHEN LORIS-MELIKOV CAME into the drawing room, Hadji Murat met him with a cheerful face.

"So, shall we go on?" he said, seating himself on the divan.

"Yes, certainly," said Loris-Melikov. "And I went to see your nukers and talked with them. One is a merry fellow," he added.

"Yes, Khan Mahoma is an easy-going man," said Hadji Murat.

"And I liked the young, handsome one."

"Ah, Eldar. That one's young, but firm, made of iron."

They fell silent.

"So I'll speak further?"

"Yes, yes."

"I told you how the khans were killed. Well, they killed them, and Hamzat rode to Khunzakh and sat in the khans' palace," Hadji Murat began. "There remained the mother, the khansha. Hamzat summoned her. She began to reprimand him. He winked to his murid Aselder, and he struck her from behind and killed her."

"Why should he kill her?" asked Loris-Melikov.

"What else could he do: he got his front legs over, the hind legs had to follow. The whole brood had to be finished off. And that's what they did. Shamil killed the youngest by throwing him from a cliff. All the Avars submitted to Hamzat, only my brother and I did not want to submit. We had to have his blood for the khans. We pretended to submit, but we thought only of how to have his blood. We took counsel with our grandfather and decided to wait for a moment when he left the palace and kill him from ambush. Someone overheard us, told Hamzat, and he summoned our grandfather and said: 'Watch out, if it's true your grandsons are plotting evil against me, you'll hang beside them from the same gallows. I am doing God's work, I cannot be prevented. Go and remember what I have said.' Grandfather came home and told us. Then we decided not to wait, to do the deed on the first day of the feast in the mosque. Our comrades refused—only my brother and I were left. We each took two pistols, put on our burkas, and went to the mosque. Hamzat came in with thirty murids. They were all holding drawn sabres. Beside Hamzat walked Aselder, his favourite murid—the same one who cut off the khansha's head. Seeing us, he shouted for us to take off our burkas, and came towards me. I had a dagger in my hand, and I killed him and rushed for Hamzat. But my brother Osman had already shot him. Hamzat was still alive and rushed at my brother with a dagger, but I finished him off in the head. There were about thirty murids and the two of us. They killed my brother Osman, but I fought them off, jumped out the window, and escaped. When the people learned that Hamzat had been killed, they all rose up, and the murids fled, and those who didn't were killed."

Hadji Murat paused and took a deep breath.

"That was all very well," he went on, "then it all went bad. Shamil stood in place of Hamzat. He sent envoys to me to tell me to go with him against the Russians; if I refused, he threatened to lay waste to Khunzakh and kill me. I said I wouldn't go to him and wouldn't let him come to me."

"Why didn't you go to him?" asked Loris-Melikov.

Hadji Murat frowned and did not answer at once.

"It was impossible. There was the blood of my brother Osman and of Abununtsal Khan upon Shamil. I didn't go to him. Rosen, the general, sent me an officer's rank and told me to be the commander of Avaria. All would have been well, but earlier Rosen had appointed over Avaria, first, the khan of Kazikumykh, Mahomet Mirza, and then Akhmet Khan. That one hated me. He wanted to marry his son to the khansha's daughter Saltanet. She was not given to him, and he thought it was my fault. He hated me and sent his nukers to kill me, but I escaped from them. Then he spoke against me to General Klügenau, said that I wouldn't let the Avars give firewood to the soldiers. He also told him that I had put on the turban—this one," said Hadji Murat, pointing to the turban over his papakha, "and that it meant I had gone over to Shamil. The general did not believe him and ordered him not to touch me. But when the general left for Tiflis, Akhmet Khan did it his way: he had me seized by a company of soldiers, put me in chains, and tied me to a cannon. They kept me like that for six days. On the seventh day they untied me and led me to Temir Khan Shura. I was led by forty soldiers with loaded muskets. My hands were bound, and they had orders to kill me if I tried to escape. I knew that. When we began to approach a place near Moksokh where the path was narrow and to the right there was a steep drop of about a hundred yards, I moved to the right of the soldier, to the edge of the cliff. The soldier wanted to stop me, but I jumped from the cliff and dragged the soldier with me. The soldier was battered to death, but I stayed alive. Ribs, head, arms, legs—everything was broken. I tried to crawl but couldn't. My head whirled around and I fell asleep. I woke up soaked in blood. A shepherd saw me. He called people, they took me to the aoul. Ribs and head healed, the leg healed, too, only it came out short."

And Hadji Murat stretched out his crooked leg.

"It serves me, and that's good enough," he said. "People found out and started coming to me. I recovered, moved to Tselmes. The Avars again invited me to rule over them," Hadji Murat said with calm, assured pride. "And I agreed."

Hadji Murat stood up quickly. And, taking a portfolio from a saddlebag, he drew two yellowed letters from it and handed them to Loris-Melikov. The letters were from General Klügenau. Loris-Melikov read them over. The first letter contained the following:

"Ensign Hadji Murat! You served under me—I was satisfied with you and considered you a good man. Recently Major General Akhmet Khan informed me that you are a traitor, that you have put on the turban, that you have contacts with Shamil, that you have taught the people not to listen to the Russian authorities. I ordered you arrested and delivered to me. You escaped—I do not know whether that is for better or worse, because I do not know whether you are guilty or not. Now listen to me. If your conscience is clear with regard to the great tsar, if you are not guilty of anything, come to me. Do not fear anyone—I am your defender. The khan will not do anything to you; he is my subordinate, and you have nothing to fear."

Klügenau wrote further that he had always kept his word and was just, and again admonished Hadji Murat to come over to him.

When Loris-Melikov finished the first letter, Hadji Murat took out the other letter, but before handing it to Loris-Melikov, he told him how he had answered the first letter.

"I wrote to him that I wore the turban, not for Shamil, but for the salvation of my soul, that I could not and would not go over to Shamil, because through him my father and my brothers and relations had been killed, but that neither could I come over to the Russians, because they had dishonoured me. In Khunzakh, when I was bound, a certain scoundrel ———ed on me. And I cannot come over to you until that man has been killed. And above all I fear the deceitful Akhmet Khan. Then the general sent me this letter," said Hadji Murat, handing Loris-Melikov another yellowed piece of paper.

"I thank you for having answered my letter," read Loris-Melikov. "You write that you are not afraid to return, but that a dishonour inflicted on you by a certain giaour forbids it; but I assure you that Russian law is just, and before your own eyes you will see the punishment of the man who dared to insult you—I have already ordered it investigated. Listen, Hadji Murat. I have the right to be displeased with you, because you do not trust me and my honour, but I forgive you, knowing the mistrustful character of mountaineers in general. If you have a clean conscience, if you actually wear the turban for the salvation of your soul, then you are right and can boldly look me and the Russian government in the eye; and the one who dishonoured you will be punished, I assure you; *your property will be returned*, and you will see and learn what Russian law is. The more so as Russians look at everything differently; in their eyes you are not harmed because some blackguard has dishonoured you. I myself have allowed the Ghimrians to wear the turban, and I look upon their actions as fitting; consequently, I repeat, you have nothing to fear. Come to me with the man I am sending to you now; he is faithful to me, *he is not a slave of your enemies,* but a friend of the one who enjoys the special attention of the government."

Klügenau again went on to persuade Hadji Murat to come over.

"I didn't trust it," said Hadji Murat, when Loris-Melikov had finished the letter, "and I didn't go to Klügenau. Above all, I had to revenge myself on Akhmet Khan, and I could not do it through the Russians. Just then Akhmet Khan surrounded Tselmes and wanted to capture or kill me. I had very few men, and I was unable to fight him off. And just then a messenger came from Shamil with a letter. He promised to help me fight off Akhmet Khan and kill him, and to give me the whole of Avaria to rule over. I thought for a long time and went over to Shamil. And since then I have never ceased making war on the Russians."

Here Hadji Murat told about all his military exploits. There were a great many of them, and Loris-Melikov partly knew them. All his campaigns and raids were striking in the extraordinary swiftness of his movements and the boldness of his attacks, which were always crowned with success.

"There has never been any friendship between me and Shamil," Hadji Murat said, finishing his story, "but he feared me, and I was necessary to him. But here it so happened that I was asked who would be imam after Shamil. I said that he would be imam whose sabre was sharp. This was told to Shamil, and he wanted to get rid of me. He sent me to Tabasaran. I went and took a thousand sheep and three hundred horses. But he said I had not done the right thing, and he replaced me as naïb and told me to send him all the money. I sent him a thousand pieces of gold. He sent his murids and took everything I possessed. He demanded that I come to him; I knew he wanted to kill me and did not go. He sent men to take me. I fought them off and came over to Vorontsov. Only I did not take my family. My mother, and my wife, and my son are with him. Tell the sardar: as long as my family is there, I can do nothing."

"I'll tell him," said Loris-Melikov.

"Push for it, try hard. What's mine is yours, only help me with the prince. I'm bound, and the end of the rope is in Shamil's hands."

With those words Hadji Murat finished his account to Loris-Melikov.

XIV

ON THE TWENTIETH of December Vorontsov wrote the following to the minister of war, Chernyshov. The letter was in French.[15]

"I did not write to you with the last post, my dear prince, wishing first to decide what we were going to do with Hadji Murat, and feeling myself not quite well for two or three days. In my last letter I informed you of Hadji Murat's arrival here: he came to Tiflis on the 8th; the next day I made his acquaintance, and for eight or nine days I talked with him and thought over what he might do for us later on, and especially what we are to do with him now, because he is greatly concerned about the fate of his family, and says, with all the tokens of sincerity, that as long as his family is in the hands of Shamil, he is paralysed and unable to serve us and prove his gratitude for the friendly reception and the pardon we have granted him. The uncertainty in which he finds himself regarding the persons dear to him causes a state of feverishness in him, and the persons appointed by me to live with him here assure me that he does not sleep at night, hardly eats anything, prays constantly, and only requests permission to go riding with several Cossacks—the sole diversion and exercise possible for him, made necessary by a habit of many years. Every day he comes to me to find out if I have had any news of his family and asking me to order the gathering of all available prisoners from our various lines, so as to offer them to Shamil in exchange, to which he would add some money. There are people who will give him money for that. He keeps repeating to me: 'Save my family and then give me the chance to serve you' (best of all on the Lezghian line, in his opinion), 'and if, before the month is out, I do not render you a great service, punish me as you consider necessary.'

"I answered him that all this seems perfectly fair to me, and that many persons could be found among us who would not believe him if his family remained in the mountains, and not with us in the quality of a pledge; that I will do everything possible to gather the prisoners on our borders, and that, having no right, according to our regulations, to give him money for a ransom, in addition to what he will raise himself, I might find other means of helping him. After that I told him frankly my opinion that Shamil would in no case yield his family up to him, that he might declare it to him directly, promise him a full pardon and his former duties, threaten, if he did not return, to kill his mother, wife, and six children. I asked him if he could tell me frankly what he would do if he were to receive such a declaration from Shamil. Hadji Murat raised his eyes and hands to heaven and said that everything was in the hands of God, but that he would never give himself into the hands of his enemy, because he was fully convinced that Shamil would not forgive him and that he would not remain alive for long. For what concerns the extermination of his family, he did not think Shamil would act so light-mindedly: first, so as not to make him an enemy still more desperate and dangerous; and second, there is in Daghestan a multitude of persons, even very influential ones, who would talk him out of it. Finally, he repeated to me several times that, whatever the will of God was for the future, he was now taken up only with the thought of ransoming his family; that he beseeched me in the name of God to help him and to allow him to return to the environs of Chechnya, where, through the mediation and with the permission of our commanders, he could have contacts with his family, constant news of their actual situation and of means for freeing them; that many persons and even some naïbs in that part of enemy territory were more or less bound to him; that among all that populace already subjugated by the Russians or neutral, it would be easy for him, with our help, to have contacts very useful for achieving the goal that pursues him day and night, and the attainment of which would set him at ease and enable him to act for our benefit and earn our trust. He asks to be sent back to the Grozny fortress with an escort of twenty or thirty brave Cossacks, who would serve him as a defence against his enemies and us as a pledge of the truth of the intentions he has stated.

"You will understand, my dear prince, that for me this is all very perplexing, because, whatever I do, a great responsibility rests on me. It would be highly imprudent to trust him fully; but if we wanted to deprive him of all means of escape, we would have to lock him up, and that, in my opinion, would be both unjust and impolitic. Such a measure, news of which would quickly spread all over Daghestan, would be very damaging for us there, taking away the desire of all those (and they are many) who are prepared to go against Shamil more or less openly and who take such interest in the position with us of the bravest and most enterprising of the imam's lieutenants, who saw himself forced to give himself into our hands. The moment we treat Hadji Murat as a prisoner, the whole favourable effect of his betrayal of Shamil will be lost for us.

"Therefore I think that I could not act otherwise than I have acted, feeling, however, that I may be blamed for a great mistake, should Hadji Murat decide to escape again. In the service, and in such intricate affairs, it is difficult, not to say impossible, to follow a single straight path, without risk of being mistaken and without taking responsibility upon oneself; but once the path seems straight, one must follow it—come what may.

"I beg you, dear prince, to present it for the consideration of his majesty the sovereign emperor, and I will be happy if our august ruler deigns to approve of my action. All that I have written to you above, I have also written to Generals Zavadovsky and Kozlovsky, Kozlovsky being in direct contact with Hadji Murat, whom I have warned that without the latter's approval he is not to do anything or go anywhere. I told him that it will be even better for us if he rides out with our escort, otherwise Shamil will start trumpeting that we keep Hadji Murat locked up; but at the same time I made him promise that he would never go to Vozdvizhenskoe, because my son, to whom he first surrendered and whom he considers his kunak (friend), is not the commander of the place, and it could cause misunderstandings. Anyhow, Vozdvizhenskoe is too close to a numerous hostile populace, while for the relations he wishes to have with trusted persons, the Grozny fortress is convenient in all respects.

"Besides the twenty picked Cossacks, who, at his own request, will not move a step away from him, I have sent the cavalry captain Loris-Melikov, a worthy, excellent, and very intelligent officer, who speaks Tartar, knows Hadji Murat well, and also seems to be fully trusted by him. During the ten days which Hadji Murat spent here, incidentally, he lived in the same house as Lieutenant Colonel Prince Tarkhanov, commander of the Shushinskoe district, who was here on army business; he is a truly worthy man, and I trust him completely. He also gained the trust of Hadji Murat, and through him, since he speaks Tartar excellently, we discussed the most delicate and secret matters.

"I consulted with Tarkhanov concerning Hadji Murat, and he agreed with me completely that I had either to act as I have or to lock Hadji Murat in prison and guard him with all possible strict measures—because if we once treat him badly, he will not be easy to hold—or else he has to be removed from the territory altogether. But these last two measures would not only annul all the advantages that proceed for us from the quarrel between Hadji Murat and Shamil, but would also inevitably bring to a halt any developing murmur and possible insurrection of the mountaineers against Shamil's power. Prince Tarkhanov told me that he himself was convinced of Hadji Murat's truthfulness, and that Hadji Murat had no doubt that Shamil would never forgive him and would order him executed, despite the promised forgiveness. If there was one thing that might worry Tarkhanov in his relations with Hadji Murat, it is his attachment to his religion, and he does not conceal that Shamil could influence him from that side. But, as I have already said above, he would never convince Hadji Murat that he would not take his life either now or sometime after his return.

"That, my dear prince, is all that I wished to tell you concerning this episode in our local affairs."

XV

THIS REPORT WAS SENT from Tiflis on 24 December. On New Year's Eve, a sergeant major, having overdriven some dozen horses, and beaten some dozen coachmen until they bled, delivered it to Prince Chernyshov, then minister of war.

And on 1 January 1852, Chernyshov brought to the emperor Nicholas, among a number of other cases, this report from Vorontsov.

Chernyshov did not like Vorontsov—because of the universal respect in which he was held, and because of his enormous wealth, and because Vorontsov was a real aristocrat, while Chernyshov was, after all, a *parvenu*, and above all because of the emperor's special inclination for Vorontsov. And therefore Chernyshov profited from every occasion to harm Vorontsov as much as he could. In the previous report about Caucasian affairs, Chernyshov had managed to provoke Nicholas's displeasure with Vorontsov for the negligence of the commanders, owing to which the mountaineers had exterminated almost an entire small Caucasian detachment. Now he intended to present Vorontsov's orders about Hadji Murat from an unfavourable side. He wanted to suggest to the sovereign that Vorontsov, who always, particularly to the detriment of the Russians, protected and even indulged the natives, had acted unwisely in keeping Hadji Murat in the Caucasus; that, in all probability, Hadji Murat had come over to us only in order to spy out our means of defence, and that it would therefore be better to send Hadji Murat to the centre of Russia and make use of him only when his family could be rescued from the mountains and there could be assurance of his devotion.

But this plan of Chernyshov's did not succeed, only because on that morning of 1 January, Nicholas was especially out of sorts and would not have accepted any suggestion from anyone merely out of contrariness; still less was he inclined to accept a suggestion from Chernyshov, whom he only tolerated, considering him for the time being an irreplaceable man, but, knowing of his efforts to destroy Zakhar Chernyshov during the trial of the Decembrists and his attempt to take possession of his fortune,[16] he also considered him a great scoundrel. So that, thanks to Nicholas's ill humour, Hadji Murat remained in the Caucasus, and his fate did not change, as it would have changed if Chernyshov had made his report at another time.

It was nine-thirty when, in the haze of a twenty-degree frost, Chernyshov's fat, bearded coachman, in a sky-blue velvet hat with sharp peaks, sitting on the box of a small sleigh of the same sort that the emperor drove about in, pulled up to the side entrance of the Winter Palace and gave a friendly nod to his comrade, Prince Dolgoruky's coachman, who, having deposited his master, had already been standing for a long time by the porch of the palace, the reins tucked under his thickly padded behind, and rubbing his chilled hands.

Chernyshov was wearing an overcoat with a fluffy, silvery beaver collar and a three-cornered hat with cock's feathers, which went with the uniform. Throwing back the bearskin rug, he carefully freed from the sleigh his chilled feet, on which there were no galoshes (he prided himself on knowing nothing of galoshes), and briskly, with a slight jingling of spurs, walked over the carpet to the door, respectfully opened ahead of him by the doorman. In the hall, having thrown off his overcoat into the arms of an old footman, Chernyshov went to the mirror and carefully removed his hat from his curled wig. Looking himself over in the mirror, he twirled his whiskers and forelock with a habitual movement of his old man's hands, straightened his cross, aglets, and large, monogrammed epaulettes, and, stepping weakly on his badly obeying old man's legs, began to climb the carpet of the shallow stairs.

Going past the obsequiously bowing footmen who stood by the door in gala livery, Chernyshov entered the anteroom. The officer of the day, a newly appointed imperial adjutant, in a shining new uniform, epaulettes, aglets, and with a ruddy face not yet marked by dissipation, with a little black moustache and the hair of his temples brushed towards the eyes, as the emperor brushed his, met him respectfully. Prince Vassily Dolgoruky, the assistant minister of war, with a bored expression on his dull face, adorned by the same side-whiskers, moustache, and brushed-up temples as Nicholas wore, rose to meet Chernyshov and greeted him.

"L'empereur?" Chernyshov addressed the imperial adjutant, directing his eyes questioningly at the door of the office.

"Sa majesté vient de rentrer, "* said the imperial adjutant, listening to the sound of his own voice with obvious pleasure, and, stepping softly and so smoothly that a full glass of water placed on his head would not have spilled, he went up to the noiselessly opening door and, his whole being expressing reverence for the place he was entering, disappeared through it.

Dolgoruky meanwhile opened his portfolio, checking the papers that were in it.

Chernyshov, frowning, strolled about, stretching his legs and going over all that he had to report to the emperor. Chernyshov was near the door of the office when it opened again and the imperial adjutant came out, still more radiant and respectful than before, and with a gesture invited the minister and his assistant to the sovereign.

The Winter Palace had long since been rebuilt after the fire, yet Nicholas still lived on its upper floor. The office in which he received the reports of ministers and high officials was a very high-ceilinged room with four large windows. A large portrait of the emperor Alexander I hung on the main wall. Between the windows stood two desks. Along the walls several chairs, in the middle of the room an enormous writing table, at the table Nicholas's armchair and chairs for visitors.

Nicholas, in a black tunic without epaulettes, but with small shoulder straps, sat at the table, his enormous body tight-laced across the over-grown belly, and looked at the entering men with his immobile, lifeless gaze. His long, white face with its enormous, receding brow emerging from the slicked-down hair at his temples, artfully joined to the wig that covered his bald patch, was especially cold and immobile that day. His

---

* His Majesty has just returned.

eyes, always dull, looked duller than usual; his compressed lips under the twirled moustaches, and his fat cheeks propped on his high collar, freshly shaven, with regular, sausage-shaped side-whiskers left on them, and his chin pressed into the collar, gave his face an expression of displeasure and even of wrath. The cause of this mood was fatigue. And the cause of the fatigue was that he had been at a masked ball the night before, and, strolling as usual in his horse-guards helmet with a bird on its head, among the public who either pressed towards him or timidly avoided his enormous and self-assured figure, had again met that mask who, at the last masked ball, having aroused his old man's sensuality by her white-ness, beautiful build, and tender voice, had hidden from him, promising to meet him at the next masked ball. At last night's ball she had come up to him, and he had not let her go. He had led her to the box kept in readi-ness especially for that purpose, where he could remain alone with his lady. Having come silently to the door of the box, Nicholas looked around, his eyes searching for the usher, but he was not there. Nicholas frowned and pushed open the door of the box himself, allowing his lady to go in first.

*"Il y a quelqu'un,"** the mask said, stopping. The box was indeed occupied. On a little velvet divan, close to each other, sat an uhlan officer and a young, pretty, blonde, curly-haired woman in a domino, with her mask off. Seeing the drawn-up, towering, and wrathful figure of Nicholas, the blonde woman hastily covered herself with the mask, and the uhlan officer, dumbfounded with terror, not getting up from the divan, stared at Nicholas with fixed eyes.

Accustomed though Nicholas was to the terror he aroused in people, that terror had always been pleasing to him, and he liked on occasion to astound the people thrown into terror, addressing them by contrast with affable words. And so he did now.

"Well, brother, you're a bit younger than I," he said to the officer numb with terror, "you might yield the place to me."

The officer leaped up and, turning pale, then red, cowering, silently followed the mask out of the box, and Nicholas was left alone with his lady.

The mask turned out to be a pretty, innocent, twenty-year-old girl,

* There's somebody here.

the daughter of a Swedish governess. The girl told Nicholas how, when still a child, she had fallen in love with him from his portraits, had idolized him, and had resolved to win his attention at any cost. And now she had won it, and, as she said, she wanted nothing more. The girl was taken to the usual place for Nicholas's meetings with women, and Nicholas spent more than an hour with her.

When he returned to his room that night and lay down on the narrow, hard bed, which he took pride in, and covered himself with his cloak, which he considered (and he said so) as famous as Napoleon's hat, he could not fall asleep for a long time. He recalled now the frightened and rapturous expression of the girl's white face, now the powerful, full shoulders of his usual mistress, Mme Nelidov, and drew comparisons between the one and the other. That debauchery was not a good thing in a married man did not even occur to him, and he would have been very surprised if anyone had condemned him for it. But, even though he was convinced that he had acted as he ought, he was left with some sort of unpleasant aftertaste, and, to stifle that feeling, he began thinking about something that always soothed him: about what a great man he was.

Even though he had fallen asleep late, he got up before eight o'clock, as always, and, having performed his usual toilette, having rubbed his big, well-fed body with ice and prayed to God, he recited the usual prayers he had been saying since childhood—the Hail Mary, the Creed, the Our Father—without ascribing any significance to the words he pronounced, and went out through the side entrance to the embankment, in an overcoat and a peaked cap.

Midway along the embankment, he met a student from the law school, as enormously tall as himself, in a uniform and hat. Seeing the uniform of the school, which he disliked for its freethinking, Nicholas frowned, but the tallness of the student, the zealous way he stood to attention and saluted with a deliberately thrust-out elbow, softened his displeasure.

"What is your name?" he asked.

"Polosatov, Your Imperial Majesty!"

"Fine fellow!"

The student went on standing with his hand to his hat. Nicholas stopped.

"Want to join the army?"

"No, sir, Your Imperial Majesty."

"Blockhead!" and Nicholas, turning away, walked on and began loudly uttering the first words that came to him. "Koperwein, Koperwein," he repeated several times the name of last night's girl. "Nasty, nasty." He was not thinking of what he was saying, but stifled his feeling by concentrating on the words. "Yes, what would Russia be without me?" he said to himself, again sensing the approach of the unpleasant feeling. "Yes, what would, not just Russia, but Europe be without me?" And he remembered his brother-in-law, the king of Prussia, and his weakness and stupidity, and shook his head.

Going back to the porch, he saw the carriage of Elena Pavlovna, with a handsome footman, driving up to the Saltykov entrance. Elena Pavlovna was for him the personification of those empty people who talked not only about science and poetry, but also about governing people, imagining that they could govern themselves better than he, Nicholas, governed them. He knew that, however much he quashed these people, they surfaced again and again. And he recalled his recently deceased brother, Mikhail Pavlovich. And a feeling of vexation and sadness came over him. He frowned gloomily and again began whispering the first words that came to him. He stopped whispering only when he entered the palace. Going into his apartments and smoothing his sidewhiskers and the hair on his temples and the hairpiece on his bald patch before the mirror, he twirled his moustaches and went straight to the office where reports were received.

He received Chernyshov first. By Nicholas's face, and mainly by his eyes, Chernyshov understood at once that he was especially out of sorts that day, and, knowing of his adventure the night before, he understood the cause of it. Having greeted Chernyshov coldly and invited him to be seated, Nicholas fixed his lifeless eyes on him.

The first business in Chernyshov's report was a case of theft discovered among commissary officials; then there was the matter of a transfer of troops on the Prussian border; then the nomination for New Year awards of certain persons omitted from the first list; then there was the dispatch from Vorontsov about Hadji Murat's coming over; and, finally, an unpleasant case of a student in the medical academy who had made an attempt on a professor's life.

Nicholas, with silently compressed lips, stroked the sheets of paper with his big white hands, with a gold ring on one ring finger, and listened to the report about the theft, not taking his eyes from Chernyshov's forehead and forelock.

Nicholas was convinced that everyone stole. He knew that the commissary officials now had to be punished and decided to send them all as soldiers, but he also knew that that would not prevent those who filled the vacated posts from doing the same thing. It was in the nature of officials to steal, and his duty was to punish them, and sick of it as he was, he conscientiously performed his duty.

"It seems there's only one honest man in our Russia," he said.

Chernyshov understood at once that this only man in Russia was Nicholas himself, and he smiled approvingly.

"Surely, that's so, Your Majesty," he said.

"Leave it, I'll write my decision," said Nicholas, taking the paper and placing it on the left side of the table.

After that, Chernyshov started reporting about awards and the troop transfer. Nicholas glanced through the list, crossed out several names, and then briefly and resolutely ordered the transfer of two divisions to the Prussian border.

Nicholas could never forgive the Prussian king for granting his people a constitution after the year forty-eight, and therefore, while expressing the most friendly feelings for his brother-in-law in letters and words, he considered it necessary to keep troops on the Prussian border just in case. These troops might also prove necessary so that, in case of a popular insurrection in Prussia (Nicholas saw a readiness for insurrection everywhere), they could be sent to defend his brother-in-law's throne, as he had sent troops to defend Austria against the Hungarians. These troops on the border were also needed to give more weight and significance to his advice to the Prussian king.

"Yes, what would happen to Russia now, if it weren't for me?" he thought again.

"Well, what else?" he said.

"A sergeant major from the Caucasus," said Chernyshov, and he began to report what Vorontsov had written about Hadji Murat's coming over.

"Really," said Nicholas. "A good beginning."

"Obviously the plan worked out by Your Majesty is beginning to bear fruit," said Chernyshov.

This praise of his strategic abilities was especially pleasing to Nicholas, because, though he was proud of his strategic abilities, at the bottom of his heart he was aware that he had none. And now he wanted to hear more detailed praise of himself.

"How do you mean?" he asked.

"I mean that if we had long ago followed Your Majesty's plan—moving forward gradually, though slowly, cutting down forests, destroying provisions—the Caucasus would have been subjugated long ago. Hadji Murat's coming over I put down only to that. He realized that it was no longer possible for them to hold out."

"True," said Nicholas.

Despite the fact that the plan of a slow movement into enemy territory by means of cutting down forests and destroying provisions was the plan of Ermolov and Velyaminov, and the complete opposite of Nicholas's plan, according to which it was necessary to take over Shamil's residence at once and devastate that nest of robbers, and according to which the Dargo expedition of 1845 had been undertaken, at the cost of so many human lives—despite that, Nicholas also ascribed to himself the plan of slow movement, the progressive cutting down of forests, and the destruction of provisions. It would seem that, in order to believe that the plan of slow movement, the cutting down of forests, and the destruction of provisions was his plan, it would be necessary to conceal the fact that he had precisely insisted on the completely opposite military undertaking of the year forty-five. But he did not conceal it and was proud both of his plan of the expedition of the year forty-five and of the plan of slow movement forward, despite the fact that these two plans obviously contradicted each other. The constant, obvious flattery, contrary to all evidence, of the people around him had brought him to the point that he no longer saw his contradictions, no longer conformed his actions and words to reality, logic, or even simple common sense, but was fully convinced that all his orders, however senseless, unjust, and inconsistent with each other, became sensible, just, and consistent with each other only because he gave them.

Such, too, was his decision about the student of the medico-surgical academy, about whom Chernyshov began to report after the report on the Caucasus.

What had happened was that a young man who had twice failed his examinations was taking them for the third time, and when the examiner again did not pass him, the morbidly nervous student, seeing injustice in it, seized a penknife from the desk and, in something like a fit of frenzy, fell upon the professor and inflicted several insignificant wounds.

"What is his last name?" asked Nicholas.

"Bzhezovsky."

"A Pole?"

"Of Polish origin and a Catholic," replied Chernyshov.

Nicholas frowned.

He had done much evil to the Poles. To explain that evil he had to be convinced that all Poles were scoundrels. And Nicholas regarded them as such and hated them in proportion to the evil he had done them.

"Wait a little," he said and, closing his eyes, he lowered his head.

Chernyshov knew, having heard it more than once from Nicholas, that whenever he had to decide some important question, he had only to concentrate for a few moments and inspiration would come to him, and the most correct decision would take shape by itself, as if some inner voice told him what had to be done. He now thought about how he could more fully satisfy that feeling of spite against the Poles that had been aroused in him by the story of this student, and his inner voice prompted him to the following decision. He took the report and wrote on its margin in his large hand: *"Deserves the death penalty. But, thank God, we do not have the death penalty. And it is not for me to introduce it. Have him run the gauntlet of a thousand men twelve times. Nicholas"*—he signed with his unnatural, enormous flourish.

Nicholas knew that twelve thousand rods was not only a certain, painful death, but also excessive cruelty, because five thousand strokes were enough to kill the strongest man. But it pleased him to be implacably cruel and pleased him to think that we had no death penalty.

Having written his decision about the student, he moved it over to Chernyshov.

"Here," he said. "Read it."

Chernyshov read it and, as a sign of respectful astonishment at the wisdom of the decision, inclined his head.

"And have all the students brought to the square, so that they can be present at the punishment," Nicholas added.

"It will do them good. I'll destroy this revolutionary spirit, I'll tear it up by the roots," he thought.

"Yes, Sire," said Chernyshov and, after a pause, he straightened his forelock and went back to the Caucasian report.

"What, then, do you order me to write to Mikhail Semyonovich?"

"To adhere firmly to my system of laying waste to habitations, destroying provisions in Chechnya, and harrying them with raids," said Nicholas.

"What are your orders about Hadji Murat?" asked Chernyshov.

"Why, Vorontsov writes that he wants to make use of him in the Caucasus."

"Isn't that risky?" said Chernyshov, avoiding Nicholas's eyes. "I'm afraid Mikhail Semyonovich is too trusting."

"And what would you think?" Nicholas asked sharply, noticing Chernyshov's intention to present Vorontsov's orders in a bad light.

"I would think it's safer to send him to Russia."

"You think so," Nicholas said mockingly. "But I do not think so and agree with Vorontsov. Write that to him."

"Yes, Sire," said Chernyshov and, standing up, he began taking his leave.

Dolgoruky also took his leave. In the whole time of the report, he had said only a few words about the transfer of troops, in answer to Nicholas's questions.

After Chernyshov, the governor general of the western provinces, Bibikov, was received, having come to take his leave. Approving of the measures Bibikov had taken against the rebellious peasants, who did not want to convert to Orthodoxy,[17] he told him to try all the disobedient in military court. That meant sentencing them to run the gauntlet. Besides that, he ordered the editor of a newspaper to be sent as a soldier for publishing information about the reregistering of several thousand state peasants as crown peasants.

"I do this because I consider it necessary," he said. "And I allow no discussion of it."

Bibikov understood all the cruelty of the order about the Uniates and all the injustice of the transfer of state peasants, that is, the only free ones at that time, to the crown, that is, making them serfs of the tsar's family. But it was impossible to object. To disagree with Nicholas's orders meant to lose all that brilliant position which he now enjoyed, and which he had spent forty years acquiring. And therefore he humbly bowed his dark, greying head in a sign of submission and readiness to carry out the cruel, insane, and dishonest supreme will.

After dismissing Bibikov, Nicholas, with a consciousness of duty well done, stretched, glanced at the clock, and went to dress for his coming out. Having put on his uniform with epaulettes, decorations, and a sash, he went out to the reception halls, where more than a hundred men in uniform and women in low-cut fancy dresses, all standing in assigned places, waited tremblingly for his coming out.

With his lifeless gaze, with his thrust-out chest and his tight-laced belly protruding from the lacing above and below, he came out to these waiting people, and, feeling that all eyes were directed at him with trembling obsequiousness, he assumed a still more solemn air. When he met the eyes of familiar persons, remembering who was who, he stopped and said a few words, sometimes in Russian, sometimes in French, and, piercing them with his cold, lifeless gaze, listened to what they said to him.

Having received their felicitations, Nicholas went on to church.

God, through his servants, greeted and praised Nicholas, just as the secular people had done, and he, though he found it tedious, received those greetings and praises as his due. All this had to be so, because on him depended the welfare and happiness of the whole world, and though it wearied him, he still did not deny the world his assistance. When, at the end of the liturgy, the magnificent deacon, his long hair combed loose, proclaimed "Many Years,"[18] and with beautiful voices the choristers all as one took up these words, Nicholas glanced behind him and noticed Mme Nelidov with her splendid shoulders, and decided the comparison with last night's girl in her favour.

After the liturgy he went to the empress and spent several minutes in the family circle, joking with his children and wife. Then he went through the Hermitage to see the minister of court Volkonsky and, among other things, charged him with paying an annual pension out of special funds to the mother of last night's girl. And from him he went for his usual promenade.

Dinner that day was in the Pompeian Hall. Besides the younger sons, Nicholas and Mikhail, there were also invited Baron Liven, Count Rzhevussky, Dolgoruky, the Prussian ambassador, and the Prussian king's adjutant general.

While waiting for the empress and emperor to come out, an interesting conversation began between the Prussian ambassador and Baron Liven to do with the latest alarming news from Poland.

"*La Pologne et le Caucase, ce sont les deux cautères de la Russie,*" said Liven. "*Il nous faut cent mille hommes à peu près dans chacun de ces deux pays.*"*

The ambassador expressed feigned surprise that it was so.

"*Vous dites la Pologne,*"† he said.

"*Oh, oui, c'était un coup de maître de Metternich de nous en avoir laissé l'embarras . . .*"‡

At this point in the conversation the empress came in with her shaking head and frozen smile, and Nicholas behind her.

At the table Nicholas told them about Hadji Murat's coming over and said that the war in the Caucasus should end soon as the result of his order about restricting the mountaineers by cutting down the forests and his system of fortifications.

The ambassador, having exchanged fleeting glances with the Prussian adjutant general, with whom he had spoken that morning about Nicholas's unfortunate weakness of considering himself a great strategist, highly praised this plan, which proved once again Nicholas's great strategic abilities.

After dinner Nicholas went to the ballet, where hundreds of bare women marched about in tights. One especially caught his eye and, summoning the ballet master, Nicholas thanked him and ordered that he be given a diamond ring.

The next day, during Chernyshov's report, Nicholas confirmed once more his instructions to Vorontsov, that now, since Hadji Murat had come over, they should intensify the harrying of Chechnya and hem it in with a cordon line.

Chernyshov wrote in that sense to Vorontsov, and the next day another sergeant major, overdriving the horses and beating the coachmen's faces, galloped off to Tiflis.

---

* Poland and the Caucasus are the two running sores of Russia . . . We need about a hundred thousand men in each of the two countries.
† Poland, you say.
‡ Oh, yes, it was a masterstroke of Metternich's to have left us the inconvenience of it . . .

XVI

IN FULFILMENT of these instructions from Nicholas, a raid into Chechnya was undertaken at once, in January 1852.

The detachment sent on the raid consisted of four infantry battalions, two hundred Cossacks, and eight guns. The column marched along the road. On both sides of the column, in an unbroken line, descending into and climbing out of the gullies, marched chasseurs in high boots, fur jackets, and papakhas, with muskets on their shoulders and cartridges in bandoliers. As always, the detachment moved through enemy territory keeping as silent as possible. Only the guns clanked now and then, jolting over ditches, or an artillery horse, not understanding the order for silence, snorted or neighed, or an angered commander yelled in a hoarse, restrained voice at his subordinates because the line was too strung out, or moved too close or too far from the column. Only once the silence was broken by a she-goat with a white belly and rump and a grey back and a similar billy goat with short, back-bent horns, who leaped from a small bramble patch between the line and the column. The beautiful, frightened animals, making big leaps and tucking up their front legs, came flying so close to the column that some of the soldiers ran after them with shouts and guffaws, intending to stick them with their bayonets, but the goats turned back, leaped through the line, and, pursued by several horsemen and the company dogs, sped off like birds into the mountains.

It was still winter, but the sun was beginning to climb higher, and by noon, when the detachment, which had set off early in the morning, had already gone some seven miles, it had warmed up so much that the men felt hot, and its rays were so bright that it was painful to look at the steel of the bayonets and the gleams that suddenly flashed on the bronze of the cannons like little suns.

Behind was the swift, clear river the detachment had just crossed, ahead were cultivated fields and meadows with shallow gullies, further ahead the mysterious, dark hills covered with forest, beyond the dark hills crags jutting up, and on the high horizon—eternally enchanting, eternally changing, playing in the light like diamonds—the snowy mountains.

At the head of the fifth company, in a black tunic, a papakha, and with a sabre across his shoulder, marched the tall, handsome officer Butler, recently transferred from the guards, experiencing a vigorous feeling of the joy of life, and at the same time of the danger of death, and the desire for activity, and the consciousness of belonging to an enormous whole governed by a single will. Today Butler was going into action for the second time, and it was a joy to him to think that they were about to be fired at, and that he not only would not duck his head as a cannonball flew over or pay attention to the whistle of bullets, but would carry his head high, as he had done already, and look about at his comrades and soldiers with a smile in his eyes, and start talking in the most indifferent voice about something irrelevant.

The detachment turned off the good road and onto a little-used one, crossing a harvested cornfield, and was just approaching the forest, when—no one could see from where—a cannonball flew over with a sinister whistle and landed at the middle of the baggage train, by the road, in the cornfield, throwing up dirt.

"It's beginning," Butler said, smiling merrily, to a comrade walking next to him.

And indeed, after the cannonball, a dense crowd of Chechen horsemen with standards appeared from the forest. In the middle of the party was a large green standard, and the old sergeant major of the company, who was very long-sighted, informed the nearsighted Butler that it must be Shamil himself. The party descended the hill and appeared on the crest of the nearest gully to the right and began to descend into it. A little general in a warm black tunic and a papakha with a big white lambskin top rode up to Butler's company on his ambler and ordered him to go to the right against the descending horsemen. Butler quickly led his company in the direction indicated, but before he had time to descend into the gully, he heard two cannon shots behind him, one after the other. He looked back: two clouds of blue-grey smoke rose above the two cannon and stretched out along the gully. The party, obviously not expecting artillery, went back. Butler's company began to fire after the mountaineers, and the whole hollow became covered with powder smoke. Only above the hollow could the mountaineers be seen, hastily retreating and returning the fire of the pursuing Cossacks. The detachment went on after the mountaineers, and on the slope of a second gully an aoul appeared.

Butler and his company, following the Cossacks, came running into the aoul. There were no inhabitants. The soldiers had been ordered to burn grain, hay, and the saklyas themselves. Pungent smoke spread over the whole aoul, and in this smoke soldiers poked about, dragging out of the saklyas whatever they could find, and mainly catching and shooting the chickens that the mountaineers could not take with them. The officers sat down away from the smoke and had lunch and drank. The sergeant major brought them several honeycombs on a board. There was no sign of the Chechens. A little past noon came the order to retreat. The companies formed a column beyond the aoul, and Butler ended up in the rearguard. As soon as they set off, Chechens appeared and, riding after the detachment, escorted it with gunfire.

When the detachment came out into the open, the mountaineers dropped behind. None of Butler's men was wounded, and he went back in the most merry and cheerful spirits.

When the detachment, having waded back across the little river they had crossed that morning, stretched out over the cornfields and meadows, singers stepped forward by company and songs rang out. There was no wind, the air was fresh, clean, and so transparent that the snowy mountains, which were some seventy miles away, seemed very close, and when the singers fell silent, the measured tramp of feet and clank of guns could be heard, as a background against which the songs started and stopped. The song sung in Butler's fifth company had been composed by a junker for the glory of the regiment and was sung to a dance tune with the refrain: "What can compare, what can compare, with the chasseurs, with the chasseurs!"

Butler rode beside his next in command, Major Petrov, with whom he lived, and could not rejoice enough at his decision to leave the guards and go to the Caucasus. The main reason for his transfer from the guards was that in Petersburg he had lost so much at cards that he had nothing left. He was afraid that he would not be able to keep from gambling if he stayed in the guards, and he had nothing to gamble with. Now it was all over. This was a different life, and such a fine, dashing one! He forgot now about his ruin and his unpaid debts. And the Caucasus, the war, the soldiers, the officers, the drunken and good-natured, brave Major Petrov—all this seemed so good to him that he sometimes could not believe he was not in Petersburg, not in smoke-filled rooms bending corners and punting, hating the banker and feeling an oppressive ache in his head, but here in this wonderful country, among the dashing Caucasians.

"What can compare, what can compare, with the chasseurs, with the chasseurs!" sang his singers. His horse went merrily in step with this music. The shaggy grey company dog Trezorka, like a commander, its tail curled up, ran ahead of Butler's company with a preoccupied air. At heart Butler felt cheerful, calm, and merry. War presented itself to him only as a matter of subjecting himself to danger, to the possibility of death, and thereby earning awards, and the respect of his comrades here and of his friends in Russia. The other side of war—the death, the wounds of soldiers, officers, mountaineers—strange as it is to say, did not present itself to his imagination. Unconsciously, to preserve his poetic notion of war, he never even looked at the killed and wounded. And so it was now: we had three men killed and twelve wounded. He passed by a corpse lying on its back, and saw with only one eye the strange position of the waxen arm and the dark-red spot on the head, and did not stop to look. The mountaineers presented themselves to him only as dzhigit horsemen from whom one had to defend oneself.

"So it goes, old boy," the major said between songs. "Not like with you in Petersburg: dress right, dress left. We do our work and go home. Mashurka will serve us a pie, some nice cabbage soup. That's life! Right? Now, lads, 'As Dawn Was Breaking,' " he ordered his favourite song.

The major lived maritally with the daughter of a surgeon's assistant, first known as Mashka, and then as Marya Dmitrievna. Marya Dmitrievna was a beautiful, fair-haired, thirty-year-old, childless woman, all covered with freckles. Whatever her past had been, she was now the major's faithful companion, took care of him like a nurse, and the major needed it, because he often drank himself into oblivion.

When they reached the fortress, it was all as the major had foreseen. Marya Dmitrievna fed him and Butler and two other invited officers of the detachment a nourishing, tasty dinner, and the major ate and drank so much that he could not speak and went to his room to sleep. Butler, likewise tired, but pleased and slightly tipsy from too much chikhir, went to his room, and having barely managed to undress, put his hand under his handsome curly head, and fell fast asleep, without dreaming or waking up.

XVII

THE AOUL DEVASTATED by the raid was the one in which Hadji Murat had spent the night before his coming over to the Russians.

Sado, with whom Hadji Murat had stayed, was leaving for the mountains with his family when the Russians approached the aoul. When he came back to his aoul, he found his saklya destroyed: the roof had fallen in, the door and posts of the little gallery were burned down, and the inside was befouled. His son, the handsome boy with shining eyes who had looked rapturously at Hadji Murat, was brought dead to the mosque on a horse covered by a burka. He had been stabbed in the back with a bayonet. The fine-looking woman who had waited on Hadji Murat during his visit, now, in a smock torn in front, revealing her old, sagging breasts, and with her hair undone, stood over her son and clawed her face until it bled and wailed without ceasing. Sado took a pick and shovel and went with some relations to dig a grave for his son. The old grandfather sat by the wall of the destroyed saklya and, whittling a little stick, stared dully before him. He had just come back from his apiary. The two haystacks formerly there had been burned; the apricot and cherry trees he had planted and nursed were broken and scorched and, worst of all, the beehives had all been burned. The wailing of women could be heard in all the houses and on the square, where two more bodies had been brought. The small children wailed along with their mothers. Hungry cattle, who had nothing to eat, also bellowed. The older children did not play, but looked at their elders with frightened eyes.

The spring had been befouled, obviously on purpose, so that it was impossible to take water from it. The mosque was also befouled, and the mullah and his assistants were cleaning it up.

The old heads of households gathered on the square and, squatting down, discussed their situation. Of hatred for the Russians no one even spoke. The feeling that was experienced by all the Chechens, big and small, was stronger than hatred. It was not hatred, but a refusal to recognize these Russian dogs as human beings, and such loathing, disgust, and bewilderment before the absurd cruelty of these beings, that the wish to exterminate them, like the wish to exterminate rats, venomous spiders, and wolves, was as natural as the sense of self-preservation.

The inhabitants were faced with a choice: to stay where they were and restore with terrible effort all that had been established with such labour and had been so easily and senselessly destroyed, and to expect at any moment a repetition of the same, or, contrary to religious law and their loathing and contempt for them, to submit to the Russians.

The old men prayed and unanimously decided to send envoys to Shamil asking him for help, and at once set about restoring what had been destroyed.

XVIII

ON THE THIRD DAY after the raid, Butler, not very early in the morning, went out by the back door, intending to stroll and have a breath of air before morning tea, which he usually took together with Petrov. The sun had already come out from behind the mountains, and it hurt to look at the white daub cottages lit up by it on the right side of the street, but then, as always, it was cheering and soothing to look to the left, at the receding and rising black hills covered with forest, and at the opaque line of snowy mountains visible beyond the gorge, trying, as always, to simulate clouds.

Butler looked at these mountains, breathed with all his lungs, and rejoiced that he was alive, and that precisely he was alive, and in this beautiful world. He also rejoiced a little at having borne himself so well in action yesterday, both during the attack and, especially, during the retreat, when things got rather hot; rejoiced, too, remembering how, in the evening, on their return from the sortie, Masha, or Marya Dmitrievna, Petrov's companion, had fed them and had been especially simple and nice with them all, but in particular, as he thought, had been affectionate to him. Marya Dmitrievna, with her thick braid, broad shoulders, high bosom, and the beaming smile of her kindly, freckled face, involuntarily attracted Butler, as a strong, young, unmarried man, and it even seemed to him that she desired him. But he reckoned that it would be a bad way to treat a kind, simple-hearted comrade, and he maintained a most simple, respectful attitude towards Marya Dmitrievna, and was glad of it in himself. He was just now thinking of that.

His thoughts were distracted when he heard in front of him the rapid beat of many horses' hooves on the dusty road, as of several men galloping. He raised his head and saw at the end of the street a small group of horsemen approaching at a walk. Ahead of some twenty Cossacks, two men were riding: one in a white cherkeska and a tall papakha with a turban, the other an officer in the Russian service, dark, hook-nosed, in a blue cherkeska with an abundance of silver on his clothes and weapons. Under the horseman in the turban was a handsome light-maned chestnut stallion with a small head and beautiful eyes; under the officer was a tall, showy Karabakh horse. Butler, a horse fancier, at once appraised the vigorous strength of the first horse and stopped to find out who these people were. The officer addressed Butler:

"This army commander house?" he asked, betraying his non-Russian origin both by his ungrammatical speech and by his pronunciation, and pointing his whip at Ivan Matveevich's house.

"The very one," said Butler. "And who's that?" he asked, coming closer to the officer and indicating the man in the turban with his eyes.

"That Hadji Murat. Come here, stay with army commander," said the officer.

Butler knew about Hadji Murat and his coming over to the Russians, but he had never expected to see him here in this little stronghold.

Hadji Murat was looking at him amicably.

"Greetings, *koshkoldy,*" he said the Tartar greeting he had learned.

"Saubul," replied Hadji Murat, nodding his head. He rode up to Butler and gave him his hand, from two fingers of which hung a whip.

"The commander?" he asked.

"No, the commander's here, I'll go and call him," said Butler, addressing the officer and going up the steps and pushing at the door.

But the door of the "main entrance," as Marya Dmitrievna called it, was locked. Butler knocked, but, receiving no answer, went around to the back door. Having called his orderly and received no answer, and not finding either of his two orderlies, he went to the kitchen. Marya Dmitrievna, flushed, a kerchief on her head and her sleeves rolled up on her plump white arms, was cutting rolled-out dough, as white as her arms, into pieces for little pies.

"Where are the orderlies?" asked Butler.

"Getting drunk somewhere," said Marya Dmitrievna. "What do you want?"

"To open the door. You've got a whole crowd of mountaineers in front of your house. Hadji Murat has come."

"Tell me another one," said Marya Dmitrievna, smiling.

"I'm not joking. It's true. They're standing by the porch."

"Can it be?" said Marya Dmitrievna.

"Why should I make it up? Go and look, they're standing by the porch."

"That's a surprise," said Marya Dmitrievna, rolling down her sleeves and feeling with her hand for the pins in her thick braid. "Then I'll go and wake up Ivan Matveevich," she said.

"No, I'll go myself. And you, Bondarenko, go and open the door," said Butler.

"Well, that's good enough," said Marya Dmitrievna, and she went back to what she was doing.

On learning that Hadji Murat had come to him, Ivan Matveevich, who had already heard that Hadji Murat was in the Grozny fortress, was not surprised by it in the least, but got up, rolled a cigarette, lit it, and began to dress, clearing his throat loudly and grumbling at the superiors who had sent "this devil" to him. Having dressed, he asked his orderly for "medicine." And the orderly, knowing that "medicine" meant vodka, brought it to him.

"There's nothing worse than mixing," he grumbled, drinking up the vodka and taking a bite of black bread. "I drank chikhir yesterday, so today I've got a headache. Well, now I'm ready," he finished and went to the drawing room, where Butler had already brought Hadji Murat and the officer who accompanied him.

The officer escorting Hadji Murat handed Ivan Matveevich the order of the commander of the left flank to receive Hadji Murat, to allow him to have communications with the mountaineers through scouts, but by no means to let him leave the fortress otherwise than with a Cossack escort.

After reading the paper, Ivan Matveevich looked intently at Hadji Murat and again began to scrutinize the paper. Having shifted his eyes from the paper to his guest several times like that, he finally rested his eyes on Hadji Murat and said:

"*Yakshi, bek-yakshi.* Let him stay. But tell him I've been ordered not to let him leave. And orders are sacred. And we'll put him up—what do you think, Butler—shall we put him up in the office?"

Before Butler had time to reply, Marya Dmitrievna, who had come from the kitchen and was standing in the doorway, addressed Ivan Matveevich:

"Why in the office? Put him up here. We'll give him the guest room and the storeroom. At least we can keep an eye on him," she said and, glancing at Hadji Murat and meeting his eyes, she hastily turned away.

"You know, I think Marya Dmitrievna is right," said Butler.

"Well, well, off with you, women have no business here," Ivan Matveevich said, frowning.

Throughout the conversation, Hadji Murat sat, his hand tucked behind the hilt of his dagger, smiling somewhat scornfully. He said it made no difference to him where he lived. One thing that he needed and that the sardar had permitted him was to have contacts with the mountaineers, and therefore he wished that they be allowed to come to him. Ivan Matveevich said that that would be done, and asked Butler to entertain the guests until they were brought a bite to eat and their rooms were prepared, while he went to the office to write out the necessary papers and give the necessary orders.

Hadji Murat's relations with his new acquaintances were at once defined very clearly. From their first acquaintance Hadji Murat felt loathing and contempt for Ivan Matveevich and always treated him haughtily. To Marya Dmitrievna, who prepared and brought his food, he took a special liking. He liked her simplicity, and the special beauty of a nationality foreign to him, and the attraction she felt to him, which she transmitted to him unconsciously. He tried not to look at her, not to speak with her, but his eyes involuntarily turned to her and followed her movements.

With Butler he became friendly at once, from their first acquaintance, and talked with him much and eagerly, questioning him about his life and telling him about his own and passing on the news brought to him by the scouts about the situation of his family, and even consulting with him about what to do.

The news conveyed to him by the scouts was not good. During the four days he had spent in the fortress, they had come to him twice, and both times the news had been bad.

XIX

SOON AFTER Hadji Murat came over to the Russians, his family was brought to the aoul of Vedeno and was kept there under watch, waiting for Shamil's decision. The women—old Patimat and Hadji Murat's two wives—and their five small children lived under guard in the saklya of the lieutenant Ibrahim Rashid, but Hadji Murat's son, the eighteen-year-old boy Yusuf, sat in prison, that is, in a hole more than seven feet deep, together with four criminals awaiting, like him, the deciding of their fate.

The decision did not come, because Shamil was away. He was on campaign against the Russians.

On 6 January 1852, Shamil was returning home to Vedeno after a battle with the Russians in which, according to the opinion of the Russians, he had been crushed and had fled to Vedeno, while according to his own opinion and that of all the murids, he had been victorious and had routed the Russians. In this battle—something that happened very rarely—he himself had fired his rifle and, snatching out his sabre, had sent his horse straight at the Russians, but the murids accompanying him had held him back. Two of them had been killed right beside Shamil.

It was midday when Shamil, surrounded by the party of murids, caracoling around him, firing off their rifles and pistols, and ceaselessly singing *"La ilaha il Allah,"* rode up to his place of residence.

All the people of the large aoul of Vedeno were standing in the street and on the roofs to meet their ruler, and in a sign of festivity also fired off their muskets and pistols. Shamil rode on a white Arabian stallion, who merrily tugged at the reins as they neared home. The horse's attire was of the most simple, without gold or silver ornaments: a finely worked red leather bridle with a groove down the middle, cup-shaped metal stirrups, and a red blanket showing from under the saddle. The imam was wearing a fur-lined brown broadcloth coat, with black fur showing at the collar and cuffs, tightly girded around his slender and long body by a black belt with a dagger hung from it. On his head was a tall papakha with a flat top and a black tassel, wrapped with a white turban, the end of which hung down behind his neck. On his feet were soft green chuviaki, on his calves tight black leggings trimmed with simple cord.

In general there was nothing on the imam that glittered, gold or silver, and his tall, straight, powerful figure, in unadorned clothes, surrounded by murids with gold and silver ornaments on their clothes and weapons, produced that very impression of grandeur that he wanted and knew how to produce in people. His pale face, framed by a trimmed red beard, with its constantly narrowed little eyes, was perfectly immobile, like stone. As he rode through the aoul, he felt thousands of eyes directed at him, but his eyes did not look at anyone. The wives of Hadji Murat and their children, together with all the inhabitants of the saklya, also came out to the gallery to watch the imam's entrance. Only old Patimat, Hadji Murat's mother, did not come out, but remained sitting as she had been sitting, with dishevelled grey hair, on the floor of the saklya, clasping her thin knees with her long arms, and, blinking her jet-black eyes, watched the burning-down logs in the fireplace. She, like her son, had always hated Shamil, now more than ever, and she did not want to see him.

Neither did Hadji Murat's son see the triumphal entry of Shamil. He only heard the singing and shooting from his dark, stinking hole, and suffered as only young people full of life suffer deprived of freedom. Sitting in the stinking hole and seeing all the same unfortunate, dirty, exhausted people imprisoned with him, for the most part hating each other, he was passionately envious of those who, enjoying air, light, freedom, were now caracoling on spirited horses around the ruler, shooting and singing as one: *"La ilaha il Allah."*

Having passed through the aoul, Shamil rode into a big courtyard, adjoining an inner one in which Shamil's seraglio was located. Two armed Lezghians met Shamil by the open gates of the first courtyard. This courtyard was filled with people. There were some who had come from distant places on their own business, there were petitioners, there were those summoned by Shamil himself for trial and sentencing. At Shamil's entry, all those who were in the courtyard rose and respectfully greeted the imam, putting their hands to their chests. Some knelt and stayed that way all the while Shamil was riding across the courtyard from the one, outside, gate to the other, inner one. Though Shamil recognized among those waiting many persons who were displeasing to him and many tedious petitioners demanding to be attended to, he rode past them with the same unchanging, stony face, and, riding into the inner courtyard, dismounted at the gallery of his lodgings, to the left of the gate.

After the strain of the campaign, not so much physical as spiritual, because Shamil, despite the public recognition of his campaign as victorious, knew that his campaign had been a failure, that many Chechen aouls had been burned and laid waste, and the changeable, light-minded Chechen people were wavering, and some of them, nearest to the Russians, were now ready to go over to them—all this was difficult, measures had to be taken against it, yet at that moment Shamil did not want to do anything, did not want to think about anything. He now wanted only one thing: rest and the delight of the familial caresses of his favourite among his wives, Aminet, the eighteen-year-old, dark-eyed, swift-footed Kist.

But not only was it impossible even to think now of seeing Aminet, who was right there behind the fence in the inner courtyard that separated the wives' lodgings from the men's (Shamil was even sure that now, as he was getting off his horse, Aminet and the other wives were watching through a chink in the fence), not only was it impossible even to go to her, but it was impossible simply to lie down on his feather bed to rest from his weariness. It was necessary before all to perform the mid-day namaz, for which he now had not the slightest inclination, but which it was not only impossible for him not to fulfil in his position as religious leader of his people, but which for him was as necessary as daily food. And so he performed the ablution and the prayer. On finishing the prayer, he summoned those who were waiting for him.

The first to come in was his father-in-law and teacher, a tall, grey-haired, seemly-looking old man with a beard white as snow and a ruddy red face, Jemal ed-Din, who, after saying a prayer, began asking Shamil questions about the events of the campaign and telling him what had happened in the mountains during his absence.

Among all sorts of events—killings in blood feuds, thefts of cattle, accusations of the non-observance of the tariqat: smoking tobacco, drinking wine—Jemal ed-Din told him that Hadji Murat had sent men to take his family out to the Russians, but it had been discovered, and the family had been brought to Vedeno, where it was kept under watch, awaiting the imam's decision. The old men had gathered here in the kunak room to discuss all these matters, and Jemal ed-Din advised Shamil to allow it today, because they had already been waiting three days for him.

Having eaten dinner in his own room, brought to him by Zaidet, his sharp-nosed, dark, unpleasant-looking and unloved but eldest wife, Shamil went to the kunak room.

The six men who made up his council, old men with white, grey, or red beards, with or without turbans, in tall papakhas and new beshmets and cherkeskas, girded by belts with daggers, rose to meet him. Shamil was a head taller than all of them. They all lifted their hands palms up, as he did, and, closing their eyes, recited a prayer, then wiped their faces with their hands, bringing them down along their beards and joining them together. On finishing that, they all sat down, Shamil in the centre on a higher pillow, and began the discussion of all the matters before them.

The cases of persons accused of crimes were decided according to the shariat: two men were sentenced to have a hand cut off for theft, another to have his head cut off for murder, and three were pardoned. Then they went on to the chief matter: considering the measures to be taken against Chechens going over to the Russians. To oppose these defections, Jemal ed-Din had drawn up the following proclamation:

"I wish you eternal peace with God Almighty. I hear that the Russians cajole you and call you to submission. Do not believe them and do not submit, but endure. If you are not rewarded for it in this life, you will be rewarded in the life to come. Remember what happened before, when your weapons were taken away. If God had not brought you to reason then, in 1840, you would now be soldiers and carry bayonets instead of daggers, and your wives would be going about without sharovary and would be dishonoured. Judge the future by the past. It is better to die in enmity with the Russians than to live with infidels. Endure, and I will come to you with the Koran and the sabre and lead you against the Russians. But now I strictly order you to have not only no intention, but even no thought of submitting to the Russians."

Shamil approved this proclamation and, having signed it, decided to have it sent out.

After these matters, the matter of Hadji Murat was also discussed. This matter was very important for Shamil. Though he did not want to admit it, he knew that if Hadji Murat, with his agility, boldness, and courage, had been with him, what had now happened in Chechnya would not have happened. To make peace with Hadji Murat and avail himself of his services again would be a good thing; if that was impossible, it was still impossible to allow him to aid the Russians. And therefore, in any case, it was necessary to make him come back and, once back, to kill him. The means for that was either to send a man to Tiflis who would kill him there, or to make him come here and here put an end to him. There was one means for doing that—his family, and above all his son, whom Shamil knew Hadji Murat loved passionately. And therefore it was necessary to act through the son.

When the councillors had discussed it, Shamil closed his eyes and fell silent.

The councillors knew that this meant he was now listening to the voice of the Prophet speaking to him, prescribing what should be done. After a solemn five-minute silence, Shamil opened his eyes, narrowed them more than usual, and said:

"Bring Hadji Murat's son to me."

"He's here," said Jemal ed-Din.

And indeed Yusuf, Hadji Murat's son, thin, pale, ragged, and stinking, but still handsome in face and body, with the same jet-black eyes as his grandmother Patimat, was already standing at the gate of the outer courtyard waiting to be summoned.

Yusuf did not share his father's feeling for Shamil. He did not know the whole past, or else he did, but, not having lived it, he did not understand why his father was so stubbornly hostile to Shamil. To him, who wanted only one thing—to go on with that easy, dissipated life he had led in Khunzakh as the naïb's son—it seemed totally unnecessary to be hostile to Shamil. In resistance and opposition to his father, he especially admired Shamil and felt the ecstatic veneration for him so widespread in the mountains. With a special feeling of trembling awe of the imam, he now entered the kunak room and, stopping in the doorway, met Shamil's intent, narrowed gaze. He stood there for some time, then went up to Shamil and kissed his big white hand with its long fingers.

"You are Hadji Murat's son?"

"Yes, imam."

"Do you know what he has done?"

"I do, imam, and I am sorry for it."

"Do you know how to write?"

"I was preparing to be a mullah."

"Then write to your father that if he comes back to me now, before bairam, I will forgive him and everything will be as before. If he does not and stays with the Russians, then"—Shamil frowned terribly—"I will hand your grandmother and your mother over to the aouls, and cut your head off."

Not a muscle twitched in Yusuf's face; he bowed his head as a sign that he had understood Shamil's words.

"Write that and give it to my messenger."

Shamil fell silent and looked at Yusuf for a long time.

"Write that I have had pity on you and will not kill you, but will put your eyes out, as I do with all traitors. Go."

Yusuf seemed calm in Shamil's presence, but once he was led out of the kunak room, he fell upon the man who was leading him and, snatching his dagger from its scabbard, tried to kill himself with it, but was seized by the arms, bound, and taken back to the hole.

THAT EVENING, when the evening prayers were over and dusk was falling, Shamil put on his white fur coat and went outside the fence to the part of the courtyard where his wives were quartered, and headed for Aminet's room. But Aminet was not there. She was with the older wives. Then Shamil, trying to go unnoticed, stood behind the door of the room, waiting for her. But Aminet was cross with Shamil, because he had given some silk not to her but to Zaidet. She saw how he came out and went to her room, looking for her, and purposely did not go there. She stood for a long time at the door of Zaidet's room and, laughing quietly, watched the white figure going in and out of her room. Having waited for her in vain, Shamil went back to his quarters when it was already time for the midnight prayers.

XX

HADJI MURAT HAD BEEN LIVING for a week in Ivan Matveevich's house in the fortress. Though Marya Dmitrievna quarrelled with the shaggy Hanefi (Hadji Murat had taken only two men with him: Hanefi and Eldar) and chucked him out of the kitchen once, for which he nearly put a knife in her, she obviously had special feelings of respect and sympathy for Hadji Murat. She no longer served him dinner, having handed that task over to Eldar, but she profited from every chance to see him and please him. She also took the liveliest interest in the negotiations about his family, knew how many wives and children he had, how old they were, and each time a scout came, asked whomever she could about the results of the negotiations.

Butler became very friendly with Hadji Murat during that week.

Sometimes Hadji Murat came to his room, sometimes Butler went to him. Sometimes they conversed through an interpreter, sometimes by their own means—signs and, above all, smiles. Hadji Murat obviously came to love Butler. That was clear from Eldar's attitude towards Butler. When Butler came to Hadji Murat's room, Eldar met him, joyfully baring his gleaming teeth, and rushed to give him pillows to sit on and took off his sabre, if he was wearing it.

Butler also made the acquaintance of and became close with shaggy Hanefi, Hadji Murat's sworn brother. Hanefi knew many mountaineer songs and sang them well. Hadji Murat, to please Butler, would send for Hanefi and order him to sing, naming the songs he considered good. Hanefi had a high tenor voice, and sang with extraordinary distinctness and expression. Hadji Murat especially liked one song, and Butler was struck by its solemn, sad melody. Butler asked the interpreter to tell over its content and wrote it down.

The song had to do with a blood feud—the very one that had existed between Hanefi and Hadji Murat.

It went like this:

"The earth will dry on my grave, and you will forget me, my mother! The graveyard will overgrow with the grass of the graves, and the grass will stifle your grief, my old father. The tears will dry in my sister's eyes, and the grief will fly from her heart.

"But you will not forget me, my older brother, as long as you have not avenged my death. And you will not forget me, my second brother, as long as you're not lying here beside me.

"Hot you are, bullet, and it's death you bear, but have you not been my faithful slave? Black, black earth, you will cover me, but did I not trample you with my horse? Cold you are, death, but I was your master. The earth will take my body, but heaven will receive my soul."

Hadji Murat always listened to this song with closed eyes, and when it ended on a drawn-out, dying-away note, always said in Russian:

"Good song, wise song."

The special, energetic poetry of the mountaineers' life caught Butler up still more with the arrival of Hadji Murat and his closeness with him and his murids. He acquired a beshmet, a cherkeska, leggings, and it seemed to him that he was himself a mountaineer and was living the same life as these people.

On the day of Hadji Murat's departure, Ivan Matveevich gathered several officers to see him off. Some of the officers were sitting at the tea table, where Marya Dmitrievna was serving tea, some at another table, with vodka, chikhir, and snacks, when Hadji Murat, dressed for the road and armed, stepping softly and quickly, came limping into the room.

They all stood up and shook hands with him one by one. Ivan Matveevich invited him to sit on the divan, but he thanked him and sat on a chair by the window. The silence that fell when he came in obviously did not embarrass him in the least. He looked around attentively at all the faces and rested his indifferent gaze on the table with the samovar and snacks. The sprightly officer Petrokovsky, who was seeing Hadji Murat for the first time, asked him through the interpreter whether he liked Tiflis.

"Aya," he said.

"He says 'Yes,' " replied the interpreter.

"What did he like?"

Hadji Murat said something in reply.

"He liked the theatre most of all."

"Well, and did he like the ball at the commander in chief's?"

Hadji Murat frowned.

"Every people has its own customs. Our women do not dress that way," he said, glancing at Marya Dmitrievna.

"So he didn't like it?"

"We have a proverb," he said to the interpreter. "The dog treated the ass to meat, the ass treated the dog to hay—and both went hungry." He smiled. "Every people finds its own customs good."

The conversation went no further. Some of the officers began to take tea, some to eat. Hadji Murat took the offered glass of tea and placed it in front of him.

"What else? Cream? A roll?" said Marya Dmitrievna, offering them to him.

Hadji Murat inclined his head.

"Well, goodbye, then!" said Butler, touching his knee. "When will we see each other?"

"Goodbye! Goodbye!" Hadji Murat said in Russian, smiling. "*Kunak bulur.* You strong *kunak*. Time—*aida*—go," he said, tossing his head as if in the direction in which he had to go.

In the doorway of the room Eldar appeared with something big and white over his shoulder and a sabre in his hand. Hadji Murat beckoned to him, and Eldar went over to Hadji Murat with his long strides and handed him the white burka and the sabre. Hadji Murat stood up and took the burka and, throwing it over his arm, offered it to Marya Dmitrievna, saying something to the interpreter. The interpreter said:

"He says you praised the burka, so take it."

"What for?" said Marya Dmitrievna, blushing.

"It must be so. *Adat so,*" said Hadji Murat.

"Well, thank you," said Marya Dmitrievna, taking the burka. "God grant you rescue your son. *Ulan yakshi,*" she added. "Translate for him that I wish him the rescue of his family."

Hadji Murat glanced at Marya Dmitrievna and nodded his head approvingly. Then he took the sabre from Eldar's hands and gave it to Ivan Matveevich. Ivan Matveevich took the sabre and said to the interpreter:

"Tell him to take my brown gelding, I have nothing else to give him in return."

Hadji Murat waved his hand before his face, indicating that he needed nothing and would not take it, and then, pointing to the mountains and then to his heart, went to the door. They all followed after him. The officers who stayed inside drew the sabre, examined its blade, and decided that it was a real Gurda.[19]

Butler went out to the porch along with Hadji Murat. But here something happened that no one expected and that might have ended with Hadji Murat's death, had it not been for his quick wits, resoluteness, and agility.

The inhabitants of the Kumyk aoul of Tash-Kichu, who had great respect for Hadji Murat and had come to the fortress many times just to look at the famous naïb, had sent envoys to Hadji Murat three days before his departure inviting him to their mosque on Friday. But the Kumyk princes, who lived in Tash-Kichu and hated Hadji Murat and had a blood feud with him, learned of it and announced to the people that they would not allow Hadji Murat into the mosque. The people became agitated, and a fight took place between them and the princes' adherents. The Russian authorities pacified the mountaineers and sent word to Hadji Murat that he should not come to the mosque. Hadji Murat did not go, and everyone thought the matter ended with that.

But at the very moment of Hadji Murat's departure, when he came out to the porch and the horses were standing ready, the Kumyk prince Arslan Khan, whom Butler and Ivan Matveevich knew, rode up to Ivan Matveevich's house.

Seeing Hadji Murat, he snatched a pistol from his belt and aimed it at him. But before Arslan Khan had time to fire, Hadji Murat, despite his lameness, like a cat, suddenly rushed at him from the porch. Arslan Khan fired and missed. Hadji Murat, running up to him, seized the bridle of his horse with one hand, snatched out his dagger with the other, and shouted something in Tartar.

Butler and Eldar simultaneously ran up to the enemies and seized them by the arms. Ivan Matveevich also came out at the sound of the shot.

"What's the meaning of this, Arslan, starting such nastiness at my house!" he said, having learned what it was about. "It's not good, brother. Have your way when it's far away, but don't start slaughtering people on my doorstep."

Arslan Khan, a small man with black moustaches, all pale and trembling, got off his horse, gave Hadji Murat a spiteful look, and went inside with Ivan Matveevich. Hadji Murat returned to the horses, breathing heavily and smiling.

"Why did he want to kill him?" Butler asked through the interpreter.

"He says such is our law," the interpreter transmitted the words of Hadji Murat. "Arslan has to take revenge on him for blood. That's why he wanted to kill him."

"Well, and what if he overtakes him on the way?" asked Butler.

Hadji Murat smiled.

"If he kills me, it means Allah wants it so. Well, goodbye," he said again in Russian and, taking his horse by the withers, he ran his eyes over all those who had come to see him off and his affectionate gaze met that of Marya Dmitrievna.

"Goodbye, dear leddy," he said, addressing her. "Thanking you."

"God grant, God grant you rescue your family," Marya Dmitrievna repeated.

He did not understand her words, but did understand her sympathy for him and nodded his head to her.

"See that you don't forget your kunak," said Butler.

"Tell him I am his faithful friend, I will never forget him," he replied through the interpreter and, despite his crooked leg, as soon as he touched the stirrup, he quickly and lightly swung his body up onto the high saddle and, straightening his sabre, feeling with a habitual gesture for his pistol, acquiring that especially proud, martial look with which a mountaineer sits his horse, he rode away from Ivan Matveevich's house. Hanefi and Eldar also got on their horses and, amicably taking leave of the hosts and officers, went off at a trot after their murshid.

As always, talk sprang up about the departing one.

"Brave fellow!"

"He rushed like a wolf at Arslan Khan, his face was completely changed."

"And he'll play us for fools. Must be a great rogue," said Petrokovsky.

"God grant us more such Russian rogues," Marya Dmitrievna suddenly mixed in vexedly. "He lived a week with us; we saw nothing but good from him," she said. "Courteous, wise, just."

"How did you find all that out?"

"I just did."

"Fell for him, eh?" said Ivan Matveevich, coming in. "No denying it."

"Well, so I fell for him. What is it to you? Only why run him down, if he's a good man? He's a Tartar, but he's good."

"True, Marya Dmitrievna," said Butler. "Good girl for defending him."

XXI

THE LIFE of the inhabitants of the advance fortresses on the Chechen line went on as before. There were two alerts after that, when platoons ran out and Cossacks and militia went galloping, but both times the mountaineers could not be caught. They escaped, and once in Vozdvizhenskoe they killed a Cossack and made off with eight Cossack horses that were being watered. There were no raids since that last time when the aoul was laid waste. But a major expedition into Greater Chechnya was expected as a consequence of the appointment of a new commander of the left flank, Prince Baryatinsky.

Prince Baryatinsky, a friend of the heir to the throne, the former commander of the Kabardinsky regiment, now, as chief of the entire left flank, immediately upon his arrival in Grozny assembled a detachment to continue carrying out the directives of the sovereign, of which Chernyshov had written to Vorontsov. The detachment assembled in Vozdvizhenskoe set off from there to occupy a position in the direction of Kurinskoe. The troops made camp there and were cutting down the forest.

Young Vorontsov lived in a magnificent cloth tent, and his wife, Marya Vassilievna, would come to the camp and often spent the night. Baryatinsky's relations with Marya Vassilievna were no secret from anyone, and therefore the non-court officers and soldiers abused her crudely, because, owing to her presence in the camp, they were sent on night patrol. The mountaineers ordinarily brought up guns and sent cannonballs into the camp. For the most part these cannonballs missed, and therefore in ordinary times no measures were taken against this fire; but to keep the mountaineers from bringing up guns and frightening Marya Vassilievna, patrols were sent out. To go on patrol every night so that a lady would not be frightened was insulting and disgusting, and Marya Vassilievna was berated in indecent terms by the soldiers and the officers not received in high society.

Butler also came to this detachment on leave from his fortress, in order to meet his messmates from the Corps of Pages,[20] who were gathered there, and his regiment mates serving in the Kurinsky regiment and as adjutants and orderly officers at headquarters. At first his visit was very merry. He stayed in Poltoratsky's tent and found many acquaintances there who welcomed him joyfully. He also went to see Vorontsov, whom he knew slightly, because at some point he had served in the same regiment with him. Vorontsov received him very affably, introduced him to Prince Baryatinsky, and invited him to the farewell dinner he was giving for General Kozlovsky, who had been commander of the left flank before Baryatinsky.

The dinner was magnificent. Six tents had been brought and placed side by side. Along the entire length of them there was a covered table, set with dinnerware and bottles. Everything was reminiscent of the life of the guards in Petersburg. At two o'clock they sat down at table. At the middle of the table sat Kozlovsky on one side and Baryatinsky on the other. On either side of Kozlovsky sat the Vorontsovs: the husband to his right, the wife to his left. All down both sides of the table sat the officers of the Kabardinsky and Kurinsky regiments. Butler and Poltoratsky sat next to each other, both chatting away merrily and drinking with the officers next to them. When it came to the roast and the orderlies started pouring glasses of champagne, Poltoratsky, with genuine alarm and regret, said to Butler:

"Our 'like' is going to disgrace himself."

"How so?"

"He's got to make a speech. And how can he?"

"Yes, brother, it's not the same as scaling barricades under a hail of bullets. And with a lady beside him at that, and all these court gentlemen. Really, he's a pity to see," the officers said among themselves.

But now the solemn moment had come. Baryatinsky stood up and, raising his glass, addressed a short speech to Kozlovsky. When Baryatinsky finished, Kozlovsky stood up and in a rather firm voice began:

"By the supreme will of His Majesty I am leaving you, I am parting from you, gentlemen officers," he said. "But always consider me, like, with you . . . Gentlemen, you are familiar, like, with the truth: one man doesn't make an army. Therefore, all the rewards that I have, like, received for my service, all the great bounties, like, showered upon me by the sovereign emperor, like, all my position and, like, my good name—all, decidedly all, like . . ." (here his voice trembled) "I, like, owe only to you, only to you, my dear friends!" And his wrinkled face wrinkled still more. He sobbed and tears welled up in his eyes. "From the bottom of my heart, I offer you, like, my sincere, heartfelt gratitude . . ."

Kozlovsky could not speak any further and, rising, began to embrace the officers who came up to him. Everyone was moved. The princess covered her face with her handkerchief. Prince Semyon Mikhailovich, his mouth twisted, was blinking his eyes. Many of the officers also became tearful. Butler, who knew Kozlovsky very little, could not hold back his tears. He was extremely pleased with it all. Then toasts began for Baryatinsky, for Vorontsov, for the officers, for the soldiers, and the guests left the dinner drunk both with wine and with the martial raptures to which they were so especially inclined.

The weather was wonderful, sunny, still, the air fresh and invigorating. From all sides came the crackle of bonfires, the sounds of singing. It seemed as though everyone was celebrating something. Butler, in the most happy, tender-hearted state of mind, went to Poltoratsky. At

Poltoratsky's some officers had gathered, a card table had been set up, and an adjutant had started a bank of a hundred roubles. Butler twice left the tent clutching his purse in his trouser pocket, but he finally could not control himself and, despite the word he had given himself and his brothers not to gamble, he started to punt.

And before an hour had gone by, Butler, all red, in a sweat, smeared with chalk, sat, both elbows propped on the table, and wrote under the cards creased for corners or transports[21] the amounts of his bets. He had lost so much that he was afraid to count up what was scored against him. He knew without counting that, putting in all the salary he could draw in advance, plus the price of his horse, he still could not cover the debt he had run up to the unknown adjutant. He would have gone on playing, but the adjutant, with a stern face, laid down his cards with his clean, white hands and began to count up Butler's chalk-written column. Butler abashedly begged his pardon because he could not pay at once all that he had lost, and said that he would have it sent from home, and, as he said it, he noticed that they all felt sorry for him, and that all of them, even Poltoratsky, avoided his eyes. This was his last evening. He need only not to have gambled, but to have gone to Vorontsov's, where he had been invited, "and all would be well," he thought. And now it was not only not well, it was terrible.

Having taken leave of his comrades and acquaintances, he went home and, on arriving, immediately went to sleep and slept for eighteen hours straight, as one usually sleeps after losing. From the fact that he asked her for fifty kopecks to tip the Cossack who accompanied him, and from his sad looks and curt replies, Marya Dmitrievna understood that he had lost, and lit into Ivan Matveevich for letting him go.

The next day Butler woke up past eleven and, remembering his situation, wanted to sink back into the oblivion from which he had just emerged, but it was impossible. He had to take measures to pay the four hundred and seventy roubles he owed to the stranger. One of these measures consisted in writing a letter to his brother, confessing his sin and begging him to send him five hundred roubles for this last time, against the mill that still remained their common possession. Then he wrote to a stingy female relation of his, asking her to let him have the same five hundred roubles at any interest she liked. Then he went to Ivan Matveevich and, knowing that he, or rather Marya Dmitrievna, had money, asked him to loan him five hundred roubles.

"I would," said Ivan Matveevich, "I would at once, but Mashka won't let me. These women, devil knows, they're so stingy. But you've got to get out of it, you've got to, devil take it. What about that devil, the sutler?"

But there was no point even in trying to borrow from the sutler. So Butler's salvation could come only from his brother or from the stingy female relation.

XXII

HAVING FAILED to achieve his goal in Chechnya, Hadji Murat returned to Tiflis and went to Vorontsov every day and, when he was received, begged him to gather the captive mountaineers and exchange them for his family. He said again that without that his hands were tied and he could not serve the Russians as he would like to and destroy Shamil. Vorontsov vaguely promised to do what he could, but kept putting it off, saying that he would decide the matter when General Argutinsky came to Tiflis and he could discuss it with him. Then Hadji Murat started asking Vorontsov to allow him to go and live for a time in Nukha, a small town in Transcaucasia, where he supposed it would be easier for him to carry on negotiations about his family with Shamil and with people devoted to him. Besides that, in Nukha, a Muslim town, there was a mosque, where it would be much easier for him to observe the prayers dictated by Muslim law. Vorontsov wrote to Petersburg about it, and meanwhile nevertheless gave Hadji Murat permission to move to Nukha.

For Vorontsov, for the Petersburg authorities, as for the majority of Russian people who knew the story of Hadji Murat, this story represented either a fortunate turn in the Caucasian war or simply an interesting occurrence; but for Hadji Murat it was, especially in recent days, a terrible turn in his life. He had fled from the mountains partly to save himself, partly out of hatred for Shamil, and, difficult as that flight had been, he had achieved his goal, and at first rejoiced in his success and actually considered plans for attacking Shamil. But it turned out that bringing his family over, which he had thought would be easy to arrange, proved more difficult than he had thought. Shamil had seized his family and was holding them captive, promising to hand the women over to the aouls and to kill or blind his son. Now Hadji Murat was moving to Nukha with the intention of trying, through his adherents in Daghestan, to wrest his family from Shamil by cunning or by force. The last scout who visited him in Nukha told him that some Avars devoted to him were planning to steal his family and come over to the Russians with them, but that the people prepared to do that were too few, and that they did not dare to do it in the place of the family's confinement, in Vedeno, but would do it only in case the family was transferred from Vedeno to some other place. Then they promised to do it on the way. Hadji Murat told him to tell his friends that he promised three thousand roubles for the rescue of his family.

In Nukha Hadji Murat was given a small five-room house not far from the mosque and the khan's palace. In the same house lived the officers attached to him, and his interpreter and his nukers. Hadji Murat's life passed in waiting for and receiving scouts from the mountains and in the horseback rides he was allowed to take in the neighbourhood of Nukha.

Returning from his ride on 8 April, Hadji Murat learned that in his absence an official had arrived from Tiflis. Despite all his desire to learn what the official had brought, Hadji Murat, before going to the room where a police commissioner and the official were waiting for him, went to his own room and recited the midday prayer. When he finished the prayer, he came out to the other room, which served him as a drawing room and a reception room. The official from Tiflis, the fat little state councillor Kirillov, conveyed to Hadji Murat the wish of Vorontsov that he come to Tiflis by the twelfth for a meeting with Argutinsky.

"*Yakshi,*" Hadji Murat said angrily.

He did not like the official Kirillov.

"Have you brought the money?"

"I have," said Kirillov.

"It is for two weeks now," said Hadji Murat, and he held up ten fingers and then four. "Give it to me."

"You'll get it at once," said the official, taking a purse from his travelling bag. "What does he need money for?" he said in Russian to the commissioner, supposing that Hadji Murat would not understand, but Hadji Murat understood and glanced angrily at Kirillov. Taking out the money, Kirillov, wishing to strike up a conversation so as to have something to convey to Prince Vorontsov on his return, asked him through the interpreter whether he was bored here. Hadji Murat gave a contemptuous sidelong glance at the fat little man in civilian dress and with no weapons and did not reply. The interpreter repeated the question.

"Tell him I do not want to talk to him. Let him give me the money."

And, having said that, Hadji Murat again sat down at the table, ready to count the money.

When Kirillov had taken out the gold pieces and divided them into seven stacks of ten pieces each (Hadji Murat received five gold pieces a day), he moved them towards Hadji Murat. Hadji Murat swept the gold pieces into the sleeve of his cherkeska, stood up, and quite unexpectedly slapped the state councillor on his bald pate and started out of the room. The state councillor jumped up and told the interpreter to tell Hadji Murat that he dare not do that, because he held the rank of a colonel. The commissioner confirmed the same. But Hadji Murat nodded his head in a sign that he knew it, and walked out of the room.

"What can you do with him?" said the commissioner. "He'll stick a dagger in you and that's that. You can't talk with these devils. I can see he's getting frantic."

As soon as dusk fell, two scouts came from the mountains, bound up to the eyes in their bashlyks. The commissioner led them inside to Hadji Murat. One of the scouts was a beefy, dark Tavlin, the other a thin old man. The news they brought did not gladden Hadji Murat. His friends who had undertaken to rescue his family now refused outright, fearing Shamil, who threatened the most frightful punishments for those who should help Hadji Murat. Having listened to the scouts' story, Hadji Murat rested his hands on his crossed legs and, lowering his head in its papakha, remained silent for a long time. Hadji Murat was thinking, and thinking decisively. He knew that he was now thinking for the last time, and that a decision was necessary. Hadji Murat raised his head and, picking up two gold pieces, gave one to each of the scouts and said:

"Go."

"What will the answer be?"

"The answer will be as God grants. Go."

The scouts rose and left, and Hadji Murat went on sitting on the carpet, his elbows propped on his knees. He sat like that for a long time, thinking.

"What to do? Trust Shamil and return to him?" thought Hadji Murat. "He's a fox—he'll deceive me. Even if he doesn't deceive me, to submit to the red-headed deceiver is impossible. It is impossible because now, after I've been with the Russians, he will never trust me," thought Hadji Murat.

And he remembered a Tavlinian tale about a falcon who was caught, lived with people, and then returned to his mountains to his own kind. He returned, but in jesses, and on the jesses there were little bells. And the falcons did not accept him. "Fly away," they said, "to where they put silver bells on you. We have no bells or jesses." The falcon did not want to leave his native land and stayed. But the other falcons did not accept him and pecked him to death.

"And so they will peck me to death," thought Hadji Murat.

"Stay here? Subjugate the Caucasus for the Russian tsar, earn glory, rank, wealth?"

"It's possible," he thought, recalling his meetings with Vorontsov and the old prince's flattering words.

"But I must decide at once, otherwise he will destroy my family."

All night Hadji Murat lay awake and thought.

XXIII

BY THE MIDDLE of the night his decision was formed. He decided that he must flee to the mountains and break into Vedeno with his faithful Avars, and either die or rescue his family. Whether he would bring his family back to the Russians or flee with them to Khunzakh and fight Shamil— Hadji Murat did not decide. He knew only that right now he must flee from the Russians to the mountains. And he at once began to carry out his decision. He took his black quilted beshmet from under his pillow and went to his nukers' quarters. They lived across the hall. As soon as he went out to the hall, the door to which was open, he was enveloped in the dewy freshness of the moonlit night, and his ears were struck by the whistling and trilling of several nightingales at once from the garden adjoining the house.

Hadji Murat crossed the hall and opened the door of his nukers' room. There was no light in this room, only the young moon in its first quarter shone through the window. A table and two chairs stood to one side, and all four nukers lay on rugs and burkas on the floor. Hanefi slept outside with the horses. Gamzalo, hearing the creak of the door, sat up, turned to look at Hadji Murat, and, recognizing him, lay down again. Eldar, who lay next to him, jumped up and began putting on his beshmet, waiting for orders. Kurban and Khan Mahoma went on sleeping. Hadji Murat put his beshmet on the table, and something solid in the beshmet struck the boards of the table. It was the gold pieces sewn into it.

"Sew these in, too," said Hadji Murat, handing Eldar the gold pieces he had received that day.

Eldar took the gold pieces and, going to a brighter spot, drew the small knife from under his dagger, and at once began to unstitch the lining of the beshmet. Gamzalo raised himself and sat with his legs crossed.

"And you, Gamzalo, tell our brave lads to look over their rifles and pistols and prepare cartridges. We'll have a long ride tomorrow," said Hadji Murat.

"We've got powder, we've got bullets. Everything will be ready," said Gamzalo, and he growled something incomprehensible.

Gamzalo understood why Hadji Murat had ordered the guns loaded. From the very beginning, and more and more strongly as time went on, he had been wishing for one thing: to kill, to cut down as many Russian dogs as he could and flee to the mountains. And now he saw that Hadji Murat wanted the same thing, and he was content.

When Hadji Murat left, Gamzalo woke up his comrades, and all four spent the whole night examining their rifles, pistols, priming, flints, changing the bad ones, pouring fresh powder in the pans, plugging cartridge pockets with measured charges of powder and bullets wrapped in oiled rags, sharpening sabres and daggers and greasing the blades with tallow.

Before daybreak Hadji Murat went out to the hall again to fetch water for his ablutions. In the hall the pre-dawn trilling of the nightingales could be heard, still louder and more rapid than during the night. In the nukers' room could be heard the measured hiss and whistle of steel against stone as daggers were sharpened. Hadji Murat dipped some water from the tub and had already gone back to his door when he heard in the murids' room, besides the sound of sharpening, also the high, thin voice of Hanefi singing a song he knew. He stopped and began to listen.

The song told of how the dzhigit Hamzat and his brave lads stole a herd of white horses from the Russian side. How the Russian prince then overtook him beyond the Terek and surrounded him with his army big as a forest. Then it sang of how Hamzat slaughtered all the horses and hid with his brave lads behind the bloody mound of dead horses and fought as long as there were bullets in their guns and daggers at their belts and blood in their veins. But before he died, Hamzat saw birds in the sky and shouted to them: "You birds of the air, fly to our homes, tell our sisters and mothers and the white-skinned maidens that we all died for the ghazavat. Tell them that our bodies will not lie in graves, but ravenous wolves will rend them and gnaw our bones, and black ravens will peck out our eyes."

With these words the song ended, and to these last words, sung to a mournful tune, was joined the cheerful voice of the merry Khan Mahoma, who cried out at the very end of the song, *"La ilaha il Allah"*— and gave a piercing shriek. Then everything became still, and again only the trilling and whistling of the nightingales in the garden could be heard and from behind the door the measured hiss and occasional whistle of steel rapidly sliding over stone.

Hadji Murat was so deep in thought that he did not notice he had tipped the jug and water was spilling from it. He shook his head at himself and went into his room.

Having completed his morning ablutions, Hadji Murat looked over his weapons and sat on his bed. He had nothing more to do. In order to ride out, he had to ask permission from the police commissioner. But it was still dark outside and the commissioner was still asleep.

Hanefi's song reminded him of another song, one that his mother had made up. This song told about something that had actually happened—it had happened when Hadji Murat was just born, but his mother had told him about it.

The song went like this:

"Your Damascus dagger tore my white breast, yet I put it to my little sun, my boy, I washed him in my hot blood, and the wound healed without herbs and roots, I did not fear death, nor will my dzhigit boy."

The words of this song were addressed to Hadji Murat's father, and the meaning of it was that, when Hadji Murat was born, the khan's wife also gave birth to her next son, Umma Khan, and she summoned Hadji Murat's mother, who had nursed her elder son, Abununtsal, to come to her as a nurse. But Patimat did not want to leave this son and said she would not go. Hadji Murat's father became angry and ordered her to go. When she refused again, he struck her with a dagger and would have killed her, if she had not been taken away. So she did not give him up and nursed him, and made up a song about it.

Hadji Murat remembered that his mother, as she laid him to sleep beside her under a fur coat on the roof of the saklya, sang this song to him, and he asked her to show him the place on her side where the scar of the wound was left. He saw his mother before him as if alive—not wrinkled, grey-haired, and gap-toothed as he had left her now, but young, beautiful, and so strong that, when he was five years old and already heavy, she had carried him over the mountains to his grandfather in a basket on her back.

And he remembered, too, his grandfather, wrinkled, with a little grey beard, a silversmith, as he chased silver with his sinewy hands and made his grandson recite prayers. He remembered a spring at the foot of a hill where he used to go to fetch water with his mother, clinging to her sharovary. He remembered a skinny dog who used to lick his face, and especially the smell and taste of smoke and sour milk, when he followed his mother to the shed, where she milked the cow and baked the milk. He remembered how his mother shaved his head for the first time and how surprised he was to see his round, bluish little head in the gleaming copper basin that hung on the wall.

And, remembering himself as little, he also remembered his beloved son Yusuf, whose head he himself had shaved for the first time. Now this Yusuf was already a handsome young dzhigit. He remembered his son as he was the last time he saw him. That was the day he rode out of Tselmes. His son brought him his horse and asked permission to accompany him. He was dressed and armed, and held his own horse by the bridle. Yusuf's ruddy, handsome young face and his whole tall, slender figure (he was taller than his father) breathed the courage of youth and the joy of life. His broad shoulders, despite his age, his broad, youthful hips and long, slender body, his long, strong arms, and the strength, suppleness, agility of all his movements were a joy to see, and his father always admired his son.

"You'd better stay. You're alone in the house now. Take care of your mother and your grandmother," Hadji Murat said.

And Hadji Murat remembered the expression of bravado and pride with which Yusuf, blushing with pleasure, said that, as long as he lived, no one would harm his mother and grandmother. Yusuf mounted his horse all the same and rode with his father as far as the brook. At the brook he turned back, and since then Hadji Murat had not seen his wife, his mother, or his son.

And this was the son that Shamil wanted to blind! Of what would be done to his wife and mother he did not even want to think.

These thoughts so agitated Hadji Murat that he could not go on sitting there. He jumped up and, limping, went quickly to the door and, opening it, called Eldar. The sun had not yet risen, but it was quite light. The nightingales were still singing.

"Go and tell the commissioner that I want to go for a ride, and saddle the horses," he said.

XXIV

BUTLER'S ONLY CONSOLATION at that time was the poetry of military life, to which he gave himself not only on duty, but in private life as well. Dressed in Circassian costume, he went caracoling on horseback and twice lay in ambush with Bogdanovich, though they did not catch or kill anyone either time. This boldness and his friendship with the notoriously brave Bogdanovich seemed to Butler to be something pleasant and important. He had paid his debt by borrowing the money from a Jew at enormous interest—that is, he had only deferred and avoided the unresolved situation. He tried not to think about his situation and, besides the poetry of martial life, sought oblivion in wine. He drank more and more, and morally became weaker and weaker from day to day. He no longer played the handsome Joseph in relation to Marya Dmitrievna,[22] but, on the contrary, began courting her crudely, but, to his surprise, met with a decided rebuff, which shamed him greatly.

At the end of April, a detachment came to the fortress, destined by Baryatinsky for a new movement across the whole of Chechnya, which was considered impassable. There were two companies of the Kabardinsky regiment, and these companies, according to an established custom of the Caucasus, were received as guests by the companies stationed in Kurinskoe. The soldiers were dispersed among the barracks and were treated not only to a supper of kasha and beef, but also to vodka, and the officers were lodged with officers and, as was done, the local officers treated the newcomers.

The regalement ended with drinking and singing, and Ivan Matveevich, very drunk, no longer red but pale grey, sat astride a chair and, snatching out his sabre, cut down his imaginary enemies, and cursed, then guffawed, then embraced people, then sang his favourite song: "Shamil rose up in years gone by, too-ra-lee, too-ra-lye, in years gone by."

Butler was there. He tried to see the poetry of martial life in it, but deep in his heart he felt sorry for Ivan Matveevich, but to stop him was in no way possible. And Butler, the drink having gone to his head, quietly left and went home.

A full moon shone upon the white houses and the stones of the road. It was so bright that every little stone, straw, and bit of dung could be seen on the road. Nearing the house, Butler met Marya Dmitrievna in a kerchief that covered her head and shoulders. After the rebuff Marya Dmitrievna had given him, Butler, slightly ashamed, had avoided meeting her. Now, with the moonlight and after the wine he had drunk, Butler was glad of this meeting and again wanted to be tender with her.

"Where are you going?" he asked.

"To see how my old man's doing," she replied amicably. She had rejected his courtship quite sincerely and decisively, but had found it unpleasant that he had shunned her all the time recently.

"Why go looking for him—he'll come."

"Will he?"

"If he doesn't, they'll bring him."

"Right, and that's not good," said Marya Dmitrievna. "So I shouldn't go?"

"No, you shouldn't. Better let's go home."

Marya Dmitrievna turned and walked back home beside Butler. The moon shone so brightly that their shadows, moving along the road, had a moving halo around the heads. Butler looked at this halo around his head and was getting ready to tell her that he still liked her just as much, but he did not know how to begin. She was waiting for what he would say. Thus, in silence, they had already come quite close to home when some horsemen came riding around the corner. It was an officer with an escort.

"Who is God sending us now?" Marya Dmitrievna said and stepped aside.

The moon shone behind the rider, so that Marya Dmitrievna recognized him only when he had come almost even with them. It was the officer Kamenev, who had served formerly with Ivan Matveevich, and therefore Marya Dmitrievna knew him.

"Pyotr Nikolaevich, is that you?" Marya Dmitrievna addressed him.

"Himself," said Kamenev. "Ah, Butler! Greetings! You're not asleep yet? Strolling with Marya Dmitrievna? Watch out, you'll get it from Ivan Matveevich. Where is he?"

"Just listen," said Marya Dmitrievna, pointing in the direction from which the sounds of a tulumbas and songs were coming. "They're carousing."

"What, your people?"

"No, there are some from Khasav Yurt, they're living it up."

"Ah, that's good. I'll still have time. I only need to see him for a minute."

"What, on business?" asked Butler.

"Minor business."

"Good or bad?"

"That depends! For us it's good, but for somebody else it's rather nasty." And Kamenev laughed.

Just then the walkers and Kamenev reached Ivan Matveevich's house.

"Chikhirev!" Kamenev called to a Cossack. "Come here."

A Don Cossack moved away from the others and rode up to them. He was wearing an ordinary Don Cossack uniform, boots, a greatcoat, and had saddlebags behind his saddle.

"Well, take the thing out," said Kamenev, getting off his horse.

The Cossack also got off his horse and took a sack with something in it from his saddlebag. Kamenev took the sack from the Cossack's hands and put his hand into it.

"So, shall I show you our news? You won't be frightened?" he turned to Marya Dmitrievna.

"What's there to be afraid of?" said Marya Dmitrievna.

"Here it is," said Kamenev, taking out a human head and holding it up in the moonlight. "Recognize him?"

It was a head, shaved, with large projections of the skull over the eyes and a trimmed black beard and clipped moustache, with one eye open and the other half closed, the shaved skull split but not all the way through, the bloody nose clotted with black blood. The neck was wrapped in a bloody towel. Despite all the wounds to the head, the blue lips were formed into a kindly, childlike expression.

Marya Dmitrievna looked and, without saying a word, turned and went quickly into the house.

Butler could not take his eyes from the terrible head. It was the head of the same Hadji Murat with whom he had so recently spent evenings in such friendly conversation.

"How can it be? Who killed him? Where?" he asked.

"He tried to bolt and got caught," said Kamenev, and he handed the head back to the Cossack and went into the house with Butler.

"And he died a brave man," said Kamenev.

"But how did it all happen?"

"Just wait a little. Ivan Matveevich will come, and I'll tell you all about it in detail. That's why I've been sent. I carry it around to all the fortresses and aouls and display it."

They sent for Ivan Matveevich, and he came home drunk, with two officers just as badly drunk, and started embracing Kamenev.

"I've come to see you," said Kamenev. "I've brought the head of Hadji Murat."

"You're joking! Killed?"

"Yes, he tried to escape."

"I told you he'd play us for fools. So where is it? This head? Show me."

They called for the Cossack, and he brought in the sack with the head. The head was taken out, and Ivan Matveevich looked at it for a long time with drunken eyes.

"He was a fine fellow all the same," he said. "Let me kiss him."

"Yes, true, he was quite a daredevil," said one of the officers.

When they had all examined the head, it was handed back to the Cossack. The Cossack put the head into the sack, trying to lower it to the floor so that it would not bump too hard.

"And you, Kamenev, what do you tell people when you show it?" asked one of the officers.

"No, let me kiss him. He gave me a sabre," cried Ivan Matveevich.

Butler went out to the porch. Marya Dmitrievna was sitting on the second step. She glanced at Butler and at once turned away angrily.

"What's the matter, Marya Dmitrievna?" asked Butler.

"You're all butchers. I can't bear it. Real butchers," she said, getting up.

"The same could happen to anyone," said Butler, not knowing what to say. "That's war."

"War!" cried Marya Dmitrievna. "What war? You're butchers, that's all. A dead body should be put in the ground, and they just jeer. Real butchers," she repeated and stepped off the porch and went into the house through the back door.

Butler went back to the drawing room and asked Kamenev to tell in detail how the whole thing happened.

And Kamenev told them.

It happened like this.

XXV

HADJI MURAT WAS ALLOWED to go riding in the vicinity of town, but only with a Cossack escort. There were some fifty Cossacks in Nukha, of whom some ten were attached to the superior officers, while the rest, if they were to be sent out ten at a time, as had been ordered, had to be detailed every other day. And therefore on the first day they sent ten Cossacks, and then decided to send five, asking Hadji Murat not to take all his nukers with him, but on 25 April Hadji Murat went out riding with all five of them. As Hadji Murat was mounting his horse, the commander noticed that all five nukers were about to go with him, and told him that he was not allowed to take them all, but Hadji Murat seemed not to hear, touched up his horse, and the commander did not insist. With the Cossacks there was a corporal with a bowl haircut, holder of a St. George's Cross, a young, ruddy, healthy, brown-haired lad named Nazarov. He was the eldest son of a poor family of Old Believers,[23] had grown up without a father, and supported his old mother, three sisters, and two brothers.

"Watch out, Nazarov, don't let them go too far!" cried the commander.

"Yes, sir, Your Honour," replied Nazarov and, rising in his stirrups and grasping the rifle at his back, he sent his good, big, hook-nosed sorrel gelding into a trot. Four Cossacks rode after him: Ferapontov, tall, skinny, a first-rate thief and double-dealer—the one who had sold powder to Gamzalo; Ignatov, serving out his term, no longer young, a robust peasant proud of his strength; Mishkin, a weakly youngster whom everyone made fun of; and Petrakov, young, fair-haired, his mother's only son, always cheerful and affectionate.

There was mist in the morning, but by breakfast time the weather cleared, and the sun glistened on the just-opening leaves, and on the young, virginal grass, and on the sprouting grain, and on the ripples of the swift river, which could be glimpsed to the left of the road.

Hadji Murat rode at a walk. The Cossacks and his nukers followed him without dropping back. They rode at a walk down the road outside the fortress. They met women with baskets on their heads, soldiers on wagons, and creaking carts drawn by buffaloes. After riding for about a mile and a half, Hadji Murat touched up his white Kabarda stallion; it went into a canter, so that his nukers had to switch to a long trot. The Cossacks did the same.

"Eh, he's got a good horse under him," said Ferapontov. "If only we weren't at peace, I'd unseat him."

"Yes, brother, three hundred roubles were offered for that horse in Tiflis."

"But I'll outrace him on mine," said Nazarov.

"Outrace him, ha!" said Ferapontov.

Hadji Murat kept increasing his pace.

"Hey, kunak, that's not allowed. Slow down!" cried Nazarov, going after Hadji Murat.

Hadji Murat looked back and, saying nothing, went on riding without diminishing his pace.

"Watch out, they're up to something, the devils," said Ignatov. "Look at 'em whipping along!"

They rode like that for about half a mile in the direction of the mountains.

"I said it's not allowed," Nazarov cried again.

Hadji Murat did not reply and did not look back, but only increased his pace and from a canter went into a gallop.

"Oh, no, you won't get away!" cried Nazarov, stung to the quick.

He whipped up his big sorrel gelding and, rising in the stirrups and leaning forward, sent him at full speed after Hadji Murat.

The sky was so clear, the air so fresh, the forces of life played so joyfully in Nazarov's soul as he merged into one with his good, strong horse and flew along the level road after Hadji Murat, that the possibility of anything bad or sad or terrible never entered his head. He rejoiced that with every stride he was gaining on Hadji Murat and coming closer to him. Hadji Murat figured from the hoofbeats of the Cossack's big horse, coming ever closer to him, that he would shortly overtake him, and, putting his right hand to his pistol, with his left he began to rein in his excited Kabarda, who could hear the hoofbeats of a horse behind him.

"It's not allowed, I said!" cried Nazarov, coming almost even with Hadji Murat and reaching out his hand to seize the horse's bridle. But before he could seize it, a shot rang out.

"What are you doing?" Nazarov cried, clutching his chest. "Strike them down, lads," he said and, reeling, fell onto his saddlebow.

But the mountaineers seized their weapons before the Cossacks and shot them with their pistols and slashed them with their sabres. Nazarov was hanging on the neck of his frightened horse, which carried him in circles around his comrades. Ignatov's horse fell under him, crushing his leg. Two of the mountaineers, drawing their sabres without dismounting, slashed at his head and arms. Petrakov made a dash for his comrade, but at once two shots, one in the back, the other in the side, seared him, and he tumbled from his horse like a sack.

Mishkin wheeled his horse around and galloped off to the fortress. Hanefi and Khan Mahoma rushed after Mishkin, but he was already far away and the mountaineers could not catch him.

Seeing that they could not catch the Cossack, Hanefi and Khan Mahoma went back to their own people. Gamzalo, having finished off Ignatov with his dagger, also put it into Nazarov, after pulling him from his horse. Khan Mahoma was taking pouches of shot from the dead men. Hanefi wanted to take Nazarov's horse, but Hadji Murat shouted that he should not and set off down the road. His murids galloped after him, driving away Petrakov's horse, who came running after them. They were already two miles from Nukha, in the midst of the rice fields, when a shot rang out from the tower sounding the alarm.

Petrakov lay on his back with his stomach slit open, and his young face was turned to the sky, and he blubbered like a fish as he was dying.

"O LORD, saints alive, what have they done!" cried the commander of the fortress, clutching his head, when he heard about Hadji Murat's escape. "My head will roll! They let him slip, the brigands!" he cried, hearing Mishkin's report.

The alarm was given everywhere, and not only were all the available Cossacks sent after the fugitives, but they gathered all the militia that could be gathered from the peaceful aouls. A thousand-rouble reward was offered to the one who would bring in Hadji Murat dead or alive. And two hours after Hadji Murat and his comrades galloped away from the Cossacks, more than two hundred mounted men galloped after the police commissioner to seek out and capture the fugitives.

Having ridden several miles along the high road, Hadji Murat reined in his heavily breathing white horse, who had gone grey with sweat, and stopped. To the right of the road the saklyas and minaret of the aoul of Belardzhik could be seen, to the left were fields, and at the end of them a river was visible. Though the way to the mountains was to the right, Hadji Murat turned in the opposite direction, to the left, reckoning that the pursuit would rush after him precisely to the right. Whereas he, leaving the road and crossing the Alazan, would come out on the high road, where no one would expect him, and would go down it to the forest, and then, crossing the river again, would make his way through the forest to the mountains. Having decided that, he turned to the left. But it proved impossible to reach the river. The rice field they had to ride through, as was always done in the spring, had just been flooded with water and had turned into a bog, into which the horses sank over their pasterns. Hadji Murat and his nukers turned right, left, thinking to find a drier place, but the field they had happened upon was all evenly flooded and now soaked with water. With the sound of corks popping, the horses pulled their sinking feet from the oozy mud and stopped after every few steps, breathing heavily.

They struggled like that for so long that dusk began to fall, but they still had not reached the river. To the left there was a little island of bushes coming into leaf, and Hadji Murat decided to ride into these bushes and stay there till night, giving a rest to the exhausted horses.

Having entered the bushes, Hadji Murat and his nukers dismounted and, after hobbling the horses, left them to feed, and themselves ate some bread and cheese that they had taken with them. The young moon, which shone at first, went down behind the mountains, and the night was dark. In Nukha there were especially many nightingales. There were two in these bushes. While Hadji Murat and his men made noise, entering the bushes, the nightingales fell silent. But when the men became quiet, they again began to trill and call to each other. Hadji Murat, his ear alert to the sounds of the night, involuntarily listened to them.

And their whistling reminded him of that song about Hamzat, which he had listened to the night before when he went out for water. At any moment now he could be in the same situation as Hamzat. It occurred to him that it even would be so, and his soul suddenly became serious. He spread out his burka and performed his namaz. He had only just finished when he heard sounds approaching the bushes. These were the sounds of a large number of horses' feet splashing through the bog. The quick-eyed Khan Mahoma, having run out alone to the edge of the bushes, spotted in the darkness the black shadows of men on horseback and on foot approaching the bushes. Hanefi saw a similar crowd on the other side. It was Karganov,[24] the district military commander, with his militia.

"So we shall fight like Hamzat," thought Hadji Murat.

After the alarm was given, Karganov, with a company of militia and Cossacks, had rushed in pursuit of Hadji Murat, but had not found him or any trace of him anywhere. Karganov was already returning home without hope when, towards evening, he met an old Tartar. Karganov asked the old man if he had seen six horsemen. The old man answered that he had. He had seen six horsemen circle about in the rice field and enter the bushes where he used to gather firewood. Karganov, taking the old man along, turned back and, convinced at the sight of the hobbled horses that Hadji Murat was there, surrounded the bushes during the night and waited for morning to take Hadji Murat dead or alive.

Realizing that he was surrounded, Hadji Murat spotted an old ditch among the bushes and decided to position himself in it and fight for as long as he had shot and strength. He said this to his comrades and told them to make a mound along the ditch. And the nukers set to work at once cutting branches and digging up the earth with their daggers, making an embankment. Hadji Murat worked with them.

As soon as it became light, the company commander rode up close to the bushes and called out:

"Hey! Hadji Murat! Surrender! There are many of us and few of you!"

In reply to that a puff of smoke appeared from the ditch, a rifle cracked, and a bullet struck the militiaman's horse, who shied under him and began to fall. Following that came a crackle of rifle fire from the militiamen standing at the edge of the bushes, and their bullets, whistling and droning, knocked off leaves and branches and struck the mound, but did not hit the people sitting behind it. Only Gamzalo's horse, who had strayed, was hurt by them. He was wounded in the head. He did not fall, but snapped his hobble and, crashing through the bushes, rushed to the other horses and, pressing himself against them, drenched the young grass with blood. Hadji Murat and his men fired only when one of the militiamen stepped out, and they rarely missed their aim. Three of the militiamen were wounded, and the militiamen not only did not venture to rush Hadji Murat and his men, but retreated further and further from them and fired only from a distance, at random.

It went on like that for more than an hour. The sun had risen half the height of a tree, and Hadji Murat was already thinking of mounting up and trying to get through to the river, when he heard the shouts of a large party that had just arrived. This was Ghadji Aga of Mekhtuli with his men. There were about two hundred of them. Ghadji Aga had once been Hadji Murat's kunak and had lived with him in the mountains, but then had gone over to the Russians. With him was Akhmet Khan, the son of Hadji Murat's enemy. Ghadji Aga, like Karganov, began by shouting to Hadji Murat to surrender, but, like the first time, Hadji Murat replied with a shot.

"Sabres out, lads!" cried Ghadji Aga, snatching out his own, and a hundred voices were heard as men rushed shrieking into the bushes.

The militiamen ran into the bushes, but from behind the mound several shots cracked out one after the other. Three men fell, and the attackers stopped and also started firing from the edge of the bushes. They fired and at the same time gradually approached the mound, running from bush to bush. Some managed to make it, some fell under the bullets of Hadji Murat and his men. Hadji Murat never missed, and Gamzalo also rarely wasted a shot and shrieked joyfully each time he saw his bullet hit home. Kurban was sitting on the edge of the ditch, singing *"La ilaha il Allah"* and firing unhurriedly, but rarely hitting anything. Eldar was trembling all over from impatience to rush at the enemies with his dagger and fired frequently and at random, constantly turning to look at Hadji Murat and thrusting himself up from behind the mound. The shaggy Hanefi, his sleeves rolled up, performed the duties of a servant here, too. He loaded the guns that Hadji Murat and Kurban passed to him, taking bullets wrapped in oiled rags and carefully ramming them home with an iron ramrod, and pouring dry powder into the pans from a flask. Khan Mahoma did not sit in the ditch like the others, but kept running between the ditch and the horses, driving them to a safer place, and constantly shrieked and fired freehand without a prop. He was the first to be wounded. A bullet hit him in the neck, and he sat down, spitting blood and cursing. Then Hadji Murat was wounded. A bullet pierced his shoulder. Hadji Murat pulled some cotton wool from his beshmet, stopped the wound with it, and went on firing.

"Let's rush them with our sabres," Eldar said for the third time.

He thrust himself up from behind the mound, ready to rush at his enemies, but just then a bullet hit him, and he reeled and fell backwards onto Hadji Murat's leg. Hadji Murat glanced at him. The beautiful sheep's eyes looked at Hadji Murat intently and gravely. The mouth, its upper lip pouting like a child's, twitched without opening. Hadji Murat freed his leg from under him and went on aiming. Hanefi bent over the slain Eldar and quickly began taking the unused cartridges from his cherkeska. Kurban, singing all the while, slowly loaded and took aim.

The enemy, running from bush to bush with whoops and shrieks, was moving closer and closer. Another bullet hit Hadji Murat in the left side. He lay back in the ditch and, tearing another wad of cotton wool from his beshmet, stopped the wound. This wound in the side was fatal, and he felt that he was dying. Memories and images replaced one another with extraordinary swiftness in his imagination. Now he saw before him the mighty Abununtsal Khan, holding in place his severed, hanging cheek as he rushed at the enemy with a dagger in his hand; now he saw the weak, bloodless old Vorontsov, with his sly, white face, and heard his soft voice; now he saw his son Yusuf, now his wife Sofiat, now the pale face, red beard, and narrowed eyes of his enemy Shamil.

And all these memories ran through his imagination without calling up any feeling in him: no pity, no anger, no desire of any sort. It all seemed so insignificant compared with what was beginning and had already begun for him. But meanwhile his strong body went on doing what had been started. He gathered his last strength, rose up from behind the mound, and fired his pistol at a man running towards him and hit him. The man fell. Then he got out of the hole altogether and, limping badly, walked straight ahead with his dagger to meet his enemies. Several shots rang out, he staggered and fell. Several militiamen, with a triumphant shriek, rushed to the fallen body. But what had seemed to them a dead body suddenly stirred. First the bloodied, shaven head, without a papakha, rose, then the body rose, and then, catching hold of a tree, he rose up entirely. He looked so terrible that the men running at him stopped. But he suddenly shuddered, staggered away from the tree, and, like a mowed-down thistle, fell full length on his face and no longer moved.

He no longer moved, but he still felt. When Ghadji Aga, who was the first to run up to him, struck him on the head with his big dagger, it seemed to him that he had been hit with a hammer, and he could not understand who was doing it and why. That was his last conscious connection with his body. After that he no longer felt anything, and his enemies trampled and hacked at what no longer had anything in common with him. Ghadji Aga, placing his foot on the back of the body, cut the head off with two strokes, and carefully, so as not to stain his chuviaki with blood, rolled it aside with his foot. Bright red blood gushed from the neck arteries and black blood from the head, flowing over the grass.

Karganov, and Ghadji Aga, and Akhmet Khan, and all the militiamen, like hunters over a slain animal, gathered over the bodies of Hadji Murat and his men (Hanefi, Kurban, and Gamzalo had been bound) and, standing there in the bushes amid the powder smoke, talked merrily, exulting in their victory.

The nightingales, who had fallen silent during the shooting, again started trilling, first one close by and then others further off.

THIS WAS the death I was reminded of by the crushed thistle in the midst of the ploughed field.

1896–1904

GLOSSARY OF CAUCASIAN MOUNTAINEER WORDS

(The speech of the Caucasus is made up of words from Tartar, Persian, Arabic, Chechen, Nogai, and other local languages. Accents have been added to indicate pronunciation.)

ADÁT Custom

AIDÁ Come

AMANÁT Hostage

AÓUL Tartar mountain village

AYA Yes

BAIRÁM Name of two Muslim festivals: Uraza (Lesser) Bairam, which ends the fast of Ramadan, and Kurban (Greater) Bairam, which comes seventy days later and commemorates the story of Abraham and Isaac

BAR Have

BASHLÝK Hood with long ends wrapped around the neck as a scarf

BESHMÉT Upper garment fitted and buttoned from waist to neck and hanging to the knees

BÚRKA Long, round felt cape with decorative fastening at the neck

CHERKÉSKA Outer garment overlapping on the chest and belted, with rows of individual cartridge pockets on each side, worn over the beshmet

CHIKHÍR Young red wine

CHINÁRA Plane tree

CHUVIÁKI Soft leather shoes, often worn under wooden shoes

DZHIGÍT Bold, showy horseman, fine fellow, "brave"

GHAZAVÁT Muslim holy war against infidels

GIAÓUR Perjorative term applied by Muslims to non-Muslims, especially Christians

IMÁM Muslim priest, leader or chief combining worldly and spiritual authority

KHAN Originally a title given to the successors of Genghis Khan; later a common title given even to very minor rulers or officials in Central Asia; Russians created the word *khansha* for a khan's wife

KIZYÁK Fuel made from dung and straw

KOSHKÓLDY Good health and peace (greeting)

KUMGÁN Tall jar with spout and lid

KUNÁK Sworn friend, adoptive brother

MURÍD One who follows the mystical-religious path of Muridis, a movement that spread through the northern Caucasus in the nineteenth century, a form of Sufism connected with aspiration for an Islamic state free of Russian dominance; used here to mean adjutant or bodyguard

MURSHÍD One who leads murids on the path

NAÍB Lieutenant or administrator appointed by the imam Shamil

NAMÁZ Muslim prayers and ablutions performed five times a day

NOGÁI A Tartar people said to be descended from Nogai Khan, grandson of Genghis Khan, settled in Daghestan, Cherkessia, and along the Black Sea

NÚKER Attendant, bodyguard

PAPÁKHA Tall hat, usually of lambskin, often with a flat top

PESHKÉSH Gift

SÁKLYA Clay-plastered house, often built of earth, with a large shaded porch in front

SALÁAM ALÉIKUM Peace be with you (greeting)

SARDÁR Chief administrator or military commander; title given to the Russian emperor's representative in the Caucasus

SAUBÚL Good health to you (greeting)

SHARIÁT Islamic written law, in the Koran and other texts

SHAROVÁRY Balloon trousers

TARIQÁT The "path" (rules) of ascetic life

TULÚMBAS A percussion instrument

YAKSHÍ Good

YOK No, not

THE PRISONER OF THE CAUCASUS

1. "Ivan" was a generic name for Russians among the Caucasian mountaineers. Tolstoy never gives Zhilin a first name.

2. *Bismillah al-rahman al-rahimi* ("In the name of God, the most gracious, the most merciful") is the opening phrase of every chapter but one of the Koran, and is also used in the call to daily prayers.

THE DIARY OF A MADMAN

1. See Matthew 7:7, Luke 11:9.

2. "Tempting" in the older, biblical sense of putting to the test, involving the risk of doubt or disbelief.

3. See Matthew 5:45 (RSV): "that you may be sons of your Father who is in heaven."

4. In the Orthodox Church, a *prosphora* (Greek for "offering") is a small roll of leavened bread offered by an individual for the sacrament of communion. After blessing it and removing a piece for the common chalice, the priest returns the prosphora to the communicant, who may share it with others.

THE DEATH OF IVAN ILYICH

1. *Vint* is a Russian card game similar to auction bridge.

2. In 1722, the emperor Peter the Great (1672–1725) established a table of fourteen ranks for Russian civil servants, rising in importance from fourteenth to first.

3. I. G. Charmeur was a well-known Petersburg tailor of the time.

4. Donon's restaurant, opened by the entrepreneur Zh. B. Donon in 1849, was one of the most fashionable in Petersburg.

5. The Old Believers, also known as Raskolniki (schismatics), rejected the reforms introduced in the mid-seventeenth century by the patriarch Nikon (1605–81), head of the Russian Orthodox Church. Historically, their relations with the civil administration were often strained.

6. The emperor Alexander II (1818–81) carried out a series of important legal reforms in 1864, establishing a new court system and trial by jury, among other things.

7. See note 2 above.

8. The empress Maria Alexandrovna (1824–80), wife of Alexander II, took over the administration of a number of charitable and philanthropic institutions, including the Petersburg Foundling Home, women's educational institutions, and three banks.

9. Johann Gottfried Kiesewetter (1766–1819), German philosopher and follower of Immanuel Kant, was the author of many works, including a manual of logic which was translated into Russian. The syllogism about Caius actually appears in his manual.

10. Sarah Bernhardt (1844–1923), the most famous French actress of her day, performed several times in Russia during the 1880s.

11. That is, combed forward in a fringe.

12. A play about the eighteenth-century French actress Adrienne Lecouvreur, by Augustin Scribe (1791–1861) and Gabriel Legouvé (1764–1812). It was one of Sarah Bernhardt's principal roles.

THE KREUTZER SONATA

1. The Epistle to the Ephesians 5:22–33 is read during the Orthodox marriage service. The final verse, ". . . and let the wife see that she respects her husband" (RSV), is translated into Slavonic as ". . . that she fears her husband."

2. The *Domostroy* ("Domestic Order") was a set of household rules (religious, social, and domestic) established in the sixteenth century. It came to have negative implications of old-fashioned patriarchal strictness and narrow-mindedness.

3. Marshal of the nobility was the highest elective office in a province before the reforms of Alexander II (see note 6 to *The Death of Ivan Ilyich*).

4. In pre-revolutionary Russia, religious education was part of the school programme.

5. The dancer and singer Marguerite Badel, known as Rigolboche, was

briefly popular in Paris in the mid-nineteenth century. She published her memoirs in 1860. The name came to mean someone who likes amusement.

6. The German philosopher Arthur Schopenhauer (1788–1860), sometimes characterized as an "atheist idealist," was influenced by Plato and Kant, but also by Hindu and Buddhist thought. Eduard von Hartmann (1842–1906), a follower of Schopenhauer, published his most influential work, *The Philosophy of the Unconscious*, in 1869. Pozdnyshev uses the term "Buddhist" in the "nihilist" sense first defined by Schopenhauer.

7. Among the Russian lower classes, hysterical women, known as "shriekers," were thought to be possessed by the devil. Dostoevsky describes the phenomenon in the chapter "Women of Faith" from *The Brothers Karamazov*.

8. Jean-Martin Charcot (1825–93) was a pioneering French neurologist who used hypnosis and "Charcot baths" in the treatment of hysteria.

9. Mnesarete, nicknamed Phryne (toad), was a hetaira of fourth-century Athens, famous for her beauty and for her high prices. The sculptor Praxiteles, one of her lovers, was said to have modelled his Aphrodite of Knidos on her. The area around Trubnaya Square and Trubnaya Street (formerly Grachevka Street) in Moscow was known for its houses of prostitution.

10. A *kokoshnik* is a characteristic Russian peasant woman's headdress, with a high, rigid front, often pointed, decorated with gold braid, pearls, or embroidery.

11. See note 1 to *The Death of Ivan Ilyich*.

12. Trukhachevsky is a perfectly plausible Russian name formed from *trukha*, which means the dust of rotten wood or, figuratively, rubbish in general.

13. Uriah's wife was Bathsheba, who was taken from her husband by King David (see II Samuel 11:2–26).

14. Vanka the Steward is the hero of a Russian folk song.

THE DEVIL

1. Tolstoy's *lapsus:* earlier the name was Pechnikov.

2. A Russian superstition which survived at least until the time of World War II, if not longer.

3. Pentecost, the feast of the descent of the Holy Spirit, comes fifty days after Easter.

4. Holy Week is the week preceding Easter Sunday, which means that the house had not been cleaned for some seven weeks.

5. See note 3 to *The Kreutzer Sonata*.

6. The *zemstvo*, a local council for self-government, was introduced in 1864 by the reforms of Alexander II.

7. See note 6 to *The Death of Ivan Ilyich*.

MASTER AND MAN

1. The winter feast of St. Nicholas is celebrated on 6 December; on 9 May there is the feast of the Translation of the Relics of St. Nicholas (the moving of the saint's relics from Asia Minor to Bari, Italy, in the eleventh century).

2. Merchants were classified in guilds according to the amount of capital they had.

3. The Advent Fast begins on 14 November and continues until Christmas.

4. The Russian stove is an elaborate construction, used essentially for heating and cooking, but also for drying clothes and even for sleeping.

5. The reference is to the school *Reader* by the well-known Russian pedagogue I. I. Paulson (1825–98).

6. Misquoted lines from the poem "Winter Evening" by Alexander Pushkin (1799–1837).

FATHER SERGIUS

1. The emperor Nikolai I (1796–1855), later referred to as Nikolai Pavlovich, came to the Russian throne in 1825, on the death of his brother Alexander I.

2. The Cadet Corps, founded in 1732 for sons of the nobility, was one of the most prestigious military schools in Russia. It furnished many generations of officers before it was closed in 1917.

3. A *dacha* is a summer residence. Tsarskoe Selo, a village some fifteen miles south of Petersburg, had been an imperial property since the time of Peter the Great. Many members of the court nobility built summer homes there.

4. It became fashionable among the Russian nobility after the Napoleonic invasion (1812) to adopt the English forms of first names.

5. The feast of the Protection (more fully, of the Protective Veil of the Mother of God) falls on 1 October .

6. Paissy Velichkovsky (1722–94) is considered the "father of the Russian elders," monks who serve as personal spiritual guides to fellow monks and laymen (cf. the elder Zosima in Dostoevsky's *Brothers Karamazov*). Amvrosy (1812–91) was perhaps the most well-known of the elders of the monastery of Optino. Tolstoy had several meetings with him during his lifetime. Paissy and Amvrosy were both canonized by the Russian Orthodox Church in 1988.

7. A hieromonk is a monk who has been ordained a priest.

8. The *proskomedia* is the preparation of the bread for the Eucharist, with special prayers, performed by the priest before the liturgy.

9. The general is not being merely ironic: the nature of monkhood is considered "angelic" in its service to God.

10. Meatfare week is the week before the beginning of the Great Lent, the forty-day fast preceding Holy Week and Easter. Meat is no longer eaten, but it is a Russian custom to pay visits and eat pancakes *(bliny)* during that week.

11. St. Anthony (Anthony the Great, or Anthony of Egypt, ca. 251–356) was an Alexandrian Christian, a leading figure among the Desert Fathers, and one of the founders of monasticism.

12. That is, a rule of prayer: a sequence of prayers and passages from the psalms recited daily.

13. See Mark 9:24.

14. That is, in the *Lives of the Saints*.

15. The first line of Psalm 68; also one of the verses sung in the Orthodox Easter service.

16. Father Sergius recites the "Jesus Prayer," also known as the "prayer of the heart," which goes back at least to the sixth century. "Pray without ceasing" was St. Paul's advice to the Thessalonians (I Thessalonians 5:17) and became monastic practice, especially using the Jesus Prayer.

17. The reference is evidently to the myth of Orpheus, who would have been allowed to lead Eurydice out of the underworld if he had been able to walk on without looking back at her.

18. See Matthew 18:7 (RSV).

19. The parable (Luke 18:2–8) tells of a judge who "fears neither God nor man," but who grants a widow's wish simply because she wears him out with her insistence.

20. In the Orthodox Church, an archimandrite is an abbot appointed by a bishop to oversee several monasteries, each having its own hegumen

(abbot), or to head an especially important monastery. The title may also be bestowed honorifically.

21. The feast of Mid-Pentecost falls on the fourth Wednesday after Easter, twenty-five days between Easter and Pentecost.

22. A near quotation of Matthew 19:14.

23. See note 4 to *The Diary of a Madman*.

24. This is the Orthodox prayer to the Holy Spirit, which is recited in church services and may also be repeated by individuals before an undertaking.

25. Preparation for communion includes fasting, prayer, confession, and attending church services.

26. So-called "internal passports" were required in Russia for travel within the country.

AFTER THE BALL

1. See note 3 to *The Kreutzer Sonata*. Balls were not permitted during Lent.

2. Elizaveta Petrovna (1709–62), the second daughter of the emperor Peter the Great, became empress after staging a palace coup in 1741. She was a woman of strong character and kept a sumptuous court.

3. In a society game, two young men would choose personal qualities and then go up to a girl and ask her to guess which quality belonged to whom.

4. Alphonse Karr (1808–98), French novelist and journalist, became editor of *Le Figaro* in 1838 and in the same year founded his own satirical magazine, *Les Guêpes* ("The Wasps"). He was famous for his wry sayings, among them the universally known *Plus ça change, plus c'est la même chose* ("The more it changes, the more it's the same thing").

5. In fact, Noah had one bad son and two good ones. When they found him drunk and exposed, the bad one laughed and pointed, but the good ones approached him backwards and covered his "shame" (see Genesis 9:20–27).

6. See note 1 to *Father Sergius*. Ivan Vassilievich uses the French form of the emperor's name.

THE FORGED COUPON

1. A detachable portion of a bank credit voucher, stating the amount of credit and usable as legal tender.

2. See note 1 to *The Death of Ivan Ilyich*.

3. People's Houses were established in Russia beginning in the 1880s as cultural centres for workers and artisans, with theatre, lecture hall, library, and tearoom.

4. See note 3 to *The Kreutzer Sonata* and note 6 to *The Devil*.

5. The feast of the Nativity of the Mother of God falls on 8 September.

6. The fast of 1–14 August preceding the feast of the Dormition (Assumption) of the Mother of God on 15 August.

7. See note 4 to *Master and Man*.

8. See Matthew 5–7, specifically 5:12.

9. The Russian word *krestyanin*, "peasant," is derived etymologically from the word *khristianin*, "Christian" in the sense of "human being," and is closely associated with it.

10. The Old Testament prophets repeatedly warned against the worship of idols.

11. See Matthew 10:8.

12. See John 15:20.

13. The Old Testament law of Moses teaches the taking of "an eye for an eye, a tooth for a tooth" (Leviticus 24:20).

14. That is, internal exile, most often to Siberia.

15. There were major semi-autonomous Cossack settlements in the south of Russia, on the Dnieper, Yaik, Ural, and Don rivers.

16. An itinerant or circuit court travelling from town to town.

17. These are the names of the first three letters of the old Slavonic alphabet, still used in church texts.

18. See note 10 to *Father Sergius*.

19. A free reference to Mark 10:21–30.

20. In Orthodox church administration, a metropolitan is a bishop or archbishop who is in charge of an entire diocese and presides over the synod of bishops of the diocese. The ober-procurator of the Russian Orthodox Church, a position created by Peter the Great in his reform of church administration, was a layman who represented the emperor and replaced the traditional patriarch as head of the entire Russian Orthodox Church.

HADJI MURAT

1. Shamil (1797–1871) was the third imam (military-religious leader) of Daghestan and Chechnya to lead his people against the Russians, who sought to annex their land. He finally surrendered in 1859.

2. Prince Semyon Mikhailovich Vorontsov (1823–82) was an imperial adjutant and commander of the Kurinsky regiment. His early service was under his father, who was vicegerent of the Caucasus. He was married to Princess Marya Vassilievna Trubetskoy.

3. Vladimir Alexeevich Poltoratsky (1828–89) began his service in the Caucasus and rose to the rank of general. Tolstoy used material from his memoirs in writing *Hadji Murat*.

4. The Avars were a nomadic proto-Turkish people of the Hun family from so-called Tartary, a vast territory in Central Asia stretching from the Urals to the Pacific. By the nineteenth century, their remnant occupied part of Circassia and was ruled by its own khan. Hadji Murat was an Avar, as was the imam Shamil. Later Hanefi is referred to as a Tavlin, which is another name for Avar.

5. The phrase *La ilaha il Allah* ("There is no god but Allah"), which states the most central belief of Islam, is sung in the call to prayer five times a day and may also be used as a battle cry.

6. Abraham Louis Breguet (1747–1823), the most famous of Swiss watchmakers, founded a factory in Paris in 1775. A great innovator, he invented the self-winding watch and the "repeater," which rings the hours.

7. See note 4 to *Master and Man*.

8. Mikhail Semyonovich Vorontsov (1782–1856) was a field marshal during the Napoleonic wars. Later he was made governor general of the new southern provinces of Russia, with their capital in Odessa. In 1844 he was named vicegerent of the Caucasus and awarded the title of prince. Between 1844 and 1853, he led a number of expeditions into the Caucasian mountains. In 1853 he retired to Odessa.

9. In fact, at the battle of Craonne, between Reims and Soissons on the north bank of the Aisne, on 7 March 1814, Napoleon led a force of 37,000 men against an army of 85,000 Russians and Prussians under the command of General Blücher and gained a clear victory, though with heavy losses.

10. Joachim Murat (1767–1815) was a cavalry commander and one of Napoleon's most important generals. He married the emperor's sister Caroline in 1800.

11. Franz Karlovich Klügenau (1791–1851), a lieutenant general, was commander of the Russian army of northern Daghestan. Tolstoy made use of his correspondence with Hadji Murat and of his journals.

12. Mikhail Tarielovich Loris-Melikov (1825–88) later became an important statesman and finally minister of the interior. In chapters XI and

XIII, Tolstoy used Loris-Melikov's actual transcript of his conversations with Hadji Murat.

13. Kazi Mullah (1794–1832) was the first imam of Daghestan and Chechnya to take up the ghazavat (holy war) against the Russians. He was killed in battle and was replaced as imam by Hamzat Bek (1797–1834).

14. In 1785, Sheikh Mansur (Elisha Mansur Ushurma, 1732–94), taking the title, not of imam, but of "preparatory mover," preached unity among the Caucasian Muslims in a holy war against the Russians. In 1791 his forces were defeated by Prince Potemkin at Anapa, and Mansur was captured and taken to Petersburg, where he was imprisoned for life.

15. Tolstoy gives his own translation of Vorontsov's actual letter. Alexander Ivanovich Chernyshov (1785–1857) was a Russian cavalry commander and adjutant general during the Napoleonic wars. He served as minister of war from 1827 to 1852 and was chairman of the State Council.

16. Count Zakhar Grigorievich Chernyshov (1797–1862), no relation to the minister of war, was a Decembrist and member of the Northern Secret Society of young noblemen whose aim was to make Russia a constitutional monarchy, if not a republic. His namesake, then General A. I. Chernyshov, was instrumental in crushing the Decembrist uprising of 1825, in which Zakhar Grigorievich took no actual part, but for which he was tried and sentenced along with other members of the Northern Society. The general did indeed try to take his inheritance.

17. The Eastern Catholic Church, Catholic Church of the Eastern Rite, or Uniate Church, existing in the Ukraine and western Russia, accepts the authority of the See of Rome, but follows Eastern Orthodox liturgical practices. The Great Schism between the Roman Catholic and Eastern Orthodox Churches occurred in 1054.

18. A prayer for health, prosperity, and "many years" of life for the person concerned is recited and sung at the end of the liturgy or on other occasions.

19. In a note to his novel *The Cossacks* (1862), Tolstoy wrote: "The most valued sabres and daggers in the Caucasus are called Gurda, after their maker."

20. The imperial Corps of Pages was an elite military school founded in 1697 by Peter the Great for training aristocratic boys in personal attendance on the emperor. Graduates had the unique privilege of joining any regiment they chose, regardless of openings.

21. "Corners" and "transports" are terms from the game of shtoss, a

gambling game similar to basset or the American faro, very popular in the eighteenth and nineteenth centuries.

22. In the biblical story of Joseph (Genesis 37–50), the young and handsome Joseph treats his master's wife with the utmost respect and prudence.

23. See note 5 to *The Death of Ivan Ilyich*.

24. Iosif Ivanovich Karganov was the military commander of Nukha. Hadji Murat lived in his house before his flight. Tolstoy was in touch with Karganov's widow, who supplied him with details about Hadji Murat's knowledge of Russian, his horses, his lameness, the appearance of his murids, and about his flight and death.

THE HISTORY OF VINTAGE

The famous American publisher Alfred A. Knopf (1892–1984) founded Vintage Books in the United States in 1954 as a paperback home for the authors published by his company. Vintage was launched in the United Kingdom in 1990 and works independently from the American imprint although both are part of the international publishing group, Random House.

Vintage in the United Kingdom was initially created to publish paperback editions of books acquired by the prestigious hardback imprints in the Random House Group such as Jonathan Cape, Chatto & Windus, Hutchinson and later William Heinemann, Secker & Warburg and The Harvill Press. There are many Booker and Nobel Prize-winning authors on the Vintage list and the imprint publishes a huge variety of fiction and non-fiction. Over the years Vintage has expanded and the list now includes great authors of the past – who are published under the Vintage Classics imprint – as well as many of the most influential authors of the present.

For a full list of the books Vintage publishes, please visit our website
www.vintage-books.co.uk

For book details and other information about the classic authors we publish, please visit the Vintage Classics website
www.vintage-classics.info

www.vintage-classics.info